THE LAMB
AMONG THE STARS

chris walley

TYNDALE HOUSE PUBLISHERS, INC.,
CAROL STREAM, ILLINOIS

the shadow and night

THE LAMB AMONG THE STARS SERIES ○ BOOK 1

Visit Tyndale's exciting Web site at www.tyndale.com

TYNDALE and Tyndale's quill logo are registered trademarks of Tyndale House Publishers, Inc.

The Shadow and Night

Designed by Dean H. Renninger

Edited by James Cain and Linda Washington

Previously published in 2002 as *The Shadow at Evening* by Authentic Publishing, Milton Keynes, England, and in 2004 by Tyndale House Publishers, Inc. under ISBN 1-4143-0067-0.

Previously published in 2002 as *The Power of the Night* by Authentic Publishing, Milton Keynes, England, and in 2004 by Tyndale House Publishers, Inc. under ISBN 1-4143-0068-9.

The Shadow and Night first published in 2006.

Library of Congress Cataloging-in-Publication Data

Walley, Chris.
[Shadow at evening]
The shadow and night / Chris Walley.
v. cm. — (The lamb among the stars ; bk. 1)
Contents: Shadow at evening — Power of the night.
ISBN-13: 978-1-4143-1327-6 (hardcover : alk. paper)
ISBN-10: 1-4143-1327-6 (hardcover : alk. paper)
1. Christian fiction, American. 2. Science fiction, American. [1. Christian life—Fiction. 2. Science fiction.] I. Walley, Chris. Power of the night. II. Title.
PZ7.W159315Sf 2006
[Fic]—dc22 2006016655

Printed in the United States of America

11 10 09 08 07 06
7 6 5 4 3 2 1

For my parents

For my parents-in-law,
with gratitude

On the basis of ecological or theological ideas that are not to be lightly dismissed, many people believe that this present world will end shortly.

But supposing, in this or some other universe, it doesn't?

And I will show you something different from either
Your shadow at morning striding behind you
Or your shadow at evening rising to meet you;
I will show you fear in a handful of dust.

T. S. ELIOT
THE WASTE LAND

ACKNOWLEDGMENTS

The idea for the *Lamb and Stars* Sequence originated in Beirut in the early 1980s as I read Iain Murray's fascinating *The Puritan Hope* (Banner of Truth, 1971) during a rather noisy part of the Lebanese Civil War. The encouragement to persist with this project during its inordinately long gestation period came from many sources, most notably my wife, Alison, and in later years, my sons, John and Mark. I would also like to thank my U.S. editors, Linda Washington and James Cain, and all the staff at Tyndale.

PROLOGUE

Listen!

This is the tale of how, at last, evil returned to the Assembly of Worlds, and how one man, Merral Stefan D'Avanos, became caught up in the fight against it.

But to tell Merral's tale we must begin with the Seeding of the planet of Farholme in the year of our Lord 3140. Eleven hundred years have passed since the long-prophesied incoming of all the children of Abraham and the spiritual renewals of the Great Intervention ended the shadowed ages of the human race. A thousand years have slipped by since the victory at Centauri ended the Rebellion and brought a final peace to the Assembly. Nearly nine hundred years have elapsed since the first of the interstellar seeding expeditions.

The location of the Seeding is approximately three hundred and fifty light-years from humanity's home planet, the blue world that is already becoming known as "Ancient Earth." Here, the long, gray, glinting needle of the Remote Seeder Ship *Leviathan-D* comes to rest around the dazzling whiteness of the cloud-wrapped second world out from the star so far known only as Stellar Object NWQ-15AZ.

Here the vast ship hangs for months, its pitted hull bearing the faded and scarred portrayal of the Lamb Triumphant on the Field of Stars, the emblem of the Assembly of Worlds. The ship spins leisurely on its axis as it watches, analyzes, and calculates every aspect of the sterile and still-nameless world beneath it.

Three times a plate slides open on one of the needle's six sides and ejects a probe. The first swings around the planet in a spiral orbit, mapping every boulder on its surface through the billows of gas and dust. The next two plunge down into the savage clouds and return days later, battered, charred, and corroded, but bearing samples of rock and atmosphere.

There is no haste. After all, on the timescale its makers work on, weeks are nothing. Patiently, the *Leviathan-D* continues to watch, listen, and gather ever more data. It measures the orbital variation of the planet to centimeters. It looks at the local sun in all the ways known to humanity and scrutinizes its output on every wavelength. It stretches out thin, sail-like extrusions to sift the dust in the space around the planet. It maps and forecasts for twenty thousand years ahead the trajectories of the largest million rock fragments within the system's debris belts. And as they hang above the endlessly simmering cloudscape, the ship's computers whisper and sing to each other as they process the data, predicting, discussing, and debating in learned imitation of the flesh and blood that made them.

The results are marginal. Positively, the spectrum, intensity, and variation of the radiation from NWQ-15AZ; the planet's orbital eccentricity; and the value of its gravitational field are within acceptable limits. As these are unalterable, this is good news. Negatively, the meteorite flux is too high, the axis of rotation too tilted, and the speed of rotation too fast. Adaptable as humans are, no civilization has ever thrived on days shorter than twenty hours and here they are only sixteen. However these things, and the sterile nitrogen and carbon dioxide atmosphere, can be altered. After further debate, the circuits reach agreement. If the Everlasting wills it, another home will be made here for humanity.

Now on *Leviathan-D* the quiet hum of long-inactive machinery starts up again. Smoothly, the vast needle breaks into two unequal parts. From the larger segment, a hexagonal disk detaches itself from the end and slides away to one side. The two halves of the needle rejoin to form a ship now a tenth shorter. The segment formed from their splitting begins to expand outward evenly, creating a six-sided aperture at its heart. As an unshielded Below-Space Gate, this hole will be the key to the future of this new world. With it, no subsequent ship will have to make the six-hundred-year-long sublight-speed journey of the *Leviathan-D*. If the Seeding goes as predicted, and this savage world is tempered enough for humanity, then long millennia hence, machinery and mechanisms to build a greater Gate with a shielded opening will come through it. Through that, in turn, will come men and women.

Carried on a column of brilliant light, the needle now withdraws from the target planet and releases two small disk-shaped satellites. One descends into a low orbit of extreme precision while the other races outward to take up position six months later underneath the rings of the nearest gas giant. When both disks are in position, the *Leviathan-D* brings into play a Local Gate linkage between the two satellites, and the disk above the planet's surface begins to slowly assume the mass of the planetary giant. The damping and correction of the orbit of the target planet begin immediately.

It is time to begin modifying the atmosphere. Two further Local Gates are released, one landing on the surface of the planet below and the other on one of the ammonia-sheathed moons of the gas giant. The Gate linkage is slowly brought on line, and a hissing and boiling exchange of gases begins.

Computer modeling of the planet for thousands of years ahead suggests that greater climatic stability can be achieved by sculpting the surface to allow linkages between what will become the ocean basins. For weeks, the Mass Blaster of the *Leviathan-D* pounds the planet with repeated energy pulses of overwhelming force, vaporizing millions of tons of rock and hewing and hammering out the channels, straits, and seaways of the future.

As the blast debris settles out of the atmosphere, the computers on the *Leviathan-D* decide it is time for a gentler but no less vital technology. In the sheltered core of the great needle, proteins are assembled and woven into helixes of genetic matter, each strand tuned and programmed to feed and multiply on the scalding gases below. The genes are inserted into biological cells and the cell cultures inserted into five cylindrical polymer cocoons. Then a panel on the side of the ship slides open and the five containers are propelled into space. There, in the shadow of the great ship, as dwarfed—and yet as consequential—as acorns before an oak tree, they linger, waiting for the word of command to send them to seed the planet.

Then, although there is no one other than God and the angels to hear, the ship speaks. In a dozen frequencies, as programmed by men and women now long dead, the solemn charge rings forth.

In the Name of the High King of heaven,
We name this star Alahir
and this world Farholme.
We of the Assembly of Worlds now command you:
Go forth and multiply.
Redeem this waste world.
Bring air and water, land and sea, day and night.
Produce a home for the Lord's people,
to the praise and glory of the Messiah,
the Lamb who was slain.
Amen.

The response is the faint, silent flickering of lights on the ends of the cylinders as, one by one, they propel themselves away, onward and down into the swirling gases below.

For a final time, a port on the ship opens and a last satellite emerges to take up a high orbit above the newly christened Farholme. This Overseer satellite is to superintend the Seeding and to attend the planet in lonely vigil for the centuries that the work will take.

The needle now begins to move. The decision has been made that what is now known as the Alahir System will be the last target on the mission schedule. The systems scanned ahead by the *Leviathan-D* show little promise. After six centuries between the stars, the survey of fifteen worlds and the seeding of six, it is time for the *Leviathan-D* to return to port. But the homeward journey will be far swifter. Using the trail of Below-Space Gates it has left behind, its journey back will take a millionth of the time and energy of the outward journey.

The ship adjusts itself delicately in space on pulses of light until one end is perfectly aligned above the axis of the Gate. In a movement of slowly gathering swiftness, the needle's tip stabs into the strangely star-free blackness at the Gate's heart. Nothing comes out of the other side. Vanishing from view, the ship slips through the hexagonal aperture with a handbreadth of space to spare on every side. A second after the tail torch nozzle disappears there is the brief, ghostly gleam of a blue aurora around the hexagon and the Gate is empty.

As the long years roll by, the Overseer satellite high above Farholme watches, without emotion, the spreading smear of green in the cloud systems as the cells begin to absorb and break down the gases. In time new types replace these, each successive generation pushing the atmosphere closer to that in which oxygen-breathing life can live without being choked, boiled, or burned.

And as life grows and increases on the new world of Farholme, the echo of the commissioning charge radiates outward through the Alahir System and beyond into the silent, unvisited spaces between the stars.

. . . *To the praise and glory of the Messiah, the Lamb who was slain. Amen.*

And time passes, not just in those petty quantities that we call days, weeks, and years, but in long centuries, and even multiples of centuries. It is now the year of our Lord 13851, and the Seeding of Farholme is ancient history to its thirty million human inhabitants; as primeval and distant to them as the final waning of the ice sheets was for the first space travelers. More precisely, using the language of a long-dead calendar, it is December 22. In short, the Feast of the

Nativity is just over two days away, and on over sixteen hundred inhabited planets the nearly one trillion citizens of the Assembly are preparing to celebrate the Incarnation.

The Assembly of Worlds now occupies a zone of space exceeding a hundred million cubic light-years; its farthest inhabited system toward the galactic edge is still Alahir with its single Made World, Farholme. Farholme retains the status that it had at its Seeding of being the farthest world, so that its thirty million inhabitants sometimes refer to their home, with a mixture of affection and gentle pride, as "Worlds' End." With the exception of its extreme position and low population, if there is a typical Made World (and only Ancient Earth is not a Made World), it is Farholme. Here the ancient, crater-pitted landscape vigorously erodes under the new regimes of water and oxygen. On it infant seas gnaw away at old impact scars, lava fields bubble and smoke sulkily as they cool under the novelty of rainstorms, barren dusty plains are slowly buried under the timorous advance of greenery, and rivers and sea and air currents are reluctantly coerced into stable and predictable courses.

But if the landscapes of the Assembly worlds remain restless this eve of the festival, its peoples, with their mutual tongue of Communal and their many dialects and historic languages, know only peace. It is, though, a peace of activity rather than a peace of rest. The Assembly is as vigorous as ever. There are always new worlds to be subdued and older ones to be stewarded. Nevertheless, this day—as every other day in the Lord's Peace that has lasted over eleven thousand years—sees no wars or strife within the Assembly worlds. And as the banners of the Assembly are brought out and checked in readiness for their grateful unfurling on the Day of the Nativity, there seems no reason why the emblem of the Lamb Triumphant on the Field of Stars may not fly at peace over an ever larger Assembly for another eleven—or eleven hundred—millennia.

Hanging high over Farholme this day, as it has for three thousand years, is the gigantic, beacon-framed hexagon of the shielded Below-Space Gate, the only link to the other worlds of the Assembly. Two thousand kilometers away from it, a dozen shuttlecraft drift gently around the Gate Station as their cargo is unloaded from the latest inbound inter-system liner. And far below their activity, night sweeps silently westward across Farholme, and as it does, the lights of a hundred human settlements flicker on.

But ultimately the Assembly is not Gates and worlds, still less banners and emblems. It is people: men and women, flesh and blood, bodies and souls. And as planets swing in their orbits, as the fabric of space is pierced at the Gates, and as atoms are broken in the forges of rocket fires, down on the surface of Farholme, a lone figure rides a horse northward into the gathering twilight of a winter's day.

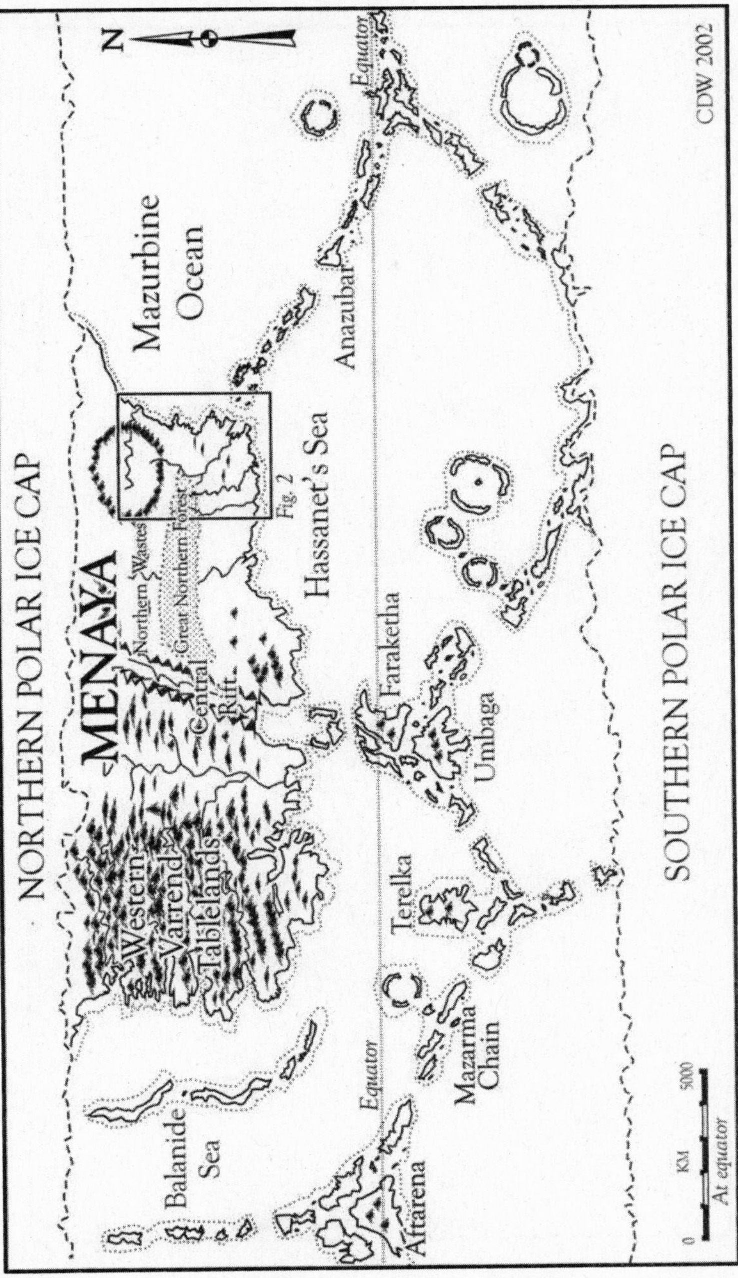

NORTHERN POLAR ICE CAP
MENAYA
Western
Varrend
Tablelands
Central
Rift
Northern Wastes
Great Northern Forest
Fig. 2
Mazurbine
Ocean
Hassanet's Sea
Anazubar
Equator
Balanide
Sea
Aftarena
Mazarma
Chain
Terelka
Umbaga
Faraketha
SOUTHERN POLAR ICE CAP
N
0
KM
5000
At equator
CDW 2002

FIG. 1

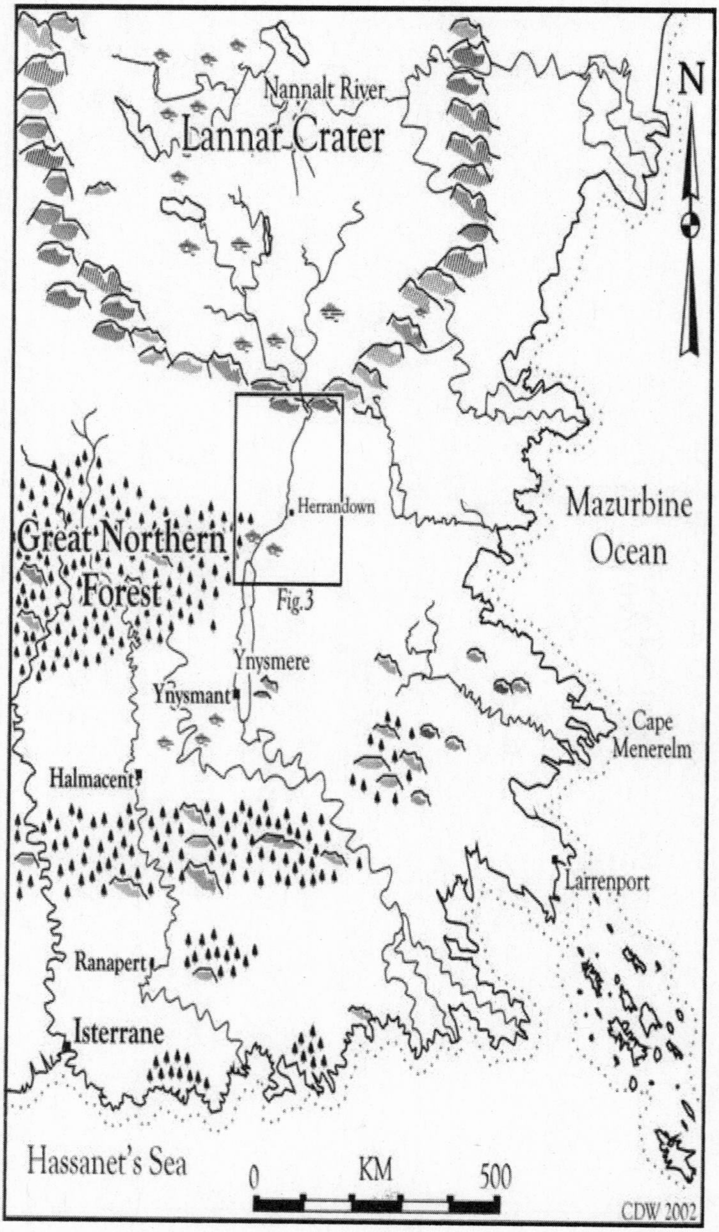

N
Nannalt River
Lannar Crater
Mazurbine Ocean
Herrandown
Great Northern Forest
Fig.3
Ynysmere
Ynysmant
Cape Menerelm
Halmacent
Larrenport
Ranapert
Isterrane
Hassanet's Sea
0
KM
500
CDW 2002

FIG. 2

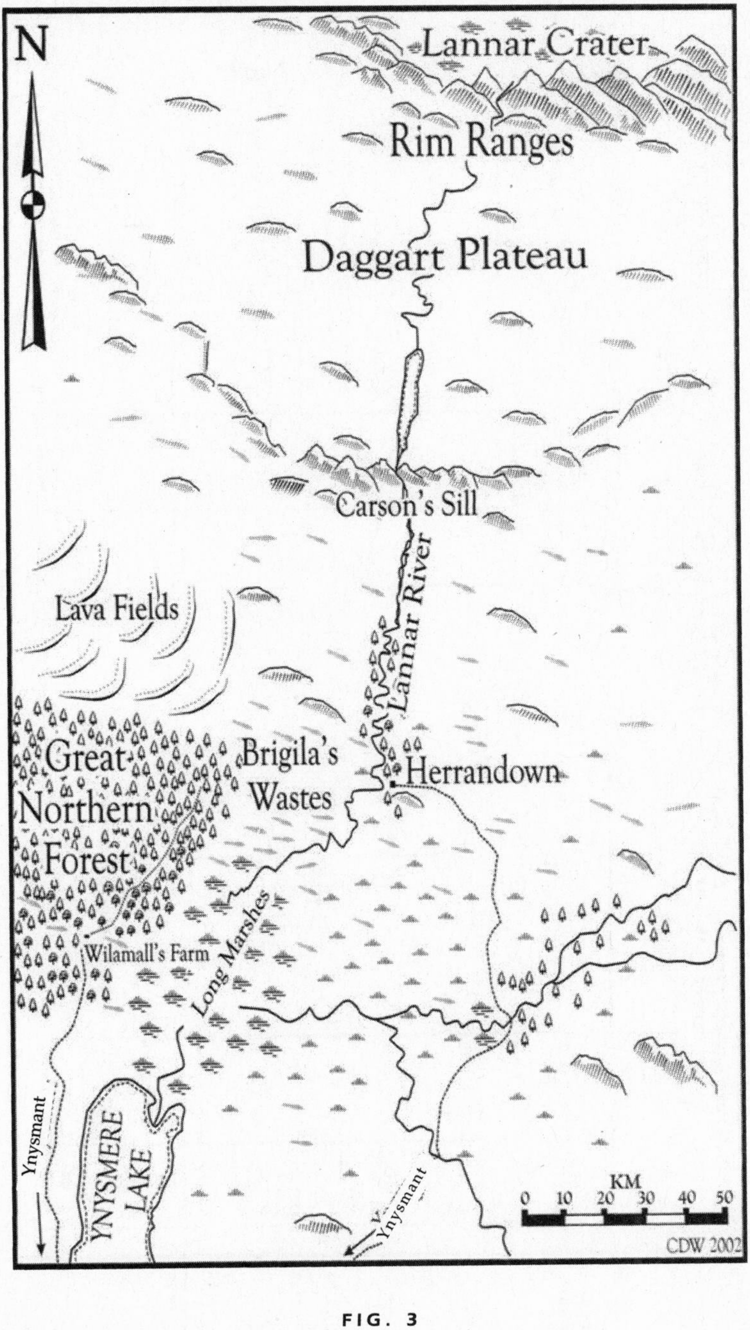
N
Lannar Crater
Rim Ranges
Daggart Plateau
Carson's Sill
Lannar River
Lava Fields
Great
Northern
Forest
Brigila's
Wastes
Herrandown
Long Marshes
Wilamall's Farm
Ynysmant
YNYSMERE
LAKE
Ynysmant
KM
0 10 20 30 40 50
CDW 2002

FIG. 3

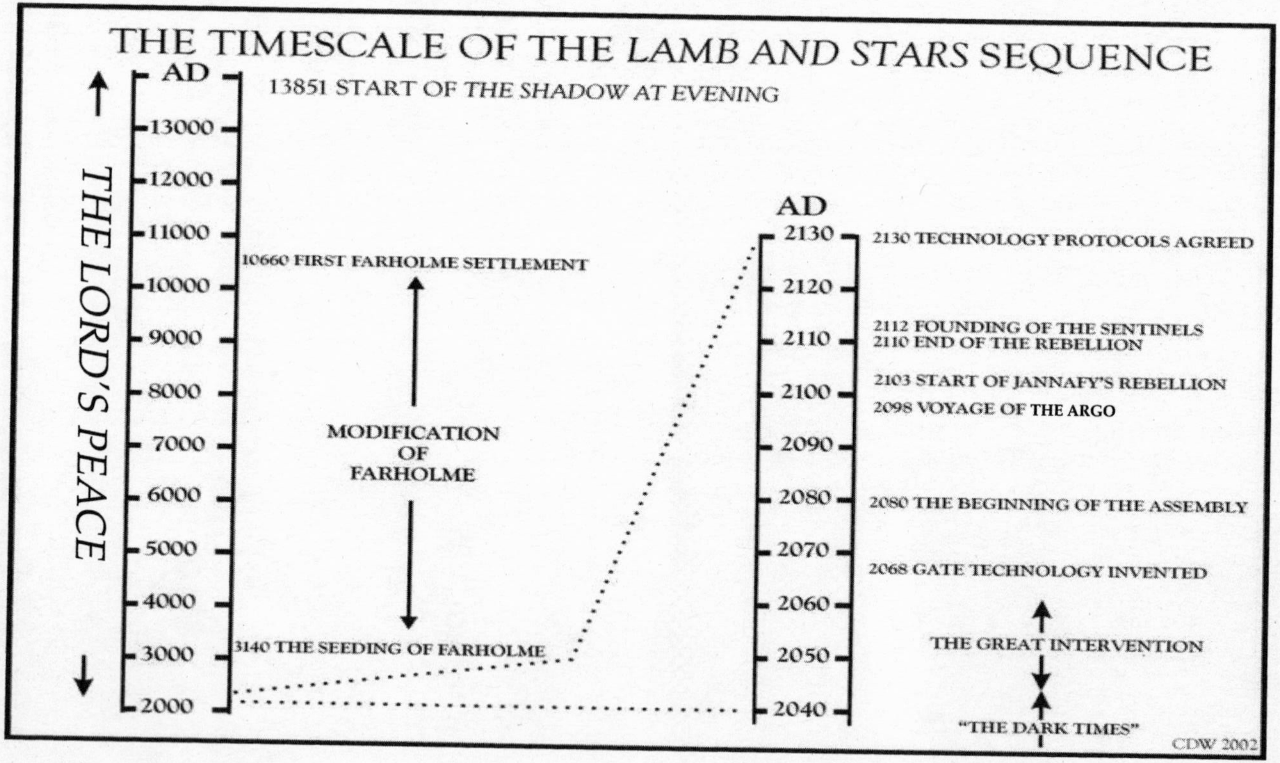
THE TIMESCALE OF THE LAMB AND STARS SEQUENCE
AD
13851 START OF THE SHADOW AT EVENING
13000
12000
11000
10660 FIRST FARHOLME SETTLEMENT
10000
9000
8000
MODIFICATION
OF
FARHOLME
7000
6000
5000
4000
3140 THE SEEDING OF FARHOLME
3000
2000
THE LORD'S PEACE
AD
2130
2130 TECHNOLOGY PROTOCOLS AGREED
2120
2112 FOUNDING OF THE SENTINELS
2110
2110 END OF THE REBELLION
2103 START OF JANNAFY'S REBELLION
2100
2098 VOYAGE OF THE ARGO
2090
2080
2080 THE BEGINNING OF THE ASSEMBLY
2070
2068 GATE TECHNOLOGY INVENTED
2060
THE GREAT INTERVENTION
2050
2040
"THE DARK TIMES"
CDW 2002

the shadow at evening

PART ONE

1

Merral Stefan D'Avanos crested the snow-flecked ridge in the northeastern corner of Menaya, the vast northern continent of Farholme, and reined in his mount. The winter's sun had just set in a great stained sphere of orange gold. He stared at the expanse of gray hills and darker, mist-filled valleys stretching northward to the ice-edged needles of the ramparts of the Lannar Crater.

Above the Rim Ranges, layer upon layer of cloud strands gleamed every shade between yellow and purple in the dying sunlight. Merral tried to absorb all he could of the sights, sounds, and smells of dusk. Down below the ridge, away to his right, crows preparing to roost were wheeling noisily around a pine tree. Far to his left, there was a moving, snuffling grayness under the edges of the birch forests that he knew was a herd of deer. Hanging in the cold fresh air was the smell of winter, new trees, and a new earth.

The beauty of it moved Merral's heart, and he raised his head and cried out with joy, "To the Lord of all worlds be praise and honor and glory and power!"

The words echoed briefly and a gust of wind out of the north dragged them away, down through the trees and bare rocks.

Silent in awed worship, he sat there for long minutes until another chill gust made him shiver, as much in anticipation as in actual cold. He bent down to his horse. "Now, Graceful," he murmured, "good girl, onward."

Obedient as ever, the mare moved forward over the frozen ground.

Merral knew it would not be wise to wait longer. The Antalfers expected him, and the nights of deep winter could be cruel this far north. Besides, as on any young world, there was always the chance of a sudden local weather anomaly. Such an irregularity might be only a few kilometers across—too small to be picked up by a weather satellite—but enough to freeze solid an unprotected man and horse in under an hour.

Merral rode on along a rough snowy trail which wound its way round blocks of lava, toying lightly with the wish that he had been born a poet or painter rather than a forester so that he could better express his love for this place and this life. But it wasn't long before he laughed at the aspiration and pushed it to one side. The Most High had made him what he was, and that was enough.

He peered ahead along the track, straining in the gloom to see the way ahead. The Herrandown Forward Colony was so small—a tree-surrounded hamlet of fifty people in six extended families—that it would be easy to overlook it at night. After some more minutes of cautious riding, he caught a glimpse of a tiny sliver of golden light in the distance. He smiled happily at the thought of his uncle or aunt leaving the shutters open so that the light would guide him in. He patted his mount, seeing her breath in the cold air. "Nearly there, my Graceful, and Aunt Zennia will have something for you."

Five minutes later he emerged abruptly from between the fir trees into the broad clearing that acted as the rotorcraft landing pad and marked the southern margin of the hamlet. As he rode out into the open, the dogs around the farm started to bark, and their dark shapes bounded across the packed snow toward him. Merral reined in as he met the dogs and, reaching down to stroke them, tried to identify as many as he could in the gloom.

"Fastbite, good dog!" he shouted. "Oh, Spotback, it's you! And Quiver, eh? Been having more pups, I hear? Brownlegs? No—it's Stripes. Look, stop licking so much!"

A door slid open smoothly in the ground-hugging building ahead. Light streamed out briefly onto the path before being abruptly blocked by the silhouette of a tall, well-built woman with long hair.

"Merral! Praise be! Children! Barrand! It's Merral! Now, mind the ice over there," she cried, half running to him. "Here, Nephew, give me a kiss!"

For a moment all was chaos as, barely allowing time for him to dismount, his aunt Zennia embraced and kissed him, while the children streamed out to hold and hug him and ask a dozen overlapping questions. And all the while the dogs, barking joyously, bounded in between Graceful's legs.

"Nephew Merral! *Welcome!*" A deep, jovial voice that seemed to echo came out of the door of the house. "Why, it's been months!"

Dogs and children gave way as the large figure of Uncle Barrand, his profile almost bearlike in the gloom, ambled over and hugged Merral to the point of pain as he kissed both cheeks fiercely and repeatedly.

"Excellent! Praise be! Your pack I will take. Thomas? Where is the boy?" His uncle's bulk swiveled around slowly. "Dogs I see, girls I see, but my only son is missing. Ah, there you are, Thomas! Good, you have a coat on. Take your cousin Merral and his horse—Graceful isn't it? Thought so—I'd know her even on another world. Take them to the winter stable. I'd take you, but I'm cooking tonight. Girls! *Wife!* It is cold. Indoors now, and let us finish preparing supper for our guest. He has ridden far. And Thomas . . ."

"What, Father?" piped the small voice from by Merral's side.

"Just take your dog into the stables. Not the whole pack."

Merral just made out a dutiful nod from the figure beside him. "Yes, Father! Here, Stripes! The rest of you dogs! You go off to your kennels! *Shoo!*" With what seemed to be regret, the other dogs drifted off obediently.

Thomas, short but well built for his seven years, took Merral's sleeve and tugged. "Cousin, we have a new stable for winter. An' I helped Daddy build it. We digged . . ." There was a pause. "Dugged? *Dug* it together in summer. Over here."

Merral ruffled the boy's black, wiry hair. "It's good to see you again, Thomas."

"Cousin, the stable is real warm over winter. We got twenty cows, fifteen sheep. When the station says it's gonna be real cold, we even send the dogs in. An' we put all our horses there, of course."

The track they followed went round the side of the low earth banks that gave some protection from the weather to the Antalfers' house and down a ramp into a mound. Merral had seen the plans when he'd come by in midsummer; the bitter cold of the last two winters had made a shelter a necessity. Inside the double sliding doors, the long, narrow structure was warm with the smell of animals. Merral led Graceful into an empty pen, made sure she had clean water and hay, and then spent time checking her over, running his hands over her legs and checking the dura-polymer hoof shields. "Good. She seems fine," he told his cousin. "Always check your animals, Thomas. They are your friends, not your servants."

The child nodded and hugged the dog, which licked his face. "Dad says that. I get a horse of my own in two years. I'm gonna really look after him." Merral nodded and patted the horse's head gently.

"Good girl, Graceful. Well done."

The brown head twisted up from the hay and rubbed itself against his hand as if in mute acknowledgement of the praise.

Merral stretched himself. "Well, I'm hungry, Master Thomas, so let's go."

Once outside the doors of the stable, Merral suddenly felt the cold anew. The wind had intensified and was swirling round the building, kicking up little eddies of snow. The last gleam of twilight had gone, leaving the molten fire of the stars and the great belt of the Milky Way splendid in the blackness of the sky above him. Despite the frigid air and his appetite, Merral paused in his stride and looked up in wonder.

"You know your stars, Thomas?"

"'Course! Well, most of 'em. Dad's taught me some. He says we should see twenty with people on 'em."

"Twenty?" Merral thought hard. The naked-eye count for Farholme was supposed to be about fifty occupied systems, but that was from Isterrane; no, the boy was right—this far north you'd see less than half of that.

"On Ancient Earth," he remarked, as much to himself as to Thomas, "they say you can see over two hundred. And almost all the remaining thirteen hundred with a small optical telescope."

"Sol 'n' Terra are over there, just below the Gate." Thomas' voice was quiet.

Merral followed his outstretched hand to the heart of the Milky Way, a few degrees below where six sharp golden points of light marked out a hexagon in the blackness.

"Yes. That's it. Sol and Terra: the Ancient Sun and Earth. Well, time to get in or we'll freeze."

Merral bent down to take the boy's hand, but as he did, his eye caught a movement of the stars. He straightened, watching the approaching speck of light as it grew in size.

"Look, Thomas, a meteor!"

As he spoke, the point of yellow light, expanding a thousandfold, tore northward almost directly overhead. Its brilliance was such that, for a few seconds, the light of all the other stars was lost.

Merral twisted round, seeing the whole snow-clad landscape flashing alight in a brilliant incandescent whiteness. In the brief moments that the light lasted he glimpsed his and Thomas's shadows form and then race away as fading, elongated smears on the snow.

Abruptly the night flooded back.

As Merral blinked, a thunderous, echoing rumble vibrated around them, the sound bouncing off rocks and snow and resounding back round the clearing. The ground seemed to shake gently.

"Zow!" yelped Thomas, his fingers flung over his ears. "That was noisy!"

Stripes howled in terror, and from near the house came the barking of the other dogs. The outer door slid open.

"Thomas? Merral? What was that?" Zennia's voice was anxious.

Merral shook himself, the afterimage of the light still haunting his vision. "Just a meteor. I think."

"Come on, Thomas. Suppertime."

They crowded into the hallway, which was bare but beautifully paneled in a light, oil-polished pine, as the double doors whispered shut behind them. Barrand's big red face, framed by his ragged black curly beard, peered out of the kitchen. "A meteor, eh? We felt the house vibrate. 'Ho!' I thought. 'Merral is doing my quarrying for me!' "

"What, Uncle? Cheat you of your pleasure?"

There was the sound of something bubbling. A look of apprehension crossed Barrand's weathered face, and he dashed back into the steam of the kitchen.

Merral took off his jacket and carefully hung it on a rack, relishing the smell of the food and the warmth of the house. He sat on a bench and pulled his boots off, enjoying the feeling of being back in a place that he had always loved. He stroked the wood of the walls gently, feeling its faint grain. Even in a society that prized the right use of wood, Barrand and Zennia's home was special. Since his first visit, Merral had always felt that the house, with its sizeable underground extension, was something that had grown rather than been built. Even if the unruliest of winds struck the exposed part of the building so hard that every timber vibrated, down in the lower parts you could feel as safe and snug as if you were inside the roots of a giant tree.

"But it was a meteor?" His uncle's face had appeared again round the door. Merral sat upright suddenly, his tired back muscles signaling their presence.

"Must have been. But the biggest I've ever seen. It was heading northward. I suppose it probably landed over the Rim Ranges somewhere in the crater."

"Oh, it'll do no harm *there*. End up as a handful of dust."

There was amusement in his gray eyes. "Anyway, you have ten minutes, assuming this new recipe behaves itself. Your usual room. Just time for a shower."

"A quick shower it is." And with that, Merral picked up his pack and climbed up the stairs to the guest room.

Some minutes later, Merral was combing his hair and wondering why a shower and clean clothes made so much difference when there was a soft knock on his door.

"Come in!" he called out. In the mirror, he saw a face peer round the door—an oval face with pale blue eyes overhung by an untidy fringe of curly blonde hair. Merral turned round. "Elana! How are you?"

Elana, the oldest and blondest of the three Antalfer girls, was something of a favorite of Merral's. He had a private opinion that she was also the deepest and most thoughtful of them. Although she wasn't fourteen until next month, Merral had felt even on his last visit in high summer that she already had one foot beyond childhood. Now she came into the narrow room and stood under a curving wood beam. She stretched delicately upright on tiptoe and gave him a beaming smile. "I'm fine, Cousin. And you are well?"

Merral looked at her carefully, recognizing in those modifications of her physique the woman so imminent in the girl. "Praise our Lord. I have gained a few more scratches and bruises since I last saw you. And some aches from riding over hard ground. But I am well."

"You rode here just to see us?"

"Sorry! No, I need to talk to your father about his quarry, so my trip here is part of work."

She stared at him, amused puzzlement in her eyes. "I thought you were a forester!"

"I still am. But there's no point in us planting a forest if your dad is going to dig a big hole in it, is there now?"

"No, I suppose not." Elana smiled. "Actually, Merral, I came to say that food is nearly served."

"Lead the way."

He followed Elana to the dining hall, noting a new painting on a wall above a stairway. He reminded himself that he must make time to look at his aunt's latest work. He might ask her to do something for his parents' thirty-fifth wedding anniversary next year. He made a mental note that when it came to planning what to do with his stipend next year, he needed to include the cost of the painting.

The dining hall lay in the deepest part of the house, and although it was the largest room, it seemed already full as he entered. Merral tried to identify everybody. On one side were his aunt, the two younger daughters—Lenia and Debora—and, of course, Thomas. On the other were Barrand's parents, Imanos and Irena, and a young couple from the next house.

Merral made his way to the seat offered to him at one end of the table. As he did, Barrand came in bearing a great pot and the chattering ceased. Quietly, everybody stood up and stepped back behind their chairs. Thomas, too short to see over the solid back of his, peered round instead at Merral.

There was silence. Barrand raised his big, gnarled hands to the heavens. "For your love and presence with us, O Lord, our protector and mighty one, and for your kindness to us, we thank you now. In the name of the Prince, the Messiah, our Savior."

A second's solemn silence was ended abruptly with a chorus of "Amen," and then the scraping and clattering of chairs and talking.

As he sat down, Merral looked around the dining room. The way the side beams sloped inward toward the floor made it easy to imagine that he was deep down in the hull of a boat. It had taken them the ten years they had been in the house to acquire just the right panels, matching in grain and tone, to complete the dining room. Along some of the roof beams, his uncle had started carving animals to what Merral recognized as his aunt's designs.

The meal was like all the many meals Merral had had at Herrandown, with lots of food, endless noisy chatter, and half a dozen conversations bouncing and jumping around and across the table. Merral was pleased to find that his own substantial appetite by no means outmatched the others at the table. In fact, everyone seemed to be happily hungry. His uncle revealed nothing about the stew other than the fact that the beef-protein had been grown locally and the girls had picked the mushrooms for it in autumn.

Barrand looked up at him. "The family, Merral? You tell us the latest."

"Well, it is five days since I left Ynysmant and I have covered a lot of ground, but when I left all were well, may the Most High be praised, and I have had no news of any change. The only thing is that Great-Aunt Namia down at Larrenport is not well. She is now very frail; she feels she will be going Home to the Lord in the spring. The doctor thinks she is right."

Imanos, a silver-haired man with an air of gentle nobility, spoke. "Namia Mena D'Avanos? The language teacher?"

"That would be her."

"Why, she taught my mother Old-Mandarin; Mama was so proud of mastering it. 'The hardest of all the Historics,' she said." He paused, smiling quietly. "I was very glad to be spared it. But she must be very old now. A hundred and twenty at least?"

"A hundred and twenty-four. But still alert and still praising."

"You'll be seeing her before she goes Home? Please, will you give her our love and blessing." His wife gently nodded agreement, her fine white hair framing a face as peaceful and still as if it had been molded.

Merral bowed his head slightly to acknowledge the taking on of an obligation. "If the opportunity is granted me, I shall indeed visit her before her death and if I do, I will pass on to her your love and blessings."

The elderly couple smiled at each other and then gratefully back at him. A few moments later Barrand, one hand tearing off a piece of bread, caught Merral's eye and gave him a broad wink. His loud voice rang down through the room, cutting across three separate conversations.

"Talking of family matters, youngster. You're twenty-six! What's happening between you and Isabella Hania Danol?"

There was a sudden silence and Merral looked at his glass, conscious that everyone was looking at him.

Zennia laughed and raised her hands in mock horror. "Oh, Barrand! Let him tell us in his own time. He's a shy lad."

"There is really nothing decided." Merral smiled. "Except that my parents and hers are meeting to discuss whether to approve that we proceed to a commitment. That's all I'll say."

"A formality, I'm sure," said Barrand, waving his bit of bread around and smiling at his girls. "We'll all come down for the wedding, won't we, children?"

"Oh yes, please. When? When?" came the chorus from the children.

"This year, next year, sometime, never," interjected Zennia. "Everything is still at the first stage. It's commitment, engagement, and *then* marriage. Now, Barrand, leave the lad alone and tell him about the cows."

"Oh, not half as much fun. But you are right. Now, what with the heat, our cows had a bad summer. . . ."

And so the meal progressed in its animated and somewhat chaotic way, with discussion of the families, farms, animals, life in Herrandown generally, Merral's travels, Barrand's musical projects, and the children's activities.

Eventually even Merral's hunger was assuaged, and slowly, and somewhat heavily, everyone (except the oldest) rose from the table and went to the kitchen to help in the clearing up. Then they went into the family room and heard the children practice their Nativity songs. As tradition demanded, two were in Communal, the universal language of the Assembly; one was in the Farholmen dialect; and one in the historic language assigned to Herrandown. Merral, whose only Historics were French and English, found the Alt-Deutsch quite incomprehensible. Then the neighbors departed, and with kisses all round the children left for bed. Eventually the "senior generation" pleaded age and departed to their own small suite of rooms.

Now the three remaining adults reclined in padded chairs in the small room above the hall and let the conversation drift. Barrand toyed gently with a dark wooden flute of his own carving, occasionally blowing a quiet note and listening carefully to it with a look of suspicion. It was interesting, Merral observed, how the contrasts met in his uncle. To look at him in his work you would think that all he could do was blast quarries and hew out tons of stone. Yet in his wood carving and his music he showed sensitivity and a delicacy of touch. But there were not two separate Barrands, but one: quarrymaster, wood-carver, and musician.

As if conscious of Merral's thoughts, Barrand looked up. "Ah, I'd ask your advice, Merral, but you singers don't understood wood instruments. I'm just not satisfied with this." He tapped the flute. "But it's a delicate business, adjusting. Easy to mar, hard to mend."

Zennia stroked Barrand's wrist, her finger delicate and thin against the muscular bulk of his arm. "All the better then, my dear, to leave it to tomorrow."

"Quite so. Although tomorrow is official work with my nephew the forester. But I will find time. My wife, as usual, is right." He carefully put the flute down. "Nephew, your glass is nearly empty. More to drink?"

"Not for me."

Then they let the conversation drift into a slower, more reflective tempo. In time, they got talking about the arts, and Barrand began to talk with his usual enthusiasm about choral music.

"Oh, Merral, I have had a struggle about what to do for Nativity. Very hard. I've always liked to do something special. It's difficult when there are so few of us, but I don't mind using re-created voices."

Merral remembered that in these small communities, the use of the preserved voices of singers in the past was not luxury in music-making, but necessity.

"As we did Bach at Easter, I thought we'd do something more recent. So it's Rechereg's *Choral Variations on an Old Carol.* You know the piece?"

"Heard of it. It's difficult, isn't it?"

Barrand nodded to his wife. "Our nephew is too busy. Not enough time to listen."

Zennia patted her husband's arm and smiled back at Merral. "Perhaps, dear, in Ynysmant they are too busy making music to listen to it. Remember our blessing of being so remote."

"Wives are always right, eh, Merral? But of course you wouldn't know. . . ." His uncle smiled, showing his powerful, white teeth. "Ho. Where was I? Ah yes, let me see. The Rechereg is very demanding. I will need three re-created voices to handle it. The great tenor Fasmiron—the voice is from 8542 when he was at his peak—and Genya Manners, one of the Lannian sopranos during the great years of their academy. She sounds more like a bird than a woman. But I'm having problems with the female alto. It's a very high part."

He looked into the distance, tapping his fingers on the wood of his chair.

"Who are you using?" Merral asked.

"For the alto?" Barrand stroked his beard. "Hmm, Miranda Cline perhaps. But does she have the range? Just ten years of singing. It was so fortunate that she agreed to let her voice be copied so she could become a re-created when she did. She came and went like a meteor. . . ."

He stared at the wall-hanging opposite. Abruptly, he looked at Merral. "Nephew! A change of subject entirely. Your meteor. Have you considered why the Guardian satellites didn't pick it up and destroy it?"

Merral thought for a moment. "It crossed my mind briefly. It seemed large enough to have done damage if it had hit anything. So the 180 East or the Polar Guardian should have intercepted it, you think?"

His uncle ran his hand through his beard again. "Me? Oh, I don't know. I've never given the Guardian satellites a thought. I know there are four, that they're as old as the present Gate, and that they destroy any meteor or comet coming in on a threatening trajectory. And that is it. They work. So we forget them. . . ." He fell silent, his fingers maintaining a gentle beat on the arm of his chair. "But, Nephew, what I was just wondering was this: Now suppose one or more of the Guardian satellites did see it, but they just plotted the trajectory and then said 'Oh, the Lannar Crater. Uninhabited waste,' and let it pass. What do you think?"

"I think I see where your logic takes you." Merral sipped the last of his drink. "With Herrandown being the farthest settlement north, that's fine, but inside a decade or two we might have a Forward Colony up to the margins of the southern Rim Ranges—at least if the winters don't get any worse."

His uncle nodded, his heavy brow furrowing. "Hmm. Exactly. I just hope someone tells the Guardians. But Nephew, surely the Guardians aren't smart enough to determine an impact trajectory to such precision that they can let it go over our heads like that?"

Suddenly tired, Merral found himself stifling a yawn. "Oh, sorry, Uncle. Yes, you may have a point but my brain is too fatigued. It would be an interesting thing to know. I'll talk to someone when I get back."

"It's not just you who is tired. Zennia looks asleep."

At her name, his wife started, opened her eyes, and shook her head so that her brown and silver hair flew around. "I'm—Oh, what an insult! I am sorry. I really ought to go to bed. If you gentlemen will excuse me."

Merral got to his feet. "I think, Uncle, if you will excuse me, I'll go too."

Barrand waved a hand dismissively. "Of course. Zennia, I'll be up in a moment. But I've just had an idea about that alto."

In the small guest chamber with its single skylight, Merral undressed. Fighting off sleep he sat on the bed, pulled the small, gray curved slab of his diary off his belt, and noting the illuminated message logo, thumbed it on, switching to speech mode.

"Today at 9:15 p.m. Eastern Menaya Time. One message: Nonurgent. Voice from Lena Miria D'Avanos." The words were flat and metallic.

Pulling out his night-suit, Merral spoke to the diary. "Play, please. Let's hear my mother."

"Message begins. . . ." The coldly sterile tones of the machine were thrown into abrupt contrast by the soprano of his mother's voice, with her haphazard stresses.

"Merral *dear*. This is not *at all* urgent. Not at *all*! But do thank Barrand and Zennia so much for their good wishes for the Nativity. Zennia's card was *lovely*. Merral, I am so blessed to have such an *artistic* sister. Lovely. I shall be writing, of course, but do please invite them down again. Those *dark* winter nights up north! Of course, I'll do it myself, but the personal touch is the thing! Oh, and Merral, I saw Isabella today. She asked after you. '*When* is Merral coming back?' she said. Father and sisters send their love too. Love from your mother."

The metallic voice returned: "Message ends. No further messages."

"Okay. Go to today's notes."

"Ready."

"Add 'Final Observations' as follows. . . . "

For the next five minutes, Merral listed what he had seen on the last part of his journey north. He would tidy up the report when he got home. Then he briefly outlined what he hoped to achieve with his uncle tomorrow before he rode south again. Finally, he switched to screen mode and continued his current evening reading of the Word before bringing his praises and concerns before the Most High.

Then Merral slid in between the sheets and lay there listening to the silence of the house and the soft creaking of the wooden frame as the night winds swirled around it. There was, he felt, something extraordinarily satisfying about being tired: the draining of energy from limbs, the leisurely and ordered shutdown of body systems.

On the verge of sleep, he realized that he had not recorded in his diary anything about the meteor. He would, he told himself, do it tomorrow. Toying with the image in the last moments of wakefulness, he played back through his mind the brief glimpse he had caught of it—the ball of light, like some great firework, racing overhead.

As he did so, it struck him that something about it was odd. But what? He ran over the vision again and again, now faster, now slower.

His last thought as he plunged finally into sleep was that, for a meteor, it had been moving too slowly.

Far too slowly.

2

That night Merral dreamed in a way he had never thought possible. Normally, if he did dream, all he would remember of it on waking was a short-lived, gentle, and vague memory. But that night his dream was of an extraordinary intensity and unpleasantness.

He was standing alone on a dark, endless sandy beach at the edge of a sullen, night-colored sea, whose slow, heavy waves never broke, but seemed to just crawl up the shore and die before sliding back with a quiet, drawn-out whisper. Somehow, there was something swollen and infected about the sea. The cloudy, sunless sky above was lit with an overcast, tepid yellow light that seemed sickly. In the far distance some dark-winged objects, which he knew were not birds, wheeled and dived ominously.

It seemed to Merral that he stood there for an age, a lone figure looking at a sick sea and a dead sky, watching the oily ebb and flow of the waters. There was an atmosphere of expectancy, a feeling that something was on its way, something impending. It was as though the waves in their slow, lapping decay were saying in words just beyond hearing, *"Wait. . . . Wait. . . . Wait. . . ."* He knew, with a strange certainty, that there was something out there in the waters. Something that was waiting out its time before emerging.

Then, in a fearful moment, he saw the faintest of movements begin far out on the water. An unhurried train of circular ripples began to spread out slowly, and the waters seemed to bulge.

As this happened, Merral felt a strange compulsion. He wanted to run away. Indeed he knew that he had to, but somehow he couldn't. Instead, half of him seemed to want to stay and to watch what was going to come out of the water. There seemed to be an invitation, a beckoning, even a command for him to stay, to watch, to somehow be present at—

At *what?* Merral didn't know. He felt trapped in lonely terror and expectation, bound against his will to watch and await whatever it was that was emerging from the growing ripples.

Suddenly Merral felt he was no longer alone. Someone else seemed to have joined him, some invisible person who tugged at him so that he was forced to turn away from the mesmerizing sea. As he turned away, he felt suddenly released from his bonds. Driven by an overpowering sense of peril, Merral began to run over the loose sand away from the rippling waters. And in his fleeing, he woke up with a start of terror.

Merral lay still for some minutes, wet with perspiration and aware of a thudding pulse in his head. It took him some time to come to terms with what he had experienced. It had clearly been a nightmare, a thing not entirely unknown in the worlds, but almost always in rare psychological ailments or in various poisoning accidents. He switched the light on and went over to the hand basin where he washed his face and checked himself over. To his surprise, he found no evidence of illness. He had no swollen glands, no spots, no pustules, and no distended stomach. Recovering something approaching calm, he went back to bed, switched off his light, and lay down, conscious of a racing pulse. He was vaguely aware of the wind gusting strongly against the walls and heavy footsteps from his uncle and aunt's room next door. Then he committed himself again into the hands of the eternal Father, the great King, the maker of the heavenly glory, and fell asleep.

This time he slept in peace.

Over breakfast, Merral's dream nagged at the corners of his mind. He had been talking over with Barrand some of Thomas's stories from school when Zennia, robed in a warm blue gown, came in and reminded the children that it was time to leave for school. As they left in turbulent good cheer, Merral's aunt sat at the table and turned to him.

She stared at him, her eyes showing concern. "Did you sleep properly, Nephew? You still look tired."

Merral put down his cup slowly, perplexed at realizing that he wanted to avoid her question. "Er, no, Aunt. No, not really. The bed was fine, but I just had . . . well, a dream."

Merral was aware out of the corner of his eye of Barrand, standing against the kitchen shelves, and as he said the word *dream*, he had the strongest feeling that a look of surprise or dismay crossed his uncle's face. But when he turned to Barrand, all he could see was a mild expression of quizzical sympathy.

"No! I *am* sorry," his aunt replied, her voice full of consideration. "You mean a nasty dream? About what?"

Merral found himself embarrassed. "Well, nothing much really. It was an oddly sort of static dream. Almost . . . well . . . a *nightmare.* I just . . ." He hesitated. "No Aunt, it's too silly, really, to talk about. Perhaps it was something I ate." Then he realized what he had said. "I'm sorry, I didn't mean to suggest that your food was—"

"No, I know what you mean," she answered, giving him a caring look.

Barrand turned to Merral. "Perhaps . . . perhaps it was the mushrooms." His normally, smooth deep voice was now ragged.

Then, as Merral watched, his uncle swung away toward the wall and began to move a plate along a shelf.

"*I've* never known them to have that effect," Zennia commented, sounding slightly puzzled. "We all had them, didn't we? Husband, you slept all right, didn't you? I do remember you getting up."

For a moment, Barrand, apparently engrossed in finding dust on the plate, didn't look up. "Oh, me?" he said eventually, in a level, flat tone. "Oh, *I* slept fine. No, nothing like that."

"Bizarre," replied Zennia. "Have you ever dreamed like this before, Merral?"

"Never, thankfully."

Barrand turned toward them, his face expressionless. "Now, don't rule out mushrooms. Fungal biochemistry is very complex. And they evolve in such a bizarre way; you get new strains all the time. There was a case some fifteen years ago: A whole community of sixty perished out in one of the Lenedian planets. Do you remember it?"

"Vaguely," Zennia slowly replied, looking at her husband as if there was something she did not recognize about him.

Barrand, who had now swung away again and appeared to be examining the kitchen shelves, nodded to himself. "Yes, well, that was put down to a rogue gene in a fungus. But anyway, no harm done here."

Merral, unsure of what to say, tried to soothe the situation. "Well, that's true. No harm done. Whatever it was, I'm fine now."

Barrand put down the plate he was still holding onto the shelf so awkwardly that it rattled alarmingly. Then without looking back at either Zennia or Merral, he said, "Excellent! Well, dreams or no dreams, we ought to get down to business, young Merral. My office in ten minutes?" But before any answer could be made, he had left the room.

Zennia stared after the departing shape of her husband with an air of puzzled unhappiness, looked at Merral, and made as if to say something. Then she seemed to change her mind and left abruptly, leaving a perplexed Merral in sole possession of the kitchen.

Eventually Merral gathered up his notes on the quarry and stepped outside. It was a brilliantly clear winter's day, and breathing in the sharp, cold air, he stared at the snow-sprinkled landscape engraved in a crisp winter fragility. As he did, the oddly unpleasant atmosphere of the kitchen seemed to dissolve in the fresh air. Soon, though, Merral felt the cold penetrate his indoor clothes, and he strode quickly down the path to the long shed huddled between earth and basalt block banks.

As he entered, Barrand looked up from where he was sitting behind a desk piled neatly with papers and datapaks.

"Welcome to my palatial office!" he exclaimed jovially, waving his great arms so wide that they nearly touched the opposite sides of the room. Merral felt encouraged that the strange mood seemed to have left his uncle as abruptly as it had come.

"Ho! Stop standing there. Do take a seat. I've lost a cross section."

Merral, however, remained standing and looked around. His previous visits had been social ones and he hadn't been in his uncle's office for years. It was a single long room with one end taken up by a south-facing window and the other walls covered with maps, diagrams, and shelves of rock samples. In one corner hung various bits of quarrying equipment, including a cutter beam and a sample corer. Despite all the objects and his uncle's apparently easygoing nature, he found it a surprisingly tidy room.

Merral's attention was caught by a small painting on one wall, apparently out of place among all the paraphernalia of work. It was a picture of an entwined mother and child peering out of the window of something he took to be an inter-system liner, as beyond them a specklike in-system shuttle was beginning reentry into the atmosphere of the green and blue planet below them. Against the margin of the picture was a Gate, its status lights green. The caption read, "A last view of Hesperian. A. R. Lymatov, A.D. 11975."

"Interesting painting," Merral observed, speaking as much to himself as to Barrand.

His uncle looked up from his papers. "Oh, that. The Lymatov. Yes. My great-grandparents were from Hesperian. But you knew that."

He stared at it as if seeing it for the first time, then wagged a finger solidly in emphasis. "Yes, now, Zennia doesn't like it. She says it's too posed. I disagree. Of course it's posed. It's a *posed* sort of painting. But it is flawed. Technically, it's wrong. They would have been seated and strapped in long before they got that close to the Gate, and the windows are too big for a liner. But I like it. Do you?"

Merral looked carefully again at the painting. He noticed that the child's arm was raised in a farewell wave that was somehow ambiguous and that the mother's posture was rather rigid and her face determined.

"Yes. I do. Like it, I mean. It's a well-established genre; you could fill a hundred galleries with them. But I find it moving. There's no father. Did he die, and are they leaving his remains there? It asks questions. I suppose he might have gone on first, but somehow the figures suggest otherwise."

Barrand gave him a knowing nod. "You always did have an abundance of brains. Yes, there is a story. A family of five was planning to go to Granath Beta. Then the husband and the other two children were killed in a freak storm. She and the remaining child went on alone."

He got up and went over to the painting, speaking quietly and intensely now. "It's always been a challenge to me. It says a lot about faith. About what the Assembly is about. What our calling as a family is. *Resolve. Faith.* You know. All those things.

"It is a well-established genre. But all genres are now." He stared at the painting. "Funny business, the Assembly, when you think about it. All the emphasis on a stable, sustainable society. The caution over innovations."

He nodded toward the horse grazing on some hay just in front of the window. "Take animals now. Like Blackmane there. He's a horse, but his genes are different from the first horse that left Earth. Or even that arrived here. Look at him: rounded extremities, reduced ears, nostril flaps, more recessed eyes, thicker hair, heavier hooves. He has adapted to this world with its cold and heat and dust."

"Of course," Merral said. "You can hardly freeze adaptation. But what's your point?"

His uncle creased his large forehead in puzzlement. "My point? Yes. Oh, I don't know. The paradox that we have frozen our culture, but that we have let life evolve. I know it's not a new thought—what is after so long?—but it has just struck me with some force."

"But, Uncle, the wisdom of the centuries is that the stable culture is best. You can't just let a culture evolve; certain limits must be defined. Long, long ago the Assembly decided the parameters in which human beings flourished and set them down. It was a choice; a fixed, conservative, and stable society over one that was open, fluid, and unpredictable."

There was a deep silence as Barrand, his large frame totally dominating the room, stroked his beard in profound thought. Then he gave a grunt that seemed to indicate mystification.

"Absolutely. What a strange idea for me to have." He shook his head. "Ho, to business! Oh, I don't need that cross section. Come and have a look at these maps and let's switch into official mode, Forester D'Avanos."

For half an hour they looked at the maps and imagery, and Merral listened intently as his uncle explained why he wanted to quarry the ridge outside the settlement rather than wait for a new access road to the already-planned quarry site fifteen kilometers to the north. Only he wasn't his uncle now. He was Barrand Imanos Antalfer, Frontier Quarrymaster, and he was presenting his case to Merral Stefan D'Avanos, Forester and head of the team that decided the citing of things such as quarries and forests. *Funny,* Merral thought, *how we distinguish official and family discussions to the extent that it would now be unthinkable for him to call me Nephew and me to call him Uncle.*

Eventually Barrand wound to a halt. "So you see, Merral, we could start in the spring and save two years. And think of the energy saving in skipping that thirty-K round-trip. . . ." He trailed off, looking at Merral.

Merral rose to his feet, walked to the window, and looked out at the bare black ridge they had been talking about.

"Barrand," he said, gesturing at the ridge, "let's go and look at it."

Zennia was free to come, and an hour later the three of them were standing on the rocky summit of the hill recovering their breath after the stiff climb up. Merral stared around. Suspended overhead was a cool, eggshell blue sky painted with the most delicate pearl brushstrokes of high cloud. To think that they were just water vapor—had the Most High ever made anything so beautiful from so little? There were one or two of the faint corkscrew twists of cloud that revealed local instability in the upper atmosphere layers, but nothing that portended trouble on his ride tomorrow.

Merral lowered his gaze. The farms, fields, and orchards of Herrandown were almost surrounded by protecting woodlands, beyond which lay rough scrub, grassland, and bare rock. To the west of the settlement the bounding fir and alder woods ran into the tree-lined margins of the Lannar River, whose path he could trace northward toward the ranges. Looking northward, from where a cold wind blew that made the eyes water, the ground became increasingly covered with ice and snow. And there, marching along the farthest skyline, were the jagged teeth of the southern Lannar Rim Ranges, gleaming a dazzling white in the sunlight. The notion struck him that this cluster of houses was a vulnerable community. *What a strange idea,* he thought. *Vulnerable to what?* "So, it's suitable rock and there's enough?"

Barrand hesitated and said, "But the ridge will be gone."

"My idea is this. I think we should work on a plan where the excavation is all on the south side of the ridge, leaving a narrow ridge to the north about this height, but we'll also give permission to excavate below ground level to make one or two long deep lakes."

Zennia smiled.

Barrand, his face wrapped in deliberation, spoke slowly, his voice warming as he did. "Ho! Yes, I should have thought of it. They'd be spectacular with vertical rock walls behind them. And they'd warm the water because of the solar radiation."

As they walked down the hill, Merral pushed those thoughts away. Zennia turned to him with a smile. "Barrand has been telling me of your recommendations. You have a gifting of vision and leadership, Merral. You would prefer to disown it, but I think you will use it in the end. If not on Farholme, then elsewhere."

"Elsewhere? I was born here, as you were and all my grandparents were. No one in our family has been off Farholme since, oh, Great-Uncle Bertran traveled forty years ago."

"Do you want to go elsewhere?"

It is an interesting question, Merral thought, *and one that I have struggled with myself.* "I have little thought of leaving, Aunt. I love this place and being here. Farholme may be Worlds' End, but this is my home." He paused. "I believe that my place is here. For the moment at least."

Zennia carefully negotiated a sheet of glittering ice and then turned again to him.

"And tell me, you are happy with the forester's life?"

Merral measured his words. "I am, Aunt. I am happy. There is the challenge of seeing Menaya change and unfold as we work on her and with her."

She smiled, encouraging him on.

"I love it," he said. "It's the combination of art and science. I look at the ground, the lava ridges, the sand sheets, and say to myself, what can I do with it? What will best bring out the uniqueness of the land? Here a beech wood, there a pine forest."

"I see the attraction; it is like painting."

"Indeed, it is art at the grandest scale." Merral smiled. "One of the great purposes of the Assembly—to take brown-and-gray, dead worlds and turn them into blue-and-green ones alive with life. Thus, we fulfill the mandate to humanity to garden what the Lord has entrusted us with."

Barrand waved an arm in agreement. "Oh, absolutely. But let *me* ask you a question. Have you *really* no ambitions beyond all this?"

A hard question. My ambition is not something I normally think of. "Uncle," he answered after a moment, "I suppose I do have one ambition. More a wish."

"What?"

Merral stopped and looked up. "Well, I would like to see the forests of Ancient Earth. To examine old woods and jungles. Ecosystems that go back, not just for eight thousand years, but millions of years. Unplanned, at least by us. Composed of a hundred thousand species in relative stability, not our five thousand in unsteady, unpredictable, and changing relationships."

Barrand grunted, but it was Zennia who spoke. "Yes, I could see that. All Made Worlds are imitations, as best as we can make, of the one original Earth. But I have heard that many of Ancient Earth's forests were badly affected in the Dark Times; they have been reconstructed."

"True. They are not as they were when our First Father and Mother walked in them. But I would like to see them once."

The house was in sight now and the dogs were coming out. Barrand, his teeth bared in a grin, turned to Merral. "And perhaps, Nephew, one day you will."

"Maybe, Uncle, but it's a long walk from here."

And as the dogs romped around them, they laughed again.

That night Merral borrowed an image projector and went up to his room early to work. He wanted to get the ideas for the ridge tidied up before the Nativity holiday and knew that there would be little time on the next day to get anything done. If he got to the Forestry offices at Wilamall's Farm by dusk as he planned, he should be back in Ynysmant by eight on the regular ground transporter. And as that would leave little time to write up anything, it was best to do it now. So he linked his diary to the image projector and used it to draw an elegant, scaled 3-D model of the proposed quarry that appeared hanging over the desk like a gray whale painted with gridlines.

As he adjusted the edges of his model, he paused. Was he really working up here just because he had to get the work done? Or was there more to it than that?

He felt there was something that he didn't understand in the house, something intangible and impalpable that he preferred to avoid; something he wanted to be away from. Somehow, the house of his uncle and aunt had ceased to be as welcoming as it had been. As he sat there in the room, Merral felt drawn to consider again the mysterious problem that had afflicted Barrand that morning. Had it been resolved, or had it simply been pushed to one side? Certainly, during the evening, his uncle had become more withdrawn and terse.

Merral was sitting there, idly rotating the diagram as he considered his uncle, when there was a gentle tap at the door.

It was Zennia, bearing a glass of warm milk for him. She smiled. "I thought you might like this before you went to bed."

"Why, thank you very much, Aunt! I hadn't realized how late it had become."

He took the glass and placed it carefully on the desk. As he began to mention his plans for the morning, he saw a glint of emotion cross her face, a look that came and went so fast that it was hard to recognize. But, fleeting as it had been, Merral felt it to be one of concern, and he knew that it confirmed his own unease. There was indeed something wrong in the house.

Zennia, apparently realizing that she had revealed some secret thing, turned sharply and made to go to the door.

"Aunt, wait a moment," Merral said. "Uncle . . . how is he?"

Zennia stopped, her hand on the door, and looked at him, her eyes showing unhappiness.

"He is tired, Merral. He's gone to bed."

"He's not unwell? Any symptoms?"

"No. Just tired." She paused as if uncertain whether to continue. When she spoke again, it was in puzzled tones.

"It seems . . . it *seems* as if he dreamed as well last night—something strange and not very nice. He won't say what." She moved again as if to go.

In his surprise, Merral said without thinking, "Oh, I'm sorry to hear that, Aunt. But I thought he said he hadn't dreamed."

Zennia, looking away from him, remained still, her only movement the agitated twisting of her fingers on the door frame. When she spoke it was in awkward, hacked phrases. "Well . . . I really can't—I'm not sure . . . exactly what he said."

There was a clumsy pause in which both were silent. Then she turned, gave him a cool, formal smile, and left, calling gently over her shoulder as she pulled the door behind her closed, "Good night and blessings, Merral."

The door was closed by the time he had begun to return her benediction.

With his mind in total confusion, Merral clicked the diary off, and the image looming over his desk instantly vanished. He sat back in the chair, arms behind his head, trying to unravel his perplexed thoughts. So, Barrand had had a foul dream too. That was curious. One bad dream in a house was odd, but for two people to have one on the same night was very mysterious. Yet the dream was not what worried him or, he suspected, Zennia. No, what was making his mind reel was that this morning Barrand had definitely said that he had slept well and had had no dreams. He had said it plainly. And Zennia's unhappiness when he had pressed her had confirmed it. She avoided answering his inquiry because she couldn't face the fact that her husband had lied earlier in the day. And with that answer came a terrible awareness: Could it really be that his uncle had lied?

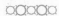

Under the thrust of the word *lied* Merral got up and paced the small room in agitation. The very word *lie* was unfamiliar. To deceive, to willfully alter truth; he knew theoretically—as everyone did—what it meant. But understood it was never practiced. You might sometimes mislead people in sport, like in Team-Ball games, where you made them think you were going right not left, but that, of course, was not lying. Nor was it lying to pull a verbal surprise, as in a joke or a riddle. And even when asked a question where the answer would be hurtful to the hearer, it was easy enough, at least in Communal—the historic languages were harder—to give an answer that allowed it to be understood that, for whatever reason, you preferred not to commit yourself. True, the idea of lying came to you on occasions, particularly when you had made a mistake. But you just pushed the idea aside. Since the time of the Great Intervention, the temptation to willfully deceive someone had had little real force. Jannafy's rebellion in the first days of the Assembly had probably been the last instance of large-scale deception.

No, Merral concluded, the idea of lying was hateful. The entire edifice of the civilization of the Assembly of Worlds was built on truth and on its counterpart, trust. The lie was the enemy to all that. As he lay down on the bed, he reflected that it was an axiom of the whole era of the Lord's Peace from the Intervention till now that no one lied. Truth had been sacred since the Dark Times, over eleven thousand years ago.

And yet, the thought nagged at Merral until sleep finally fell on him; the conclusion seemed inescapable.

His uncle had lied.

3

Merral was up early the next morning, and after donning his jacket, slipped outside to look at the weather. Although the sun should have been rising there was only a dull glow in the east, and in the gloom he could faintly make out that during the night the wind had changed and was now coming out of the barren wastelands of the west. At least, he comforted himself, from that direction neither rain nor snow would come.

When Merral entered the kitchen he found Barrand sitting at the table. There was an unhappy look on his face, and after the briefest of greetings he blurted out, "Merral, I'm so sorry about yesterday! The whole thing was ridiculous! Zennia said you were worried because I seemed to have, well—*contradicted*—myself. It could, I suppose, seem like that. The fact is that . . . well . . . I did dream, it's true. But I had—I suppose—pushed it out of my mind. When you spoke about having a dream, I began to remember it, but I was unsure about it." Here he paused, as if uncertain what to say next. "I mean I was unsure about whether I had had a dream. If you follow my meaning."

Uncertain how to respond, Merral just nodded, and his uncle went on in an unsteady fashion. "So, anyway it was just later on in the day that it all came flooding back. And when I said in the morning that I hadn't dreamed, it was, well . . . true then. But I mean, it wasn't a major dream anyway. So the whole thing is nothing serious. I wouldn't want you to get it all out of proportion."

I need to think about this, Merral thought, recognizing that his uncle seemed to be in serious difficulties.

"I think I understand, Uncle. But actually, if you'll excuse me, I'd better have breakfast and be off—if that's all right with you. Graceful and I have a long way to go today."

A look of relief seemed to cross the gray-blue eyes. "Yes, yes. Now tell me your plans while I get some food out for you."

Fifteen minutes later as he came down the stairs with his pack, ready to leave, Zennia was waiting at the outer door. She smiled rather distantly at him. "Your uncle has explained everything, has he? A sort of delay in recognizing that he had had a dream. It all makes sense now. Something about nothing."

Merral hesitated. "Yes, I hope so. I'm glad you've got it all sorted out." He kissed her on the cheek. "I must be away, Aunt. Give my love to the children. I'll be back this way soon."

There was the clatter of feet on the stairs and a slender figure in a fluffy pink robe with a straw-colored mop of hair bounced lightly down the stairs, ran over, and clutched his hand.

"Bye, Cousin Merral. Don't get talking to the trees now."

Merral gave Elana a hug, noticing as he did that she was already nearly up to his shoulder. "Bye, Elana."

There was a heavy thudding on the stairs and Thomas leapt down, slid across the wood floor like a skater, and wrapped his arms around Merral.

"Cousin! You nearly left without saying good-bye."

Laughing, Merral disentangled himself from Thomas's clutches and lifted the boy high so that his head nearly touched the roof. "Owf! You are getting too heavy to do this."

"Have a safe trip, Cousin Merral. Look after Graceful." Thomas giggled as, with a playful tickle, Merral put him down.

"I will. And you look after the dogs!"

Merral turned to his aunt. "I'd best be off before the rest of the family comes down."

He raised his hand. "A blessing on this house." Then he pressed the door switch and, as it slid open, stepped out into the raw grayness of the dawn.

It was still little more than half-light when, ten minutes later, Merral rode Graceful southwest from the hamlet. The route he had planned was a long one. He intended to travel first west over Brigila's Wastes, keeping south of the still-barren lava seas, then south along the Long Marshes before swinging back through the eastern tip of the Great Northern Forest. From there, a track should allow him to make Wilamall's Farm, the most northerly forestry base, by midafternoon at the latest. There he would leave Graceful in the stables while he took the daily overland transporter down to Ynysmant. There were more rapid routes home from Herrandown, but Merral wanted to see as much as he could. Sampling and observer machines made regular survey trips across these lands, and drones flew overhead to monitor for changes, but he knew that there was no substitute for walking or riding the ground.

Fifteen minutes later, having carefully crossed the solid ice of the Lannar River on foot and ridden up the sparsely wooded western bank, Merral squinted across at the wastes before him and wondered why he had been so zealous.

Ahead was a desolate and empty landscape across which a cutting wind whistled hungrily around him. Facing into it, he found that there was little escape even with the glare goggles on and the face baffle of his jacket up round his nose. As he rode on, with Graceful picking her way across the frozen tussocks, he decided that there was little to choose between the west and the north wind. While lacking the polar chill of the wind from the north, the west wind had its own cruel character. Here every turbulent gust that struck carried a reminder that it was drawn across five thousand kilometers of treeless waste, much of it a dry, salty, and sandy desert. At least, he reminded himself, in winter there was still enough moisture to remove the dust. In summer, the dry and baking west wind was filled with dust, silt, and static, and became the scourge of machinery and men's lungs.

Merral, trying to keep his face averted from the wind as much as he could, found little compensation in his route. Here only the thinnest skins of frozen soil and turf covered hard black volcanic rock. There were patches of powdery snow and, every so often, dangerous stretches of colorless ice over which dismounting was necessary. The only vegetation was clumps of rough tussocky grass with occasional straggly bushes of hazel and willow. Given the scarcity of the vegetation and the harsh weather, Merral found no surprise in the fact that he saw little life in the wastes. Every so often he put to flight a party of migrating tundra hares, pale in their winter coats, and once he came across a herd of grazing reindeer, which stared at him stupidly before turning away and shuffling off to resume their foraging. Once a pair of great Gyrfalcons circled above him, ghostly below the clouds, then drifted away southward. But that was all he saw.

Soon he found that he was in a featureless landscape where the gray of the ground faded into the softer grayness of the sky to give an elusive and unchanging horizon. Merral decided that here he could not afford to be lost and set his diary to check the route: a thing he rarely did. So his progress was marked by periodic noises from the diary, a deep long beep for a deviation to the left, a short high one for one to the right, and a bell-like chime for a correct course. Like all Forestry horses Graceful understood the signals enough to steer herself. So together, horse and man progressed slowly over Brigila's Wastes, the silence broken only by the whistles of the wind, the clip-clop of Graceful's hooves, and the occasional interruption from the diary.

For the first half hour or so, Merral was preoccupied by what had happened at Herrandown. He was unsatisfied by what both his uncle and aunt had said this morning. Something odd, alarming, and even wrong had happened yesterday. But what? No hypothesis he could invent would make any sense. In the end, Merral reluctantly decided that Zennia and Barrand must be right: It was some sort of psychological oddity that they had mishandled between them so that it had become completely distorted. After all, human beings were complex. On that basis, Merral pushed the affair out of his mind.

Yet as he rode on, he felt a strange feeling of disquiet that seemed to have nothing to do with the weather. More than once, he found himself looking around or even over his shoulder, as if some invisible shadow had fallen upon him. But, other than the gently undulating bleak surface under him and the gray billowy sky above, there was nothing to see.

Eventually, Merral forced himself to concentrate on studying the ground and trying to get a feel for these barren lands. He found himself pondering over the wastes, aware of how widespread this sort of landscape was in Menaya. *Here, I can believe this is a half-finished world, with this ripped veneer of soil and scrub over lava and rock outwash supporting, at best, a handful of species.* But that thought came to him as more of a challenge than a criticism. God willing, within a few years there would be trees over much of this area, and with them, a much greater diversity of plants and animals. The issue was how to do it.

As the brown reeds of the marsh's edge came into sight, Merral checked his location from the diary and ordered the active navigation off. He would swing southward down the flanks of the marshes up to the edge of the Great Northern Forest. Not only was there no danger of losing his way here, but the presence of patches of marsh and swamp made such an automated navigation worse than useless.

Merral picked his way along the slope just above where the reed beds started, watching carefully for patches of thin ice. As he rode down along the marsh's edge his journey became easier. The wind blew now at his side rather than into his face, and the sky lightened overhead so that there was enough sunlight to cast a faint shadow. Here there was life: birdsong from within the reed beds, the whistling of the dwarf swans on the lake, and the piercing cries of the gulls. A reed heron scuttled away in front of him. In the distance he saw a herd of gray deer, a pair of otters slithered away into an ice-free patch of water at the sound of Graceful's hooves, and a Raymont's musk ox lurched across his path.

As he drew near the edge of the forest, he crossed the distinctive tracks of a half-ton hexapod surveyor. They were fresh and going south with a purpose rare in surveying machines, and Merral wondered if it had been programmed to return to base before Nativity so that the samples could be unloaded before the break. Wilamall's Farm would probably be busy today.

An hour or so later Merral stopped and took another bearing. He wanted to be certain of striking the forest edge south of the limits of the rough lava flows. At the ragged edge of the forest, he reined Graceful in and took a last look over the Long Marshes, a great sea of tan reeds swaying gently in the wind as far as the eye could see, broken only by snaking waterways clogged with brittle ice. He would, he decided, come by again in summer and camp and linger.

Today, though, there was something about the wastes that he found peculiarly unwelcoming, and as he entered under the shadows of the trees, Merral found himself rejoicing even more than usual. He had always loved woods, even in winter when the rowans and gray alders were bare and only the pines were green, and even these impoverished and marginal forests with their gale-tumbled trunks. So he didn't mind that, with the branches low to the ground and the land rough, his journey was a slow one. It took well over an hour's skillful riding to reach the support road, as he skirted around areas of impenetrable scrub and avoided the deeper streams while trying not to depart from his compass bearing. Even so, he was wondering about taking a location check when suddenly he was out of the trees, and the track—a rift of dead, yellow bleached grass between the high trees—lay before him. The road had been made two centuries or so earlier to ease the passage of the ground transporters bringing in the first trees for this part of the forest. Since then, it had been cleared periodically to maintain a line of access into the forest.

Merral dismounted, letting Graceful graze on the remains of the grass. Then, listening to the wind whistling through the treetops, he looked at the track for signs of recent passage of men or machines but found nothing. Any woodland sampling and observer machines were too delicate on their feet to leave traces on hard ground, and if any humans had come through here lately, they had used some zero-impact machine such as a gravity-modifying sled, a hoverer, or, like him, a horse. He was not surprised; he was too far away from any homes for stray visitors and he knew that the current schedule of the Forestry Development Team did not include any visits in this area. No, today the woods were his and he was glad of it. He loved the solitude and was always glad of the opportunity to sing his heart out to heaven's King.

He remounted and set off southward, starting to sing as he went. Today, though, for some strange reason, he found a lack of spontaneity in his singing, and it was only by dint of discipline and effort that he kept himself going. But for the next three hours, as he rode slowly along the old track as it wound its way down and round a succession of valley flanks and ridges, Merral sang, working his way twice through the entire Nativity section of the Assembly songbook. It was not, he knew, the greatest singing, and there was little in it of the quality that Barrand's re-created voices would have, but it was genuine and, with a deep gratitude, he offered it up to the One who was the Light above lights.

But even in the singing Merral was keeping a careful eye on the forest. In general he was pleased with what he saw, finding almost all the trees, apart from those felled or beheaded by ice storms or wind gusts, in a satisfactory state. No, he concluded, after its two centuries of history this wood would pass—at least at first glance—the highest test of a Made World woodland and be taken as an original forest of Ancient Earth, albeit one with some unfamiliar species. A closer inspection would, of course, show a much more limited diversity of plants and animals, and some oddities as species adapted rapidly into the new and unoccupied environmental niches. Everything took time, and you couldn't just throw a world together and hope it would work. Everything had to be checked, its every possible interaction with everything else modeled and predicted. And even then things went wrong; like the fungal species that digested dead wood on one hundred and sixty worlds but which, on the hundred and sixty-first, suddenly became one that digested living pine trees. But as they said, "every world sown was new lessons reaped." What had taken a thousand years on the first Made Worlds now took under half that. But there was always room for improvement and no world was ever truly Earth.

As he rode south, Merral noticed, with faint surprise, that his spirits seemed to lift. He put it down to the gentle lifting of the temperature and to getting away from the bleak emptiness of Brigila's Wastes. Yet it was funny, he reflected, that he had never felt such a change in mood before. But he soon shrugged off his puzzlement; introspection was not something that he, or any of his world, ever indulged in for long. He stopped once for food in a clearing overlooking a stream, setting Graceful free to find what she could to eat among the blanched and withered grasses. Then, mindful of the short winter days, he set off again. Yet as he did so, a strange, fleeting thought came to him that he had an anxiousness to be home he had never had before. It was still another oddity for him to consider.

By four in the afternoon he had approached Wilamall's Farm and other tracks joined his. At one junction, Merral waited while a woodland surveyor, six smaller undergrowth analyzers docked onto its back, ambled past on its eight long, metallic legs. As it passed him the machine stopped and turned its slender head toward him. The two large glassy eyes looked at him without expression. Merral raised his right hand vertically to reassure the surveyor that he needed no assistance. The machine raised a front paw in dumb mechanical acknowledgement and continued on its way south.

The sun was hanging low on the western hills as Merral came out of the forest and saw below him the fences, roofs, and domes of Wilamall's Farm. Down by the labs a line of gray samplers full of plant fragments for testing waited with perfect patience to be unloaded, and over by the transport offices, other machines were being garaged. As he watched, a pale long-winged survey drone descended gently through the air overhead, extruded legs, and with a smooth glide, came to rest on the small landing strip.

Merral was met at the gate by Teracy, the assistant manager, who, after warmest greetings and high praise for a recent project he'd undertaken, told Merral that he had a place booked on a freighter going south in half an hour. Wasting no time, Merral took Graceful over to the stables.

A large, stooped figure in a dark gray jacket walked over awkwardly from the small office by the stables. His left foot dragged behind him.

"If you please, Mister Merral!" the man sang out loudly in a voice as rough as broken wood.

"Jorgio!" Merral replied, delighted at seeing the broad, tanned, and twisted face of his old friend, who served as gardener and stable hand at Wilamall's Farm. "Greetings! It's good to see you."

"Greetings indeed." Then, careful to avoid crushing a bloodred cyclamen sticking out of his breast pocket, he squeezed Merral in a forceful embrace. Returning the embrace, Merral caught the faint odor of animals, stable, and gardens, and suddenly his earliest memories of meeting Jorgio came back to him. He had been five or six, and he had been taken one cold spring day to see the new lambs near the edge of the cottages where Jorgio lived. At first, he had found the man's large and deformed figure intimidating. Yet, within minutes, Jorgio had put him at ease and they had been friends ever since. Merral had no idea exactly how old Jorgio was; he assumed he was in his sixties but found it hard to tell.

They released each other, and Jorgio, his amber-brown eyes gleaming softly, gave Merral a thick-lipped and skewed grin and then turned his large, bald head toward Graceful. He whistled to her in a strangely out-of-tune way. As she trotted over to Jorgio, it came to Merral again that everything about Jorgio, from his legs to his misshapen shoulders, was asymmetrical. Occasionally he felt his logic was unusual as well; Jorgio seemed to have an odd perspective, almost as if the childhood accident that had damaged his body had also curved his way of thinking.

"Graceful, let's have a look at you," Jorgio said with a surprising softness of tone. "There's long miles you have covered."

He bent down and ran his rough, veined hands over the mare's flanks. Watching him as he made soft whispering noises, Merral knew that it was not just affection that he had for this man; it was also respect. He had long felt that, as if in some form of compensation for his distorted body, the Most High had given Jorgio special gifts. He was an excellent gardener, capable of making things flower in the poorest of soils, and had a deep affinity with animals. His curved logic wasn't wrong; it was just different.

"It's a real blessing to see you, Mister Merral," Jorgio said, glancing up at him. "It really is."

"And for me to see you."

It is interesting, Merral thought, as Jorgio looked over the mare, *how we deal with people like Jorgio, these accidents of life. We always seem to find them something in which they can fulfill themselves, whether it is tending gardens, painting our houses, or minding our horses. He and I do a job, get the same food and housing, have the same stipend to give away or use, and only the Judge of all the Worlds knows which—if either—of us is the more valuable.* Jorgio looked up, his mouth skewed open in a smile. "It is north you've been, eh?"

"Indeed so. As far as there are farms, Jorgio."

"Thought so."

In an uneven singsong Jorgio whispered words to the horse. Then he gave Merral a clumsy wink. "Let me stable Graceful here and you and I'll take some tea together."

"Ah, I'm sorry, old friend. I'm afraid I shall have to skip the tea. I've been put on the next freighter out. Twenty minutes. But I'll help you stable her."

"Tut, tut! No tea with me? If you please, you youngsters are too busy by far. Here, lass, give me a hoof. I'll talk to your horse instead." He stroked a flank. "Good girl, good girl."

Suddenly, as if caught by a thought, Jorgio lifted his face up briefly, his brown eyes showing puzzlement. "Do you know, Mister Merral, as I've been praying for you lately?"

"You have?" Merral replied, struck by the intensity in his friend's face. "Well, I value that. I truly do."

Jorgio was now peering at the hoof. "Tut, tut. Ice and sharp rock are nasty things for a hoof. Even with dura-polymer coatings. If they're all like this I'll get new coatings put on 'em. But after Nativity."

He looked up again at Merral, the angle making his face seem even more distorted. "Funny, it was. I haven't been sleeping well lately. Restless. For two weeks now. The other night, last night, I think. Anyway, I'm lying awake in my bed. You've seen my room, haven't you? Nice it is. Cozy; you can see it now. Oh no, you're off away, aren't you? Anyway, middle of the night the King just says to me, 'Jorgio Aneld Serter.' Full name like. So I sits up in bed and says, 'Your Majesty, present and correct!' Well, there's not a lot else to say, is there?"

Sometimes Merral found it hard to know whether Jorgio was trying to make a joke, but this didn't sound like one. "I suppose so," he said, patting his friend on the back. "Not much else indeed. But go on."

Jorgio let the hoof drop to the ground and stood up, screwing his face up as he struggled to remember something.

"So, well, the King, he says, 'That Merral Stefan D'Avanos, he's in a spot of bother right now. I think you ought to pray for him.'

"'Well, right you are, Your Majesty,' I says, and then he's gone. So I starts asking the Most High to look after you. Half an hour I reckon I prayed. Hard work it was, like wrestling with a bear. Not that I've done that, but you takes my meaning. I was in a regular sweat when I finished. I don't know what the bother was." He scratched a crumpled ear. "Never had that happen. You know what it was about?"

"Last night? I was safely asleep indoors last night at the Antalfers. But *wait*. . . ." Something like ice seemed to run up his spine. "When was this? *Last* night?" Merral stared into Jorgio's eyes.

"Aye, last night. . . ."

"You're sure?"

The old man wrinkled his weathered face and bit his bottom lip in puzzlement. Then he grunted. "Tut. No! I'm sorry. It wasn't. It was the night before."

Merral stepped back, feeling as if a chill hand had touched him. "No, it wasn't a bear," he said, suddenly both chastened and grateful. "But it was something. I don't know what it was. And I'm very glad you prayed. Very glad."

For a moment, Jorgio stared at him, as if waiting for an explanation. Merral found himself oddly disinclined to say anything about his dream and suggested instead that they stable Graceful.

Ten minutes later, having said farewell to Jorgio, Merral was still oscillating between puzzlement and thankfulness as he made his way down to the loading bay. There, floodlit beneath the weather shelter, he could see the brick red, faceted bulk of the six-wheeled Light Groundfreighter with the code *F-28* stamped on its side by the Lamb and Stars emblem.

He was striding toward it when his attention was caught by a slender female figure with long black hair tied back walking ahead of him with a strangely familiar pace.

"Ingrida Hallet!" Merral called out.

The woman spun round smoothly and gave a little cry of recognition. "Why! Merral D'Avanos!"

They hugged each other affectionately. Ingrida had been a year above Merral at college, but they had been close friends. Separating himself from her embrace, Merral stepped back and they looked at each other.

"I heard you were here," she said. "I gather you've been riding around up north. Going all right?"

"Fine, but no room to relax. The winters could be warmer, the summers cooler. But what brings *you* here?"

"Ah." She smiled brightly. "You don't know? Of course, you've been out of touch and it's not been posted yet. I've been asked to work here. Forestry Assistant and so on. So I decided to come and look round on my Nativity break."

"Oh, but I thought I'd heard that you were going south. That you'd got the rainforest assignment they have been wanting to fill. I was wrong?"

She shook her head in an amused way and grinned at him mischievously. "Oh, we talked it through. The board thinks this is more suitable. I'm inclined to agree, although this—"she gestured to the farm complex—"will be a bit of a backwater when the enlarged Herrandown village is up and running and the new Northern Forest extension is the front line. No, I think the tropics job requires more than I have got. There's a better candidate."

"I'd be surprised; tropical systems are tough. But I'm sure you'll get on fine here. I like it up north myself."

She gave him the grin again, only this time he felt laughter was just below the surface. "Not too much, I hope."

"Sorry, I don't understand."

"Oh, Merral, you haven't changed. Not a bit! You are the last person to recognize your gifting. *You* are the one they want for the tropical assignment."

In his astonishment, Merral struggled for words, aware that a man in rust-red overalls was waving at him from the side of the freighter.

"Me? This is all news to me. I've always seen it as *your* job."

"No. You are outgrowing here. Ask anybody." She patted him on the shoulder. "Anyway, take it with my blessing, Merral. Do a really great job. Look, that's your driver, you'd better go. Swing by sometime. Love. . . ."

Then Ingrida was gone and the hatch door on the freighter was opening.

The six-wheeler took four hours to cover the one hundred and eighty kilometers to Ynysmant, slowed down by patches of ice on some of the ridges, a track washout, and a herd of golden deer that refused to move. Merral spent most of the time in conversation with the driver, Arent, who was an enthusiast for this particular Mark Nine Groundfreighter, which he'd driven for thirty years. Merral liked enthusiasts of any sort, even if wheeled, winged, or finned engines of transport were not a personal interest.

Yet, in a strange way, Merral was glad of being forced to concentrate on Arent's lengthy discourse on the advantages of the Mark Nine over the old

Mark Eight. There was too much crowding into his tired brain now and he was glad of a relatively simple distraction. The prospect of the tropical forestry posting was staggering. When, a few months ago, he had originally heard about it, he had expressed regret that it hadn't come up two years later when he felt he might have been ready for it. Tropical forestry was held up as the great challenge in his profession, and only those who had proved themselves in temperate or cold realms were asked to serve in it. The saying was that cold or temperate forest work was like juggling with three balls; but with tropical, it was eight. The many more species gave a multitude of interactions, and everything happened so fast. He wondered whether Ingrida had made a mistake. In the meantime, he forced himself to follow Arent's explanation of why it would take at least another twenty years of careful design before it was worthwhile producing the Mark Ten Light Groundfreighter.

They were winding through the beech woods on what Merral knew was the last ridge before Ynysmere Lake when Arent looked upward through the transparent roof panel. "Tell you what, the clouds have cleared and we are ahead of schedule. Let me put her on nonvisual waveband sensing and slow the speed."

The rapid flickering of the tree trunks in the headlights eased. "Now we cut the lights. We should get a great view of the stars and the town."

Merral had seen it done before, but found it as impressive as ever. For a moment everything outside was total darkness and then gradually his adapting eyes made out the stars, high, sharp, and diamond brilliant above the rushing black smear of branches, and ahead over the ridge, the golden beacons of the Gate and the sharp, clear pinpoint that was the gas giant planet Fenniran were clearly visible.

Arent looked upward and spoke in hushed, reverent tones. "Nativity's Eve, Merral. I always feel somehow that high heaven is that bit nearer tonight. But I suppose that'd be the sort of thing you learned folk would smile at?"

"Oh, 'learned folk' indeed, Arent!" Merral laughed. "This night of all reminds us of the folly of that idea. I recollect that it was to shepherds in the fields the angels appeared, not to the wise in Jerusalem. Anyway, I'm not as learned as you are on your F-28."

"True enough."

"And you may well be right, I suppose, Arent. High heaven may be nearer to us tonight—but we have no instruments to measure its proximity." Then, without thinking, he added, "Or that of hell either."

He sensed Arent's face, looking curiously at him in the darkness. "Sorry, Merral. Did you say something?"

"Sort of. . . ." He paused, puzzled at where the words had come from. "But I didn't mean to."

There was a long silence as the road flattened, and then they crested the hill. Ahead and below them in a sea of blackness appeared a cone of tiny twinkling points of silver light, as if some sort of faint human echo of the glory above.

And as he looked carefully at the town of Ynysmant perched on its steep island in the lake, Merral could see how the reflection of the lights shimmered as the lake's dark waters stirred in the wind.

Home, he thought, and the word had a peculiar taste of welcome to it that he felt it had never had before.

Merral left the freighter at the island end of the causeway, thanked Arent, and half walked and half ran up the winding steps into the town. With it being Nativity's Eve there were many groups on their way to parties and concerts, and Merral picked up a sense of excitement in the air.

The lights were on at his house, a narrow three-story unit in the middle of a sinuous terrace with overhanging eaves. Merral pushed open the door, vaguely surprised to find the hall and kitchen empty. There was ample evidence of recent cooking with a tray of small jam cakes on the side table, and the smell made him realize suddenly how hungry he was. Putting his bag down, he took off his jacket and slung it on a chair. He was suddenly aware of feeling tired and sweaty. It had, he decided, been a long day. Eventually the smell of the cakes was too much for him and he helped himself to one, putting it whole in his mouth and finding it as delicious as he had expected. As he stood there, he heard talking in the general room beyond and, swallowing the last cake fragments, pushed the door open.

His mother, dressed in a skirt and blouse patterned with flowers, rose from her chair suddenly at his entry. She gave a little cry of "Merral," came over, and kissed him warmly. As they broke free from each other, he saw behind her a thinly built, dark-skinned man of medium height wearing a neat blue formal suit rising from a chair.

His mother took his arm and stretched it out.

"I'm so *glad* you're back. Merral, let me introduce you to—I think I have the name right—Mr. Verofaza Laertes Enand."

The young man smiled gravely and gave a slight bow. "Indeed," he said. "Verofaza Laertes Enand, *sentinel.* A pleasure."

Merral stared at him, hurriedly trying to wipe crumbs off his lips with his left hand. The name made no sense. There was only one sentinel on Farholme, an old man, and this was not him. Besides which the man's accent was out of the ordinary, but somehow familiar. Merral felt he had always known it.

"Merral Stefan D'Avanos," he said, awkwardly swallowing the last fragments of cake as he shook hands. Then he looked at the guest. *"Sentinel?* Here?" he asked. "But have you replaced old Brenito? He's not . . .?"

The man stood back, his smile slightly awkward, even shy. *He's young,* Merral thought, *probably my age—midtwenties.*

"No, he is alive and well. I have traveled farther than your capital."

Merral realized that he had answered in Communal, not the Farholmen dialect. He was suddenly aware of his mother tugging his arm and speaking to him in a quiet intensity of excitement. But even as she spoke he knew what she was going to say, for he had understood why the accent was familiar and why he had known it since childhood.

"Merral," she said in an awed voice, "he's come from Ancient Earth."

4

Merral stared at the stranger. At college, he had once been in a meeting that had been addressed by someone from Ancient Earth, and he had met pilots and others who had trained there. But he personally had never as much as shaken hands with anybody from there. Indeed now, as he scrutinized the visitor, he felt there was something unusual about him. The suit had a strangely severe line, the black curly hair was cut in a peculiar way, and the rich dark brown skin was darker than any he had seen on Farholme. On their own, these things were merely oddities; taken together they said that the visitor was not from his world.

Merral realized that he was staring too much. "I'm sorry, Verofaza. You have taken me by surprise. . . ."

The other man smiled wryly. "It's Vero. Everyone calls me that. I gather you've been traveling all day. That makes us both travelers."

A kind comment, and one that makes me feel more at ease. He found himself warming to the stranger. "I find it generous that you can put my miserable two hundred or so kilometers in the same category as your three hundred and fifty-odd light-years."

"Nearly four hundred in total. I kept careful count." He gave a little shudder. "The only place they could find was on a long route combination."

"It is a mere twenty million million times my journey."

Vero grimaced vividly. Merral decided he had a very mobile face and that he could make a great clown or mime actor.

"I try not to think of the distances like that, Merral. A light-year is somehow manageable; ten trillion kilometers isn't. Please, why don't we sit down?"

"I'm sorry," Merral said. "I should have asked you."

"It's not a difficulty. And you don't mind me using Communal? I seem to understand your dialect easily enough, but I wouldn't dare try and speak it."

Merral felt that the visitor's warm, deep brown eyes were watching him keenly. "There is no problem. Yes, Farholmen dialect has not yet seriously diverged from Communal. Although there are trends. As a sentinel, I expected you to wear your badge."

"The Tower against the Sky?" He smiled. "Oh, I should do, but I find it a bit of a nuisance. Everybody points you out: 'Look, Mum, there's a sentinel.' It's a tradition—not a rule—to wear it. And I choose not to. But I will wear it tomorrow."

Merral turned to his mother, who was still standing nearby. "Mother, will you not sit with us?"

She shook her head, letting her braided, silver-flecked brown hair bob on her shoulders. "No, no thank you, Merral. I'd *love* to, really. Your father has been delayed at the depot and I really *must* get the rooms ready. And *really,* I have to finish off some things for supper and the meal tomorrow. And would you like something to drink? Perhaps another cake?" She gave him a knowing nod.

Merral, suddenly feeling rather sheepish, wiped his mouth again. "Er, yes. Both please, Mother. I've been traveling since dawn."

She turned to their guest. "Perhaps Vero, a drink of something for you?"

He nodded formally. "Thank you. Just a glass of your excellent water please, Lena."

She bowed slightly, patted Merral on the shoulder tenderly, and left the room.

"Are you fasting?" Merral asked.

The stranger's face acquired a slightly pained look. "Not really. Over the past two weeks I have been through five Gates. And I have found out that I do not like them. I think that my stomach is still several light-years behind in Below-Space and trying to catch up. In fact, I wonder if I will ever be reunited with it."

"You found it unpleasant? People vary, I gather."

"Yes. Very disorienting. Have you ever been though a Gate?"

"I've never even been in Farholme orbit."

"Lucky you." Vero stretched himself back in his chair and flexed his long, smooth brown fingers against each other as if concerned that they were all present and working. "Five Gates in thirteen days, Merral. There was a lot of turbulence between the Nelat Four Gate and Rustiran. You could feel the whole Normal-Space tunnel being buffeted. A weird feeling. And weightlessness wasn't much better. Or takeoffs." He wriggled his face in an almost childlike look of disgust.

Merral found himself enjoying his visitor. "I have lots of questions, you know," he said.

Vero closed his eyes and shook his head slowly, as if trying to fight off a headache. "Ah, that I can imagine. But I'm here—well, in Ynysmant—for three days, and I promise I'll try and answer some at least. In time. Actually, I'm here to ask questions myself."

"You are?"

"Yes."

Merral waited in vain for any further clarification then asked, "What sort?"

Vero flexed his fingers again, stared at them, and then smiled with wide eyes at Merral. "Ah, that is the problem. But my first question is, what sort of journey did you have?"

Merral was just on the point of answering when his mother came back bearing a small wooden tray with two glasses of water and a plate of small cakes. She put them on the low table between the chairs and gave a glass to Vero, who bowed his head in acknowledgement.

"Thank you indeed." Then he took the glass carefully, held it up toward her as if making a toast, and sipped it delicately.

Merral's mother smiled at him. "And it's our *honor* to have you. But, not wishing to interrupt your conversation, I'd better remind you, Vero, that it's not long before you're expected at the house of Former Warden Prendal. There is a party, with a meal and dancing."

"You are right, Lena." Vero glanced at his watch. "And the evening is going. I'd better get ready. Is it far?"

Merral put down his glass. "Ten minutes' walk, a bit more. I'll take you. In say, fifteen minutes?"

"Done."

Somehow, Merral made time in those few minutes for a shower and a change of clothes. He also managed to wonder why there was a sentinel visiting Farholme, why he had arrived here in Ynysmant, and what exactly sentinels did. Then he grabbed his winter jacket and met up with Vero, who was standing self-consciously by the door in a long, thick brown coat that went down to his ankles. Vero caught Merral's glance.

"Ah yes. The coat. Well, I was near the Congo Position when the Sentinel Council suddenly asked me to go. It was all a last-minute rush. So I was actually on the way to the launch site when I realized I'd be arriving here in winter. The only winter coat I could get was one from a very tall Nord-European. It is far too long, isn't it?" He glanced down at it again in an embarrassed way and then looked up at Merral. Suddenly, they both found themselves laughing.

Merral shook his head in mirth. "What a mess, eh, Vero? They send you four hundred light-years to the end of the Assembly through Below-Space five times and with expenditure of enormous amounts of energy, and all with the wrong-sized coat! Oh, I love it!" he chortled.

Vero shook with laughter. "Do you suppose . . . ?" he spluttered, pausing for breath between stifled snorts of laughter. "Do you suppose . . . ? No. . . . It's too funny." Here he suddenly seemed to control himself. He turned to Merral with a perfectly solemn face and, in an intensely serious voice said, "My friend, do you think that perhaps I ought to go back and get one that fits?"

Then the facade of seriousness cracked and he broke out with a croaking laugh. Merral, unable to control himself, burst out into renewed peals of laughter. Eventually he clapped Vero on the back and ushered him out the door. Guffawing with mirth together, they set off up the hill.

By the end of the street they had quieted down enough for Vero to begin asking Merral various questions about Ynysmant, such as how big it was and how long he had lived in it. Apparently satisfied, he then said with a quiet intensity, "Now tell me, Merral, are people happy here?"

At first, Merral wondered whether he had heard the question correctly, then he considered whether it was a joke, and then finally he asked for clarification. "Is that an Ancient Earth question? I mean—excuse me for saying it—it barely makes sense."

Vero stopped in his tracks, obviously thinking hard. "Yes, I know what you mean. But look, are they contented? Do they long for, well . . . what they cannot have?"

Merral heard himself laughing again. "Want what they cannot have? Vero, this may be Worlds' End, but we aren't stupid. I mean, what would a man or woman want with something that was not theirs to have? You'd drive yourself crazy. It'd be like . . . well . . . I don't know—a lake wishing to be a mountain or a bird wanting to be a fish."

For long moments the only sound was their feet on the cobbles and muffled singing from an adjacent house. Then Vero spoke, but this time it was in a puzzled, reflective tone. "See, I don't even know enough to know where to begin. This whole thing is . . ." He sighed. "Very difficult."

They walked on without speaking between the high painted walls of the houses and in and out of pools of light and shadow. Barely audible celebratory music and laughter seemed to seep through windows and doors.

"Vero, why did you come here, to this town, to us?"

"Because it seemed right. My task was to visit here and to write a report. It's my first task as an accredited sentinel."

A cold gust of wind whistled down an alleyway, and Merral was aware of his friend shivering.

"What sort of report?"

There was the faintest of pauses. "On how Farholme is doing. There are specific questions but . . . well, it's very open. Anyway, after I disembarked at

Isterrane two days ago, I visited Brenito, who had made the request for a visit. And he said I ought to start looking around 'from the outside in.' "

"And we are one of the farthest towns out. So you came here?"

A shaft of light caught the dark, lean face, seemingly huddled down in the shelter of the coat's high collar.

"Here. And of the thousand doors it seemed right to knock on that of your house."

"Well, Vero, I hope it was."

"I feel it was. I feel that we are to be friends."

"Yes, I think it will prove to be so."

He led Vero up a narrow brick path that wound round onto a footbridge that brought them high along the side of the hill so that they looked down over the spired and steepled houses. The only illumination now lay in the directed-downward light of the active yellow strips that switched themselves on as they approached and off as they walked away. Above them they could see the stars flung out across the night sky. At the very top of the bridge, Vero put out a hand in front of Merral.

"May we stop a moment please? I would like to see where Earth is."

Merral pointed out where in the Milky Way, if they had had a telescope, they would have been able to see Sol. Vero was silent for some moments, then he leaned back against the brick parapet of the bridge and stared at Merral.

"So much of your world I find familiar. Which is as it should be—the Made Worlds are made to be as much like Earth as they can be. Then suddenly I catch a glimpse of something that reminds me where I am." He shook his head. "And the stars do that all the time. It is almost overwhelming. I can't recognize a constellation. And no moon. Ever."

"Sorry, no visible moon. Just a small invisible Local Gate with enough mass to give the tides to stir our oceans. That's all."

"No, it's not the same. Our moon is something really special, Merral." He sighed. "Yes, I can believe those three-hundred-odd light-years now."

He seemed to shudder. "And tomorrow is Nativity. Strange to think, Merral, this will be the first one I have had away from my family. And on this side of Ancient Earth I could not have gone much farther away. Actually, it's the cold that I find odd. Nativity at home in Africa is always hot."

For a moment Merral said nothing, trying to put himself in the other's shoes, imagining himself transported somewhere with a warm Nativity, strange languages, and alien stars. He could sympathize, and he reached out and put an arm around the stranger.

"I understand." He paused, trying to think of the words. "And yet, friend Vero, if God is infinite what does three-hundred-odd light-years compare to the infinity that is his? And doesn't Nativity itself promise that we will have the Most High with us?"

Vero clasped his arm tightly in return. "You are right, Merral. I'm sorry for expressing myself that way. It was a mastery of my mind by my heart. Perhaps I should explain—it's no excuse—that we sentinels are supposed to be different. In our training we are encouraged to be sensitive, to be intuitive, to be able to listen to what others cannot hear, to see what others cannot see. And it takes its toll. Particularly after five Gates."

Yes, Merral thought, *I can see that it could. And yet, are you so different from me? Perhaps with your training I would be as you. Maybe the way of upbringing I have had has suppressed such feelings, or rather channeled them elsewhere. But deep down I have them, and if I too were all the worlds away from home tonight, then I might well feel as you feel.*

"No, I understand. I really do. But why are you trained that way? Sentinels are not exactly an important thing here. We know you watch and guard, but for what?"

Vero answered thoughtfully. "Your question is delicately ambiguous. 'For what' indeed? For what do we search or for what purpose? Ah. . . ." Here he sighed gently. "Both are valid questions that even we inside the sentinels ask. Or at least I ask. And neither has a simple answer."

Merral felt there was a curious hint of uncertainty or even doubt in his voice.

"Well, tell me as we walk on."

Vero began to speak using a tone of voice that indicated that what he said had been long thought over. "The sentinels were founded in 2112 by Moshe Adlen, just after the end of Jannafy's rebellion. Moshe Adlen was from one of those Jewish families whose conversion to the Messiah marked the very start of the Great Intervention. Incidentally, you do call it the Great Intervention here?"

"Of course. . . . I mean, why not?"

Vero shrugged. "Every so often someone reminds us that what we call the Great Intervention is really a misnomer and wants to change it. The real Great Intervention in human history, they say, occurred when the Most High took on flesh, died, was raised from death, and returned to heaven. You've heard the view?"

"Oh yes. But then you can argue that the events of revival, repentance, and conversion that we term the Great Intervention were, in a way, merely the outworking of that earlier event."

"Exactly; the two-thousand-year-long infancy of the Church finally ended." Vero nodded. "Here too, Farholme seems orthodox. But back to Moshe Adlen—he was a teacher of theology in a university when the Rebellion broke out, and he joined up. He fought against the rebels and was at the final battle at Centauri, and saw what had happened to the colony. He believed that the Rebellion could have been foreseen. He went to Jerusalem and stood before the three symbols the Assembly created to await the Great King: the empty throne, the unworn crown, and the unwielded scepter. And there he took a solemn oath to the Most High that, in as much as it was humanly possible, he would see to it that no such thing should happen again. So he founded an organization, first to help him, and eventually to perpetuate his work."

As the visitor paused, Merral spoke. "Some of this I knew or had been told and had half forgotten. But surely, Vero, we are nearly twelve thousand years on. Do you still hold to the same vision?"

They were now winding round the sides of the gardens of the elevated levels of the town. The light from the houses was splintered through the bare branches of the trees.

Vero answered slowly, the words coming out as if he was thinking afresh about the issue. "A sharp question. There has been a modification in some ways. We hold the standard view that, since the Great Intervention, the founding of the Assembly that followed, and the ending of the Rebellion that marred its infancy, we are in the era of the Lord's Peace as predicted by the prophets of the Old Covenant. The glories of the Most High King are proclaimed already on nigh-on sixteen hundred worlds and a dozen Cities-in-Space. Evil is constrained to a shadow of what it was before the blessed Intervention. We get ill, we suffer loss, we die, but these things do not preoccupy us and mar our existence as they did our distant forefathers. And we believe that this pattern will persist until the end, when the King will return and evil will not simply be bound but will be destroyed and the fabric of the universe will be transformed. But into what, we—as ever—only foresee faintly."

He paused. "That much you on Farholme believe too?"

"Yes. Of course."

"Quite. If anything else were the view here, then Brenito or the Custodians of the Faith, who monitor what we believe, would have warned us of it long ago. Now when the King's Son will return and all things will be renewed is, as it has ever been since the days of the apostles, a mystery. There are two main views. Some say that it may not be long delayed, and there are others that think that the King's Peace may yet continue for many more thousands of years. Some among the sentinels even speculate that the Assembly of the Firstborn may itself not be complete until the whole galaxy is under his name. After all, did not our Lord plainly say that, at the end, the elect would be gathered 'from the ends of the heavens'? Indeed, it may be that in the history of the Assembly, all that we have seen so far may simply be the first chapter."

"Whether we are at the dawn or evening of the Assembly is sometimes discussed on Farholme," Merral replied softly, "but we are mostly too busy about the present to be concerned about a distant future. Such questions are not a specialization here. I personally hold no opinion on the timing of the Messiah's Return other than to await it with certainty and hope."

Vero paused in his stride and gestured up with his arms. "Good. And I hold no fixed opinion. Indeed, there is no contradiction. We plan for a much greater Assembly but we are prepared that the Return and the Remaking may take place before tomorrow dawns. But, on either view, most people consider that rampant evil is a thing of the past."

He turned, and Merral could see his eyes shining in the faint light. "Now here, the sentinels interject a note of caution. You see, we believe that the devil—the enemy—is not dead, just cast down; he is not destroyed, but merely bound. We find no guarantee that, even under these conditions, evil cannot return. We insist that the Assembly must watch, listen, and pray. That is the only task of the sentinels: to watch out for a new rise of evil." He paused. "Well, that's the theory."

"I see," answered Merral, struggling with the concepts. "We are nearly there—it's just up these stairs. I suppose I understand that. But what exactly are you looking for? Do you know, when I first heard about sentinels as a child, I thought you watched out for aliens."

"Aliens?" Vero laughed gently. "No, they have never figured in sentinel thought. Even in Moshe Adlen's day humanity had realized they were alone. The probability of intelligent life elsewhere had become vanishingly small. Bacteria, yes, but nothing else. And everything since has confirmed that view."

"Oh, it was a childish fantasy of mine. But what are you looking for?"

Vero's answer was slow in coming and strangely hesitant when it came, "We do not know. Anomalies, oddities, changes."

"Sounds like everything and anything."

There was a long—and to Merral, very significant—silence before Vero spoke again. "Ah . . . that is the problem."

How interesting. He seems to have his reservations. But Merral felt it would have been ungenerous to pursue the matter and gestured Vero onward.

Soon they turned down a small, narrow street with a single line of trees down the middle and flanked on each side by winding terraces of four-story houses. He began checking the names at the doors, but in the end the sound of the dance music gave away the location.

"Interesting, Vero, but I'm still only a little wiser. Anyway, here we are."

"Hello! Guests!" he called in as he opened the door. Vandra, the former warden's wife, squeezed past a crowd of relatives and neighbors and came down the hall to greet them. In the next few minutes, Merral found himself immersed in a sea of introductions and repeated requests to stay for food and for the dances. The hosts had opened the doors between three adjacent houses to make a single, long, extended room, but even so, it was still full and barely large enough for the dancing. As Vero was introduced, Merral gradually slipped back so that he stood against the wall. There he stood watching as the next dance started. When the dance—a very formal West Menayan one involving two lines of partners and some complex foot movements—had finished, Merral made arrangements for someone to bring Vero back. Then, pleading tiredness, he offered his apologies and left.

Winding his way back home, Merral considered what Vero had told him about the sentinels, noting that even after his answers he actually knew only a little more about why Vero personally was here. From that he moved on to think how strange it must be to spend your life doing something so vague and ill-defined. It all seemed so very different from his own work with its all-too-tangible trees, rocks, and lakes, and only slightly less solid plans and schedules. But it was strange how talking to Vero had made him vaguely desirous of seeing beyond his own world's horizons. Perhaps one day he would have an excuse to go through the Gate. But in the meantime . . .

Here he began to think about the news of the tropics post that Ingrida had told him was to be his, and he was still working out the implications of this when he entered his house.

His father was taking his outdoor shoes off in the hallway. Seeing Merral, he stopped what he was doing and, one shoe on and the other off, hopped over and kissed him. Merral felt his father's beard tickle him, caught the distinctive workshop scent of oil, and rejoiced in the happy memories it brought back.

"Son! My, but it's good to see you! It's been a week."

Merral stood back and they examined each other. *My father looks tired. But then if he's only just finished work, he has a right to.*

His father, as if conscious that his appearance was under review, swept his thin, untidy, and graying hair back and stroked his silver-tinted beard. "Sorry I'm late, but it's been one of those days. Things break down without regard to it being Nativity's Eve."

"Everything all right?" Merral asked, hanging his jacket up.

"Oh, eventually. We had fun repairing a leaking hydrogen tank on an old lifter. A Series Two had a lot of hard use on the delta, so you can imagine the mud. Took off the tank, flushed it, washed it, dried it, tested it, found the hole, fixed it, tested it with nitrogen—fine. So we tested it with hydrogen—fine. Flushed it again, put it back on. Tested it finally with hydrogen again, and what do you know? Well, it leaks! So, we repeated the entire procedure all over again. But anyway, we fixed it by seven o'clock."

My father's tendency for using many words has not deserted him, but I love him for it. "You must be tired," he said.

"A bit. But you've had a long trip yourself. It went well, I take it? How are Zennia and Barrand?"

In a flash, Merral decided that he would not say anything about the difficulties there. Indeed as he thought about them, he now seemed to have trouble discerning what those difficulties were exactly. From here it all seemed such a vague matter. "Oh, everything seems all right with the colony—more or less. It's been a hard winter. They send their love."

"Good, good. Well, you've met our guest. Quite a surprise, eh?"

As he spoke, the door opened and Merral's mother came into the hallway.

"I thought I heard both of you. Stefan *dear,* I do hope you aren't too weary?"

They kissed affectionately and he put his arm around her shoulder, a gesture that always struck Merral as awkward, given his father's shorter height.

"Fine, my dear. And your day went well?"

"*Excellent.* Somehow there were no last-minute crises in Housing Allocation this year; no one's long-lost relatives with six children suddenly deciding to spend Nativity in Ynysmant. Mind you, I always think it so seasonal to have housing crises at this time of the year. There's such a precedent. And I miss the satisfaction of sorting them out. But one can quite live without them. . . . Supper is ready."

As they ate, Merral listened to the news of the town and of his three sisters, all of whom were now married and lived away with growing families. Feeling tired, he was content to listen to the conversation rather than to lead it. Whether it was because of his tiredness or for some other reason, it seemed to him that he had never seen his father and mother with such clarity. It was almost, he fancied, as though they had portrait frames around them. His mother, apron now off and hair flying loose around her face, was apparently all brightness and glitter to the extent that you might have thought she was shallow minded. Then abruptly, as when a crack in a brightly painted surface reveals pure metal underneath, she would make some comment that revealed a hard, acute mind. Merral thought it strange that she and the much less impulsive Zennia were sisters.

Merral turned his attention to his father. This evening he was, as ever, a source of verbose—if amiable—stories and anecdotes, large portions of which seemed irrelevant and some of which were so diffuse that he lost his way. But here beneath the dryness, grace and good sense gleamed at depth. And Merral saw that while each partner saw the weaknesses of the other—and, he presumed, themself—they were accepted in a spirit of amused love. Merral was also conscious, but less clearly so, that the same benevolent acceptance was turned toward him.

Over dessert they discussed the guest. His father was enthusiastic. "Well,

Merral, I must say, I think it's great. With the girls away we easily have a spare place for tomorrow."

His mother leaned over. "Stefan *dear*. Of course we have a place for Vero. We could take half a dozen guests. And there's *plenty* of food. I've made sure. *Especially* for Vero. No one is going to come all that distance and go back hungry."

Merral, trying not to laugh with happiness, was moved to suggest that it was probable that Vero wouldn't be going back immediately after the meal and that he was unlikely to be short of food after Nativity lunch. "Indeed, it's problems of overeating that are more likely."

As if prompted, his father started wiping his dish with a fragment of bread, only to catch a look of disapproval—tempered by merriment and fondness—from his wife. He put the bread down, winked at her, and turned to Merral. "I hope you get on with our Vero. He's a long way from home and they all say that the Made Worlds are strange for those born and bred on Ancient Earth. 'Disturbingly like but unlike,' someone has said. All that distance must take a toll too, and I can give that floating from Gate to Gate business a miss. If you do have to do it, say to move somewhere else—like a new world—that's all right, but it's a dreadful way of transport. I prefer my feet on the ground, or at least on wheels. But, charity apart, he must know a lot. There may be some question over how valuable sentinels are, but there's no doubt that they train their people well."

"But Father," Merral asked, "why is he here?"

His father stabbed at a stray bit of cheese with his knife. "The problem, my son, with foresters as a profession is that they don't deal nearly enough with machines. With machines you have to be precise, verbally logical. 'Why is he here?' is inadequately structured. In a word—it is ambivalent. Do you mean, *on* Farholme, *in* Ynysmant, or *at* our house?"

"All of them, my good and respected father. I believe in economy of words."

"I can't think where you got that from!" interjected his mother with a chortle.

His father smiled with good humor. "Thank you, my dear. Vero's bright, highly thought of, and just finished well above average in his tests. Incidentally, Merral, I have been hearing excellent things about your plans for the northeastern forest advance. Oh yes—economy of words—so I won't tell what I heard. Anyway, as I understood it, old Brenito said that there was something that needed looking at in Farholme—or words to that effect—and so out he comes and here he is."

"Well, I wonder what needs looking at?"

His father shrugged his shoulders. "On that I have no idea."

"Still," Merral said, "I suppose that answers a little bit more of my questions."

"The rest you will have to ask him. And if he is so minded he may give you an answer. Now let me make some coffee."

They had coffee sitting round the table and, after a brief and unsuccessful attempt by his father to try to interest them in the detailed scope of the planned new workshops, his mother spoke. "Merral, your father and I had a *lovely* meal with George and Hania Danol. . . ."

Ah, I wondered when that was going to come up.

"I used to know George years ago," his father said. "Funnily enough, he was an engineer on the first of the workshops. I suppose we shall soon have to call them the *old* workshops. . . . Sorry, my dear, I digress."

She patted his hand, cleared her throat, and started again. "And, *of course*, the conversation soon turned to you and Isabella. Did we approve? Did we consider that your relationship should be approved, so that you could proceed to making a commitment to each other? Well, it was a *very long* series of conversations."

His father coughed slightly. "There was a lot of appreciation of your talents. . . ."

"In fact, Merral, *that* was the only problem." His mother paused. "Oh dear, really, I'm not doing this well. *Problem* isn't the word. You see, at the end of it all, both we and George and Hania felt . . . well . . . undecided. Isabella is a super girl and very solid and stable. She has such a gift with children, and it's no wonder Education rates her highly. If your life were to lie here in Ynysmant or even just in eastern Menaya alone then she would be just the person. And yet we all felt that your path may run, as it were, higher and steeper. To Isterrane. Or beyond."

Or to the south, Merral thought, trying to take in what his mother was saying. "Well I suppose that's true," he answered. "I am happy enough here, but I do not know what is in store for me."

"Quite so," answered his father, sipping his coffee and staring at his son.

"So," his mother said slowly, "there was much to discuss. For ourselves, we would love nothing more than to have you and Isabella commit to each other and to have you married and living near us, especially with the girls so far away. But we are *very* concerned that the path that is yours to tread may be too much for Isabella to bear. Perhaps in a year the way will be clearer; after all, she is only twenty-three. And she is changing." She sighed and looked at his father.

His father nodded. "So, Merral, to come to the point. Rather unusually, not one of the four of us felt it right to take any steps in that direction. At least, not at the moment. We decided to review things again next summer. I hope that isn't too disappointing."

Merral felt shaken by a confusion of emotions. *So, they are not going to approve that Isabella and I make a commitment to each other. We stay as close friends but not—at least not yet—exclusively committed to each other. How strange. I had somehow assumed that they would approve.*

I see the reasoning, and I suppose, reluctantly, I approve it. Commitments and engagements are always with parental approval; that is how things always have been.

His father was talking again, thoughtfully and with a soft intensity. "You see, Merral—and it's a funny thing to say about Ynysmant—we have become here a place on the edge of maturity, perhaps, you might even say, of stability. The weather's not as predictable as it could be, and there's always the odd earthquake and ice storm, but it's as safe and cozy a place as anywhere in the Made Worlds now. Why, I was hearing only today that the engineers say the Gulder Swamps are now stable enough that they can begin the new monorail route to Halmacent City next year. No more twenty-hour bus trips on bad roads. Anyway. . . . Oh yes, *this*," he waved his arms around, "is Isabella's world. But we are not convinced it is yours. You see—oh, how can I express it?"

He put his cup down, got to his feet in agitation, and paced over to the end of the room. There he swung round to face them and leaned stiffly back against the wall, his face a picture of concentration. Merral saw his mother's eyes following him with understanding.

"I've never said this to you before, Merral, for fear I was misreading the signs. Son, you're a rare breed. At times I wonder if you really are my offspring. Of course you are, and if I search hard within me I can see bits of you in me. Or the other way about. Something like that. But in you everything has come right. You have the vision, the energy, the drive. You can lead men and women too. The youngest forestry team leader ever in Menaya, I gather. I have no idea where you will end up. But I doubt, very much, you will stay a forester here for long."

There was an expectant silence. Merral bowed his head to signify acceptance. *I am surprised and yet unsurprised.*

"Father and Mother," he replied, choosing his words carefully, "I thank you for the care and consideration that has gone into your decision. I am both honored and humbled by the confidence you have in my abilities. I trust that I will not disappoint you. With regard to Isabella, while a part of me might wish otherwise, I appreciate both your judgment and your motives."

His mother grasped his hand with great warmth. That gesture seemed to close the matter, and after some minutes of general conversation, Merral, feeling suddenly tired, decided to go to bed. After kissing his father and mother good night, he went upstairs to his bedroom.

His head was reeling with a hundred thoughts, most of them contradictory, centering on Isabella and on his future. But he felt that, in some strange way, things had worked out. The message from Ingrida about his pending appointment had prepared his mind for his father's views on his career. Equally, being with Vero had aroused within him a renewed desire to see beyond the horizons of this one infant world. No, he could indeed see the wisdom in what they had said. He would have to talk more with Isabella; there was time, and you didn't rush into any of the stages that lead to marriage. From those thoughts he drifted into thinking about what it would be like to work in the tropical ecosystems and whether they were as hot as everyone said.

However, as he was undressing for bed, a strange, unsettling notion came to him about something else. It was so unnerving that he stopped still, his shirt half on and half off, trying to deal with it. Two things had come together. First, Vero had said that the only task of the sentinels was to search for a return of evil and had implied that he had been hastily summoned. Second, according to his father, Brenito had called for someone, saying there was something that needed looking at on Farholme. Now, if you put the two ideas together you got—the fear that evil was breaking out on Farholme.

His mind rebelled at the thought. It was too staggering for words. After eleven thousand years the sentinels were still looking for evil. And surely now and here wasn't likely to be the time or place. No, the obvious answer was simple but sad. Brenito was old and failing in his wisdom, and Vero had been brought here on a wasted journey. After all, if it had been seriously thought on Ancient Earth that evil was breaking out in Farholme, then they wouldn't have sent out someone so young and inexperienced.

Would they?

5

Next morning Merral awoke to the clamor of trumpets and drums. He lay in bed for some moments listening to the fanfares rolling down from Congregation Hall and echoing over the rooftops, streets, and courtyards of Ynysmant. Then, as every year, there came the answering trumpet blasts and drumrolls from the Gate House and the flag stand on the promontory.

"Nativity Morn," he whispered to himself, quietly rejoicing in both the meaning and the familiarity of the day.

As the fanfares echoed and counter-echoed across the town, Merral rose, drew aside the thick insulating curtain, and opened the window. He shivered briefly in the fresh air and then leaned his head out. The winter's sun was shining obliquely out of a clear sky over the orange-and-brown-tiled roofs, turrets, and copper green spires, leaving the narrow, winding streets below in shadow. From the highest towers and spires, flags—mostly of scarlet and gold—fluttered gently in the breeze and, as he watched, others were raised to join them. Down beyond the roofs, Merral could see the wave-rippled dull gray waters of Ynysmere Lake, with white gulls wheeling over it and catching the sun. Far beyond, still hazy in the weak morning light, lay the grays and greens of the rolling hills that stretched northward.

Merral stared into the distance, hearing the fanfares and drumrolls rise to passionate ringing climax and then die away. After a few moments' silence, from down by the promontory the tolling of bells great and small began, sending pigeons flying skyward. As the sound swept through the town, other bells of different pitches and timbres joined in, until Ynysmant seemed awash with their joyful pealing. Slowly, one by one, the trumpets and percussion sounded, adding new levels and colors of sound. Intoxicated by the music, Merral just stood and immersed himself in the surging and swelling of the melody until, slowly and irresistibly, the music built itself through a series of crescendos up to a final culmination of exultant blasts of trumpets over a thunderous echoing roar of drums and tolling bells. Slowly, the music died away in ebbing ripples of sound until finally the silence was broken only by the gentle flapping of the flags in the breeze.

Merral stood savoring the dying echoes of music and the cries of the gulls as they swung over the rooftops until he was suddenly aware that, even in his night-suit, he was cold. He closed the window and returned to his bed. There he knelt and spent time in praise for all that the festival meant. The tradition of missing breakfast on Nativity Morn to spend time in private worship meant that he was in no need of haste.

Indeed it was more than half an hour later that, dressed in his best brown jacket and red trousers, Merral went downstairs. He took the stairs so silently that none of the three people in the general room heard him, and he paused on the landing to look at them. His father, looking splendid in the primrose-and-silver tunic of the neighborhood band, was polishing his trombone. His mother, dressed in an ample dress of a rich purple fabric, was pacing the room, staring at a vocal score she held and silently mouthing words. Vero, dressed in a rather drab gray suit in which he seemed ill at ease, was seated at the table running a finger under some words in the old family Bible.

As he came down, they shared Nativity greetings among each other, and his mother put her score down on a table and came over and kissed him. His father, for once with immaculately groomed hair and tidy beard, beamed affectionately. "Very nice, Merral. Very nice, you look. Are you singing this morning?"

"Not in the choir. Being up north meant that I had to miss the rehearsals; next year maybe."

"A pity, but anyway, we need someone to accompany Vero up to the hall."

Vero glanced at Merral with an apologetic grin. "The kind people of Ynysmant have asked me to do one of the readings. I've pleaded shyness and an uncouth accent. But it's no good."

Merral caught sight of the badge on the suit: a gold circle around a stone tower rising up against a blue sky.

Merral's mother caught his eye. "He's doing the Luke 2. It's very appropriate, son. About the shepherds watching their flocks. Just like sentinels."

Vero wagged a finger theatrically. "Ah, but I trust you note, Lena Miria, that what the shepherds were watching for, was not what actually happened." He paused thoughtfully. "In other words, they were watching for the wrong thing. It is indeed appropriate, for it is a humbling passage for sentinels."

Merral's father spoke quietly, his words slow. "Well, I must say, things do have a way of catching us all out. Talking of which, Merral, your mother and I must be down at the Lower Square in ten minutes. So you two follow on down. I've made sure that they are reserving a place for both of you up near the front of the hall. It's easier for Vero to get up and read."

When his parents had gone, Merral sat down facing his guest.

Vero grinned happily at him and stretched out his legs in a gesture of relaxation. "Your parents have made me very welcome."

"Of course. Now tell me, did you have a pleasant time last night?"

"Ah yes. Everyone was so busy wanting to talk to me that I didn't have to eat anything. I had no idea that merely being from Ancient Earth was enough to make me a celebrity."

"Well, we are a long way out."

"Yes, so I realize. The end of the line. I feel there should be a big sign out there in space. 'You are now leaving the Assembly. May the angels go with you!'" He smiled. "So, my stomach and I have been finally reunited. What about you? Did you get a good night's sleep?"

"Good, although I had an interesting discussion with my parents that I'm thinking through."

Vero leaned back in his chair, his face attentive. "Really? May I ask what about?"

"By all means. I was expecting them to approve that my friendship with a girl named Isabella Hania Danol go to commitment. But rather to my surprise, they feel that—at the moment—they cannot make any such decision. So, it's all up in the air for six months."

"Oh?" There was a look of sharp inquiry. "Have they changed their mind about the girl?"

"No. It's that . . . well, it's odd. . . . They think that I may be moving on from here and that she may not be so well suited to such a move. They see me as a frontiersman or something."

"I like that!" Vero smiled. "I think of everyone here as a frontier person. But are you?"

"A frontiersman? Well, I'm happy in my job. I could want nothing more. But we shall see. I am open to the will of the Most High."

Vero nodded. "Well said. Incidentally, everyone speaks highly of you. Or they did last night."

My reputation again. How can I escape it? Or should I even try?

"Anyway," Vero continued, "there's no approval about you and this young lady. Not unheard of. But how do you feel about it?"

"Well, odd, Vero. You see, it raises all sorts of issues. But I suppose they have a point. I am fond of Isabella; we have a close friendship, and I would have liked it to have gone deeper. But I accept their views."

"Of course. Is she in Forestry or Forward Planning?"

"Isabella? No, she's an educational advisor. She monitors the progress of twelve- to fourteen-year-olds against Assembly standards. You know the sort of thing?"

"Indeed. I find it a very interesting subject."

"Well, I'm not sure I do. But it hardly has anything to do with being a sentinel, does it?"

Vero gave a brief smile and uttered the faintest of sighs. "Moshe Adlen said that sentinels were never to overlook anything. Which is fine in principle, but tough in practice. But one model for how we think is this: Imagine the Assembly as being a complex but beautifully balanced mechanical machine going at a vast speed. Like, say, a hydrogen turbine. Now if, within that machine, one part was to suddenly grow even slightly larger, what would happen?"

Merral threw his hands apart. "Explosive disintegration."

"Exactly. So it is with the Assembly: Stability and balance are vital. And the Assembly has within it a number of mechanisms for ensuring that no part gets larger than it should. One of those mechanisms is education. Through it the Assembly tries to make sure that no world gets unbalanced, perhaps by becoming all artistic or all scientific. It's hard, but things like this are partly our concern too. On one model, as the Assembly grows, the more probability there is that a minor imbalance could become catastrophic. Hence a sentinel's interest in all stabilizing mechanisms."

"I see. Well, you may have a chance to meet Isabella."

"I hope so. But take heart. I'm sure it will all work out." He smiled sympathetically. "Of course, I can say this because we sentinels normally never marry before our early thirties. So, I have all this ahead of me." He furrowed his forehead. "Although that too is something that I have asked questions about."

"Do you like being a sentinel?"

There was a pause. "My likes are immaterial. I was born to the job, as was my father and so on before him."

"Do you question it?"

Merral caught a sharp, thoughtful glance from his companion. "Yes, I do sometimes." He paused. "Not seriously, of course. That would be akin to the sin of grumbling and worthy of investigation itself. But I do ask questions. One of my lecturers said to me: 'Verofaza, as someone committed to preventing rebellion, you do a very good job of imitating a rebel.' I have a reputation. If it was not a disrespectful thought, I would say they had sent me to tame me. You can imagine it, can't you? 'What shall we do with Verofaza Enand?' 'Oh, I know—let's ship him off to Worlds' End.'"

Merral laughed. "But what do you question?"

There was a delicate, almost embarrassed, laugh. "I thought it was me who was supposed to ask the searching questions! But . . . " Vero seemed to choose his words carefully. "You see, in all our time, now nearly four hundred generations of sentinels, we have sat and watched and listened and—"

"Found nothing?"

Vero's head seemed to nod almost imperceptibly in agreement. "More or less. Some argue that evil was trying to break through in the trouble on The Vellant in 12985. It was certainly a very odd malaise, a whole community seized by paranoia and delusions. But we alerted the Council of High Stewards in time."

"What happened there? I've not heard of it in the history files."

"It never made it there. They rotated the population out, checked the air and water, and reviewed the diets. Then things settled down."

Merral felt that there was a rough and uncomfortable edge to Vero's answer. "So, were the sentinels right?"

There was a long pause, as if Vero was making a painful choice. "The currently prevailing view, which is—I think—the correct interpretation, is that the problem was primarily biological. And not spiritual." He gave a quiet little awkward chuckle. "You are thinking it is not much to show for a hundred and seventeen centuries of labor, is it?"

"Well, I suppose I was."

"I would—I think—find it hard to disagree. And I refuse to talk about some of the other cases we have gotten involved in." He shook his head firmly. "The toad plague on Saganat. The library anomalies on Tegranatar. The so-called psychic triplets of Limaned. Best forgotten. Please!"

"I see. But, Vero, surely you shouldn't question what you do? If you are called to do something, then you do it. Whatever happens—results or not. Here on the Made Worlds we build and plan and sow, but we do not know whether or not we will be successful."

"Ah, well said." Vero smiled ruefully. "Oh, I suppose the last two weeks of travel have made me question my vocation a little more."

"Who knows—perhaps your vigilance has been a factor in the preservation of the Lord's Peace."

"A useful rebuke. *Perhaps* indeed. We do not know."

Merral heard, far away, echoing up through the streets, the renewed sounds of percussion and brass. "Time to go. You'd better get your coat. The weather looks nice and the forecast is good, but you never know."

"It is proverbial. 'Beware the weather in the Made Worlds.'"

Outside the house the street had become crowded with people dressed in their colorful best and with an air of exuberant noisiness. All the neighbors wanted to make Vero's acquaintance, and many people on the other side of the street pointed him out to their children. Gradually the sound of the procession became louder and the talking in the crowd died away to be replaced by an eager silence. All eyes turned expectantly to the end of the street. Suddenly, amid raucous laughter, two dogs raced around the corner, wheeled briefly around to look at what was following them, and hurtled up the street, egged on by the cheers and whoops of the crowd. After them, but in a far more dignified manner, came the procession. Three flag bearers led the way, the first held aloft the great Lamb and Stars banner of the Assembly; the next the gleaming blue sphere on a black field for Farholme; and the third Ynysmant's flag, the stylized cone of buildings above a blue lake. After them came the first of the uniformed musical groups, supplied this year by the music college, and following them, the first singers. Three green gravity-modifying sleds borrowed from Agriculture followed, bearing those who by reason of age, pregnancy, or injury could not walk with the procession. After them came his father's band, and Merral and Vero were rewarded by a wink over the trombone. Walking behind them were the first long lines of townsfolk, more flags and banners, and then his mother's choir. Eventually it was time for their street to join the procession. Merral and Vero fell in with the other families.

Half an hour later, they were filing into the vast space of Congregation Hall on the top of the ridge. Merral found the seats allocated to them, scanning the crowd as he did for Isabella. There was no sign of her, but as the hall was such a tumult of people he felt it was not surprising. As he settled into his seat he noticed that Vero was looking around at the roof and walls with an expression of unease. Their eyes met.

"Those are high-load beams. And the doors are airtight and sealable." His voice was low and curious. "A refuge?"

"Of course it is," Merral replied in surprise, but it was only as he answered that the significance of the question registered. "Oh, sorry, Vero. I forgot you're from the only planet that doesn't need them. Welcome, inhabitant of Ancient Earth, to one of the Made Worlds. Yes, it's a refuge, with two months' food, air, and water for the whole town underneath us and a landing zone on the roof."

"I see," Vero said, his voice somber. He looked around pensively.

It's strange to think that it's new to him, Merral reflected, *when it's one of the first things we learn in the Made Worlds. That it may all go wrong and we may find ourselves huddled in here for weeks, breathing, eating, and drinking our recycled wastes while they get the rescue shuttles in through the Gate. And we always know that sometimes even refuges may not be enough.*

"Do you know much about Yenerag, Vero?"

"You read my mind. Standing in a refuge cannot fail to remind me of Yenerag. A thousand years after the planet's core failure, and the volcano eruptions that buried sixteen cities in ash—*sixteen*—in three days. Fifty thousand people remain entombed in Yenerag's refuges until our King of kings returns."

Merral shifted in his seat, feeling in some way that such thoughts were unworthy of Nativity Day.

"It could all go wrong, couldn't it?" Vero said suddenly.

"Yes, we live with that reality." Then a thought came to Merral. "But Nativity helps."

"How so?"

"The universe is so vast and unforgiving that the only way this whole venture of ours—spreading ourselves over thousands of light-years—makes sense is if God is indeed with us."

"A fair point."

Suddenly, with an increasing rapidity, silence descended on the hall. From the floor three people took the stage and stood still, every eye on them. Merral prepared his heart for worship. Then, away behind them at the door of the hall, the trumpets sounded four loud, open chords and, with the echoes dying away, the congregation stood for the invocation.

Almost two hours later the benediction ended the service. Slowly people got to their feet and began to talk and embrace one another.

Merral turned to Vero. "I hope that wasn't too strange for you?"

Vero shook his head gently and returned a warm smile. "No, that was fine. It seems to me that there's nothing wrong with your services."

Merral wondered whether there was supposed to be and was trying to phrase a question on those lines, when someone came to Vero and introduced himself, and then a moment later Merral's attention was occupied by an old school friend. He had just finished his conversation a few minutes later, when he felt a hand gently grasp his elbow.

"Happy Nativity, Merral D'Avanos!"

Merral turned to see Isabella at his side. How typical of her to slip up to him so unnoticed. They looked at each other, and he noticed how her long gray-blue jacket seemed to offset her dark, almost black, eyes.

"And to you, Isabella Danol. I was looking for you earlier."

"I was at the back." Isabella brushed a strand of her long, straight black hair away from her face. "The Earther who read—the one who is staying with you, I missed his name—Vera something, wasn't it?"

"Vero. It's short for Verofaza. I hadn't realized till I met him that on Ancient Earth men's names can end in *A*. 'Verofaza Laertes Enand, sentinel' is how he introduces himself. Yes, he was one of a number of surprises yesterday."

"I can guess one of the others," she answered, a hint of regret darkening her soft voice.

"Yes, Isabella. My parents told me when I got back. I'm still thinking that one over, but what with Vero and the service today, I'm afraid I haven't really digested it. Six months' wait before approval."

Merral looked at her, realizing that she was revealing no emotion in her expression. *She wouldn't here, and not so soon.* It would take something like an hour's walk in the park to find out what she really thought.

Then she spoke again, her voice businesslike. "If then. But I understand. Do you have any first reactions?"

"Well . . . actually, thinking about yesterday, Vero was the second of three surprises. We were third. The first was fairly reliable news that I am going to be given a tropics posting." He watched her face as he said it, but other than the faintest lifting of a fine dark eyebrow, she kept any feelings hidden.

"You'd like that, wouldn't you?"

She knows me so well. "It's a challenge. Very demanding and horribly hot, especially if it's Umbaga or Faraketha. Oh, I haven't really thought about that news either. But it does seem that my path may be away from Ynysmant before long."

Isabella said nothing immediately but nodded gently. When she did speak it was in a voice that he could barely hear over the chatter in the hall. "Our parents seem to have assumed that this sort of thing might happen." Isabella joined her delicate fingers together in front of her mouth. She might have nodded, but if so it was so faintly that Merral couldn't be sure whether she had.

"We will talk more of it another time," he added, thinking, *Isabella, it's so hard to read your emotions even though I know you very well. It's as if I have to tune my senses to maximum to pick up the signals you give out.*

She smiled delicately. "Yes, I'm sure we will. And I'd like to met Vero if I can."

"Of course. He wants to meet you. But any particular reason why?"

There was a moment's hesitation. "I have a certain professional curiosity, Merral. There is a school of thought that says that Ancient Earthers and Made Worlders have differing psychologies. Actually everyone agrees on that—it's just how far the differences go. Made Worlders are more assertive and outgoing but at the same time less secure. Partly that is society, partly it is environment."

"I've heard that, but you aren't going to profile him here?"

"No! Of course not!" She laughed. "But it would be nice to talk to him."

"Well, come on, I'll introduce you."

They walked to where Vero was talking with a young man. At a suitable point Merral made the introductions, to which Vero responded with the utmost formality and a slight bow. Isabella smiled at him. "I hadn't realized Ancient Earth had so much civility."

Vero smiled shyly at her. "It hasn't really, but training instilled in us the idea that in a strange culture it is better to be overformal than the opposite."

"And we are a strange culture?"

Vero gave an oblique grin to Merral. "No, madam, not entirely."

They all laughed, and Isabella turned to Vero. "Have you found Nativity here as you expected it to be?"

Vero paused, thinking through the answer. "I can answer both yes and no. I had assumed it would be like home and in some ways it is like that. But there are differences. For example, with us there is silence on Nativity Morn until we are assembled. And there are other things."

As he went on and listed differences, Merral found himself standing back and treating the conversation as if he were a spectator. *It is interesting how Isabella is able to draw out of Vero what she wants.* He watched how she kept her intent, almond-shaped eyes on him and how she encouraged him with the slightest movements of her head.

Merral's thoughts were interrupted by a member of the Team-Ball squad he played for who wanted to pass on news of a match that he had missed. When they parted after ten minutes or so, Merral realized that the hall was now nearly empty. He walked over to where Isabella and Vero were still deep in conversation.

"Sorry to interrupt, but, Vero, we must go."

"You are quite right." He gave a little bow. "Isabella, I hope we meet again."

"And I too. Merral, you will be in touch soon?"

"Of course."

As Merral and Vero walked down from the hall in silence, Merral felt that his new friend seemed deep in thought.

"You had a good discussion with Isabella?" he asked.

"Yes. I think, though, she found out more about me than I did about her."

"Well observed. She is both an acute observer of others and a private person herself."

"I can believe that. A striking face—but you know that. Her family isn't recently from Earth? I mean in the last five generations?"

"No, Farholme for four generations on both sides. Antakaly before that on her father's side, I think; Marant on her mother's. Why do you ask?"

"Because out on the worlds, most racial genes have been fairly well diluted and yet, at a glance, she appears to have fairly pure Chinese features. It's more typical of Earth. Did you know that?"

"That on Ancient Earth there had been much less intermarriage across the races? Yes, I'd heard that. I mean, you are much darker than anyone I know on Farholme."

Vero raised an eyebrow in amused acknowledgement. "It has been pointed out. Well, it removes the temptation to go disguised among you. Anyway, Isabella asked some penetrating questions."

"She would do that. And what was the hardest she gave you?"

Vero shook his head gently. "Ah, you have something in common. She asked whether I had found what I came for."

Merral looked sideways at his companion. "To which you said . . . ?"

"To which I said . . . 'No, and I'm no longer sure what I'm looking for.'"

"That sounds bad."

"Perhaps. But then if it isn't here, then not to find it is surely no bad thing."

"I suppose not."

"I am on the point of coming to a decision. But I need to think more about it. I will talk more about this to you later."

They strode on and Merral caught his companion glancing up at the sun.

"You look puzzled, Vero," he said.

"Disoriented. It's just slightly wrong; it's too red."

"Yes, our sun is slightly cooler than Sol. You'll adjust."

"Maybe. Do you ever call it 'Alahir'?"

"As in 'I see Alahir is setting'?" Merral laughed. "Hardly. In formal astronomy, maybe, but to us it's just the sun. Makes sense to me."

Vero shrugged. "Yes, it makes sense. We never call our sun 'Sol,' except under the same circumstances. But I find it hard. I suppose it is as if you were a child and your mother died and your father married again. You might have a hesitation about calling the new woman 'Mother.'"

Merral felt that the observation revealed how deeply Vero felt that he was away from home.

They walked down the west steps and Merral asked his guest whether he had appreciated the service.

Vero paused. "Yes, it was very good."

"I vaguely noted that you were paying careful attention to what was going on."

"Yes. Well, I suppose I had thought that if there was anything untoward, it would show itself here."

"And it didn't?"

Vero seemed to bite his lip. "I saw, heard, and felt nothing to raise an alarm. It was reverent, orthodox, and all the rest. As you would expect."

"You seem almost disappointed."

He shook his head. "No, on the contrary, I suppose I am relieved. But I am puzzled. Anyway, I'll discuss that later." He paused. "Incidentally, the choir was very good. I'm gifted—if that is the word—with perfect pitch, and a failure to hit the right note hurts. But it was painless on that account. A credit to Farholme."

"I'll pass it on. Now we'd better hurry or we will be late for the meal."

Much of the rest of the day was spent in festivities and eating. There was an apparently endless round of visits of friends, relatives, and innumerable children, and numerous rounds of food and drink. Then there was the time of giving presents. Merral gave his father a new map and his mother a brooch and received sweets and a scarf in return. There were any number of family stories, and presumably because of Vero, almost any incident even vaguely concerned with Ancient Earth that had happened in the last five generations was brought up. Surprisingly, the one everyone found funniest was that of his father's Great-Aunt Margarita, much given to precise and painstaking management of every detail of her affairs, who at a very advanced age had finally managed to travel to see her family on one of the worlds on the other side of the Assembly. On the way back she had found the strain too much and had gone Home to the Lord without warning. But as she had been such a quiet passenger and much given to sleeping, it was many hours before anybody noticed she had stopped breathing, with the result that the death certificate had written on it under "Location" the words, *Not known within fifty light-years.*

Then there were games, including a long and noisy one called Cross the Assembly. Vero revealed, with a certain awkwardness, that when he played it on Earth, everybody hated getting the Farholme card because you could never get to anywhere from it and it was so far from a decent Gate node. The news that, even in games, Farholme had a reputation as Worlds' End was greeted with a great deal of amusement.

Sometime about nine Merral found himself yawning. He felt he had not fully recovered from his long and tiring northern trip and, making apologies, he went upstairs to his room. As he began to undress he put his diary on the table and noted that a nonurgent text message had been transmitted an hour ago. He flicked it on and read the message as it slid across the screen.

```
Merral,
The Rechereg choral went fine. I hope you enjoy the attached
performance. I did use Miranda Cline after all.
Give my love to your family,

Happy Nativity,
Barrand Antalfer
```

There was a sound file attached, and switching it through the room speakers, Merral began to play it as he rinsed his face in the basin and put on his night-suit. He was about to switch it off when there was a tap at the door.

It was Vero. "Not asleep then? Good. Look, sorry to interrupt, but I was going to tell you that I have decided to leave tomorrow." He paused. "Wait—

I know this music." He started waving his fingers slowly in time to it, his face a study in concentration. Suddenly his face acquired a look of recognition. "Of course! Rechereg's *Choral Variations on an Old Carol.* The old carol being the truly ancient 'Child of Mary, Newly Born.' Very fine. Where did you get the recording?"

Merral, his tiredness gone, sat on his bed and gestured to the chair opposite. "Please. My uncle up at the Forward Colony at Herrandown sent it to me today. He did it himself."

Vero nodded appreciatively. "A good job. Re-createds?"

"'Fraid so. They can barely make a string quartet up there. Some good names. Shall I play it back from the beginning?"

"No, tempting though it is. But I wouldn't mind a copy."

"No problem. There are all the details on the file."

Merral switched the music off and ordered the file to be copied.

"Thanks," said Vero. He looked around the room and gestured to a small glass egg perched on a stand on the table. "A personal creation of yours?"

"Yes," Merral said. "It's a tree."

Vero stared at him. "I've known aquaria, fantasy cities, snowscapes, but a single tree?"

Merral gestured at it. "It's unique. I call it a castle tree. There's a spare pair of glasses there. Put them on and let me show you."

Merral found his imaging glasses on the shelf above his bed and put them on. "Log on to castle tree; real time," he ordered, and in seconds the darkness of the lenses cleared, and Merral saw himself near the top of a low hill. The sky above was a brilliant pale blue, and all around, stretching as far as he could see, lay long, dry, brown grass buffeted under the force of a wind he could neither feel nor hear. At his feet was a bare stone surface etched with the words *Castle Tree; Merral Stefan D'Avanos; Farholme. Simulation 4.2b. Elapsed Real Time: 26401.3 hours. Elapsed Simulated Time: 52021.2 years.*

A soft, glistening light at his left showed him that Vero had joined him.

"I see no tree." Merral found the room acoustic of Vero's voice strangely inappropriate with the open scene around him.

"Lock your position with me."

Merral touched the glasses frame and accelerated forward, flying over the blur of the grass toward the crest of the hill. He stopped dead at the summit and heard a gasp from beside him.

Perhaps a kilometer away from him a mass, like some vast broad tower, rose up into the sky. It was pale gray and speckled with green and the summit was strangely serrated as if made up of a thousand spires.

"What is it?" Vero said, his voice ringing with incredulity. "A building? It's enormous."

"It's a tree. But I felt it looked like a castle; hence the name. Do you think it looks like a castle?"

"I have seen the ruins of castles, but they were never this size. Yes, the shape is right. But a tree?"

Merral touched the frame of the glasses again and he and Vero flew onward over the featureless grass. As they did, the awesome size of the tree became more apparent. He could soon begin to make out the great spreading branches of greenery extending from the uneven wall of silvery bark.

Finally, Merral came to rest at the base of the tree beneath a great bent branch and amid great snakelike roots that burrowed deep into the ground. Dead leaves blew around them and strange insects with long silver wings flickered silently past.

"It's more than enormous!" he heard Vero say, in awed tones. "It's bigger than any building. It must be the size of a town."

"Look up," Merral said and swung his gaze upward. Through the gigantic spreading branches that lay overhead, the great tree trunk towered as if it were an overhanging cliff. At the very top, the trunk and branches passed into wreaths of mist.

He heard Vero gasp. "How high is it?"

"About three hundred meters. Three, four times higher than any living tree. But the volume is something else. Let me show you an aerial view."

Merral touched the glasses again and heard a sharp intake of breath from Vero as they raced upward, passing soundlessly through smears of green and brown branches and foliage, up through the mist patches, until finally, they were high above the highest branches.

Merral looked down. Through the wreaths of low cloud and mist, the vast, hollow inner heart of the tree was clearly visible, and below the outstretched inner branches he could make out the gray waters of a lake.

"The tree is a tube?"

"No, a spiral." Merral began a slow swoop down over the foliage. "I designed this tree. It's like nothing in nature. The size is really incidental; I wanted something that would grow in places where there are high winds and frequent dry periods."

"The Made Worlds."

"Exactly. So it starts low and grows sideways as well as upward. But in growing sideways it makes a spiral like snails do. The result is an enormously strong structure—more like a hill than a tree."

Merral tilted his head and dived under some of the topmost fronds.

"Yow!" Vero exclaimed. "Gentle with the maneuvers, my friend. I know it's not real, but no one has told my stomach. The water in the middle? How does that get there?"

"Sorry." Merral slowed his motion. "It's a design feature. The core of the spiral slowly rots, so you get an inner water body. The branches drain down into it. It acts as a reservoir. And do you see how the inner branches are so much bigger and more delicate? They are protected from the winds."

"Elegant."

"Thank you. Seen enough?"

"I'd like another browse sometime. At my own pace. But it's wonderful."

The image went dark and Merral took off the glasses.

Vero was staring at him, blinking. "So, that is what you do in your spare time?"

"Yes. It's my relaxation. I spend my spare stipend in setting it up and renting computer time. That sort of personal creation system is pretty heavy in processing time."

"I can imagine."

Vero put the glasses carefully down on the table. "How long has it taken you to create that?"

"Five years. The early attempts were disasters. Finding a way for a tree to pump water that high is hard work"

"Could we make it for real?"

"It works, if that's what you mean. The world in this creation is accurate. But it is beyond our skill and—as you know—well beyond the gene-engineering limits we impose. Bacteria, fungi, some crops, yes. But to create totally new trees? Hardly."

Vero nodded agreement and Merral continued. "Actually, the real problem is that it takes time. A castle tree would take three thousand years to get to that sort of size. It's hardly suitable for a Made World."

Vero closed his eyes. "A pity. But a wonderful vision, my friend. The city-sized tree. I shall treasure that image: the D'Avanos castle tree."

There was a moment's silence between them before Merral said, "And what do you do with your stipend, Vero? Give it all away?"

Vero smiled. "Ah, there has been much discussion about that. We Sentinels have toyed, as other organizations have, with having no money, but we think Assembly policy is right. Free food, lodging, clothing, and welfare, and a standard stipend for all on top to spend or give away. Totally money-free societies are dull; how can you give a present when it cost you nothing?"

"I'm sorry I didn't have time to get you anything today."

"Send me some castle tree images; they will do."

After a moment's silence Merral spoke. "So, you are off tomorrow? That's sooner than you had expected."

Vero flexed his legs and seemed to look at his shoes carefully. He spoke slowly. "Yes. Sooner."

Merral said nothing, and eventually Vero leaned forward on the chair, his hands clasped together, and looked up.

"What I'm about to say is really for sentinels. But that's advice, not rules. Do you know why I am here?"

"Not really; I have ideas."

"Well, two weeks ago, Brenito—who is very respected, by the way—made an urgent call to Earth with a warning. We only have that happen every century or so. He simply said that he had had a vision that Farholme was under threat."

"But what sort—?"

Vero raised a hand and gave a mock grimace. "Exactly our problem. I don't want to go into the details. But he couldn't clarify the danger. 'Under threat,' that was all. Physical, spiritual, mental? He had no idea. So they weighed it all up and, bearing in mind that he is a hundred and five, they decided to send me. Well, everybody else was busy or had commitments."

"You drew the Farholme card?"

Vero smiled slightly. "I suppose so."

"What other options did they have?"

"A full threat evaluation team. So I'm here to try and find what the threat is and whether there is anything really wrong." Vero looked at his feet again.

"And?"

He looked up. "Well, I have to say it's a tough assignment. You see, everything is strange here. The sun, the clouds, the buildings, are all peculiar. I can barely understand the dialect, and some aspects of your society are totally alien to me."

"Really? Such as?"

"Don't sound so surprised. Many things that you take for granted. Like that thing you are wearing now."

"My night-suit? What's wrong with that?" Merral looked down at his one-piece winter suit, trying to find anything odd about it.

Vero grinned and shook his head as if in despair. "See? You don't even realize it! That orange thing is an active thermal suit designed to protect you if you are forced to evacuate your building overnight or it collapses on you. It is visible on almost every waveband from ultraviolet to infrared and has a passive signal emitter so they can find your body under ten meters of titanium or magnesium-cored concrete debris. And it has your name and career and specialization encoded on it should they need to decide whether you are a priority to resuscitate when they find you. *That's* what's wrong with it."

Merral found himself looking at his night-suit in a new way. "Oh," he said.

"On Ancient Earth, Merral," Vero continued, "we sleep in whatever we want. Some of us choose hopelessly impractical soft, fluffy things in pastel colors called pajamas or nightshirts. And we can choose and go to bed with a reasonable confidence that there will still be an atmosphere we can breathe in the morning."

"I see. I suppose that could make a difference. . . ."

"A *difference*?" Vero laughed. "Oh, it does. Believe me. But you see that's what I mean. How can I find out what is wrong here when even your night clothes are odd!"

Merral raised a hand. "Sorry! But you Ancient Earthers are the odd ones out numerically!"

They laughed together until Merral managed to ask whether Vero had found anything.

Suddenly becoming quiet, the sentinel shook his head. "Nothing. Nothing to alarm me, nothing to persuade me that there is something wrong. But then I don't know what I am looking for. No one does. So I have decided to go tomorrow to Isterrane, and there in your capital I will try to see what ideas Brenito has. I may come back here, or I may travel around. But I do need to talk to Brenito."

"I see. Do you think he has made a mistake?"

There was a thoughtful pause. "You are nearly as bad as Isabella with your questions. Yes, I am beginning to think it possible that the good Brenito may have overreacted. I have so far found nothing remotely odd or peculiar. Nothing at all. I'm glad of the chance of seeing Farholme. But I see, I feel, nothing."

"If he has, what will you do?"

"Stay around for a bit, just in case. It was a long journey out, and without an emergency, it will be hard booking a passage on the route back in hurry. I need to write a report, anyway. I will be suggesting better ways of handling this sort of thing. Asking some hard questions."

"Sounds radical."

"*Radical?* That is a familiar word to me. 'Where, Verofaza, is the boundary between being radical and being rebellious?' That was the dean of political history. Anyway, I shall find somewhere that reminds me of Earth and sit down and write a long review."

He stood up. "I'd better leave you. I hope to be off on the early flight, so I'd better be in bed soon too. I'll be in touch."

As Vero stood by the door, Merral went over and shook his hand. "Vero, I'm afraid I wish your mission total failure. But when Brenito confesses to having let his fruit juice ferment, come back and see what we are doing here. And I'll take you out of the town into the country. That's what you should see."

Vero grinned and shook his hand firmly. "Let's indeed hope we can do that."

Then with a quiet "Blessings," he left the room.

After Vero had gone, Merral switched the light off, prayed, and then lay down and closed his eyes. But Vero's conversation had disturbed him and would not leave his mind. He wondered about the odd things that had happened at Herrandown. *Perhaps I should have discussed them with Vero.* However, as he considered them, it all seemed too unlikely to be of interest. The entire case hung on Barrand's words and now he was pushed to remember exactly what it was that he had said. No, there must just have been some misunderstanding there. One or both of them had overreacted, and Vero's arrival at the same time was just a coincidence.

Then he thought about the eleven thousand years of peace that the Assembly had had and that put his mind at rest. After all, one of the many lessons taught by that awesome span of history was that almost all potential crises had ended up being very much less than that.

Quite plainly, there was nothing to worry about.

6

One morning some three months later, Merral looked up from his work on the map of the proposed northern extension of the Great Northern Forest and gazed out of his office window. The view looked eastward over the waters of Ynysmere Lake, and Merral had positioned his desk so that whenever he glanced up he saw the water and the rolling hills beyond. In winter, it encouraged him to come in early and catch the sunrise. But today the only view he had was one of a buffeting dull gray wetness in which it was hard to distinguish between the spray of the breaking waves, the blowing rain, and the clouds above.

Wondering at the weather, Merral shook his head. Winter had dragged on this year, and spring was more a fickle, fleeting guest than a permanent resident. Dry, sunny weather would come, and for a few days spirits would lift, windows would be opened, and jackets left at home. Then abruptly, out of the north would come a bitter whistling wind, or cold, soaking rains would blow in from the ocean far away to the east, and winter would be back. He consoled himself with the certainty that spring and summer would come in the end. Besides, he thought with a certain amusement, if the tropics posting—now almost certain—did come through, then he would doubtless miss the longs wet winters of northeastern Menaya.

He bent over the map again, but as he did so, the diary adjunct link on his watch pulsed gently three times. He glanced at his diary lying on the desk and saw that the screen confirmed an urgent and private call. He tabbed an acknowledgement back, and then got up and closed the door, trying to remember when he had last had such a message. He sat down and rotated the diary so its lens could image him and ordered it to open the link.

The image that flashed onto the tiny screen was that of Barrand and

Zennia. They were sitting at the desk in his uncle's cluttered narrow office. The moment he saw them, Merral knew something was wrong. Zennia was plainly agitated, her face pale and taut, her eyes constantly flicking toward her husband while she clasped and unclasped her slender hands. Barrand, by contrast, was sitting still, but his hands were tightly folded together and his stern face had a determined look.

"Greetings, Uncle Barrand, Aunt Zennia."

"Greetings to you, Merral. Thank you for your prompt response."

His uncle's voice had a strange formality, and his aunt's smile seemed weak, strained.

"Ah, Merral. Thank you," Barrand continued. "I'll come straight to the point. We have a problem here. It's very odd. We need some advice."

"I'm ready to help all I can. Tell me all about it."

Barrand looked briefly at his wife, as if for encouragement, and then turned back to the screen.

"It's Elana. The day before yesterday, you remember? It was dry. At least with us. The first such day for a week. What a winter, eh? Anyway, she went out into the woods above Herrandown. Just northwest of us. There she says she saw something." He paused, clenching his hands tight and glancing at Zennia. "Now she describes it as like a small man, only brown and shiny like a beetle. It scared her badly—"

"She's still scared," Zennia cut in.

Merral's mouth dropped open, and he snapped it shut. "Sorry, Uncle. Try it again. She saw what?"

"Something like a small man, only brown and shiny like a beetle." Zennia nodded.

Merral tried to visualize what she had described but failed. "I mean—an obvious point—this isn't some sort of . . . well . . . story?"

Barrand shrugged, but Zennia shook her head strongly and turned to the screen. "Merral, I *know* my daughter. And if she did make up a story, she scared herself silly doing it. And us. She came running in, screaming. She won't go outside alone and is sleeping next to our room."

They looked at each other. *I have,* Merral realized, *a potentially serious problem up in Herrandown.* Maybe it was already past the potential stage. Usually able to say something in any situation, Merral suddenly found himself floundering. "Look . . . ," he said, "how big did she say this creature was?"

Zennia spoke. "She said it was about her height."

Merral became aware that he was staring blankly at the screen. "Baffling, quite baffling," he responded and realized it sounded banal; but what else could he say?

He paused for a moment. "Well, you both know the problem, I'm sure. We have an inventory of every species on the planet; we may not know numbers exactly but we know what we have. And all the brown, shiny, beetle-like things we have are small enough that you can hold them in your hand. In fact, anywhere in the Assembly to our knowledge. At least to mine."

Barrand shrugged and threw his arms up in bemusement. "Merral, I know. But she's convinced she saw something."

Zennia nodded. "And I think she did."

"Aunt, how is Elana otherwise?"

"Physically fine. The nurse can find nothing wrong. There's no evidence of hallucinatory activity; it's not associated with a fever. Blood tests, neural activity all read normal."

Merral found himself admitting defeat. "Uncle, Aunt, I have to say I'm baffled. Absolutely. She just saw it and ran away?"

Barrand gestured to his wife to speak.

"No; it was staring at her from behind a bush, she says. It realized it had been observed and ran away."

Merral was silent. He threw up a quick request to heaven for wisdom and tried to run through the various options. He had to have more time.

"And what do you two think?"

Barrand shifted on his seat. "I don't know. . . . I suppose it must be nonsense—a dream or something. . . . I went to have a look, but I could see no sign of it. I haven't searched the area thoroughly. But—"

Zennia nudged him into silence and she spoke. "Elana saw something, Merral. And we think there's more to it than that."

Technically, Merral told himself, the guidelines were such that in the rare event of a psychological problem with a colony, a forester would call in specialist help. In his case, Ghina Macreedy. Of course, if it was something in his forests that had caused it then that was a different matter. But this was a curious affair and they were family. Perhaps, too, if it could be dealt with quickly, then a deeper crisis could be avoided.

Barrand was stroking his beard restlessly. "Yes, I'm afraid, Merral, there is something odd here. Or there may be. . . . The animals are agitated, especially the dogs. Particularly since we lost Spotback."

"Spotback! I never knew you'd lost him. He was a good dog. How did that happen?"

"A good question. We saw him one morning about five days ago heading northward from the farm. Then he just vanished."

Suddenly, Merral knew that at least his aunt and possibly his uncle had worked themselves into a highly concerned state. And recognizing that, Merral knew what he had to do.

"The other families?"

His aunt shook her head. "Elana is the only one that's seen it. The others feel the same as we do. You can call them."

"Perhaps. I'll see."

There was one last question he wanted to ask. "What does Thomas think?"

Barrand's face looked pained. "Our son Thomas is, I'm sorry to say, acting scared. He will only play outside the front of the house. And he comes inside well before dusk."

So he's affected as well. That settled it.

"Look, I think I'm going to come up and see you. I'll see if I can't get one of our fast Recon vehicles and be with you tomorrow. Just for a day. Talk to Elana; take a look around."

Zennia's hazel eyes showed gratitude. "Oh, thank you, Merral! We'd feel better for that. See if you can make sense of it. You think it's a good idea, Barrand?"

There was a pause "Ho! Why not? Better our Merral than a host of people we don't know. We might be able to solve it. Yes, come up. As soon as possible."

Then, with abbreviated family news, they closed the conversation.

After the call Merral did nothing immediately but sit staring at the rain and waves, thinking through what he had heard. It was troubling. Forward Colony families were always selected for their ability to handle remote small communities and few facilities. For them to be so uneasy was extremely odd. The whole thing defied analysis. Merral decided that the most likely cause was that Elana, perhaps helped by her active imagination, had had some sort of waking dream or hallucination.

But, whatever its cause, the event had generated some sort of real collective anxiety. And that needed a rapid resolution. Not only were the Antalfers his family, they were also a good team with a lot of experience. If they had to be rotated out, they would be hard to replace.

After ten minutes, Merral got up and walked down the corridor to where his director was working and put his head around the door. Henri was in his thinking pose. He was reclining in his chair, with his lean arms behind his head and his feet up on the desk, staring at the giant map of northeastern Menaya that occupied most of the opposite wall. At the sight of Merral he swung his legs down and gestured him in with a wave of an arm and a genial smile. "Merral! Come in, man. Take a seat." Ten years in Ynysmant hadn't blunted Henri's distinctive Tablelands intonation.

Closing the door behind him, Merral took the proffered seat. "I hope I'm not disturbing any deep thoughts?"

Henri stroked his carefully trimmed brown beard and stared at him with his closely spaced, deep-set dark eyes. "Thoughts? Yes, I'll say so. We have just lost a hexapod; got washed away at the Grandell Cleft. It's how to recover what's left of it. And the weather this winter. . . . Ach!" He frowned. "When I started here, they were worried about polar ice sheets shrinking; now they are expanding too fast. This planet is like an unbroken horse; it runs this way today and tomorrow that. But this winter—it's been so long—means there is the danger of us all being way behind schedule. Summers are short enough in our northernmost zones. I'm thinking of ways of saving time when the weather does improve. My other issue is how to replace you, assuming you go. You'll be missed, man. Really missed."

"Sorry. I'll miss being here."

"Ach." He smiled. "Not with this weather. . . . Anyway, what can I do for you?"

"We have a problem at Herrandown." Merral paused, trying to work out how to tell the story.

Henri clucked sympathetically. "Man, that's bad news. I've got your quarry team ready to go to the ridge. But tell me about it."

Very carefully, Merral explained the substance of his call that morning while Henri listened attentively and without comment. "So you see, Henri," Merral ended, "I'd like to go up and check it out personally. I think that way we can best reduce the strain on the family."

Henri nodded. "I can see that. If you can fix it." He stared a moment at the wall-high image of Mount Katafana. "Yes. Ghina is out south; otherwise, I'd suggest you take her. You really ought to go with someone with some psychological background. I mean, that's what you think it is, I take it? Psychology?"

"There doesn't seem much other option, does there?"

His director thought briefly. "No," he asserted, shaking his head. Then Henri looked at the image again and Merral remembered that his boss was planning to climb Mount Katafana this year.

"No, man. I'm at a loss to think of any other explanation." He gave his beard a further stroke and stared at Merral. "You've got much experience in talking to troubled fourteen-year-old girls?"

"Not really. Although I know the girl at the center of the problem." Then an idea struck him "Mind you, I know someone who has experience."

A look of gentle amusement came onto Henri's face. "Ah yes. I should have thought of her. Yes, see if you can get Isabella Danol to go with you. Get a Recon vehicle booked now. Check that they've still got the winter tires. Normally, by now we'd be starting to grapple with dust, not mud. But not this year. Oh no."

"Thanks, Henri. Thanks a great deal."

Merral turned to go. As he did, Henri spoke again in a low voice. "One last thing, man—if it turns out to be serious, then just ask for help. The Antalfers deserve our best efforts."

Back in his office, Merral had an idea. He pulled off his diary and asked it to call "Anya Salema Lewitz, biologist, location unknown." Moments later the response came from the Planetary Ecology Center in Isterrane where a man, who identified himself as Anya's assistant, answered. He apologized and said that she was in a conference, but expressed the confident opinion that she would call him back as soon as she was free.

Merral had better fortune with Isabella, who was in her office. "Isabella, I have had a problem this morning that you may be able to help me with. It's right in your age group. The Antalfers; you remember them?"

She nodded, her thin face thoughtful. "Of course. Barrand and Zennia out at Herrandown. She is your mother's younger sister."

"But very different. My mother wouldn't last a week in Herrandown. Zennia's much more placid. Or she was. Anyway, their oldest girl—Elana—has had a disturbing experience. Two days ago she claims to have seen a creature her size in the wood. It was brown and shiny, hard-skinned, like an insect."

Isabella said nothing for what seemed a long time. In fact, Merral thought that if it hadn't been for the slight frown on her face he would have assumed that she hadn't heard. When she did speak, it was very softly. "Poor thing. Is she all right?"

That's Isabella: cautious and concerned. Everybody else, me included, leaps in and says the thing can't exist. She thinks of the girl first.

"Apparently, she's pretty unhappy."

"So I should imagine. Hmm. How old is she?"

"Just fourteen. Becoming a young lady."

"I see. And this thing was her size?"

"So she claimed. Of course, as you know, there is nothing like that. What do you think?"

Isabella put her head on one side for a moment and looked back at him for some time before answering. "Sorry, Merral, I can't judge that. It's odd, and there isn't enough data, I'm afraid. I mean, I'd have to be sure that such a thing *was* ruled out. It has to be an illusion? I mean, it's not an escape of something, is it?"

"No. There are no such things in or out of captivity."

She nodded. "Thought so. Well. . . ." She paused, leaning back as if trying to get the best position to think in. "You would have to know her up-to-date psychological profile. And a lot of other things."

"Such as?"

"Physical health, recent diet, allergies, mental state, etc. It's fairly common for temporary and mild psychological perturbations to occur in puberty. But seeing things is a bit odd. I think there would have to be something else. Hmm." She lapsed into silence.

That is what she would say; she wouldn't be so highly rated if she had made an instant diagnosis in a case like this. But then, who could?

"Look, Isabella, I'm going early tomorrow for the day to see them and to try and sort out what's happening. Henri has okayed a fast Recon vehicle. Can you come up with me? We'd be back early evening at the latest."

There was a moment's pause and then the faintest hint of a smile. "Yes, if I work this evening. I'd like that, Merral. It sounds like you might need some help."

"All right. Meet me at the end of your street at half past six tomorrow."

Anya Lewitz called back just before lunch. She grinned at him from the screen of the diary before he'd even said a word. With her broad, freckled face, sky blue eyes, flaming red hair, and perpetual dynamism, Merral had always thought her pretty in a rather obvious way ever since he met her in college. The image he saw offered nothing to change that view.

"Merral D'Avanos! Where have you been? Still up to your waist in bogs planting trees, eh? Growing roots? It's been so long since we met up. When was it?" The voice was as bright and cheery as ever.

"The last round of planning for Northern Menaya; you were talking about the problems with the introduction of mammals from different Terran continents into a world with a single supercontinent." He remembered that she had had her red hair shorter then.

"Ah yes, the old purity-versus-practicality debate. Do you have either American or Eurasian faunas or do you do what we've done here and just mix them up and see what does best? Yes, I remember it. I'm now on reconstruction work, actually."

"Reconstruction? I sometimes think that I'd like to be involved in that—restoring species and environments that humanity destroyed in the past. That's valuable."

"Oh, nonsense!" She snorted. "So is planting trees, Merral. Bringing back the dodo is neat, but you can't breathe dodos. In fact, I'm told they are rather ugly and stupid."

"True, trees play a pretty important role in the great scheme of things. Anyway, I enjoy my work so I'm thankful."

"That's good."

There was a slight pause.

"Anyway, Anya, the reason I'm calling you is that I have an odd situation." He hesitated again, feeling strangely certain of how his question would be received. "See, I have a girl here on the edge of the Great Northern Forest who claims to have seen something strange. She says she saw a creature like a small man, with a hard, shiny brown skin like a beetle. Is this a case for zoology or psychiatry?"

"The latter, I'm afraid. No question." The response was immediate, and Anya's smile radiated confidence.

"No other possibilities? I mean, Farholme was, of course, dead when it was seeded."

The red hair bobbed as she shook her head emphatically. "The last bacteria here died out a billion years ago; about average for this sort of world. And there is no evidence that anything beyond the usual simple forms developed. And everything was sterile here long before *Leviathan-D* arrived."

"As I thought. And our existing beetles?"

"The biggest beetles on Farholme could fit in the palm of your hand. On the tropical islands." She sighed. "I'm afraid you are talking psychiatrist. Sorry."

"Well, it's what I concluded too. They are my forests. But, as a matter of interest, what would you need to be convinced otherwise?"

She looked surprised. "I'd need a specimen, dead or alive. You've got a full description? skin or cuticle samples? still or video images? even a drawing?"

"Not at the moment. You have all the data I have. I hope to interview her tomorrow. Oh, the thing ran off when she saw it."

The blue eyes flashed with amused exasperation. "Oh, you tree experts! Learn to describe movement! Try to improve on that 'ran off' line. Did it lope, bound, slink, or scuttle? And please—on how many legs? From the description it could be two, four, six, or eight."

"Okay. Thanks for the tip, Anya. I'll remember that. But I suppose it is a hallucination? You've not reconstructed Cretaceous beetles?"

She smiled and tossed her head. "I'm sorry, especially for the girl. No, the Reconstruction Mandate has strict limits. You know them, but I'll remind you. It has to be a species made extinct by man, so we are still arguing over whether or not we reconstruct the mammoth. I'm voting yes, incidentally. But I'm afraid your guess is right. I can state categorically that it was an illusion. For a start, physics gives a finite size to insects because of their breathing mechanism. If you doubled our oxygen levels you might get them a *bit* larger, but a meter-plus high? No hope! And they never look human unless . . ." She moved closer to the screen. "Say, how many legs do *you* have up there in Ynysmant?"

Merral laughed. "You haven't changed, Anya. I have just the usual."

"Sorry, it sounds like a waking nightmare. Talk to the psychology crowd.

But if there is any hard data, and I mean *hard*, Tree Man, let me know, and I'll get the lab ready. And I'll lay in a ton of triple-strength cockroach killer. Incidentally, what's this I hear about you and the tropics?"

So it's news in Isterrane too.

"True, Anya. It's being worked on. Almost certainly I'm being posted to Faraketha at the end of summer. Do you know it?"

"Hot, hot, and hot. And that's the cool season; you'll sweat off a few kilos in days. Actually, I've only flown over it. It's very poor quality at the moment, mostly very low diversity jungle. I'm no expert, but I think you ought to use a vortex blaster on it and start over again from scratch."

"I've heard it's an option. But I need to take a look."

"Actually, in fact, I'm going to be working with the Madagascar Project on Terelka. That's only five hundred kilometers south. But milder."

"You are going to be on that? I'm impressed. That's a grand vision."

Anya raised her hands in excitement. "Maybe too big. It's still in the design stage. But here, we think we can risk the ecological purity approach. Specific reconstruction of a whole long-gone subcontinental ecosystem. Lemurs, small mammals, birds, reptiles, vegetation—the lot. It will take a millennium before we know if we have achieved a viable re-creation." She laughed sheepishly. "Sorry, Merral, I get excited."

"That's how it should be! Well, I'd better get on with my work. I'll hope to catch up with you soon, Anya. But thanks for the opinion. It confirms what I think."

"Apologies about that," she said, shrugging. "Giant anthropoid beetles would be interesting, but I think we'd know if they existed. Blessings, Merral."

"Blessings, Anya." The image faded away.

Merral could only make time for a trip north by working extra hours, so he stayed on at work until early evening. The idea of a community running from shadows dogged his thinking; he felt certain that there was something about the story that was familiar. Just as he was about to leave the deserted building, the answer came to him: Vero. Vero had talked of a sentinel investigation on a world where there had been a problem with a community. It would be useful to see that data. But where had it been?

Through his diary, Merral located Vero. He was on Aftarena Island on the other side of Farholme. With the time difference, he would be asleep for a few hours yet. Merral left a message on Vero's diary, ordered the building lights off, and walked home across the causeway.

Vero returned the call just as Merral was getting ready for bed. He quickly pulled his night-suit on, sat within view of the diary and switched on the screen. Suddenly the dark, lean face of Vero appeared. He was wearing a lightweight, short-sleeved shirt, and there was bright, low-angle sunlight streaming behind him.

"Merral! It's been quite a few weeks. I'm sorry I haven't called before," he said with an apologetic smile.

"Vero, greetings. No problem. You wouldn't be wearing that shirt in Ynysmant today. Or this week for that matter."

"I've heard your weather's been poor. Aftarena is very nice. I traveled around a lot after I left you, just looking around. And I've ended up here. I like it—it's my sort of climate."

Merral noticed that his Farholmen dialect was now almost perfect.

"I'm glad for you. What we have at the moment would make you miserable. You have to be born here to put up with it. And congratulations on your Farholmen, Vero. It took me a bit to realize that you were speaking it. You sound like a native."

"Not quite."

"It's fine. Anyway, I was calling to ask you about something we talked about. The world where there was the collective disorder and some thought it was evil, but it was just biology after all—where was it?"

Vero twitched his nose and scratched his tightly curled hair. "Ah, that's just an interpretation. Sentinels have debated ever since it happened—which was in 12985, maybe '86. And it was on Vellant. But isn't it rather an unusual topic for a forester?" His face had acquired a look of curiosity.

Merral wondered how much he should tell. "Yes," he replied carefully. "The thing is, I have a Forward Colony where things are getting a bit odd. It could simply be the bad weather. But I thought your case might provide a lead in."

Vero's brown eyes widened and he opened his mouth to speak. Then he shook his head as if trying to dislodge a thought. "Look, I'll send you the best reviews I can find."

"Thanks. Anyway, how is the visit going?"

"Interesting. I'm enjoying it."

"So you haven't found anything anomalous yet."

Vero blinked. "Well . . . just maybe."

"Can you tell me?"

The brown face on the screen stared at him.

"Er, yes. In fact, I was thinking of calling you about it anyway. It's an odd thing. I've been uncertain how to proceed on it. Can I ask you some questions first, questions that may seem irrelevant?"

"Go ahead."

Vero shifted in his chair and then leaned toward the screen. "The Technology Protocols—you would rate them as important?"

A strange question indeed. "More than important—*vital.* The Technology Protocols make us masters of technology rather than the other way about. It is generally believed that the Assembly would have self-destructed without them."

Vero nodded slightly. "Now, can you remember how the Preamble goes?"

"Testing my memory eh? Well, the final A.D. 2130 version has, 'The Assembly of Worlds believes that, in his providence, God has provided technology so that, in some measure, the effects of the Fall may be lessened in this life. However, the Assembly also believes that, precisely because of our fallenness, technology can be abused to the detriment of an individual and his or her God-given personality. The Assembly therefore solemnly covenants that the only technology that will be accepted is that which can be shown will not lead to the loss or damage of individuality or personality.' How was that?"

Vero nodded again. "Flawless. Now, Protocol Six?"

"Six? Oh that one. The shortest. 'The rights of an individual to be protected from direct or indirect technological abuse are not extinguished by death.'"

There was a further nod. "And, Merral, you understand that to mean—what?"

"Well, I have to think back to college. It's mainly that there is to be no rewriting of history. Because it's banned, it's hard to think of an example. Yes, I know, to alter a visual file to make your partner in a Team-Ball game look like a famous player of the past. I must admit I've never understood why it was in the Protocols. It's never seemed a big thing to me."

"You are fortunate. Sentinels have to spend time studying the times before the Great Intervention, and I can tell you there were many serious instances of this problem. But that's the end of my questions."

Vero paused, flexed his long fingers, and sighed quietly. When he spoke it was in a hushed and solemn tone. "I ask you these things, Merral, about Protocol Six, because there is some evidence that it may have been breached."

It took some time for the significance of the last word to sink in. *Does he mean here on Farholme?* "Not here? Surely not? . . . I mean, breach of the Protocols is—" Merral ran out of words as the import of the statement sank in.

Vero leaned back in his chair and Merral was aware of the palm trees behind him. "Was *serious* the word you were looking for?" he suggested quietly.

"I suppose so. I was actually trying to find a more major word."

"You would be right to do so." The face on the other side of the world was grim.

"You'd better tell me about it."

Vero rubbed his flattened nose between his hands and then stared at the screen.

"Sorry, Merral. You won't like this. A voice has told me that there is a problem. Do you know whose?"

Merral, now feeling too perplexed to even try to answer, just shook his head.

"It was the voice of Miranda Cline." Vero paused to let the name sink in and then repeated it, as if listening to it himself. "Miranda Cline. Although dead these three thousand years, she still speaks."

"*The* Miranda Cline? The alto? The one my Uncle Barrand used on his Nativity piece?"

Vero nodded, unhappiness imprinted on his expression. "The same, Merral, the very same. In fact, the problem is precisely the audio file you gave me—the one of Rechereg's *Choral Variations on an Old Carol.* The one with Miranda Cline as alto."

Merral gasped. If it was barely believable that anyone could breach the Protocols, how much more unbelievable was it that such a breach was linked to his uncle? It made no sense at all. But then, nothing at Herrandown did anymore.

Vero was speaking quietly and apologetically, almost as if he was confessing something himself. "See, Merral, I got round to listening to that recording again recently. I liked it, especially Miranda Cline. I'd never heard her sing as well. And one evening here, with nothing much to do, I called up the background to it from the files in the Library and found that there was an interview with Rechereg himself. There he mentioned that the alto part was very hard and very high. And as I heard that, something clicked: something that I should have known. Because I knew about Miranda Cline. While she was unparalleled in the lower and midrange, she kept out of the topmost ranges. She was the classic, low second alto. Yet in the file you gave me she sings right up to top *G* and holds it firmly without breakup for two seconds."

There was silence between them. Outside his room, Merral could hear his father and mother talking softly as they went up to bed. Their world seemed a long way away.

Merral heard himself speaking slowly. "So you are saying that there is no way that her natural voice could have reached that high. But perhaps it was someone else?"

Vero nodded. "Excellent, Merral. That is quite the line I am taking. The file says it is Miranda Cline and it sounds like her. But there could be a mistake. There are a thousand re-created voices."

Merral closed his eyes. "No, he said he was thinking of using her. And when he transmitted it to me the covering note said that he had used Miranda Cline after all." A faint voice seemed to cry out within him that he was condemning his uncle.

Vero stirred. "Well, it could still be a mistake. An error of the machinery. I'm going to have the file checked." He stared at his fingers, as if seeing them for the first time. "I suppose it is just possible that there was some sort of coding error. I'd prefer any alternative to what I'm afraid I think is the case."

"Which is," Merral stated dully, scarcely able to phrase the words, "that Barrand altered her voice in complete defiance of the Sixth Protocol."

Vero looked away, as if unable to face him, but signified his agreement by the tiniest nod of his head. "You see," he said slowly, after a moment, "re-createds are at the limits of what we allow. They willingly give their vocal skills to be copied so that their voices can be reused later. But there is a commitment that we do not abuse that gift. Some re-created voices come with specific restrictions of the donors. Falancia Wollan, for instance, felt that her voice was unsuited to dramatic works like opera. But this is something else." His face became somber.

"Vero, what are you going to do?"

Vero turned slowly back to face the diary. "I shall transmit the file to my office on Ancient Earth. They have the ability there to take the waveforms to pieces. To definitely say whether it was hers and whether or not it was altered. I will do it in the next few days. I needed to talk to you first."

"If it is an alteration?"

Vero shook his head. "Merral, I have no idea. There are no precedents on file. We can hope that it is some sort of psychological problem and treatable." He looked profoundly miserable and after a moment went on slowly. "It all seems so . . . well, disproportionate. A few seconds worth of a single note on a file from a singer who is long dead. I'm sorry, Merral."

As Vero fell silent, Merral felt caught between his own unhappiness and that of his friend. But the issue was plain and he felt it right that he restate it. "It is not a light thing, Vero. And you as a sentinel know it, even if we use re-created voices more here than you do. To be one is an honor, to give your voice for things like the Forward Colonies and the ships. Voices are special. That's why no machine, no diary even, is ever given a human voice, although we could easily do it. The sovereign Lord made Miranda Cline unable to reach those top notes. To have altered her voice so it did—if that's what happened—is a lie, a twisting of truth."

Vero nodded his head gently and seemed to stare for long moments into infinity. "You know, they always say to sentinels at graduation, 'Always pray that you spend your entire life without being needed.' I always thought it funny." Then his focus shifted back to Merral. "But what do you think? Tell me that your uncle's hardware is set wrong, that he's deaf . . . that in the transfer one note got changed by some distortion of the electromagnetic field—*anything*. Tell me, Merral. Tell me!"

"I need to think Vero. Wait a minute. Please."

With his mind reeling, Merral tapped off the video and sound and sat back in his chair. This was too much. He had been worried before Nativity at the possibility that his uncle had lied, he had been made uneasy by this morning's news, and now this. Three things. His options were very limited indeed.

He reached for the diary and the image of Vero in a pale shirt with the brilliant sunlight behind him returned.

"Right. Vero, let me be open with you. I think something is wrong up at Herrandown. I have some other evidence—"

Vero raised a finger. "A question—which you may, of course, refuse to answer. The Forward Colony with the collective instability you mentioned?"

"The same."

Vero shook his head slowly. "Oh dear. Oh dear."

After several moments, Vero spoke again. "On the positive side, Merral, it's fairly isolated. And, at least it's localized. So far. But what to do?"

"Well, I'm going up there tomorrow for the day. I think, though, your fears are probably right. I think it highly probable that he has willfully modified the voice parameters."

Vero rubbed his face. "I do not know what to advise. This is surprising. I assumed that there was nothing here. But now. . . . No, we need more information. I will wait to hear from you before I do anything. Look, Merral, can you meet me in Isterrane two days from now? No, wait—that will be the Lord's Day. The day after, then?"

Merral hesitated, then spoke. "Yes, if you like. If you think that it's that important?"

"My friend, my reading of the data is that we have either a psychological crisis infecting one individual and probably others—which is what I hope it is—or—" He shook his head.

"Or what?"

There was a long silence in which Merral became strangely aware of the perfect stillness in the room, a stillness so deep that he felt he could hear his heart beat.

Vero's voice, when it spoke out of the diary, almost surprised him. "Or, I do not like to say. But I cannot rule out that we are seeing the start of something so significant that . . ." He tailed off and then shook his head. It was only after another long pause that he spoke again. "No, I will not speculate. Keep this to yourself, Merral, for the moment."

"I see. I will abide by that."

"Oh, and be careful when you go to Herrandown. Look out."

"Look out for what?" Merral asked.

"I only wish I knew."

They stared at each other, a tension somehow transmitted around the globe. Finally, Merral forced himself to say the words. "Vero, I need to know. Finish what you said earlier. Or what?"

Finally, as if being dragged out of the depths, the answer came back, syllable by painful syllable.

"Merral, if what I fear is the case, then the rules we have lived by for over eleven thousand years may be on the point of changing."

7

The weather on the journey north to Herrandown next morning was dull and overcast, although thankfully dry. There was little to see on the road, whose route had, after all, been planned to avoid the more exciting landscapes. Even so, part of the road had been washed away in one place by a rogue stream, and the little Recon vehicle had to make a brief and muddy detour that fortunately added little to the journey time.

As they rolled slowly along a marshy stretch with the pale sunlight trying to penetrate the drifting mists, a particularly protracted silence fell upon them. Merral looked at Isabella, feeling that her slight figure looked incongruous in the large passenger seat of the Recon.

"No regrets about our parents' decision, Isabella?" he asked, catching her eye, wishing to hear her voice as much as to get an answer.

She paused, stretched her legs out and then smiled softly back at him. "No. Not really. Your tropics job is almost definite, and the more I hear of it the more I think I may be best off in Ynysmant. But also, yes. It would have been desirable, in many ways." The smile grew slightly wistful. "Of course, I think that maybe things could still work out between us."

She fell silent again and then she looked back at him. "And you, Forester D'Avanos?"

He thought for a moment. "The same. This is how things are. I could wish otherwise, but what would be the point?"

Ahead of them, a road repair machine sensed their approach, pivoted its body clear of the road on its four hind legs, and turned its head toward them. Merral raised a hand toward the machine and the silver head nodded slowly in acknowledgement.

"Just so," Isabella said. "What would be the point?"

Just after ten-thirty the Recon rolled up to the top of a rise on the road and Herrandown came into view. Merral paused the vehicle and switched the power off. He stared down at the sleepy little cluster of houses and fields surrounded by trees in their tentative fresh green foliage. *What do I expect to see? A dark cloud? A visible shadow?* But there was nothing.

He started the power up again and they moved on down quietly to the houses, where he parked near the rotorcraft pad and switched everything off.

The dogs came running out and carefully encircled the machine. *Poor old Spotback. I do wonder what happened to him.* As he opened the hatch and got out on his side, the dogs edged warily nearer, yapping vigorously at him. Merral stopped, struck by their behavior. It was extraordinary how they seemed much more cautious than in the past. *Perhaps, they know better than we do what is going on.*

His thoughts were interrupted as he was suddenly compressed in an embrace by his aunt. "Oh, Merral! Thank you for coming. We are so grateful. . . . We don't know what to think—"

She stiffened suddenly as Isabella appeared round from her side of the machine.

"Aunt," said Merral, sensing the awkwardness, "I brought Isabella. She has more experience with young girls."

A look of incomprehension, or even annoyance, passed over his aunt's face, only to be replaced swiftly by a smile. "Oh. Yes. I see." She grabbed Isabella in a firm and hasty hug.

"And thank you for coming too." Zennia turned to Merral. "Elana is in her room. The other girls and Thomas are at school. Come on in and I'll get you both a drink. Barrand is on his way down from the ridge. He wasn't expecting you so soon. He's making the most of the dry weather."

Leaving Isabella to look at some recent paintings, Merral went into the kitchen. "Aunt, I want to apologize. I should have warned you that I was bringing Isabella."

She shook her head. "No, it doesn't matter. It's just that—"

He waited for an answer and reluctantly she continued. "I was hoping, I suppose, that we could keep it within the family. If you know what I mean. Elana's problem. It's . . . well . . . a *sensitive* matter."

"But, Aunt, if she has a problem, then it affects the community. And it may be that the problem isn't with her."

"But it particularly affects us. It will not look good."

Puzzled, Merral replied, "Who cares?"

"*We* do, Merral, I'm afraid."

Oh dear. We never used to worry about what others felt about us. What has *happened here?*

When they had passed on all the news and finished their coffee, Zennia took them up to the room they had moved Elana to. Pleading work, she left them there.

Elana was lying faceup on the bed reading a book projected onto the ceiling above her head. She switched it off abruptly after they entered, half got up, and then slumped back onto the bed. Her face was pale.

"Cousin Merral! I heard you might be coming."

He kissed her. "I've brought Isabella to see you. She heard you weren't well."

Elana gave her a mischievous smile. "Some excuse! Hi, Isabella."

After a few minutes of news and pleasantries, Isabella sat by the bed and said in a matter-of-fact voice, "You had a nasty time the other day I gather, Elana."

"Hmm, yes."

"Would you mind—if it doesn't hurt too much—telling me and Merral about it? Slowly. You went for a walk, didn't you?"

Gradually, bit by bit, the story unfolded. Merral, sitting to one side, watched both as they talked and was impressed by Isabella's gentleness and the slow, steady way she worked at the questions. When, as frequently happened, Elana dried up, Isabella would quietly and softly try another angle. The story that emerged, however, was little more than an elaboration of what Merral had already heard. Elana had been on her own, climbing the path to the north-northwest of Herrandown, when she saw the beetle man in the bushes. He made no noise but just stared at her. When she screamed, he vanished.

After praising some paintings on a desk nearby, Isabella managed to get Elana to do a drawing. After some minutes, she had produced a result that, while being crude, was enough to give an impression of what she was trying to describe. The overall picture was of a vaguely manlike figure. It had a narrow face with two eyes and mouth on top of a body with a chest that appeared to be made of plates.

"Like a suit of war armor from the early Dark Times?" Merral asked, but the concept was unknown to her. Further questions revealed a firm and unshakable view that there had only been one pair of hands and legs and that the body casing was brown and shiny, like a beetle's.

"Or like wood?" Merral asked, wondering whether the whole thing was a bizarre illusion based on a fallen log.

"Oh no," she said in firm voice. "Not like wood. Not really. I suppose the surface, the shell, looked like polished wood—dark wood." She gestured to the varnished planks on the wall opposite. "But you see, Merral, the bits moved together, like they do on an insect."

Merral and Isabella shared a bemused glance.

After a few more questions that seemed to elicit nothing new, Elana began to be restless. "Please, Merral, Isabella . . . I'd rather not talk any more. It was horrid!"

Isabella looked at Merral, who reached over and patted Elana gently on her shoulder.

"Thanks, young lady. You'll soon be better. The weather is improving no end. We'll see you before we go." With a few general comments they slipped out, closed the door, and went back downstairs. Halfway down Merral turned to Isabella, expecting her to say something. She merely shook her head.

"Go on," he said.

Isabella shrugged her shoulders. "What do *you* think?"

"Me? I have no idea. If it wasn't impossible, I would believe her. But it's your opinion I value. What do you think?"

"A convincing vision," Isabella remarked gravely. "It's no game or joke. She is certain that what she saw is real."

"Which is different from saying that what she saw was real."

"Quite so. And that is out of my area."

"And into mine. But well done anyway. You did better than I could do."

"Thanks."

They were talking with Zennia a few minutes later when Barrand came in from outside, his gray overalls heavily stained with reddish brown mud. He greeted them all with smiles. If Isabella's arrival had been news to him, Merral thought that he did not show it.

"Sorry, sorry. Business as usual here. Merral, here, give me a hug. I'm expecting your quarry team any day. Isabella, how lovely to see you. Let's give you a hug too. Excuse the dirt. Thank you both for coming." He sank into a chair heavily and breathed out loudly. "Ohh, I'm getting old. Not enough exercise this winter. How was your journey?"

"All right: a washout at about the thirty-five kilometer post."

"Ah, there. A wild stream again. But a lot of mud?"

"Of course."

There was a long silence that Merral felt obliged to break. "Uncle, we had a long chat with Elana."

There was the faintest hint of a frown on his uncle's face. "Ah yes. So how did you find my eldest daughter?" To Merral his tone sounded strangely lacking in compassion.

Merral looked at Isabella, who hesitated a moment before answering. "Well, Barrand Antalfer, I'm no specialist, but I would think she'll be all right in a few days. She's had a nasty shock."

"I'm glad to hear what you think." Barrand nodded impassively and then looked at Merral. "You are both staying for lunch, I take it?"

There was an awkward pause. Merral looked at Isabella and could see her staring at his uncle as if summoning up courage to say something. Eventually, though, it was Merral who found himself breaking the silence.

"Uncle, Elana said she saw it about this time of day. As the issue of the lighting is critical, can we go and see where it . . . where she had the incident? Could we go and have a look? Now?"

Barrand pursed his heavy lips. "To see the place. Well, yes. I don't see why not." There was a curious hesitation. "Both of you? Anyway, I suppose I'm already in outdoor clothes."

He's either acting or he doesn't care, Merral decided. *And either is bizarre. What is going on here?*

Five minutes later, they were walking up the muddy track to the hill. It was still cold, but the clouds had thinned so that there was enough sunlight to cast faint shadows. Under the trees, however, the shadows remained deep. Some of the spring flowers were out. There was a fine display of little yellow daffodils in places, and along a rockier patch bright pink cyclamens glowed.

Barrand, still apparently cheerful, led the way. "It began to rain shortly afterward. It's been a rotten spring. The worst I can remember. The children have been indoors a lot."

"Elana said it had been one of the first good days." Isabella's voice was unobtrusive.

"Just so. Now, it was up here."

They turned up a slippery path between stringy pines and old, brown, straggling brambles. The way narrowed and they fell into single file.

"Can I go ahead?" Merral asked. "Stop me when we get there."

"Be my guest."

They made poor progress, as every so often Merral would stop to look at the ground. There were few clear impressions. Once he felt he could see a child's footprints, and in another place, boot marks that belonged to Barrand.

They kept on for another hundred meters. Here the trees had grown higher, and behind the shrubs and bushes flanking the path, a heavy darkness lay under the lower branches. Merral stopped, gestured for silence, and strained his ears as he listened. He soon heard the noise of scrabbling as a rabbit fled, far away a distant buzzard mewed, and somewhere nearby there was the faint hum of a power saw at another farm. Carefully, Merral breathed in, but he could only smell the new flowers, the clean aroma of the pines, and the faint odor of the new young garlic.

Nothing he heard or smelled was wrong or unfamiliar. Objectively, there was nothing alarming, nothing untoward. And yet, he had an inescapable feeling that something was not right.

They walked on, gradually climbing up above the hamlet. Despite being chilly, the day seemed oddly oppressive, and Merral felt keenly that he wanted the clouds to open and the sun's rays to break through. He glanced around, noticing Isabella's pinched and strained face, while Barrand bore an expression of unnatural unconcern.

The trees now were hanging over them and Merral looked up at them, feeling disoriented. These woods were somehow unfriendly. The idea puzzled him. It was, he knew, intellectually a nonsense concept. There were no unfriendly woods. They were bright woods and dark, even just possibly gloomy woods, but *unfriendly* was not an appropriate adjective. But yet, today, in defiance of all he knew, he felt that the word seemed appropriate.

Suddenly they turned a bend in the path and there was a gap in the trees to the right with a view overlooking Herrandown with all its patchwork of gray-roofed buildings buried to varying extents in the ground.

"Here,"—Barrand's voice was flat and without emotion—"in those trees. She said she saw it there."

Merral's gaze followed his gesture. The bases of the trees were obscured by brambles, young grass, and some scrubby hawthorn bushes. He went up to the spot and looked carefully, feeling even more out of his depth. He could find nothing unusual. *What am I looking for?* Suddenly the whole expedition seemed stupid. After all, he thought, supposing there was another creature there, what would he say to it? "Oh, hello, do you realize you have frightened a girl?" And what language would he use? Communal, Farholmen, pre-Intervention English or French? He felt vaguely stupid staring at a clump of perfectly ordinary brambles. *Genus* Rubus, he told himself, as if finding taxonomy a safe retreat from this imponderable puzzle. *And don't ask me the species name; it's probably another new form. We can travel to the stars, but one hundred and twenty centuries after Linnaeus first gave organisms such names, the humble bramble still mocks any attempt at a usable field classification.*

"Well, any ideas?" There seemed a hint of impatience in his uncle's voice.

"None worth stating, Uncle. Let me see if I can get into the woods behind this. You stay here so I know where I am."

Merral walked back into the trees with Isabella following silently behind him. He picked up an old branch and used it to clear a way through the fringing scrubs. Once through the marginal growth, the undergrowth thinned out. Merral paused to let his eyes adjust to the gloom, which was broken locally by patches of brightness where the light entered through the fractured pine cover.

He sensed Isabella come close alongside. He whispered to her, "What do you think? You are very quiet."

"You are asking the wrong person. Woods aren't my thing and I've got plenty to think about." She frowned, her eyes half closed. "But you think there's something wrong, don't you?"

Merral realized that he might have known she would have detected that. "Wrong, yes. But what sort of wrongness and where? I have no hard data. Let's just listen."

So, with pauses to listen, they moved quietly through the trees. Ahead something dark moved among the trees and Merral froze instantly, his hand swinging up to make Isabella pause. A moment later he relaxed and began breathing again as the squirrel saw him and ran up the trunk. Beckoning Isabella on, he made his way slowly round toward the strip of yellow light that marked the boundary of the path. Beyond the trees he could just make out Barrand in his dark gray jacket.

It must have been about here. There was a feeling of anticlimax. There was nothing to see, no sign of a track or trail. He looked around. The view to the path ahead was obstructed by the combination of the low branches and the brambles. She had imagined it all, she must have.

He called out, "So, Uncle, can you see me?"

"Not well. Go further right, though." Merral moved obediently that way but could see nothing.

"About here?"

"Yes, I think so."

For a moment, Merral was nonplussed, finding that here there seemed to be only undisturbed branches. Then he remembered Elana had called what she had seen a "little man." He squatted down.

Suddenly, through a gap in the bushes, he had a clear view of Barrand's ruddy face framed by vegetation.

"How interesting," he muttered, his voice sounding as if it were from a distance. He turned to Isabella. "You have a look."

Merral stood up and stretched his legs, trying to think clearly. He realized now that he had been assuming all along that Elana had imagined the whole thing. But the gap in the branches made that harder to believe.

He heard a sharp intake of breath from Isabella and then her voice, low and intense, drifted back up to him. "Oh. That adds a different dimension. I hadn't realized . . ."

Alerted by her tone, Merral knelt beside the bush again. "What hadn't you realized?"

"That you can see everything."

As she slid out of his way, he looked beyond her. Barrand had walked away, and beyond the path, glinting in the weak sunlight, stretched the buildings of Herrandown. All of them.

He bit his lip. "Oh my. Oh my," he said, almost under his breath.

The implications sank in one after another, like a succession of stones thrown into still, deep waters. There had been something here. Whatever had been here had been intelligent. It had also, it seemed, had a purpose—that of watching the hamlet. He swallowed, his throat somehow dry. An intelligent purposeful watcher: race or kind unknown.

"Isabella, say nothing to Barrand," he hissed, pitching his voice as softly as he could. He didn't want to alarm his uncle and aunt further.

He heard Isabella answer, "I won't," and recognized a quavering note in her voice.

Suddenly a minute color difference just in front of his face caught his eye. He focused on it. It was the yellow cut end of a tiny branch, thinner than a rose stem. But what had it been cut with? Merral looked around on the ground and found what he was searching for. Carefully, he picked up the other part of the thin branch and stepped back.

"What is it?"

"Whatever . . . whoever was here . . . no, that makes no sense." He paused in desperation. "Anyway, there is a branch here which was cut in half. Somehow."

He held the branch end under a shaft of sunlight and looked at it, noticing a strange, sharp, oblique cut. Aware that his hand was shaking, Merral imaged the cut as best he could on his diary.

Isabella watched him in silence. He saw that she had moved to stand with her back against a tree trunk as if it gave her protection.

Merral spoke to her, his voice little more than a whisper. "We'll talk later. I'm confused."

She nodded sharply. "And I . . . I feel strange here."

He forced a smile, trying not to put his unease into words. *I can understand that strangeness; I've been in these woods for years and I have never felt as I do today. I want to get out, and I want to be in the warmth and coziness of urban Ynysmant surrounded by people.* Forcing those thoughts away, he carefully cut off the end few centimeters of the stem with his knife, put it in a sample bag, and sealed it.

If it came here, then there will be a path to and from this place. Having worked with some of the larger mammals like deer, Merral knew a little of tracking. As he looked into the depths of the woods, he felt he could make out a possible trail between bushes running down into a depression.

He called out to Barrand. "Uncle, we are just going for a walk into the woods. Ten minutes?"

The deep voice boomed back. "Yes, yes. If you need to. Fine. I'll wait here."

Slowly, Merral walked back into the woods, looking for any clue as to what had passed this way. Within a few paces he began to have doubts that there was a trail. Surely he was fooling himself into believing that these depressions were footprints? Might it not simply be the trail of a lynx, a fox, or even a deer?

Yet what he felt might be the trail went west in a fairly straight manner and started to drop down toward the Lannar River. A few dozen meters on, just as he was on the point of giving up, the trail suddenly became very obvious. He found crushed grass stalks and what might have been small and rather angular footprints. But of what creature he had not the slightest idea.

"How much farther, Merral?"

He looked at Isabella, aware from her face as well as her tone that she was unhappy.

"Just another minute or two!" he called out and was rewarded by a fixed, determined smile. *She's right though. We should be going back.* Anyway, the going was becoming rougher, as the trail was now leading down into a steep-banked tributary that fed into the main river.

A large fallen larch trunk partly blocked the way and Merral stooped to get under it. The branches had been snapped off in falling so that the underside of the trunk was punctuated by a series of jagged, splintered protrusions.

"Be careful, Isabella, mind your head."

Merral stopped, his attention grabbed by strands of brown hair hanging on a sharp broken branch. He peered at it carefully in the poor light, just able to make out that the fibers were long, coarse, and wiry. Isabella came and peered at it. Merral pushed her hand away as she reached out to touch it.

"No," he told her, "You'll contaminate it. I'll take it for analysis. We'll get the DNA out and it will tell us what we have."

"Of course. Can you do it?"

"Not here, but I'll get the main lab in Isterrane to do it. An old friend of mine, Anya Lewitz, will organize it."

He imaged the hair on the diary, and then carefully wrapped a sample bag around it. As he did he bent over and put his nose to the mouth of the bag. There was a faint, pungent odor, a smell of something unpleasantly rancid, as if food had been left out in warm weather.

Isabella gestured. "Let me. . . ." Her nose wrinkled in disgust. "Ugh! That's horrid! What creature was that from?"

"I really don't know. There's nothing I can think of here that it's from. And look at the height above the ground. Whatever it was is probably as tall as you or me. Taller, if it was stooping."

Isabella shuddered and looked round.

Merral rubbed his face, as if trying to see the situation more clearly. Not only did this fit nothing in his experience or training, it fit nothing that he had ever heard of.

"It makes no sense at all. It wasn't from what Elana saw, but from something else."

Could there be two unexplained creatures? That seemed hard to believe. He wondered whether two impossibilities were more or less probable than just one.

However a more pressing issue was the need to decide what to do next. Merral paused, weighing up all the options. Should he try and pursue the trail? Take a dog or two and follow it? There would be no problem for a dog following a creature with such a smell. But he was not equipped for a trail that could lead to a day's walk or more, and he had to be back home today in order to be in Isterrane the day after tomorrow. Besides, something like that would raise the status of the whole affair and would inevitably make it a major crisis. And, if it was a false alarm, then harm might be done to his uncle's family. He made his decision.

"Isabella, we will go back now. Anyway, we said ten minutes."

"A good idea," she answered, relief in her voice. "What are you going to do?"

"I will take advice in Isterrane. In the meantime, I think we are neutral about what we have seen. The data, after all, needs analysis." Merral began to walk back toward where his uncle was.

"I suppose you are right."

Barrand was sitting on a tree trunk whittling away at a piece of wood with a knife. "Ho! I was wondering where you had both gone to."

"I found something that might have been a track and I picked up some samples for analysis."

Barrand seemed almost uninterested. "Some faunal anomaly, I'll bet. Well, we'd better get back for lunch."

Lunch was an oddly subdued affair, especially by comparison with the other meals he'd had at Herrandown. Elana preferred to stay and eat in her bedroom. Barrand and Zennia were pleasant and affable, and the food was good and plentiful, but Merral felt a tension. Every so often Merral noticed glances between his uncle and aunt that hinted that all was not well between them.

After lunch Barrand and Zennia disappeared into the kitchen to make coffee, leaving Merral and Isabella alone in the small family room that he had sat in with his aunt and uncle just before Nativity. That reminded Merral that he really ought to try and raise the issue of the recording. It was not a prospect that appealed, and thinking of the best way to approach it began to occupy his mind. While Isabella sat looking at a portfolio of his aunt's paintings, Merral got up and, trying to clarify his thoughts, opened the window and leaned out, enjoying the fresh spring air.

As he did he realized he could hear what his aunt and uncle were saying. *The kitchen window must be open,* he thought, and the breeze came from that direction. A second or two later he realized that the conversation was also very animated.

His uncle's voice, loud and ill tempered, drifted past. "You shouldn't have got me to bring him in. It's something *we* can handle."

It was such an extraordinary tone that for a moment Merral wondered if it really was his uncle.

Then his aunt replied and, to his distress, her manner was similar. "*We* handle it?" she seemed to snap. "*We* haven't a clue—least of all you. There's something wrong here, Barrand. I keep telling you."

There was a snort, as if an animal were loose. "Don't be a fool, woman. There's nothing wrong here but hysterical women."

"Hysterical? I like that!" His aunt's voice seemed to vibrate with rage. "The real problem is a man—a man who is too proud and too stubborn to admit that there is something badly wrong here!"

Merral, suddenly ashamed both of eavesdropping and of what he was overhearing, abruptly closed the window. He stepped back into the room wondering if his face was burning. He was staggered, even shocked. The words he had heard made sense, but the tone was like nothing he had ever heard before. Things like it were alluded to in the old literature, but for it to happen between a husband and wife? It was hardly credible.

"What's wrong?" Isabella asked.

"I have heard . . ." He paused, finding himself in agonized consternation. "No, I can't say. . . ." He looked at her. "What's wrong here, Isabella? I'm convinced everything is. Badly."

Isabella opened her mouth to speak and closed it abruptly at the sound of approaching footsteps.

The subsequent coffee was a very quiet, even embarrassed affair in which almost nothing was said. After it Merral and Barrand left Zennia and Isabella and went over together to the office.

The big man closed the door, sat down awkwardly at his crowded desk, and stared over his papers at Merral.

"Tell me, Nephew," he asked, "what will your verdict be?" Merral felt that there was a wary, defensive look on his uncle's face.

Merral did not answer immediately, his mind instead running over a range of possible answers. Eventually he spoke. "Uncle, I need to take some advice. I am a forester. I am not convinced that the problem lies in my area. If it does, it goes beyond my knowledge. Frankly, I have no idea what is going on."

Barrand nodded and leaned back in his chair. "So what are you going to do?"

"The day after tomorrow I will go to Isterrane and talk to some people there about your situation."

A clear look of unease crossed his uncle's face. "It's going to go *that* far? I was hoping that it could be sorted out easily. Here. Or at worst, Ynysmant."

"I had hoped so too, but I think not. I think I need specialist advice. You see, there is always the possibility that the wrong action may make matters worse."

"I suppose so." His uncle shifted his large frame heavily in his chair. "Well, to be honest, Merral, I'm rather regretting my call yesterday. Zennia pushed me into it. Elana had this thing, this vision. By taking it seriously, we have just made matters worse."

"You don't believe her?" Merral asked.

"Believe what?" There was a hard-edged incredulity in his voice. "That she saw a creature that doesn't exist? I wouldn't say it to her face, of course. No, let's just say I'm frankly skeptical—very skeptical. Female hormones, I'd say."

Feeling unsure what to say, Merral said nothing.

"See, Merral," his uncle continued, leaning forward slightly, "I would rather that we kept the whole thing low-key. Not blow it up. This girl of yours, Isabella, now—very nice, don't get me wrong—she may talk and we might have the colony here closed down. And we've worked hard."

He gestured widely with his arms, got up with a lurch of the chair, walked to the window and peered out of it.

"It's not easy here, you know. 'The blessings of isolation,' I think my wife said." He made a strange, almost mocking noise. "Maybe, it has its curses, though. Fifty of us. All together, and such a lousy winter. I wonder if you people in Ynysmant really understand. . . ."

He swung round and shook his large head angrily as if trying to break free of something.

"Strange, Merral. I've never felt this way before. Very strange. Sorry to take it out on you, too. It must be the weather. It's just . . . well . . . in a word, *tough* here."

He paced the floor as if trying to find words to express his feelings. He paused at the Lymatov painting and stared hard at it. "We were talking about this last time, weren't we?"

Merral nodded.

"Well it's saying different things to me now. It asks a question. Is it worth it? Is the whole venture"—he threw his arms wide as if to encompass the colony—"the sacrifices, the blood, the suffering. Is it all worth doing?"

For some time Merral's perplexity was so great he could say nothing. Eventually, feeling compelled to speak, his reply was hesitant.

"I have to say, Uncle, that this question has been debated, well, ever since the Intervention. The verdict has always been that it is. It *is* all worthwhile."

"Well then," his uncle said, in a tone that suggested he was unconvinced, "in the event of the entire Assembly of Worlds versus Barrand Imanos Antalfer I guess I must be wrong." And he sat down so heavily in his chair that it protested. "Sorry," he said, but his tone denied his words.

There was a heavy silence in the room. Merral, wishing he was elsewhere, plucked up his courage. "Uncle, before I go. There is one more thing. I hate to mention it. But I have a question about your concert at Nativity. The one with the Rechereg."

Merral found it impossible to identify the emotion that his uncle's face suddenly acquired.

"Oh yes. *That*. Did you like it?"

"Very much. But Miranda Cline . . . she seems to have sung at a higher pitch than she was able to in life."

Very slowly, almost as if drugged, Barrand nodded his head. "Ah, that. *That*. I'm surprised you noticed." He shrugged.

"My attention was drawn to it. But her range *was* altered?"

His uncle gave a long, low sigh. "In a way, yes. In a way, no. See, she would always have liked to sing higher. I've read her biography. That's the thing. So I was acting—shall we say—in her best interests."

"But we don't know what she actually thought. Or what she thinks now. And the Technology Protocols say that—"

"Oh yes." There was a clear note of irritation here. "Number six, isn't it? But I think she would have agreed."

In the hanging silence that ensued, Merral realized that he was becoming tempted to say that the affair didn't matter. But he knew it *did* matter. He tried to think what to say next but was spared by his uncle. "Look, I was in a hurry and I didn't think it would give offense. But I will destroy the file."

"Probably the best thing." But it was more than a matter of giving offense, Merral knew. It was wrong.

The silence returned, only to be broken again by his uncle's voice, now quiet but vaguely truculent, as if he was trying to reassert himself. "But maybe, Merral, we need to remember something."

"What?"

"That the Technology Protocols were made by men, not God. They're not Scripture."

Merral suddenly realized that they were now in very serious and very deep waters. He knew that he had to get out of the conversation without giving in.

"No, they aren't. True. But they are part of the fabric of the covenant of the Assembly of Worlds, and there has been no serious discussion of the removal of any part of them for over ten thousand years."

Merral decided that he really couldn't get into an argument. He had to talk to Vero about this.

"Anyway, Uncle. I've had a long day. We can discuss it all at some other time."

"Oh, perhaps so. Anyway, you'd best be going."

Barrand got to his feet, his bulk seeming to dominate the office.

"Look, I'm sorry about the business with Miranda Cline. It was stupid. It's just been a long winter." He sighed heavily. "You'd best go. I suspect it will all blow over here. A proper spring is nearly here and summer won't be far away. And I'll feel better when I get the quarry started. But thanks for coming."

Merral chose his words carefully. "Uncle, be assured of this. I support you, and I'm available whenever you need me."

They walked slowly back to the house where they were greeted by Thomas, now released from school, who leapt on Merral with a boundless energy and demanded to clamber over him. Merral put up with it for a few minutes and then deposited the child on the ground. Not only had Thomas become heavy today, his heart was not in it. Instead, he hugged him and let him go. As he looked at him, he realized how much he wanted to have children of his own someday.

"So, Thomas, how are things?"

"Not good, Cousin. Not good at all." He gestured with a stubby and rather dirty hand to the surrounding woods. "There's something bad out there. Real bad. You're gonna fix it, aren't you? You are, for sure. Do you promise?" His round face was troubled.

"Well, Thomas, promises are made to be kept. So it's a serious business to make them. I won't promise to do what I may not be able to. But what I will promise, Thomas, is this. . . ." He paused, thinking of the binding significance of his words. "I am going to do everything to find out what's bad in the forest. I promise."

"Thanks. Thanks. Find out what's in there."

He looked thoughtful for a moment, and then he whispered something to Merral in a voice that was so quiet that no one else heard it.

And what Thomas said so appalled and disgusted Merral that when he went over everything that he had seen and heard that day, it was Thomas's comment that alarmed him most of all. And when, the day after, he journeyed to Isterrane, it was still a preoccupation.

Again and again, the words that Thomas had whispered to him came back to him. Endlessly, he saw the little lips move and heard the voice whisper to him.

"Find it, Cousin Merral, find it. And when you find it . . . *kill it.*"

8

As the short-haul passenger flier made its unhurried descent through thick but patchy clouds into Isterrane Airport, Merral peered out through the window. As it was fully loaded, the pilot chose not to land vertically, but instead to come in on a gentle curving descent northward over Hassanet's Sea. Although slower, this approach to the landing strip was Merral's favorite as it offered him better views, and today he was not disappointed.

As they dipped below the clouds, his first sight was of the warm blue waters of Isterrane Bay with the high gray cliffs and green woods of the western headland rising beyond. Moments later as they swung round, the sloping red-tiled roofs of Isterrane could be seen, broken up into segments by the green of the fields and parks which ran into the very heart of the city. As the flier came in low and straight for touchdown, the gleaming pale gray wall of the hundred-meter-high anti-tsunami barrier that guarded the seaward margin of Isterrane suddenly seemed to loom up above the town's skyline.

I wonder what Vero makes of that, Merral wondered, remembering the sentinel's unease at Congregation Hall's role as a refuge. *But we must do things like this; on our unstable Made Worlds there is always the risk of some submarine landslide, volcano, or earthquake suddenly displacing a million tons of water landward. And a hundred other perils.* But, as the thought came to him, Merral found his reflection becoming somber as he realized that he had—for all its risks—always found his world vaguely reassuring. True, it had its hazards, but they were all mapped, cataloged, and known. And yet, in the last two days he had come to wonder whether Farholme was such a known world after all. Could it be possible, he had puzzled, that they might have overlooked something? Might it be that there was something not mentioned in the Catalog of Species loose here? Something so strange that no light could be shed on it by all the millennia of knowledge of the Assembly?

Both the atmosphere and space segments of Isterrane Airport seemed busy. Away down to the west, on the long rendered-basalt runways of the space strips Merral noted the white squat hulls of three general survey craft and two of the much larger in-system shuttles. Probably as a result, he found there was a lot of land traffic leaving the port, and the allocating computer almost immediately found him a seat in a vehicle going past the Planning Institute complex. So it was barely twenty minutes after landing that Merral was able to let himself into the guest room that had been issued to him. He unpacked his things, briefly admired his view of the Institute's mixed woodlands and the lake with the high white fin of the Planetary Administration Building rising behind it, and then sat down at the table with his diary to try to contact Vero.

The image that he received showed him immediately that his friend was not yet in Isterrane. The picture was shaking. Vero's face was too close to the screen, and behind him were the unmistakable green furnishings of a long-haul flier. Even as Merral extended a greeting, Vero's eyes closed as if in pain, his face bobbed sharply, and there was a thud as the transmitting diary bounced. The brown eyes opened and Vero gave an unnatural smile. "Merral! I am just being reminded of something I once read but had long since forgotten."

"What was that?"

The face jerked again.

"Ah! That atmospheric turbulence on the Made Worlds can be very much worse than that on Earth. And much less predictable. Oh, here we"—the image jarred and the dark skin seemed to acquire a paler tone—"go again. I'll never complain about the Gates again. Never! Look, Merral, I'm six hours away. Where shall I meet you?"

"The Planning Institute. I'll be there all this afternoon."

Vero nodded weakly. "I'll come straight over as soon as I land. *If* I land. . . . Look, I'm going to switch off. On Earth it's very rude to be sick on screen. Oh no!"

The screen went blank. After a few moments of praying for Vero, Merral called Anya Lewitz. She winked at Merral and gave him a broad smile that seemed to split her freckled face. "Tree Man! You made it in from the wilds. Welcome to the big town." There was a boisterousness to her manner that Merral found engaging and heartening.

"Nice to be here and to see you, Anya. I have something for you."

"Great, put it on a lead and walk it over. What does it eat?" Merral's concerns seemed to diminish in the presence of Anya's seemingly boundless good cheer.

"Sorry, it's dead. No, just a couple of samples."

"Shame! You're at the Institute?"

"Yes . . . how did you . . . ?"

"That decor. Terribly dull. No wonder the planet is such a mess; you guys can't even paint your own walls coordinated shades of blue. Look, get on over straight away. We are at the south end of the center. I want to catch up with your news and I've a meeting in a couple of hours."

Using the Institute's transport allocation system, Merral very quickly found himself a lift to the western side of the city, where the various offices, laboratories, and nurseries of the Planetary Ecology Center occupied most of a park the size of Ynysmant town. From the main entrance, he walked along the long, covered path to the Reconstruction Project Station. There, after stopping briefly to marvel at the wall-size holograph system that was today showing *The Blue Whales of Marsa-Mena*, he was directed up to Anya's office.

This turned out to be a charming, extended second-floor room under a high-pitched wooden roof, with wide glass windows and a balcony overlooking the city. For all its size, the room seemed full. The walls were covered with maps and images of animals, the shelving loaded with equipment, datapaks, models, and books, and the spare table and bench space were covered by papers and charts. In one corner of the room a model of a giant sloth, almost Merral's height, stared at him with a haughty air. In the far corner some tree hamsters in a large cage ran up a branch and peered at him with some uncertainty.

Anya gave him a hearty hug and a moist kiss on the cheek. *Very nice,* Merral thought, surprised at the strength of his feelings. She gestured in her lively way to a seat at a low table. They sat down, and she looked at him in the evaluative way old friends do after an absence of years. Merral felt that Anya's notorious playfulness and exuberance had been slightly tempered with growing maturity, but not entirely lost. *No, she has just learned how to tame it.*

Over coffee, they shared news of families, friends, and jobs. Anya's face brightened. "Oh, and while I remember, tonight—come over for a meal. The building over there, Narreza Tower. Fifth—that is, top—floor. It's at my flat; my older sister is in town. You know Perena?"

"Yes, you introduced me at the beach once. The pilot?"

"Ah, a Near-Space Captain now. Anyway, Space Affairs is letting her off for the night, so she's cooking. Theodore will be there too. You've met him?"

"No. I don't think so."

"Tree Man, you've been out in the bush too long. Theodore is a good friend of mine. He's with Maritime Affairs, works on deep-sea currents. Anyway, you'd be more than welcome."

"Thanks. But I've got a guest myself coming in from Aftarena. I'd better look after him. He's from Ancient Earth—truly a long way from home."

"Ancient Earth? Really, oh, you must bring him. Perena would like that. She finished her training there. But who is it?"

"One Verofaza Laertes Enand, sentinel."

Anya wagged her head slowly and seriously as if reading a lot into the answer. "Ah, a sentinel. You are keeping interesting company. I'd heard we had one visiting. Bring him, though. What's he doing?"

A good question, and one that I wonder if Vero can answer.

"Well, he's writing a report. But it's complicated. Ask him yourself, though."

"Oh, I will."

There was a pause and Anya glanced at the clock on the wall. "Time flies, I'm afraid. Now, your problem. Tell me about it."

"It may be something or nothing. I'm involved professionally and also because it is family. I have an uncle at Herrandown, a Forward Colony up toward the Lannar Crater. It's his eldest girl who says she saw it . . . this thing."

"Yeah, the more I thought about it the stranger it became. She is sticking to the story, I take it?"

"Oh yes. I'm certain she believes in it. She did a drawing. Look at this." He summoned up a scanned copy on his diary screen and turned it so Anya could see it.

Anya looked at it in silence, her bright blue eyes examining it carefully. Finally, she shook her head. "Like nothing in reality and precious little I've heard of in fiction. I'm no wiser. It's more humanoid than I had thought. But what do *you* think, O great expert of the Great Northern Forest?" Merral noticed a searching look to her face that belied the teasing tone.

"Me? Well to be honest, I'm embarrassed by it. I really don't know. I was set to dismiss it, but then we found that where she said she had seen it there was evidence that something had been there. Watching Herrandown. And it was a good surveillance spot."

Anya looked at him with surprise. *"Watching* Herrandown? How far away?"

"Two kilometers."

She shook a finger at him and grinned. "Oh, Merral, so it's intelligent now. With long-distance vision. Some cockroach! We'd better evacuate the planet quick and blow the Gate behind us. That will give the human race forty years minimum to work on insecticides before it makes the next Assembly world. Assuming it doesn't go faster than light too."

Merral laughed.

Anya shook her head merrily. "Any other data? These samples . . ."

"The branches had been cut to clear the view. I got a sample." He reached into his bag, pulled out the carefully wrapped sample, and handed it over to Anya. "The right angle cut is mine."

She took the clear bag in her hands and held it up to the light. "You've looked at it?"

"Not really. It's not my area. What do you see?"

"Not much. But let me look at it under a lens." She got up and took it over to a desk where a large microscope stood. Merral got up and joined her as the cut piece of wood came into focus on the screen.

Anya peered at it. "Hmm. Need to do comparative studies. But it was a scissors action. From both sides at once; you can see the pressure points on either side. Could be a tool, I suppose. Tiny scoring or scratch marks. See there?" She pointed to part of the image. "Probably two finely serrated scissor blades. But big. That branch is five millimeters thick. Size of my little fingertip."

She paused, puzzlement in her tone. "Let me see the girl's sketch again."

Merral called it up and Anya enlarged the area around the creature's hands. "Odder still." The note of puzzlement was deeper and darker now. "I had assumed that the hands were badly drawn. Let me get a printout."

A few seconds later, they were peering over a sheet of paper.

"Look, Merral."

"So?" he asked, noting that there were fingers sketched on each hand.

"The thumb."

Merral looked again. "Odd," he said. "It's not really there. As a thumb that is. Just another long finger but oddly wider. Is it an accident of drawing?"

"I think not. See how they are symmetrical? Both hands are alike. It suggests a real memory. But interesting . . ."

"How so?"

Anya gave Merral a distant, abstracted smile and held up her right hand with the fingers aligned together. Then she swung her thumb in and out against the fingers in a snipping motion.

"I see," said Merral, in surprise. "You think that . . . ?"

She shook her head so that her fine red hair flicked over her shoulders. "It must be coincidence." She stared out of the window for a moment, then turned back to him. "No. I refuse to fuel silly ideas. I'll get one of our animal people to look at it."

She put it carefully down, but Merral noticed that her thoughtful look had not evaporated.

"What else?"

"Only this," Merral said as he handed over the second specimen.

She looked at him in feigned bemusement. "No, *no*, Tree Man. That's *hair*. Normally only mammals have it."

He smiled. "Oh gosh, Anya, I'd forgotten that. But joking apart, I don't recognize it, and I've seen all our wildlife. That's my job. What's odder still is that it was caught on an overhanging branch above the trail. About a meter seventy-five off the ground, so you can read that as a minimum height. It could have been an even larger creature if it had been stooping."

Anya rubbed her forehead. "So this little anthropoid arthropod suddenly sprouts hair and doubles in size. Oh dear."

Merral shrugged. "Oh, I know."

Anya sucked her lower lip in. "So, we have *two* new beasts. The human cockroach and a big hairy thing."

"That is a conclusion I've tried to avoid drawing."

Anya put the sample down carefully and leaned back in her chair.

"I can see why. Of course, it could be that there was a monkey that sat on the back of the cockroach. There, have you considered that possibility?" She grinned at him.

"No."

"Well, at least we can get the DNA out of this. Assuming it has any. I'll give you the results tomorrow."

She looked at the hair and then back at Merral. "Well, if it's real, then we have a problem, to put it mildly. Everything we do depends on us knowing exactly what fauna we have here. We always worry about new strains, some new mutant mouse with an insatiable appetite perhaps, but a totally new mammal—let alone a physically impossible mega-arthropod—is totally off the scale. And if it's a nightmare or a delusion we need to keep it in check. We don't want people fearing new creatures. You are certain that it isn't a joke or prank?"

Merral ran the question over again in his mind for the thousandth time. "Oh, Anya, I'm totally unsure. The whole thing says that she really saw something. But it just can't be. And yet . . ."

In this room, with Anya's blunt common sense, his fears seemed to almost vanish. Almost, but not quite. He hesitated.

Anya leaned slightly toward him. "There's more than what you've told me, isn't there?"

"Yes, but it's not really biological. More spiritual or psychological. Something's wrong, though."

"So you called in the sentinel?"

"Uh, no. A wrong guess there. He sort of wandered in. A coincidence. In fact, I'm not at all convinced that he can help. Maybe. What do you know of them?"

"Sentinels? A bit. They have contributed to the Reconstruction Debate. Genetic alteration or manipulation has always been an issue with them."

"I hadn't realized that."

"They are concerned about anything that erodes the human."

"Interesting. That fits with what little I know."

"Anyway, bring your friend tonight."

"I will. Just at this moment he may not be feeling like eating much. But by tonight things may be better."

Anya looked at the clock. "Well, my meeting starts soon. I'll drop these into the lab on the way over."

She picked up the specimens and, apparently catching his unspoken question, answered, "Should have the results tomorrow morning. The whole mystery solved. Anyway, see you tonight. Top floor, Narreza Tower—say, seven-thirty? Cheers, Merral. Great to see you again." She patted his shoulder gently. "It really is."

Suddenly she was gone and Merral was left in the room. Feeling strangely elated, he echoed her statement in his mind with approval.

Yes, Anya, it is great to see you again.

Half an hour later Merral was back at the Planning Institute. There he had a light lunch and met some old colleagues with whom he shared routine news. Finding he still had time to pass before Vero arrived, he sat down in his room, switched his diary through to the wallscreen, and logged in to the Library. The traditional image of the interior of a vast, high-vaulted building with an almost infinite number of shelves appeared on the wall.

What to look up? Merral asked himself. He had so many questions, but where did he start? Psychological disturbances, perhaps? He pushed his finger on the diary as if to walk to the behavioral science section, but as the file-laden aisles with the ghostly figures of the other users sped past him, he began to have second thoughts. There was so much there. Even within the psychology section. Where to begin? He lifted off his finger and found himself halted in front of a bay of a dozen shelves packed with virtual datapaks. The top of the bay was clearly labeled "Assembly Psychology: The Years A.D. 4000–5220: Section 32, The Schools of the Varantid Worlds. Bay 510 out of 870." With the renewed realization of exactly how much data there was available for him, Merral felt suddenly daunted. Access to all of humanity's knowledge didn't seem to help him.

Perhaps, he wondered, he should ask one of the virtual librarians about beetles? or sentinels? or Protocols and their abuses?

I don't know where to begin. He exited the Library and switched off the link. He borrowed a canoe and for the next few hours paddled around the lake at the center of the Institute's extensive grounds, enjoying Isterrane's warmer climate and trying—*and failing*—to put the pieces of the puzzle together.

In midafternoon, alerted by a faint noise high above him, he looked up to see the gull-like long-haul flier come in to land, the wings extending fluidly outward into landing mode as he watched. He paddled over to land, handed back the canoe he'd borrowed, and went back to the center to wait.

Half an hour later Vero arrived. He lowered his heavy bag to the ground and gave Merral a hug. "Good to see you again. And very good to be on solid land," he said with feeling.

"You'll get used to our atmosphere's fluctuations."

Vero shuddered. "Fluctuations! There are gaping holes in your atmosphere. I doubt I'll ever get used to it. Where can we talk?"

"My room?"

"No," Vero said firmly. "I need fresh air. Let's walk around the grounds."

"Fine, leave your bag in the office here. Incidentally, you are invited to a meal tonight. Let me tell you about it. . . ."

Once out under the trees, Vero turned to Merral, his brown eyes wide and solemn. "Look, I'm taking this seriously. I want you to tell me everything that has happened at Herrandown. Everything, every detail. In order. I'll just listen, although I may need to take a record later."

So for the next hour Merral found himself recounting first the request for help from his uncle and aunt, and then the details of his and Isabella's visit to Herrandown. Vero listened and nodded and occasionally asked for a clarification or a repetition. When Merral described the discovery that the site where the creature had been seen overlooked the settlement, Vero looked at him in an agitated way. "You're sure? Overlooking all of them?"

"Of course. It was what made me think there might be something in it."

"Yes. It raises a number of issues. . . ." His face acquired a worried look and for a moment he seemed to be on the point of saying something. "No . . . ," he said, as if addressing himself. "We will discuss that issue later. Continue."

A second point that excited a particular interest was the conversation that Merral had overheard between his uncle and his aunt. It was something that Merral had felt reluctant to mention; in the end he decided that he had to. Besides which, the business had so troubled him that he was glad to share it with someone. Vero frowned darkly when it was described to him and asked for it to be repeated. At the end of the repetition there was a silence in which Vero just shook his head sadly.

Merral broke the silence. "Vero, I almost can't believe I heard it. A noisy, aggressive dispute between husband and wife. Repeating it now, it sounds incredible. Can I be making it up?"

They had stopped walking and Vero rubbed his face wearily with his hand. "You have every right to be disturbed by it, my friend. No, you can't be making it up. For me, it is in its way all too familiar, I'm afraid. As a sentinel we are encouraged, no—required is better—to study personal relationships before the Great Intervention. You, of course, have the Scriptures too, so you know something of this, but we have to look at such things in more . . . depth." He looked embarrassed and after a brief hesitation, went on. "If *depth* is the word. No one now would read or watch such things out of choice but it does—we believe—no real harm under controlled conditions. So what you heard is familiar to me." He rubbed his long fingers through his tight-curled hair. "Familiar, but no less worrying."

Merral then told how his uncle had reacted when confronted with the question of modifying the re-created voices. He and Vero had stopped on a wooden bridge over a stream that fed into the lake and were leaning over it, staring down into the clear water and watching the trout dart about below them.

"So Barrand then replied, 'We need to remember something. The Technology Protocols were made by men, not God. They're not Scripture.' "

Vero seemed to jolt upright as if an electric current had been applied to him. "He said *what?*"

"That 'the Technology Protocols were made by men not God. They're not Scripture.' "

Merral saw that Vero was giving him a look that seemed close to incredulity. There was a long silence and then he spoke very slowly and softly. "*That* was said by another. But a very long time ago. . . ." He shook his head as if stunned. "Extraordinary! Very alarming! But go on."

They set off walking again and eventually, with the account of young Thomas's injunction to kill whatever he found, Merral ended his tale.

"Can you believe it, Vero?"

There was a long sigh from Vero. "Believe it? Yes, I think I can. But I can't explain it." Then he fell silent.

A six-legged transporter robot carrying flasks paused deferentially to let them walk past. "So now tell me, what do you think? And what am I supposed to think?"

Vero stopped and turned to Merral. "As to what you think, you must decide that. For myself, I think many things. Before you told me all this, I was going to say that I was worried that it was serious. And now I know that it is serious. But there are questions."

"Such as?"

"Everything. What's happening? Why? Why there? More importantly, what do I do?"

"Isn't that easy? Don't you just call your people on Ancient Earth?"

"Yes, I have considered that. I am close to doing it." His face radiated unease. "But there are problems. Supposing we have a full-threat evaluation team come in and I am wrong? We will have done damage to your uncle and his family, damage to Herrandown, and damage to the sentinels." He sighed. "The problem on The Vellant that I mentioned did us some harm. And the other cases. There is an old, old story about the boy who cried wolf. You have heard of it."

"Indeed."

They were standing near a fence overlooking the lake. Vero tapped the wood impatiently. "But you see, it's all so different from anything we might have expected."

"Which was?"

"We have been looking for a slow shift in opinions, for subtle changes across a world. So small that only statistics would show. Not for a sudden, isolated event like this. Least of all one with such bizarre manifestations. No, it's too strange. I need more evidence."

He drummed his hands on the fence and stared over the water before looking at Merral with sharp, inquiring eyes.

"When do you get the results back from Anya?"

"Tomorrow morning, she said. Why?"

"What I think is this . . . no, wait. Can you get me a large display of the area? A remote image—decent scale."

Merral gestured to his diary but Vero shook his head. "No, something bigger, projected would do. I need to visualize the area."

"No problem. There's a free office near my room. I can call up the most recent satellite image—that would be last week's—and overlay places on it."

"Good." Vero shivered slightly. "I feel it's getting cool outside here. Let's go inside. I think my blood got used to the tropics."

Ten minutes later Vero was staring at a projected image that covered most of a wall. It was grainy but clear enough for the individual buildings of Herrandown to be seen. He moved around it, touching parts with a light pointer.

"Your uncle's house is here? Yes. That's the new building for animals in winter. The office. Good. As I'd pictured it." Vero stared at the image and then continued. "And the woods here—this sort of crescent around the side of the hamlet—they run down to the river. The Lannar."

Merral noted that his friend seemed to have rapidly grasped the area's geography.

"Now," Vero said, "show me where the sighting was. And where you found the hair sample."

Merral pointed out the two localities and Vero stared at them.

"There is less woodland up here than I thought," he commented. "Other than the plantations, it's all confined to the rivers. Where it is quite dense, but otherwise the area is quite bare."

"We are working on it. But in summer it gets very dry with the westerly wind out of the interior. So the best-established woods all follow the rivers."

"Your trail runs north and, if it went along the river, that runs north–south too. And the dog was last seen going north too. North, north, and north."

Vero magnified the image until the woods around Herrandown were a tiny patch of green in a vastness of pale browns and grays, and the sharp arc of the southern mountain ramparts of the Lannar Crater appeared at the top of the image.

Vero turned to Merral. "I mean, do you know what happens in the north?"

"I thought I did. It's a pretty active area. The Lannar Crater averages a rating of eight on the Stellman Scale of geomorphologic activity for Made Worlds. That's out of a high of ten. Isterrane is around two; Herrandown, four something."

"It's unstable?"

"Let's say, stabilizing. The crater is only about a million or so years old. So it was still pretty fresh at the Seeding, with steep walls and a lot of impact fragments around. When the atmosphere switched to being oxygenating and water-rich in the Eighth Millennium there was an enormous lot of weathering and erosion."

"As everywhere on Farholme."

"Yes. But more so here. Pan out to show the whole crater."

Vero nudged the controls so that the entire circle of the Lannar Crater slid into the center and the brown-smudged blue of the sea edged onto the right of the image.

"At first," Merral said, "the crater just filled up with a great pile of debris and became a mass of lakes and swamps but, oh, about two thousand years ago, the crater walls began to be breached by river erosion. The Lannar is the southern system, but you can see the important Nannalt river system going out east into the Mazurbine Ocean."

"The big brown smudge here?" said Vero, gesturing to a protrusion into the sea.

"Yes. The Nannalt Delta. Anyway, so it's still adjusting to massive changes in its drainage. Some of the swamps are drying up; there's a lot of river erosion. I've seen the images, Vero; some areas are almost unrecognizable within a year."

Vero stared at the map again. "That helps me. But it has been visited?"

"Yes. The odd botanical, geologic, and zoological trips. I've flown over. But it's wild country. We tend to leave it alone and let the satellites keep an eye on it for us. There are only thirty million people on Farholme and there's a lot of areas with more promise."

"So, you have no plans for it?"

"No. Not unless winters warm up a lot. Along the higher parts of the Northern Rim glaciers are growing. You can see them on the image. They've done remote seeding of trees and plants, but it's an area we have left to itself, particularly while it settles down."

"So, it isn't visited regularly?"

"No. This isn't like Ancient Earth, Vero. We have no shortage of wildernesses or work elsewhere. There is no archaeology, no undiscovered animals or plants."

Vero gave him an odd smile. "That's what you used to say."

"True. But what are you thinking?"

Vero put the pointer down and began to pace backward and forward. "I am building a delicate chain of logic. Too delicate, but I must go on. Let us suppose that there is something here, something—what shall we say?—exotic. Yes, that's the word. Then it must hide, breed somewhere. The best guess would be to the north. To the south, east, and west are bare open wastes. But the river valley offers cover along its length well into the crater. Do you follow my train of thought?"

"I do not dissent from it. I was thinking vaguely along those lines but was going to wait for Anya's results."

Vero sat down at the table and stared at the image. "Merral, my suggestion is this: Tomorrow, if Anya comes up with anything strange . . . indeed, anything unaccountable at all . . . then the trail you picked up must be pursued immediately."

"It will be cold. Nearly a week old. But I see that you think it can only go one way."

"Correct. Our creature, assuming we have one—or even two—is furtive and loves cover. It has been seen and knows it. I do not think it will venture out into the open. It will have taken the river. It probably came south down it and retreated back up it." He adjusted the image so that it showed the entire length of the river from Herrandown to the Southern Rim Ranges.

"Well, true enough. Brigila's Wastes is no home for such creatures," Merral answered as he tried to assess Vero's line of thinking. For all the unfamiliarity of the concepts, he found it made a sort of sense.

"I think, Vero, that I agree with you. If the results are odd then I will get permission and take off up the river for a few days."

"Can it be done quietly?"

"Yes, I can travel light on foot. If necessary, I can get food dropped to me. I could probably get most of the way up to the Ranges without needing that. But it's rough going, Vero. Remember our landscape is still in an unfinished state."

He gestured to the image, wondering if the yellow and red gashes of landslides and mudflows were as visible to his friend as they were to him.

Suddenly Vero spoke quietly. "And if you do, I will come too."

Merral laughed. "You? Please, Vero. There are no guest rooms there. It's well, tough country. We would be walking, perhaps with a pack animal. You are . . ." He hesitated. "Well, you show no evidence of being able to travel in this country."

Vero stood up. "I may surprise you. I have done my share of walking and camping on Ancient Earth. We have our jungles and mountains too."

On impulse, Merral squeezed Vero's upper arm. To his surprise, he felt muscle.

"Well. . . ." He paused. "I must say, Vero, that company would be acceptable. Strange. . . ."

Vero was looking at him with curiosity. "Why strange?"

"Because I have spent a lot of time in the last five years on my own in woods such as these. I have camped in solitude in all seasons. I have spent as much as a week without talking to a single person. I have never felt the slightest unease or fear. I watch out for bears and I pass by wolf packs. But that is caution, not fear. Yet since Nativity, on the last few trips, I have felt—" Merral hesitated, trying to find the words. "No, I can't describe it, Vero. Only that I have been glad to be back home. Behind walls and doors."

Vero looked at the image again and then turned it off. Then he spoke aloud in a quiet but penetrating voice. "Another tiny thread of evidence. A forester feels uneasy in forests. All tiny threads, but wound together they are forming a solid rope. But attached to what?"

"I have no idea."

"Me neither." Vero handed the diary back to Merral. He rubbed his forehead. "Sorry, I'm tired; it was a twelve-hour flight. I may get some sleep. And definitely a shower before this meal tonight. Brenito will put me up. I'd better be off now."

Merral arranged for a lift for Vero, and then the two of them went to the doorway.

Vero opened the door and then stopped, his long fingers tapping on the glass. "You know . . . ," he said, then paused as if in doubt. "No, I ought to say it. There is one more thing. I am reluctant to mention it, but I am worried about the possibility of danger."

"To who?"

"To your uncle and his family. You see, my dear Forester, you must become a sentinel with me, at least in thought. You and I must ask questions that no one has asked for thousands of years. Try this. What purpose had this creature—assuming there was indeed one—in watching Herrandown?"

Merral felt slightly cold, as if a draught of air had come through the door. "I'm sorry, I hadn't thought that through. I had assumed just curiosity. As when we watch deer or birds. But you mean that it could be with evil intent? with malice?"

The words *evil* and *malice* had a strange, archaic flavor to them, as if they had just been dug up out of the ground.

Vero gave him no answer except a little shrug of his shoulders.

But was it necessarily so, Merral considered, that these terms were fit only for a museum? Maybe the sentinels had a point; perhaps evil was only sleeping. It was not a thought that he cared for. Merral hesitated. "Surely not, Vero? All our history says not. Frontier communities are at peril from floods, bush fires, earthquakes. And such like. But not creatures in bushes. Real or imagined. Over ten thousand years of history and sixteen hundred worlds say the same thing. These things do not happen. That is the rule."

"Is it?" asked Vero softly, with a raised eyebrow.

"Yes. It is statistically improbable that such a rule will come to an end here in Herrandown and in our time. All our history says they are safe."

"I know, Merral, I know. You see, I can use your argument too. There have been—I was working it out last night—nearly three-quarters of a million sentinels since we were founded. All were looking for what I look for. Logic and statistics say to me that I should not be the one to find what they looked for and failed."

Vero paused and turned his brown eyes on Merral. "History does abide by rules, but those rules are set by the Everlasting One. And he can change them if he chooses. And he does not have to alert us first. The revivals of the Great Intervention happened quite unexpectedly, in Earth's darkest hours. The Holy Spirit gave no warning that he was starting a work unparalleled since Pentecost."

"I suppose not. . . ."

"Besides, consider logic itself. If there is a first time for everything, then logically the first time must happen to someone."

"But to my uncle and his family?"

Vero looked at him thoughtfully. "Assuredly to someone's uncle and family."

9

For many reasons, the meal that evening was an event that firmly embedded itself in Merral's mind. When he remembered it later—as he often did—it always seemed to him that it marked the end of something. When he tried to define exactly what it was that it ended, the answer was always "the Peace."

Anya's flat was small and low-roofed, with numerous wall hangings in warm shades of brown and green which made it seem even smaller. Merral felt that the apartment had been hastily tidied and was reminded that Anya had always put neatness well down her list of priorities. Despite the fact that Vero and Merral were, to a greater or lesser extent, strangers who had become last-minute guests, there seemed no sense of awkwardness at their presence. Merral, at least, soon felt at home, and he sensed that Vero had relaxed. Yet somehow, despite being welcomed, Merral found he was more analytical than usual and, at intervals, he caught himself looking round the candlelit circular table at the others and seeing them, as it were, for the first time.

Perena Lewitz sat to Merral's right. Although Merral had met her two years before, he never really got to know her, and he found it fascinating to compare her with her younger sister. In many respects he felt that she was a muted version of Anya. Physically the hair (which, as a concession to work in weightlessness, she wore short) was auburn rather than red, the eyes were a grayer shade of blue, and the face was less freckled and less immediately pretty.

The pattern persisted in the character, in that while Anya was the sort of person everyone noticed immediately, Perena's quieter, more introspective personality meant that it took time for her existence to become apparent. She seemed content to be an observer rather than a participant. It struck Merral as typical that when Perena was quietly persuaded into admitting that she was close to being the Farholme Space Affairs champion in old-time chess, Anya should loudly state that the game bored her to distraction and that anyway, she always lost within minutes. Along with Vero, Perena seemed to be one who was most happy to be dragged along by the flow of the conversation rather than to seek to mold it.

Round to the right of her was Theodore, a big, barrel-chested, and deep-voiced man with short blond hair and a pale moustache. He was plainly in high spirits and was given to frequently nodding his head to signify agreement and shaking it vigorously to denote dissent. On one or two occasions he clapped Vero on the back to make a point, once catching him unawares so that he nearly choked on his drink. He and Anya could easily have dominated the entire conversation, and Merral felt that both of them were deliberately holding back to encourage the others.

Beyond Theodore was Vero. To Merral he seemed very much subdued, and for much of the time he sat slightly back from the table as if physically distancing himself from the conversation. Merral felt that he was finding it hard to resist the temptation to withdraw into himself and slip into the shadows. Whether the cause was tiredness, the effects of his flight, or his worries, Merral could not be sure. But he saw no evidence that Vero was not fully attentive to what was going on. Although his mobile fingers would often reach out and toy gently with some item of cutlery, his deep brown eyes seemed to track the conversation carefully around the table as if he was scared of missing something. *I wonder whether this is his temperament or his sentinel training? And anyway, after so many generations, could the two be distinguished?*

Between Vero and Merral sat Anya, who, despite her sister's role as cook, was very much the hostess. Whenever the conversation flagged, she drove it on with an anecdote, joke, or provocative statement. Every so often she shook her long hair and the highlights in it glinted in the light of the candles. Merral found himself enjoying watching her face for the sheer animation and joy of life in it. Again, he felt that there was something he found very attractive about her. Once, the thought came to him suddenly that, under other circumstances, there might have been the possibility of something developing between them. The idea so disturbed him that he rejected it immediately and found himself in such a momentary state of consternation that he had to ask Theodore to repeat a question.

The fact that three of the five around the table were relatively quiet did not stop the conversation from moving rapidly and freely. There seemed to be no agenda, no concerns, no preoccupations.

Midway through the evening, Merral suddenly found himself thinking about how he appeared. *I have reviewed my friends, but how do they see me? How do I appear to them? Strange,* he decided. *I've never worried about how I seem to others before.* It was almost as though he longed for a mirror in which to see himself. Was he becoming self-conscious? These odd thoughts vaguely troubled him. He felt he was worse than some adolescent. He resolved that when the Herrandown problem was resolved he would take some leave. A week just walking the beaches, cliffs, and woods of Cape Menerelm might help clear out these funny ideas. His reverie was interrupted by Anya asking Vero if he found the food satisfactory.

Vero delicately wiped his mouth before answering and smiled. "The food is excellent, Anya, and a credit to Perena's cooking skills, but I am, I fear, still recovering from having lost and gained several hundred meters of altitude in under a second this morning. Repeatedly."

"All our fault, Vero," rumbled Theodore. "The seas are too shallow. We still can't get the current systems stable. Heat transport is unbalanced. That's what gives you all that turbulence."

Anya winked at Merral. "For the benefit of our new guests, Theodore is the expert on the thermal properties of the deeper sea basins. He wants to use a Mass Blaster to deepen them all another kilometer."

Theodore gave a wide grin. "Only some. It's not really feasible now. But it would have helped when they were knocking Farholme into shape."

Merral nodded. "I've heard that. But it was the early days in making worlds then, Theo. They were still struggling with how to slow rotation speeds so we didn't have to live around a sixteen-hour day. Contouring ocean depths was an imprecise science. We know better now."

Perena looked across at Vero. "Well, I sympathize," she said, her quieter voice somehow cutting across the table in a way that Theo's louder tones did not. "I've seen those equatorial storms bubbling up and I've often given thanks that I'm in vacuum. But space is different. . . ."

She paused, rotating the stem of her glass between her delicate fingers. The company looked at her and she continued, but in a tone of voice that almost sounded as if she was talking to herself. "In fact there are times when you would like some turbulence. It's the sense of void that is striking about space. Of being supported by nothing. Absolutely nothing."

Anya gave her sister a bemused look. "Oh, for a Near-Space Captain you feel a lot. You are too much the poet."

Perena shrugged and smiled as if at a private thought. Then in an even quieter voice she said, "But vacuum kills quicker than either air or water."

There was a brief, stiff silence, and then Anya, in a voice that seemed a fraction too strident, asked, "So Vero, how do you like our world?"

Vero thought for a moment. "For myself, I think I have been surprised how familiar things are. But then, of course, that is the very goal of making worlds. We are—as we have found out—a species that is adapted for one world. To live elsewhere on a lasting basis we must re-create our homeworld as best we can. The standard for every Made World is Ancient Earth. The Assembly has shunned novelty; we cannot take too much strangeness."

"So, what do you miss?" Anya asked.

"I miss the history of Ancient Earth and the richness of its species, but there are many compensations. Above all, I enjoy the freshness, the excitement—the challenge—of Farholme. This is, indeed, a new world."

With nods of agreement the meal continued.

After everybody had finished eating, Perena suggested they all go on the roof. "It is the first clear night we have had for weeks. I need to see the stars."

"You'd think," Anya commented, her blue eyes glinting conspiratorially at Merral, "that she saw enough of them at work."

They clattered up a narrow spiral staircase, lifted a hatch, and clambered onto a flat roof bounded by a metal railing. The sky was clear and the stars shone as brilliant chill points of light. Theodore and Anya walked off together down to the end of the roof and stood looking over the lights of the town.

Perena, looking up, spoke quietly to the slight figure standing beside her. "So, Sentinel Vero, what do you think of our stars?"

"I like them better here than from Aftarena."

"Really? It's not that different in latitude."

"Ah, Perena," he replied, and there was a wistful note in his voice, "from here I can see the Gate."

Merral watched his hand stretch out across the stars and point to the golden hexagon of light high above them.

"Ah yes. I had forgotten that." Perena's voice was sympathetic. "And that means a lot to you?"

"Yes . . . it does mean a lot to me. I have missed it these last three months. Through *there* is home, family, friends. And my father is rather elderly and not in good health."

"I understand. And you would wish to be going through it soon?"

"I suppose so, but duty declares that I should stay here."

"Yes, duty," Perena sighed. "This side of heaven, duty and desire are often in tension. But in my experience they mostly overlap."

"Mostly," he said. "For which we give thanks. It was not always thus."

Merral heard rather than saw Perena reach out and briefly touch Vero's shoulder. He marveled at the paradox of humanity. *We have the strength to sling ourselves between stars and yet at the same time the weakness that, when we do, we end up lamenting our absent loved ones. And yet it is perhaps appropriate to remember the weakness,* he thought, *lest we think we are more than we are.*

Perena spoke again quietly. "There is a ship coming through the Gate in a few minutes. The inter-system liner *Heinrich Schütz,* inbound from Bannermene with Farholme being—inevitably—the last port of call. Heading back inward in six days' time if I remember rightly."

She walked over to a low cabinet, opened it, brought out a fieldscope, and swung the lenses up to her eyes.

"Yes, the status lights are on the slow red flash."

Merral strained his eyes hard at the six golden lights of the beacon satellites.

A minute passed and they stared at the same spot. Merral remembered his own surprise when he had first visited the other hemisphere of Farholme and found the Gate, with its geostationary orbit forty thousand kilometers over the equator due south of Isterrane, absent. *We grow up with the Gate and its beacons,* he reminded himself. *It is the first thing in the night sky they show us as children. After all, Sol and Terra are not easy to find. "That's the Gate, Son," they say. "Through that your parents, grandparents, or whoever came from other planets and, ultimately, Ancient Earth. Through that, not just people but all our messages go. That's our umbilical cord." And as you grew up you realized just how important the Gates were.*

Merral still remembered the shock of the surprise he had had as a ten-year-old when he had worked out that if, instead of the two-day Gate trip they had taken eighty years earlier, his great-grandparents D'Avanos had set off from Menedon on the fastest ship available, they would still have been en route to Farholme. As someone had said, after the cross—and it was a long way after—the hexagon was the geometric symbol of the Assembly.

Perena's voice broke into his thoughts. "Here we go. Rapid flashing."

He could hear the latent excitement in her low voice. Merral stared up at the hexagon waiting for the flash as the awesome energies involved in taking the shortcut through Below-Space were balanced. As he watched, an abrupt wave of iridescent deep violet blue rippled out from the core of the Gate, briefly masking the fringing beacon lights, and then faded away.

Perena gave a little grunt of pleasure and put the scope down. She turned to Merral, the starlight reflected in her eyes. "Sorry, I get a thrill from that."

"You love space, Perena?" Merral asked.

She sighed happily. "Yes, I do. It's not for what it is itself. Space is nothing, truly nothing. But I see it as the nothing that holds the Assembly together. If that statement means anything." She paused and looked heavenward. "And I love the whole thing, the Assembly, the Gates, the stations, the whole great system of things. Not forgetting, especially, this tiny, insignificant, half-finished little planet. And, most of all the One who made it and sustains it."

Then she turned her face back to Merral and he caught in the half-light an amused grin, almost as if her declaration had embarrassed her.

There was a gentle tap on Merral's arm. He turned to find Vero hugging himself for warmth.

"I'm sorry. I find this a bit cold. I'm going to go down to check the possibility of us getting on the first flight to Ynysmant early tomorrow. Would you be able to do that?"

"Yes, I suppose so. But I thought we wanted to talk to Anya?"

"She can reach us easily enough. There is nothing to detain us here." He dropped his voice. "Sorry, Merral, but I've been thinking over all you said again. I'm becoming frustrated by these fragments of evidence. I think we need to take some action. Everything points to Herrandown and the area to the north of it. My mind is becoming fixed on this Lannar River. Anyway, if we leave it too late the trail could be too cold."

Merral thought quickly. "Yes. I take your point. Let's see if we can do it. You check if there is a flight."

Anya and Theodore seemed also to find it cold and followed Vero down, leaving Perena and Merral alone on the roof. They stood there leaning on the rail for some time, engaged in desultory conversation as Perena pointed out the trail of tiny glinting points that marked the processed cometary ice inbound from Far Station to be stored as fuel for the ships at the Gate and Near Stations.

A faint orange flash at the edge of his vision caught Merral's attention.

"Meteor! Small one to the south. Oh, but it's gone."

"Ah, it burned up before I could see it."

Seeing the meteor jogged Merral's memory. "Perena, three nights before Nativity I was up at Herrandown and there was a very big meteor that came overhead. Going north, with a noise like thunder. Some ground vibration. It was almost as bright as day for a second and it quite shook the ground. Scared the animals."

"That *is* big." She sounded intrigued.

"I was wondering—well, we all were—why the Guardian satellites didn't eliminate it before it came in. They can't have just assumed that the north was uninhabited, can they?"

He saw her shake her head. "No. They deal with such things well beyond Farholme. Typical Assembly policy to play it safe; it allows a second or even third chance to get them. It's spectacular if you are close enough to see it happen. I saw it once. I was near the north polar one. It warned us and we had—oh—fifteen minutes to get clear. There was no real risk. But it was a pretty impressive sight. It instantly vaporized about a cubic kilometer of nickel iron asteroid."

"I don't understand why they didn't get this big one. But then I don't really understand the mechanics of it all."

"Well, they have a hierarchy. Within a hundred thousand kilometers of Farholme they watch everything larger than a small boulder; beyond that they track everything house-sized or larger as far out as Fenniran or as Alahir's corona. Larger blocks are tracked to the system's edge or, if they are comets, well beyond. Anything coming in fast on a Farholme or Farholme Gate impact trajectory they blast. Pulsed protons, UV laser cannon, Mass Blaster. They are actually more worried about the Gate in some ways. With an open Gate you could patch up or evacuate a damaged world. Without a Gate . . . " She shrugged.

"Okay. But—and I've never thought of this before—suppose it's a ship or incoming probe?"

"Oh, these things are smart, Merral," she replied with a broad smile, and for a moment he was reminded of her sister. "They know where every ship of ours is. They need to. In fact for slower ships or static structures, like a Weather Sat, they may protect them if they detect a meteor is inbound. So the only risk is to an unscheduled ship or a probe coming in fast on a particular trajectory. That's unlikely. But if it were to happen the Guardian would always check on the ship identity codes."

"So have you any idea why it let this one through?"

"No. But they always work. There would have been a reason. I've flown the flights that service them. There are endless backup systems. Look, give me the details and I'll run it through the Guardian files and we'll see what happened."

"Twenty-second December, around five-thirty eastern Menaya time. Above Herrandown going north."

Perena noted the details in her diary, and as she put it away, she shivered. "I'm getting cold too. It's all right for you; you work outdoors. Let's go down."

As they returned to Anya's apartment, Vero broke off a conversation with the others and came over to Merral. "There is a freight flight tomorrow at 6:20 a.m. with space for two. You can manage it?"

"Yes, but there goes my relaxing morning. But certainly. I'll call my parents to make sure that they'll be expecting us tomorrow night."

"Do tell them that it will be for a single night. And give them my love."

The news of their early flight seemed to precipitate the end of the evening. Amid thanks to Perena and Anya, the five split up.

As Merral made to leave, Anya grabbed his hand lightly. "And take care up north. Cockroach men or not, it's tough country. We can't afford to lose you."

He squeezed her hand. "I'll be back. God willing. Whatever's out there."

Then they parted.

On the way back to his room, Merral thought about Anya in a mood that oscillated between pleasure and concerned perplexity. It was one more thing, he said to himself, which had to be sorted out soon.

The flight next morning was uneventful. Mist shrouded much of Isterrane on takeoff and low cloud hid Ynysmant on landing. Merral went with Vero straight to the Planning Institute, and after dropping their bags in his office, they both went over to see Henri, who was engaged in drawing a sequence of graphs on his desk. He turned off the monitor as they came in and gave both of them a warm welcome, his deep-set eyes asking unspoken questions about Vero. After introductions and pleasantries, Merral carefully explained what he wanted.

Henri sat back in his chair and looked from one to the other in a thoughtful manner.

"A week's trip, fine. But a rotorcraft tomorrow? There's not much time to arrange it. . . ." He ran his hands through his thinning hair. "*Ach*, we will have to reschedule other things. But . . . if you really think this is needed?" There was a questioning note in his voice.

"I do." Merral found himself surprised at both the abruptness of his answer and the certainty it carried.

There was silence for a moment and then Henri shrugged and smiled. "Fine, man. I'll arrange it." He stared at a wall map a moment and then looked back at Merral. "In fact, in some ways, I'll be glad of it. The Quarry Logistics Team is up there now and I've already had one comment about Barrand."

A stab of concern pierced Merral. "Is he—are they—all right?"

"Well, yes. But he's put a bolt on the house door."

There was a sharp intake of breath from Vero and Merral turned to him. "A what?"

The dark face was clouded, and Vero spoke in a low, expressionless voice. "A *bolt*. A catch openable from one side only. Like you'd use—I assume you do here—to stop children from getting into machinery. You put it high against a door."

"I see," Merral said, trying to imagine the mental state that would need something like that. He turned back to his director. "You mean, Henri, that he bolts himself—his family—in?"

"At night, I gather. And he walks around with a big stick, too. That's about it."

There was a long silence that eventually Henri broke with hesitant words. "I'm sorry . . . I'm on the point of sending the psychologist up. I was waiting to hear from you. Your uncle is, I suppose, scared." He looked inquiringly at Vero. "Sentinel, do you know why?"

Vero pursed his lips and shook his head slowly. "Everybody thinks I do, but I'm afraid it's not the case. I'm as much in the dark as anybody else. But I *am* determined to find out."

"Good, good." Henri's face expressed a continuing unease. "I don't like it at all. I'll let you get everything ready. Help yourself to gear. I'll arrange the craft for dawn."

After leaving Henri, Vero returned with Merral to his office where they called up maps, photographs, and computer reconstructions of the Lannar River system.

Vero gazed intently at the detailed imagery. "How accurate is this?"

"The resolution is two meters. It's accurate but misleading. I find that it's the fine grain on a landscape that takes time. These images never show things like brambles, thorns, and mud. But you get the overall trends."

"Your surveying and monitoring machines—do they ever get this far north?"

"Infrequently. It's a long way. Sometimes it may get looked at as part of some special project; for instance, we had a region-wide beaver survey last year and the Lannar was covered then. But not much else is done. A drone probably cruises over once a month looking for oddities. As Herrandown develops we will survey it more."

"So, it's little known." Vero looked at the map. "How far would we get in four days?"

"Day one would be around thirty kilometers in the narrow, densely wooded meanders from Herrandown. Day two would be, say, another thirty kilometers in the more open section where the river braids itself. All being well, that would bring you to the foot of Carson's Sill. Now, that bit's tricky."

Vero gestured at the image. "I can see that."

"Yes, that leads up to the Daggart Plateau, which lies in front of the Rim Ranges. That's a climb of at least eight hundred meters—probably nearer a thousand—up and over a lot of steep ledges. Tiring. But then you are on the plateau at the top. With that long lake, the Daggart Lake." He paused. "So that's an easier walk along that. Say we do twenty kilometers that day. Day four, what? Another thirty kilometers along the plateau to the edge of the Lannar Rim Ranges proper. Would I be right in thinking that you would not wish to go farther?"

"Yes," Vero answered as he peered at the image again. "It gets very steep then. Four days will be enough." He flexed his fingers. "Yes, my guess is that we will be ready for pickup by then. One way or another."

They looked at each other. *Funny,* Merral thought, *I can't easily visualize what sort of answer we might find to this set of problems. I wonder whether he can.*

Vero tapped his diary. "I'm puzzled that we've not heard from Anya. It's nearly lunchtime."

"Let me call her."

When she came on screen, Anya looked harassed. "Oh, sorry, you guys. You did well to get out of town and not to wait. The results are a bit of a mess. I can't decide what's going on. I'm going to get a second opinion. And our bug scholar has only just come in from out of town."

"Any hints?"

Anya flashed Merral a smile, but he felt it was the forced expression of someone under pressure.

"Insufficient data, Tree Man. I'll call you as soon as I have anything."

Merral and Vero ate lunch outside, sitting under a large apple tree and looking across the lake to where Ynysmant rose up out of the water, its roofs gleaming in the sun. They were both silent, as if the burden of the expedition north had crushed the desire for conversation.

They were crossing back through the compound after lunch when a rough cry rang out. "If you please! Mister Merral."

Merral turned to see a familiar, bent-backed figure lurching across the compound toward him.

"Jorgio!"

Merral hugged him. As he did, he caught again the smell of earth and animal and he felt sorry that, since their last meeting just before Nativity, he had not made the time to go up to Wilamall's Farm. "Let me introduce you," he said. "Jorgio Aneld Serter—gardener, stable hand, and old friend—this is—"

"Verofaza Laertes Enand, sentinel. But—more commonly—Vero. Delighted to meet you."

The two of them shook hands and looked at each other. As they did, Merral saw a strange expression passing across Jorgio's face: a look that was almost one of recognition.

"If you please, Mr. Vero; you are from Ancient Earth?" Jorgio asked.

"News about me must have been spreading," Vero replied with a quiet laugh. "Or is it my accent?"

A smile appeared on the leathery face. "I was told to expect you."

It was Vero's turn to look puzzled now.

Jorgio turned to Merral. "I was looking for you. I have a message for you and Mister Sentinel here. I assume he's come to sort out what's wrong."

Vero looked startled. "Excuse me, Jorgio—before you give us this message—what *is* wrong? I gather the weather hasn't been good."

Jorgio stared at him, his thick lips protruding. "Tut tut! No. Not *just* the weather. Much more than that. There've been all sorts of things wrong. Here and there. As you know."

"*I* do?" Vero stared back at him with an air of intense interest. "Would you like to tell me what you think is wrong? But please, let us sit down."

"What's wrong?" Jorgio said with a pout as they walked over to the seats at the edge of the compound and sat down. "Why, if you please, all manner of things are wrong. Birds, insects, animals. Even the woods are wrong, now. You see, I dream, Mister Vero. I dream in odd ways."

"I see," Vero said gently. "And in your dreams, what do you see?" He leaned forward as if straining to catch every nuance in Jorgio's words.

Jorgio rubbed a hand over his smooth bald head before speaking. "Since Nativity, in my dreams, I have seen shadows under the woods. *Cold* shadows. Things you don't want to see. Eyes, claws, teeth. Things that creep and slide." He seemed to shudder and fell silent.

Vero threw a glance at Merral, and in it Merral recognized a mixture of fascination, fear, and wonder.

"Jorgio, do you know what—*who*—is behind it?" Vero asked delicately.

Jorgio stared ahead. "Evil is back," he said bluntly.

"Can we be sure?" Vero whispered.

But instead of answering, Jorgio turned his head toward Merral. "You know how the Lord speaks to me? Special ways. Mostly, how I can help people. Anyway, last night he came to me as I was sleeping. 'Jorgio Aneld Serter,' he says, 'I want to show you something.'"

Jorgio cleared his throat. "'Amen, Your Majesty,' I says, 'lead on.' Next thing is that I am in this great big room—enormous, it is—with these dark wood walls. And standing on the floor are all these candles. Set on stands. Must have been over a thousand of them and they are all lit."

Jorgio wiped his face with the back of a hand. "Then he says to me, 'Jorgio, whose is the Assembly?'

"'Yours, sir,' I says. 'It is your work.'

"Then he says, 'Do I have a right to test my work?'

"'Of course,' I answers. Because he does—he is the Lord.

"'And test it I will,' is what he says. Then suddenly a door opens and a wind blows and candles start flickering and I think they are going out."

Out of the corner of his eye Merral saw Vero staring with wide eyes at Jorgio. "Extraordinary," he murmured. "Quite extraordinary."

Jorgio spoke again. "Anyway the Lord speaks again. 'Let me tell you what will happen,' he says. Then suddenly, before I could see whether the candles would blow out, the picture changes. And it's as if I am a bird—like one of them gray kites we get round here—flying around and looking down at a farm. It's beautiful. All on its own. Surrounded by trees and fields of wheat and the sun is shining on it. Then I see that there is a storm brewing. Big, thick, black clouds that go up in the sky forever. But it's not a good storm, it's a bad storm; it hates. The wind gets up; the clouds move toward the farm; the sun goes in. The trees start shaking and the rain starts and there's thunder and lightning. And the Lord says to me, 'Will it stand?' And then the clouds sweep across it and I can't see it anymore.

" 'Your Majesty,' I says, 'who do I tell?'

" 'Tell Merral D'Avanos and his friend from Ancient Earth,' he says.

" 'What do I tell them?'

" 'Tell them what you saw. Tell them to watch, stand firm, and to hope.' And then, suddenly, I'm back in my room."

For a moment there was a still silence. Then Vero shook his head. "An amazing account. The candles . . . you think they were the Assembly?"

Jorgio stuck out his lip and his brown eyes tightened. "I'd say so."

"And the farm?"

"I reckon it's us. *Farholme*."

"And a storm approaches. Any ideas about that?"

"No."

Vero turned sharply to Merral. "My friend, what do you think?"

"Me?" Merral heard what was almost a note of protest in his voice. "I'm not capable of analyzing this just yet. I need to think."

"The wisest thing. But remarkable. Thank you, Jorgio. I—we—want to think very carefully about what you have said. Merral and I are going north tomorrow. To look for what is the problem. Do you have any advice?"

Jorgio's soft brown eyes looked uneasily at Merral and then turned to Vero. "No. Only that I feel that things have changed round here." Then he looked up at the sun. "I must be on my way. Going back up to the farm now. I will pray for you. But remember that things have changed."

Then he rose to his feet and, with an odd and awkward bow, made his way over toward the vehicle depot. "Extraordinary," Vero said, staring after Jorgio. "Quite extraordinary. Has he done this before?"

"Once . . . last Nativity. He said that I had been at risk up north and that he had prayed for me. I didn't know what to make of it."

Vero stared after the departing Jorgio and shook his head. "A very striking man. How did he get to be like he is?"

"The story I heard is that when he was a child there was some landslide. Must be fifty or sixty years ago now. Down by the coast. His parents were killed; he was badly injured. They did the best for him. But he was always different. He has always been—in his rather different way—a godly man."

Vero nodded agreement. "You know how we sentinels are supposed to be able to sense things? I felt when I faced him that he was a man who knew more than I have ever learned. I had a sense that—somehow—what sentinel training tries to produce over years is what he already has."

"You think he is naturally gifted with some insight?"

"*Supernaturally* would be better. It is a gift of the Most High. We must reflect on his words as we go north. I do not trust myself to speak of what they may mean. The vision of the candles and the farm is chilling." He paused and then in a half whisper, as if to himself, muttered, "And evil is back." He frowned.

"Vero," Merral asked slowly, "how could evil come back? Would that mean the end?"

Vero looked at him. "Maybe. But maybe not. Jorgio talked of a testing, which is not necessarily the ending. But evil? You are aware that no one, not even the wisest person, knows how evil works. We never have. Not even in the twentieth and early twenty-first centuries when evil was so rampant. We all know that following those events that we abbreviate to the 'Great Intervention' evil became less pressing on us. In a well-worn phrase we 'felt a partial reprieve' from the effects of the Fall."

"But could that be revoked?"

"Merral, it's the Lord's Assembly, not ours. I never heard of any guarantee that this protection from evil was eternal. It has been assumed to be his gift to his people. And, as such, I suppose he has a right to withdraw it."

After a few moments of silence, Merral felt it was time that they returned to their preparations and went over to the stores. A silent Vero, deep in thought, followed him.

Merral already had much of the equipment he needed for himself, but finding suitable boots and a backpack for Vero was less easy. Merral found reassurance in the competent and familiar way in which his friend handled outdoor gear and the sensible suggestions he made about what to take.

Sometimes, however, what he said made Merral think. At one point Vero, his head deep in a supplies cupboard, asked in a low, thoughtful tone, "Merral, if you had to defend yourself from a hostile animal—say a deranged bear—what would you do?"

"It's a rare threat. We coexist pretty well. But sometimes, if you meet one of the big tawny bears and get between them and their cubs, they get ugly and try and take a swipe. And if you have to bring one in for any reason, say for a veterinary or biology study, we use neuro-potent tranquilizer guns. There's one up there."

Vero pulled out the box and read the instructions. Then he looked up at

Merral. "I think we should take it and a few cartridges. Put the dosage on maximum."

"Yes . . . I suppose that makes sense."

In another cupboard Vero found a lightweight, twin-eyepiece fieldscope with a variable magnification and low-light capability. "Ah, this looks useful. What do you use it for? Normally."

"Counting deer herds. Wolf packs at night—that sort of thing. It's useful but it weighs half a kilo or so. You seriously want to take it?"

"Yes," Vero answered firmly. "It may help us to keep a distance."

Merral found himself shrugging agreement.

A few minutes later, as Merral was checking a suitable tent, Vero came over to him carrying a short red tube. "I see you have some of these excellent bush knives."

"Careful!" Merral raised a hand in caution. "That blade is sharp. It's molecularly tuned to cut through wood. They are useful for clearing ground."

Vero pointed it away from himself and cautiously slid a catch. Slowly but smoothly, a dull gray blade slid out in three nested segments extending to an arm's length, before it locked open with a soft, precise click.

"I have seen them used in Aftarena. I think we should take two." Vero's tone suggested that it was not a negotiable point.

"Two? There isn't that much bush but, well, you may be right. They weigh little. But be careful in their use. They can take a hand off and without a surgeon nearby—that is likely to be permanent."

Vero slid the catch again and the blade slid softly back into its handle. His brown eyes looked impassively across at Merral. "I know," he said quietly, "but we may need them."

"What for?"

Vero hesitated, seeming to weigh his words before continuing, "Merral, I do not know what we face. I was concerned before today. But after talking with Jorgio I am even more concerned. There is an expression that I am reluctant to use. It has been thankfully obsolete for most of our history. . . ." He stared at the knife for a moment. "But yes, I must—there is no other. Merral, out there, this time, you—we—may be among enemies."

10

When Merral and Vero had agreed on a pile of equipment and supplies that they felt was the maximum that they could carry over rough terrain for four days, they took the two backpacks down to the rotorcraft hangar and stowed them on board their allocated machine.

Then they went back to Merral's house, which was empty as his parents were still at work. Vero put down his things in the spare room, lay down heavily on the bed, and stared at the ceiling.

"Nice to be back here, if only for a night."

"Better enjoy it. The beds out along the Lannar River won't be as good."

"I can put up with a lot. Sentinel colleges are notoriously Spartan. How is your castle tree by the way? You are still working on it?"

"It's fine; with it running on sped-up time, it's had three winters and summers since you looked at it. Still growing. Mind you, I need now to work out how it reproduces."

"Any ideas?"

"I think it needs to have flowers and insect pollination. That could be fun visually. Imagine the whole outer surface of the tree—tens of kilometers square—all covered with flowers."

"Let me know when you do it. It should be quite a sight."

"I will," Merral said. A moment later he was struck by a thought. "By the way, should we spend any time with the Antalfers? Don't you want to interview my uncle?"

Vero stretched out his arms. "A point I have been thinking about. Only briefly, if at all. Barrand may simply be a symptom of something. Besides—"

He sat up and gave a deep and impatient sigh. "Besides, Merral, I need *data*. Real data. More than twisted notes on a piece of music. Contact, an image, an *identification*. I do wish Anya could come up with something. Anyway, this evening I'm going to put my notes in order. Before we travel."

Before Merral could comment, the downstairs door was heard opening.

Vero smiled. "Well, it can wait. I think we'd better see your parents. And if I know your mother, I think there will be food."

Vero was not disappointed, and after hearty greetings and the sharing of the most pressing news, food was brought out. They had no sooner started to eat than Merral's father, visibly tired from work, came in and joined them. His mother bubbled on about life in Ynysmant, and his father, rambling as ever, talked first about machines and then his Historic, Welsh, and confused everyone in trying to explain the three basic types of the *cynghanedd* form of poetry. As a result there was little space for Merral or Vero to reveal their own concerns.

Halfway through the meal, there was a knock at the door and Isabella came in. She beamed at all and then gave Merral a shy, almost secretive, smile. Merral rose from his seat and kissed her on the cheek.

"I heard you were both in town," she said.

Vero bowed. "Nothing is overlooked in Ynysmant, that is sure."

"I'm afraid," Merral said, "that this is purely an overnight stop, Isabella."

She looked sideways at them. "So you must be going back up to Herrandown. There's nowhere else to go." Merral sensed a vague disappointment.

"Sorry," he replied. "We should be back in a week. Probably very much less."

"I see. . . ." Now the wistful note to her voice was unmistakable.

"Isabella, are you free at all tonight?" Merral asked.

"I have to look after Eliza. That's my youngest sister, Vero; everyone else is out. It's too late to change."

Vero coughed quietly and they looked at him. "Er, Isabella, I was only saying to Merral earlier that I need to work tonight. So, if you and he were to meet, you would not be depriving me. Besides, we *are* going to be seeing quite a lot of each other over the next few days."

Isabella looked from one of them to the other but said nothing.

"In fact, your arrival has rather caught us by surprise too, Merral," said his mother. "I should have said last night when you called but it quite slipped my mind. We are due out this evening, to see the Berens. They are leaving to be with their eldest and his family on the coast. *Permanently.* Tomorrow. It's very sad for us. So we can't really miss it. Can we, Stefan?"

His father shook his head gravely. "No. I mean you can come with us. But Merral, if you want to go with Isabella . . . and I'd understand . . . well, feel free. And if Vero wants to work here, then well, that's fine."

"I see," Merral said, somewhat relieved that he did not have to disappoint Isabella, "the decision seems made. So, Isabella I'll come over for an hour as soon as I can."

The Danols' house was in a freshly painted, narrow, four-story terrace high up the eastern end of town. By the time Merral arrived, young Eliza had been put to bed, and Isabella ushered him up to the main family room on the topmost floor with its sparse decor and pale, polished pine floors. As Isabella prepared coffee, Merral went out onto the balcony and looked out at the view over the choppy gray waters of Ynysmere Lake, above which the gulls swooped, their wingtips gleaming red in the rays of a setting sun that seemed to bleed through rips in the clouds.

I feel troubled, Merral acknowledged as he looked out over the warm, glowing tiles and brickwork, the spires, roofs, and deep shadow-filled streets of his town.

He stood there looking at the town he had grown up in. As he did, he had a brief and terrible presentiment—too ill defined to be a vision—of everything before him slowly crumbling, as if Ynysmant were sliding brick by brick into the lake. It was almost as though its buildings and houses were just dissolving into rubble, like snow under warm rain. Merral shuddered and clutched the balcony rail. In a flash of cognition, he sensed that his concern was not the loss of his town but of his world.

A gust of wind blew from the north, and he shivered. He went back inside to the Danols' room and sat down on the sofa, trying to soothe his mind by staring around at the abstract paintings and the carefully spaced pottery items on the high glass shelves until Isabella returned.

There, as the last rays of the sun fled the nearby towers and twilight fell, Merral and Isabella sat together on the sofa with their coffee and talked of the news from the town and of the worlds.

Yet as they talked, Merral found that instead of his strange mood being allayed, his unease persisted, but it was now focused in a different area. In particular, he sensed that Isabella was in some extraordinary, fey mood that seemed to defy analysis.

She leaned back into the corner of the sofa and stared at him with her deep dark eyes as if she was watching for something.

"Are you glad to see me?" she asked in her gentle but searching voice.

"Very much so. I would have got in touch with you after supper."

"I know that," she answered, stroking her long, straight black hair.

"I've been pondering our relationship, Merral," she announced a minute later.

"I would have been, Isabella. But I've been busy." Merral slowly put his cup down. "Still, please tell me what you have been thinking."

"Well, it's odd. Hard to put into words. Do you see it going anywhere?"

"Going anywhere? Well it's sort of frozen, isn't it? We can hardly do anything without the approval of our parents."

"No," she replied, but he felt that a strong suggestion of doubt hung over the monosyllable.

"You sound like you don't believe it."

"Hmm." She twisted a lock of her hair. "I'm just exploring things. I mean the whole commitment routine—the traditional formula. Trying them out in my mind. You and I are *special* to each other, aren't we?"

"Special? Yes, we are."

She snuggled next to him, and he was oddly aware of the warmth and softness of her body. "I agree," she said.

There was silence for some time, a silence deeper than conversation. In it, Merral began to think about the relationship between himself and Isabella. Then his mind drifted, drawn away by the thought of the journey he faced tomorrow. *Where will we be in twenty-four hours' time?* A vague feeling of foreboding came into his mind. *What will we be facing? And what did Jorgio's vision mean? Could there really be something in the north? Some sort of wild, malign presence?* Merral wanted to condemn the idea as folly, to throw it out of his mind, but felt he could not. It was strange how the very phrase *the north* was acquiring an edge to it. It was almost as though it conveyed the same sort of chilling force on the mind as the north wind did on the flesh.

He was suddenly aware of Isabella's eyes scrutinizing him. As if sensing that she now had his attention, she spoke in a firm but insistent voice. "The whole thing is ridiculous. We can do nothing."

With an effort, Merral directed his thoughts toward Isabella. "It's the way it is. A parental decision. We wait—what—another three months?"

"And then, will they say yes?"

"Possibly. My parents are very fond of you."

"And mine of you. They would let me go with you as your wife to your jungle project if necessary. Even if we rarely got the chance to come back here."

"I'm sure they would. But that, well, just wasn't the point."

"Yes, but it seems so, well, *sad* that our parents won't approve of us being committed to each other."

"Sad? I suppose it is. I hadn't seen it that way. But I don't see that we can do anything about it. Except wait."

"And hope."

"I suppose so," he answered, wishing that the pending journey wasn't overshadowing all his thinking.

"I was wondering . . . ," Isabella said, a few minutes later.

"About what?"

"About an alternative."

"How do you mean 'an alternative'?"

"Hmm . . . ," she replied, as if having difficulty trying to frame the words. In the silence that followed, she nestled closer to him. Merral found it undeniably pleasant with her soft, slight weight against him. In fact, he decided, pleasant was an understatement. There was an excitement about it, a sense of an anticipatory promise. Suddenly marriage—and all that it brought with it—seemed to be something that wasn't merely attractive to him; it was something so compelling that he felt himself hunger for it.

Isabella reached out, put her soft hand over his, and squeezed gently. "You think it will work out for us?" she inquired in a low, urgent tone.

"I hope so."

"You'd like it to work out?" There was an almost pleading intensity to her voice. He paused, aware that her eyes were wide and soft and tender.

"Yes . . . ," he said. *Funny,* he wondered as the word slipped out, *should I have said that? That yes? I should have qualified it with "if it's right."* But now other thoughts flashed through his mind: *this feels so pleasant, it seems so right, Isabella is my best friend, our parents will surely approve, and our being linked together is inevitable.*

"You see," Isabella said, looking at him, her mouth so red, soft, and close that he could sense her breath. "I was thinking that—on that basis—we could have a private understanding between us."

"'A private understanding between us?'" he echoed, a shadow of disquiet trying to intrude into his mind but making little progress against the whirling torment of emotions.

"Yes. An *understanding*—just between us—that we are, really, sort of committed to each other. Privately. Just waiting for the approval to come."

Part of Merral's mind wanted to tease out further what she meant by an understanding. After all, what was the point of waiting for their parents to make a decision if they were to preempt it? But another part of his mind was preoccupied by the delicious fact that she was very close to him. He could sense her warmth and feel her breathing. She stroked his hand.

"You agree?" she asked, her mouth suddenly welcoming, her white teeth shining in the fading light.

Suddenly it didn't matter; the approval of their parents seemed something he could take for granted.

"Yes," he answered, almost to his own surprise. "I suppose—"

But Isabella had interrupted him by kissing him on the lips. He yielded to her, and the world seemed to explode into something he had never imagined that flooded his brain with sensations for long, immeasurable seconds.

"Oh, Merral," she whispered, her face pressed against his so close that he could hear her breathing and feel her heart beat. "I do love you. *Thank you.*"

Only the committed or the engaged kiss like that, he realized.

Suddenly an urgent note of alarm sounded over the surging flood of excitement and sensation that was flowing through his mind. In a moment's flash of intuition, he realized that he had initiated something—he was now not quite sure what—without the thought and seeking of God's will that was required.

He pulled himself back from her, the urgent words forming in his mind: *Lord, forgive me. Give me wisdom. Protect me, us. From doing anything foolish, anything wrong.*

"Is everything all right, Merral?" she asked sharply, sensing his consternation.

Suddenly there was a triple pulse from the diary adjunct on his watch.

"Sorry, Isabella," he answered, somehow both relieved and frustrated by the interruption. "I'm expecting a message."

He glanced at the screen and saw that the call was from Anya Lewitz. He tabbed an acknowledgement and stood up, shaking himself and brushing his hair smooth with his hand. Then, trying to focus his mind on what Anya might say, he went over to a nearby table, sat down rather unsteadily, and unclipped his diary. He angled his chair so that the background was a blank wall and flicked the screen on.

Anya peered at him over her disorganized desk. She looked weary, and there was little trace of her normal ebullience.

"Hi, Merral. I hope I wasn't disturbing any family reunions."

"No. Not at all," he replied, somehow glad that it was a question he could answer honestly. "No family reunions. But I've been waiting for your results."

"Well, they have come in. At last." She answered slowly. "They are odd. *Very.* I'd like to talk to both you and Vero about them. Is he there? Or shall we get a three-way discussion going?"

Merral paused, suddenly feeling that he needed to be out of this place. He needed time to think about what was happening—what had already happened—between him and Isabella. "Can you hang on twenty minutes or so, Anya? I'm not with Vero. I think we both need to discuss these things."

"Okay, I'm around."

As soon as her image had faded on the screen, Merral called Vero to say that he would be over straightaway. As he clipped the diary back on his belt, he was conscious of Isabella at his side.

"A problem?" she said.

"Sorry, I need to go back down and talk with Vero. We are waiting for some analyses. It may affect our plans for tomorrow."

"I see. I understand." Her voice strongly suggested that while she might understand, she wasn't happy about it.

"Thanks."

"No, thank *you*," she said, and suddenly kissed him softly and fleetingly on the lips.

As he walked back down quiet winding streets to his parents' house, Merral struggled to try and impose some order on the turmoil of his feelings. Somehow, inadvertently, without seeking the Father's will, he had made some sort of promise of an understanding of commitment to Isabella. A promise that he was not quite sure he understood the significance of, and one he was not sure that he should have been involved with. But surely it hadn't been a real commitment, had it? He frowned. It was more, he decided, that it had been a sort of commitment to a commitment. He was unhappy with that as a phrase, but it expressed how things were. And put like that it didn't seem quite so dreadful. But he realized that this was another thing that seemed odd. Was all of Farholme now running so oddly?

Back at the house Merral pushed the matter of Isabella out of his mind, telling himself that he needed to concentrate. He joined Vero at the table and called Anya with a diary linked to a wallscreen.

"Okay, you guys," said Anya, rubbing her face in a gesture of tiredness. "It's been a long, long day. Part of the delay has been because I wanted to check the result with Hamich Bantys and he is on the Mazarma Chain and ten hours behind us; I didn't want to wake him." She stared unhappily at the screen. "I take it, Sentinel Vero, this isn't a test to see if we are alert?"

Vero just shook his head.

Anya sighed. "Sorry, just a desperate last resort. Okay, the DNA results are odd. We've checked the machinery and it seems to be running fine, but it doesn't add up. First of all, it is an unknown species; it has never been recorded. We know its high-level taxonomy—I'll come on to that—but it seems to be a novelty. Now, as you know, Merral, the Standard Operating Procedure with a novelty is straightforward."

"Get the Genetic Innovation Team to look at it. We did it with a new thistle last year."

"Exactly. We'd just say that a new species or subspecies has emerged and ask for a GI investigation. Catch the thing—or sample it—and decide whether it is going to be a blessing or a curse." She paused. "But this is quite off the scale. We have the DNA analysis, but on the line where we should have species, subspecies, and any matching results from the database, we get merely that it's mammalian *definitely*, anthropoid *definitely*, and hominoid *probably*."

"Hominoid?" Vero asked. "So that includes apes and man?"

"Exactly."

"Ah."

"Ah indeed. Unlike thistles or parrots—incidentally, Merral, that new Great Blue variant is making a real mess down on Anazubar—hominoids do not tend to share their genes across species. And in Menaya, of course, there is only one living hominoid."

"Us," Vero said, his face wearing a disturbed look. "But is it known outside Farholme?"

She shook her head. "Not in the entire Assembly. I've even checked it against the few reliable genetic records of Neanderthals and the like. No match."

"Most odd. So is it a new species?"

"It's a theoretical possibility. Hamich agrees. But . . . well, that raises all sorts of problems. There seems to be a lot of human code there, but there are also biochemical and genetic peculiarities." Anya bit her lip, evidently nonplussed. "Oh, I don't know. There may be some decomposition . . . or some contamination. But then, the biomarkers seem to be negative on that."

Vero threw a puzzled glance at Merral, then turned back to look at the screen. "Anya, would you like to speculate what has happened?"

On the screen Merral saw Anya start to open her mouth and then shut it abruptly. "No," she said firmly. "Speculation in the absence of adequate data is not appropriate. And could be dangerous." She stared at Vero.

"I understand you, Anya Lewitz," responded Vero firmly. "I am as reluctant as you are to jump to conclusions."

"Good," she answered, and to Merral's ears she sounded relieved at not having to deliver a final verdict. "Anyway, tomorrow I will make a Gate call to the best person in the field, Maya Knella on Anchala, and will transmit the data to her for a third opinion. I was wondering, Vero. . . ." She paused, as if uncertain about whether to proceed. "Yes, in view of historic sentinel concerns, if there might be someone else you think I should consult."

"Ah," Vero's head rocked gently as if something had become plain. "A generous and thoughtful gesture."

He paused. "No, I think I can wait. I hope to get more data in another forty-eight hours. I fully appreciate your desire that we do not jump to conclusions."

Merral felt that there was an emphasis to his last words.

Anya nodded slightly in response. "Which brings me to the cut branch." She sighed. "What a pair of specimens! Our invertebrate expert is sure that whatever made it was something with very large jaws or mandibles. He suggested some sort of crab and was worried about what we had evolving in our seas. He was nonplussed when I said it was six hundred kilometers inland and in a wood. 'Well, it would have been twice the size of any crab known here,' he said. As if that helps."

She paused for her words to be understood, and then, with a strange look, went on. "So he is scratching his head too. But well, it may be worth mentioning that he estimates that whatever did it could put a lot of force into a shearing action. It could take an arm off, he thought, if it had the gape for it. It could certainly cut through most unarmored synthetics thinner than a centimeter. I thought you should know that."

"I see," Vero said. "I was rather hoping for one puzzle to be solved. I now find that I have two unsolved puzzles."

There was silence and eventually Merral asked. "Is that all?"

"You guys want *more*?" There was a smile and Merral felt the old Anya was back.

Merral shook his head. "*No.* Many thanks. You work on your data, Anya. We'll try and get you some more up country."

"You are going after it?"

"Or them. A hunt. The first hunt for any totally unknown land organisms for—how many thousand years?"

"Twelve or so. I don't know. But take care. Incidentally, Perena is based at the Near Station from tomorrow for some low-orbit Central Rift surveys—they want to check the volcanic activity. I'll get her to watch out to the east. So smile when you look up."

"Will do. Thanks for your help."

"Thanks for a challenging problem. And keep safe, Tree Man. And you, Mr. Sentinel."

Vero bowed slightly and the screen went blank.

Merral leaned back in his chair and stared at his friend. "Now, Vero Laertes Enand, do you know what is going on here?" He was aware of a strange sharpness in his voice.

Vero looked thoughtful, shifted his lean body in the seat, and rapped his fingertips together twice as if summoning something. "Merral, I have a bad feeling. But I am worried about deceiving myself. I wish I had someone else here with my background to talk it through. If you will excuse me, I want to keep my thoughts to myself. I think things are moving to a head, and we will know better in a day or two what is happening."

"Well, if that's the way you think is best, then I won't argue." Merral thought for a moment. "But I think you know what is going on better than me. There was something that passed between you and Anya."

Vero shook his head. "No, I do not *know*. I *suspect*, but I cannot believe it. And as for Anya? Yes, I fear I know what she saw. But what it means and how it got here at Worlds' End is quite beyond my understanding."

He got up and paced the room. After some moments he turned round and stared at Merral. "But oh, I find it too hard to believe. We will see. Oh dear."

He sat down, steepled his fingers, and stared at them, his smooth brown forehead now furrowed. There was a long silence which Merral did not feel like breaking.

Suddenly Vero got to his feet and stood upright with a stern face.

"Merral, my friend. I owe you an apology for not telling you more. I think—no, I fear—we are on the edge of something so awful that I cannot even begin to understand what it means. But I cannot be certain. The trip north will tell us whether I have found something that is beyond even the sentinels' nightmares." Then he paused and spoke in harsher tones as if to himself. "Yet it makes no sense! None at all. Oh, I must be wrong. *I must be.*"

Then he shrugged and looked back at Merral. "Anyway I must spend the next few hours making a report. I do not wish to be dramatic but I will file it in a closed format with Brenito, with instructions that if I do not report back from our expedition it is to be transmitted to Ancient Earth immediately."

Merral went to the door, finding it difficult to know what to say. "As I have said before, I hope you are wrong, Vero."

"I hope so too."

Merral opened the door to go, and as he was about to slip through, Vero spoke again. "Try to get some sleep. You will not get as much as you like tomorrow."

"How so?"

"I fear we must adopt an ancient policy that has not been needed for long years."

"Which is?" Merral asked, with a sense of foreboding.

"We will have to take turns at keeping watch."

Herrandown seemed deserted in the bright, early-morning sunlight as the rotorcraft pilot landed, and for a few moments, Merral found himself uncomfortably worrying whether some disaster had overtaken the Frontier Colony. Then he saw his uncle's bulky form emerge from his house and stand watching them. His posture was strangely rigid, as if uninvolved in what was going on.

The pilot swung her tight-clipped blonde head round into the passenger bay and smiled.

"Have a nice walk, fellas. I hope the weather holds. You're keeping your diaries on?"

"Yes," Merral answered, "but emergency contact status only."

"Good enough. Just so the Met Team can warn you if the weather throws a wobbly. It's been a bad year that way. Anyway, I'm off back. Hope you enjoy our countryside, Mr. Vero. It's not Ancient Earth, but it does for us."

Vero paused long enough in pulling on his backpack to bow slightly. "Thank you, Anitra. I'm sure it will do for me, too."

Then the doors opened and they were on the ground. With a gently rising whistle the rotorcraft soared away southward.

Merral looked up to see Barrand standing before them, his expression one of puzzlement mingled with unease.

"Ho, nephew. Again!"

Merral found little warmth in his uncle's tone and was struck by the stiff and cool nature of his embrace.

"And a guest. Another guest." Wasn't there a sharp edge to the voice here? Merral tried to suppress the idea.

"Uncle, can I introduce . . ."

"Verofaza Laertes Enand, *sentinel.*" Vero extended a hand in formal greeting.

Barrand took it with a sort of sideways glance at Merral. "Ho. A sentinel now! Am I in trouble, then?"

Merral found the tone strange, as if his uncle had started to make a joke but had changed his mind halfway. He took his uncle by the arm. "Uncle, we are just passing through. At very short notice. Vero wants to see the north so we are going for a long walk. It suits my purposes to examine the area north of here on foot."

"I see."

Merral sensed an almost-open hint of suspicion in the voice. "So, Uncle," he said, trying to adopt a tone of levity that he did not feel, "we are going to be rude and just say 'hello' and then 'farewell.' "

"As you wish. Well, come in for a few minutes. The children are heading off to school soon so it's all a bit chaotic. It is probably best you don't stay. Things are settling back to normal here."

His uncle glanced at Vero, and Merral felt that his expression seemed to ask, "How much do you know?"

"I'm glad to hear it, Uncle."

They strolled over to the house in silence. Merral found his aunt and the children at the door and made the introductions to Vero. As he did so he found himself analyzing them, almost fearing the worst. He felt that his aunt looked tired but otherwise well. Elana seemed brighter than she had been, and Thomas appeared to have regained his former good spirits. *Perhaps the shadow has lifted off this community.* But as they moved inside, Merral caught sight of a welded metal loop against the door frame. Vero's eyes met his and there was a barely perceptible shake of the dark face.

They spent barely half an hour inside the house, and during that time

Merral felt that there was little said in the conversation of any significance. It was almost, he felt, as if no one wanted them to stay for long. Merral watched for any evidence of problems, but saw little that was obvious. However, it appeared to him that his uncle and aunt were now no longer the vibrant, large-scale characters they had always been to him. They now seemed to be in some way drained, and even shrunken figures, with faint shadows around them. He found himself wondering whether Vero would see anything awry.

Eventually, with good wishes and unbending embraces and handshakes, Merral and Vero were waved off up the track out of the hamlet.

When they were out of sight of the house, Merral turned to Vero. "Well, what do you think?"

Vero said nothing for a few moments and then looked at Merral with a raised eyebrow. "Most odd. They were watchful."

"Interesting. Of what? Of us?"

"No. Of themselves. Let me explain. Of course, I have never met them before. This is my first Frontier Colony, indeed my first Made World. But it is a characteristic of the Assembly that we speak what is on our minds. That we say what we think, without regard for anything other than charity. You agree?"

"But of course," answered Merral, once again wondering at the extraordinary perspective that Vero brought to bear on so many things. "Is there any other way?"

"Ah, that is the interesting thing. If you read the pre-Intervention literature or watch—if you can stomach it—their imaged data, so much of what they said was to actually disguise rather than reveal."

"To disguise—"

"Oh, come on! It comes over in the Book. For instance, when King Herod says he wants to worship the baby Jesus as well. It is a pretense."

"But he was an evil man."

"However, the principle still stands. Anyway, with your uncle and aunt I detected a watchfulness. They thought before they spoke."

"True. I suppose I had noted a lack of freedom, perhaps. But I hadn't seen the significance."

Vero adjusted his backpack and looked across with thoughtful eyes. "It was there all the same. But as I said yesterday, I didn't come here to investigate the Antalfers."

"Yes, I suppose that's fair."

Vero gave Merral a thoughtful look. "Come on; it's a long walk to the Rim Ranges."

He shook his head ruefully. "And besides, who knows what we will meet on the way?"

11

As the track out of Herrandown began to steepen and the weight of their packs made itself felt, Merral and Vero fell silent. As he strode up the slope, Merral reminded himself that he had been here with Isabella only a few days ago. And as she came to mind, he realized how perplexed he was there. What was going on? And yet it wasn't just her; his own feelings seemed to have polarized. A few weeks ago, there had been just a low, deep friendship. Now at least two things had happened. His feelings for her seemed to have evolved into an intensity of desire that almost scared him. And yet another part of him was counseling caution and almost screaming that there was something wrong. It was a conflict that he could not easily resolve. And to make it all worse, he had already made some sort of promise to her.

Abruptly he saw that they had come to the point where Elana had seen the creature. Merral gestured to Vero to stop and his friend looked at him expectantly. "It was here?"

"Yes."

"I thought so." He stared around at the view. "Yes, a fine vantage point. And on a day like this, a particularly pleasant view of a charming spot."

Merral agreed. There was a hint of white blossom on the apple trees now and the other trees were covered in fresh greenery. Over the whole scene the sun shone out of a perfect blue sky flawed only by the faintest high-altitude haze.

Turning their back on the view, they moved into the woods, and Merral paused at the site where he had found the cut twig. Vero took off his pack and spent a few minutes looking around the site and seemed vaguely satisfied.

"I am no bushman, and the trail is very cold and has been overprinted by others—I presume you and Isabella. But let us go on."

Cautiously, letting his eyes adjust to the lighting under the trees, with the gloom broken in places by brilliant shafts of light, Merral led them on, trying to avoid trapping his pack on the branches.

They paused briefly at the site where they had found the hair and then moved onward. Now, beyond that part of the trail that he and Isabella had examined, Merral found himself being more watchful. It was not just that the traces they were following were now faint, it was that, somehow, he found himself anxious not to come across anything unexpectedly.

The trail was still visible as a line of broken, buckled grass, vague imprints in dry soils, and torn and snapped stalks and twigs. Once, Vero stopped to examine the dents in the ground. He looked up at Merral. "Hard to be sure, isn't it? But I feel there was something heavy through here."

Merral gestured to a clumsily broken branch just above his head.

"Big, too."

"So it would seem." Vero looked up and grimaced. "I'm not sure I want to meet it in a bad mood."

"I'm not sure I want to meet it in a good one."

"True." Vero stroked his chin. "You know, I have seen wild gorilla tracks on Earth and, although smaller, they looked similar." Then he stared ahead, at the way the trail went straight along the valley side. "But were they ever so purposeful?" he added in a baffled tone.

Over the next hour, Merral led them on at a steady pace as they went northwest under the trees, dropping slowly down toward the Lannar River. He felt a need for urgency. The trail was already very cold and he knew every extra day would make following it harder. Another rainstorm—perfectly possible within the next few days—could make following the trail harder or even impossible. Besides, they could ill afford any delay; in order to allow them to travel faster they had taken only enough food for four days.

Finally, they started to come to the edges of the wood, so that the trees became absent from the valley ridges and were confined to the base and flanks of the stream valley. There, under the shade of a gnarled, flute-barked oak, they stopped to drink water and have a mouthful of food. Vero wiped the sweat from his face and flicked a fly away. "Forester, what do you think of the track so far?"

"Interesting. Whoever—*whatever*—made it is no fool. Down in the gully itself it is very muddy and the going would be slow."

"Yes. But why not take the ridge route? You'd make faster progress there."

Merral looked up at the bare, grass-covered ridge. "Yes, a puzzle. Perhaps it isn't that smart."

Vero looked at him carefully. "Now if you had sentinel training like me—that curious way of bending your brain so that you see nothing as it really is—you might think that the ridge would be avoided because you would be open to being seen from above."

For a moment, Merral stared at Vero, then he looked back at the ridge as it lay open to the sun. "What a very curious idea. So our watcher doesn't like to be watched?"

"A suggestion. That's all."

Then they moved on down the stream flanks toward the Lannar River. As the morning passed, it began to be warm and humid under the trees, and Merral began to be conscious of a sweaty feeling along his back as the weight of the backpack pressed on him. Every so often he stopped, gestured for silence, and as Vero dutifully froze, listened carefully. There was the noise of flies, distant birds in the trees, and increasingly louder as the morning passed, the liquid rustling of the river. But he heard nothing unusual.

"And what do you think, Sentinel?" he asked at one point.

"Seems like a normal temperate wood to me. Of course, it's subtly different. That beech, for example; the trunk seems wider and more ridged while the branches are stubbier. I presume that's an adaptation. A bit short of animal life, though."

"Oh, give us time, Earther!" Merral said with a laugh. "Just remind yourself that if we went back a mere twelve thousand years here you would have been choked by carbon dioxide, slowly dissolved in an acid rain, and fried on rocks as hot as any home oven. Your world has had far, far longer. In another few thousand—the Ruler of All permitting—Farholme will match old lady Earth."

Vero smiled and made a little bow as if to admit defeat. "No, you are right. Forget the Gates, forget the Library, forget our Cities-in-Space. Of all the wonders we have done with the Most High's permission, the Made Worlds are the greatest. To have turned near-molten rubble and poison gas to soil, woods, flowers, and air is—by God's grace—our race's finest achievement."

And yet, Vero's point is true enough; I still long to see, someday, the woods of which these are the copies.

After half an hour they stopped to get their breath back and took their backpacks off.

Vero turned to Merral. "Jorgio's vision. What do you think about it?"

"I found it made me very uneasy. It's like nothing I have ever heard of. And, well, visions are not my line." Merral patted a birch trunk. "Trees, yes; visions, no."

"If we assume that it was genuine, then how do you interpret it?"

Merral thought for a moment. "The candles are the Assembly and the farmhouse is Farholme. That much seems beyond doubt. And in both cases, as a testing, a threat is being unleashed."

"Exactly. But a threat of what? Where?"

Merral shrugged and Vero continued. "There the vision stops and our insight fails. If we knew what we faced it would be easier to obey the charge to watch, stand firm. And perhaps to hope. But visions never tell all." He sighed. "I desperately want to talk to Brenito about all this and will do when I get back. But, in the meantime . . ." He fell silent.

"I think we need to focus on the task ahead. So let us move on. And watch," Merral said and, putting his backpack back on, set off. Vero followed him.

Ten minutes later the trees began to open out. Vero touched Merral's arm lightly and whispered, "I think we should be careful down here. We will soon be out into the open."

"I agree," Merral answered with reluctance. "Although the track still shows no sign of being younger than four or five days."

Merral listened again, but heard nothing to alarm him. Nevertheless, he felt uneasy. An intangible *something* seemed to be present. *Why is it that I don't like these woods?*

Vero seemed to sense his unease. "You're not happy, are you?"

"Ah, you talked earlier about our Assembly transparency. No, I'm not happy."

"May I make a suggestion?"

"Of course."

"From now on have your tranquilizer gun ready. I'm going to wear my bush knife."

Merral suddenly realized what lay behind Vero's interest in the knives the previous day. "A *weapon!* You're planning to use it as a weapon?"

"Not planning, *please,*" Vero looked vaguely hurt. "Preparing, perhaps. As a last resort."

For a moment, Merral could not say anything as he tried to grapple with the concept of a weapon. No, he decided, this was too much. It was important to impose some limits on what were plainly excesses in sentinel thinking, and now was as good a time as any.

"Look, Vero," he said firmly, "we need to think about this. We have no evidence at all that these things are hurtful, harmful, or even hostile. If they are sentient and can communicate, we either talk to them or bring in those men or machines that can."

As he heard his words, he knew that he had pitched the tone all wrong; it came out abrasive and critical. Under his dark skin, he felt that Vero was blushing. Eventually his friend spoke quietly. "You are—of course—right, Merral. I was . . . I suppose, letting my imagination get ahead of myself."

It was now Merral's turn to feel guilty. "Sorry, Vero, I guess I don't know what's up here either."

He patted his friend on the shoulder. *He's overreacting.* But then it occurred to him that, nevertheless, to follow such a trail as this into the open might not be the wisest thing. "Okay, what do you suggest?" he asked.

"Hmm. I recollect that in the past, when there was the risk of a . . . *confrontation*, it was considered unwise to do the expected thing."

"Yes," Merral replied, wondering about the use of the word *confrontation*. "The same rule applies in a Team-Ball game."

"Quite so. So, could we go south a little way and reach the stream bank at a new point? That way we come out into the open at a different place."

Merral noted with unease the apparently bizarre way you had to think when you believed there might be enemies around.

As quietly as they could, parting the foliage softly with their hands, they made their way to a point a hundred meters downstream of where the trail would have struck the river. There, Merral motioned Vero to stay, took his pack off, and gently edged his way through a clump of young willows and bright yellow flowering irises down to the pebble strand. There he peered out of the greenery carefully. The Lannar River here was around thirty meters wide, although, he guessed, nowhere now more than waist-deep. Although it had been a wet spring, the river was now at a much lower level than at the height of the winter floods, so that a sizeable strand of rough pebbles and gravel lay on either side of the water. The other side of the riverbank was tree lined, and to both north and south, the river disappeared round meanders within a kilometer or so. Feeling on alert, Merral looked once up and down the river quickly and then again in a slower, more careful scrutiny. There was nothing to see apart from some ducks out on the deeper part of the stream. Equally, apart from the soothing, bubbling flow of the water, there was little to hear except an irregular plop as a fish leapt.

Merral moved out of cover. There was an abrupt splash nearby and he felt his heart beat faster. With relief he saw a stream vole swimming away into the depths. Moments later, the ducks took off, their wings rattling against the water.

Slowly, Merral regained his composure and beckoned Vero to join him. "A false alarm. There is nothing here."

Vero was looking up the stream. "We have to decide how to follow this trail now. These pebbles will show no tracks, and we will be very obvious walking along the stream. Anyone watching would see us half an hour before we arrived."

"I take your point. I presume whatever we are following walked along under the bank; they would be covered by trees that way. I suppose if we walked above the level of the bank we'd cover more ground quickly."

"I agree."

For the next two hours they traced the Lannar River northward. So wide were the meander loops here that, although they walked a long way and cut off some meanders entirely, their progress north was not very great. The going along the riverbank was, however, generally easy. Other than a few birds and a glimpse of some tri-horned red deer, they saw nothing. They stopped once for a quiet, frugal, and brief lunch and then kept walking.

As the afternoon wore on and the sun began to sink, Vero raised a concern that was troubling Merral: Could they be sure that they were still following the trail? Shortly afterward, though, they came across a part of the river valley where the edge was marked by a large sandbar.

"Look," whispered Vero. "Tracks."

There, faintly cutting across the edge of the coarse sandbar just by the side of the trees, were impressions of footprints, clearly traceable for a length of about a hundred meters before they were lost in coarse gravel. Looking carefully around them, Merral and Vero slithered down onto the bank and took their packs off.

"*Creatures* plural, Merral," Vero announced dully as he peered at the footprints, the wonder and apprehension in his voice barely concealed.

"Yes," Merral answered in a strange, distant voice, as his mind grappled with the awesome, unbelievable awareness that he was dealing with reality, not illusion.

Merral squatted down and, staring at the tracks, reached out and stroked the edge of one gently with his finger, watching the black sand grains roll over into the depression.

"It's *real*," he said, looking across at Vero, whose wide brown eyes stared back at him with an inexpressible emotion. "Vero, let me make a confession."

"Feel free. But I think I have my own."

"I now realize that, until this moment, I didn't—in my heart of hearts—really believe in this. I don't know what I expected. I suppose I still believed that there was another more rational explanation. That it was a hallucination, a trick. Anything but this. . . ."

"Yes, I agree," answered Vero slowly. "I suppose I am more conditioned to be prepared for this, but I too find this an extraordinary moment. I, too, have had my doubts. As you have known. Maybe I have doubted too much. But come, let us examine these prints quickly and be on our way. We have some way to go, and I want to find a safe camping spot for the night."

It was odd, Merral thought, how *safe* had now acquired a meaning that it had never had before.

Vero gestured at the line of tracks. "Let's spend a few minutes separately and then get back together and share our conclusions."

Agreeing, Merral began looking at the prints and imaging them on his diary. The most striking tracks were a series of deep, widely spaced footprints with a rough similarity to a bare human foot. Wordlessly, Merral tried to match the pace. Even striding, his footprints were only two-thirds the distance apart of the older prints, and furthermore, penetrated to only just over half their depth.

To their side marched another set of prints with a much lighter impression and a very much shorter pace. In fact, they were so closely spaced that they reminded Merral of those made by a child. Curiously, the prints were bounded by sharp, angular sides and seemed not to have any clear imprint of toes.

Eventually Vero looked up from imaging them.

"Okay, Sentinel," Merral said, "you tell me what is going on."

"Going on? I wish I knew." Vero shook his head. "What I can tell you is what you yourself know. There were two creatures. The larger one has feet not dissimilar to ours, walks upright, weighs as much as you and I together, and must be—I'm guessing—as high as if I sat on your shoulders."

"And, I presume, the hair Isabella and I found comes from it."

Vero nodded. "A fair guess. If the sand were Earth quality—sorry, but it's true; it's very coarse—we might have seen signs of the fur. The other type is half the size; no, more like a third. And much, much lighter. The foot structure is, however, odd. It's bipedal too, but where are the toes? Or was it wearing shoes?"

"I don't feel so. And presumably this is our beetle-like man."

"Yes," said Vero, with a frown. "Elana is vindicated. But it is odd."

Then he looked around at the open river. "Merral, I know these are strange tracks and we could study them more, but I think we should get back off the stream. We are just too visible out here."

Merral found that he needed little encouragement to get back under the shelter of the trees. Together they clambered back up onto the grassy bank, picked up their packs, and set off again, walking thoughtfully northward.

By late afternoon there was no doubt that both were tiring. Merral checked how far they had traveled and was far from disappointed. Indeed, he realized that he was secretly pleased with the way that Vero had borne up. His light build plainly concealed a considerable toughness.

After some discussion, Merral and Vero singled out a tree-capped hill that rose sharply above a river bend ahead of them as a suitable place to overnight. Vero examined it with the fieldscope from a distance.

"It seems fine. The banks are too steep to climb up from the river. That will make keeping watch easier."

Whether as a result of his words, his tone of voice, or both, Merral felt a shiver of disquiet. It was, he found himself thinking, both a novel and an unwelcome feeling.

Slowly and carefully, they made their way round up to the summit of the hill where, under the silver-barked birch trees, they found an almost-flat surface covered by heather and bilberry. There they took their backpacks off and, following Vero's suggestion, made a survey of the immediate area. Their examination showed that, apart from an apparently active ground squirrel set nearby, there seemed to be no life larger than a bird or rabbit in the area. The hill allowed a good view in all directions, and taking the fieldscope, they went and looked northward from the edge of the hill.

The air was clear and they could see as far as the southern Rim Ranges. With the low-angle sunlight picking out features with dark shadows, the nature of the landscape ahead was clear. For some time Merral and Vero gazed at the scene, looking at parts in detail with the scope and comparing what they saw with the map they had with them.

Not far north of the hill the landscape changed. The rolling terrain they had passed through became a broad, open plain of coarse grassland broken by dispersed patches of fresh green woodland and drabber marshlands. Through it the Lannar River flowed, no longer in a single meandering unit, but rather as an array of separate channels weaving their way in and out of each other in a complex silver braid, producing a mosaic of small, pine-covered islands. Behind this, the ground rose sharply up to the Daggart Plateau, a feature marked by a broad, steep escarpment in which lines of black cliffs could be seen. *Carson's Sill,* thought Merral as, with the fieldscope on maximum power, he could make out the white thread of the waterfall down it. And behind the escarpment and beyond the Daggart Plateau, the Rim Ranges, with high, incised, and still-snowcapped peaks, marched across the horizon, firmly marking the edge of the Lannar Crater proper.

As Merral looked at the scene, he found himself feeling very mixed emotions. One part of him was simply satisfied at the distance they had traveled today. Another part of him—he wondered whether he could call it the "old Merral"—rejoiced in the sheer beauty and grandeur of the view. And yet he realized there was another emotion: one that tainted the view and marred his enjoyment. He tried to isolate the unfamiliar feeling, seeking to name it and wondering if he had the vocabulary for the task. It was, he finally decided, *foreboding*: a feeling of unease, bordering on fear, about what lay ahead.

"See anything?" Vero asked softly.

"Anything unfamiliar? No. It all looks normal to me."

"But does it feel normal?"

"No, Vero, no," answered Merral with a shake of his head, but he did not elaborate on his answer.

Back in the heart of the cluster of birch trees, they sat down and stretched out on the heather. Vero rubbed and stretched his back, as if trying to soothe pained muscles.

"I'm out of practice, Merral. I hope I didn't hold you back?"

"Not at all. You did well for a—"

There was an inquiring smile. "For a what?"

"For a man from Ancient Earth." But as he said it, Merral realized it was an odd thing to say and an odd thing to think in the first place.

Vero seemed to sense his consternation and the smile slid off his face. "Ah," he said, "you seem surprised at the thought."

"Yes, I am. The idea just came to me that the inhabitants of Ancient Earth were, in their way, old and decrepit. Tired. That sort of thing. Sorry."

Vero stiffened and looked at him searchingly, concern written across his face. "Merral, can I ask you to think carefully? Have you ever had that thought before? Or anything like it?"

Merral paused. "No. Never. I have awe and honor for Earth's history. I suppose we look on it as the infant church looked on Jerusalem. A mother to whom we owe a debt we cannot repay, even if we now have a life of our own."

"Good. But a supplementary, if I'm allowed one. Was there another thought with it? However distant, however unpleasant?"

"An associated idea? You mean if I had continued the train of thought?" He hesitated. "Well, I suppose, it might have gone that Ancient Earth is made up of tired old men and women, and that the new worlds are now the future. It is offensive, I'm afraid."

There was a raised eyebrow. "Have you ever heard such statements before? Ever read of them?"

"No, not that I can remember. They are—embarrassingly enough—mine alone."

"I wish they were. Something very like them was said a long time ago."

"By who?"

"General William Jannafy. In a talk to his council. Around 2102. It was a famous quote: 'The tired, timid, old men of a decrepit Earth stand in pathetic contrast to the brave vigor of our new worlds.'"

"*The* Jannafy? Of the Rebellion?"

"The same. Just before declaring his independence from the new Assembly."

"Then it must be coincidence. Or I've picked it up from a forgotten history lesson."

Vero was staring at him. "Perhaps. But Barrand also effectively quoted Jannafy. That the Technology Protocols were made by man, not God, and that they were not Scripture. Jannafy said something very much the same as part of the debate on the first versions."

"I remember." *And,* Merral thought, *I remember too your alarm when I mentioned it.* "But, all that was long, long ago."

"I know," replied Vero with a weak smile. "Everyone says that. It's the standard answer."

Then he fell silent and would say no more on the subject.

Eventually, as the sun touched the horizon, Vero spoke out. "I think we must make our preparations for the night. I think it would be better if we do not use any lights."

I suppose, Merral thought, *it's part of being a sentinel to find danger anywhere.* He was deciding that it could get wearisome, then he remembered his own moments of unease earlier and thought of the footprints. *No, it might be better not to be taken by surprise by an ape-creature, even if it was benign.*

"As you wish."

They rapidly erected the ultra-light two-person tent and quickly made a stew from the reconstituted supplies.

As they ate, Vero poked at the food with a fork. "I suppose I had hoped that your camping food might taste better than ours. I think I shall soon get bored of this."

"There is little option. We could catch and eat ground squirrel if you wanted."

Even in the gloom, Merral could make out the grimace.

"As a forester do you have to do that? Killing animals?"

"It's part of our training," Merral said. "I've had to do it once or twice out of necessity, and we sometimes have to cull weak or sick animals. Or when we get a species that has acquired bad habits. We had some wild boar a few decades ago, they tell me: gentle creatures, ideal for the Made Worlds. Then suddenly they evolved a taste for young trees. It couldn't be allowed, so there was a Menaya-wide boar hunt. They still talk about it. But yes, I've eaten deer and so on. I don't care for killing, of course, and my experience of real meat leads me to believe that our plant protein versions taste just as good."

"Well, they are supposed to be indistinguishable at the molecular level. So you could kill?"

"It depends what." Merral hesitated, realizing that they were no longer talking about food. "Why, what are you thinking?"

"You are on guard tonight while I sleep. I suggest you take both a bush-clearing knife and your tranquilizer gun."

"Well . . . okay, if it helps you sleep better."

Merral could see the glint of white teeth as Vero smiled. "You are uncertain, aren't you, my friend? One part of you is afraid but another part refuses to let you be so." His voice was sympathetic.

"Yes, I suppose that is so. I partly think you are being ridiculously overdramatic and then—"

"You think of the footprints and what has happened to the Antalfers. And you think of what Jorgio said which makes no sense."

"Pretty much so."

"And I am the same."

Above their heads, a bat fluttered through the darkness, and Merral looked up to see the first stars.

"Vero, tell me something. I gather that what is happening does not conform with your models. So how did you expect things to happen?"

"*Expect* is too strong a word. The broadly preferred model runs something like this: You may perceive the Assembly as being in some sort of stasis with a fixed but slowly expanding state as the worlds are made. In reality, it is far more complex. There are rhythms, pulses, cycles, waves. We have a whole branch of sentinels that just looks at them. For instance, the seeding projects occur in pulses—as every child knows—and that has a major impact. But there are slow, subtle changes in such things as demand for migration and allocation of resources. There are also ill-identified things that we can only describe as being the 'mood' of the Assembly. Sometimes, it breaks the surface."

"Like the innovative three hundred years from 8120?"

"Yes, and the much less adventurous thousand years before it. I mean, how many Eighth Millennium painters or musicians can you name? Worthy men and women, but no geniuses."

"So, there are these cycles."

"Yes, cycles and pulses, and we have tried to chart them. And these great cycles work continuously within the Assembly all the time. With their peaks and troughs. Now suppose that, just once"—Merral was conscious of Vero gesturing in the darkness with his arms—"the crests were to coincide. Like the waves of the sea—the waveforms might peak together and you might get a catastrophic wave."

"So that the Assembly might be vulnerable to an internal disruption. Through a coincidence of natural events?"

Vero sighed slightly. "We could argue about 'natural events' and 'coincidence' forever. But the point is that we have been thinking about an internal phenomenon, something felt widely and traceable back to a combination of large-scale ordinary processes. This here, this Farholme phenomenon, is the exact opposite. It is localized—really just one family—and appears to be externally caused by something that—whatever it is—is not ordinary."

He paused, evidently choosing his words with care. "This is part of the problem for me. If this is a genuine event, it suggests we have been badly wrong. And if we have been wrong here, where else are we wrong?"

Suddenly, Merral remembered that they had to contact Anya, and a few minutes later her blue eyes were peering at them out of the diary screen. "Hi, guys. Well, there's hardly much point being on video mode as I can barely see your faces."

"Sorry, Anya," Merral answered. "But we can see you fine. Anyway it's a quick call. Do you have anything for us?"

She seemed to swallow. "Well, yes, I have. You fellows may not like this. But you may be on a wild-goose chase. I was going to call you, but I thought you might still be swinging through the trees. You see, I called Maya Knella on a truly lousy Gate line. The signal to Anchala must have gone round the Assembly several times, and it's only a hundred or so light-years away. Look, she is dismissive. She thinks we have cellular decay as well as faulty hardware."

Vero spoke before Merral could say anything. "Sorry, Anya. *Faulty* hardware?"

Anya's face acquired an uneasy expression. "Yes, Vero. She says there is the possibility that the analyzer was miscalibrated before being sent out to Farholme. She has heard of something similar."

"Anya, I can't believe she said that!" Merral snapped, unable to control himself. "That the Assembly could allow such a thing to happen!" He turned to Vero, his face just visible in the reflected glow from the diary screen. "Can you credit that?"

Vero answered in a flat tone, as if he was restraining himself. "It is indeed an odd suggestion and I agree it is very worrying. Anya, this Maya Knella is good? You know her?"

"Well, we've never met in the flesh, Vero. I've been at screen symposia she has spoken at. She is good—the best. I was . . . well, shocked myself."

Vero was speaking again, and Merral felt that he was pushing gently. "So she doesn't think there is anything wrong here? No strange, exotic, alien forms?"

Anya, after opening and closing her mouth as if struggling for words, spoke slowly. "She was—I have to say—incredibly negative about it. She implied that any other option was preferable."

"I see," answered Vero. "Was she negative about your work, in any way?"

Anya looked at the screen thoughtfully. "She did not go out of her way to affirm my competence. It was all rather odd. . . ."

Feeling irritated at this turn of events, Merral nudged his friend. "Show her the images, Vero," he said quietly.

"Not yet," Vero whispered under his breath.

"Hey, what images? What have you guys seen?"

Vero gestured out of the range of the camera for Merral to be silent. "Oh, just some tracks, Anya. We'll show them to you sometime. I need to think about them properly. Run some enhancement, computer comparison, and so on. But, I suppose, we must follow our expert geneticist's advice. Still, it's a nice stroll. Look, we'd better shut down for the night."

Anya peered at them. "Okay. Well, I'll check out the equipment here. But it's odd."

"Yes, it is odd. And Anya . . ."

"Yes, Vero?"

"Er . . . don't spread what Maya's saying around, will you? If it's true, it's very bad news. If it's not then, well—she's made a fool of herself."

There was a hesitant pause. "No, I'll keep it private."

The light of the screen vanished, and Merral and Vero were left alone in the dark.

Vero spoke first. "To spare you questions, no, I don't know what is going on. But I do not believe this Maya Knella. She is covering something up. She must be. Perhaps there the solution lies. Perhaps there is a problem on Anchala, too. Perhaps the Assembly has let something loose. I must find out—" He stopped suddenly. "Merral—my most tolerant friend—I am babbling. Would you mind sleeping first? I couldn't sleep and I need to think over all that I have seen and heard today. It's now nearly eight, and first light will be—if I remember—at six. I'll take watch until one and wake you."

Merral agreed, laid out his things where he could find them in the dark, slipped inside the thermal sleeping bag in the tent, and adjusted its insulation settings.

The last thing he was aware of before sleep took him was a glimpse of Vero, hunched under the tent fly sheet and, apparently deep in thought, silhouetted against the evening sky and staring resolutely northward.

12

Merral felt that no sooner had he fallen asleep than his shoulder was being shaken gently and Vero was telling him that it was one o'clock and time for his watch.

"Glory! I must have been tired," he muttered, realizing that the darkness was complete. "Anything to report?"

"Puzzled badgers, or what passes for them here. I watched them through the fieldscope on infrared. A fox went down along the riverbank; some bats and an owl circled overhead a bit."

"Fine. I'll wake you at six."

The air was cool now and Merral pulled on his jacket, scrambled out of the tent, and sat on a soft tussock of heather peering into the darkness and listening to the noises of the night. After a while, he felt unable to sit still and, moving slowly to avoid tripping over tree roots, got up and went to the edge of the hill. There, under the light of the star-filled heavens, he could only make out the faintest outline of the landscape ahead. He could see the moving gleam of reflected starlight from the river's waters, and in the farthest distance, he thought he could make out the glint of light on the distant snowy peaks. Otherwise, impenetrable night surrounded him. He listened carefully but heard nothing untoward. The badgers snuffled down below him; away to the east a fox barked, and somewhere a nightjar chirred.

Using the fieldscope on the infrared and image enhancement modes, he scanned the area but saw little new. He put the scope down and sat there listening, trying to make sense of things.

Suddenly, he was conscious of a noise in the air above him, a quiet fluttering sound that was little more than palpitations on the edge of audibility. He glanced up to see something scudding through the air just above the trees, briefly blocking out the starlight as it passed. Using the fieldscope again, he tried to follow it but failed to see it. He decided that either it was too fast for him to follow, or for some reason the scope could not image it.

He put the instrument down and used his eyes as it came round again as if circling above them. It was plainly a bird of some sort, and Merral decided that it was probably the owl reported by Vero. But he found himself quite unable to identify which of the five possible owl species it might be. Then, abruptly, it was gone.

The rest of the night was uneventful, but Merral felt ill at ease, looking here and there at the slightest noise. He often looked up at the Gate, watching for the dull shimmer of the Near Station or for the faster-moving twinkle of the other satellites. For some reason the evidence, however far away, of his fellow humans seemed to give him comfort. It was with a strange and unaccustomed sense of relief that he watched the sun rise and the darkness vanish.

After a perfunctory breakfast, Vero and Merral set off again northward, dropping down carefully from their hill toward the river. They made good progress, and within an hour or so of their start, they had reached the point where the broad, open plain began. Now, as the river flowed in a number of wider, sandy channels separated by clumps of trees, they had to decide which to take. Despite a careful watch, they had seen no further signs of tracks. In the end, Merral agreed with Vero's suggestion that the middle channel was the best option.

Merral found that the going seemed harder than it had on the previous day and that, as they strode along the sand and gravel bars, his legs were tiring more easily. As the hours passed, he found himself sweating strongly and wiping his brow. In spite of his tiredness and the effort of walking, he maintained a careful watch on the deep shadows under the pines that crowded together on the gravel and pebble mounds that lay between the stream channels. But he saw nothing.

Increasingly, though, it was precisely the fact that he saw nothing that began to concern Merral. There was too little life. There were trout jumping in the water, in the distance he sometimes heard a woodpecker, and every so often a squirrel would bound away through the treetops. In general, though, there seemed to be a scarcity of mammals or birds, either because they had moved away, or because if they were there, they were hiding. Both hypotheses gave him cause for concern. He did not mention his feelings to Vero, who had been largely silent since breakfast, but noticed that his friend now kept the collapsed bush knife attached to his waist within easy reach.

Toward the end of the morning, Vero stopped suddenly and wrinkled his nose in disgust. "I smell something. Something nasty."

Merral sniffed cautiously and agreed. Ahead of them, three black crows flew up leisurely from a tall larch tree standing on its own on a bank of brown sand.

Without a word, Merral began to walk cautiously to the tree, his eyes sweeping this way and that. He felt suddenly tense.

"Merral!" Vero whispered, his voice thick with emotion. "There is something in the tree."

Midway up the larch, a dark, formless shape lay sprawled stiffly amid green branches. As Merral tried to make out what it was, he saw Vero, his hand on the knife, slip off his pack. Not knowing what to do but aware that the time for deliberation was now over, Merral took off his pack, pulled out the tranquilizer gun, slotted in a cartridge, and thumbed the dose level up to the maximum setting of five. Vero, his eyes scanning round warily, merely nodded agreement.

Together now, they slowly walked to the tree. As they came closer, Merral could see a confusion of tracks on the sand at its foot. The stench was stronger now: a disgusting, repellent odor of decay.

Cautiously, they walked up under the tree. As they did, Merral became aware of the faint, high-pitched sound of buzzing flies above them. He stared up at the object in the branches, seeing a scrappy bundle of disheveled black fur out of which white objects protruded. Bone white objects.

"They'd lost a dog." Vero's voice, rich in disgust, broke the silence.

In a flash of sickening revelation, Merral knew what he was looking at. "Spotback. The Antalfer's dog. Poor thing." He felt a surge of anger.

"On Ancient Earth dogs do not climb trees." Vero's voice had an odd, strained tone. "On Farholme, is that rule now broken too?"

Merral looked at the tree, noting that the dog's body was nearly three times his own height above the ground.

"No, Vero, our dogs do not climb." He heard a coldness in his own voice that surprised him. "Stand watch while I go up and get him down."

He handed the tranquilizer gun to Vero and with some effort climbed the tree and levered the body out with his boot.

By the time he had descended, Vero—his face furrowed in disgust—was already imaging the body. He looked up at Merral, his eyes wide in horror. "Before you look at it, see what you make of those tracks."

He gestured to the left.

The prints on the coarse sand were of low quality and confused, but it was possible to make up some sort of dreadful story out of them. There were paw marks and the two types of prints they had seen earlier, all mixed in as though there had been a considerable melee. Then there was a rough depression, dark with dried blood, and a confused, dragging trail into another deeper and bloodied hollow in the sand, which was surrounded by the large footprints running all around in strange, intense, deep impressions. At the base of some of the prints was a dark stain.

"A fight," Merral observed, trying to sound calm. "Spotback attacked them, I'd guess. Or they attacked him. Here a wound, possibly fatal to Spotback. Then the dog crawls here. But all these prints . . .? Was the creature dancing in triumph?"

Vero gestured back at the body. "Take a look."

Merral bent over and looked at the corpse as Vero joined him and poked delicately at the pile of fur and bone with a stick. He realized that the bones were crushed into white slivers, the skull shattered into a dozen or more fragments.

Suddenly, here by this open river with the sun shining and the wind softly ruffling the green needles of the larch tree, Merral felt sick. For a moment he thought that he was going to have to go behind a bush and vomit. Then he controlled his feelings and looked up at Vero, his nausea now mixed with anger.

"It *stamped* on the dog," he said, his tone dull.

"I am no expert in such things. But I would say so. A repeated, angry stamping." Vero's tone was icy.

"Although it might be useful to try to work out the weight of the creature that did this, I think there is no point in getting this taken back to the lab. It's probably too late for a useful analysis. It's at least three days old, badly decomposed, and has been eaten by birds."

Vero looked at him. "As for the weight, I'd guess in excess of a hundred kilos. As much as two big men. I mean, could you have thrown that dog up there?" He gestured up at the tree.

Merral stared at his friend, seeing the sweat and dust on his face and noticing the strain in his eyes. "No. He was a decent-sized dog. Twenty kilos, maybe. It was a big creature that did this. Consistent with the footprints. Think of a big man and double his size."

"For a creature that doesn't exist, according to what this Maya Knella says, curiously substantial. Odd. Very odd."

"And very nasty," Merral added. He found himself looking around, trying to peer into the shadows under the distant trees as if expecting to see something. He felt an urge to shiver.

"Vero," he said, "I've seen enough."

They buried the dog under a rough pile of basalt pebbles. Merral paused as he put on the last stone. *It is strange,* he thought, *how this has annoyed me: to kill this dog in such a way and then just fling the body away as if it were rubbish.* Whatever these creatures were, he decided that he already felt very ill inclined toward them.

Then, more positively, he told himself that he would get Spotback's name put on something here, some ridge or hill, when the naming commission came up this far north for the minor features.

They picked up their packs and set off again. Merral, however, did not put the tranquilizer gun away but attached it to his waist, where it banged against him annoyingly. As they walked on he found himself more than once wondering how fast he could operate it and whether it would work against such creatures. *And supposing it didn't,* he asked himself, *how quickly could I get out my bush knife?*

And, as he tackled these thoughts, he wasn't sure which disturbed him most: the idea of the unknown creatures or the anger they had aroused within him.

Merral and Vero pushed on throughout the day along the sandy margins of the river channels, taking only the briefest break at midday. They said little to each other but set a steady pace, their eyes and ears alert for any signs of the creatures. Merral noticed how they kept to the edges of the river and that when they approached large boulders they carefully circumvented them lest something be behind them. Irritated by the tranquilizer gun but with no inclination to put it back in his pack, he found himself carrying it awkwardly on his shoulder.

In the afternoon their steady pace was rewarded by good views of the steep black rock walls of Carson's Sill and the dense dark greenery of conifer woods that clung to the slopes in patches along it. And, as the afternoon wore on, the tiered rock face of the plateau edge with the white vertical slash where the Lannar River plunged down in a series of waterfalls rose before them, and it began to dominate their thinking.

"It has been climbed?" asked Vero in doubtful tones, as he stared through the fieldscope at it.

"Of course, or I wouldn't have taken this route. By Thenaya Carson first, oh, two centuries ago, and about every decade since. But not by me. It's around eight hundred meters from the base to the lip of the scarp."

"With packs, and on that surface, it won't be easy."

"The trick, I'm told from the files, is to go up well away from the river. There is a lot of loose debris and the spray from the waterfalls has smoothed the rocks, so it makes for treacherous climbing. The western side is supposed to be fine, if it hasn't slipped. There's a lot of erosion going on."

"Ah, the Made Worlds again," commented Vero with a tight smile.

"Sorry. But it will be a hard climb and we will be exhausted at the top."

"I'm tired at the thought. How much longer until we stop today?"

"Can you manage another hour?"

"Yes, Forester," Vero answered, amid a wipe of his brow, "but it can't come too soon."

They walked on, and half an hour later, as they were walking through a narrow section with high dark stands of the woodland pine on either side, Vero caught Merral's gaze. "I have noticed you listening a lot. You ought to be more at home here than me. What do you feel?"

Merral stopped, listening again to the silence around them. "*Feel?* I don't know. I'm worried that I'm talking myself into seeing and hearing things that don't exist. What with the dog, and Jorgio's warning . . ." He prodded a pebble tentatively with his foot. "But there just doesn't seem anywhere near as much wildlife as I would expect. Not here. Maybe, not since last night. The odd rabbit and the squirrel, that's all, and they seem to keep their distance. Normally, I'd expect to get within feet of them. There are fewer birds, too."

Merral looked up to see, high above them and too far away to identify, a stiff-winged brown shape circling above them. "And there's the odd buzzard. But little else."

He found it hard to put his feelings into words. "But I have to say that sometimes . . . sometimes I feel that we are being watched. Do you?"

"Yes, I do," answered Vero without hesitation, looking ahead at the ridge before them. "I was trying to avoid saying it, but I have an uneasy feeling about this Carson's Sill and what lies beyond it. I am wondering if I should just have asked a full Sentinel Threat Evaluation Team to come in and go through the whole area. With both ships of the Assembly Defense Force sitting in low orbit."

"I have to say," Merral said, "that for the first time in my entire life I consider that the Assembly may have been wise in retaining two military vessels. Not that I ever gave it very much thought."

Vero wiped the sweat off his hands on his trousers. "Yes, persuading the Assembly to maintain two armed cruisers and a hundred crew as a Defense Force on constant readiness has been a priority of the sentinels since Moshe Adlen's day. It has not been an easy task."

Then he looked at Merral. "I have not said this before, but the existence of the Assembly Defense Force makes my position tricky."

"How so?"

"This would be their first intervention ever. News of it would go throughout the Assembly, and if it was for a false alarm, then it could be unfortunate for the sentinels. But we may well have to call them anyway."

And with that he gestured Merral onward.

By five o'clock they had reached a point where the ground had begun to rise toward the sill. Here, with the cliffs looming over them, Merral decided to stop. They had made good time and there was no way that they could climb the sill today. He had already assessed the ascent as requiring at least three hours, and with the evening fast approaching and their growing tiredness, it made sense to camp at the base and tackle the climb when fresh.

They found a suitable spot for camping. A landslide from the cliff had left an enormous mound of debris, within the angular boulders of which there had been enough fine material to make a poor soil in which stunted and tilted fir and spruce trees had grown. At the top of the mound was something of a hollow surrounded by small young firs, and Merral felt that it afforded a perfect site for camping.

In the depression, they put up the tent and then took turns bathing in the river below. As one bathed in the clear but icy river waters, the other sat by on a rock with the tranquilizer gun and a bush knife keeping watch. The troubling thought came to Merral that the very idea of keeping watch would have been inconceivable only a few weeks ago. Now, he realized ruefully, they had slipped into practicing the habit almost as a routine.

Then, refreshed by their baths, they climbed back up to the tent and, for some minutes, lay back on the soft heather enjoying the warm, gentle late-afternoon air and watching the swifts dart above them, hearing their screeching over the echoing rumble of the waterfalls and rapids. Then, taking the fieldscope and with the map in front of them they turned to look up at the rock face, trying to decide which route to take.

As Merral stared at the bulwark of rock that was Carson's Sill, he felt his spirit sink. It was an uncompromising vista; the lines of vertical cliffs of black lava seemed stacked one above another, crag hanging upon crag. Where the towering ranks of the cliff faces were broken, massive piles of sharp-edged rock fragments radiated downward and outward in vast cones of scree. Merral noted that, amid the frequent patches of firs, whole trees were toppled over or had been splintered by rolling rocks, and in the debris piles, fragments of trunks stuck out at crazy angles. The only consolation he could find was that he could see no sign of any creatures on the cliffs.

"Tough," commented Vero with a frown. "It's like looking up at your castle tree. Only the absolute necessity of my following this trail encourages me to persist."

"I agree, and I'm afraid there is another factor," Merral added, gesturing up at the sky where high in the atmosphere fine, wispy spirals of cloud were drifting westward. "I think we will find the weather changing tonight. It looks like rain coming in from the east."

"How bad?"

"Well, if it is going to be a cyclone we'll be warned by the Met Team. But we need to think about a wet-weather path."

Vero gave a theatrical groan. "Beware the weather in the Made Worlds!" he muttered.

In fact, as they looked up at the cliffs, they soon realized that their choices were limited. The Lannar River had cut something of a gorge through the top part of the plateau edge so that on either side the ground rose through forested flanks up to steep, flat-topped summits several hundred meters higher.

Merral pointed to the V-shaped notch of the stream that was sharply defined against the skyline. "So, Vero, the easiest route is to go straight up to that gorge on the plateau and then on to the Daggart Lake."

"The easiest, no doubt . . . ," answered Vero slowly and Merral sensed his disquiet.

In the end, they agreed that there was only one suitable route, an easily followed line which took them in a slow, zigzag fashion over the shiny black lava blocks, up through clumps of spruce and fir, and then upward to the western side of the gorge at the crest.

They returned to the tent and, as the shadows lengthened, ate in silence.

As the sun began to set, the gathering clouds acquired hues of purple, red, and gold so that the sky began to look like some astonishing experiment in flowing and shimmering colors.

"Ah," mouthed Vero in appreciative wonder, "you do have awesome sunsets here."

Merral smiled. "There are two explanations. One is that it is God's compensation for our being a Made World. The other is that it is the combination of abundant high-altitude dust—inevitable in this stage of our world's making—and a complex and still partially unstable multilayer atmosphere."

"May it always be that your world never divorces the two explanations."

Then, as the light faded and the stars came out, Merral said he was going to call Anya. Vero stopped him. "I think . . . ," he began hesitantly. "I think we might want to avoid saying anything very much about today's discovery."

"Fine, but why?"

"Just a feeling. We will see her in a day or two. You see," he sighed, "she is inclined to believe this Maya Knella. I think there is something very funny there. However I want to talk over with Anya exactly what was said and see the conversation replayed."

"I see."

"So I think we should play it down. We say we had a good day's walk and that's all."

The issue of withholding information made Merral uneasy and he nearly said something, but, in the end, he remained silent. These were strange events and the old rules seemed no longer to hold. *"Things have changed,"* Jorgio had said, and he felt the truth of that. If only, he found himself wishing, things would stabilize long enough, he might see his way to understanding what was going on and working out how to respond to it.

When Anya's image came on the diary, it showed her still in the office. She smiled at them.

"Good to hear from you. I noticed you made good progress earlier. What's new?"

"Bits and pieces, scraps of data," Merral answered. "We are still puzzling. Tell you about it when we get back, another day or two. Anything new on your end?"

She shrugged, her freckled face showing open puzzlement. "Well, I just can't square Maya's statement with what I've seen." Vero nudged Merral's arm and then spoke. "Anya, it's Vero. Nice to talk with you."

"Hi, Sentinel. You shouldn't call people so late. With your complexion I can barely see you in this light."

"True. I guess I'm designed for nocturnal camouflage," he joked, then changed his tone. "But look, Anya, this thing with Maya . . . I think we'll talk it over together when we get back. In the meantime, just don't let it bother you."

"Okay, but it's still odd." She paused. "Oh, yes, I checked with the Met Team people. Rain tomorrow over your area. Ninety percent probability by dawn. But passing over rapidly."

"Thanks, Anya, saves me checking. We suspected it. But it will be a wet climb tomorrow."

"You'll do it. Take care. We'll be in touch the same time tomorrow."

The screen darkened.

For a few moments, they sat in darkness. Merral looked up to the escarpment to the north of them, now only visible as a high, brooding mass of black against the hazy stars.

"The rain is confirmed, Vero."

"I'm used to it, as long as it isn't too cold," Vero answered, stretching himself. "Do you want first or second watch tonight?"

"I'll take second. I'm more used to the rain. But now, after seeing the remains of Spotback, I am under no illusions about a watch being a good idea."

"Yes, sadly, it is needed." Vero got to his feet. "Which reminds me, what did Anya mean about noticing us 'making good progress'? How did she know?"

Merral found himself wondering at his friend's surprise. "By monitoring my diary's location signal, I presume."

"What? Your diary broadcasts out?" Vero's voice was incredulous. "Without you telling it to do so?"

"Yes, foresters, farmers—anyone who works out in the wilds—always set their diary to emit a location signal." Merral was puzzled at Vero's tone. Suddenly a realization came to him. "Of course, you probably don't need to do it on Ancient Earth. I think it's every sixty seconds or so. Any satellite or plane can pick it up. If an accident happens, they know where to find me. Standard practice in all the low-population worlds."

A snort came from Vero. "You mean we have been radiating our position ever since we came? And I have been worried about keeping under cover!" Merral could see him shaking his head. "But why, oh *why* didn't you tell me?" His tone was now one of extreme irritation.

"Why should I?" Merral answered sharply, feeling on the edge of anger and trying to control himself. "We are dealing with animals. Aren't we? You mean to tell me that you think we face *things* with the intelligence and technology to pick up a tight-band EM signal?"

"Maybe. . . ."

"So why didn't *you* tell *me?*" Merral asked, his anger now supplemented by a definite unhappiness at the idea that what they faced might be far more than some sort of clever animal.

"Because I wasn't sure. And I am still not sure. . . ."

A sullen silence descended between them, and suddenly they both apologized at the same time.

"Sorry! I'm—"

"—No, me too."

Vero patted Merral on the shoulder. "My fault. Naive Earther that I am. I should have thought. Can you switch the thing off?"

"Yes. And I will do it now." Merral unclipped the diary and spoke to it. "Diary. Menu Command: Location signal—disable until countermanded."

The manufactured voice responded in its flat lifeless tones, "Location signal is now disabled."

Merral put it back on his belt. "So, my sentinel friend, you don't think it's animals we face? You feel there is an intelligence here?"

"It is a possibility. No more. One of many possibilities that I have thought of and some that I haven't." He sounded rueful. "Probably among the ones that I haven't thought of is the correct answer."

Merral waited for some elucidation of the possibilities, but Vero seemed disinclined to give them and said nothing more.

After some time Vero spoke in a low voice. "You get some sleep." He paused, as if listening to something. "It is quiet here, isn't it?"

"Yes," Merral said listening again. "It is. Or is it my imagination? There should be more noise. Keep a good watch, my friend."

When Vero woke Merral it was raining. The air seemed thick with the incessant soft, gentle dripping of water as it trickled off the needles and branches of the firs to tap on the roof of the tent.

"What have you seen?" Merral grunted sleepily as he pulled his jacket on. In the pitch blackness of the night, he sensed his friend shedding a damp outer jacket under the fly sheet and clambering through into his side of the tent.

"I don't know," Vero answered with a strangely unsettled tone. "There isn't even any starlight now. It's pitch black and I find it very disorienting. I was careful not to go too far from the tent. In case I got lost. I wish you'd been there. . . ."

"Why?"

"I heard . . . or I thought I heard . . . sounds."

"Wind perhaps?"

"No, no. Not the wind, not the river. It was different—as if it was voices."

"Voices?"

"So it sounded to me. . . . Distant voices, as if the wind had brought them. . . ." Vero seemed to shudder. "But, as I think I told you when we first met, we are trained to be sensitive, to be able to listen to what others cannot hear, to see what others cannot see. Tonight, I wished I had not been so trained. . . ."

Merral reached out, found his friend's arm, and squeezed it gently. "You can get to see and hear things in wind and rain. Did you think they were human?"

There was a shudder. "I hope not. . . ."

"Anything nearer?"

"No, I checked around on the scope in infrared. It's too dark for anything else. Some deer by the river. I think I saw another owl."

"Again? Get a good look?"

"No. I couldn't seem to image it in infrared."

"Maybe the feathers are effective insulators. So they may not radiate enough heat to be picked up. Well, it's a theory. Anyway, let me go out."

"Watch well, Merral. The knife, the gun, and a couple of flares are under the tent awning."

"I hope not to need them. And you sleep soundly, Vero."

In the long, weary, and uncomfortable hours that followed, Merral found himself frequently thinking of the pleasant evenings and nights he had spent in the countryside in the past. Tonight, in the rain and the dark, he felt as if they might have been on another planet. Merral, trying to analyze his feelings, decided that the darkness was one factor. The night was pitch dark, unbroken by stars or even any flash of lightning, and at one point he found that he literally could not see his hand in front of his face. With the infrared mode set on the fieldscope, he could at least make out the general landscape and see the vague glow of his sleeping friend in the tent. While that was an improvement, the strange effect of seeing things in a ghostly monochrome only seemed to make him feel more disoriented. The rain, he felt, was another factor. It was a soft, wetting mist of a rain that not only fell, but also drifted up, under, and somehow even inside things. Despite the excellence of his garments, Merral very soon found that he was getting wet. So he stood up, feeling the cold water drip and ooze down inside his clothes, and felt miserable.

He knew, though, that it was neither the dark nor the rain: There was another factor, and that was hard to define. There was an atmosphere of unease, of some sort of inexpressible hostility that got on his nerves. Merral realized that he was close to reaching a level of fear that he had never known existed. Everybody was familiar with some levels of fear; you might have a fear of being crushed by a falling tree, a fear of falling off a cliff, or a fear of being caught in a forest fire. Yet that was, he realized, something normal, natural, and even good. Now, though, he sensed he was close to something deeper: a darker, wilder fear that threatened to overwhelm all logic. Was this, he thought, what they had called *terror*?

So Merral prayed for himself, for Vero and their mission, and for the strange things that were happening on Farholme. But—and he found this the most depressing thing of the night—there seemed to be no answer to his prayers. The act of praying seemed to him to be almost futile, and his words seemed cold and lifeless. It almost seemed—and he hardly dared frame the thought—as if the throne of heaven was vacant.

Through what was left of the lonely night, Merral saw and heard nothing, although once he felt sure that, over the soft, steady drip of the rain off the branches, he could hear soft, slow wing beats above him. And when, at last, dawn broke, it seemed to bring little comfort, with the blackness around merely being replaced by a formless and clinging wet grayness.

Damp and cold, Merral woke Vero and together they ate a cheerless breakfast in the tent, folded it up, and loaded the packs.

Under the gentle gray rain they set off toward the cliffs, picking their way slowly up among the wet boulders, rough grass, and tall dripping pines and spruces that obscured the cliff ahead. As they did, Merral looked around, acknowledging to himself how different things looked in the rain. In front of them, above the green-steepled firs, wisps of white cloud drifted across, obscuring the grim ramparts of rock that rose up behind. To their right the cloud, mist, and rain mingled with the spray of the waterfalls, as the Lannar recklessly and noisily plunged downward off the plateau. The very top of the plateau was obscured by a wreath of pale clouds.

After a quarter of an hour of stumbling and sliding in the mud, they came to something of a clearing and were able to take stock of the task ahead.

Merral tilted his head over to Vero. "Well, any trail is now lost, but it hardly matters. There is only one way ahead and that is the way we chose last night."

Vero nodded, shaking a large drop of rainwater off his snub nose. "Yes. But Merral, I have to say that I am worried about what we will meet on this hill. I think—I *feel*—that there is something up there. And that that something is not friendly to us or the Assembly."

He stretched out a dripping hand and pointed to the cliff. "May I make a small suggestion?" His voice was unsure. "I have studied, as all sentinels must, something of the distasteful science of warfare. Your reading of the first part of the Word will have been the nearest that you will have come in this respect. After thought last night, I have decided that I do not like the route you suggest." He traced the line up the slope with a wet finger. "It is too obvious. The gorge at the top is a mere fifty meters or so across. We will climb over the sill edge there onto the plateau, tired and weary. It would be an ideal place for us to either be seen or . . ." He paused. "Meet opposition."

"You mean it's a fine site for a . . ." Merral ransacked his memory. "An ambush. Is that the word?"

"Exactly so." Vero wiped water off his face. "Now, it seems to me that if we kept over to the left we could come onto the plateau at a higher level. Perhaps a hundred meters higher. It's hard to assess it from here. It would make for a tougher climb, but we are also more under trees. And we would not be as obvious."

"Vero, I'm beginning to feel that we are in some pre-Intervention tale."

The wet brown face seemed to wrinkle with some deeply unpleasant emotion. "I hope, my friend, you do not speak truer than you can imagine."

There was silence, and then Vero raised his head and spoke loudly in a firm voice that rang out around the trees and the rocks. "Our Father, who is the defender and ruler of your people, we fear this place and what is on it. Protect your children and go before us now. In the name of the one who is both Lamb and Shepherd. Amen."

"Amen."

There was silence, and then a dripping hand touched Merral's shoulder. "Now, to the climb. . . ."

The slope was harder than Merral had imagined. He was tired, and even though the route they took was one of a series of oblique traverses, it required continuous exertion. Where there was soil, the rain had reduced it to a soft, greasy mud so that they found themselves slithering without warning. Fortunately, the firs and scrubby bushes meant that they rarely slid down for more than a few meters. Their hands and legs soon became muddy and, inevitably, as they tried to clear the rain out of their eyes, the brown mud was transferred to their faces. Where there was only wet, loose rock, they found they had to test every step carefully lest a block roll away under their weight. Despite the drifting rain, they found that under the effort of climbing they soon warmed up, and the high humidity meant that it was not long before sweat was running off them. A few hundred meters up, Merral called a halt and sat down heavily on a slab of rock, panting for breath.

"Vero," he muttered eventually, when he had the spare energy to speak, "the idea of sliding down and asking for a ride back home in the belly of some warm, dry rotorcraft seems very attractive."

His companion grunted. "I sympathize entirely."

Then Vero looked up to the crest of the sill above them with determined eyes. "But I believe we must climb this. And, increasingly, I think we must be in a position where we can find such weapons as we have easily."

For an instant, Merral felt himself on the edge of rebellion. The words "I'm not climbing this cluttered with a bush knife and a tranquilizer gun" framed themselves in his mind. Then he pushed the thought aside and, without a word, pulled out the bush knife from his pack and attached it to his belt. With some difficulty, he was able to put the tranquilizer gun in his jacket pocket.

Then they set off again, and as they climbed on upward, weaving their way between crags and trees, slipping in the mud and bruising themselves against the rocks, Merral found the climb beginning to blur in his mind. The wet pine needles, rough tree trunks, chocolate-colored mud, and protruding razor-edged black lava blocks seemed to merge into a single slope that ran on upward forever. When, gripped by the risk of slipping down hundreds of meters to the scree below, Merral tried to watch his feet, he found instead that he walked into sharp branches that poked at and whipped his face and hands. When he concentrated on avoiding the branches, he lost his footing and slid.

Once, when they had stopped and were trying to get their breath, there was a great crash and a slab of rock fell down on the other side of the river, plunging noisily downward in a damp cloud of dust and debris. Merral and Vero stared carefully at where it had fallen from, but there was no sign of anything other than natural erosion having caused its fall.

"Beware the weathering in the Made Worlds," grunted Vero as he looked up at the crags above them, but there was no humor in his voice.

Increasingly as they climbed on, Merral became conscious of how his legs and back ached, how his lungs hurt, how he wanted to stop, and how water—he had ceased to care whether it was rain or sweat—was running down his back and chilling him. And when he looked down and back he saw, through the veil of rain and mist and cloud, a dizzying drop through green lines of trees and sheer rock ramparts to the braided, tarnished-silver line of the river.

Slowly though, they made progress, and finally, after nearly three hours of climbing up the sill, Vero nudged Merral. "Not far now," he gasped. "We are at the level of the gorge."

Merral looked to his right to see that they had indeed reached the sharp notch through which the river tumbled urgently. He breathed a silent phrase of thanks, and a few minutes later, they pulled themselves over a final rock level. There, below the wet and drooping branches of the fir trees, they could see that the ground fell away gently northward and that several hundred meters ahead of them lay the still black waters of Daggart Lake with dense pine forests clustered around it. To the left the ground rose up steeply through more trees to a steep-sided, flat-topped summit.

Weary, heedless of the rain, Merral slumped down flat on the wet mossy ground. He had to lie down, he had to rest, and he had to adjust his backpack.

Vero tapped him gently on the shoulder. "No! Don't lie down. You are too vulnerable. Sit!"

In a sudden surge of emotion, Merral felt certain that Vero was going mad and a wave of anger rose in him. *I have had* enough *of this crazy sentinel lunacy.*

He was about to say something when he looked up at Vero's mud-stained face and saw his mouth drop open and his eyes widen.

Suddenly, Vero was on all fours, cringing low on the ground.

"Stay down!" he hissed in a fierce, urgent tone.

Merral, still lying flat, pressed himself against the ground.

"S–slowly," Vero whispered, a hint of a stutter in his words, "look behind you."

Merral rolled over and stared toward the lake.

Along the water's edge, dark tall figures were moving.

For a second *figures* and *moving* were the only words that came to him because his eyes could not make sense of what he saw. The figures were large, walked on two feet, and had an upright stance, but they were not—and he knew it instantly—human. It was not just that they were a dark brownish black in color and were covered in hair, but that they had the wrong proportions, the wrong posture, and the wrong motion. Their arms seemed to reach well below the waist, there was an odd stooping character to their stance, and they had a peculiar loping gait that no human legs could ever have imitated. There was an oddity too about their heads that, at this distance, he could recognize but not define.

Merral realized with a sharp thrill of horror that these were definitely not men. But then neither were they apes; not only was the shape wrong, but there was a purposefulness, a sense of mission in their motion that he had never seen in an ape.

"Vero," he heard himself whisper, "what *are* they?"

He saw that the figures were moving toward the sides of the gorge overlooking where the river began its plunge over Carson's Sill. "I–I wish I knew," Vero answered in numbed tones. "I know less now than I did. But if I do not know what they are, I can guess what they are after. . . ."

He stared at Merral. "They are after us."

13

Merral gaped at the creatures again, oddly aware that his throat was dry. The creatures were big, nearly half as high again as a big man, and they appeared to have powerful muscles. It was all too easy to imagine one stamping on a dog and hurling it effortlessly high into a tree.

Suddenly Merral became conscious of his heart pounding in his chest, his skin tingling, and his stomach twisting on itself. The deep fear that he had sensed existed last night now seemed very close. *I am really afraid,* he realized.

"T–time to get out, Merral," Vero whispered in shaken tones. Merral found a strange comfort in the fact that his friend was also very scared.

"Yes, a good idea. I have a reluctance to try and dialogue. How many do you think there are?"

"Six at least. The source of the hair you found. . . ."

Merral rolled away and looked to their left. He forced himself to ignore the thudding in his chest and to reason out what to do next.

"We must plan, Vero," he said, surprised by how level his voice sounded. "We cannot be picked up here easily by any plane or rotorcraft—there is too much vegetation. And we are too near those things for my liking."

Vero, still staring down to the lake, just nodded.

Merral looked up through the trees. "We must climb again, I am afraid. See how this hill is flat topped?"

"Yes. . . . They are dropping into the gorge."

Merral looked round to see the last of the creatures lowering itself over the rocks with a disturbingly human motion of the forearms.

"Yes, but we must move. They will find out shortly that we are gone and will trace our route."

Vero looked up at the summit, his face bizarrely transfigured by the mud. "It's another few hundred meters up. It's steep at the top. Can we climb it?"

"I hope so. I can see a crack of some sort. I think we call for a rescue pickup as soon as we can get up there. We'd better go."

They set off and Merral led the way, trying to avoid making any noise and vigilantly looking ahead between the trees. He was aware of Vero following closely behind him. They wound their way up through the firs, and soon the view of the lake disappeared behind the wet foliage. With the initial shock now waning, Merral asked himself, *Do they have a sense of smell? How far can they see? Could they track us up this way?* Mindful of his fear, conscious of tired limbs and of the soft rain wetting his face, Merral forced himself onward.

Ahead through the trees, he could see two house-size blocks of pitted, charcoal black lava that had come to rest after rolling down the hill. In between the great rocks, Merral could now see properly up to the top of the hill. The cloud was slowly lifting, and he could make out a steep, bare slope of broken rubble capped by a slablike expanse of rock. In the thick lava unit that formed the top of the hill, there was a dark, slitlike fracture in which small trees grew. Merral motioned Vero to stop, noticing that on his tired face the rain was running down and mingling with the mud. *I must look like that.*

"Look, that's the way, Vero," he said as he carefully looked up the hill. "Through this gap in the rocks, up to the crevasse, and then on to the summit plateau."

"I can see. But what if the top is occupied?" Vero's voice was urgent.

For a brief moment, a spasm of despair ran through Merral's mind. "No," he answered after a moment's evaluation of the possibility, "I think it's unlikely. It's bare rock. They like cover."

"So we believe," Vero answered stiffly. "But anyway, we have little choice."

"I'm tempted to call in a rescue now. What do you think?"

Vero thought. "Not yet," he said, pulling off his backpack and taking out his water bottle. "I must have a drink. I don't want to use a signal here. On the chance they can locate us on it. Besides, if the top is occupied, we may want to retreat back to somewhere else." He hurriedly swallowed some water.

Merral flung his own pack off his back, pulled out his own bottle, and took two hasty mouthfuls. "Fine, but let's keep moving. They may have realized by now that we aren't coming up through the gorge."

"Yes." Vero slung the pack on one shoulder and started to walk ahead.

Merral replaced his own bottle in his backpack and put it back on his shoulders. He was about to follow Vero when he stopped. Somewhere there was a noise: a faint scrabbling that made his spine shiver. Merral looked around, conscious of the darkness under the firs about him. A dozen paces ahead Vero was starting to wind his way between the high, overhanging dark rocks.

There was another noise.

Something dropped down from the top of the rocks. Something that, in the fraction of the second before it struck the ground, appeared to Merral to be like a child wrapped in shiny brown rags.

"Look out!"

Vero turned as the shape fell toward him and stepped back awkwardly. The creature landed lightly on all fours ahead of him and sprang upright.

Now the shape became clear to Merral, as if the image had just focused. It was a small creature, smaller than Vero, with squat brown legs, long arms, and hands that seemed to swing and thrust as it hopped strangely forward. Despite the small size, there was an air of menace and aggression about it.

Merral began to run toward Vero. As he did, he saw the creature suddenly bound forward with a surprising speed, holding its hands out in front as if they were weapons. Vero sidestepped clumsily, swinging his backpack off his shoulder at the brown thing. The pack struck the creature on the chest with a thud and it staggered back, flailing its arms and displaying oddly flattened hands. As Merral bounded forward, he realized that he had no strategy.

With a wild chirring noise, the creature flung the pack aside and sprung to its feet with a bounce. It began to advance on Vero, who had moved back against the side of the left-hand rock. There, realizing that he was unable to retreat farther, he reached for his bush knife. As he pulled it out, the creature leapt at him. A polished brown arm flicked out and, even as the blade extended, the knife was swept clean out of Vero's hand. It whistled overhead and rattled down against the rocks. Vero yelped and snatched his hand back. From the creature came a strange, high-pitched hissing noise.

Suddenly the creature seemed to recognize Merral's approach. It swiveled its head and looked at him with small eyes as black as shadows. Merral, coming to a halt just in front of it, could see that the head was small, vaguely reptilian in its profile, and covered with brown, waxy plates. It was like nothing he had seen or imagined.

With a fast but somehow ungainly shuffle, the creature turned round to face him, its legs clattering woodenly against the stones, its arms opening wide. Merral was oddly aware of details: the rain dribbling down the carapace, a yellow scratch on a chest plate, the black, lidless, deep-set eyes with a ring of plates around them.

The strange and terrible thought that he had to fight it came into Merral's mind. Reality seemed to have fled. Merral fumbled for the bush knife, his hand closing tight on the handle, his wet fingers reaching for the release button. With a sharp click the gray blade extended. He held it out and moved toward the thing. As if recognizing danger, the creature raised its strange arms high.

Now, as they faced each other, Merral saw the creature properly for the first time. Yet he felt that even now he saw it only as series of impressions of separate parts, as if its unfamiliarity made it impossible to see as a whole. He was struck by the polished-wood appearance of the creature and the massive segmented platelike sheets over the front of the chest that fused into a single hard vertical ridge along the abdomen. What made the most impression on him, though, was not the grotesque physical appearance, but the sense of malignant intelligence in the recessed, tar black, resinous eyes. What he faced was not simply an animal.

The hands moved slowly, and Merral saw that there were three fingers vaguely like those of a man and then a thumb and forefinger whose matching flat inner sections made a pair of blades with serrated edges like a pair of wire cutters. As he watched, the creature seemed to flick them open and shut almost as if to demonstrate them. It came to Merral as a cold fact that the gape was quite wide enough to take off an ankle or a wrist. Various deep, hissing noises came from the wide horizontal slit of the mouth, and Merral wondered if there was a language in them.

As the thing inched closer, making an odd clicking noise as its plates rubbed together, Merral waved the dull metal blade uncertainly in front of him. He saw new details: the swollen and armored joints of limbs that approximated elbows and knees and the clawlike feet that pivoted oddly at the ankles.

"*Lord*," he prayed aloud, "I don't know what to do."

The creature took another rolling step forward, its body swaying slightly from side to side. Then it lowered itself down on bended leg joints.

It sprang.

Merral leaped aside, swinging the blade out as he jumped. The blade struck a plate on the creature's arm and, with a dull clatter, bounced off. Merral landed awkwardly on the wet grass and slid into a half crouch. In a strange hopping motion, the thing was bearing upon him. *I must not get knocked down.* With his left hand he found the edge of a rock and pushed himself upright. As he did, the creature lunged again.

Merral swung his right boot up to ward off the attack. But the creature's hand swiveled, opened, and seized his ankle. There was a sudden, sharp stab of agony and Merral kicked hard. The bladed hand opened wide and his ankle flew free. A new hiss came from the creature, and Merral wondered if it was a note of triumph. Now, less than a meter away, he was aware of a strange, unpleasant odor that brought back memories of college biology laboratories.

"Hit it, Merral!" Vero cried. And Merral, conscious of a surging pain in his foot, began to raise the blade again. But, as he lifted the handle, it came to

him with a sharp clarity that his opponent was too armored. He had to find a weakness.

The creature moved again, this time in a crablike crouch with the head tilting and swaying this way and that, as if calculating the next attack. The broad mouth opened into a wide oval to show matching rows of sharp-pointed, brown teeth.

It is in no hurry. In a new pitch of alarm, he noticed vivid red on its left hand. A quick glance down showed blood on his right ankle and he realized that he was hurting there.

I must strike, but where? He stared at his opponent, suddenly noticing the beads of water running down the smooth surface of the creature's skin. *Skin or shell?* he asked himself and pushed the question aside. The creature seemed to stretch its head, and for the briefest of moments, Merral saw a patch of wrinkled soft yellow tissue between the hard brown plates of the neck and chest. Then the thing moved slowly toward him again, and Merral realized that he could not retreat. He knew it was going to attack again and he felt certain that this time it would go for his face or neck with those scissorlike blades.

As if from nowhere Vero appeared, bearing down on the creature with a branch in his hand. He swung it down hard on the thing's head but it was a clumsy weapon, and as it descended, the creature suddenly turned sideways. The blow landed on the armored shoulder and bounced harmlessly off. But as it did, the thing turned its flattened head upward, exposing again the yellow patch. Suddenly, with a force and speed he did not know he had, Merral stabbed the blade forward into the exposed gap. For a fraction of a second, the blade struck shell and met an unyielding resistance. Then—just as Merral thought he had failed—it shuddered, turned, slipped a fraction sideways, and with an appalling sucking sound, plunged deep down into the soft tissue.

Everything happened at once.

The creature reeled back, striking the rocks with a cracking sound; the blade was snatched out of Merral's hand; a high-pitched loud rasping scream echoed out of the red-foaming mouth. The bladelike fingers began flapping and clattering in desperation at the knife embedded in its throat.

Merral stood back, clutching the rock behind him, aware of fresh crimson drops on his wet legs. He shook uncontrollably and gasped for breath.

I have killed, was the thought that pounded again and again through his brain.

Over everything the terrible screaming—surely more human than animal—was continuing.

Suddenly Merral was aware of a wild-eyed Vero shaking him. "Quickly! Now! Let's run while we can!"

Above his agony, Merral somehow recognized the truth of what was being said and began to move. He took three steps forward and looked at the creature that was now writhing like some monstrous broken insect on the wet grass.

Merral hesitated. Then, from far below, came strange bellowing howls.

"Quick!" Vero was snatching at his hand.

Merral began to run, vaguely conscious that his right ankle was on fire. He saw that Vero had recovered his bush knife and now had it ready with the blade out.

"What was it?" gasped Merral.

"Save your breath. But well done!"

Well done? Merral thought, in an astonishment that cut through his appalled and confused state of mind. *Well done! An intelligent creature is dying—is already dead perhaps—because of my action. Do we applaud such things?* Then he realized that he had had no option.

He pushed the idea out of his mind and, trying to ignore the sharp pain in his ankle, began to run as fast as he could.

They were beyond the great rocks now and were coming out of the edge of the trees. Ahead lay the open, desolate scree of the hill and above that stood the final black wall of the cliff. The cloud was lifting and the rain seemed to be dying away.

They stumbled out onto the wet piles of broken angular rock, heading for the narrow dark cleft that cut through the upper cliff. From below them, amid the trees, they heard a series of booming bellows followed by high-pitched chattering.

Merral moved forward with a new urgency. But increasingly, as they ascended over the rough blocks of the scree, pain took over: the pain of his lungs, the pained tiredness of his limbs, and, above all, the pain of his bleeding ankle.

Suddenly, Vero turned, saw him lagging behind, and threw down his torn backpack.

"Quick, Merral, let me have your pack," he said amid gasps, the sweat, mud, and rain on his face barely masking a look of intense fear. "We'll throw away mine and anything we don't need. . . . Let me carry it. Quickly!"

Merral, trying to take any weight off his injured ankle, passed the pack over and watched as Vero feverishly threw out the tent and camping equipment, spare clothes, and much of the remaining food. Vero, his eyes nervously searching the dark margin of the trees below, stuffed in some things from his own pack, which he then threw away. Putting the remaining backpack on his back, Vero turned to Merral.

"Does your foot hurt?"

"Not badly," Merral replied, his voice uneven. "I'd like to wash the cut, though."

Vero looked round. "Not here. That . . . *thing* came out of nowhere. If we can make the top we will have some respite. How fast would a pickup be?"

"Ten, twenty minutes. Make an emergency call and they will be in fast. It depends whether a ship is in the air."

"That will have to do. Anyway, it's only another ten minutes climb. You'll be in a nice sterile rotorcraft inside half an hour. Meanwhile, let's go."

They climbed on up over the unstable blocks, hardly daring to look behind. Slowly, the top cliff became closer.

The wound in his foot nagged at Merral as he moved on over the uneven ground, giving him a jarring agony at every slight twist of his ankle. Not having the pack helped, but he wished he could take some painkiller. Over his pain, he became aware that it was no longer raining and that the cloud was lifting.

Soon, though, they were in the cleft of the rock and its dark walls engulfed them. *There had better not be anything here,* thought Merral. *I cannot fight again.* But here all was silent and up at the top of the crevasse was open sky.

The crevasse was steep and strewn with boulders, and soon they were reduced to scrabbling on their hands and knees. Finally, they came to the top of the cleft, where the way to the summit was blocked by a final sheer wall of smooth gray-black rock, twice as high as a man. At one side, a pile of loose blocks of rock suggested a precarious way to the top.

Merral waited at the foot of the cliff while Vero cautiously ascended and vanished from view over the edge. After a few anxious moments, he peered back over the edge and extended a hand down.

"Fine. Smooth, level, and deserted. An ideal landing spot. Come on up."

Using his hands to help him, Merral scrambled over the blocks and, with Vero's help, hauled himself onto the flat tabletop. His breathing was coming hard and fast and sweat was dripping off him.

"Vero, that was horrible!" he gasped. "Horrible! What was that thing I killed? Should I have done it?"

"Merral, priorities!" Vero shook his head. "Yes! But let me call for help and then we'll patch up your foot. Then we can discuss what we have come across."

He slid his diary off his belt. "Watch down below while I call us a ride home. Keep your head down."

Merral crawled forward and looked down below at the dull rocks passing into the conifer woods with the gray lake waters beyond. Tattered wreaths of cloud drifted like smoke over the treetops as a weak sunlight tried to break through. There was nothing else to see, and the noises seemed to have died away.

Behind him, he could hear Vero talking in a low, urgent way. "Diary! Priority message to be repeated until countermanded. All emergency frequencies. Priority override all other traffic. Message thus: 'Rescue immediately. Emergency.' " Vero paused. "Diary, transmit!" There was a slightly longer pause. "Transmit!"

With a terrible feeling of foreboding, Merral looked around to see Vero staring at the gray block, his expression a mixture of puzzlement, frustration, and alarm.

"Diary, transmit!" Vero looked at Merral. "Incredible! Of all the times to have the first diary malfunction of your life." He stared at the object in his hand in bemusement.

"Merral, you try yours while I run diagnostics. A general emergency call will do. See who we can call down."

Merral pulled out his diary, noting the dull green status light glowing normally on the diamond-coated screen.

"Diary, emergency rescue call! All available frequencies!"

He waited for the red signal light to flicker. Nothing happened. Merral, vaguely conscious of Vero tapping his screen, could barely believe what had happened. "Vero! Mine, too. But they always work! Always!"

Vero nodded furiously and kept flicking his finger at his screen. "It cannot or will not transmit. It is unheard of." His voice was strained.

He put it away suddenly and, after scanning the plateau around them, turned to Merral, his face a strange, sickly color under the mud.

"My friend, I apologize. Again." He gulped and shook his head. "I believe I have made a major error. A very major one."

Then, without explaining further, he bent down, slipped toward the edge, and peered over. He slid swiftly back and stared at Merral, his brown eyes wide with anxiety.

"I have indeed made a serious error. I'd been prepared for one or two creatures, even a few. But I had assumed they were dumb animals, perhaps let loose. But this technology! We cannot do this. Although blocking diary transmissions on a dozen frequencies is not a skill we have sought."

He shook his head and then said, "Perhaps we can get a message through. Low angle to Herrandown. . . ."

He peered forward again, looking over the edge of the cliff, and suddenly stiffened. "We'd better." There was a chill edge to his words that made Merral crawl forward and join him.

Far down below them, just emerging from the trees and approaching the backpack they had left behind, were three tall, dark, and ominous figures. *The creatures we saw down by the lake,* Merral noted dully, *the things with the fur and long limbs, the things with the height and the muscles: the things that kill dogs by stamping on them.* As if suddenly conscious of being watched, the creatures stood still in their tracks and looked up at the cliff. There was a curiously regimented similarity in their movements that seemed almost uncanny to Merral. For a moment, he stared back at their faces, feeling he could make out large, dark brown, impassive eyes. Then, suddenly aware of his peril, he ducked his head out of sight. Perhaps a minute later, he peered over the edge again cautiously. The three figures had turned and were now moving back under the trees. There they stopped and stood in a fixed manner looking up again at the plateau.

"Ah! They have stopped their pursuit." Vero's voice was full of relief.

"But for how long?"

"I don't know. We have probably only a temporary respite. Try this for a hypothesis: They do not like being out in the open in daylight." He paused. "So, we may have till night before they pursue us."

Merral looked around, seeing that the clouds were thinning fast and that he could make out the disk of the sun clearly now. He was now casting a faint shadow. He glanced at his watch and saw that it was now just after eleven o'clock. There were nine hours before darkness.

"Perhaps," he said. "Alternatively, Vero, they are just waiting for reinforcements. They need to be sure we are trapped. But I know nothing about how these creatures think."

Vero shrugged. "I know no more than you. I really don't. These events have taken me by as much surprise as you. We face the unknown together." He shook his head again and ran his fingers through his wet black hair. "I feel I have failed us badly. In letting us come out here to be so vulnerable. The evidence, of a sort, has been available for some days. Perhaps before. Oh, what a fool I've been!"

He stared out at the dripping green forests below them and the cloud-wrapped sharp peaks of the Rim Ranges to the north. Then his voice was more resolute. "But we have not totally failed yet. We must fight. We have got to warn Isterrane, the sentinels, the Assembly. And to do that we must think. 'Tell them to watch, stand firm, and to hope.' That was the message we had." He shook his head. "I fear we have failed on the first, and the last seems a challenge. But stand firm? We can but try."

He fell silent, squeezing his forehead as if trying to encourage his thoughts.

"I must look at your ankle. How does it feel? Your trousers look horrid. I take it that most of the blood isn't yours?"

"No," Merral answered slowly with revulsion. "It belongs to the thing. . . ." He touched his ankle and winced. "Painful. But it has stopped bleeding."

"Okay." Vero looked around. "I'd better check how we stand first. The way this hill is, I think that we can be attacked from only a few places. You keep an eye on our pursuers while I go round."

Vero set off walking round the circumference of the summit. Merral glanced up every so often from watching the creatures below to see that his friend kept a sufficient distance from the edge so that he couldn't be seen. Vero periodically dropped to his knees, crawled forward, and cautiously looked over the edge. The smallness of the summit area they were on was such that he was able to stay within calling distance all the time. *In fact,* Merral thought, *you would have difficulty playing a decent Team-Ball game on this flat plateau without the ball falling off.*

Below, the strange creatures continued to do nothing. Merral tried to call them *animals* in his mind, but the word did not seem right. He was certain that whatever they were, they were more than animals. The word *creatures* seemed more appropriate, but he wondered exactly whose creatures they were. Had they been fashioned by God, man, or the devil? If they were produced by either of the latter, he felt less guilty about killing one. But could the enemy make such things? And in this age of history?

His thoughts were interrupted by Vero's return. "Still there?"

"They haven't moved. So what's our situation?"

"Hmm. Well, we could be in a worse situation. There is really only access on two points: one we came up, and the other—almost opposite—on the western side. At our south, we go straight off the entire Daggart Plateau. It's a nasty drop: hundreds of meters. The north end appears vertical too, of course not as high. So, I think we only have two points to guard. But it's pretty bleak here. No water, no vegetation—just rock. Still, we must be grateful that it is not scorchingly hot. Although it is warming up."

"No caves? lava tubes?"

"Other than the fact that there is a low ledge on the southern side, what you see is all we have."

Merral surveyed again the flat, almost horizontal, plain of the summit surface. There were cracks in it in which a mouse or even a fox might hide, but nothing larger.

"Now," said Vero, "let's look at your foot. Do you think we can get the boot off without a painkiller?"

"Let's try."

Merral flinched as the straps were undone and Vero pried the boot off. He looked down to see that his sock was a mass of blood.

Vero reached into his jacket pocket and pulled out a small medical kit. He bent down and peered at the ankle.

"In the Divine mercy, the thing seems to have struck your boot more than your ankle, so it was unable to close tight around it. That extraordinary blade finger-thumb arrangement was sharp, but the wound is by no means as deep as it might have been. Here goes."

Vero carefully exposed the flesh of the ankle and stared at it. "Not too bad. It has almost stopped bleeding. But you can see that it has actually cut partly through the dura-polymer shell of the upper boot sleeve. You would think it had been done with a knife."

Vero washed the wound with a small amount of water, powdered it with a multi-potent wound powder, and then closed it with a self-suturing tape.

"That should be fine, unless they use some slow-acting toxin unknown to science. Let's hope it washed its hands regularly."

"Ugh!" said Merral, relieved that the wound was no worse. "Actually, that feels better already. I think I'll try and put my sock and boot back on. This isn't terrain for going barefoot in."

Vero went and peered over the edge again and came back while Merral was painfully putting his boot on.

"They are still waiting under the trees. Like machines. How do you feel?"

"The wound's okay," Merral answered. "But inside I feel lousy."

"I'm not surprised. I'm pretty shaken."

"I was terrified, Vero! I mean it; it was extraordinary! But there was more than that; I killed something there. Something sentient, alive, thinking. More than an animal. It's awful!"

Vero scratched an ear thoughtfully. "No, we—*you*—had no choice. I am totally convinced it was evil. But I understand your feelings. It was, though, an impressive action of yours. I would have slashed and slashed until I was exhausted. Why did you strike it there?"

"After my first blow bounced off, I realized that it was armored, shelled. Then—I suppose—I realized that there looked like there was thinner or missing armor just below the throat. I guess it made sense too; you can't have thick armor everywhere. So when the opportunity came . . ." He ran out of words.

"You have a gift."

"A gift! That is the stupidest thing you've ever said. A gift for killing!" Merral was surprised at the force and bitterness of his own voice.

Vero flinched and then began to speak again slowly. "But, my friend, if evil has returned in force, then there may be a place for such things. Many of the Old Covenant writers praise such skills."

Merral, calming down, remembered some of the troubling verses in the Psalms that he had passed over as "of mainly historical significance only."

"Maybe," he muttered.

"Besides, even though you were terrified, you analyzed the situation brilliantly and acted on it. To evaluate rightly and to act in a crisis is a gift."

"Well, if you say so."

"I do. I was a failure."

"Come on, Vero. You were badly shaken. And you distracted it so that I had a chance."

"Teamwork, Forester. Just like your Team-Ball games. But let's see what we have to defend ourselves with."

Vero took his jacket off and began opening the one remaining backpack. "Three flares," he announced and laid out the three stubby tubes next to his bush knife.

"And I have the tranquilizer gun," Merral said, taking off his jacket and finding the gun in his pocket.

"I'm relieved. I thought we had left that behind." Vero shook his head ruefully. "You know, it was a folly of mine leaving that pack behind. We had extra water in it, spare food, other things. . . ."

Merral felt sorry for him. "Vero, you can't blame yourself. This is a unique situation. We needed to get out of there quickly."

"I suppose you are right." Vero frowned. "Funny, I've never really felt guilty about anything before. Perhaps this spiritual atmosphere—whatever we call it—is getting to me too."

He was silent for a few moments. "But enough about the past. We have few weapons to defend us. Let us make twin stockpiles of rocks at either possible site of attack. Gravity can aid us. We must be prepared to use them to dissuade any attacker."

He looked up at the sky. "I do think, though, it will be the night when we are attacked. Whether they fear the sun or whether they are just wary of being caught on any satellite or plane images, I do not know."

Over the next half hour, as the remaining clouds disappeared and the top of the hill began to become warm in the sunshine, they scoured the surface of the plateau for hand-sized fragments of rock. They piled these up above the two points on the cliff edge where it seemed possible that an attack could come. Twice, Merral and Vero tried to make emergency calls, but each time, although incoming signals could be received, their diary messages out seemed to be blocked. They did find out that over distances of a few centimeters they could transmit between diaries, but beyond that any signal was disrupted.

"Formidable!" Vero commented. "I think whatever frequency we broadcast on they pick it up and absorb the signal within a few microseconds. I wonder what other technology they have? No wonder they are happy enough sitting under the trees waiting."

Then they took out the fieldscope, which somehow had not been left behind, and spent some minutes watching the creatures below. With the sun now shining with undiminished force, their pursuers had retreated a few meters farther back so that they were under the shade of a large pine. Merral watched them with the scope, trying to assimilate some understanding of what they were. The strange heads of the ape-creatures, with their angled, almost noseless front and the marked overhang of the skull at the rear, struck Merral as odd. *It is almost as if a human skull had been sculpted in wet clay and then—somehow—a board pressed against the front so that the whole upper part was deformed backward.* Once he caught a glimpse of a wide-open mouth with two arcs of large, dirty whitish teeth. *Are they vegetarians or carnivores?* he wondered unhappily.

Vero spoke quietly. "So, Forester, what do you think?"

"These ape things—I am struggling for a name—seem much less strange than the other kind. These seem to be bad imitations of humans or gorillas. The other thing seemed just, well . . . weird. These I would classify as mammals, which fits with the DNA results. But what do you think?"

"I agree these things look like mammals, but do they—I ask you—have the organs diagnostic of mammals?"

Merral scanned the three as they sat on the ground. "I see no breasts. Perhaps all three are male?"

"Ah. But do you see any indication of the diagnostic organs of maleness?"

"Interesting. No, there seems to be an absence of external genitalia of any sort. I should have observed that. Are they sexless?"

Vero shrugged. "I do not know. If they are, that raises other questions. But this morning's other creature?"

"Not as easy," Merral answered, overcoming a reluctance to think about his assailant. "Definitely animal, but I can go no further. It fits into no known category of biological classification. There were elements of mammal and insect in it. That beetle-like exoskeleton is what puzzles me."

"And me. What do we call these two sorts of creature?"

Merral thought for a moment. " 'The naming of animals'? These things are 'ape-creatures.' "

"I agree. And 'cockroach-creatures'?"

"No. I am unhappy about *creature.*"

Vero nodded. "Very well. I suggest that we borrow the Ancient English word *beast.*"

To Merral, the word had echoes of the Dark Times with its wars and horrors, but then he realized that any such allusions were now strangely appropriate. "So be it," he agreed.

"The cockroach-beast: the puzzle creature, the fusion of man and cockroach."

"A disgusting thought."

"I agree. Anyway, I shall take some images of these ape-creatures and dictate some notes. God willing, I will be able to transmit it to Anya in some way. And then onward. . . ." Vero paused and gestured with a thumb in the vague direction of Isterrane. "It just occurred to me: when will Anya start to get concerned about us?"

"No earlier than eight, when she finds she cannot get through to us."

"What do you think she will do?"

"I don't know," Merral answered slowly. "We can only hope she gets worried and asks for a search team to come in. Fast. Then we fire the flares and they pick us up."

Vero nodded thoughtfully. "Let us indeed pray it is so."

While Vero linked his diary to the fieldscope and imaged the ape-creatures, Merral walked slowly around the perimeter of the hilltop, conscious of his aching ankle. He was becoming uneasily aware that the summit that he had thought might be their refuge was now in danger of becoming their prison. He paused at the southern edge of the cliff, noting the ledge that Vero had seen, and gazed southward over the dizzying drop off the plateau. Far below he could see where they had camped the previous night and traced the river southward until it disappeared into the haze. His eye caught the dark crescent-winged swifts as, with their effortless mastery of the air, they soared, dived, and raced noisily off the cliff edge. Merral decided that at this moment he would have given a lot to be able to fly as they could.

As he watched, the swifts suddenly scattered in every direction with wild screaming noises. Merral glanced up to see, high above him, a large, stiff-winged bird gliding round in slow circles. *A raptor of some sort,* he thought, shading his eyes as he stared at it. He decided it was a buzzard and was puzzled by the reaction of the swifts; unlike some of the faster falcons, the slow buzzards posed no threat to swifts. He made a mental note to discuss it with Lesley Manalfi, the Planning Institute's head ornithologist, then reality flowed back and he realized that he had more pressing biological problems than aberrant bird behavior.

"Now what?" he asked Vero on his return.

"Now, we sit and wait and think and pray," came the solemn answer. "We have almost no water left, a little food. And no shade."

Merral sat down beside him and pulled his jacket over his head to gain some protection from the sun. So as the hours passed and the rocks around grew warmer, Merral sat there hunched under the jacket with the sweat dripping down his face, conserving his energy and praying, in a way he had never remotely imagined he would ever have to, for deliverance.

14

By late afternoon Merral, feeling hot and increasingly thirsty, decided to try and distract himself. He turned to Vero, who still had his jacket over his head. "Let me ask you what you now think these creatures are."

"Ah. As you know, I have had a number of theories. I make the total five. One theory has been destroyed over these last two days. Namely, that the whole thing was a collective psychosis."

Merral tapped his bandaged ankle gently. "I have evidence that renders that untenable."

"Rather a shame. It was the easiest view to hold." There was a thoughtful pause. "Theory two was that it was a direct incursion of the demonic. Obviously, we have little data on how that might occur. . . ." He paused. "But did you feel it was a demon you grappled with this morning?"

Merral thought about what he had seen and felt in those terrible few minutes. "No, I don't believe you can kill demons with a bush knife. But, having said that . . ." He stopped, finding himself unable to continue for some moments. "Having said that, I felt in some way that that cockroach-beast was more than an organism. I felt there was anger in its actions, even hatred. Evil." Merral caught a sympathetic nod of agreement from his companion and went on. "I cannot express it," he added. "Not yet. Ask me again after the memory fades."

And, for a few moments, Merral sat still, staring at his shadow on the baking black rock and trying to put out of his mind the weird jumping motion, the sound of the plates clicking together, the hateful organic smell, and those staring, bottomless, tarlike eyes.

Vero spoke suddenly, seeming to choose his words carefully. "I agree. It's all too tangible. But I share your hesitation; there are some strange effects.

Something has come into the worlds. I hope we can get it out. Or that, at least, it will not spread . . ." He tailed off midspeech, his face full of unspoken worries.

He slid over to the cliff edge, peered over carefully for a few moments, and then slid back. "Still under the tree." Then he leaned back gently, putting his hands behind his head, and stared up at the sky. "So we scrub theories one and two. Now theory three is that these are aliens. We are, after all, on the edge of the Assembly. 'Worlds' End' and all that. A thought which must have struck you?"

"Indeed, and been rejected," Merral replied. "These creatures do not seem to me to be alien. Certainly not the ape-creatures. And all our experience is that the probability of intelligent alien life is very small. That Earth stayed stable long enough for such life to develop has always been assumed to be a direct work of God. And, of course, despite claims, we have never found anything more than simple algae or bacteria. And no alien artifacts or signals." He paused. "At least such was the confident view I was taught. But my confidence is being eroded right now."

Vero, still staring upward, nodded. "I agree. We may have become too confident. But I can't see these things as alien. The DNA evidence seems against that too."

"No. Not aliens. They are simply not alien enough. Which leaves you where?"

"With two related possibilities. Either theory four . . ." Vero shaded his eyes a moment. "Funny buzzards you have in your world. I've been watching this one for a bit."

"Probably the same one I saw earlier. But go on."

"Ah yes, theory four. Here we have a genetic mutation of humanity. More precisely, two mutations. Natural events occurring due to some accelerated biological process; a supercharged evolution."

Merral's answer came slowly. "No, again. All we have here is microevolution, the same as you have. Some of it pretty dramatic, but it is limited. Yes, we have new species, but they are recognizably related to what was imported here. Variation on places like Farholme is about what you would expect for a world with new niches. That buzzard you are watching is probably a living example. That strange flight pattern is probably because it's moving slowly into a new niche. Another hundred generations and it will probably be more like a condor. And, as you know, human genetic change here, while it occurs, is slight. But these things . . ." He hesitated, wondering how to express his feelings. "These monstrosities would be a major jump—or a series of major jumps—beyond anything we can imagine. Anyway, the whole Assembly would hear and mourn if any parent here produced an ape-creature or a cockroach-beast as offspring. A truly horrible thought. Try me with your last one."

Vero was shading his eyes again and squinting as he looked upward at the buzzard. "Hmm. Strange how he keeps the sun close enough behind him. Yes, theory five is similar, but says that these things are deliberately gene-engineered."

"What?!" Merral could hardly contain himself. "That we have produced these things?"

"Well, that someone has." Vero had shifted his gaze sideways so he could look directly at Merral. "This is my preferred option. Reluctantly."

Indignation and unbelief seemed to flood into Merral's mind at once. "But that," he protested loudly, "is totally against everything the Technology Protocols allow. Gene-engineering up to plants—if needed—is allowed. But no further. That's enough. That's about the most fundamental breach possible. I mean, we were upset enough about modifying a long-dead human voice, but that is nothing. Nothing at all in comparison."

"Ah. . . ." Vero's voice had a sharp edge to it. "You too made the link. How interesting. This is one reason why I was trying not to feed you with my ideas."

"The link?"

"Between altering a re-created voice and genetic manipulation of human cells."

"Oh, there is no link!" Merral felt himself getting irritated. "Your overactive sentinel imagination!"

"Sorry. I'm not saying your uncle did this, too. But—what shall we say?—a spiritual climate in which one can happen is a climate in which the other can happen. Both are rebellion."

Merral could merely shake his head. "The idea that anyone could create that fiendish creature that attacked us is beyond me. Why?"

"It may have advantages that we do not have." Vero rolled over so he could face upward again. "For instan—*wait a minute*!" His voice sharpened and he froze. "Oh, the idiots we are!"

Something's up, Merral realized. *But what?*

"I wish I hadn't left my pack," Vero announced suddenly in a voice that was oddly louder than normal. He turned sideways to face Merral and began whispering with exaggerated lip movements. "I think the bird is not right. A mechanical observer of some sort. Pretend to have a conversation with me and take a look."

It took Merral a second or two for the bizarre concept to be understood.

"It's not your fault, Vero," he said loudly as he looked upward, narrowing his eyes against the brightness of the sky. "We needed to make a quick getaway, so it was quite reasonable."

He looked at the bird out of the corner of his eye. Yes, Vero was right. There was something wrong about it. It wasn't that it was a buzzard practicing to be something else. It was something else pretending to be a buzzard.

Vero was speaking. "Yes, but I shouldn't have left the water."

Merral made his mind up; all the evidence fit. He rolled over and looked at Vero. "You are quite right," he whispered. "I should have spotted it."

"It's called surveillance, and we don't want it," Vero muttered between clenched teeth. "Any ideas how we remove it?"

Over the next few minutes, in quiet asides interjected into a loud conversation about why, and why not, they should have left the pack, they plotted how they should get rid of the circling watcher above them.

"Right," announced Vero. "I'm going to see if I can get any more decent images of the ape-creatures below."

"Fine, a good idea. I shall sit here and save my energy."

As Vero walked over, peered over the margin of the cliff, and toyed with his diary, Merral leaned back next to the tiny pile of weapons and looked upward at the sky.

The bird drifted over Vero.

Still staring upward, Merral reached out slowly until his fingers wrapped around a flare tube. The bird seemed preoccupied with Vero and slowly descended to within four or five meters of him. Without looking at what he held in his hand, Merral rotated the two setting rings to give the shortest range and the maximum intensity. The flare wouldn't last for a long time, but it might be enough. If he was accurate.

One-handed, he pulled off the tab that protected the firing button.

"Hey, Merral!" Vero shouted, walking toward him, "wait until you see this."

Vero came over with his diary and put it down next to Merral, who rolled over as if to look at what his friend had in his hand.

"Ready?" whispered Vero.

"Yes."

Still staring in apparent fascination at the screen, Merral held onto the flare, carefully avoiding the recessed button. He listened until he was sure that he could hear the gentle sound of slow wing beats and see, faintly reflected on the polished screen, an image of the circling bird.

Suddenly, Merral rolled over, swung up the flare tube, aimed it, and pressed the firing button.

There was a brief, ear-piercing screech as the flare shot up, a brilliant flash of silver light, and a simultaneous bang.

As Merral leapt to his feet, he heard a falling, fluttering sound that ended in a gentle thud as the bird struck the rock nearby.

Vero bounded over and put a foot on its neck. The bird writhed and flapped; he twisted his foot sharply and the creature became still.

Vero bent down, picked up the buzzard by its wingtip, and dropped it on the rock at Merral's feet. It lay there as a curiously stiff, broken mass of brown feathers with no hint of motion.

"Pooh! It smells!" Vero said, wrinkling his nose. He bent over the bird and began poking it tentatively with a tiny pocketknife. As he did, Merral caught sight of a fine silver tracery that glinted in the sun.

"You see," Vero stated in flat, almost numbed tones, "it is a machine imitating something. A simulacrum." He looked sharply at Merral. "I presume this the first thing of its kind you have seen?"

"Of course! I have never dreamed of such a thing. The Technology Protocols forbid it. All our machines proclaim that they are machines."

"As throughout the Assembly. Since that far-off year of 2110 when the Rebellion ended." There was a strange, grim satisfaction in his voice.

Merral swallowed, squatted down, and looked in wonder and puzzlement at the creature. True, there were feathers and claws. But the beak was fixed half open, the eyes were empty holes, and beneath the vacant sockets was a pair of tiny, glinting lenses that ran back into wires.

Vero, who had been prodding gently with his knife, abruptly paused and muttered. Then he poked again. "An odd technology. Very odd. Look!"

Merral peered closer, seeing where Vero had stripped off a part of the skin and feathers and exposed a filigree of delicate silver wires wrapped over a gray substance in which thin white tubes were embedded. An unpleasant, rotting smell came from somewhere.

Vero glanced up at Merral with a worried expression. "It's not at all what I expected. There are bits of dead bird here."

"Dead?" Merral asked, suddenly aware where the foul odor was coming from.

He stared at the bird, catching sight of a tiny wisp of smoke. "Look out!"

There was a tiny crackling sound and a burst of yellow flame began to play around the body. Vero and Merral hurriedly stepped back as a black-edged golden flame flickered rapidly over the body, giving a cloud of acrid stinking smoke that twisted upward.

Flapping away the smoke with disgust, Merral stared at Vero. "What happened? Did you short-circuit it?"

"No. I don't think so." He looked thoughtfully at the fire, which was already sputtering out. "I think it was a mechanism to prevent us from taking it away and analyzing it."

"So they have clever machines, too. Do we have the power to do this?"

Vero was staring at where the abating flames were revealing a blackened skeleton over which melted wires drooped. "Extraordinary, quite extraordinary," he muttered, a great disgust evident in his tones. "The power? Maybe. The desire? Thank God, no. Disguise has never been our way. And to do it by using a dead bird? That is something very strange. No, far worse than strange. . . ." He tailed off.

"Well spotted," commented Merral, "I thought it was odd. It has been watching us for some time?"

"Yes. Probably listening, too. But good shooting on your part. You got the wing."

"I stunned it. I suppose it was that odd owl we saw."

"Yes." Vero nodded, still staring at the pile of wire and bone. "We should have realized it wasn't flesh and blood when we couldn't pick it up on the infrared."

"Of course."

Vero scratched his chin. "And what was the power source? I saw no fuel or energy cells. Odd."

Then he stood up and turned to Merral. "This bird thing is, it seems to me, every bit as significant as the other creatures. But a discussion about what it portends must wait. We *must* get a message out. Our own safety—even our survival—is quite immaterial."

Merral looked at him and realized that he was perfectly serious. Then, as he thought about what they had encountered that day, he realized that Vero's judgment was right. "I agree, reluctantly. The message must get out. That is all that matters."

Vero reached out and patted his arm. "Thank you for your support. Now we have only limited time. In under three hours or so the light will begin to go. Let us think through our options. We might be able to make a run for it now, down the other side and through the woods. How well can you walk?"

"I suspect short distances. But I am unenthusiastic. We might have to walk a long way for a diary to work. Possibly Herrandown, in fact. Not an easy task with enemies at our heels."

Vero frowned. "Well, it was one idea. Perhaps we must just hope that Anya realizes there is a problem when she calls us."

Then he sat down and fell silent.

At five o'clock they divided the last of the water, had some food, and for the fiftieth time tried—and failed—to send a signal out. Then they returned to watching, Vero taking the west side of the plateau and Merral the east.

Merral, wishing, among many things, that they had more water, sat dry-mouthed near the edge of the cliff, moving forward every few minutes and peering down to the trees. There the three dark figures continued their seated vigil, and only the occasional slight movement revealed that they were not statues. The lower angle of the late-afternoon sun had enlarged their shadows and somehow seemed to increase their menace. As he stared at them, an alarming thought struck.

He rolled back away and walked slowly over the hot rock to the other side of the summit where Vero was squatting down, peering over the edge. Vero glanced back at him and gestured him down with an unmistakable urgency.

Merral's heart sank. He dropped to his knees and crawled alongside his friend.

Vero grimaced. "Well, we don't have to worry about making a run for it down here. Look."

Merral carefully looked down. Here, too, the sheer cliff face ended in a long, bare rock scree which, amid more large tumbled boulders, ran down under dense trees. Now, in the shadows of the trees and the boulders, five large figures were standing still, like distorted and blackened imitations of humanity. At their feet, equally immovable, half a dozen smaller, brown figures were clustered. Although they were too far away for him to be certain, and he was squinting against the light, the indelible impression Merral had was that all of them were staring up at the cliff.

For a moment, Merral could say little, so great was the internal turmoil this scene caused him. A part of him, detached from the cold waves and billows of emotion that buffeted him, was able to recognize that he was again deeply afraid. *What I am feeling today is true fear. What I have only read about before, I now experience.* This time, though, he knew it was different; with the cockroach-beast he had been scared, but he had had no time to think about his emotions; he had to act. *Now, I have fear and cannot act, and I can feel the fear seeping into my mind and corroding my thinking.* But, even as he thought this, another part of his mind intruded and said that he must think, and that now was not the time for analysis of his feelings.

He swallowed. "Yes. Interesting. Eight ape-creatures and six cockroach-beasts. I don't suppose sentinel training gives you any idea what to do next?"

"No," Vero muttered. "Not at all. The vision Jorgio had seems the best guide here: watch, stand firm, and hope. And, at the last, to die well and take as many with you as you can."

"I hate to add trouble to trouble, but before long, perhaps ten minutes or so, my side of the hill will be in total shadow."

"Shadow!" Vero winced. "I had forgotten. They might prefer that to darkness. I was hoping for another hour or two at least. What a mess we are in!"

"Perhaps we can hold them off until tomorrow with stones."

"Perhaps. Would they see one of these flares from space?"

"If they knew where to look they would see one. But if they knew where to look they wouldn't need a flare."

"We need a bigger flare, then." Vero screwed his eyes up. "Wait! There may be a way. If I can remember—"

"Listen!" Merral interrupted, as from over the eastern side of the hill came the faintest rattle of stone on stone.

They ran to the edge. Below, in the darkness of the ravine they had come up, two of the dark ape-creatures were climbing up with smooth, confident moves, their arms and feet working together in a powerful and coordinated motion.

Without hesitation, Merral picked a brick-sized basalt fragment and hurled it down. It hit the wall just above the head of the leading ape-creature and shattered. There was an angry rumbling growl, and the creature paused in its ascent and looked up.

They were separated by no more than twenty meters, and Merral could see the face clearly despite the shadows. It seemed to him that, despite its flattened appearance, the face was more human than ape. The large brown eyes seemed to stare at him, and Merral decided that if the face conveyed any emotion at all, it was of a cold intelligence and a determined and calculating hatred. He knew with absolute certainty that it was useless to try to communicate with this creature.

"Throw another!" cried Vero, letting fly with a rock himself. This, however, was way off target and clattered away harmlessly down the ravine.

Merral looked around and found, a few strides away, a large rock slab, the size of a kitchen tabletop but thicker.

"Quick, Vero, help me push this."

Together they tugged and heaved until the slab was at the cliff edge. Then, putting their shoulders to it, they pushed until it started to hang over the edge.

From below came a high-pitched series of wordless squeals and grunts that conveyed alarm. Merral pushed and suddenly the block began to wobble. He pushed again and the rock fell over the edge.

There was a series of booming and echoing crashes as the slab fell and bounced down the cliff. They peered over the edge in time to see it displace other rocks and cannonade down the gloom of the ravine in a gathering tumult of fragments. At the bottom of the cliff, the debris cloud exploded outward down the scree in a turbulent dark cloud of fragments. Stray rocks could be seen careening clear of the debris flow and bouncing up into the trees.

Then the rising dust cloud covered their view.

"Very satisfactory," Vero announced in admiring tones, as the sound of crashing and clattering blocks died away.

Merral, nonplussed at the effect of combining one large rock, gravity, and a fifty-meter drop, said nothing. *What have I maimed and injured now?*

As if in answer to his question, a howl of agony came from below. Although there were no words, it seemed to Merral that it conveyed an intelligence greater than any animal had. He shivered.

Slowly, the dust died away and they could see one creature standing at the edge of the trees apparently unharmed, while another sat nearby nursing a bloodied and useless arm. Of the third, nothing could be seen until Vero pointed out a red smear under a gray block of rock.

"One ape-creature and a cockroach-beast dead so far. Another wounded." Vero's voice was dry.

"Ugh! You make it sound like a sport that way."

"Unintentionally. But men once did, you know."

"I know. 'Saul has killed his thousands, David his ten thousands.' But that was another age of the world, Vero. I do not rejoice. I am answerable to their maker for those that I have killed."

Vero bowed his head slightly. "I am rebuked by your sensitivity. But I do not think that you will stand in judgment before their maker."

"You mean . . . ?"

"Simply, I do not believe that God alone made them. I believe their maker may have far more to answer for at the Final Judgment than you."

"You may be right," Merral said, wondering whether that diminished the magnitude of his killing them. "May the Most High grant us the leisure and security to debate the point further. But how do things stand now?"

"Well, this side now seems to me much less climbable than it was."

Merral looked down. Sure enough, the top part of the ravine was now cleared of boulders and was vertical for the last ten meters.

Vero rubbed his face with his hands. "Now, it has come to me that there is a slight hope. But only a slight one and it is fraught with problems."

"Go on."

Vero tapped a finger on his diary. "Do you realize how much energy these things use in the ten years between energy cell replacement?"

"No. A lot, though."

"Yes. Well, there is a way of realizing it all, of venting it all in a few milliseconds."

"You'd have an awesome explosion. I've never heard that."

"I was told it was the fourth best-kept secret in the Assembly."

"The other three are?"

"I don't know. The third is probably what the first two are." Vero's face twisted into a grin and Merral had to laugh.

"The results are spectacular?"

"So it's claimed. Mostly visible light, but a lot of electromagnetic wavelengths get a hefty kick. I was told you could see it on the moon. If you did it on Ancient Earth, that is." He paused, stroking his diary thoughtfully. "Non-nuclear. Just. I think that's what they said."

"You think?"

"Well," he sounded embarrassed, "the whole technique was given as a sort of passing comment at the end of a lecture. A piece of curious information. Any brighter ideas?"

"No."

"Well, I'll try it. It will take some time to do. It's not an easy trick. For obvious reasons."

"So I would hope."

"Quite. Now, Merral, if I may, can I download all my data onto your machine? I wonder if you could check the other side. Just in case they try the same trick."

Merral handed over his diary, and as Vero made the orders for a full data download to be made, he went over to the western side and peered into the gathering shadows, trying to see if there was any change in the positions of the ape-creatures and cockroach-beasts. Unnervingly, they were standing in silence exactly as he had last seen them. In frustration—and was it also fear?—he threw a block of rock at them, but it fell short and clattered away into the trees with no effect.

He returned to Vero.

"Still there and still out of range. But what's your plan?"

Vero looked up, his eyes showing tiredness. "We need to wait for darkness so we can guarantee being seen. If I can trigger the reaction, we will have a short delay. We find a spot where the energy can be channeled upward. Then, we get down onto that ledge at the south end. Put our fingers in our ears and, well—let it go. Hopefully, one of your satellites will notice a firework that size. You think so?"

"If it is as big as you say, I should think so. We are always on the alert for forest fires or volcanic eruptions. The Northern Menaya Monitor will pick it up unless it's helping Perena watch the rift volcanics. But will they act on it?"

"Ah. A key point. Will they?"

"They may send someone over."

There was a silence and Vero looked doubtful.

He knows, thought Merral, *as I know, that it probably will not be enough.* But as he considered Vero's suggestion, an idea came to him.

"There might be a way of making it of more benefit to us," he suggested.

Vero raised an eyebrow. "How so?"

"If the model you proposed for their interception of our signals is correct, then a blast of such a size might overload their blocking system. At least briefly. If we could get a message out immediately afterward . . ."

"*Yes!*" Vero nodded urgently. "That might work. Let's do that. Anyway, data download is now complete. I feel happier about losing my diary now."

He handed back Merral's diary and slid open the access panel on his own. He started muttering to himself. "Now you set the toggles. Blue to green, yellow striped to orange . . . and that down, that up. Or is it the other way about? It was such a joke when I was told it. The most useless piece of information ever. Now I close the back and reset. Thus. Now, input the following codes." His forehead puckered in thought.

"Diary! Go into deep internal level four. Password is Gedaliah. Reveal battery temperature. Now, cycle energy cells one through eight."

The metallic voice that responded seemed startling in the quietness. "Under current parameters this will eventually give potentially dangerous thermal conditions in energy cells. Require authorization for procedure."

"This is the first tricky bit. Diary! Password is Eleazar! Aha, looks good."

"Authorization accepted."

"Proceed."

Vero sighed and slid the diary back on his belt.

"So far so good. Let us hope that after that failed assault, our enemies stay down at the foot of the hill for some time."

"How long before it works?"

"I can't remember. A couple of hours, at least. Anyway, we can't do anything until dark. I suggest we get some more images of those cockroach-beasts through the fieldscope. If we do get out, such evidence will be invaluable. Then we just sit and wait. And pray."

An hour later Vero came over to where Merral was lying down, peering over the edge at the immobile tableau of creatures below.

"How are things on your side?" Merral asked, drawing back from the margin.

"Only the one ape-creature left; the injured one has gone somewhere else."

"Your diary?"

"At least thirty minutes, I'd guess, but it is definitely heating up."

Merral gestured westward where the remains of the morning's storm clouds hung on the horizon as the last of the rain emptied itself into the wastes on Interior Menaya. The red sphere of the sun was dropping rapidly toward them. "A fine sunset," he commented.

"I would prefer dawn," sighed Vero.

"And so would I. I feel that this side is where the attack will come from.

It's a wider front. I can see various places for them to try and get up. But hopefully they will wait for darkness."

Vero got down on his knees and moved cautiously to the edge of the plateau. The setting sun had put a warm orange glow on the rocks and at the same time exaggerated both the darkness and the length of the shadows so that it was not easy to see what was happening down below among the trees and rocks.

"There are more," hissed Vero.

"Yes, I didn't feel it worth telling you," Merral added as he joined him. There were now at least six of the tall dark figures standing rigid and staring up at them, and perhaps slightly more of the cockroach-beasts, their shorter stature making them hard to distinguish from the shadows of the rocks. *It is unnatural,* Merral decided. *Both types behave like men in many ways and yet they seem to have little individuality. To act as regimented machines is not at all like us. What creatures are they?* He wondered whether Vero was right in thinking that they were modified humans and, if so, what had been taken out of them—or put in—to make them so different.

"Well, I hope they stay there longer," Vero said as he backed away. "Let me know if anything happens. I'm going to sit back from the edge and check the diary."

Merral lay down and waited, trying not to stare at the setting sun lest it damage any night vision. Finally, the lower edge of the sun dropped behind the clouds and a warm twilight started to descend. He leaned forward, stared down into the gloom, and saw that nothing had changed.

Something caught his attention. Hanging back behind the ape-creatures and all but hidden in the gloom under the trees was something new. He peered at it, recognizing another anthropoid figure, but one with a different, smaller, and somehow more familiar shape. As he strained his eyes Merral felt that, despite a size midway between the ape-creatures and the cockroach-beasts, there was somehow a presence about the figure as if it was superior to those beasts: almost, it seemed, as if it was their master.

"Vero," he called out, "there's something odd—"

There was a violent hissing and bubbling next to him. Something spat angrily and stung his right hand.

"*Get back!*" Vero shouted.

Merral threw himself backward, landing awkwardly and painfully on his hip. He was aware of a strange heat around and a smell of burning in the air.

Vero was ducked down behind him, pointing with an urgent hand at the lip of the cliff. An arm's length from where Merral had been lying the rock edge was glowing a livid scarlet and spitting vapor and drops of lava. Bubbles of rock were forming and bursting with an intense popping noise.

"What was *that?*" Merral asked as the color of the rock returned slowly to black.

Vero nodded, as if to himself. "One of a number of things capable of transmitting enough energy to melt rock. An infrared laser, a portable pulsed particle beam, something like that. Probably would just explode flesh and blood."

"So they are no longer unarmed." Sucking his hand where a small drop of molten rock had struck, Merral cautiously got to his feet, and together they moved back into the middle of the plateau. Could he be certain of what he thought he had seen? He was about to speak when there was a pulsing on his wrist.

Merral pulled his diary off his belt so fast that he nearly dropped it. On the screen, Anya was staring at him from her laboratory bench.

Thank you Lord, thought Merral in exultation, *she's called early.* "Anya! Anya!" he shouted at the diary.

To his horror, he saw her face acquire a blank, puzzled look.

Her voice was clear. "Say, what's up with you guys? Merral's location signal goes off. Now, I'm having problems even making contact."

Vero was beside him now, peeping over his shoulder at the image.

At least, Merral comforted himself, *she will realize that there is enough of a problem to call for a search tomorrow.*

She stared at the screen. "You know guys, I'm getting worried."

"That's it Anya! Go on. You get worried! *Really worried!*" Merral heard himself speaking aloud.

Without warning, another voice sounded from the diary. Although it was weirdly familiar, for a moment Merral could not recognize it.

"Sorry, Anya. We have had diary problems. Some trick of Vero's, trying to transmit data. Seems to have fused circuits on both."

Merral heard a gasp from beside him. "*Now* what are we up against?"

"Yes," the familiar voice went on, "we lost both vision and location."

"Okay, Merral. Apart from that, how is it going?"

Merral? In a dreadful, appalling moment of revelation, Merral understood why the voice was familiar. It was his own voice!

"It's not me!" Merral yelled in fury, "Anya, *it's not me!*"

"Hi, Anya," came from the diary. It was Vero's voice, but so convincing that Merral had to stare at the wide-open mouth of the startled figure next to him to be sure he wasn't hearing his friend. "Sorry. I just used too much power. Stupid sentinel trick. Anyway, we are fine."

Merral was on the point of saying something when Vero silenced him with a sharp wave of the arm.

"Oh yes," went on the voice from the diary, "we are fine. We are beyond

Daggart Lake. We'll call you tomorrow night. We aim for pickup the day after. Look, we'd better shut down now, while we still have a signal. Good-bye."

It was Vero to the syllable.

The machine spoke again. "I agree. This is Merral saying good night, too."

There was a faint look of consternation on Anya's face.

"Well, okay. Sleep well. Talk to you tomorrow. Bye for now."

The screen went dark. There was a long silence, and finally Vero spoke, his numbed voice suggesting he was still absorbing the impact of what he had overheard. "Well, there have been a couple of times today when I thought we might get out of this alive. I am now repenting my optimism. It was very clever."

"Clever? It was diabolical!"

"Exactly so."

"How did they do it?"

"They have been monitoring us. Easy to do. They have had hours to prepare a voice duplicate. That will be how they did Maya Knella, of course. Anya said it was a bad transmission."

"You mean they *faked* a Gate call?"

Vero laughed quietly and bitterly. "Merral, don't you see? Whoever—or whatever—is behind this can do almost anything. They can bend and break genes to suit themselves, they can create imitation birds, and they can mimic people. Intercepting interstellar communications is a little thing. And not only do they have the means, they have the will." He seemed to shudder. "They appear to have no barriers. I would have to think carefully, but I am certain that they have broken all of the Technology Protocols and some that were never even thought of."

"I had no idea. . . ."

"No, neither had I," Vero replied, looking troubled and seeming to struggle with something. Then, without warning, he slammed a fist into the palm of his hand.

"No! We will not yield without a fight." His face acquired a determined look. "They are not immune. We will stand firm. By grace, we may win through. But everything hinges on us calling in help. We can't rely on Anya anymore. We are on our own."

He struck his fist in his palm again in resolve and turned back to Merral. "What do you think?"

"Vero, I am reeling from this morning. And this afternoon." Then Merral paused, thinking of the right words to express what he wanted to say. "But I will gladly die here if we need to. We must fight. For the Assembly and for the King."

Vero clapped him on the back. "Good! I feel better listening to you. We may have had nearly twelve millennia of peace, but if we have to fight a last stand here then I feel you—at least—will do no worse than any heroes of the distant past. And I will do what I can."

"We will try." Merral added thoughtfully, "I—well, I suppose my own feelings are mixed. I do not mind, or fear, dying, but I do not relish it. And I wish I had not killed."

"I understand, but we must do what we are called to do. Anyway, let us prepare for an early attack. I think you had best take charge of the weapons. These things seem to be your expertise, not mine."

"As you wish," Merral answered as Vero crouched back down over his diary.

Merral went over to their few belongings, put on his jacket, and stuck the two remaining flares in one pocket and the tranquilizer gun with its two cartridges in another. He grasped the knife and clicked the blade in and out, reflecting that this—plus all the rocks he could throw—was all they had. Against adversaries who outmatched them in numbers, technology, and weapons, he knew it wasn't enough.

As he grappled with the thought, he turned to watch the sunset. There was a narrow gap in the clouds at the bottom, and in it a tiny ruby-colored sliver of the sun shone out. As Merral watched, it slipped down below the horizon and, almost instantly, the shadows about him seemed to thicken.

For a strange moment, an extraordinary desire seemed to seize hold of Merral. It was a desire to lament his lot and his pending death, to grieve for himself and Vero and for the loss his saddened family and Isabella would feel. At the heart of this compelling desire was a dark yearning to give in and to admit that the whole thing was hopeless. As he grappled with the emotion, Merral tried, and failed, to label it, until suddenly the word came to him. *Despair*, he thought with a sudden recognition. *That's what I am close to. Today I have met four strange things: ape-creatures, cockroach-beasts, terror, and despair. And will death be the fifth stranger I meet?*

Then he looked up into the sky and saw that the stars were coming out and that southward the six beacons of the Gate were becoming plain. Heartened, he praised the All Highest; hope returned and the despair fled.

As he turned to go back to Vero, he remembered that the last warrior to set out to fight for the Assembly had been Lucas Ringell in 2110. He had gone to the Centauri Station to take on Jannafy and the rebels, well trained, surrounded by his troops, and armed and suited with the best defensive and offensive equipment the Assembly could devise.

And as Merral remembered that, he was suddenly aware that all he had was two flares in one jacket pocket, a tranquilizer gun in the other, and a knife. Not one of them had even been designed as a weapon.

Suddenly, the irony of the situation struck him and, in spite of all his fears, Merral smiled.

15

As Merral approached him, Vero looked up, his face inscrutable in the gloom. "Nearly there," he said, his voice an urgent whisper. "It's at 37.5 degrees Celsius and lots of warnings."

Vivid red letters were scrolling across Vero's diary screen.

"Ten minutes before it is at the right temperature. Perhaps . . ."

Merral noted the uncertainty.

Then Vero spoke again. "Can you prepare a message for transmission the moment this goes off? Continuously repeating. Every emergency frequency."

Merral slid the diary off his belt and chose his words. "Diary! Prepare for a transmission on the maximum emergency frequencies and with maximum output and repetition of the following message: 'Emergency. Under attack from non-Assembly forces. Request immediate pickup from transmission location. Landing zone 100 by 160 meters and flat.' "

When, he wondered, was the last time—other than in some play or reenactment of the Rebellion—that anyone had uttered anything like those words *under attack from non-Assembly forces?*

He paused the diary and looked at Vero. "And how do I warn about the possibility that they will use weapons? My military terminology is minimal."

"Ah. How about adding, 'Attackers have beam weapons capable of damage to ships'?"

"Thanks," replied Merral as he laid the message out and checked it. Then he looked around. Night was falling quickly and it was already too dark to distinguish colors. A strange, unwelcome thought came to him. For the first time in his life, night was no longer a welcome, restful darkness in which the stars and the Gate shone, but a time when things moved, when evil stirred. What did one of the Psalms say? "You will not fear the terror of the night." With a barely restrained shiver, he realized that he now understood it.

Vero interrupted his reflections. "Up to 38.5 degrees and more warnings."

"What happens then?" Merral asked as he scanned the gloomy edge of the plateau, his mind already halfway to investing shadows with motion.

"We walk over to the ledge there." Vero gestured south. "You drop over, get under the ledge, and sit ready to hit the transmit button. I pull out the safety fuse—tricky in the dark—give a final code word, and the thing goes into a chain reaction. I put it down and run and join you. We put our fingers in our ears and close our eyes tight. And pray."

"*How* long after the last code before we get the bang?"

"Not long."

"How long?"

"Er, ten seconds. Perhaps twenty."

"You've *forgotten?*"

"Yes."

After a moment, Merral laughed. "Oh the Glory! What a useless pair we are! I'm glad I believe that the Most High graciously governs our affairs. That the fate of the Assembly might hinge on us alone would fill me with extreme terror!"

Vero echoed the laughter. "An amusing thought. I must—" He stiffened. "Wait! I hear something. It's too soon. We aren't ready."

From the western edge of the summit, where the top of the plateau was a black silhouette against the glowing and simmering purple sky, there came a faint scrabbling noise. The thought came to Merral that only brief hours ago he would have interpreted such a sound as that of a fox or badger. Now, and here, it could only be one thing.

On instinct, Merral thrust his diary to Vero. "You send the signal. I may be busy."

Then, cautiously in the dark, he ran toward the edge. Well to the left of where he had been before, he dropped down onto his knees and slid warily to the edge. He peered over carefully, half expecting to feel the hot and fatal blast of the beam weapon.

The sheer flank of the cliff was now in deep gloom, illuminated only by the waning sunset, and for a moment Merral could see nothing. He was about to run back and get the fieldscope when, with a quiver of alarm, he suddenly saw that, down to his right at the base of the slope, there was movement.

Within moments, he knew that there were at least three ape-creatures moving up the cliff. Their movements were measured and unhurried, and there was a confidence that suggested the darkness did not bother them.

Merral slid back away from the edge and turned toward Vero. "They're on their way up," he called. His mouth was now appallingly dry and he was aware of his hands shaking.

"Try to give me another five minutes."

"I'll try."

Merral slid back to the cliff margin, lay down on the rough rock surface, and prayed for help and protection. Within moments there was a further noise from the cliff below.

Suddenly, Merral felt a strange calm descend upon him. He knew what he had to do. Making sure there were some stones within reach, he coolly pulled out one of the flares and, acting from memory, rotated the settings onto short range and long duration. He primed the tranquilizer gun, flicked the safety catch off, and put it down on the ground with a surprisingly steady hand. Then he picked up the flare and waited until the first of the ape-creatures was within a few moments of reaching the top. He aimed and fired, raising a hand immediately to protect his sight.

There was a loud whoosh, and as a dazzling silver light flooded the rock surface, he glimpsed the creature turn toward him, the white teeth of its open mouth gleaming in the brilliant metallic light. As the flare struck the rock above its head, the creature instinctively lifted an arm to protect itself. Then, as the incandescent flame slithered down onto it, it gave a wailing scream and fell backward with arms flailing. It plummeted downward; the screaming ended with the sound of something smacking in a ghastly, sodden way against rock.

"Forgive me, Lord," Merral muttered, appalled at both the act and his own coolness.

Down at the base of the cliff, the flickering, sinking flare illuminated two more climbing ape-creatures. In a curiously detached way, Merral seemed to watch himself as he coldly picked up the tranquilizer gun and sighted on the next creature. As its big hands reached for a rock ledge, he pulled the trigger. There was a hiss as the dart fired. Merral ducked his head down low and flicked the last cartridge into the chamber.

He looked up, only to see that his target continuing its upward climb.

I must have missed, he realized dully, and sighted again, anxious to make the most of the fading light of the flare. As he squinted through the eyepiece he saw the thing suddenly twist its body. Then it leaned backward, flung out a desperate arm to steady itself, missed, and toppled down the cliff. This time there was a heavy thud, a slithering sound, and a succession of softer thuds. Simultaneously heartened and sickened, Merral risked a longer glance below. In the ebbing light of the flare, he could make out two other huge forms moving to the base of the cliff below and starting the climb upward.

He was reaching for the rocks, intending to throw them, when he suddenly became aware of a sizzling sound, as if he had his ear next to a frying pan. Immediately to his right the line of the cliff edge began to hiss and glow in an intense cherry red color. Merral jerked himself backward. A whiff of scalding, dusty air enveloped him and he saw that where he had been lying was now a mass of bubbling molten rock. He crawled away from the edge carefully. He had one flare left, and after that, only rocks and the blade. But if he couldn't get near the edge, even rocks would be little use.

How was Vero doing? Merral looked backward. In the darkness, he could just make him out bending over the diary's illuminated screen, his face lit by a furious red glow. *Hurry up,* he mouthed, *oh* hurry.

Beyond Vero something moved.

His heart thudding, Merral strained his eyes, scanning the starlit blackness of the surface. Along the northern edge of the summit the brilliance of the five bright stars of Reitel's Crown caught his eye. *I imagined it.* There could be no threat there: it was too steep.

The stars were blotted out.

"Vero, behind you!" Merral shouted, realizing that, once again, they had underestimated their opponents.

He began to run forward, aware that he had to put himself between Vero and the attackers. Still moving, he reached for the last flare and fired it. As he pressed the button he regretted it; the flare hit the ground and screeched along the rock surface before bursting into a blinding silvery flame. Beyond its blaze, two dark gigantic figures—each like some animated caricature of a man—were fiercely illuminated. Vero turned, realized his peril, and began to run to the south end of the cliff.

As Vero ran past him, Merral dropped to one knee, braced himself, and fired the remaining cartridge in the tranquilizer gun at the front creature. Seeing them for the first time at eye level, he now realized how big the ape-creatures were. It was a good shot and Merral saw it hit home in the chest. But his satisfaction was short-lived as the creature ripped out the cylinder, gave a horrid yell, and threw it away.

Suddenly he was conscious that behind him, Vero was shouting. "Now, Merral! Now!"

Merral began to run unsteadily over the rough surface after him. As he ran, he was aware that the creatures were following him, skirting round the flare. Ahead of him, he saw that Vero, illuminated only by the fading glow of the western sky and the light of the sputtering flare, was now standing at the very end of the cliff. Merral came to a stop next to him, aware of the drop down to the ledge just beyond and sensing more than seeing, far below that, the darkness of the plains and the feeble glint of the Lannar River.

"N–nearly!" Vero gasped. "It's almost on overload. When I shout, jump. Not too far. Hold them off until then."

"Okay. Tell me when."

Marveling again at his steady tone, Merral turned to face his enemies. The two pursuing him had come to a halt next to each other. They stood, just a few meters away, silhouetted against the dying glow of the flare like an enormous matching pair of bizarre statues. To his left the sky bore the last faint purple glow of the sunset. The creatures began slowly edging toward him, their steps almost matching, as if in some crazy dance. Over to the left and behind them, Merral could suddenly make out more movement. At least five of the ape creatures had now made that ascent. A cold dread seemed to grab hold of him.

The left-hand creature facing him made another move. Merral, still waiting for Vero's word, hurled the empty tranquilizer gun as hard as he could at it. The creature ducked and the gun went over its head and rattled to the ground beyond. Merral pulled out the bush knife, clicked it open, and held it out in front of him. Suddenly, on a wild impulse, he decided he should not fight these beings in silence. Their very monstrosity aroused his wrath and indignation.

"Creatures!" he yelled as loud as he could, his dry voice somehow echoing on the open summit. The shadowy forms seemed to freeze. "This is not your world! It belongs to the Lord Messiah, the Slain Lamb, the One who holds the stars of the Assembly in his right hand! In his Name I defy you! Go, or I will slay you!"

There was a cracked but enthusiastic "Amen!" from behind him. Then, as the words died away in the darkness, the light of the flare sank until it was little more than a glow.

Was there a hesitation among the creatures? Merral wasn't sure, but they made no move forward. Did the value of such challenges come in improving the morale of the defender or in intimidating that of the attacker? Or was it just something that had to be done? After all, had not David so challenged Goliath? Merral marveled at the irrelevancy of his questions and pushed them away. *How do I fight these things?* Positively, unlike the cockroach-beasts, they were unarmored. Negatively, their long limbs meant that they could grab his throat while all he could contact would be their hands and arms. And, if he did get close in, he knew he ran the risk of being crushed. *My only assets are speed and a sharp blade.*

Abruptly, the two creatures ahead separated and began to swing round at Merral from both sides. *A simultaneous attack,* he thought bleakly. He was aware of an urgent muttering from Vero behind him, as if his words could encourage the diary into self-destruction. The two were now barely an arm's length away. He could smell them now—an unnatural decaying smell, as if something within them wasn't working properly.

I must protect Vero. "Vero, stay where you are!" he shouted. "I have to know where you are!"

Merral took two steps to the right, aware that his ankle hurt him, and was gratified to see that the two ape-creatures followed him with a perfect symmetry. *Good, they want me.* He was relieved that he could treat it like a Team-Ball game. *That's right, don't think of what is involved.*

"Right!" shouted Vero. "Nearly there! Very nearly! Oh, come on!"

The flare was out now and the only light was the dull waning glow from the western skies. Merral stretched out his right hand and swung the blade in as broad an arc as he could. He felt a strange certainty that Vero had failed, but it almost seemed irrelevant. His one task now was to grapple with these things. With a low throbbing grunt, the creature on the left lunged forward.

Merral leapt backward and sideways to the right, sweeping hard with his blade at the same time. As the creature lurched past him, his blade connected with a forelimb, biting deep into soft, sinewy tissue, clinking on—and through—bone and out through flesh. There was a high-pitched scream and something struck the ground at Merral's feet with a sickening thud. He jerked the blade back, but before he had recovered his balance he saw, outlined against the stars, the second creature charging at him with its arms flailing wide.

Merral threw himself to the left, ducking low as he did, and the outstretched arm swung over him, foul rough fingers glancing over his back. He slashed at the creature, but the knife arced only through air and struck nothing. He staggered to his feet, aware of his first attacker writhing amid screams on the ground. The second ape-creature lurched to a halt, wheeled round clumsily, and came back toward him, its head low and its arms wide as if to claw him. Merral dodged again as a long arm swung out widely at him in the blackness. Despite his efforts to dodge it, the flat of the great hand connected with his shoulder. The force of the blow sent him reeling onto the hard, uneven rock.

Before he could regain his footing, he was aware that that creature was standing astride him, its feet almost touching his face, the stink of its fur enveloping him. Amid an awful bellowing, the creature raised a shadowy foot high, and Merral had a sudden terrible remembrance of the crushed remains of Spotback. As the foot hung there above him, Merral unhesitatingly put both hands on the knife handle. With every bit of energy he possessed, he lunged upward with the blade to where the great torso blocked out the stars.

"The Lamb!" he cried, amid a chill anger. The blade plunged deep and the creature's bellowing flowed into a hideous scream. It toppled over and the momentum tore the blade out of Merral's hands. As he tried to roll clear, a hot fluid pumped out all over him and a rough, stinking fur thrashed against his face. Everything went black. Then Merral was aware that he was free of the writhing hulk and Vero was tugging at him and yelling to make himself heard over the screaming.

"It's fused! It's fused!"

Wiping blood out of his eyes, Merral staggered onto all fours. He was aware of Vero throwing the diary and he saw it spin over his head as a pulsing, angry red block. As he moved toward the edge, Merral glimpsed in the red beating glow other figures now on the plateau. Large and small.

An army.

There was the ledge. He half jumped and half fell down onto it. Vero was pushing him down under the lip and he rolled in. Gasping for breath, aware of blood in his mouth, Merral dully remembered what was supposed to happen and turned facedown against the rough rock. Then he closed his eyes and put his fingers in his wet ears. This was the end.

"Lord, I commit myself to you," Merral said quietly. He realized he had never properly said farewell to Isabella or his—

The world stopped.

Sense, feeling, thought, time, *life*. All ended.

At first there was only light. Brilliant light, the light of creation, a light that seemed to penetrate through rock and bone and eyelids. There was nothing else, and it seemed to Merral inconceivable that there ever had been anything else or could be anything else. Then there was the noise. A deafening noise on every frequency from the lowest vibration to the highest screech. A noise that bypassed the eardrums to pummel every bone, muscle, and organ in his body. Then there was the wind: a wind as solid as flesh that tore at his clothes and whipped at his hair. A wind that seemed to want to blow him off the ledge to Herrandown.

Gradually, the light, noise, and wind ebbed away.

Merral opened his eyes slowly and rubbed them to see around him a bizarre winter landscape of snowlike ash lit by a diffuse and flickering red light. A pale figure coated in a fine gray debris coat was squatting beside him stabbing at the diary.

Over the ringing in his ears Merral could—somehow—make out Vero yelling, "Transmit! Transmit!"

He looked up to see a billowing column of dust high above them, glowing in lurid oranges and yellows and casting strange, pulsating shadows over the landscape. In the background, he could hear the diary echoing the message. *"Emergency! Under attack from non-Assembly forces. . . ."* It was getting through! *". . . have beam weapons capable of damage to ships. Emergency message ends!"*

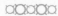

Vero turned an ash-plastered face toward him. "It's gone successfully!" he shouted with a sort of manic triumph. In the background Merral could hear the message being repeated. Vero was speaking again now, his voice seeming distant and distorted. "You look awful, Merral. Truly awful." He reached out and carefully touched Merral's shoulder. "Are you all right?"

"Yes," Merral answered slowly, shaking his head to try and clear the noise out of his ears. "I think so. But you look like a corpse." Suddenly he heard a voice, crackling and varying in volume, coming out of the diary.

"Merral D'Avanos, Assembly ship *Nesta Lamaine* has received your message. Fireball seen. Captain is evaluating your situation now. Are you okay?"

Vero handed him the diary. Merral wiped the dust off the screen and spat to clear his mouth.

"Yes. Yes. Just about. We are on the south end of the cliff—Uh-oh!"

The screen was flashing the "Unable to transmit message" sign. He showed it to Vero who merely shook his head. "As I expected. A temporary overload. Well, we got our message out."

The diary crackled to life. "We have lost your signal. Captain advises we are coming down to you. Standard Operating Procedure is to do a Farholme orbit first. This will give two hours—"

"Two hours!" Vero shouted.

"—before we can get to you. Just hang on. Out." The signal light faded.

Merral tabbed the transmit button and shouted at the slab, "Two hours is too long! Forget Standard Operating Procedure! Make it faster!"

But the diary refused to transmit.

The gloom was descending again as above them the eerie light was fading. Merral was aware of Vero waving his hands in protest. "Can't they get in faster?"

"I know! The only ship around, this *Nesta Lamaine*, must be in high orbit or something. But I'm surprised. . . . Can we survive?"

Vero blew his nose. "Maybe, but only if there are no more attacks. You're sure you are all right, Merral? There's blood on you."

In response, Merral tried sitting up. He ran his hands over his chest and felt them come away in a disgusting mixture of dust and blood. "Praises, I think it's not mine."

"Let's get back on the main ledge then," Vero said. "We need to see if our attackers have gone."

They scrambled slowly back onto the main rock ledge of the plateau. The light from the dust cloud had almost dissipated now, but they could see that the once flat surface now bore a gentle circular depression a half a dozen meters across that was glowing a dull crimson color. They were alone on the summit.

In the growing darkness, Vero's voice was quieter now. "Those ape-creatures are very agile. To get up the northern face that we thought was impossible was an extraordinary feat."

"Yes," answered Merral slowly, suddenly feeling incredibly weary. His throat was dry, his ankle hurt, and he felt unspeakably sickened by what had happened.

As the night seemed to slip back around them, Vero coughed and spat. "Ugh! Dust! Incidentally, Merral, do you realize that you may have done what Thomas wanted you to do?"

"Sorry? Oh, you mean kill whatever had taken Spotback? Well, if it was one of those—and I hope there aren't many more—then maybe I did just that." In fact, he found the idea of little comfort.

For a few minutes they were silent. Some of the dust slowly settled around them, but much remained in the air, dulling and diffusing the light from the stars. Eventually, Vero spoke slowly. "Assuming—just assuming—they can rescue us, we must do some urgent thinking."

"You mean what happens next?"

"Yes. What we do. Earth must be told: told fast and told securely." But he said no more and fell silent.

A few minutes later, Merral's eye was caught by a moving beam of light cutting up through the dusty air from the ground just to the west of them. Carefully, a new dread rising in his exhausted mind, he and Vero picked their way slowly over the ash-draped rocks to the western edge of the hill. Not far away under the trees, a light was drifting leisurely toward them, swinging from side to side as if searching out a pathway for feet between the rocks and tree roots. Behind it, Merral could just make out dark figures, and from their height and gait he knew they were not human.

Vero sighed. "More trouble. Not our rescuers."

"Yes," Merral answered, surprised how drained of emotion he felt. "They will be here in a few minutes. Watch, stand firm, and hope."

"The hope bit is getting harder to do. And nearly two hours before the ship arrives. . . . I wish now we had got a full message out." Vero gave a little grunt. "Huh, I really thought we were going to make it."

Then he reached out and patted Merral affectionately on the back. "But let me say—while I have the chance—that you did wonders here tonight. Remarkable. That challenge. Epic stuff. Worthy of a painting in the style of the Thirteenth Millennium romantics: 'Forester D'Avanos Faces the Ape-Creatures Alone."

For a brief moment, Merral felt like pointing out that a really authentic picture would have to be done in shades of blacks and dark grays. But he hurt too much.

Vero seemed to drift away into silence, and Merral, torn by his own memories of the day, tried to put his thoughts in order. They had a few minutes yet; the moving light had yet to approach the edge of the trees. Merral prepared himself to crawl to the edge and hurl rocks down until—inevitably—he was overwhelmed.

Then, abruptly, the light went off. In the distance below, near where the beam had been, Merral could hear voices, but what they said, and even whether or not they were human, he found impossible to tell. He began to crawl toward the cliff edge, wondering if he could find any rocks in the darkness to throw.

"Listen!" whispered Vero.

At first Merral could hear only the ringing in his ears.

Then he was able to make out a faint whistling noise in the air coming from the south. He stared into the darkness. Whatever it was could not be the rescue ship; that had to be ninety minutes or more away on the other side of Farholme. For a moment, he saw nothing.

Low in the southern sky the hazily twinkling stars were obscured by a shape that was growing larger every second. Merral, seized by a feeling of stark horror, stared at the blackness as the expanding silhouette rose above the cliff.

Then from his belt his diary bleeped and a dry male voice echoed around. "This is Assembly ship *Nesta Lamaine!* Prepare to board immediately! Beware hot external surfaces!"

As the shadow eclipsed more stars, four columns of white flame burst out like waterfalls of light, throwing up dust into the air. Blinking, his ears adjusting to the newly unleashed storm of sound, Merral could now make out the stained white-plated hull of a general survey craft. He wanted to cry for joy.

The ship tilted and lowered itself down vertically, thin legs extruding through the pulses of shimmering heat. A smell of steam and fumes and waves of warm air rolled over them. Above the glare of the engines Merral could make out the green light of the cockpit and the dull orange glow of heat around the stubby wings. A line of cold blue light opened in the underside of the ship and grew as the hatchway ramp lowered to within a handbreadth of the surface. Stumbling, trying to shield their eyes from the dazzling intensity of the thrusters, Merral and Vero clambered up the ramp.

"Go! Go!" shouted a voice, and a firm hand grabbed Merral's arm and hauled him into the hold. The craft swayed and bobbed like a boat on rough sea, the ramp closed, and Merral felt vibrations under his feet. Then he heard a succession of noises: the hissing of pistons closing the hatch, the tolling of a warning bell, the clamor of a siren, and then the thudding bellow of sound as the thrusters kicked in.

A big man in the deep blue Space Affairs uniform pushed Merral into a seat and strapped a belt around him. Then he was pressed first down and then sideways into the bucket seat as the ship began a series of violent motions, tilting sharply, first one way and then the other.

"Emergency maneuvers," grunted a low voice behind Merral but he was too deep into his seat to see who it was.

Without warning, a brutal rattling noise sounded underneath them. The ship wobbled briefly and, for a second, the lights dimmed. A new set of alarms sounded. With renewed force, the ship seemed to be thrown across the sky, until at one point Merral was on his side and all round him he could hear creaks and the sound of equipment sliding about in lockers. As the wild lurching motion continued, Merral twisted his head and caught a glimpse of Vero slumped in an adjacent seat, covered from head to toe in pale dust, a dirty hand over his mouth and a look of utter misery on his face.

Then it was over.

The ship stabilized, the sirens faded out, and the background creaks died away.

"I feel sick," mumbled Vero.

"Not surprised! That was rough." The cheerful voice came from behind Merral. "But can you hang on while I check out your friend? He looks bad."

Whom is he referring to? Merral looked at his jacket where the crimson blood was now brown. The crew member, a stocky, bearded man with green eyes, took his wrist and applied a diagnostic unit to it.

"It's not *my* blood," Merral protested, as he felt the DU's probe gently penetrate his skin. "Except for around my right ankle," he added.

"Good. Good, you can talk, and better, it's largely not yours. Otherwise I'd have to start putting some replacement in." He glanced at the readout. "Your vital signs are good. But you're dehydrated."

A door slid open and a slender figure with short auburn hair in a night blue uniform slid in, one hand cupped around an earpiece.

"Welcome aboard the *Nesta Lamaine*," Perena said in a quiet voice. "Oh, are you all right, Merral?"

"Well, Perena Lewitz!" Vero said, a smile cracking the dust on his face. "We *are* greatly obliged."

"Perena! I should have guessed it was you," Merral added. "And yes, I'm fine. I think."

Perena glanced at the crewman. "Matthew, is he really all right?"

"Yes, Captain. Pretty much so. It's largely surface blood. But he's dehydrated."

She smiled with frank relief. "Then I should have made you wash first. And do excuse me if I don't even shake hands." Then she frowned. "But then whose blood is it, if it isn't yours?"

"Ah. I think—" Merral caught Vero's gesture and fell silent.

"Perena," Vero interjected, "we need to see your sister about that. I think she knows something. But it's an odd story. And a worrying one."

Perena wrinkled her nose. "*You* don't look much better, Vero. Matthew," she ordered, "get some water for these guys to drink and perhaps a damp cloth to wash with." She looked at them again. "I guess a hot shower with disinfectant is what's really needed."

The crewman nodded assent and left the hold.

"Many thanks, Perena," Merral gasped, realizing how glad he was to finally be off that besieged hill and in the ship. "That felt like an interesting bit of flying."

"I agree," Vero said, "even if, at the time, I may not have appreciated it. Where did you learn it?"

"It's called the Yenerag Maneuver. It's pretty specialized and normally envisaged as being for the evacuation of people from active volcanic sites—"

Perena raised a hand and seemed to listen to her earpiece. "Roger!" she snapped. "Continue on present course and speed, but watch those strain warnings. Maintain the self-sealant pressure."

As she spoke, Matthew came in with water.

"Sorry, guys. It's busy time here. Matthew, can you run up to the bridge as soon as you can? Amira may need help. I'll be up in a moment."

He gave Merral and Vero water and cloths and then left. As he did, Perena turned her cool slate blue eyes on them.

"Thank you for the appreciation. My computer is less amused and is telling me we have suffered major damage to the port lifting undersurface and minor to the starboard. From the nature of the damage and the speed of the impact, the computer has deduced that we were hit by multiple small meteoroids. It is clever enough to be puzzled as it realizes that we were flying in normal altitude near the ground and that meteoroids do not fall upward from a planetary surface. It is *not* clever enough to deduce the explanation. And, in truth, neither am I. It might be useful to know what hit us."

Merral looked at her. "A beam weapon of some sort. High temperature, portable. Hot enough to melt rock."

The eyes widened and she shook her head in incredulity. "Seriously? My ship really was fired on?"

"Yes. As we warned you."

Her face acquired a look of astonishment mingled with unease. "And what does that mean?"

"Mean?" Vero shook his head. "I wish I knew. To start with, it means we need to have a meeting. You, us, and Anya. As soon as we land. Somewhere quiet."

She nodded thoughtfully. "Fine. The self-repair systems are in operation and we are heading at high subsonic speeds—which is as fast as I dare—to

Isterrane. I can't really spare you the time anyway now. In fact, I'd better get back to the bridge."

Vero, rubbing dust off his face, spoke again. "What have you said to anybody so far?"

"Nothing much. I've been too busy. Wait. . . ." She raised a hand again, her absorbed face showing she was getting another message. "Okay, Amira, I'm coming up. We'll get Matthew to check the R3 coolant levels manually. Initiate clearances for possible emergency glide landings at every strip between here and Isterrane."

She looked back at Vero. "Well, I've said we've got you. I've been a bit busy to do anything else. I'm afraid your alert about non-Assembly forces is being treated as evidence of delirium. Like the Youraban shuttle pilot who—oh, a century ago—was adamant that he was being attacked by thirty kilometer-long space octopods."

Vero nodded. "I remember that. May I suggest, Captain Lewitz, that you try to land as far out of sight as possible. Encourage the crew to keep silent. We don't want a panic."

"A panic?" Perena arched thin eyebrows. "No. I suppose you may have a point. I'll call Anya and have her meet us."

She turned to the door.

"Perena?" Merral asked. "Just one quick question. You said you would be two hours in arriving. You were a half an hour. I don't understand."

She reached for the guide rail and turned to him. "*I* didn't think it was delirium. And the mention of 'non-Assembly forces' and 'weapons' alarmed me. So, at first I felt it best not to say when I would arrive, and then I thought harder and decided that it might be safer—and quite legitimate—to mislead." She looked faintly amused. "I have, after all, played a lot of old-time chess."

"So you lied?" Vero asked, raising a dusty eyebrow in alarm.

"Vero, please!" Perena winked at him. "If you remember my communication, I told you that the Standard Operating Procedure would take two hours. I ignored the SOP and just corkscrewed in. Not pleasant, I may say. And risky, and we probably lost a centimeter of ablatative material off all my underside plates. So, do thank my crew. At worst, I misled you and your . . . enemies." She frowned at the last word.

Then a new message came on her earpiece and she winced. "And even then it was a near thing. But"—and she gave a heartfelt sigh—"by the King's grace, we did it."

An hour later, after a landing marked by a series of bounces and an odd slewing motion, they were on the ground at Isterrane.

16

As the ramp to the compartment swung down, Merral and Vero got to their feet. There was the smell of fresh, clean air with the hint of the sea, and through the doorway, Merral could see the black of the fused basalt runway below glinting under the lights of the landing strip.

Then there was the sound of feet running up the gangway, and a red-haired figure in sweater and trousers appeared. A freckled face, blue eyes blinking in the light, peered up at them.

"Hi, guys!" Anya called out, her voice soft and concerned, and Merral sensed a seriousness to her that he was unfamiliar with.

"So, you had an interesting trip," she whispered, staring at him and Vero with her eyes open wide.

With a strange throb of emotion, Merral realized that he was very pleased to see her.

"An understatement," Vero commented in pained tones, gently shaking off dust.

Anya looked them over again and shook her head. "Well, if you think I'm going to hug and kiss either of you—especially you, Merral D'Avanos, when you look like an accident in a blood bank—not a hope. As for you, Sentinel Enand, you look like you failed to get out of a quarry before blasting."

Merral looked at Vero and then down at his bloodied clothes and decided he didn't know whether to smile or shudder.

Perena's slim figure slipped in through a doorway. As she embraced her sister, she gestured to Merral and Vero. "Have you ever seen anything more disgusting?"

Anya shook her head as Perena continued urgently. "My poor ship needs a trip to Bay One for full damage assessment and repair. I've arranged for these guys to clean up at the medical center. Take them over, let them shower off, fix them clean clothes. Issue them some standard Space Affairs suits. I've asked for Doc Larchent to see them. He's under instructions not to ask questions." She gave a grimace. "Excuse me, all, I've got some weird holes to look at. See you later."

She turned to make her way down the ramp onto the runway.

Anya hooked a thumb downward. "Out, you guys, follow me. We've an ambulance here and we'll go in by the back way. And Merral," she said, giving him a crooked grin, "if that is your blood, you ought to be dead and I want you for science. And if it isn't, well, then I want your clothes for science."

Merral clapped Anya on the back. "Only the ankle blood is mine."

She looked hard at his clothes, her eyes widening. "I'm glad of that. The rest is the blood of one of these insect-creatures?"

"There wasn't just one creature, Anya. There were many of them. And two different kinds; there was an ape-creature as well."

She stared wide-eyed at the garments for a moment before looking up at him with a colder, businesslike look. "You have both kinds of blood on you?"

"Oh, yes." Merral smiled. "I went to some trouble to get good samples for you. The left ankle and trouser leg is from the cockroach thing; the jacket and shirt blood is from an ape-creature. My contribution is the right lower leg and the sock."

"Excellent." She shook her head in mock reproof. "But next time, Tree Man, you might remember that a drop is adequate."

"Enough of the repartee, you guys," Vero said. "We need to meet together as soon as we have cleaned up. There is a long, long chat we have to have, and some hard decisions to make."

As Merral and Vero walked unsteadily and stiffly out from under the general survey craft to where the ambulance hovered gently on the strip, they could see a cluster of people looking up and shaking their heads at the underside of the stubby wings. Above them, beams from handheld lights were picking out a cluster of a dozen or so fist-sized holes with blackened edges.

Vero tapped Merral gently on the shoulder and bent his face toward him. "My friend," he said, and Merral heard the anxiety in his voice, "I ask you to pray for me. I need to make decisions now. They are hard decisions, because a wrong move now could be disastrous. If, on the summit, the weight of the struggle fell on you, it now falls on me. We will meet and discuss after you have been fixed up, but already I have to decide." He sighed. "It is not easy."

As he spoke, Merral realized that this was something he had overlooked. Vero was right; action had to be taken, but choosing the right action would be far from easy.

The ambulance whispered through the back of the medical center. There Merral was divested of his clothes, allowed a hasty but wonderful shower, and then taken in a bathrobe to a room where he had a brief medical examination by a doctor and a nurse. His ankle was examined and the wound opened, cleansed thoroughly, and then microsutured. A bruised shoulder was treated, the small burn to the hand covered, and his eardrums examined.

As the doctor gave Merral a third different anti-infection agent, he stared at him with puzzled eyes. "I've been told not to ask questions, Forester D'Avanos, but that is an interesting wound on your foot. I've never seen anything quite like it."

Their eyes met.

"Yes, it is interesting."

Realizing that he was not going to learn anything more, the doctor just shrugged. "It should give no more trouble. Call me if it shows any inflammation."

Aware of the doctor and nurse watching him curiously, Merral headed to an adjoining room where he took a new set of clothing, including a shirt and overalls in the dark blue colors of Space Affairs. Then, feeling more human, he was shown to an empty refectory where he helped himself to fruit juice and sandwiches from a fridge. A few minutes later Vero joined him, and together, with the minimum of conversation, they ate and drank gratefully. As they were finishing, Anya came in, and this time there were embraces all round.

Then, with the gentle night air with its hint of impending summer drifting through the cab, Anya drove them across the runway in a small Space Affairs transport. Merral realized he had conflicting urges within him. His body simply wished to go to bed and sleep off recent events, while in his mind there burned the stronger longing to take action, to warn Farholme and the Assembly.

"Where are we going?" he asked Anya as they overtook the *Nesta Lamaine* being towed slowly across the runway.

"My sister asked me to take you to the Engineering and Maintenance Complex."

Vero leaned over to Merral. "While you were being patched up, I went and sorted some things out with Perena. We have set some things in motion. We need to talk in a place where we can be sure of not being overheard or having equipment intercepted. She suggested one of the engineering rooms. They are all underground."

They stopped at the end of one of the runways where a series of wide entrances and narrow doors was cut into a low hill. Perena was waiting for them and led them to a closed door.

"Captain Perena Lewitz and three colleagues," she announced to a panel at the side, and the doorway slid open.

"You have security?" Vero asked her in surprise as Perena led them through.

"Security?" The door slid closed behind them. "It's *safety*. That alone. There are vacuum chambers, laser cutters—any number of radiation-emitting processes. You can't have just anybody walking around here. Otherwise we would have space-besotted children being fried accidentally every week."

She gestured to a weighty array of warning notices on the walls and then stared at a screen. "But it's almost empty. A few engineers checking some circuits for motors in Bay Three. Six technicians preparing Bay One for *Nesta*. That's about it. Eleven o'clock in the evening is not the time for routine work."

They walked down two flights of stairs and along a lengthy corridor. At a heavy glass window at the end she stopped and peered in at a large, well-lit chamber with a vacant center space and an array of machinery around the perimeter. "Bay One," Perena observed. "Home for *Nesta* for the next few days at least. We'll have to replace a dozen undersurface plates and make sure there are no leaks. Put her in vacuum for a day or two." She stroked her chin gently. "Extraordinary," she whispered in wonderment. "Battle damage."

Then they moved on into another corridor. At the end of this was a heavy door marked Communications Isolation Room, and a notice warned that no diary communication was possible within the room. A datascreen by the side proclaimed that the room was unoccupied.

Perena opened the door and gestured them in as the lights automatically flickered on. "Make yourselves as comfortable as you can. I need to make sure we are left alone and that any com-links to this room are switched off." She gave Vero a meaningful look. "And, check on some other matters. There'll be water, coffee—everything—in the office next door." Then she left.

The laboratory was small, with a low ceiling, and empty apart from banks of equipment and testing racks. They found a table in a corner, cleared it of testing units, and pulled up chairs. Anya and Vero made coffee while Merral put his ankle upon a box.

They had barely sat down with the cups when Perena came in and closed the door behind her. She nodded at Vero. "Maybe," she said, "in an hour we will know. Just after midnight."

Then she pulled a chair up and sat with them. Merral realized that she was looking expectantly at him. He glanced around and saw that everyone else was as well.

Vero nodded at him. "I think, Merral, that you'd best start things off. It seems to be the general feeling."

"Very well. But I don't know where to begin. I am certain, though, that we should seek the blessing of the Lord first. We have been spared so far in an extraordinary way. Yet we are up against something so enormous . . ." He paused, his thoughts almost overwhelming him. "So enormous, that what we decide here tonight may have unimaginable consequences."

They bowed their heads and Merral prayed. He gave thanks for deliverance, made a fervent plea for future protection, and then petitioned for clarity and guidance in their discussion. After the resounding "Amens" he looked around and saw, as he had expected, that they were all still looking at him.

Merral turned to Vero. "You asked me to start, but if I am not mistaken, Vero, this is your hour. I know you do not understand everything, but I believe you've thought these things through more than I have. Also your background has better prepared you."

Vero looked around with a troubled face and gestured his reluctant agreement with the least of nods. "Very well. Although I must say Merral has shown a remarkable practical ability. He seems to be a born soldier."

Merral made a murmur of protest but Vero continued. "He is unhappy with that word, I know. Indeed, if he were happy with it I would worry. Anyway, let me begin, because I think there are things that I need to say. Then I will let Merral tell you what we have seen. But we must be urgent; we have decisions to make, and I think we must make them within the hour."

He paused and seemed to stare ahead solemnly into the distance for a long, heavy moment. "We have a problem. I wish I could tell you all about what that problem is—where it comes from, what it means, and how it might be countered. Description, analysis, prescription. But I cannot. I am not even sure whether there is one problem or many. To some extent it is not our task to solve it. That can be done by others. But we do need to make urgent decisions, and make them now."

There were nods of assent and Vero continued. "Let me state the problem. Something is in the north—something evil, something unknown, since at least the beginning of the Assembly. And maybe not even then."

As he spoke the words, Merral's memories of grappling in the darkness with the ape-creatures and the dreadful encounter with the cockroach-beast were stirred again. He grabbed the table's edge.

Vero stopped, creased his forehead in thought, and then went on. "There are, I think, three distinct aspects: First, there are now on Farholme two sorts of new creatures, both unknown to the Assembly. Merral will describe them. Both are intelligent and very hostile."

Merral saw the sisters share glances with each other.

"Second," Vero continued, "these creatures are connected—in some way—with a technology that is beyond ours in the area of weapons and communications." He leaned forward, his thin figure tense. "And third—and worst of all—there is an evil influence loose. A spiritual influence that corrupts. . . ."

As the words sank in, Merral stared around. In the whole history of the Assembly, he wondered whether there had ever been such a meeting as this.

Anya and Perena shared looks of silent astonishment. Then Anya turned to Vero and shook her head in such a firm gesture of denial that her long red hair flew over her shoulders. "All of this seems too much to believe. I *know* this world."

Vero tapped the table thoughtfully with his fingers for a moment. "I sympathize, Anya, and your skepticism is valuable. But, partly to help you to believe and partly to explain why we meet here, can you call up the conversation you had, what—six hours ago? When you called to make contact with us? Remember, it was just voices."

"Sure. I was impressed, Vero," she replied with a look of amusement as she pulled off her diary and put it on the table. "I've never heard of anybody managing to wipe out the main functions of two separate diaries. I was very surprised when I heard it."

A strange, ironic smile crept across Vero's face. "Your surprise, Anya, was—I'm certain—exceeded by mine. But then it has been a day of surprises. And more. But play the conversation. Please."

Evidently mystified, Anya searched for the file on her diary, and then the room was filled with the sound of her call to Merral and Vero while the sentinel stared at his fingernails. When the transmission ended, she turned to Vero. "So? Why that?"

There was a delay, then Vero lifted up his large brown eyes and stared at her. "Because, in fact, neither Merral nor I spoke." The words were hushed.

Perplexed, Anya looked at her sister, then back at Vero. "Yes, you did. We all heard you."

Catching a minute gesture from Vero, Merral turned to her. "Anya, that was not us. I testify to it. Our own diaries had been blocked for the best part of a day. Whatever it is . . . no, whoever *they* are, they duplicated our voices."

Anya's face paled. "But that *was* you. . . . I don't believe it. I *can't* believe . . ."

The troubled silence was broken by Perena's gentle and thoughtful voice. "Sister, it might help to remember that *something* burned holes right through five centimeters-thick thermoceramic plates on my ship. At a guess, by generating a local temperature of at least twelve hundred degrees C. And *something* cut off these guys' diary signals within seconds."

Anya, a determined skepticism on her face, merely shook her head again in exasperation and said nothing. Merral caught a tremor in Vero's fingers and knew that he was finding the meeting difficult. He prayed for him again.

Vero sighed, then looked up at Anya, his dark face strained. "I understand your reluctance to believe something so disturbing, so almost impossible. But, Anya, you must. We must all understand what we face. Now, if you could play us another diary clip. I want you to show us the interview with Maya Knella about the samples."

Anya breathed out heavily, as if in exasperation, and then pointed her diary at the wallscreen. "Very well. . . . But, as I told you, it was a bad line."

A few moments later they were looking at a grainy image of a middle-aged woman with a heavy-boned oval face, her jet-black hair tinged with gray and held in place by a silver hair clasp, and wearing a long red dress with a green leaf pattern. The background was a laboratory. The image jumped and flickered, the sound bounced up and down in volume, and there was a marked time delay between question and answer. What the woman said was more or less as Anya had reported: a denial of anything peculiar in her sample data and a suggestion that the equipment might be failing.

"F–freeze it, please," Vero ordered. "Now window the previous conversation you had with her."

"But . . . that was about a technical aspect of gene transmission in mammals. It was about nothing relevant."

"Please," Vero asked, casting a glance at his watch. "If I am right, it is an issue of greatest significance." Moments later, Maya Knella appeared again below the first image.

"Ah!" There was a note of relief in Vero's voice. "Freeze that, too!"

"I thought you wanted to hear it."

"It is not necessary. When was this?"

"About ten days earlier."

"Yes," Vero said quietly, as if to himself. "And what do you see, Merral?"

"Same woman," he answered, failing to see any cause for Vero's excitement. "But in an office this time. She's got a different dress."

Vero got up from his seat, walked over, and peered at the images, one inset inside the other.

"No, she hasn't," he said, gesturing with an outstretched finger. "This is a gray dress with brown leaves. The pattern is identical. Only the color is changed."

His finger jumped from one image to another and back. Merral heard a gasp from Anya.

Vero continued staring at the image. "See, too, that the hairstyle and combing is exactly the same. But the hair clip here is gold."

"But—," Anya protested, looking at everyone in turn as if trying to elicit support. "But the background is different."

"Standard shots of a laboratory," Vero added, his voice terse, as if he was anxious to move on. "Easy enough to provide. Careful analysis would probably show discrepancies in the angle of the shadows between her and the background."

Anya, now half standing, was leaning forward over the table, staring intently at the sentinel with an expression that seemed to fluctuate between confusion and dread.

"So, Vero," she said, her voice full of perplexity and fear, "you are saying that I never talked with her a second time. That it was made-up. That they just . . . Surely not?" She stared at the screen and Merral saw her swallow. "That they just took an old conversation we had . . . and modified it?"

Vero pursed his mouth and nodded. "S–sorry," he said.

"No!" Anya snapped and, blank-faced, sat down suddenly in her chair. She put her face in her hands for a moment and then looked around, her expression one of shocked stupefaction. "I'm appalled . . . ," she said slowly. "I mean, it smashes everything we stand for: ethics, Technology Protocols, decency—everything!"

Anya's misery was so evident that Merral was struck by a strangely potent—and perturbing—desire to comfort her by hugging her.

Anya stared at Vero with resentment in her eyes. "But . . . how did they know to do it to me?"

Vero wrinkled his nose. "I'd guess they knew because you had told us you were going to call her when we were in Ynysmant."

Anya gulped. "They listened in?"

"At a guess."

Her face flushed. "No . . . ," she continued, her face showing that she was fighting desperately not to believe what she was being told. "It can't be! I mean, how did they get the old conversation with Maya?"

Merral, who had just worked out the answer, decided that she was not going to like what Vero was going to say. But, in fact, it was Perena who told her the answer, her blue-gray eyes filled with a cold anger. "I'm afraid that they went through your files, little sister. I'd imagine when you were asleep they just contacted your diary and pulled off what they wanted and prepared the duplicate."

Anya's face and posture showed that the disbelief had vanished, to be replaced by an anger just short of fury. "That's just . . . well, I've never heard anything so . . . wrong!" She stood up and struck her fist on the table. "I'm absolutely furious. Why, I've never been so angry! To invade my privacy. To fake that call. And I was beginning to think that Maya Knella's reputation was undeserved!" She sat down again, a look of simmering anger on her face. Suddenly a look of guilt appeared. "Why, I ought to apologize to Maya."

A hint of a wry smile played across Vero's mouth, "Amid this tale of enormous evil, I'm touched by your concern about your thoughts. Anyway, the hour is late and we have much to go through. But now you believe it, eh?"

Anya was silent for a moment and then moved her head slowly up and down in unenthusiastic affirmation.

"Now we can move on. Only, when it came to faking our forester and me," Vero said in a measured tone, "they did not have the time or data to do the job properly. So, they just faked the sound."

Perena, who had been leaning forward over the table, suddenly looked up, her eyes carefully moving round the table. "I am as horrified at all this as my sister," she said in her quiet but forceful voice, "but this means that they must have some entry into the Gate circuits. Either at the Gate itself, or—surely more probable—at one of the Gate signal relay stations." Merral saw that she was doodling with a finger on the tabletop. Then she stared at Vero. "But you see," she continued gently, "as our student of ancient history here will confirm, the Gates are the central nervous system of the Assembly. Those who control Farholme Gate control Farholme."

"Well said," responded Vero, "and that was one lesson learned in the last military action the Assembly took. In the Rebellion, because Jannafy had seized the Centauri Gate, the Assembly Force had to travel at sublight speed to get there. It took Ringell and his men six years. Once they had the Gate, they were home in an afternoon. Sorry, but it is an episode that has been on my mind much lately."

Anya grimaced. "I really don't like that phrase, 'the last military action.'"

Vero shrugged. "Nor do I, Anya, but you saw the blood on Merral. He and—to a very much lesser extent—I fought today. *Fought* . . ." He hesitated, apparently suddenly hit by the significance of the word. "I, we, fought. Not as in sport, or as in a metaphor, but in reality, a bloody reality." He stroked his chin, as if realizing that he needed a shave, and then continued. "But, if I may say so, I have a greater—if more subtle—concern, which I feel I must express."

Merral stared at him, thinking that he needed a week to absorb all this and what it signified. But Vero was right, decisions had to be made and made tonight.

"My concern is this: They must know that they can't sustain such a scheme forever. Sooner or later Maya and Anya will correspond by paper—or even meet—and the trick will be apparent."

There was silence as the implications sank in, then Vero continued, his face now bearing an expression of foreboding. "I think it is one of two things. Either it is a desperate measure or it is a short-term strategy . . . until—"

"Until what, Vero?" queried Perena in a keen and worried tone, her head slightly on one side.

"Frankly, I don't know."

Everyone was looking at each other. *We are all out of our depth,* Merral realized. *None of us is stupid and yet here we haven't got a clue.*

Vero sipped at his coffee and stretched back in his chair. "That's me finished, Merral. But I want us all to realize at the start of our discussion that there is no question that we face a powerful foe. And also, that we cannot now trust any diary conversation. It has occasionally been a theoretical sentinel concern that our communications in the Assembly are totally open. But we have never been able to justify the use of any encrypting practices."

"Encrypting?" Anya queried.

"As in code. And not genetic. You scramble a message and disguise it so that only a recipient with the correct digital key can read it. You might do it with a personal diary."

A look of anger erupted across her face. "Yes. That makes me so—" She shook herself in a barely restrained emotion. "No, continue."

"Merral, over to you. Tell them exactly what happened."

"Very well," Merral said. "Although I'm at a loss to know where to start."

Vero shrugged. "Just begin where you first noticed anything odd."

Merral thought hard. "I would say just before Nativity."

Vero started. "*Before* Nativity?" he queried sharply.

"Yes. At Herrandown. I had a nightmare of something evil coming out of the sea. And I think—in hindsight—my uncle did, too. But he denied it."

Perena lifted her head and stared piercingly at Merral. "When 'just before Nativity'?"

"Three nights before. The twenty-second."

"The night of the meteor?"

"Yes."

"What meteor?" Vero threw a sharp glance at Merral. "Why didn't you tell me?"

For a fraction of a second, Merral was tempted to be angry. "Sorry, Vero . . . I hadn't assumed it was significant. This is Worlds' End. *Nothing* happens here. Or did."

Perena looked at Merral. "If I may interrupt. I believe that it is significant. I have been doing some checking up. For about a week before the night Merral is speaking of, one of the Guardian Satellites had been tracking a sunward meteoroid of around two thousand tons apparent mass. As soon as it was noticed, its trajectory was calculated—of course—and it was determined that it would miss Farholme by at least fifty thousand kilometers and eventually hit the sun. There was nothing alarming about either its size, speed, or path, and obviously, no action was necessary, so they just kept a regular watch on it. Just in case it broke up or did anything odd." She looked at Vero. "I should say that, at any one time, there are a dozen of this size of thing within a few million kilometers of Farholme, but they just let them through when they are certain that they are going to miss. It's a minimum intervention policy. So, the existence of this particular moving block of rock wasn't even flagged to the human supervision office in Isterrane."

Vero nodded and gestured for her to continue. "So, it was routinely tracked every fifty minutes. The last reported sighting was at 4:20 p.m. Central Menaya Time. It was still coming sunward and nearly at the point of closest approach to Farholme—estimated to be at one hundred thousand kilometers out—but was still behaving itself. When the Guardian checked again at 5:10 p.m., it expected to find it sunward of us, but it was absent from the predicted path."

"Ah!" muttered Vero. "How interesting. But I interrupt."

Perena looked at the wall clock. "Yes, we must watch the time. Machine logic being what it is, they looked around for it and, having failed to find either it or fragments, they did the electronic equivalent of shrugging their shoulders and got on with life as usual. Remember, only the presence of a meteoroid is a problem, not an absence. They did, however, tag the case to the supervisors just in case it was the first hint of a malfunction. They assumed it was and rescheduled the next overhaul sooner."

"So," Merral said, "the meteoroid changed course and came to Farholme where I saw it coming in."

"Oh, I wish you'd told me, Merral," Vero interjected. "I might have been more suspicious."

Merral, feeling tired, sighed. "It was just a meteor, Vero. An incoming pile of rock and metal. It's not rare here. It's different from the solar system: for a start we have two debris belts, one on either side of Fenniran. It was just larger than usual."

Vero looked at Perena. "And let me guess: it wasn't a meteoroid, it was a ship."

She gave him a strange, subdued smile. "Not so fast, my friend. In theory, yes, it could have been a ship, mimicking a meteoroid. But there is a timing point. It had gone by at 5:10 p.m. Central Menaya Time and Merral saw his object come in ten minutes earlier at around 6:00 p.m. Eastern Menaya Time. Incidentally, confirmed by a record of a small and poorly defined shallow-focus earthquake around two hundred and fifty kilometers north of Herrandown at 6:02 p.m. But there is a major problem."

"What?" asked Vero, looking crestfallen.

Merral spoke slowly. "I see it. It had to change course, travel over a hundred thousand kilometers, and decelerate into a landing mode in under fifty minutes."

Perena looked appreciatively at him. "Good. Let me translate. If we are right in linking the meteoroid in space with Merral's meteor, then it did what our fastest unmanned ships would take at least a half a day to do in around twenty minutes. It pushes engineering beyond anything we can envisage."

Vero closed his eyes. Merral decided that he was imagining what it must be like to be in a ship doing that sort of a maneuver.

"So there may be a ship there," he said slowly. "I was beginning to wonder about that. But can we find it?"

Perena looked at him, her face expressionless. "That is the next task. I have already ordered satellite imagery over the Carson's Sill area from the next overflight."

"Which is when?" Vero asked.

"In an hour or so. Not the best resolution, but it may show something. There's a better one midmorning."

A silence fell and Merral realized that, once more, everybody was staring at him. "Then," he began again, "other strange but apparently unrelated things happened. . . ."

For the next few minutes he described, as best he could, these other things. At Vero's prompting—and then only reluctantly—he outlined how his uncle had altered a re-created voice and how, in a subtle way, things had begun to go wrong at Herrandown. He then went on to explain, largely for Perena's benefit, how Elana had been scared by seeing a creature, and how he and Isabella had gone to investigate and found evidence that there had indeed been some sort of strange being there.

At this point Vero interrupted. "Merral, excuse me, I think this is the time for us to find out what Anya saw when she looked at that strand of hair."

Anya wrinkled her nose as if smelling something distasteful. "Well, the most obvious interpretation was that it was a mixture of two natural genetic codes: human and ape—probably gorilla. Along with some unknown, but probably artificial, segments. It was not a result I was happy with. I would have preferred almost any other interpretation."

Merral looked at Vero, who nodded gently and pursed his lips. "That would fit our ape-creatures."

A frown darkened Anya's face. "I can't believe that these things exist. But you really saw them?"

"I'm afraid so," Vero answered. "And more. . . ."

She shuddered and then looked at Merral. "Go on then. I need to hear what happened when you went north."

Reluctantly, Merral told of what had transpired over the last few days. He began with the meeting with Jorgio and his vision of the testing of the Assembly, with the command to watch, stand firm, and hope. Then Merral went on to tell of the trip north. At times he paused and had to be encouraged by Vero. In places, notably where it came to bloodier dealings, Vero had to draw out the events from him sentence by sentence. And as he recounted the tale, Merral was aware of a growing intensity to the atmosphere in the room. *It is as if the shadow has spread over us.* Where appropriate they ran the images from Merral's diary, and both Perena and Anya took copies of the images of the ape-creatures and cockroach-beasts and stared at them. When it came to the description of the imitation bird, there was horror and disgust and, despite

Merral's invitation, Vero declined to talk about it. "Later," he demurred, "later. . . . In daylight perhaps."

Then, with the aid of more substantial encouragement from Vero, Merral reluctantly told of the last half an hour on the summit. With the account of the rescue by Perena's ship, he fell silent.

It was Anya, looking round the table with broad and worried eyes, who broke the ensuing silence. "A tale that is darker than I can understand. I wish it was a vision or even the result of hallucinations. . . ." She paused, her fingers locking and unlocking. "But, as with the Maya Knella incident, I *must* believe it. We have the images, the testimony, the genetic data from the hair, and will shortly have the blood results. And there is Merral's wound. . . ." She shook her head.

Perena spoke, her voice full of a restrained bewilderment as if she were thinking through a dream. "Like my sister, I would like to try and dismiss it all. But then I think of the holes in my ship." She gestured over her shoulder in the direction of Bay One.

Vero, who had been staring at his hands again, looked up. "Good, but unfortunately it is more than what we believe that is the problem. It is how we are to act. Thank you, Merral, for your account. It is, I think, obvious to you, Perena and Anya, how extraordinarily able my friend here was when it became necessary to fight these things. It is, I believe, a most significant and encouraging matter that our first contact with these things should have involved Merral."

Merral, wondering whether to protest, was aware of Anya looking at him with admiration, and the unsettling thought came to him that he found her attention pleasing.

Vero raised a finger. "Merral, time is moving on and delay may not be good for us. But I feel there may be more questions. And I want us to have all the data we can have before we decide what to do. Anya, comments on the biology?"

Anya bit her lip and shook her head. "Yes. I suppose. We have two sorts of—let's call them 'intruders.' You say, Merral, you saw no evidence of male or female with either?"

"That's right," Merral agreed. "It was less clear with the cockroach-beasts, I suppose. And we saw fewer of them."

Anya nodded. "Size variation of any type?"

"No. Each species—if that's what they were—seemed the same size."

"Like identical twins?"

"Yes."

"So they were probably cloned. Bred somehow in vitro."

Vero threw her a puzzled glance. "That's a very old phrase. I suppose it predates even basic genetics. In glass. Outside the womb?"

"Yes, laboratory generated. Very intriguing." She looked around. "Well, that does me. I'm still absorbing it all."

Vero nodded and looked around. "Thanks. Any other points about what we face?"

Perena stirred. "Just one, Vero. A question. The creatures you describe are so low technology they do not seem to use tools. But whatever weapon was fired indicates advanced technology, as does the interception of the Gate call. And maybe the ship—if it was indeed a ship—that landed. I don't see how it fits together."

Before Vero could answer, Merral spoke. "There is one more piece of the puzzle that may help. I should have said it earlier. Just before the weapon was fired the first time, I saw something in the shadows, standing back. It was a different creature."

Vero opened his mouth wide. "You mean a third type?"

"No. Sorry, Vero, I meant to tell you but, well, I was too busy afterward. I think it was a man."

"A man!" Anya's voice echoed round the room, but it was plain that the others were equally surprised.

"Well, I can't be sure," Merral answered, feeling challenged. "It just, well, looked like one."

"A man?" Vero's tone expressed surprise. "That would confirm an outlandish speculation of mine. . . . But to answer Perena, a just-conceivable scenario might be something like this: These creatures are created, I'm afraid, merely as servants. The technology and the weapons belong to the creators, not the creatures. The classic pre-Intervention slave economy."

Perena looked thoughtful. Then she glanced up at the wall clock and Merral followed her gaze to see that it was nearly midnight.

"Vero," she said, "I indicated that I would call again at twelve."

"Ah yes. But we have nearly finished. Let me tell you what I think. And then I will make a proposal."

He frowned and then looked around, his smooth face tired. Merral suddenly felt that he had a glimpse of what an older Vero would look like. "A common theme emerges. Does anybody else see it? Or is it just me?"

There were puzzled looks. "Only that horrid things seem to have been done all around," Anya offered.

Vero nodded and rose to his feet, walked to the end of the room and stood there against a battery of equipment. He stretched his limbs and frowned. "It is that boundaries have been broken. The boundaries between humanity and animals, between living things and machines." He stopped and his face showed an expression of disgust. "But there may yet be a darker twist. The bird thing. You all expressed revulsion. And rightly so. It masqueraded as a living creature. It was a machine imitating life, in contravention of all that we have ever maintained about such facsimiles. In doing so, it crossed a boundary. But there was worse. It was built on a dead bird."

Perena shuddered. "That . . . I do not—or cannot—understand."

Merral caught a look of extraordinary repulsion on Anya's face.

"Yes," Vero said, "and we can but hope they can shed light on it on Ancient Earth. But this is yet another boundary broken. And this, this monstrosity is perhaps the greatest of the breaches. The boundary between life and death. To raise the dead is the prerogative of the Messiah alone. And this—most assuredly—was none of his handiwork. On the contrary."

In the silence that followed, Vero tightened his lips and looked around the room. "But you see, this is part of a pattern too. From Merral's dream onward, through the problems at Herrandown, there is a second theme. A theme of spiritual corruption unparalleled in the long years since the Rebellion, and maybe since the start of the Great Intervention. If I had to choose between the visible genetic abominations we have seen and the less visible spiritual problems, I would choose the latter as the most worrying. But the linkage of the two is most terrible."

Merral looked at him. "So, what do we do?"

Vero smiled. "Ah, ever the man of action. In fact, I have made a decision for myself." He looked at Perena. "Can you check for me now?"

She rose gracefully. "There's a diary link point outside. Excuse me." She left the room.

Vero walked forward and leaned on his chair back. "I need to talk with Brenito as soon as I can. Then we need to meet with the representatives here, but that would take a few days to organize. And, in the meantime, Earth must know. This matter is quite beyond us here and it raises issues that affect the entire Assembly. This matter must go straight to an emergency session of the Council of High Stewards. They will doubtless summon the whole Congregation of all the Stewards, the Farholme Delegate, and the Science Panel. I have no doubt, too, that the Custodians of the Faith would be consulted about the spiritual aspects."

"And the sentinels?" Merral asked, awed at the realization that this matter would have to go so high and so quickly.

"If asked." Vero looked thoughtful. "But, oddly enough, we have served our purpose in this matter. Or very nearly. We only ever existed to watch and alert. This we have done. It could be, perhaps, that in this case we might have done better, but that is for discussion at another time."

Merral could faintly hear Perena outside talking on her diary.

"Do you think you can safely call Earth?" Anya asked.

Vero shook his head. "How? We cannot trust Gate communications. Your attempt to contact Maya Knella has taught us that. The files must be hand carried to Ancient Earth as secretly and fast as we can manage."

Anya nodded. "Yes, I can see that. But the council and everybody—what do you think they will do?"

"I think I can safely say they will rapidly muster the entire Defense Force and bring them in. There are only two ships, and even by Assembly standards they are elderly, but they—and their men—will be enough to search the north. Beyond that, I do not know."

The door opened and Perena came in and smiled at Vero. "Done. Two."

Vero seemed to breathe a sigh of relief. "So, I propose to leave for Earth on the next ship. The *Heinrich Schütz.* It departs the Gate Station at 10 a.m. Central Menaya Time the day after tomorrow—no, tomorrow now. In just thirty-four hours time. We will take tonight's in-system shuttle."

"*We?*" Merral asked, a bizarre speculation suddenly forming in his mind.

Vero walked round from his chair and grasped Merral gently on the shoulder.

"Yes, soldier," he said, "*we.* I want to take you too."

"Are you serious?" Merral gasped, his mind reeling. To Ancient Earth! He had hoped to go someday, but today? In barely hours?

Vero's smile seemed weary. "Yes, for one thing, they—whoever *they* are—probably expect us to stay here and meet up with the representatives. But the four other representatives need to fly in, so we can hardly summon a meeting today and, as tomorrow is the Lord's Day, they ought to know that we will not have any real meetings for two days. They may also be in disarray after their losses."

"But why me? To Earth?" Merral asked. "All that way?"

He was suddenly aware that he must sound stupid, and he realized that Anya was staring at him, her face a mixture of amusement and envy.

"Merral," Vero commented, "I need you. I cannot answer all the questions that will be asked. And the testimony of two is stronger than one. You have also seen and grappled with these things. If I went alone there might be a concern that it was my allegedly fertile imagination. Besides, this way, we take duplicate data. But don't you want to go?"

"Yes. . . . *No.*" He gulped. "I mean, I haven't really thought it through yet. And my family and Isabella. And Henri at work. I need to talk to them."

Vero looked at him, his brown eyes showing concern. "I understand exactly. But just think what has happened to us today. And think what is at stake. It is beyond computation."

Merral thought for a moment and swallowed. The words *Ancient Earth* seemed to thud in his mind. "No, you are right. We need to go."

Vero raised a finger in warning. "Oh, and Anya and Perena can give farewells and apologies once you are gone. But, in the meantime, no diary calls."

"Okay," Merral answered. "But I need things. I mean, I'm not prepared. Anyway, there's a waiting list for places."

Vero looked at him. "You need little. Perena has sorted the places out. I wasn't sure she could do it for both of us so I delayed telling you. It would hardly have been fair to disappoint you."

Merral turned to Perena. "So that is what you were up to! But how have you done it? It must have taken one of the representatives to get you on with an urgent priority status. There's always a waiting list for spare seats."

Perena grinned. "There's one power equivalent to the representatives in such matters and that's Space Affairs. For whom I work. And you are traveling on an urgent mission."

"But you didn't tell them? Surely not?"

Vero was smiling now. "No," he said, "but while you were getting your wound dressed, Perena and I talked about this. She suggested that, in view of the curious and alarming problem occurring to General Survey Craft *Nesta Lamaine* today, it was appropriate—even a necessity—to send the plate samples to Earth. On urgent-priority status. You and I will hand carry them for her."

Perena interrupted with a gesture. "But you *will* be taking plate samples and I would like an assessment—fast. *Please.*"

"I see," Merral replied, his brain still spiraling furiously around the concept, "but won't they know if they control the information networks?"

Vero looked at Perena.

"There were," she said, "two Space Affairs engineers going—Sabourin and Diekens. They have been asked to stand down and go on the next flight." She looked at the floor, as if embarrassed. "Unusually, their names have not been removed from the manifest. Even more unusually, they are keeping quiet about the fact that they are not going. You, er—just replace them. You are even dressed for the part."

Vero gave her a look of amused respect. "Captain Lewitz turns out to have an aptitude for duplicity—I think that is the word—that worries me. It must be that chess." He wagged his head. "Be careful, Perena, that it does not get you into trouble."

"We are all in trouble now." Perena's face had acquired a wry expression. "If it is a gift, then I trust I may be careful how I use it. But the hour seems to require it. Oh, and Vero, I ought to warn you, it won't be comfortable. Space Affairs are ruthless in making their own people take the roughest seats. And in an inter-system liner, the crew seats are down just above the engines."

Vero winced. "Vibration as well. But at least only for forty-eight hours." Then he sighed, and Merral was suddenly aware of how tired his friend was and how much he was forcing himself into the giving of these orders. Vero turned to the sisters. "Oh, Perena and Anya, you ought to try and get in touch with the representatives and ask for a meeting in two days' time."

Anya nodded. "Anwar Corradon is the current chair of the Farholme representatives; I vaguely know him. My perception is that he is an unusually intelligent and thoughtful man."

Vero looked around. "That, then, is the proposed plan of action. Are all in agreement with it?"

Everyone looked at each other and nodded.

Vero looked around. "Fine. Then let me suggest the following. I think we all need at least some sleep." He looked at Perena. "If you, Captain Lewitz, can get some of those damaged tiles cut off and packaged up. And check any satellite imagery when it comes in. Oh, and any chance of a new diary for me?"

"I can get you one," Perena said.

"Thanks. Anya, if you could look at those DNA samples. Perhaps a preliminary analysis? And prepare some duplicates for Merral to take to Earth. And can I get copies of that Maya Knella data too?"

Anya nodded.

"And finally, I need to talk to Brenito. I have many questions and some he may be able to answer."

"What about me?" Merral asked.

"And you?" Vero smiled. "You rest that ankle. But I wouldn't be surprised if Brenito might want to see you."

"When do we meet again?" Perena asked.

"Here? Ten-thirty tonight? To give us all the maximum time to do what we have to do."

As they left the room and began to walk up the corridor to the exit, Merral overheard Perena outline the journey to Vero, and suddenly he felt that he was in a dream. "You will be at Bannermene tomorrow noon. From there, you are booked on from Bannermene Inward Gate to Namidahl a couple of hours later. Namidahl is, of course, on the outer ring and you go one Gate clockwise to the Finent Node. From Finent there's a lot of traffic and depending exactly when you arrive, you should be at one of the Terran Gates with no more than two Gate jumps. Stress the urgent-priority status. So, all being well, in just over forty-eight hours traveling, you will be on Ancient Earth."

Merral felt his mind reel at the prospect. This was not a game of Cross the Assembly; this was the real thing. They were talking about his journey.

"Where are we sleeping?" he asked. Suddenly feeling overwhelmed with tiredness, he had a desperate need to lie down.

Perena patted his shoulder. "There is a spare room in the pilots' quarters for you and Vero. I'll get you another set of spare clothes each too."

Perena drove Merral and Vero to the quarters at the edge of the complex of landing strips and showed them to the spare room at the far end of the building. It was small and its basic furnishings gave it the air of a room that was only used as a place for people to sleep; yet it was, they agreed, quite adequate.

After Perena left, Vero sat on his bed and put his head in his hands.

"Are you all right?" Merral asked, conscious that his ankle was still hurting.

"That meeting . . . I wasn't sure I could manage to lead it. I knew I had to, but it was not easy. Thanks for your support." He rubbed his face. "I am out of my depth, Merral. Making decisions; giving orders. All that sort of thing. I am an ideas person."

"You did well."

"If I did, it was by the grace of God. But we will see what happens. You nearly threw me twice, you know."

"How? I didn't mean to."

"You sprung two new surprises. That you had seen a man and that there was evidence of a ship."

"I apologize."

"No, no, it wasn't your fault. In fact, I am sure that they will help to resolve things. But I need to think about them." And with that he fell silent.

17

When Merral awoke after a troubled sleep, it was midmorning. Vero had gone and there was a handwritten message on the table. *Gone to see Brenito. Back around midday. Suggest you stay out of sight and don't make diary calls. Vero.*

Merral rose, showered, and dressed his ankle again. There was food on the table and he made himself some coffee. He looked out of the window, but the quarters were at the end of a side runway and there was little to see other than bare rock baking in the warm spring sunshine. In the end, Merral went and lay down on his bed and stared at the ceiling, trying to make sense of what had happened.

Just after midday, Vero returned with food, drink, some more clothes, and a replacement diary. After checking that Merral's ankle was healing, he announced that if Merral felt he could manage it, Brenito would like to see him.

"I would be fascinated to meet him," Merral said. "His summons for help set so much in motion. And if I don't have to walk far, my ankle will be fine. How was your meeting with him?"

An odd expression slid across Vero's face. He frowned. "He listened. He was very disturbed about almost every aspect of our trip north. A number of things particularly alarmed him: Jorgio's vision, the creatures—of course, the imitation buzzard, the manipulation of the Gate and diary transmissions. Especially the bird. When I told him it wasn't a robot but was actually based on a dead bird, his eyebrows nearly flew off his head. And it was the first he had heard of Barrand's alteration of a re-created voice too. So, there was plenty for him to think about."

"Any answers?"

Vero seemed to stare at the wall.

"No, not really. He thought a lot, but he is a very cautious man. He said he was going to sleep on it when I left. He sleeps a lot. But no blinding answers. Maybe this afternoon will be better."

"You seem disappointed."

"Hmm. Oh, I suppose I had built my hopes up too much. Frankly, Brenito was far less help than I expected. I'm glad we will be at Earth in a few days; I need some answers and I think they may be able to give them to us. Incidentally, he took a special interest in my account of your exploits. 'Oh,' he said, 'I'm glad you found yourself a warrior. That's something, at least.'"

Merral shook his head. "I reject that title. I'm still very unhappy about what I did."

"I—as you know—have a different opinion," Vero answered, tilting his head. "As does Brenito."

Merral shook his head. "Nothing pleases me more about this trip to Ancient Earth than the prospect of handing over responsibility for all this. Vero, I want to turn the clock back. I want to go back to my trees."

"Indeed. I have decided I want to write and teach. May it be soon, for both of us. But in the meantime, let us eat."

After they had eaten lunch and Vero had restored his data to his new diary, they drove over to Brenito's cottage in a small four-seater that Vero had borrowed from Space Affairs. They had the windows open, and Merral, reveling in the smell of blossom and spring, found himself wondering whether Ancient Earth would smell the same. As they drove, Vero began to tell Merral more about Brenito.

"He was very distinguished in his day as an academic historian. On Ancient Earth he wrote several studies of early sentinel history under his full name of Brenito Camsar. He was a bit of a collector of things too, as you will see. Then in retirement, he felt he wanted to spend his last years doing something else. So he came out to replace Lars Mantell, who was sentinel here."

"I see. I just call him 'Brenito'? Not 'Sentinel Camsar' or something?"

"No, he's informal enough. I call him 'sir' out of deference. You need not."

They drove toward the headland on the southwestern side of Isterrane, and every so often there were glimpses of a cornflower blue sea down valleys or over fields. Then abruptly they turned off down a pale white track between silver-skinned poplars whose new leaves rustled in the breeze. At the end of the track, nestled between two low hills, was a wooden house painted white with faded yellow shutters.

After Vero parked, they walked through a neat vegetable garden set between trimmed hedges to a blue wooden door upon which Vero rapped his knuckles loudly.

There was the sound of movement in the house, and after a few moments, the door slowly opened to reveal a large, stooped man in an old gray suit with a faded sentinel badge on the left breast and a shirt that was open at the neck. Merral had seen images of Brenito before, but seeing him now in the flesh, nearly filling the doorway, he was surprised by how big a man Brenito actually was. Once, he must have been an imposing figure, but now any muscle had turned to fat. His face was a mass of creased flesh dominated by strangely pale gray eyes capped by faint white eyebrows, and his tightly cropped white hair was little more than a pale stubble.

Behind Brenito, Merral glimpsed a corridor filled almost up to the ceiling by glass cases, cabinets, framed images, and prints.

The old man looked from Merral to Vero, and then back again with hooded eyes. Then he leaned his jowled face toward Merral and smiled knowingly.

"Ah, welcome, Merral D'Avanos," he said in a heavy, resonant voice with a hint of a non-Farholme accent and slowly extended a large, soft hand. Merral noticed that he wore open-toed sandals through which large toes protruded.

Merral bowed and took the hand. "Sentinel Brenito, it is my honor."

A wry expression played across the heavy mouth. "Ah, come, let's not worry about honor, Forester. If we ever get to that, the Assembly is in a real mess."

Merral felt that if the voice was that of a man who had lived for a century, the sharpness of the riposte indicated a mind that had no weaknesses in it.

"Now, Verofaza," he added, "you come on in too. You look tired."

"I am slightly, sir, but it will pass."

"As do all things under heaven. I'm making tea. Excuse my clothes. But do take our hero through and give him a seat."

Merral felt that the dry, humorous tone went some way to easing the burden of his being termed "hero."

Vero led Merral to a long side room. Sunlight streamed in through the large glass windows at the far end, and Merral caught a glimpse of the sea, dazzling in its blueness. But his eye was drawn away by the extraordinary collection of mementos and antiques that dominated the room. A hundred items clamored for his attention: an ancient space helmet, fragments of exotic machinery, maps of strange worlds, signed images of men and women, and piles of old paper books. On one wall behind glass was a worn blue flag with the gold-encircled stone tower of the sentinel insignia in the middle.

"Take a seat," Vero said, motioning to an armchair of such an age that Merral wondered if it was another heirloom.

"Why, it's almost like a museum," Merral said, carefully moving his ankle past a plant pot mounted on a thruster nozzle and lowering himself gingerly onto the chair.

"History is part of sentinel culture," Vero said. "The past must not be forgotten lest the future be lost too."

"I can see that. But, for example, what is this?" Merral tapped a dusty, black metal box on a shelf.

From somewhere in the room a voice speaking in Communal rang out. "This is the navigation unit of the Assembly Seeder Ship *Vladimir Hengstra*. This ship seeded a total of thirty worlds from 2245–2585. Do you wish further information?"

Merral smiled. "No, thank you," he said to the unseen responding machine.

He turned to Vero. "I see. Everything is labeled. That voice is familiar."

"The younger Brenito. . . he recorded labels for all these things."

The door opened and the old man came in ponderously, carrying a tray on which were cups, a teapot, and a sliced cake. As Vero helped him put it down on the table, Brenito stared at Merral.

"Interesting, isn't it?" he said slowly. "The past, that is. But now, ironically, at the end of my earthly life, I find it is the future that preoccupies me. Now help yourselves. I still do a little cooking, and I hope the cake is to your satisfaction."

Then with sighs and gentle groans, Brenito seated himself in a massive wooden rocking chair that creaked under his weight. He turned to Merral. "First of all, thank you for coming. Increasingly, I have the belief that in summoning Vero here, I have played the part allotted to me. Now it is the task of Earth to deal with it and answer the questions. I have really, I suppose, asked you here to satisfy my own curiosity." He paused. "And yet I also want to tell you both something of what I think is going on."

"You know?" Vero asked with an urgent enthusiasm.

The big hands opened wide. "I have a hypothesis. No more than that. But as I thought about what you told me this morning, some ideas have come to me. And those tentative thoughts may give you something to think about as you travel. But first things first. Forester, shall I tell you why I summoned help?"

"Please."

"It is easy to tell: I dreamed of a field of stars and of a great red dragon that walked across them, swallowing the stars up one by one." The pale gray eyes gleamed at Merral. "The dream was repeated three nights running. It was a very powerful dream, like nothing I have ever had. And I knew that the stars were symbols of the Assembly worlds, and I knew that the first star to be swallowed up was Farholme. So I asked Earth for help. And so Verofaza came."

Merral looked at Brenito for a moment before answering. "I see. You have heard of the dream or vision that Jorgio Aneld Serter had?"

Brenito gave a slow nod and stared up at the ceiling for a moment. "The testing of the Assembly. The candles shaken by a gust of wind, a storm unleashed on Farholme. The command to watch, stand firm, and to hope. The similarities are marked, are they not? A threat to the Assembly, beginning at Farholme. But Jorgio's vision is more explicit and, I think, on Earth they will be very concerned about what it means."

Then he fixed his eyes on Merral. "Now, please, would you tell me your account of matters? If you could begin at Nativity?"

Merral began to summarize what had happened to him since Nativity. He was prompted every so often by Vero, who seemed otherwise anxious to retire into the background.

As he spoke, Brenito sipped his tea in an oddly delicate manner and listened, nodded, and frowned. Other than to dryly murmur things like "fascinating," "how curious," and "most alarming," he made little comment. Finally, when Merral had finished, he put his cup down shakily on the table.

"Quite remarkable," he pronounced. "Hearing it the first time from Verofaza was remarkable, and this second time from you is no less so."

Merral looked at the big man. "Sir, what is going on?"

Brenito made no answer but slowly rocked backward and forward. The creaking of the chair seemed to mingle with the sound of seagulls mewing outside. Then suddenly, Brenito lifted his head and stared at Merral with a strange, troubled smile.

"Ah," Brenito said slowly. "I researched the early history of the Assembly, years ago. Strictly, my period was 2120–2510, and the Rebellion was not in my scope. But you had to understand it; it cast a shadow over those years. For sentinels, as you know, it still casts a shadow. Now, I found much in your accounts that reminded me of the Rebellion, and I know that Verofaza has felt the same. When Verofaza and I discussed these matters earlier, the subject of the Rebellion kept coming up. It is almost as if Jannafy's 'Free Peoples' have crept back. But, as my young colleague here can tell you, they cannot."

Vero stared at the floor for a moment as if making a final deliberation and then looked hard at Brenito. "Sir, two points: First, the Rebellion was ended in a manner that would ensure its total termination. And all the accounts suggest a total annihilation of everything that Jannafy had set up. To use a horrid word, there was *sterilization*." Vero hesitated. "And second, the sentinels were set up shortly afterward to guard against any resurgence of what Jannafy had proposed."

Brenito nodded. "Oh, I agree. And across the length, breadth, and depth of the Assembly there has not been the slightest hint of anything surviving these last eleven thousand-odd years. Until . . ."

"Until now?" Merral said, feeling almost surprised at the sound of his own voice.

"Indeed," Brenito said and looked at Vero. "Briefly, for my benefit and for the benefit of Merral here, rehearse again the tale of the ending of the Rebellion."

Vero glanced at Merral. "I believe he knows it well, sir."

"That is as may be, but tell it again." Brenito sat back in his rocking chair, closed his eyes, and folded his hands over the expanse of his stomach.

Vero cleared his throat and began to speak. "Very well. With the rebels in command of the Centauri Colony and the Centauri Gate, the decision was taken, very reluctantly, to end the Rebellion militarily. The assault fleet was assembled and sent in late 2104; it arrived, apparently unsuspected, after an unparalleled six-year journey in 2110. Surveillance indicated that the colony had indeed been destroyed with massive loss of life and a new orbiting laboratory station made. Preparations were plainly advanced for colonizing missions elsewhere. The decision was made by Fleet-General Denion to attack, try to release any prisoners, and then destroy the complex. A previously untested poly-element fusion explosive device was armed and fitted to the frigate *Clearstar* under Captain Lucas Ringell."

Merral noticed that at this name Brenito opened one eye and looked across at him. Vero continued, his voice dry and factual. "Ringell and his men forced an entry into the station and established from the computer that there were no surviving prisoners. There was heavy fighting, with Lucas Ringell in the forefront and many casualties made worse by the loss of air pressure as the hull was blasted open. Finally, in an end chamber they faced William Jannafy himself. In the resulting fight, Ringell shot Jannafy and killed him. In the meantime, General Denion had retaken the Gate. The assault fleet regrouped and exited through the Gate an hour before the device exploded."

"Yes. A fair—if terse—account of humanity's last battle. And the results were what?" Brenito's eyes remained closed.

"The ship *Nighthawk*—incidentally, Merral, with Moshe Adlen on board—returned through the Gate a week after the explosion when the worst of the radiation had faded. They found that the devastation was even greater than predicted and that nothing but fine dust remained of the complex." Brenito opened both eyes and nodded at Vero to continue.

"And just over four years later, when the light reached Earth, the flash of the explosion was detected by even modest ground-based telescopes. The Rebellion ended with a bang. Nothing survived. The end of the story."

Brenito leaned forward to the teapot and carefully poured himself another cup. Then, sitting back in the chair, he looked hard at Vero. "Perhaps." His voice rang out in the room.

"I'm sorry?"

"You said, Verofaza, that it was 'the end of the story' and I said 'perhaps.'"

Vero stared at him. "Could you elaborate, sir?"

He sipped again at his tea. "Let me go back. There were many causes of the Rebellion, although only a few are now spoken of. Jannafy, for all the evil he produced, was a clear thinker. At least, at the start. He looked at the earliest versions of such things as the Technology Protocols and foresaw—perhaps better than his contemporaries—the society that they would produce. He saw that the Assembly would be stable but that the cost of that stability would be a restriction on what could be done. To him that was an unacceptable cost; he demanded total freedom. The name of 'The Free Peoples,' chosen by him for his followers, reflected that demand. That much, Forester, you know?"

Merral nodded.

"It is the part of the story that is generally told. Yet beneath Jannafy's general request for freedom, there were, if I remember rightly, two specific issues. The first issue, about which I know little, and which may—only *may*—not concern us, was to do with Below-Space exploration. You need to talk to your pilot—what was her name?—about that. She may know more."

"Perena Lewitz," Vero said. "But—if I may, sir—we don't explore Below-Space. We never have. The Gate system is a linkage of Normal-Space tubes carved through the upper levels of Below-Space. We travel through Below-Space, not in it."

"Oh, I know that, Verofaza," Brenito said. "But it was an issue. You talk to Perena Lewitz. And when, on Earth, you have found out what the issue was, come back and tell me. And bring this young lady with you."

Merral caught the hint of a faint flush of embarrassment on Vero's face. "Er, thank you, sir. She would, no doubt, be fascinated by much that is here. You have so many old things."

"Ah, at times I feel like an exhibit myself," Brenito said, and in his slow, heavy words Merral detected a great weariness. "Now the second specific grievance of William Jannafy—'that restless mind' as he was called—was what became called 'The Alternative Proposal.' Have either of you heard of it?"

Vero and Merral shook their heads.

"Briefly, it was this: At the end of the twenty-first century, as the Assembly was forming, the whole process of making worlds fit for humanity was in doubt. They knew we could reach them—if slowly—they knew we could alter their orbits and do all sorts of things, but with the atmosphere-modifying organisms then available it looked as if it would take forever—well, many tens of thousands of years—to produce worlds where men and women could live under an open sky. So some people, including Jannafy and those associated with him, came up with what he labeled 'The Alternative Proposal.' The phrase that came to be linked with it was 'to fit humanity to the worlds, not the worlds to humanity.' In short, they proposed major modifications of our species to produce new forms. These forms included—if I remember—beings modified to handle higher radiation exposures, heavier gravities, or even low oxygen levels. The modifications were to be genetic or mechanical."

Vero furrowed his brow. "I've never heard of this. Not in as many words. It sounds appalling."

"No," Brenito said, "you wouldn't have. If you had done further studies, Verofaza, it would have come up; it is on the postgraduate syllabus. But it is in a class of knowledge that, while not hidden, is not broadcast. You could find out about it freely in the Library, but you would have to know it was there. Now, you may wish to debate the wisdom of that on Earth, but there it is. Anyway, after the Rebellion there was no desire to have the idea discussed again. And as for it being appalling, well it is, but Jannafy presented it with a great deal of skill. Anyway, the proposal was resoundingly defeated and so—at least, we have always assumed—it passed into history. But it was over these two matters in particular that Jannafy and his supporters decided to forcibly secede from the infant Assembly. And from that came the Rebellion and its suffering."

There was an intense silence that was broken by a weary sigh from Brenito. "I am tired. But perhaps you now follow my train of thought. These creatures, as you describe them, seem to be exactly what Jannafy would have created. . . ." He stopped, staring into the distance. "And yet nothing survived. Nothing. Or so we have been told."

Vero gazed at Brenito, a range of emotions—consternation, bewilderment, even anger—crossing his face. "Sir, you believe that—somehow—something of what Jannafy and the rebels created has, despite everything we have been taught—survived? For so long? But where? How?"

Brenito sighed again. "Verofaza, it is a hypothesis only. Whether it is true is for Earth to decide."

"But, sir, isn't it obvious that the rebels were destroyed? We know that Jannafy was killed. I mean, I've seen the vid-clip from Lucas's shoulder cam. Once, out of curiosity. The helmet shatters, and blood droplets float everywhere in the vacuum. He was dead."

"Just so."

Vero continued. "And no one else could have escaped in the couple of hours before the blast. And they could hardly have outrun it."

"Oh, Verofaza, I know the objections—all of them. But—and you can tell the Sentinel Council this—I do believe that, somehow, the ghosts of the Rebellion have come to back to haunt us. And if they ask whether I mean ghosts literally you can tell them that old Brenito isn't ruling that out either. Not after that awful dead bird thing."

"I will, sir," Vero said with a slight bow of his head.

"Good. And another thing. Don't let them focus totally on these beasts and creatures. It will be easy to do because you now have the DNA and the images. But it's the invisible things—the spiritual dimension—that may be the biggest threat. We can eliminate these monstrosities with swords or a vortex blaster. But spiritual evil is less obvious and far more contagious. And it is harder to remove."

"I will remember that, too."

"And finally, on Earth I want you to look at the records—the primary sources, mark you—on the Rebellion. They might give clues. What was in the laboratory? I assume no one knew, but is that true? If anyone looked at the lab it would have been the crew of the *Nighthawk*, so you might want to look at Moshe Adlen's records."

"But they were published, weren't they? Aren't they in the Library?"

"Only an edited account was ever published. And, interestingly enough, the foreword to his *Accounts of the Centauri Military Expedition* says somewhere that this 'is all the material that he felt appropriate to publish.' The central sentinel office holds all Moshe Adlen's records in their vaults, and my memory is that when I looked at them—oh, fifty years ago—I found more in them than I had expected." Brenito rubbed his stubbly hair. "In fact, I made copies of parts, and probably still have them somewhere. If we had time—and if I could find them—I would show you the difference."

"That I will certainly do."

Brenito closed his eyes and shook his head slowly. "Oh, I'm sorry. I'm rather tired."

Vero rose to his feet. "I'm afraid I—we—have exhausted you, sir. We must go."

"I am getting frail. I sent a message the other week, but, Verofaza, if you could—when you have a moment—pass on the fact that it is time to find a successor for me."

The old man rose laboriously out of his rocking chair and stood upright, his big body gently swaying. "Of course, who they choose may well depend on how this matter turns out. But yes, I think I need to lie down. You can see yourselves out."

He turned to Merral. "Forester D'Avanos, I presume you will be returning to Farholme. When you come back, I would hope to see you. I would love to hear your account of the deliberations. And as a warrior—oh yes, I know you refuse the title—there is much here that would interest you."

"The Lord willing," Merral replied as they shook hands, "I will return. But I am not sure that what you have in mind will interest me. My concern is to get back to forestry."

There was a wry, slow nod. “May it be so. But don’t go back until we let you go. Please! We may need you.”

Brenito extended a hand to Vero. “And you—young Verofaza—I suppose you will not be coming back unless there is something—or someone—to bring you back.”

Vero’s face suddenly became void of emotion. “I have no idea, sir, what happens to me after the next few days. There are many issues for me to resolve. My father is not well. But I hope to be in contact with you at least fairly soon. I would like to return.”

“I understand. Do have a good trip. I will be praying for your deliberations.”

Vero turned toward the door and took a step forward. Then he turned back to face Brenito.

“Sir,” he said, his face turned to the ground, “I have a confession to make.”

Brenito looked surprised.

“You see, sir,” Vero continued hesitantly, and Merral glimpsed his fingers wrapping and unwrapping themselves, “I confess that I have entertained, well—doubts, about the worth of our calling. The thought had often come to me, until a few days ago, that what we sentinels were doing was a waste of time. That we were watching for something that would never happen.”

Then he looked up at the old man. “Suddenly, I find I have resolved my doubts. About what the sentinels do. We were right to watch. Moshe Adlen was right; those generations of sentinels—my ancestors, your ancestors—were right. Evil *was* lurking.”

Brenito stared at him and nodded almost imperceptibly. Then a wide smile split his face. “I am so glad to hear it, Verofaza. Your doubts were no secret. In fact, when I asked Earth for someone to be sent, I asked for the most skeptical person they could find.”

“You knew?” Vero looked startled. “But why?”

Brenito shrugged. “We didn’t want someone imagining evil where there was none, did we? We couldn’t afford that. Not again. You were sent here because of your vices, not because of your virtues. I hope that amuses you.” He stared at Vero and smiled broadly again. “Well done, anyway.”

A grin crossed Vero’s face and he bowed his head. Then he turned and, followed by Merral, left the room.

They had driven barely a few meters from the house when Vero began to laugh aloud.

“He knew all along! Merral, he knew! I would say that that was the funniest thing I've heard for a week, but that would be faint praise. Oh dear. I was sent here because of my vices, not because of my virtues. . . ."

Then, with a great reluctance, he seemed to push his amusement away. "But, Merral, my friend, do you think he's right? About the Rebellion?"

Merral stared at the poplars before answering. "Perhaps. Nothing else fits. Although I find it hard to come to grips with it. To believe that we got it all wrong? That—somehow—Jannafy's people escaped and have been hiding out somewhere for thousands of years?"

"I agree it's hard to take in. One of the things that I have taken for granted ever since I first heard the story of the Rebellion was that it was distant history. It was over. Every human being everywhere was part of the Assembly. But now?" Vero shook his head. "Now, I'm not sure I take anything for granted. Perhaps, I am not skeptical enough." He looked at Merral with his brown eyes wide. "I think that's the lesson, isn't it? Remember that what you think can't happen, may happen. Assume nothing. Rule nothing out."

Then Vero turned the vehicle out of the avenue of poplars onto the main road. "But, Merral, I rejoice that it is not my battle anymore. I will willingly hand it over to whatever council of wise men and women the Assembly comes up with. With very great gratitude. And I imagine you agree?"

"I do indeed, Vero. Let's hand this over to others as soon as we can."

That night Vero and Merral arrived at the isolation room before either of the women. Vero had brought with him the travel case that held his possessions. After all, he said, there was no certainty that he would be returning to Farholme. Merral, in contrast, simply had a small holdall that contained little more than the spare clothes he had been issued.

Shortly afterward, Anya and Perena arrived bearing parcels. After greetings and inquiries about Merral's ankle, everyone sat down.

Vero gestured to Merral. "Take over. Now you know as much as I do."

Merral glanced around. "Thanks. I think it's best we go round in turns. Who wants to start?"

Anya raised a hand, reached down to the floor by her, and put two identical packages on the table. With her face creasing into disgust she pushed the packages over to Merral. "Take them away, Tree Man and Earther. Duplicates. I don't want to see them again. Let someone else deal with them. They are horrid!"

Merral looked at her. "Samples of DNA and the datapaks?"

"And the Knella images."

"What do you want to say about them? The samples?"

Anya leaned back in her chair, her sky blue eyes looking hard at Merral.

"I got three different types of DNA out of your dirty clothes. Of such things is science made. Only one is human." She smiled. "Relax, Merral, you are one of us." There was laughter, but Merral felt that it was forced and shallow.

Anya shook her head. "The other two, however, were not human. Now, I have only done a preliminary scan; after all, they will put a whole team on this on Ancient Earth." She frowned and gestured with a finger at the packages. "There is no doubt that what you carry with you will cause an outrage. It confirms what I had first suggested. The ape-creature has three genetic components: gorilla, human, and what must be artificial code. The cockroach-beast parallels it; it has human and arthropod genes and, again, artificial code."

"There's no doubt they are a creation? Not a mutation or, well, a natural hybrid?" Merral asked, knowing the answer even as he spoke the words.

"No. Simply, no. First, the human DNA is similar in both cases: as if it was taken from the same stock. In fact, the human component is odd. Natural human DNA is rather florid, baroque; it has lots of extra bits on it. This is lean and neat: a sort of optimized human genetic code. Very odd."

Merral caught the imprint of distaste on Vero's face as Anya paused, looked around, and then continued. "Second, on the basis of your descriptions, I did a quick check for where the genes for reproductive organs would be in man and gorilla. They are absent. They cannot make themselves; they must be made."

Vero stared at her. "Forgive me, my biology is basic. These are organisms?"

"In one sense, yes. Of course they are. But I think I see what you are getting at. Unless they clone themselves they are basically—I'm sorry, this is such a negative thought—little more than biological tools."

Out of the corner of his eye, Merral saw Perena's face twist into an expression of disgust.

"And the cockroach-beast?" Merral asked.

"*That.*" Anya made a grimace. "Let me correct something here. I had thought that it was some sort of giant invertebrate with an exoskeleton. In fact, it seems, at first glance, rather similar to the ape-creature. I would guess that it has, basically, a human skeleton, but a thickened cuticle instead of skin as an outer covering, a sort of organic armor. Of course, then you have to make all sorts of changes to allow for movement and sweating, but I could see how it might be done. But . . ." She shrugged. "This is beyond me. Professionally, I would be interested to know what they come up with in a more detailed analysis, but personally I would be happy never to see or think of this again. I feel I need a shower."

There was silence and Merral looked around the room. *Things now are very different from last night; then we were reeling with shock and frightened; now we are more in control and our fear has turned to revulsion and anger.*

Merral looked at Vero. "Do you want to say what we learned today?"

"No," he said. "Not yet. I want to hear what Perena has to say."

Merral looked at Perena. "Captain Lewitz, anything to report?"

Perena gestured to two oblong packages that she had leaned against the wall. "Your tile samples. Hand carry them, please; there are addresses on them. I checked for radiation and there is none." She gave a shrug of her slight shoulders. "We need to know what did it. Urgently. And what is the range of such weapons? Can I suggest that once you have gone through the Gate, I get a ruling issued giving a minimum altitude for flights over the Carson's Sill and Lannar Crater area? Perhaps three thousand meters?"

Merral looked at Vero, who nodded agreement. "Good idea. Anything on the imagery?"

Perena put her diary on the table and tapped the screen. "Here. I haven't had a chance to look at it in detail."

A landscape appeared on the wallscreen. *Thermal imagery,* Merral decided, as he looked at the browns and yellows of land cut by the cold dark blue of the lakes, ponds, and rivers. Any large creatures or a ship should show up. Used to interpreting such maps for forestry purposes, Merral saw the anomaly quickly.

"There!" he snapped, pointing a finger at a cluster of small red dots and an orange oval outline to the north of the lake.

"Well spotted," Perena said with a nod. "Four kilometers from where I picked you up. I got an enhanced blowup."

A second image, but with a more grainy texture, filled the screen. There was a large, clearly marked orange oblong with four bright yellow points at the rounded corners. To the left of the oblong were five dull red dots, two of which were smaller than the others.

"The intruder ship?" Vero said, excitement in his voice.

"*An* intruder ship," Perena said. "It is only thirty meters long. A bit shorter than my *Nesta Lamaine*."

"Too small, right?" interjected Merral. "There were at least twenty creatures."

"Exactly," Perena said, in her quiet, unruffled way. "It's far too small to be an in-system machine, let alone one capable of inter-system travel. To me, this looks to be much more like the size of an Assembly ferry craft. That would be my guess. Carried inside a ship and used for local flights within the atmosphere."

Merral scrutinized the image carefully and caught Perena's eye. "Can you make anything of it technically?"

"A bit. It needs enhancement and an assessment by an aerospace engineering team. One other bit of data is on another image taken ten hours later. The ship has gone, but there are four scorch marks at the corner of the outline. But if I use imagination and assume that it uses a similar technology to what we have, I think here it's just landed." She nodded at the image. "Let me tell you why: The hot spots suggest four engines at the corners that are still warm. Confirmed by the corner scorch marks seen on later images. They suggest a vertical capability, probably with chemical engines. There is no hint of gravity-modification technology or anything even more exotic. There is little aerodynamic shaping; the front is only just slightly more pointed than the rear. So I read that as a low-speed craft, say Mach 2 or 3 maximum. I also find it interesting that there is no evidence of heating on what we presume are the front edges of the machine. So, no evidence of atmospheric entry. My guess is something small, subspace, and subsonic."

"And that it hasn't traveled far?"

Perena gave a pained smile, "Vero, you are asking me to pile supposition on guesswork. But normally a ferry craft wouldn't be used for a journey of more than about fifteen hundred kilometers."

Vero, leaning back in his chair, gestured at the image. "Perena, you make it sound just like one of our ferry craft."

Perena gestured at the packages by the wall. "I could be wrong. I have put copies of these for you to take; I want a team of engineers to look at them. But I *was* surprised at how familiar it seemed. It does not seem alien—whatever an alien ship would look like. But remember, it almost certainly cannot be the parent ship. You can see that by the comparison with the figures."

"I was going to ask about those," Merral said. "Are they human-sized? Bigger, smaller?"

"I did a rough check. The two smaller figures are within the range for human beings. The three others are something else."

"Ape-creatures?"

"So one presumes."

Vero looked up at Perena. "You think they are evacuating what is left of their forces?"

She nodded. "Feasible."

"And we have no idea where they have gone? where the mother ship is?"

"None. It's a big place up there, Sentinel. What? A million square kilometers?"

"Could you find it the same way?"

Perena shrugged. "It depends on how big the ship is and whether it is hidden. Remember playing hide-and-seek as children? If they don't want to be found, then it could be hard."

"This showed up fairly easily," Vero said, nodding at the image.

"This was probably an emergency mission." Perena's tone was terse. "And the area we were searching was vastly smaller."

Merral looked at Vero. "Well, that is a task for the Defense Force. But your turn, Sentinel. You'd better tell everybody what we learned from Brenito."

Vero started to summarize the conversation they had had with Brenito. When he came to Brenito's references to Below-Space exploration, he stopped and looked at Perena. "Can you help here? He thought you could."

Perena stared at her fingertips for moment before answering. "It is a part of space-flight history that I know little about, and I have never heard of Jannafy's name in connection with Below-Space exploration. But then, I wouldn't read too much into that. What do I know?" She hesitated before answering, apparently choosing her words. "The story is something like this: As soon as Gate technology was devised in 2068 there were efforts to use a single Gate as a portal to Below-Space. It was attractive. Building Gates gave us access through Below-Space, but to be able to fly within it would open the universe to us. Spatial physics theory suggested that enormous distances could be traveled very easily, giving speeds that were effectively ten or twenty times that of light. And the deeper you went into Below-Space, the faster you went."

Perena paused again, and as she did, Merral felt struck by the quiet, cool, and unflustered way she dealt with things. She continued. "At first, remote probes were sent, but very few returned. They confirmed the theory that the vast distances and vast speeds were possible, but there were problems. Navigation was hard. Anyway, in the last quarter of the twenty-first century there were—I think—twenty human missions, with two- to five-person ships. They were all failures. Most never returned. Two came back with dead crews, and finally, one ship returned with a living crew. But they were in a poor state and died shortly afterward. The ship was called the *Argo*. I know that because there is a tradition—which still exists—that no ship is ever to be called by that name again." Her face had acquired a troubled look. "Which is odd, really, because we have lost other ships. Anyway, after that, there was a decision to abandon the research. Then there was the Rebellion, and ever since we have been content to travel through Gates. After all, once they are set up they work very well."

She looked at Vero. "I was quite unaware that Jannafy wanted such research continued. I had assumed the Rebellion was over generalities, not specifics." She frowned. "But it fits with the man: rebellious, bold, and—as events showed—someone who could be reckless with human life. I would be interested to research that data. Mind you, much of the material may have been lost in the Rebellion. The Experimental and Projects Unit on Mars was devastated."

"I will make inquiries too," Vero added. "And it may only be of passing relevance. But the thing that Brenito told us that I feel is of real relevance was about Jannafy and 'The Alternative Proposal.'"

As Vero repeated what Brenito had said, Merral watched Anya and saw that as the details were recounted, her eyes widened with evident shock. The way she kept looking at the packages she had placed on the table earlier suggested that she had made the same connections as he and Vero had.

When Vero had finished, he looked at her. "So, Doctor Lewitz, comments? Please."

Anya stared blankly back at him. "I'm appalled . . . stunned. I find it hard to imagine how someone actually proposed making the very things that I—no—we have been so horrified about. But. . . . No, the time gap is too great. Even if we allow that Jannafy didn't just propose but *did* make these things—perhaps in the Centauri Lab—all those thousands of years ago . . . could . . . ?" She frowned. "No, the Rebellion was brought to an end."

Vero spoke in a low but audible voice. "Yes, history says that nothing survived. Jannafy and his followers were killed. Their labs were vaporized in the biggest artificial explosion ever created."

Anya nodded agreement. "No, for these things to have survived and got out here is too much. It must be coincidence. Mustn't it?"

But her questioning glance received no confirming response, and finally Merral, after looking at the clock, broke the silence. "Our time has gone. We'd better get over to the terminal to check in. Thankfully we can soon pass the burden of all this to Earth. But it has been helpful to discuss these things here. Vero, would you summarize what you think is happening?"

Vero stared ahead. "For me the strands of evidence suggest that something survived from the rebels. Whether some of Jannafy's followers, his teachings, or even—just possibly—something of what he created. But where, when, and how will, I think, be much debated over the next few weeks." He sighed. "As will be the still harder question of what is to be done."

Merral rose. "And that, I suspect, ends the Farholme deliberations on these matters."

"Indeed," Vero said with a nod as he rose. "Well, Forester, it's time for us to travel."

18

While the sisters went inside the terminal to try and ensure that formal embarkation procedures could be avoided, Merral and Vero found seats some distance from the building. Merral stared into the night. Away to his left was the main part of Isterrane City, where only a few lights remained in this first hour of the Lord's Day. Ahead, within the space terminal itself, there were lights and movement as families gathered for the imminent departure for the Gate. And to the right, spotlights picked out the curving fuselage and wings of the shuttle lined up on the runway.

"Two in the morning is an awkward time for a flight," Merral commented, as a wisp of vapor from the ramjets drifted upward and caught the light.

"I know, but to minimize the time people spend floating around at a Gate Station waiting for connections, someone has to start at a bad hour. And being the end of the line, it's Farholme. Anyway, today it suits us perfectly. We will be out of the system by midday."

Vero stopped, sniffing the night air. "I wonder," he said, "whether I will come back. I suppose they may just say, 'Thanks, Sentinel Enand, but we'll handle it from here.'"

"Do you want to come back?" Merral asked, looking at the lights of Isterrane and thinking with a sudden pang of emotion of his own town and his family.

"I've grown to be quite fond of Farholme; Worlds' End isn't that bad a place. And I have grown fond of the people; particularly you, Anya, and Perena." Vero paused, and Merral read much into his momentary silence. "But I need to go back. Above all, my task is not quite finished; I have to be sure that all this is sorted out. Then I will think of my future. I need to see my father."

Suddenly, Merral found his longing for his family more than he could bear. "Vero," he blurted out, "I need to leave a message with my parents. And Isabella. May I?"

Vero hesitated. "It will be just after one in Ynysmant. So they will all be asleep. Oh, I guess so. Just leave a message: say you are going on a private trip, that you are going to be out of touch. Whatever words you can find. But remember that your call may be monitored."

That alone, Merral thought wearily, *is cause for concern. Is privacy the first victim of these events? Until this is resolved, will anyone ever again have the confidence that his or her conversations are their personal and private affair?* He suspected from her earlier outrage that Anya would have agreed.

A new thought struck him. "What about giving them a contact? In case they need me."

"Ah. Oh, tell them to get in touch with Anya. She can pass it on. In two days she can give your address on Earth. Diaries are switched off on shuttles and liners anyway."

Merral found the mental image of his mother hearing that her youngest child—her only son—had gone halfway across the Assembly without telling her, almost overwhelming. That would raise a few eyebrows permanently. Few, if any, people in Ynysmant had been to Ancient Earth, and no one he had ever heard of had gone at a day's notice.

Merral found himself staring into the darkness as yet another new thought struck him. "But when am I coming back?" he asked, all too aware of the consternation in his voice.

"Back?" He saw Vero shrug his shoulders. "If they move quickly, you could be back in days with the Defense Force ships. They don't bother with waiting at Gate Stations. Just in one Gate and out the next. You could do Earth to Farholme in twenty-four hours. You'll feel lousy. But it can be done."

So I could be back in a week, Merral thought and wondered if he would see anything of Ancient Earth other than offices. He walked a few meters away from the seat, called his mother's diary, and was told—inevitably—that she was asleep.

"Hi, Mother and Father," he dictated. "Vero and I just got back safely from the north. But I have some urgent work to do. I will be out of touch for a few days. You can reach me through Anya Salema Lewitz at the Planetary Ecology Center. Love to you and the rest of the family. Merral."

When, however, a minute later he called Isabella, he was surprised to find that she answered in person. "Oh, er, hi, it's Merral," he spluttered. "I thought—"

"Merral! Where are you? I've been getting worried." Her smooth voice radiated concern, and the message he had prepared—similar to that sent to his mother—evaporated from his mind.

"Why, Isabella, I thought you'd be asleep. It's after one o'clock with you."

"Yes," came the answer. "I was just about to switch the diary off. I've been lying awake. Why don't you switch to visual? I'm decent."

Hearing her voice with its inviting, affectionate tone, Merral felt a desire to confide in her. He wanted to tell her the awful truth about the north and the awesome news that he was on his way to Ancient Earth. But he couldn't. *After all,* he told himself unhappily, *even now they might be listening in.*

"I'm under starlight. It's not worth it," he answered. *Just as well really,* he thought, remembering that he was wearing a uniform that was not his.

"Fine, Merral. We stay on audio then. But I have tons of questions, *tons.*" She paused. "I mean, the screen says you are in Isterrane. But how did you get there from Herrandown?"

"Ah. We had a lift from a general survey craft."

"My! That's a very odd way to travel. But it went well? What did you find out?"

With something of a shock Merral understood that the perception that he valued in Isabella was now turned against him.

"Well . . ." He paused, aware in the gloom that Vero was stirring, as if he had just realized that this was a live conversation. "Well, we have a lot of data. But it would be premature to say anything. I hope to be able to sort everything out soon."

"So, no beetle-men?" The tone was curious.

Merral hesitated. "That would be telling. But I can't talk too long. Look, I have to go away for a week or so. Work." He felt the word sounded unconvincing.

"Without coming back to Ynysmant?" She sounded shocked, even affronted. "But where? Faraketha or Umbaga?"

"No. But I can't say."

"You can't say! And you're calling me now. Truly strange. So, can I call you when you get there?"

"Er, you can try. You can get me through Anya Salema Lewitz at the Planetary Ecology Center in Isterrane."

"So this Anya Lewitz knows?" There was a hint of misgiving in her voice.

Merral could see Vero coming over to him.

"Yes, that's the way it is. Look, I have to go. Sorry."

There was a pause before Isabella answered, a pause only the merest fraction of a second long.

"Apologies accepted," she said, in a cool way. "Have a good trip. I mean, are you traveling a long time? More than a day?"

Merral was aware that Vero was waving his hand disapprovingly at him. He reached for the Terminate tab.

"Sorry. Can't say. Call Anya in forty-eight hours. Bye!"

Then he switched off.

"Sorry, Merral." Vero's tone was flustered and apologetic. "I mean . . . well . . . I wouldn't ordinarily intrude, but I thought you were just going to leave a message. I was worried you might give too much away."

"No, my apologies," Merral sighed. "Of all the times! She was still awake. I only told her I was going to be traveling for a bit."

"Did you mention how long?" There was alarm in Vero's voice.

"I suppose that I implied a couple of days. They could hardly . . . could they?"

"Oh, they could. You can get anywhere in Farholme in less than that. And why from here, Isterrane Strip, an hour before the Gate shuttle goes? If they were listening . . ."

"Sorry," Merral sighed. "I'm tired, Vero. I hope that wasn't too much."

"Well, maybe there's nothing they can do. We may have damaged them badly. Let us hope so."

Merral slid his diary back on his belt and sat down on the seat.

"How are you feeling?" Vero asked.

"The ankle aches but it's okay. I'm just tired. And numbed, I guess. The idea that next time I sit out under stars they will be those of Ancient Earth. It's all too much."

"I know. You'll find it a shock. But I think you will manage it better than me."

Then they fell into a long silence. Merral found that his mind was still racing. For some time, he sat there watching the activity around the shuttle as hatches were closed and the control surfaces on the flaring wings and twin tail were flexed. As Merral stared at it, the thought struck him that he now knew that this was not the only type of vessel to have transited Farholme's atmosphere over the last months.

New questions flooded his mind. What did this other ship look like? Did it have the same age-old lines as this? Was there just one? Did it, too, refuel in space from cometary ice, or did it have some novel energy to fuel its awesome speeds? If so, then why had it come in so fast, when it might have done so in near silence? As he stared at the vast white vessel, he was suddenly struck by the notion that the biggest issue centered on the fact that, whatever adorned the sides of its hull, it was not the emblem of the Lamb and the Stars.

He decided that he had thought long enough about the intruders and tried instead to comfort his mind with thoughts of Ancient Earth. He pictured its clouded pearl blue surface, its history, its knowledge, and its peace. He imagined the Council of Stewards: wise, concerned, and helpful. He allowed himself to picture the inevitable and solemn commissioning of the Defense Force and their proceeding at maximum speed to Farholme to render assistance.

Then realism took over, and he decided that his time would be more sensibly spent in prayer. He committed himself, his journey, and those he would leave behind into the hands of the almighty Father.

A few minutes later Perena and Anya came back. After sharing out the packages between them, they walked into the Embarkation Terminal. Merral found that there were fewer families waiting to see loved ones off than he had expected. But then, most farewells would have been said earlier in homes or at formal or informal parties. *How strange to have missed all that.*

Through the high windows, Merral could see what he assumed were the final checks being completed on the shuttle. Through its small round windows, they could see passengers taking their places silhouetted against the cabin lights. Merral noticed the name *Shih Li-Chen* inscribed beneath the cockpit in Communal and what he took to be the Old Mandarin script. Shih Li-Chen, he recollected: poet, church leader, and—unsurprisingly for early twenty-first-century China—martyr.

Perena, standing next to Vero, gestured at the ship. "Normally, I would have shown you around and introduced you to the crew."

"Next time, Perena," Vero replied. "For now, the fewer who know who we are, the better."

Perena turned to Anya, who had been standing quietly by, staring out of the window, her usual ebullience apparently subdued by the impact of the night's news.

"Sister, you want to say good-bye before I see these guys into their seats?"

Anya smiled at Vero and Merral. "Safe traveling, guys. I really wish I was going for the ride."

"Personally," Vero muttered in an aside, "I wish I could miss out on the ride."

"It's a pity we can't all go," Merral said.

Anya wrinkled her nose. "Your plants will wait, Tree Man, but my animals won't. But I'll pray that you get some good counsel on Ancient Earth, and I look forward to seeing you come back with the Defense Force. Both of you."

Then Anya hugged them both in turn, and Merral fancied that her hold on him was longer and firmer than he might have expected. And was it too, he wondered briefly, more appreciated by him than it should have been? Merral was aware that, behind all the awesome news they had to take with them, there lay other personal issues that had to be resolved. His thoughts were interrupted by Perena gesturing them toward a service tunnel.

Carrying their baggage, Merral and Vero followed her along the tunnel. An approaching luggage hexapod moved to one side as they approached it, raising a forelimb in a mechanical gesture of acknowledgement. They passed it and walked through a complex hatch system that led to the rear crew compartment of the shuttle. The compartment was compact, low-roofed, and rather basic, and Merral felt that, with the six or more people in uniform in it busily packing equipment, it seemed almost cramped.

Perena smiled at someone by the door who Merral took to be a steward. "The two seats for Sabourin and Diekens, please," she said, while Merral looked around, taking in the soft cream and yellow seating, the small portholes, and the neatly labeled hatches, ducts, and containers extending around and along the curved walls and between the seats. It occurred to Merral that if he had taken after his father and had had a greater affection for mechanical means of transport, he would have known far more about the shuttle and had some idea of the function that everything served.

The steward checked a listing and pointed to a pair of couches in a corner by the rear wall. Perena came over with them.

"I must go," she said, almost under her breath, "but my prayers go with you."

She hugged Merral and turned to Vero.

Suddenly, Perena's reserved and cool expression slipped, and Merral caught an emotion of fear and strain on her face that he had never seen.

"Vero," she whispered as she clutched him tightly, and Merral could only just make out her words. "We need help."

"I think help will be here soon," Vero replied in a near whisper.

"Please," she begged, her subdued voice suddenly thickened in urgency. "I can feel it. It's a spiritual concern. I feel—somehow—that there is something hateful here. Make sure help arrives."

Then she released Vero and her face seemed to regain a look of calm nonchalance. A crewman settled down into an adjacent couch and a female voice warbled from a loudspeaker somewhere. "Captain here. Five minutes before takeoff is initiated. All ground crew, please leave now."

"Vanessa Lebotin," Perena said, apparently forcing her mouth into a smile. "She nearly beat me at old-time chess only the other month."

"Perena," Vero said softly, "I note your concern. I agree. I will do all I can. See you soon."

Perena closed her eyes briefly, nodded, and then suddenly—as if to avoid revealing any emotion—turned, wove her way through the other dark-blue-uniformed personnel, and left by the hatchway.

Vero looked at Merral and sighed. Then he sat down and began to adjust his couch and, amid the sound of hatch doors closing and pumps whirring, Merral followed suit.

As Merral lay there, he decided that he should have said farewell to his family better. *My father, with that love for transport machinery that I do not share, would doubtless have endlessly briefed me about the types of shuttles and their engines and what to look out for. My mother would have worried and flustered and forced me to take spare clothes. Instead, here I am, knowing almost nothing about where I am going and what I am doing when I get there.*

He turned to Vero who was reading the instructions on a small packet marked "For Travel Nausea. Adult Strength."

"A stupid question, Vero. Where exactly on Ancient Earth are we going?"

"Incidentally, when we get there you just call it Earth. It's not pride; it's just that there isn't any chance of confusion. Anyway, where we land depends on which of the five Terran Gates we come out of. That depends on getting the best connection, just as in Cross the Assembly. From what Perena said, Beijing III is the most probable. If so, we take the long-haul passenger flier to Jerusalem. It is late spring there, too, so the weather should be fine." He paused and gave a little dry laugh. "Just as well; I've left that coat behind. Do you remember it?"

At the memory of Vero's ridiculous coat and their first meeting, Merral felt an amusement stained only by a fierce longing to be back in his own bed in his own house.

Then the takeoff launch instructions began. There was the hymn of the Assembly and the appeal to the Lord of the heavens for mercy and protection. After taxiing to the longest runway, there were the final commands, the rising vibrating roar of the engines just behind his head, the brief race down the runway, and the little skyward bound. Amid a rumbling vibration the ship flew upward and southward. Within minutes, though, they were in level flight, and with Merral watching their journey on the wallscreen, they crossed Hassanet's Sea at ten kilometers altitude.

Just as Merral felt himself sliding into a doze, Vero nudged him. "Hold on. We are over the equator now. Serious acceleration is about to begin any minute now."

The ship swung round to face eastward and tilted upward, with his seat rotating under him in response. Seconds later, there was a double warble from the speakers and a booming roar engulfed the cabin, making the storage cabinets rattle and the roof fixtures sway. Merral, forced down into his couch under the acceleration, closed his eyes and tried to think of something more pleasant.

Within a dozen minutes, the force and the vibration had waned, and out of the window, Merral was able to see sunlight glinting on the wingtips.

Dawn in space. It gave him an odd feeling.

He watched as Vero slowly took hold of his sleeve, lifted it, and let it drop. But it didn't drop. It floated there, devoid of weight.

Extraordinary. Zero g.

And he fell asleep.

When Merral woke up later, it took him a long time to come to terms with where he was. Only when he stared out of the porthole to see the blackness of space and the sharp pinpricks of stars and felt his limbs float up against the restraining straps was he sure that it really was not just a dream. For a moment, he thought they had stopped because of the silence; then he heard the distant hum of the engine pumps.

Aware of a full bladder, he unstrapped himself and, mindful of the fact the only experience he had of zero g was ten minutes in a traveling simulator as a student, made his way carefully to the lavatory cubicles. Then, grateful for the fact that, despite the costs of the technology, created gravity existed in shuttle washrooms, he drifted back over to the window. Everybody else in the compartment seemed to be busy, either working on their couches or, like Vero, asleep. *At least,* Merral reflected, *traveling among people who do this on a weekly basis, I don't have to queue to look out of the window.*

As he stared through the gold-tinted glass, at first all he could see was the stars, perfect and clear against the flawless blackness. *The night sky,* he told himself, before remembering that this was the permanent reality of space. By tilting his head he could just make out the blue and brown curve of Farholme below, its edges blurred by the atmosphere.

A few minutes later the starscape rotated slowly, and Merral reached out for the wall for some sort of stability. Now, hanging above the eternal black backdrop, the sprawling silver tubes, spheres, and cylinders of the Gate Station came into view. Merral stared at it, blinking at the brilliant glitter of the silver foil-coated block of captured comet at the edge of the fuel processing section and tentatively identifying the central station complex. There, protruding delicately from the middle of the cylinders, like a mast on a homemade raft, was the matte, titanium gray, stub-ended long column of the intersystem liner. With its hexagonal cross-section, Merral realized that it looked like an enormous pencil.

But was it really enormous? The scale was impossible to tell, and for a moment, Merral had a fancy in which all he was looking at was merely some tiny but immaculately crafted model a few centimeters across. Then, floating over the fuel storage tanks and casting a tiny distorted pitch-black shadow below, he made out the shape of a general survey craft, some sister vessel to the *Nesta Lamaine*, and the sense of scale became apparent.

Then there was another course change, and one by one the dazzling bronze yellow Gate beacons rotated into view. He peered at the midpoint of the six beacons, straining his eyes until he saw, glinting dully, a minute metallic object. *The Gate*, he said to himself in awe. *I can see the Gate with my naked eye!*

The call came to return to seats before deceleration, and he drifted back and buckled himself in.

With what Vero sleepily remarked was "typical Assembly caution," it took fifteen minutes from the first gentle echoing tap of the *Shih Li-Chen* docking with the Farholme Gate Station until, to the accompaniment of various whistles and hisses, the hatchway opened to reveal a corridor into the station. Floating over to the exit, laden with their bags and the plate samples, they left the *Shih Li-Chen*, drifted into one end of the gravity transition corridor, and walked out of the other at the ferry car system.

After ten minutes of travel down tunnels and along corridors with only the briefest of glimpses of space and stars, Merral and Vero were unloaded at the lower entrance to the *Heinrich Schütz*. They walked into the gravity transition corridor and at the other end floated their way out into the crew and technical section.

As Vero asked for the locations of the couches for Sabourin and Diekens, Merral looked around in awe. He had, he supposed, been unimpressed by the interior of the *Shih Li-Chen*, which had seemed little more than an exaggerated and overlarge general survey craft. But this was different.

Merral knew, of course, that the *Heinrich Schütz*, as an inter-system liner, was one of that order of vessels known as the "Great Ships." Other than their size, the distinguishing feature of their order was the fact that their designers had had a freedom to work denied to them in the lesser craft that had to fly through atmospheres. He had seen many illustrations of the interior design of the Great Ships, but to be inside a real one, rather than a simulation, was somehow a very different experience. The results, honed over generations, were, to Merral's eyes, an outstanding and eye-catching triumph.

His first thought as he looked around was that it reminded him of being in some enormous and fantastic seashell with a spiral-curved floor sweeping upward above him and linking fluidly with the walls and the central column. The impression of being in a natural organic structure was aided by the scarcity of straight lines, the pale milk-and-honey coloring, and the smooth porcelain texture of the walls. Abundant lighting, whose source appeared to be everywhere and nowhere, lit the interior so that the whole ship seemed to glow as if it were a translucent shell illuminated by sunlight.

Then, suddenly, Merral's point of view changed, and he saw himself at the base of a high ancient tower with a vast snowy marble ramp sweeping gracefully through buttresses and archways up a score of levels in smooth, gentle, stepless curves. In the end, he concluded that both views were true; the interior was both organic *and* architectural.

"Over here." Vero's voice intruded into Merral's contemplation.

"Sorry. I was just taken aback by it. It's beautiful."

Vero gave his friend an amused grimace as he gestured to a pair of couches. "It's some compensation for the turbulence when we go through Below-Space. But I have to admit that the Assembly designers were surely right in thinking that a purely functional form was not an adequate response to the privilege of traversing Below-Space. You were told Horfalder's maxim?"

Merral tugged himself forward on a strap and floated over to where couches protruded at the edge of a fluted ridge curving out from the towering central column. "Horfalder? I remember something, but you tell me."

"She was head of the design team for the Composer Class; she said that as the average distance covered by an inter-system liner between Gates was equivalent to around fifty years of space flight, the least they could do was create a structure that you could live with for a half century. Even if you were only in it for a few hours."

Merral looked around again, considered Horfalder's wisdom, and found it good. Then, having stowed his holdall and the plate sample in a compartment under the couch, he lay down, trying not to float off, and stared around again. Now, though, as he looked harder, he realized that underneath his first complementary images of the shell and the tower he could see the ship as a machine. As he stared upward he could imagine the twenty-odd levels above him as distinct compartments, and glancing around he could see, concealed in one way or another, all the lockers, access panels, handholds, and information screens that such a ship needed.

With the final preparations being made around him, Merral strapped himself down and found a switch that lowered a screen down just in front of his eyes. On it he was able to read about the composer Heinrich Schütz, and he marveled again that anybody could have dedicated music to the Almighty during a war that lasted thirty years. Then as he chewed the simple food that was passed around, he glanced at the explanatory section on the ship itself.

He could easily imagine how much his father would have enjoyed reading about the Composer Class (prototype built in 9101, the *Heinrich Schütz* being the twenty-fifth of the second series) and its lifespan of around a thousand years before a complete renovation was needed. Yet now, more than ever, he found himself with little appetite for machinery or mechanics. With more interest, he went through the elementary introduction to Gate travel with a well-done and elaborate version of the traditional analogy of the two ways of getting across a narrow but deep estuary.

Travel in Normal-Space, it reminded him, was analogous to the long, slow journey round the edges, while the Gate travel was like taking a shortcut through a tube running directly through the waters. It was a familiar illustration, but now, on the verge of taking that shortcut, it had a new relevance. The illustration was developed to explain some of the Below-Space features such as the notorious turbulence, which was here portrayed as being analogous to the buffeting of the estuary's water against the tube. Then, balking at a treatment of plasma engines, Merral allowed the screen to retract.

Eventually, just before ten o'clock, the last door closed and Captain Bennett gave her welcome from the speakers. After that the Assembly hymn was played and there was the traditional solemn appeal to the sovereign Lord on undertaking Below-Space travel, with its acknowledgement that such travel was a privilege and its request for safe arrival.

At exactly ten o'clock, just as the "Amens" were dying away, there was a dull thud as the linkages detached themselves. Slowly, Merral heard a gentle low-frequency rumble begin behind him and his couch began to sway ever so slightly. He lowered the screen to where he could read it and checked the flight plan. They would swing in a wide arc clear of the station to align themselves exactly above the hexagon at what was known as the burn-point. There, at 10:40, the plasma engines would ignite at full burn to start the rapid straight-line acceleration that would give them the ten-thousand-kilometers-an-hour speed needed to coast quickly along the Normal-Space tunnel linking the Gates. At 10:55 they would enter Farholme Gate, emerging a mere ten and a half minutes later at Bannermene Gate. Forty light-years away.

Merral lay back, feeling pushed slightly down into his couch by the acceleration's comforting semblance of gravity that a wall sign declared to be 0.6 g. He was still tired, and in his brain a thousand thoughts seemed to be chasing each other.

Some of the dozen people around him in this part of the Space Affairs section were busy monitoring the ship and the passenger levels, while others were plainly relaxing or sleeping. One or two were walking buoyantly from the lift section in the middle of the ship.

Eventually Merral closed his eyes, wondering if he was tired enough to sleep through both burn-point and the Below-Space transit. He was aware that some people claimed to have slept through Gate passage, but most stayed awake due to the buffeting and those various psychological effects such as disorientation that were common, but which still eluded comprehension. Merral tried to get his mind to relax and encouraged it to concentrate on nothing. *Imagine a white snow field,* he told himself, *during a blizzard.*

"Sentinel Enand? Forester D'Avanos?" The voice was urgent.

Startled, Merral opened his eyes to see a man in a dark blue uniform bending over him, clutching the side of the couch.

"Yes? I'm Merral D'Avanos," he answered, wondering with some alarm how this man knew his name.

"I'm Charles Frand, Second Communications Officer." The angular face with a thin black moustache had an expression that seemed to request immediate action. "Captain Bennett needs to see you both now. There's been an odd message. Can you both come forward to the bridge please? Immediately. We will be at burn-point in minutes."

A look of profound alarm crossed Vero's face as he gingerly unstrapped himself. "Odd . . . ," he murmured.

Together, they walked unsteadily across the floor to the elevator tube, aware of others watching them. As they accelerated up through the central spine of the ship, Vero, gripping a hold-bar tight, stared at Merral. "I don't like it," he muttered. "I don't like it at all! There is barely half an hour before we leave the system."

The door opened into the high-roofed command cabin. Merral was vaguely aware that the spiral theme continued here, with the space being dominated by a single sweeping floorway that ran in a smooth curve from the base up to the vaulted ceiling. On this grand sweep was a series of pastel-colored consoles all facing one high, flat wall, on which an enormous image of the Gate appeared. Merral felt sure that the screen surface must match a plane of the hexagonal outer surface.

"Created gravity here, careful," Officer Frand said. "Captain's up to the right. Blue console."

Gripping the sculpted handrail, they walked up the gentle sweep of the floor. As they did, Merral looked across at the screen, recognizing that the image was a computer-generated illustration showing the Gate from an oblique angle. Incomprehensible data readouts shimmered around the edges of the screen.

A lean woman with blonde hair in a tightly coiled braid rose stiffly from her seat and turned to them as they approached the cluster of three consoles grouped on the top of the slope that evidently formed the bridge. *The captain,* Merral thought, seeing the two yellow flashes on her shoulders.

She greeted them with an abrupt and rather cool handshake.

"Captain Leana Bennett," she announced in a precise, truncated way that mingled authority with perplexity. Looking at her tanned face with its fine etching of lines, Merral realized she was his mother's generation, but of a very different character. There was a tautness and precision about Captain Bennett's frame, face, and manner that told you immediately why the Assembly trusted her with over three hundred lives and an almost priceless ship.

"And you are not Engineers Sabourin and Diekens. Rather, you are instead a sentinel and a forester. How very irregular." She looked sternly at them for a second with piercing dark brown eyes. "But that can wait. This came in five minutes ago. Comms, show it, please." She pointed to a small screen on one of the adjacent consoles.

A flickering image of Perena Lewitz appeared. "Captain Bennett, this is Perena Lewitz, Captain of the *Nesta Lamaine*." Merral strained to hear the voice, which was slightly distorted.

"This is very urgent. I am unable to access you through normal channels. I have just received an unusual message, which I think I trust. It says that your ship must not enter the Gate. Repeat: not enter the Gate. There is a peril there. The problem is related to Sentinel Enand and Forester D'Avanos who are occupying the couches of Space Affairs Engineers Sabourin and Diekens. They may be able to explain the situation. But, I repeat, I have been warned that your ship must not enter the Gate. I suggest you return to Gate Station and—"

The image on the screen froze, broke into lines of static, and faded away.

"Return to Gate Station?" Vero whispered in alarm. "But we *have* to go through. . . ." Then he stopped and stared at Merral, his eyes glinting. Intuitively, Merral knew they both had the same thought: *Is it her*?

Vero turned to the captain. "I suppose the message is, well—authentic?"

"Authentic? That's an odd way of putting it. Charlie?" The captain turned stiffly to Officer Frand who gestured his bewilderment with a shrug and an opening of his hands.

"Captain, gentlemen," he said, "all I can say is that it came in just now by one of the backup communications links. One of the old laser systems. Out to the Gate Station and then bounced on to us. It's hard to verify. I mean, we take these things on trust. But—" He turned a perplexed gaze to the captain. "Why wouldn't it be authentic?"

"Don't ask me, Charlie." She looked bewildered. "Why are these men not Sabourin and Diekens? This is beyond me. But it looked and sounded like Captain Lewitz to me."

"Two minutes to burn-point, Captain," came a quiet voice from the console to the right. Merral glanced at the wallscreen to see that they were now nearly face-on to the hexagon and that in the bottom right corner, one set of digits had just counted down below 120.

"Helm Officer," the captain responded crisply, "proceed as scheduled."

Then her brown eyes turned back to Vero and Merral, shifting from one to the other in careful scrutiny. "Naturally, I immediately tried to contact her. I also instigated a check on the Gate and have asked Gate Control for a full update."

With a quick gesture of a finger she summoned a slight young man with cropped brown hair from a console at a lower level. He bounded up energetically toward them with an active datasheet in his hand. Then she lifted an inquiring eyebrow at Officer Frand, who had been checking an adjacent console screen with another officer.

"Captain," Frand said, "still no response from her diary. It's apparently switched off. But it's the Lord's Day and meeting time, so there's no surprise there."

"Yes. Except if she did try and call us." Captain Bennett turned her troubled face to the man who had just arrived. Merral noticed a neat yellow hexagon badge on his blue overalls.

"Gateman Lessis," Captain Bennett said in an urgent way. "review the Gate systems. In view of this message."

The Gateman turned to her, his back straight. "Captain, I report that the Gate seems normal." The tone was intelligent, confident, and unruffled. "I have reviewed all our data and that from Gate Control. All readings are within normal limits."

Merral had the impression of a man with a sharp mind, thorough training, and total mastery of his field. He would, he told himself, have expected nothing less.

"Thank you, Mikhael. Please stay for a moment. So you see, gentlemen, I have a real problem. I know Perena slightly but there is not enough evidence for me to abort. Indeed *no* evidence. If we return to Gate Station it will be at least six hours before we can reenter the Gate. That will throw up a lot of problems for connections." Captain Bennett turned pensive eyes first on Merral and then on Vero. "Do either of you have any new data?"

"Captain," Merral appealed, "I need to talk to my friend here. For a moment only."

The captain flicked a glance at the screen. The image now was of a fully symmetrical hexagon, and in the corner of the screen the seconds counter now stood at ninety seconds.

"You have just over a minute," she said politely, and turned to peer at the Gateman's datasheet.

Merral and Vero took a step back and faced each other.

"Vero, is it a trick?" Merral asked, searching to see any indication in his friend's eyes as to whether they should trust the message.

"It must be. . . . Surely it's a trick to stop us from leaving?"

Merral forced himself to think. He was aware that he was tired, aware that it was a complex matter, aware that the seconds were ticking away, but also aware that he had to make a right decision. It sounded like Perena, but now he did not automatically believe anything on a screen. And to be summoned back now? *Lord, grant wisdom and overrule if we get it wrong.*

A sudden revelation struck him. *Supposing I look at the problem the other way about, as with an inverse logic? Think like a sentinel. Put myself in the shoes of the intruders. If I wanted to stop this ship, would I have done it this way?*

"No!" he blurted out, suddenly certain. "It's a genuine message. The intruders would have faked a direct message to the captain. To do it this way makes no sense."

"Right." Vero blinked nervously. "Yes, I back you."

They turned to face the captain, who was looking expectantly at them.

"It's a real threat," Merral said with as much urgency as he could muster. "Believe me. It's unparalleled, but it's real."

Behind her he could see the screen saying there were twenty seconds left. The captain's cool, unflustered eyes flicked to Vero.

"Yes," Vero added, "a genuine warning of genuine peril. Please return to Gate Station."

Captain Bennett bit her lip and glanced at the screen. "Gateman Lessis, you are completely happy with the Gate status?" Her face stared at him, as if seeking the slightest hint of doubt.

The Gateman paused, blinked, glanced at his datasheet, and returned the stare with wide, confident eyes. "Captain, all the information I have suggests no hint of anything untoward." He glanced at the image as more words tumbled out. "If I may say, the last significant Gate problem was a generation ago and half the Assembly away. That was only a Class One failure and automatically fixed within hours. The Gate's reputation for reliability is well merited, Captain. As you know. There are at least two levels of duplicate safety mechanisms on every system."

The seconds scrolled down to zero.

The captain looked at the screen, shook her head, and then gestured to the man at the console to her right.

"Helm Officer," she ordered, "initiate burn."

19

Merral stared at the wallscreen as the figure of *00:00* was replaced abruptly by *15:25* and a new countdown started immediately.

Captain Bennett turned around to face Merral and Vero with a face that bore an uneasy expression. "My apologies," she sighed. "But under standing orders I had no choice. Now"—her tone acquired an inflexible edge—"I need you off the bridge, please. Acceleration will be building up in the passenger area. But I will need a full explanation at Bannermene Gate Station."

"Yes, of course," Merral answered, trying to suppress feelings of frustration and alarm. "But I still think there is a risk. Can we still abort?"

"I'd rather not," she said, shaking her head. "Composer Class ships aren't built for maneuvers at speed."

The look on her face seemed to Merral to say as strongly as possible that the interview was over. *So that is that,* he thought despondently.

"Gateman Lessis," she ordered, "you can return to your station." But as the man started to move away, Vero stretched out his hand to block him. "Don't rule anything out," he said in a voice so low that Merral barely caught his words.

"Captain," Vero inquired in a voice that was both firm and gentle, "that image on the screen is a simulation. Can we look at the Gate directly?" Merral looked up at his friend, surprised at the determination on his face.

She frowned. "Optically? Yes, we have a scope linked to it. But the navigation simulation mode is much more appropriate."

"Of course," came the polite response. "But can we see the Gate? On screen? For just a minute?"

Captain Bennett stroked a bronzed cheek. "Give them two minutes,

Gateman, and then send them back down. It's too late after that anyway." She smiled distantly at them and then turned back to her console.

As she sat down, Mikhael Lessis touched the datasheet and the image changed to one of a black, star-strewn sky in which a blurry graphite gray mass hung. It shuddered slightly, came into focus, and then slowly expanded to fill the screen.

"We are still over a thousand kilometers away, so there is some vibration." The Gateman's voice was matter-of-fact.

Merral stared at the smooth metal surfaces, trying to grasp the size of the structure. Only the tiny yellow marks on its dully gleaming surface that indicated the access points for visiting service vessels gave any idea of the vastness of the construction. He could see the sutures between the segments where, long ago, the Gate had been put together, and the brilliant green lights, now rapidly flashing to signify their imminent entry. Then he stared wonderingly into the still, eerie blackness at the heart of the hexagon. There was something awesome about the structure, with its palpable size and its aura of vast age. *If we had idolatry,* Merral thought, in a strange mental aside, *men and women might worship such a thing.*

"Seems all right to me," commented the Gateman, looking at Vero. "You see, Gates *never* fail. Because we can't have them fail, we don't allow them to fail." The tone was of total cool confidence. "That's what Gate engineering is about. Perfect reliability."

Merral found his attitude exasperating, but reminded himself that this young man had seen neither the falsified images of Maya Knella nor the horrid monstrosities they had met at Carson's Sill. *This man believes that the impossible does not happen. We know now that it can.*

Vero nodded thoughtfully. "Of course, only God is perfectly reliable," he answered as he scrutinized the immense mass of metal.

"I was meaning in human terms," came the defensive response.

Merral couldn't see Vero's expression, as it was fixed on the screen, but he knew that he had found nothing untoward.

Vero, biting his lip, gestured at the image. "I'd like to look at each segment. Please, one by one. Just briefly." There seemed to be an unshaken determination in his voice, and despite his own dejection, Merral felt admiration for his friend's attitude in the face of defeat. He felt he could only hope that Perena—if the message had indeed come from her—was somehow wrong.

The Gateman shrugged. "One," he said in a flat tone and tapped the datasheet.

The screen filled with a smooth, almost glassy, gray surface broken by a few minor debris impact marks and faded yellow and red markings and lettering. The thought occurred to Merral that there was less aging than he would expect for a three-thousand-year-old structure.

"Two."

Another surface appeared at a different orientation, but with similar features. Merral realized they were going clockwise.

"Three."

The image switched again, but other than the angle and subtle differences of marking, it might have been the same segment as the previous two.

"Four."

Now the alignment of the segment was back to that of the first one. *Nothing again,* thought Merral with a mounting feeling of inevitability. *Nor will there be on the rest. It looks as if, for good or evil, we are going through the Gate.* The numbers on the bottom of the screen showed him that that would now be in under twelve minutes.

He began to wonder how easy it was going to be to return to his seat in the crew section with the acceleration now building up below them.

Captain Bennett was turning toward them with a frown. Their time was up.

"Five." Another segment, exactly the same. Just like—

A fine line of intense electric blue light writhed round the edge of the image.

"Stop!" Vero's shout turned all eyes to the screen.

Merral was aware of the Gateman staring open-mouthed and of Captain Bennett turning round sharply to the image.

Another line of iridescent blue arced crazily over the smooth, still, and ancient surface of the Gate. Merral felt that there was somehow something shocking about it, as if he was seeing an act of violation or even desecration.

There was a rising murmuring around the control room.

"Gateman!" snapped Captain Bennett, rising stiff-backed from her seat, apparently transfixed by the image. "Did you see that?"

"Yes . . . Captain." The Gateman's tone was one of utter stupefaction. Merral observed in a strange, detached way that he was seeing yet another person realize that the boundary between the possible and the impossible was now being penetrated.

The Gateman continued to gape at the screen as more lines of blue curved round the surface. "There's another. And *another*. It's some sort of electrical discharge. . . ."

"So it seems," returned the captain almost brusquely. "Can you assure me it's harmless, Gateman?"

"Harmless? I have no data on that. . . . I really don't know, Captain." His eyes flicked nervously down to his datasheet. "But the Gate signals indicate plainly that it has no malfunctions." The confidence was oozing away now.

"My eyes, Gateman, tell me otherwise." Captain Bennett's voice was icy and determined. "Helm Officer, take us clear of the Gate. Minimum deviation. Mr. Lessis here will want some detailed images as we fly past, I'm sure. Say about a hundred kilometers away to be safe. And then plot us a course back to the Gate Station."

She turned sharply round on her heels, her face a mask of disbelief. "Gateman, find out what the verdict is from Gate Control. And tell them I want to know why they didn't tell us there was a problem."

As Gateman Lessis, his face pale and his eyes wide, turned away to talk into his datasheet, the captain swung back to her own console.

Merral felt a gentle change in the ship's direction, and moments later the captain's words were echoing around the cabin. "Captain Bennett here to all crew and passengers. I regret to tell you we have identified—" there was the briefest of pauses— "an apparent technical anomaly at the Farholme Gate and are returning to the Gate Station. In the meantime, I urge you to stay in your couches. Hopefully, we can reschedule our journey within a few hours. Thank you."

She turned and briefly gazed at Vero and Merral with puzzled and unhappy eyes before swiveling back to look at her readouts. Merral found the idea that they were going back to the Gate Station something that gave him both relief and concern. A moment later Gateman Lessis walked over to the captain with a nervous face. "Captain, they are looking into it. But they assure me that the Gate monitor systems are still giving perfect readouts. On my insistence they are going to switch to visual themselves."

"Perfect readouts in spite of problems?" Vero had leaned over toward Merral. "I've heard that before," he murmured.

There was another flicker of blue light on the screen, and Vero stepped forward and tapped the shoulder of the Gateman. "Excuse me, do you have any model for what's going on there?"

Mikhael gave Vero a worried look. "No, not at all. I don't know. It's not normal at all. Of course. It's against everything I've ever heard of or been taught. The diagnostics aren't telling us anything." He looked up at the screen. "I mean . . . No, there goes another discharge."

He rubbed his bloodless face as if unable to believe what he was seeing, and Merral felt a twinge of sympathy for him.

"Crazy." His tone was almost one of outrage. "There must be a major overload on some circuitry. It just doesn't make sense." He clenched his fists in frustration. "The Gate's internal monitor should have switched to backup circuits before this even happened. Straight away. And told us. But at this rate we will have a Class Two failure."

Vero peered at him. "A Class Two failure? What would happen to any ship going into it?" Merral noted an urgency in Vero's questioning.

"The Below-Space link is severed and you go straight out the other side.

Harmless but embarrassing." His face wore an expression of total perplexity. "And also almost unheard of. A Class Two failure has happened only twice ever in a production Gate." Gateman Lessis nodded to himself thoughtfully, as if the words had gone some way to giving him reassurance. "And both of those were, what, ten millennia or more ago. As there are nearly two thousand Gates and on average they are five thousand years old, that is one Class Two failure per five million working years." He looked at Vero, a veneer of confidence trying to reestablish itself. "Approximately."

"Of course. Impressive." Vero glanced at the screen. "Forgive me. But what about a Class Three failure? What happens there?" There was an intensity in the question that grabbed Merral's attention. *Vero has sensed something that I have not,* he realized. *He is not content to simply go back to the Gate Station.*

"Most odd. Damping doesn't appear to be taking place." The Gateman was looking at the screen. "But it should be. Sorry, Class Three failure? There the ship hits the Gate. We've never been able to create that in remotely realistic simulations."

"At ten thousand kilometers an hour?" Merral asked in alarm, wondering if that was the peril that Perena had alluded to. It certainly sounded as if it would fit in that category.

"Yes, or thereabouts," the Gateman answered in vaguely dismissive tones. "But it's just impossible."

Mikhael suddenly tapped a corner of his datasheet. The visual image of the entire Gate now appeared on the wallscreen. It was larger than it had been and crisper.

We must be nearer, Merral decided.

There was a flicker of blue tracery on the segment at the top of the hexagon; then another echoed it along the bottom segment.

"That was on Five *and* Two, Gateman Lessis," said the Captain sharply.

"Yes. It isn't being damped. But it should be." There was now a note of bewilderment in the voice.

"What should be is no longer the issue," the captain retorted gently.

"On segments One and Four now as well, Captain," called up a voice from below. Merral stared at the screen, seeing faint moving coils of blue light around most of the Gate.

Vero cleared his throat. "Sorry to interrupt, Gateman, but is there a Class Four failure?"

His body rigid, the Gateman stayed staring at the screen as if glued to it. He shook his head. "No, not in the real world." His tone denied any possibility, however slight.

Merral saw Vero shake his head in frustration. Then he seemed to breathe in deeply and took a step toward the man. "Look, Gateman Lessis, you have already admitted that *this* is impossible." Exasperation was thick in his voice. "What *is* a Class Four failure?"

The Gateman continued to gape at the screen and just shook his head again. "It's hypothetical. Every level of fail-safe mechanism would have to be overruled."

Merral saw that the countdown on the corner of the screen had scrolled down to nine minutes. Suddenly, Vero reached out a hand, grabbed the Gateman's shoulder, and turned him round so that they were face-to-face. "What is a Class Four failure?" he shouted.

The captain stepped forward to separate them, anger flooding her face. "Sir, whoever you really are, this is my ship." In her voice, consternation and anger were mixed. "This is an outrage. . . ."

To his surprise, Merral found that he had stepped forward to meet her so that there was a strange cross-shaped symmetry with the four of them. *As if this were a dance.* His eyes locked with hers.

"And so, Captain, is that!" Merral snapped, pointing at the screen.

Over the entire hexagon a wreath of faint moving blue lines now hung, as if someone was scribbling frantically over it with a blue pen. The Captain glared at him with a look of indignation, then flung a glance back at the screen. The glance, however, seemed to become locked into a stare. Merral followed her gaze. The image showed a foreshortened Gate with the hexagon distorted and the top of the upper segment now visible. The captain opened her mouth slowly, but her curt words, when they came, were not to either Merral or Vero.

"Gateman Lessis, I order you to give this man this information. What is a Class Four failure?"

The Gateman swallowed. "In theory, Captain, gravitational instability builds up. Cycles and pulses between segments. And ultimately the Gate . . . blows up."

For a moment, the concept seemed so outlandish that Merral refused to accept what was being said and found himself sympathizing with Lessis's reluctance to mention it. A Gate, *this* Gate—*their* Gate—was something permanent, fixed, fundamental to existence. For it to "blow up" was as meaningless as talking about the angles of a circle.

Beyond his unsettling thoughts, Merral was aware of a brief moment of intense silence among them. For a fraction of second, he saw the captain, barely an arm's length away, turn to him with her brown eyes wide in a strange and terrible surmise.

"Captain . . . ," he heard Vero say, "I think—"

But he had no need to say anything because the captain was already running back to her desk and issuing a flurry of orders in tones that demanded instant obedience.

"Helm Officer! Maximum deviation and speed without compromising hull integrity. I want us to be at least a thousand kilometers away. And facing away from the Gate to minimize radiation effects."

There was a crisp acknowledgement and she took a brief breath. Merral, reeling at the concept of the Gate being destroyed and all its implications, felt the hull vibrate as power was applied. "Comms!" she snapped. "Emergency alert to Gate Station, Isterrane, and all ships that the Gate is going to blow up. Possibly within minutes. Repeat it. Have all ships and stations go to minimum radiation exposure profile. Crews to shelters. Use the solar flare drill, but make sure they realize that it's the Gate, not the sun, that is the problem. Have all rescue services on alert."

Merral noticed that on the wallscreen the perspective on the Gate was already changing as the ship's path began to curve upward. A sheath of blue flickering light was embracing the whole structure now, and as he watched, he saw the light had begun to pulse.

Around him an urgent wailing siren sounded. "Passengers and crew, alert. This is Captain Bennett." The voice was strained. "A possibility of a major Gate incident has emerged and we are accelerating out of the way at high g. Remain in your couches and strap yourselves in. Internal hull barriers will be automatically extruded shortly to provide airtight segments." There was a pause. "I would value your prayers."

For a second, a brief, intense, and awed silence seemed to fall over the cabin, only to be swept away in a wave of activity.

The Gateman looked up from examining his datasheet. "Captain, the Gate readouts now seem to reflect reality and—"

"About time," she interjected.

"—the Gate is in trouble. Serious trouble." Merral felt that the breathless and awed voice was barely recognizable as that of Gateman Lessis.

The whole ship was vibrating softly now, and every so often sharp little shudders shook the frame. Merral found a support bar and held on to it. They were almost directly above the Gate now, the entrance hidden by the upper segment. Blue pulsing flickers of light were embracing the entire frame.

Captain Bennett seemed to notice it. "Helm Officer! Give us everything you can. Even if you do bend the hull. We need to be farther away."

She looked around the cabin. "Crew," she called out, "everyone take a seat and strap yourselves in. Created gravity may be unsustainable shortly."

Then, pale-complexioned but still very plainly in command of herself, she turned to Merral and Vero. "There are seats there." She gestured to the rear wall. "Oh . . ." A thought seemed to strike her and there was the briefest flicker of a smile on the wan face. "If we don't make it, my genuine apologies. To you both."

Vero, stepping back to the seat, bowed. "Apologies accepted."

Moments later, as Merral was belting himself into the seat, the vibration reached a new pitch of intensity. *This is a dream,* he told himself desperately, *a hallucination, an artifact of the ship's computer. After all, the Gate exists and the Gate must exist. Without the Gate . . .*

Merral was conscious of the wall behind him vibrating. On the wallscreen he saw that they were still looking down on the top of the Gate, surrounded in its blue haze. But he had no idea how close they were. On the bottom of the shaking image he saw the now meaningless timing numbers reach zero and then begin to run down from 10:32. *The time we would have taken between the Gates.* He prayed that, even now, the endless backup circuits and fail-safe switches within the Gate would snap into operation.

They must. The Gates were the Assembly.

There was a tinkling chime and over the mounting rumble of noise a machine voice announced, "Created gravity termination five seconds away."

There was the sound of frantic activity as seats were adjusted and equipment secured, and then Merral was aware of an invisible something pushing on his chest and legs. His arms felt heavy and his head touched the soft pad on the wall behind him. There were thuds and bangs all around the cabin as unsecured objects slid around. The image shuddered and went out of focus. There was a cry of pain from somewhere.

The vibration seemed to multiply, growing louder and deeper and occurring at more frequencies. Over it were now transposed various rumbles, creaks, and groans. Orders were being shouted. The screen image came back into focus slowly, a furious blurred squall of a thousand blue lines that pulsed inward and outward like some great slow heartbeat.

The cabin lights flickered and then dimmed for a moment. Merral glimpsed flashing yellow and red lights on the panels of the consoles. He could see the captain, bracing herself against the desk and hurling orders. The entire ship was quivering angrily now, and he had a terrifying vision of the long structure vibrating like a twig in a storm. Suddenly something broke free above him and crashed down in a pile of fragments in front of him.

The vibration continued. He slowly and painfully turned his head to see Vero, his face distorted by the acceleration, with his eyes closed, his hands clenched on the seat edges, and his mouth moving.

Merral began to pray intensely, aware of the smell of smoke, the shuddering of the whole ship, and the almost deafening compound noises of the different sirens and alarms. Nearby a side panel tore loose with a bang and vomited out wiring.

On the screen image, thrashing from side to side, there was an image of the pulsing blue slab. But now the beating was faster and faster, every pulse brighter, every gap between the pulses shorter.

"It's going!" came a yell. *The Gateman*, thought Merral dully, feeling, in some strange confused way, that the catastrophe focused on this one figure.

The screen flashed a dazzling brilliant white that cast shadows around the cabin. Above the vibrating, roaring groans of the ship, Merral heard a single united awed gasp and knew that his own mouth was open and that he had contributed to it. Blue lines slowly returned to the screen as the whiteness faded. Now, though, they were less frantic, more leisurely, and their pulse seemed to be weakening. For a fraction of a second, a wild hope seized Merral, only to vanish as he saw that underneath them there was no Gate.

Awestruck, unable to comprehend what had happened, Merral stared as first one, then another, then many sharp-edged gray fragments raced outward through the waning blueness. He could hear an inconsolable gasping sobbing from somewhere in the cabin.

"The Gate has exploded," intoned Vero, his voice clogged with emotion and barely recognizable.

Numbed, Merral stared ahead to the consoles, aware of action and orders as, despite the appalling vision, the ship raced onward. Barely audible over the cacophony of sirens and ship noise, Merral could hear the captain's distorted announcement: "*All crew!* The front of the debris cloud will reach us in approximately one minute. Prepare for possible damage to hull and engines. God be with us all."

Merral closed his eyes and waited, trying to close out the brutal bombardment of sound and vibration. *The Gate has gone.* The thought rang in his mind again and again but he could barely make sense of it. It was a simple, factual statement, but he felt vaguely that the news of his own death would have been less shocking. *Be with us all, Lord.*

Something struck the ship.

There was an awesome, tearing hammer blow that broke through all the noise of the vibration like a thunderclap in a rainstorm. In a wild, explosive flurry of fragments, something burst up through the floor, ripped through the cabin, and struck the roof.

And kept going.

Most of the lights went out. A deafening screaming whistle began and a gust of air sucked across Merral. Through half-closed eyes, he could see, caught in the rays of light from the few remaining sources of illumination, debris being whipped up roofward in a whirlwind. Above him, at the apex of the spiral of dust and fragments snaking up through the weird twilight, Merral could see a hole. He was aware of a new screaming in the cabin, the screaming of men or women in extreme pain.

There was a popping sound in his ears, and he realized that through the gap in the roof he could see points of light.

Stars.

In his mind, Merral heard Perena's voice, eons ago and worlds away: *"But vacuum kills quicker than either air or water."* The sounds were dying away now.

So this is it, Merral told himself in the encroaching quietness of the vacuum. How very strange to face death twice in a few days. And, even as the idea came to him, Merral noted his ability to think irrelevant thoughts.

Then, beginning to gasp for breath, he began to make a final prayer. As he did he was aware that above him something was being extruded into the cavity from every side. The vision of stars died away as the hole seemed to shrink to nothing. Sound came back, and with it the noise.

But he could breathe.

Lights flickered back on, and the wallscreen image slowly came to life. But the image it displayed was now a schematic plan of the *Heinrich Schütz,* and two words in brilliant red, *Pressure Crisis*, hung on top of it. Of the twenty or so sections, six were a flashing red and the rest were either a pale or dark blue. As Merral watched, one by one the flashing red blocks were replaced by shades of blue until, within minutes, all were dark blue.

The words *Pressure Restored* flashed across the top. From somewhere came a cry of praise.

Still absorbed in appalled reflection on what had happened to the Gate, Merral was only peripherally aware of how, over the next few minutes, the acceleration died away, the created gravity came back on, one by one the sirens and alarms stopped, and the screaming died away into a dull, sobbing whimper.

Numbed, Merral undid his straps, uncertain of why he did so, and got to his feet, shaking fragments off him. There was debris all around: bits of wall, thermoplastic sheet, portions of tile, shards of metal. In the roof, an ugly brown resinous mass bulged downward, showing where the hole had been plugged.

Merral turned to look at Vero, who was sitting up, his head between his hands, his face a picture of blank desolation. He was shaking. Slowly, as if in a dream, he patted Vero on the shoulder. Then, picking his way between debris fragments, Merral walked toward the three consoles on the bridge. At a gaping head-sized hole in the floor he paused and looked down, only to see that it had been blocked between decks by the same automatic sealant system that had closed the breach in the roof.

Disjointed fragments of sound seemed to drift into his mind from the frantic talking going on around him. A particular phrase seemed to be repeated and rang out again and again like a chorus. Somehow, though, its meaning failed to register with him.

He walked on. Gateman Mikhael Lessis was sitting down with his back to the guardrail, with someone bending over him, administering medicine to a bared upper arm. Merral glimpsed an expression of total vacuity on his face and a meaningless twitching of the lips. *I hope he gets better quickly and gets back to work.* In that instant, the appalling revelation struck him that there was no hurry at all for a Gateman to recover.

Staggering forward, almost overwhelmed by the thought, he came to the bridge area, now crowded with people. Merral glimpsed the captain slumping over her console with her hands to her head, her hair loose and hanging over a shoulder. As if sensing his approach, Captain Bennett turned her face up toward him, revealing tear-filled eyes.

"How is it?" Merral asked, and the words seemed to sound in his ears as if they had come through a wad of cloth.

She just shook her head. A man behind her with a single flash on his dusty uniform answered in slow, numbed words. "Five dead, twelve seriously wounded. Thirty with minor injuries. A lot of damage to the engines . . . but, God willing, we'll make it back to Gate Station."

Captain Bennett looked up at Merral with moist and appalled eyes.

"Sorry," she said, her voice almost a sob. "I have a son on Marant." It came to him that there was an odd exactness to her words, as if she were speaking in a foreign language. She swallowed and spoke again, but this time she said just two words: "Fifty years."

Fifty years.

With a stunning blow of horror, Merral realized that this was the phrase he had heard repeated—the words that had been on everyone's lips. Forty light-years from Bannermene at the maximum of eighty percent light speed. Was there ever a more simple, rigid, or cruel equation? Suddenly, as if a dam had burst, Merral realized the import of the loss of the Gate, and he reached out for the edge of the console to support him.

Fifty years, at a minimum, before there was any physical contact of any sort with the rest of the Assembly. Fifty years for a Made World to survive on its own with no external advice, no brought-in equipment, no emergency resources. Nothing out, nothing in, only long decades of silence. In forty years' time they would get the first message—already nearly half a lifetime old, doubtless with condolences, a promise of prayerful support, and probably a tentative timescale of sending a new Gate. But nothing until then.

He was aware of the Helm Officer speaking into his console and turning to Captain Bennett. “Gate Station, Captain. They are okay—just. They want to know where we are going to dock: main or engineering segments?”

The captain looked at Merral, her face bearing an infinite weariness, and then she turned back to her navigator.

“Main,” she answered, and her faint voice sounded as if were from a continent away. “Engineering can wait. We aren’t going anywhere for a long time.” She put her head in her hands. “Not for half a century.”

20

On the evening of the following day, Merral cautiously made his way down to the observation bay in the crew section of the Gate Station. There he floated, his hand only a few centimeters away from a grab rail, and looked down on the browns, greens, and blues of Farholme as the night spread slowly over the Mazurbine Ocean toward Menaya. In the last dozen hours, he had found that there was something soothing about being here and watching his world. The magnificence of the view both distracted and comforted him, and whenever the enormity of what had happened threatened to overwhelm him, he calmed himself by forcing his mind to identify all the places he knew on the globe below.

The passengers who needed urgent medical treatment had been ferried back to Isterrane as priority, and Merral and Vero had been allocated berths with the crew of the *Heinrich Schütz.* In the last few hours, the *Shih Li-Chen* had returned to the Gate Station to bring back the remaining passengers and crew.

To his surprise, Merral had found that the delay had not been a problem. In part, it was because he had been in too much turmoil to think about it, but also because he was vaguely aware that it was probably as easy to come to terms with the new situation in the seclusion of the Gate Station as anywhere on Farholme.

As Merral stared down over the planet, his mind kept coming back to the events that had overtaken him and his world during the last few days. The loss of the Gate was so catastrophic that he had had to struggle not to let it push the other matters out of his mind. He wondered whether his ancient ancestors, so used to wars, rampant evil, and catastrophes, had handled such things better. *Did they just shrug their shoulders, pick themselves up, and get on with life?* If so, he envied them that, at least.

He forced himself to stare out of the glass again. From this vantage point Merral could see almost all of Menaya, apart from the extreme western Tablelands and the most northerly parts of the ice cap. South of Menaya, he noticed a swirling cluster of storm clouds gathering over Hassanet's Sea, their shadows black on the silver-tinged sapphire waters. It would, he decided, be wet and windy in Isterrane by dawn. Along the eastern coastlands, evening was falling, and inland he could make out the green swathe of the Great Northern Forest, and at its very eastern end, the tiny dirty blue smudge of Ynysmere Lake. North of the forest, the Northern Wastes stretched in lifeless shades of gray and brown almost across the entire continent, passing ultimately, on the edge of his vision, into the gleaming featureless white of the polar ice fields.

As he hung suspended there, Merral realized that even gazing at this tranquil scene gave him no ultimate escape from his problems. Normally—especially when faced with things to think about—he would have looked forward to walking out into the wilds and being alone among the forests and lakes that he could see so clearly, but so distantly, below. Only now, the wilds were no longer the invigorating and innocent spaces they had been; they had become in his mind—and perhaps in reality—haunted and shadowed places. With this somber thought, his eye was drawn inevitably to where the low-angle light was etching in black the vast broken circle of the Lannar Crater and the Rim Ranges.

There was a noise to his right, and a slight, slim form dressed in dark blue slipped down through the far opening of the observation bay. With a fluid motion, the figure glided smoothly toward him, almost like a diver cutting through water, extended delicate fingers, caught a strut, and with a practiced ease, swung to a stop an arm's length away.

"Perena!" cried Merral, lunging forward to hug her. He missed and, arms flailing, started spinning.

Retaining her fingertip hold on the strut, Perena stretched out a hand, caught him, and pulled him over so that he could reach the handrail. Then she wrapped an arm around him and hugged him. They hung there staring at each other.

"It's gone," he heard himself whisper, and he realized he sounded like a child. "The Gate's gone."

Perena lifted her gaze upward through the gold-tinted glass to where the hexagon would have been. "Yes," she replied, and there was strain in her voice. Then she added, quietly but defiantly, "Nevertheless, the King still reigns."

"Amen!" Merral answered, but felt it was an effort to say it.

Perena gave him a smile, at once determined, weary, and sympathetic. "I'm glad you agree. But it's a hard thing to say."

Funny, he thought, *she looks older now. But then perhaps we all do.*

"What are you doing here?" Merral asked, realizing how pleased he was to see her. "I thought you were getting your ship fixed?"

"I came up as extra crew on the *Shih Li-Chen* just now. They have a general survey craft here, the *Eliza N'geno,* they want bringing down, and I'm assigned as co-pilot."

She sighed and glanced down at Farholme. "A new ruling, as of this morning. All ships are to have co-pilots. Ship safety is now a priority. We can't afford to lose a single vessel from now on."

"I'm afraid I've been a bit too absorbed to take in much of the news from elsewhere. What's it like down there?"

She shook her head. "Hard to summarize. It's taking time for it to sink in. No real lasting panic, of course. Resignation, acceptance, grief: especially where families have been broken up. The day after tomorrow has been declared a solemn day of petition and fasting."

"That I had heard. But what do they know?"

She stared out of the window again at the planet below. "Only that there was a Gate malfunction on an unprecedented scale. There is no hint of intruders, or of it being deliberate—I think that is the word. To those that know of it, my warning is being put down to a premonition. I have a reputation, it seems." She smiled a shy, secretive smile. "Apparently, out of the whole of Space Affairs, I seem to be the one person that everyone feels a visionary warning might have been granted to. I don't know whether to be personally flattered or collectively ashamed."

"And was it a vision? We owe you a lot."

For a second she continued gazing out of the window. "No," she said in quiet way as she turned back to Merral, revealing a curious, thoughtful expression. "Not in a conventional sense. Something very strange happened. But I will tell you of it when Vero is with us. And how is he?"

Merral detected a deep concern in her voice and he chose his words carefully in answering. "It's been bad for everybody. But for Vero it's been an especial blow. He's said little since it happened and I've left him on his own. He's been in the chapel a lot." Merral remembered how he had last seen Vero, a brooding and disconsolate figure floating in the corner of the chamber the station congregation used for worship.

"Poor Vero," Perena said, with a sigh of sympathy. "I've sent a request for him to come and meet us here. Incidentally, the provisional statistics are that ten thousand Farholmers are trapped out of the system and just over a thousand people are trapped in. Both cases are awful."

"I can imagine. The only family member I have lost contact with is a great-uncle on Mamaria, and I've never met him. I've been asking myself, how would I take being told that I would be an old man before I had any sort of communication with my family? And Vero's father is elderly and frail."

Perena bowed her head as if in resignation. "It's tough. And how are you handling it? How's the ankle?"

"The ankle is fine, especially when I'm weightless. As for the rest, I'm trying to digest it. Bit by bit. I'm spending time in here. I find staring at Farholme consoling in some way. As if having a perspective on the planet gives me a similar perspective on my problems."

"Yes." She gave him a determined smile. "But they're *our* problems. We are together in this."

"Thanks. That is one of the things that makes it bearable. How's Anya?"

"Numbed and quiet. Which is an unusual state for her. She has lost—no, that sounds like they are dead—but you know what I mean—colleagues and friends. We all have."

She paused. "Of course, in a way it's worse for us four. Everybody else thinks it was some appalling, unexpected accident. We know—or we strongly suspect—that it wasn't that."

Merral felt himself clench the handrail. "No!" he answered, and he was surprised at the bitterness in his voice. "It was an attack! It was a deliberate, malevolent destruction of the Gate! Perena, when I think of it, it reminds me of the attack on Spotback. Multiplied a millionfold!"

"Yes," she said in barely audible tones, "and we must act. Look, I've also been sent up here to bring you both back personally. Anya's arranged a private meeting between Representative Anwar Corradon and us tomorrow. But I'd like to talk to you and Vero first."

She cocked her head sideways and listened. "Sounds like him."

There was a clunking noise from along the corridor. A pair of flailing legs descended out of the roof hatch, a groan, and a moment later, the rest of Vero awkwardly followed.

Perena launched herself toward him, smoothly curling into a tight ball and then unrolling with a final neat twist. She came to a stop with her feet against a wall strut and stretched herself out so that she lay horizontally across the corridor.

A sickly grimace appeared on Vero's drawn, weary, and unshaven face. "Perena Lewitz, the Queen of the Zero G Circus," he said in a subdued voice.

Then he smiled solemnly. "But it is very good to see you. However, bearing in mind my delicate stomach, could you please go the right way up? I would feel better about hugging you."

Perena walked down the side of the wall, stood vertical, and then reached out slender arms and hugged him. Nervously, Vero clasped his arms about her and held her tight.

"Well, Vero," she sighed as they separated, "I could wish you were safe home. Yet it's good to see you too. Very good. And I'm glad you are in one piece. The King does indeed reign."

"Yes," he answered in a hesitant tone, staring at the observation window and Farholme beyond it. "To deny that would be a greater disaster than the loss of the Gate." But Merral felt there was more determination than enthusiasm in his voice.

Then, with his legs hanging out untidily behind him, Vero hauled himself slowly along the guide rail until he was alongside Merral. As Perena made a precise glide to join them, Merral gripped his friend's arm.

"Are you feeling better?" Merral asked, heartened at Vero's appearance.

"Yes, I suppose so. It's been a bad twenty-four hours though. Extremely bad. The only way I have kept going is by trying to work out what's happening."

Vero drifted slowly forward and then peered dubiously through the glass at the stars, his gaze moving along the Milky Way until it found the location of Ancient Earth. Then he stopped and sighed deeply. "I am telling myself that I mustn't do that. Home is now down there." He gestured to the world below.

Merral felt a pang of sympathy for his friend. "We may be able to do something," he muttered.

"No." There was a sad and dogmatic shake of his head. "Don't encourage any false hopes. I have heard the commentators. And I checked it out myself. There is no chance of you—I mean *us*—making a new Gate."

Perena gestured down at Farholme. "We have the plans in the Library."

"No, Merral, Perena," he answered. "They are there to satisfy curiosity alone. Shielded Gates—Gates of any sort—are just too big. I hadn't realized a full Shielded Gate is nearly two million tons in mass. There's one factory that makes them—in the Solar asteroid belt. Even then it takes ten years to fabricate just one. A world of thirty million people can't do it. We can't even make an unshielded one."

"No," Merral admitted, "I suppose not."

"So you see, I'd better make the most of it. Become a Farholmer." He scrutinized the world below. "Hi, home," he murmured in an unconvinced tone. "Will you have me?" he asked Merral.

"Of course." Merral patted his arm. "Anyway, we are citizens of the Assembly, not of planets. But for your insistence yesterday we would have lost everybody on the ship. We owe you a lot."

"We still lost five, or whatever the toll will finally be."

"I know, but it could have been much worse. And I had given up. You didn't. Why?"

Vero rubbed his face with his mobile fingers. "I had a terrible thought, a presentiment, that what I had done with the diary it might be possible to do with the Gate. Get into the circuitry and rearrange it. Turn the power against itself. I tried to push the idea to one side, but the phrase came back to me: 'Don't rule anything out.' As the Assembly we have never really built in safeguards against . . . sabotage." He shook his head as if the word stung. "We sentinels should have insisted that it was always a possibility." He stared silently outward. "I derive no pleasure at all from being right."

Merral turned to Perena. "You realize that we weren't sure it was you?"

"But Merral believed it was," Vero interjected, "and persuaded me it was genuine. And I just didn't want to give up. I guess I was really hoping that—by playing for time—you would get through again." Then he frowned and bit his lip. "But I wish we could have saved the Gate."

Merral stared out of the glass and thought hard. "Yes. But it seemed so impossible." He peered up to where, at the edge of the window, the three remaining Gate beacons hung equidistant from a smudge of dust that obscured the stars. "I still barely believe it. You heard poor Gateman Lessis. 'They never fail.' We never believed they could. And by forcing us to look at the visual images, you saved the ship."

"I suppose so . . . ," Vero said dully, as if distracted by the vision of the world below. He stared down, his eyes squinting as he peered toward the planet's surface.

Merral knew what he was looking at. "I know," he added, following his gaze to the edges of the Lannar Crater, now half flooded with black night. "My eyes keeping looking there too."

Vero nodded and turned to Perena. "Farholme will manage?"

For a moment, she didn't answer but merely tapped delicate fingers thoughtfully against the glass. "The short-term prognosis—that is, over months—is fairly good. But the big issue is the long term. There are a number of teams being set up to study the implications. There are so many unknowns, but the provisional word is that—if the Most High wills—Farholme may well survive fifty-plus years of isolation."

"Merely 'may well'?"

"Assembly caution," she answered with forced humor, and Merral realized that there were aspects to the Gate loss that she was still trying to come to terms with.

"Will you keep flying?" Vero asked her.

"To a lesser extent. We need to work out how much we can actually afford to do. Space flight is a major area—maybe *the* major area—where the worlds rely on the Gate system to supply spare parts. We have some supplies, but we can't make fuselages or ion engines here, let alone gravity-modifying engines or Gates. Fortunately, Assembly engineering has always gone for having long times between servicing. Of course, we don't need in-system shuttle flights or a Gate Station now. And we can recycle bits of the *Schütz*. It all may help."

"I see." Vero looked at Merral and then back at Perena. "We need to talk. I have some ideas; I think they are outrageous, but this situation is so extraordinary that it needs some explanation."

Perena gave a slight nod of affirmation. "If we have to see Anwar Corradon tomorrow, we need to decide what we are to say. And I would like to think that we have not just questions but also answers."

"Exactly," Vero said. "So first, the warning, Perena. Can you explain about it?"

Perena gazed back at him. "Explain? No, but I can tell you what happened. That was a strange matter. Very strange." Her eyes seemed to focus on something invisible that was a long way away, and Merral sensed again the depths that there were to her. Vero leaned forward unsteadily, his weary face showing an intense curiosity.

"Very well," she said softly. "After I left you I decided to stay over rather than go back into town, so I just grabbed some things off the ship and took a berth at the pilot's center. Yesterday—was it really only yesterday?—I decided to look at the *Nesta* before going over to the morning service. So I went over to the Engineering and Maintenance Complex and checked in. When I looked at the status screen at the entrance, I saw that there were a couple of people around the main offices but no one in Bay One. I'm certain of that because I'd asked that no work be started without me being there, and I remember feeling reassured that this was the case. Anyway, it was the Lord's Day. So I walked down to the entrance to Bay One, glanced at its status screen, and saw again that no one was there and that the bay was at normal temperature, pressure, and radiation. In E and M Complexes you always do that. Just in case. You don't want to walk into vacuum."

She paused, as if mentally thinking through her account. "So I went through the airlocks, put the lights on, and wandered up to the port lifting surface." She gave a tiny smile as if thinking of a private joke. "I suppose I wanted to reassure myself that the holes were really there."

She paused and closed her eyes as if uncertain about what to say next. "They were. I was staring at them when I saw, under the fuselage, that there was someone on the other side of the ship."

Merral heard a sharp intake of breath from Vero. Perena continued. "From where I was standing I could really only see a pair of legs, and the way the light was, it was impossible to make out anything about them. It was as if someone else had come in and was looking at the other lifting surface. I was, as you can imagine, pretty puzzled. After all, I had asked that no work be begun before I had okayed it and it was the Lord's Day. And I had not heard the door open. So I walked over and peered round the nose."

She hesitated. "There was someone there. He was standing up and looking at the underside almost as I had been doing. Now, whether it was a trick of the lighting or something else . . . I have to say I can't give any sort of real description." Now her words came slowly, in a labored way. "I had the impression of a tall, dark figure. Almost a silhouette. A man, I would say. Yes, definitely."

She paused, and Merral was oddly aware that beyond the tense silence he could hear the faint hiss of the ventilation system. "He was—or he seemed—oddly dressed. As if he wore something like a loose, long black coat and seemed to have a hat of some sort. But it was hard to make out. He always seemed on the edge of my vision. And I am fairly certain that he cast no shadow; there is a lot of lighting in Bay One. He was just peering at the underside of the wing as if he was curious. No, more than that; as if he disapproved of what he saw."

Vero opened his mouth to speak, closed it, and gestured for Perena to ignore him.

"I suppose," she said, as if speaking to herself, "I knew that there was something wrong. Well, not wrong, *weird.* I think I shivered." She gave a little swallow. "Then he turned toward me and spoke. And it's hard to describe his voice, but his way of speaking was incredibly striking. As if the words were just pressed out of the air. . . ."

She fell silent, staring at the planet far below and Merral could see her reflection in the curved, coated glass.

"What did he say?" Vero asked, as gently as if he were talking to a child.

"He said this: 'Captain Lewitz, night is falling. The war begins.' But I can't give any sense of the sheer weight of the words."

She paused again and moved her head so that she was looking carefully at Merral and Vero, as if weighing them. " 'Night is falling. The war begins.' "

Vero asked, "Do you understand what he meant at all?"

She looked at him blankly. "Not then." Then she looked to where the Gate had been. "But I do now. Or think I do."

Perena turned back to Vero and Merral saw there were shadows under her eyes. "I wish I could describe the voice. It was human in its words, but not in its sound. It was emotionless; I felt there was no flesh and blood, no lungs and larynx involved, but that it was not—most definitely not—a machine voice." She shook her head. "If it was a vision, it was a remarkably concrete one. Anyway, so I said, 'Who are you?'" Then she paused and sharply corrected herself. "*No.* I said, 'Who are you, *sir?*' because there was such an authority in the voice. Then he answered me. 'I too am a captain, and I too serve.' He paused, as if to let the words sink in, then he said, 'I have been sent by our Lord the King as an envoy to you. I am to warn you that the enemy is seeking to regain his authority over your worlds. His power extends to Farholme Gate. Even now he seeks to seize your friends.' "

Merral felt himself reach for the grab rails. He glimpsed Vero gulping and, for a moment, wondered if he was going to vomit.

Perena swallowed and when she spoke again there was a great emotion in her voice. "I was nearly sick with fear, but I said, somehow, 'Can I stop it?' There was another silence and then he just said, 'You may be able to stop the ship entering Farholme Gate.' Then he seemed to start to walk away toward the rear of the *Nesta*. There he turned briefly to me. 'And remember, Perena, whatever happens, the King reigns. And stand firm.' Then he was gone."

"Gone?" Vero's voice shook and Merral was aware of his hands twitching.

She raised her eyebrows. "He just wasn't there. In the chamber. Did he move or did he vanish? I don't know."

She turned and leaned her head back against the glass and looked at them, her face pale and intense. "For a moment I froze. Then I started shaking and I had to lean back against an undercarriage leg to brace myself. I prayed. Then I realized that you were going through the Gate in just over an hour. So I raced up to the complex offices and asked if anybody else had been in Bay One. They looked at me as if I was deranged. 'Of course not,' they said. I ran to the Gate Control office. I must have been a sight for them to see. I told them to stop the *Schütz*. Turn it back, whatever. Then the fun began." She sighed, rubbing her chin gently. "They were very kind, they all knew me, but they said, 'Why?' Of course, I was in a mess, because all I could say was that I had met someone or had a vision of some sort. So they looked at each other and checked and rechecked all the Gate signals while they got me a chair." She wrinkled her face up in a rueful smile.

"Visions, I now realize, do not appear in the manuals. Nor do angels. Anyway, the Chief of Operations—a nice man—said, well, they had Standard Operating Procedures and, of course, there was nothing they could do. There was no basis to order any diversion. So I thanked him and walked out. Of course, I couldn't get you on the diary. Then I remembered something, so I walked through to Communications and sat down at the desk where they had the backup systems. There was no one about there so I sent the message that you got. I saw how it was cut off after a minute, so I just went outside and sat on a step and prayed. Half an hour later, I heard this extraordinary commotion from the Gate Control Office. I ran in. . . ." She took a deep breath. "You cannot imagine the atmosphere there. But eventually we realized the ship was safe, if damaged. As you know, a number of Gate fragments perforated it, but you were going so fast by then that their relative speed was pretty low."

She looked at them with an oddly respectful look. "I trust both of you have given thanks for great mercies. Despite our ships' excellent self-sealing abilities, most space travelers who see the stars with naked eyes find that it is the last thing they do see in this life."

Vero bowed. "I think that neither of us will overlook that."

For some moments, nobody said anything, and in the silence Merral heard the clatter of equipment echoing from one of the station's corridors. Finally Vero, his weary face marked by a bemused expression, spoke. "Extraordinary, quite extraordinary." He looked at Merral. "Are you reminded of something in Perena's account?"

"Jorgio's dream, of course. Of the testing of the Assembly; to watch, stand firm, and to hope."

"Yes," said Vero. "But Perena, I keep thinking about this appearance—this apparition. I do not have the words. What was it?"

She closed her eyes for a moment before opening them. "I wondered if it was a hallucination. I was tired and stressed. But there was a curiously solid quality to the appearance. As if it had come from somewhere else. And there were other things; I felt a moral aspect to the envoy. I felt under judgment in some way. It was—" she stared at her fingers and Merral wondered if she was blushing— "a not entirely welcome feeling."

"Was it an angel?" Vero asked. "In the Scriptures, an envoy and an angel would be the same word."

Perena shook her head. "I would not wish to claim—or deny—that he was an angel."

"That angels guard the Assembly," Vero said slowly, "is an ancient statement of faith. That, in this age of the world, they do not appear to human beings, is a statement based on equally ancient experience."

"In this age of the world?" Perena said in a sharp voice. "But if I understand Jorgio's vision—and mine—then this age of the world may be ending."

Vero stared out into space for a moment. "Perena," he said, and his tone was troubled, "I stand corrected." Then he turned to her. "Thank you twice over. Your encounter not only saved our lives; it has added another significant piece to the puzzle."

She shook her head. "There are two more things I must tell you. First, yesterday evening I did a check on the *Argo*. The ship that in 2098 went into Below-Space with a living crew and returned with a dying one."

Vero bent closer as if to hear better, swayed, overcompensated, and began to spin. Perena grabbed his arm and steadied him.

"Take it easy. No sudden movements. Anyway, very little of the *Argo's* voyage was made public. The crew names, dates of injection into Below-Space, and recovery; that sort of thing. There are some comments on the properties of Below-Space, and they provide our only real eyewitness knowledge of what happens there. The comments were that, as the remote probes had suggested, some wavelengths of electromagnetic radiation travel through

Below-Space. At the upper levels you could make out stars and planets in shades of gray, but as you went deeper, it became opaque quickly. But with depth they reported a progressive and remarkable degree of mental disorientation with hallucinations and eventually delirium. Which, sadly, proved irreversible."

"Is that it? That tells us little." Vero looked disappointed.

"No, the oddity is this: That is all that was reported of the mission of the *Argo*."

"But there must have been a full report published."

"No. I checked. The full report on the voyage of the *Argo* is one of the few documents never put into the public domain in the entire history of the Assembly."

"Really? Why?"

"Ah. I then ran a search on rumors and fables of early Assembly space flight. There was one record to do with the *Argo*; simply an early post-Rebellion rumor that it had encountered 'Powers.' "

"*Powers?* Not 'power problems'?"

"The wording is precise, if ambiguous. *Powers.* With a capital letter."

"Surely it was just a tall tale?"

"The obvious conclusion but for one very odd fact. The *Argo* Review Commission, made up of a dozen men and women, met in closed session in 2099. It met for a week, adjourned, and then resumed with an enlarged board of six extra people. It met for another month. They made two recommendations: first, that the *Argo* report must remain forever unpublished, and second, that no further attempts were ever to be made to explore Below-Space. Gate links were fine, but going outside them was not."

"Odd." Vero stared at Perena with tired eyes. "Why did they enlarge the board? To put on more psychologists?"

An odd, distant expression crossed Perena's face "No, Vero, it wasn't psychologists. It was theologians."

"Theologians?"

"The six extra people were the Custodians of the Faith."

Merral suddenly felt cold. "Perena," he said, "they felt that there was something *wrong* in Below-Space?"

Perena paused, looked at Vero, and began again. "I think—and it is partly a guess—that they concluded that in deep Below-Space there were spiritual forces, elemental powers. Influences. Something like that."

Vero frowned and shook his head. "It has always been a belief that, if allowed to, human beings always go too far and become, either directly or indirectly, involved with evil powers. That is why we have checks and controls. But I had never heard that it might be so literally true. Nevertheless, Perena, I am not sure I see how this affects us now. We have more pressing problems."

Perena looked at him, her eyes troubled. "I have not finished. I have another piece of information for you. But let me first ask you a question: Assuming the intruders did destroy the Gate, why did they do it?"

Vero opened his hands wide. "It's obvious. They wanted to kill us. To stop us getting through with the news."

"I am not so sure." The voice was quiet.

Vero gave her a look of astonishment. "There are few things that I now take for granted, but that was one of them. I mean, isn't it obvious?"

"Surprisingly, no. Did either of you notice when the explosion happened with respect to your scheduled entry into the Gate?"

"I did," Merral said. "Now you mention it, it was after entry time. A few minutes later."

"Yes." Perena's firm tone brooked no argument. "It exploded at 11:07. You would have entered at 11:02, so that by then you would have been exactly midway between Gates."

Vero stared at Perena in astonishment. "I had never thought . . . What would have happened?"

"A good question and one the spatial physicists—there are two of them here—will have to work on. It has never happened. But the Normal-Space tube would have collapsed instantly and you would have dropped out into Below-Space. At the deepest point of your traverse, you—"

"—would have done what the *Argo* did." Vero's voice trembled.

Merral suddenly felt an urgent longing to be on the ground and to never, ever leave it again.

Vero, swallowing hard, was staring at Perena, his eyes open in a wild surmise. "What did this envoy say about what the enemy wanted to do again?"

"He said 'The enemy wishes to seize you.' Not destroy . . ."

For a moment Merral could only close his eyes as a wave of fear and horror broke over him. He felt his body shake.

When he opened his eyes, he saw that Vero had drifted over to the window and was gazing down at the planet. There was a long silence.

Finally, after perhaps a minute, Vero spoke. "I see why you told us this, Perena. It is horrific but is also suggestive . . ."

Vero stared toward Ancient Earth and wagged a finger slowly in that direction. Then, still looking outward, he began to speak in a slow-paced and almost dreamy voice. "Perena, Merral, let me tell you a story. About something that happened—or may have happened—a long, long time ago. As we know, frustrated by the restrictions of the infant Assembly, William Jannafy and his followers rebelled and, after much bloodshed, took control of the Centauri Gate and the colony. There, free from the restrictions of the Assembly, Jannafy encouraged exploration and experimentation into areas that had been forbidden. He had human beings altered genetically and joined with animal tissues to suit his ends—had new races made. And he sent ships deep into Below-Space. There . . ."

Vero paused, his brown eyes focused on infinity. "There they found more than they had bargained for." He hesitated. "What shall we call them? *Powers, elemental spirits?* Perhaps the older word *demons* might be better. Was Jannafy influenced by them? Did he do a deal with them then? Maybe even he held back from that. I do not know. But then, in the sudden assault at Centauri, he was slain and his men saw that their end was hours away. They chose to save themselves by fleeing to safety through deep Below-Space." He shook his head. "And what price, I wonder, did these Powers and influences exact for safe passage?"

Merral shuddered as Vero paused to let his words sink in. "So in my story, the remains of the Free Peoples fled through Below-Space to the edge of our galaxy. There they survived. But now they were bound to the Powers and they were no longer free. From them they learned—or were taught—new things, such as how to make dead creatures live again and how to use them for their ends. And as the millennia passed, their hatred of the Assembly showed no lessening."

Then Vero turned round suddenly to face them and raised his voice. "And now, they have returned to the Assembly. After long years, Jannafy's descendants are back and they bring evil with them."

Vero paused and gave Perena a questioning look. "Is this—or something like this—what you think happened?"

"Yes," she whispered, and there was fear in her eyes.

Vero turned to Merral. "My friend, you have just heard this story. But tell me, do you think it may be true?"

An urge rose in Merral's mind to deny it all, to protest that Vero's words were nonsense, a wild fiction. But he could not.

"Vero," he heard himself eventually say, "I wish I could say it was false. But what you say has a ring of truth to me."

Vero nodded but said nothing more, and in the end it was Merral who broke the silence. "So, if this tale is true, what are we to do?"

A shadow of a grin crept over Vero's face. "Ah, our soldier here asks about action. I rejoice we have you with us, Merral. I truly do. But, please, answer your own question."

Merral knew what he had to say. "If this is the case then, once more, the Assembly must fight them."

"Amen," whispered Perena.

"We fight," Merral said, aware that he was repeating himself. "We have no option. However awesome the odds and however terrible the enemies we face."

"Indeed." Vero turned to look out of the window. "The first step is that we need to find the source of these creatures. Somewhere down there is a ship."

Merral was aware that all three of them were looking where the line of night was now creeping to the westernmost edge of the Lannar Crater.

Perena gestured to the western Rim Ranges, their valleys deep in shadow. "The satellite data is coming in, but I have to say that if there are intruders there, then they are hidden. Anya and I had a quick examination yesterday; we found no settlements or landing strips."

"They will be hidden," Vero said with confidence. "Our opponents know the techniques of war. On a vast, unknown, and sparsely populated planet like this, they could find many hiding places."

Merral stared silently down, struck now by the scale of things. He felt he was seeing the immense bleak brown wastes, the vast rolling green forests, the dark pinnacled mountains, and the ever-expanding marshy deltas for the first time. *How odd, for a world entirely made by mankind, that there is so little evidence of our race's presence. Here pinpricks of light in the new darkness, there a gleaming vapor trail left by some long-haul passenger flier, elsewhere a few small, extended star shapes of the cities. So much of this world,* he thought, *has been left to evolve its own way, and all we have done is sow, watch, and—where needed—prune.* Now what he would once have seen as a glorious challenge had become an ominous threat. Farholme, and especially humanity on Farholme, suddenly seemed terribly vulnerable. *We would be threatened enough by our enforced isolation,* he thought, *even without this intruder threat. With it, we seem to be in such a great peril as to make our future a dubious matter.*

Merral spoke aloud. "Even if we were the entire Assembly, to encounter such an opposition as we fear that we face would be daunting. But as one world?"

"Yes, but we have had the encouragement of Perena's visitor. If he was not an angel himself, then his counsel was angelic. The King *does* still reign. We are to watch and stand firm. And to hope."

Merral said, "I will hold onto those words. I am grateful for them. Nevertheless we face an almost overwhelming task."

"True," Perena said, looking at her watch. "But we need to return to Farholme. There we will gather together and decide what we do. And I must go see Captain Bennett. Can I meet you both at Shuttle Dock Two in an hour? The *Eliza N'geno* will be refueled by then."

Vero nodded. "Good. We need to be back down. Anyway I'm not sure I care for this view; it's too overwhelming. Besides I want to lie down, or whatever is the equivalent when there is no down. Merral, see you at the ship." He turned to Perena and cautiously bowed his head. "Captain Lewitz, my thanks for your news and for your encouragement. And," he sighed, "for your sympathy."

Then slowly and clumsily, aided by a gentle push from Perena, Vero exited up through the hatchway. Perena shook her head as his feet scrabbled for a hold on a rung and then disappeared out of view.

She looked back at Merral. "Staying here?"

He nodded. "Yes, for a few more minutes. I just want to admire the view a bit longer. I may not get the chance again for a long, long time."

Perena nodded slowly. "True enough. But you can't stay much longer; the sun will come in at the window, then the glare will wipe out everything."

Merral stared down at the blue, brown, and green hemisphere below and sighed. "Perena," he said slowly, "you know what I have just thought?"

"No, tell me."

"Vero has lost his world and is going back now to a new one. But less obviously, I think, we are too."

"Yes," she said and her voice was barely audible. "You are right. What did Jorgio say? 'Things have changed'?"

"Indeed they have. But it is not just the Gate that has gone. It is the old Farholme. The world we knew has ended."

"Yes," she said, leaning her head against the window, and he realized that she had shed many tears recently. "I know. I fear that we will find that soon nothing is the same. But we will fight, Merral. We mustn't give in."

He found that her voice had a strange quality of resolution in it that challenged and encouraged him.

She nodded to herself, then bobbed over and patted him gently on the back. "Look, I must go. We need to start the prelaunch checks. See you at the shuttle dock."

"You will."

She touched him on the shoulder and then slid away and pirouetted up out of the hatchway with the grace of someone to whom the absence of gravity was a joy.

In the silence that followed, Merral stood suspended in the chamber, staring down at the world. He watched for several minutes as twilight followed by night continued its silent and inexorable creep across the planet. He absorbed trivial details now: the smoke from the rift system volcanoes, the brown smudge of a dust storm careening across the Northern Wastes, and the light shimmering on some infant upland glaciers. Ynysmant—with his parents and Isabella—now lay in darkness, its feeble light output too small to be visible from up here. To the west, the sun had just set over Ranapert and Halmacent Cities, where pinpricks of light were forming in the purple twilight. Farther west still, the daylight was coming to a close on Isterrane, and on either side of the city the wooded headlands stood proud in the golden evening light. In the extreme west, the late afternoon shadows were lengthening over the high and rugged Varrend Tablelands with their vast lakes and coiling rivers.

Merral thought about the people that were within his field of view. With a sweep of his head he could see where half of Farholme's entire population lived. *And tonight,* he said to himself, *they will all be looking skyward for only the second day in their history to see the Gate gone and the beacons broken. And all except the very youngest will know that no Made World has ever been as alone as Farholme is now*. But of all that population, he knew that there were only four of them who realized that the threat was far more terrible than the peril of mere isolation.

"My world," he whispered, and he heard the words ring with a compassionate intensity. "I'm sorry we didn't bring back help. I'm sorry that Perena and Vero and Anya and I are all that there is. Apart from the King."

He paused. "Lord," he said in a tone so soft that he could barely hear himself, "I don't really know what is happening. And I don't know what we face, and what I've heard and seen scares me. Especially because everyone seems to look to me for a lead. But Lord," he went on, suddenly aware of his reflection in the glass, "I love this place and I hate what has happened to it. And if you can use me to save it or restore it, then I offer myself to you." He bowed his head.

Do you mean it? something—or someone—seemed to ask. Was it, Merral wondered, an inquiry that he was asking himself, or was another asking him? He hesitated, thinking of the terror of the fighting he had been involved in already, and of the possible cost.

He had no choice. He exhaled heavily. "Yes," he said, "I mean it."

It was time to go to the ship, descend to the planet, meet Anwar Corradon, and prepare for whatever the future might bring. He drifted to the hatchway and reached up to put his fingers on the lowest ladder rung.

He took a last look at his fragile and beautiful world below.

"I promise," he said aloud. "I promise."

Suddenly, a brilliant ray of sun, unheralded by any forewarning in the dustless vacuum of space, slid into the compartment, filling the far corner with a brilliant yellow-white glow.

"Amen," muttered Merral.

Then, with a sharp tug on the rung, he propelled himself toward the shuttle dock.

the Power of the Night

PART TWO

21

It is like being at the prow of a ship, thought Merral Stefan D'Avanos, as he gazed southward out of the rain-drenched windows of the Planetary Affairs building at the sodden houses, roads, and parks of Isterrane below.

Beyond the high gray wall that protected the city from storm and earthquake waves, he could faintly make out the angry white breakers of the ocean's edge. *A storm. How appropriate. A storm has been unleashed on this planet—the Gate has been destroyed and Farholme is isolated from the rest of the Assembly. And we must face what it brings. Do the others feel this?* Merral turned around slowly to stare at the three figures who sat round the dark wood table, awaiting the arrival of Representative Corradon. Vero, dressed in a green jacket and trousers with a definite non-Farholme cut, sat at the far end of the table, staring abstractedly at the large mural of the woodlands of the High Varrend that filled the end wall. Merral sensed that the bland expression on his face barely concealed a profound dejection. Vero reminded him of a lost child. But then, wasn't that exactly what he was? It would take forty years for any message to reach them from the Assembly, fifty years for a ship to come. In what sense did a family continue to exist after half a century of total separation? To the right of Vero sat the slight but erect figure of Perena Lewitz. Dressed in a deep blue space pilot's uniform, she was staring out of the windows, her expression unreadable. Merral knew the uniform was unnecessary for this meeting and suspected that it was an act of defiance against events. The Gate might be gone and, consequently, her flying curtailed, but Perena would wear the uniform nonetheless. There was always something insubstantial and reserved about Perena, and here, amid the gathering storm, both qualities seemed emphasized.

Perena's sister, Anya, sat next to her, and Merral noted the contrasts between them. Anya, with a heavier build and longer, redder hair, wore a beige pullover and trousers that teetered on the edge of informality. She was staring at a pile of papers with a deep frown, and as she shuffled them in evident consternation, he felt a longing to put his hand on her shoulder to reassure her. Vero rose and joined Merral at the window.

"My friend," he said lightly, the accent of Ancient Earth plain in his voice, "I have made a decision to keep some of my suspicions quiet."

"Which?" Merral was aware of the others listening.

"Up there," Vero said, gesturing skyward to where the hexagon of the Gate had hung, "I made guesses. I guessed that, despite everything that our history has told us, elements of Jannafy's rebellion somehow escaped destruction at Centauri in 2110. I guessed that they survived, fled, developed in ways we cannot imagine, and now, over eleven thousand years later, they have come back."

"Where, on the very edge of the Assembly, we have encountered them."

"Perhaps."

Perena had joined them now, her face showing curiosity. "But why do you wish to keep these guesses silent?"

"I simply have no proof. It is all speculation." Vero shook his head. "Our tale is extraordinary enough without my adding to it. I think we had best stick to facts. Theories can wait."

Anya leaned back in her chair. "Makes sense, Vero. I barely believe it myself. But, Merral, reassure me—you will take the lead in any discussion? Please?"

Merral hesitated. "I think it is Vero who should speak. He has had suspicions longer than any of us that something was wrong. He is a sentinel."

"No," Anya replied, the ghost of a grin on her face. "Be realistic. The story of your meeting with the intruders is so incredible that they will only believe it if it's told by someone with as little imagination as a forester. This is *your* job, Tree Man."

Vero turned to Merral, a faint smile trying—and failing—to break through his dejected expression. "Yes, you, Merral, should lead. I am both a stranger to Farholme and a sentinel."

Merral noted a slight gesture of accord from Perena. "Very well," he said.

There was the sound of echoing footsteps outside the room. The door slid open, and a tall man wearing a dark gray suit entered, paused, and looked around with alert blue eyes. Merral instantly recognized Anwar Corradon, representative for northeastern Menaya and the current Chairman of the Farholme Committee of Representatives. He had heard the representative speak at ceremonies and conferences, and along with all of Farholme, he had watched his short but momentous broadcast the previous night.

This close, Merral was suddenly struck by how much Corradon looked the part. In his midsixties, he had the sort of face that sculptors and painters liked: long and rather angular, dominated by a well-defined, almost aquiline nose, and thick, wavy black hair with silver streaks. With his looks and bearing, Corradon would have stood out in a room full of people. There was something about his calm, positive manner that seemed to reassure that, however bad things were, they could be sorted out.

"Good afternoon," he announced in a precise and resonant voice as he looked around. He gave a rather sad smile, and for the first time Merral felt there was a hint of the strain he must be feeling. "In the last few hours, I have wished, for the first time in my life, that I was neither a representative nor chairman of the Farholme Committee. Yet this—" here he raised a hand skyward with a slightly theatrical gesture—"happened on my shift. And we must all do the tasks we are called to."

Corradon smiled at Anya. "Now, Miss—sorry—*Doctor* Lewitz, I know. And I can guess this is your sister, Captain Perena Lewitz, but the others here . . ." He shook his head.

"Let me," Anya said. "This is Sentinel Verofaza Laertes Enand of Ancient Earth."

"Ah, our visiting sentinel," Corradon said as they shook hands. "I'm sorry, Verofaza. It's hard to know what to say, I'm afraid."

"I get abbreviated to Vero, sir." Vero hesitated. "Yes, I'm afraid I will be a guest of Farholme for a long time." He seemed to struggle with his emotions.

"Fifty years." Corradon shook his head. "My deepest commiserations," he said in a voice barely more than a murmur. "Another lamentable story. But if there's anything I can do, let me know."

"Thank you, sir."

The representative turned to Merral.

"And this," said Anya, "is Forester Merral Stefan D'Avanos of Ynysmant."

"A forester?" Bushy eyebrows rose in surprise. "I think I have heard your name." He offered Merral a firm handshake. "It's a small planet." A rueful smile slipped across his face. "I was in agriculture once, before they decided that I was more gifted at management. Until this happened, I had not regretted the change."

The door opened.

"Ah, here is Dr. Clemant."

A younger man, also wearing a gray suit, entered the room, closing the door carefully behind him. He stood in front of the door, looking around with deep-set dark gray eyes as if he was trying to fully evaluate the situation before taking another step into the room. The newcomer was shorter than Corradon and had a pale, round face accentuated by neat, pitch black hair parted precisely down the middle.

Merral, who judged the newcomer to be in his forties, felt struck by his watchful and reserved expression.

"And may I introduce," said the representative, "Dr. Lucian Clemant. Until yesterday, Dr. Clemant advised me on planetary social trends. He has now been given the role of crisis advisor."

Doctor Clemant bowed formally and gave a stiff smile. "An unprecedented title for an unprecedented situation," he said in a deep but rather unemotional voice. *He is a private man,* Merral decided. *You couldn't fail to notice Corradon, but you could easily overlook his advisor.*

"I have no idea of the purpose of this meeting," Corradon said. "Anya insisted it was vital. So I took the liberty of inviting Lucian. Please, everybody, introduce yourselves to him and then—without further ado—let's take our seats. As you can imagine, we are busy people at the moment."

Clemant nodded and moved around rapidly, giving brief handshakes, repeating each name carefully as he heard it.

When all were seated, Corradon nodded to Anya.

"Representative, Advisor," Anya began awkwardly, "thank you both for seeing us—"

"Oh, Anya, we can be on first-name terms."

"Thank you, sir. But this is a serious matter. We seek you as Representative. Formality is appropriate."

Corradon and Clemant exchanged glances, and Merral felt that the advisor's watchful gaze suddenly seemed to become sharper.

"Formal it is then, Dr. Lewitz," Corradon said. "But before you begin, let me give you a status report, so you know where we stand. We have, by the grace of God, weathered the immediate crisis. Communications across Farholme, for example, will shortly be fully restored. The shock of the blast weakened the diary network, and the inevitable usage surge in the wake of the accident overloaded what was left. But it should be back up in an hour."

He glanced at Clemant and got a nod of confirmation. "And, thankfully, the Admin-Net has stayed up." Merral sensed relief in his voice. It was understandable; almost everything to do with running the planet, from the registration of births to the requisitioning of road repairs, went through the Admin-Net. If that had been wrecked, Farholme would have been incapacitated.

"May I ask, sir," Vero said, "about the state of the Library?"

Merral remembered that Vero hoped to use the Assembly's vast store of information to try to obtain clues to the mystery of the intruders.

"Lucian?"

Clemant, who was sitting with his hands placed neatly before him on the table, gazed at his fingers for a moment before looking up at Vero. "The Library? Well, we hold copies of about 63 percent of the Assembly data stock here. Those files are, of course, intact. I have ordered an inventory of what is missing. I suspect the losses will mostly be specialist files to do with other worlds. It will not be back on line today, and tomorrow is, of course, the day of prayer and fasting. But it will—I am told—be back on line the day afterward. Does that help?" The advisor turned toward Corradon to indicate he had finished and then returned to staring at his fingers.

"Thank you," Vero said.

Corradon looked around. "So, that is encouraging. Long term—well that's another matter. A whole new global set of priorities will have to be sorted out. There are endless meetings being arranged, and I can only hope that tomorrow will help clear all our minds. But there are grounds for optimism."

Corradon paused and stared at the end wall. "I have to say that I sympathize with those who have found this event personally traumatic. Our youngest son . . ." He paused, struggling against some deep emotion. "His fiancée was on agricultural training on Pananaret. . . ." The public persona seemed to crumble slightly. "The wedding was to have been this autumn. It is almost unimaginable. Already you can see the problem that is emerging." His voice was slow and strained. "Does he stay engaged to her for the next fifty years? Or does he treat it like a death?"

Corradon continued to stare out at the rain a moment longer and then turned back to them, his face once more the picture of assurance. "But such decisions *will* be made." Then he looked sharply at Anya. "So, Dr. Lewitz, if, as you say, you and your friends can cast light on this calamitous accident, we will hear you out. But otherwise—if you will excuse me for saying so—other needs are pressing."

"Sir, it was not an accident."

Corradon's eyebrow shot upward. The advisor stiffened.

"*Not* an accident?" The representative frowned. "I hope you can both clarify *and* justify that statement."

Anya nodded. "Yes. But, please, let me hand you over to Forester D'Avanos, who has been involved from the start. I will let him tell the story."

Merral, aware of the intense and unfaltering gaze of both the representative and his advisor, began his account. He started four months earlier, just before the Nativity celebrations, when he had visited the Forward Colony of Herrandown and seen what he had taken to be a large meteor going northward, toward the area of the Lannar Crater.

Here Clemant silently raised a finger to pause him, drew a control pad out from the table, and pressed buttons. The woodland scene on the far wall disappeared, to be replaced by an image of the whole of Menaya. Merral, recognizing it as a customized digital composite, was struck by how the green areas of woods and cultivation seemed no more than some artist's daubs over the blacks, grays, and dirty browns of the lava fields, ash flows, and sand deserts.

Feeling conscious of the shortage of time, Merral quickly continued. “While I was at Herrandown I felt there was something wrong— something I couldn’t identify. Anyway, I returned on the eve of Nativity to Ynysmant to find that Vero had arrived at my parents’ house.”

At Vero’s name, the advisor again raised a finger in interruption. “Sentinel Enand, if I may ask . . . why are you on Farholme? Isn’t Brenito Camsar our sentinel?” His tone was cool.

Vero’s gaze seemed as steady as the advisor’s. “Yes, Brenito Camsar has been your official sentinel for—I think—twenty-two years. He requested help. He had had a vision that Farholme was under threat. I was sent in response.”

Clemant, still staring at Vero, tapped his chin thoughtfully. “A threat? As long ago as Nativity? Remarkable. . . . Anyway, please continue.”

Choosing his words, Merral explained how, two weeks ago, his cousin Elana had reported seeing a creature that she described as half insect and half human above the Herrandown colony and how his own brief investigation had suggested that there had indeed been something there. As he spoke, Merral saw how the expressions on the faces of the representative and his advisor began to shift from puzzled interest to marked unease. Merral then mentioned results Anya had obtained from the DNA analysis of the strange fur sample he had found and how the results implied that, in total contravention of all Assembly practice, the creature had an apparent mixture of animal and human DNA. As he spoke, Merral found himself comparing the faces of Corradon and Clemant; while Corradon’s expression displayed alarm, horror, and shock, his advisor’s face simply showed a cool astonishment. *Corradon is outraged,* Merral noted. *His advisor seems to see this as nothing more than some extreme intellectual challenge.*

Then, as Merral went on to mention Vero’s discovery that his uncle had apparently willfully altered a re-created voice, the advisor leaned over and whispered something into the representative’s ear. Merral caught the word *miriam* or something like it, but it made no sense.

Corradon paused as if in thought, turned to the map, nodded, and then motioned Merral on with his account.

As Merral recounted the story of his trip north up the Lannar River with Vero, Clemant smoothly enlarged the wall image to show the river’s path. When, with halting words, Merral described the discovery of the two types of intruders, the representative suddenly strained forward over the table toward Merral.

“You are *serious?*” he asked, his blue eyes strangely wide. “This is not some vision or illusion? There really *are* strange creatures loose on our world?”

“I am afraid so,” Merral answered, suddenly aware of the tension in the room. "I wish it were a vision. But we saw them clearly. And I have a wound from one, and we have provisional genetic results from blood samples of both and images."

Corradon shook his head in bewilderment, looked at Clemant as if for reassurance, found none, and leaned back in his chair. "Continue," he said in a tone that indicated he had been badly shaken. "I did not mean to interrupt. Nor, of course, to suggest that you had not got your facts right. However, I had no idea that you were going to tell us anything of such appalling importance."

Mindful of the passing time, Merral rapidly told the account of how they had spent the day on the hilltop at Carson's Sill. Here, although he was inclined to skim over the violent and bloody encounter with the intruders, Vero kept interrupting him and prompting him to expand on various details. Then, alarmed by the intensity of his memories, Merral recounted how they were attacked at nightfall and, at the last minute, rescued by Perena with her ship. He then explained—as economically as he could—how, once back at Isterrane, Perena had arranged for them to join the inter-system liner *Heinrich Schütz* in order to leave the system and get to Earth rapidly. Perena took over and showed her satellite image of the intruder ferry craft near Carson's Sill before outlining the appearance of the mysterious envoy and his warning to her. Finally, Merral concluded with how the inter-system liner had narrowly escaped being destroyed.

"And that is our tale," he said. "We felt you ought to hear it."

The representative took a deep breath, placed his head in his hands, and stared silently at the table in front of him. Merral found himself impressed by the man's control. In the silence, he was aware of the gusts of rain being flung at the window. Then Corradon looked up at Perena, his face pale. "This envoy, this strangest of figures, can you repeat what he said to you? His words were . . . ?"

Perena gave the tiniest of nods. "'Captain Lewitz, *night is falling. The war begins.*' The words will not easily be forgotten."

"Excuse me, Captain Lewitz," Clemant said, his dark eyes scrutinizing her, "can we be sure that this was an *objective* occurrence?"

Perena returned his gaze, her face revealing no emotion. "As opposed to a subjective vision? *No.* It *could* have been a hallucination. But as it preceded—and predicted—one of the most dramatic events in Assembly history, I think we ought to treat it seriously."

The representative nodded.

"You have never had anything like this before?" continued the advisor.

"No," said Perena. "Space Affairs gives me a yearly psycho—"

"Lucian, what's your point?" Corradon's tone was sharp.

"Sir, I just want to distinguish qualitatively between the biological data and the ship damage, which can be considered as hard data, and this report. Which is of . . . of an *appearance.* It could be a vision."

Perena looked across at Clemant with what Merral felt was a gentle curiosity. "I considered the vision hypothesis myself, sir, but after examining the evidence I felt it was an objective appearance. And I do not feel that the creature I met with was human." Her voice remained even-toned.

Corradon looked up at the wall clock. "Please," he said, "discussion of exactly what, or *who,* Captain Lewitz saw can wait. The fact that this envoy predicted the Gate loss and allowed us to save almost everyone on an inter-system liner validates it for me. Whatever, or whoever, it was. And it makes the announcement of a war and 'night' worrying in the extreme."

"There was another warning." Vero's voice was quiet but firm. "From a man who dreams and who has visions. He told Merral and me—independently—that he had foreseen the testing of the Assembly and a storm unleashed on Farholme. He gave us a command 'to watch, stand firm, and to hope.'"

"To watch, stand firm, and to hope," Clemant echoed slowly, his round face a mask. Then he looked at Merral with something that hinted at a frown. "Forester, I wish we had known these things. Had these anomalies been reported . . ."

"In hindsight, sir, I erred. But—"

Corradon waved a hand in dismissal. "Never mind now. I'm afraid we have another meeting in five minutes with the Epidemiology Council. Anya—Dr. Lewitz—please tell me more about the biology of these creatures."

"Sir," Anya said, slipping her diary off her belt and putting it on the table, "there are two sorts of organisms that we have evidence for. Both seem, I'm afraid, to be heavily modified humans."

She clicked on her diary, and after a terse command, the map on the wall was replaced by the images Merral and Vero had obtained through the fieldscope. Merral stared again at the strange creatures with their brown, polished-woodlike carapaces, their weirdly jointed limbs, and the platelike covering of their heads and chests. As he watched, the horror of them came back to him, and he was barely able to suppress a shudder. He heard a sharp, appalled intake of breath from Corradon and saw his advisor shaking his head in incomprehension.

"These," said Anya, her voice dark-edged with a note of disgust, "are the ones that we call cockroach-beasts. About 1.5 meters high, with a chitin-rich, rigid outer skin casing. I thought it might be like fingernail cuticle but it's different, apparently generated from insect DNA segments. It's not actually a true exoskeleton, as apparently they do have a vaguely hominid bone structure underneath. It's more an organic armor."

The advisor opened his mouth and closed it again sharply.

Anya showed a few more images. "You can see they are bipedal; they have stereoscopic, forward-facing vision. The insect appearance is purely superficial; they are mammals. Not arthropod eyes either, which is consistent with Elana Antalfer's report that one was watching Herrandown. Distance vision, you see. The hands are strange; the finger and thumb give a scissorlike cutting blade. It's apparently efficient, as Merral found out."

Merral, trying to suppress his memories of the attack, observed a look of stunned incomprehension on the face of the representative and his advisor.

"These we just call ape-creatures," she said, flicking a new image on the screen. Merral felt his stomach squirm again at the sight of the tall, dark-furred beasts with their strange, backward, displaced heads and their peculiar stooping stance. "Bigger, around 2.2 meters tall. These seem to have a mixture of ape and human DNA, but with some innovations. The data is preliminary."

The representative, his jaw moving up and down, gestured at the image. "Ape and human DNA *intermixed*. I find the concept appalling and the reality, well . . . are there *no* limits?"

"A profound question," Vero said in a low but insistent voice.

"This data has not gone to Ancient Earth?" Merral turned to see the advisor staring at him.

"No," Merral answered. "We were taking it with us when the Gate exploded."

Clemant shook his head. "Putting aside—for the moment—the extraordinary irregularity of your journey, why didn't you just transmit all this data as soon as you had it?"

Vero spoke before Merral could answer. "S-sir, I take responsibility. It was because we found out that the signals through the Gate were being intercepted."

"Intercepted?"

"I'm afraid so," Merral said, feeling he needed to protect Vero. "We can show you the evidence, but the intruders were able to intercept and modify Gate signals and diary calls."

Vero raised dark, mobile fingers. "A-and if I may interrupt. Please, we must all assume from now on that all our calls can be overheard. Nothing of what we have said here today must be transmitted."

Corradon and Clemant exchanged wide-eyed glances.

The silence was broken by the advisor's deep voice. "Let me summarize. *One:* you believe that non-human—or modified human—creatures have landed in northeastern Menaya. *Two:* they have at their disposal technologies beyond us: in communications, genetics, and weapons. *Three:* they are hostile. And *four:* they are behind the destruction of the Gate. Is that a fair summary?"

Merral was conscious of nods of agreement around him.

"But *f-five*—" there was determination in Vero's voice—"we must not neglect the spiritual dimension. The disturbances in Herrandown, the modified re-created voice. The feeling of evil we have felt. Above all, the warnings of this envoy. Indeed, the very fact of his presence."

Clemant, his face inscrutable, said nothing.

The representative rose. "We must go," Corradon said. "Although after this, I do not feel like another meeting. I need a chance to think and pray."

He stared at Vero for a moment before shifting his gaze to Merral. "But I have, of course, one more question: What do you suggest I do? You have had more time to think about things."

Merral, suddenly finding himself unclear about what he was to say, looked at Vero.

"To be honest, sir," Vero replied, "I think that, at this precise moment, you should do nothing. Until we can meet again the day after tomorrow."

"Nothing?"

"Yes; we too need time to think and pray. I do not think a day's delay will make any difference. I also fear there is a real danger that we may make a wrong decision."

"But surely," Corradon asked, "it could be dangerous to delay?"

"Possibly, sir, but we do not know where the intruders are. And your north looks very big to me."

"I agree with Vero," Merral said. "We need to keep quiet. For the moment."

Corradon looked at Clemant, who gave an unhappy shrug. "Sir, I agree," he said in a low voice. "We need to be very careful. There are issues here that we need to discuss before we act."

"But shouldn't people be warned?" Corradon asked, smoothing his streaked hair. "I have a responsibility."

"Ah, but warned against what, sir?" Vero was frowning. "We do not know how many intruders there are. Or even whether they are a threat beyond the Lannar Crater area. Besides, everyone is so shaken at the loss of the Gate that another shock may cause panic."

An intense expression of alarm briefly appeared on Clemant's face before vanishing.

"Hmm. What about the other representatives?" Corradon asked. "I must talk with them. Can I call them?"

Vero shook his head. "Sir, I do not think you should use diary transmission to talk of such things. None of us should; it may be intercepted. Are you meeting them soon?"

"They are all gathering here in two days for what are scheduled as several days of crisis meetings."

"Sir," Merral said, catching a nod from Vero, "I suggest we meet with you earlier that day. Would that be possible?"

Corradon looked carefully at him and then glanced at Clemant for support. "Yes."

"And, s-sir," Vero interjected, "if I might make a request, can we meet somewhere more isolated? We have no idea what the power of the intruders is, but we cannot rule out being overheard or noticed here. It was an old rule for meetings to do with strategy to be carried out in secret places."

Corradon shook his head with wearied astonishment. "I had not thought that it was possible to get worse news than the loss of our Gate. But *this* clearly is. This event . . . no, these *events*, are almost too terrible for words. Indeed, the combination of this and our isolation . . ." He paused as if reluctant to finish the sentence. Finally, a degree of composure returned to his face. "I'm sure we can find somewhere suitable to meet. Can't we, Lucian?"

Clemant gave a slight nod of agreement.

The representative walked to the door with a determined step. "Come, Dr. Clemant, we must leave or we may have to make an explanation. And that would not do. Everybody, nine o'clock the day after tomorrow. And then we must take some action." Then he gave a small bow of his head and swept his gaze around the table. "Forester, Sentinel, Doctor, and Captain—my greatest thanks."

Then, with his advisor following him, Representative Corradon left the room.

Perena, anxious to get back to her ship to oversee the repairs, drove them back in her borrowed Space Affairs four-seater. She dropped Anya at the Planetary Ecology Center and Merral and Vero at Narreza Tower, where she and Anya had their apartments. Perena had found Merral and Vero an empty fourth-floor two-bedroom apartment there; an out-of-system visitor was going to occupy it in a fortnight's time, but that wasn't going to happen now.

As they drove, there was almost total silence in the vehicle. *Somehow,* thought Merral, gazing at the somber, wet streets that seemed to echo his mood, *we have crossed another boundary. Until just now, only four of us really knew what was happening. Now we are six, and the two new people have the power to act.*

Now we need to decide what to do.

22

Vero sank heavily onto a sofa and leaned forward, squeezing his head between his hands. Then he looked at Merral with urgent eyes.

"Tell me, my friend, did I make the right decision?"

"About what?"

"Telling Corradon not to do anything. For the moment."

"I think so. We all need time to consider matters. And I can't think of anything we can do at the moment."

"I suppose so." Vero sighed. "But God grant we make the right decision when we do meet again." He stared out of the window at the rain and then shook himself. "I need to talk to Brenito. I have some ideas I need to bounce off him. But what do you propose to do this afternoon?"

Merral thought for a moment. "Now that the diary network is apparently operating properly, call up various people."

"Okay, but from now on we must always watch what we say."

"Of course," Merral answered, reminded of his own incautious conversation with Isabella just before their flight.

Vero paused, as if in thought. After a while he said, "Are you going to call Barrand?"

"Yes. The last thing he heard from us, we were walking northward. I don't want him trying to follow. Any suggestions as to what I say?"

"You can't say much. But—I suppose—you could suggest that he and the other families don't stray into the woods, that they take the dogs with them, and that they stay indoors at night. They might want to have the quarry team move closer. Into the settlement."

"Do you think there's a risk to them?"

Vero shrugged. "Oh, my friend, you know as much as I do. If the intruders can destroy a Gate, they are powerful enough to put us all at risk. But it may not be so simple. . . ." He paused. "Look, I'd better go. I hope Brenito may have some ideas. I have no idea when I will be back."

As Vero rose and left, Merral watched him, feeling that his thin figure was visibly bowed under the weight of events.

Alone in the bare apartment, Merral sat on a chair by the window and gazed across at the wet orchards; shiny, red-tiled roofs; and thick gray clouds that twisted across the sky. He checked his diary and found that, as Corradon had promised, the network was now working. For a moment, he stared at the screen, wondering again what to say if anybody asked him where he had been when he had heard about the Gate explosion. Because he and Vero had been on the *Heinrich Schütz* under the names of other men, only a handful of people knew that they had nearly been caught in the Gate's explosion. Merral realized that he could not now admit to having been on his way secretly out of the Alahir System without raising more questions.

For some time, he pondered the novel and rather unnerving problems that this raised. His only real knowledge of being less than totally honest came from the old literature, and he realized that he had never appreciated how treacherous untruth was. He now saw that if you merely failed to reveal a particular truth, it could become necessary, simply in order to protect that, to tell a new and much stronger untruth. And then to protect *that,* still further duplicity was needed. And so on. One small misdeed bred others until there was a whole swarm of multiplying complications that seemed to have no limit. In the end, he simply prayed that he would not have to reveal too much.

He called his uncle first. Barrand was glad to hear from Merral and seemed satisfied by Merral's statement that they had finished the trip safely and now had a lot of data to analyze. When Merral suggested the precautions that Vero had proposed, his uncle hesitated. "Since you passed through," Barrand said, "the air seems to have cleared. But better play safe; I will do as you suggest."

Merral then called his mother, who was plainly thrilled to hear from him. The implications of the Gate loss to her seemed to go no wider than how that event had affected Ynysmant, and with her usual gusto, she recounted how two neighbors had relatives caught beyond the Gate. It was all "just so *dreadfully* sad." His father was well, she said, but was now going to be even busier at work repairing things. Then his mother inquired after Vero, sent her sympathy, and made Merral promise to tell him that he could be considered part of the family. "We could sort of *adopt* him, really," she said breezily, "for the duration."

"Mother," Merral replied, trying not to laugh, "that's a nice idea, but he hardly needs adopting. And 'the duration' is fifty years plus. But I'll pass on your concern."

He then called Henri, his director at the Planning Institute. When Merral began to give his careful summary of the trip, Henri cut him short. "*Ach,* it probably doesn't matter now," he said, giving his beard a sharp tug. "Man, even keeping Forward Colonies like Herrandown going is now open to question."

Finally, and with a strange reluctance, Merral called Isabella. She was in her office. Straightening her long black hair, she beamed at him with a tired face.

"Merral!" she cried. "So you are still in Isterrane? I thought you were going away."

He caught a sharp gaze of inquiry in her dark eyes.

"Ah. Isabella, the loss of the Gate has changed everything. So I'm here for a few more days. Then back home, I presume." He paused. "Anyway, how are you?"

She shook her head and breathed out heavily, as if unable to express her feelings. "Shaken, in a word. Coming to terms with being out of a vocation."

The realization that Isabella could indeed hardly assess educational progress against Assembly standards when there was no link to the other worlds struck Merral sharply. It was yet another area in which he hadn't given thought to the implications of the Gate loss.

"Yes, I suppose that's true—"

"You mean you hadn't realized it?" Isabella stared at him, as if offended that it hadn't been at the forefront of his mind.

"Sorry," Merral replied, feeling embarrassed. "I suppose there are just so many areas that the Gate loss has had an impact on that I hadn't thought of that. And I'm afraid I've been busy on other things too—"

She shook her head ruefully. "Oh well. Anyway, I'm sitting here thinking the unthinkable. What do I do? Now we are separate. Isolated." She threw her hands up in a gesture of uncertainty and insecurity.

"Isabella, we are all having to come to terms with that. It's not going to be easy."

"Absolutely, and there's the whole psychological dimension. It's potentially scary."

It's even scarier than you think. "I can sense that, but tell me what you believe."

"It's stood everything on its head. We all grow up with the same sort of mental picture of the Assembly. It's like some great, spiky, three-dimensional shape amid the darkness of the stars, and we at Farholme are on the very tip of one of the protrusions. Yet we are always part of it; that's what the word

Assembly means. Worlds' End we may have been, but we always looked in to the center, and we always belonged. . . ." She paused. "But no longer. We are *isolated.* We will have to come to terms with that. Psychologically, it's going to be a very interesting fifty years. *Very* interesting."

I might have known that Isabella would see more deeply than me. He picked his words carefully before he answered her. "Isabella, you have to say to yourself that it's temporary. It's not permanent. And ultimately nothing has changed in the great scheme of things. That's what we have to hold on to." He paused. "The King still reigns." *Perena said that,* he reminded himself.

Isabella seemed to think over his words, and then her face brightened. "Yes, you are right. But it may be difficult for some to adjust. Anyway, when will I see you here?"

"I may be back in Ynysmant the day after tomorrow. Or the day after that, all being well. There's a lot of things to be done here."

"We must meet up as soon as you get back. There's a lot to talk about. About *us.*"

"Yes," Merral said, trying to disguise an unwelcome feeling of apprehension as he closed the link.

Merral was sitting at the table, eating and trying to find a new angle on events, when Vero came in. He took off his wet outdoor jacket and, wiping the water off his dark curly hair, came and sat down gently on the chair on the other side of the table. Without explanation, he took a small package out of his pocket and put it down beside him.

Merral pointed to the pasta he had recently made, and Vero found a plate and helped himself.

"So, have you been outside?" Vero asked after giving thanks.

"Briefly, a walk around the block. I thought it might help me think."

"You've got the picture of what people are feeling then?"

"I was quite impressed. The crowds I met seemed to be taking a positive attitude to it all, really. Is that what you found?"

"Pretty much," Vero said, "but it's early days. I'm not sure how deep or long-lasting the resilience will be."

"Isabella was saying that there's got to be a massive psychological adjustment."

"Indeed," Vero said, midmouthful. "And that makes our dealing with the intruder situation even harder. We must tread warily."

"Yes. And how was your meeting with Brenito?"

Vero swallowed and frowned. "He sends his greetings. He is more shaken by the loss of the Gate than I expected. He feels—as I do—responsible for not sending the warning while we had a chance. But we had—I suppose—a profitable meeting. . . ." He wiped his mouth with a napkin and seemed to stare at the wall.

"You don't seem very convinced."

"Hmm. Oh, I suppose I had my hopes too high. He wants me to set up a meeting with Jorgio. Fine, we will travel out to meet him at Ynysmant. But otherwise—"

"He wasn't much help?"

Vero frowned. "Exactly. . . . In the end he said, 'Well, I shall be interested to see how you handle *this,*' and just looked at me."

"I thought *he* was the official sentinel for Farholme? The point that Dr. Clemant was making this morning."

"I know. But Brenito is a hundred and five and ailing. He also talked about you. 'You know,' he said to me, 'I sensed that Merral would be a warrior; I was puzzled when I saw him head to Earth.' "

"I don't much care for that."

"Didn't think you would. 'That forester and this Jorgio are your assets,' he said."

"Jorgio, maybe. I'm less sure I fit in the asset category. But did he have any solid ideas?"

Vero's face creased into a deeper frown. "Sadly, no. I tentatively outlined some possible actions, and he thought that they were reasonable under the circumstances."

"What possible actions?"

Vero looked away briefly. "I'd rather not say now, Merral. Not just yet. I need to think and pray over them before we see Corradon and Clemant again. At the moment, I'm not even sure that I agree with them." His face became overcast with uncertainty, and for some time he poked at the pasta. Then he looked at Merral. "Do you know what I obtained this afternoon?"

"I have no idea."

Vero pulled the paper bag over and, with an ironic flourish, pulled out two small, yellow, hard-backed notebooks. "It was hard to get them. I am just so unsure about how much our diaries can be explored without our knowledge. But I suspect even the intruders will not be able to spy on pen-and-ink notes. One is for you."

Merral gazed at it wordlessly for a moment before he could bring himself to take it.

"Thank you."

"You see," Vero added, "I have decided that when we next meet with Corradon, he will ask us what we want. That will be the point to make specific requests. I am now going to spend some time making a list so that when they ask, I can say exactly what we need. But exactly what? . . . What dare I ask? What should I ask?"

Then, after helping himself to more pasta, he went and sat down on the sofa, leaned back, folded his hands behind his head, and began to stare up at the ceiling. Eventually he found a pen and set to writing in the book in a tiny, neat script.

Stimulated by Vero's action, Merral spent some time thinking about what his own role might be in trying to deal with the intruder threat. Not long after nine, both of them acknowledged tiredness and, after washing up the supper things, retired to their rooms.

Merral had held high hopes that the Solemn Day of Prayer and Fasting would shed some revelation on the questions he had, give some comfort, and grant guidance for the future. But none of these happened. And when, at last, Merral slept on the night of that Solemn Day, his slumber was a turbulent one, interrupted by strange, eerie dreams of a curious intensity. In the last of these, and the only one about which he could remember anything, he became aware that he was standing on a high, bare hill in a vast, arid landscape of browns and grays under a sky as white as bone. As he looked down the slope below him, he could see, working their way up toward him in slow, steady strides that never faltered, two figures in the gray, plated space suits of the early Assembly. Finally, they stood just before him on the summit, and as he peered into the reflective metal visors, he saw that he could see nothing, not even a reflection of himself. Then one visor slid away downward and Merral found himself gazing into the dark, hairy face of an ape-creature with snarling yellow-white teeth. As he leapt back in horror and fear, the visor on the other slid away sideways to reveal the shiny brown, woodlike plates and dark, gleaming eyes of a cockroach-beast. As the creatures raised their arms and closed on him, Merral woke and sat bolt upright, clutching his heaving chest.

Unable—and unwilling—to return to sleep, and with dawn less than an hour away, he rose and quietly showered. Then he sat and watched as the rays of the rising sun shining through torn clouds struck first the highest buildings and masts of Isterrane and then slid lower until the houses, trees, and finally the grass were baptized with a fresh, golden light. And as Merral watched, the horror of his dream seemed to fade into oblivion.

At half past seven he and Vero went up to Perena's apartment to find Anya there, sorting out the breakfast.

"Perena's gone to collect some images," Anya explained. As they helped to make breakfast, Merral found himself intrigued by how different Perena's apartment was from that of her sister. Where Anya's had been crowded to the point of clutter and covered with green and brown wall hangings, Perena's flat was bare and neat with cream walls. Aside from some small abstract sculptures on glass shelves and a large glass chess set, the only decoration in the main room was a large watercolor of a night scene on one of the ice moons of Fenniran, with what Merral took to be Farholme glinting in an upper corner.

As they were about to eat, Perena arrived.

"So," Vero asked as they greeted her, "have you found something new?"

"No," she said, and her face showed unconcealed disappointment. "They have vanished. We have a program for finding a lost ship or its wreckage. I had put all the most recent images of all of northern Menaya through it just after we met the other day, and the machines spent all yesterday scanning them. Nothing. I have that single thermal image of the shuttle taken the morning after your attack and that is all."

Vero grimaced. "I was hoping we would have something concrete for today's meeting."

"I too." She looked at her chess set. "It's hard to make a strategy when you don't know what pieces are in play."

"Agreed. And no idea where they have gone?"

"None, Vero. They could easily be in an area the size of your Northern America."

"But it can be found? by a manual search?"

She stared at him. "Perhaps. You'd look for thermal, magnetic, gravitational anomalies. Get imagery and scan every square kilometer visually. You'd have to know the area and the terrain. It could take weeks."

"But it could be done?"

"Unless they make themselves invisible."

Merral realized that everyone had turned to look at him. "Are you suggesting I do it?"

"Perhaps," Vero said, waving a hand dismissively. "But we will see what the meeting brings."

Over breakfast, Anya asked Vero whether he had had any new thoughts. He paused for a moment before answering. "Only this: I am puzzled about these intruders. They seem both powerful and weak; confident and hesitant at the same time."

"Explain that," said Anya. "They scare me; I'll be honest. To destroy the Gate . . ." She shuddered.

"Yes," said Vero thoughtfully, "they can destroy a Gate and they can modify and fake our communications. We mustn't forget that. Yet—" he tapped the table with a finger—"yet, their dealings with us have badly failed so far. Merral and I are alive and well. Their losses were heavy."

"God was good," said Perena.

"Amen and amen," Vero agreed. "But you see what I mean. It's all very odd. It suggests that they may have only a limited power. They may not even know as much as we imagine they know. But what do you think, Merral?"

"Me? I am as puzzled as you are," Merral replied. "But I take your point, Vero. I know nothing of warfare, but I know something of sport. I have a feeling—no, more than that—that what happened was not the carrying out of carefully planned tactics, but rather a desperate response to something going wrong."

"Fair point," muttered Anya, and no one seemed inclined to disagree.

A few minutes later, Vero pulled his yellow notebook out of his pocket. "Now," he announced, "we need to decide what we want from our meeting. I think it would be helpful for you, Merral, to lead again, and I think it would also be very helpful if we agreed what we wanted beforehand."

Merral saw nods of accord from Perena and Anya and gestured his assent.

"Thanks," Vero said. "Now, in the few minutes left before we must leave for the meeting, let us decide what it is we wish to ask. I should say that I have my own requests, but for the moment I would prefer to keep them quiet."

"Any reason?" Merral asked.

"They will be controversial." He gave a deep sigh. "So controversial I think it is only fair that I alone bear any blame."

23

The Planetary Affairs building gleamed like a great white sail in the fresh sunlight. A clerk, who was expecting them, led them down a series of stairs and corridors, ushered them into a small, windowless, white-walled room and closed the door on them.

Merral looked around. Crates and boxes had been neatly piled at the back of the room to make space for a single, long, lightweight table and six white folding chairs, and along one bare wall was hung a huge administrative map of eastern Menaya with towns, roads, and airstrips overlain on the topography.

Merral disliked the room; it was small and seemed to hem him in. His mind slipped away to the open woods and forests depicted on the map, and he found himself heartily wishing that he was back at his old job, with the sound of the wind in the trees and the dappled light breaking through fluttering leaves.

His daydreams were no sooner begun than ended, as the door opened and Representative Corradon and Advisor Clemant joined them and took seats round the table.

Merral found himself looking at Corradon. There was a hint of tiredness in the blue eyes, and the representative's bearing did not seem quite as erect as it had been.

Clemant's face was inscrutable, yet his tense posture and his sharp gaze hinted at a deep concern.

After the briefest of greetings, Corradon stared hard at Merral. "So," he said, "I have had some time to think about matters. First though, have you anything new for us?" His words were slow and seemed to hang in the room.

Merral gestured at Perena. "Sir, Captain Lewitz has looked further for the ship."

"And?"

"All I have," Perena said apologetically, "is what I showed you before. There is no obvious trace of an intruder ship. It could have left Farholme, but I believe we would have spotted that."

"I see," the representative said. "I had hoped we would have a location. But finding it is something we badly need to do." He glanced at Clemant, and Merral saw some look of concern pass between them.

Corradon looked around. "You may be surprised to learn that the information flow in this meeting may not be one way. I—*we*—want to reveal something to you."

Merral saw Vero's face register surprise.

"Just after Easter this year we had a short-lived incident that we could only classify as an extraordinary sociological anomaly. I thought of mentioning it the other day, but Lucian and I needed to think more about it. I believe it is important."

He turned to his advisor. "Lucian, please tell them about the *Miriama*."

Clemant rose, walked to the map, and gestured at a coastal town on the southeastern corner of Menaya. "The *Miriama* is a physical oceanography vessel—Type Six. It operates out of the Oceanography Center at Larrenport."

At the word *Larrenport,* Merral had a sudden image of the town as he remembered it: the serried rows of windswept white houses clinging to the cliffs on either side of the great semicircular scoop of the bay.

Clemant's factual and precise voice drew him back to the present. "It has a crew of ten. Normally it operates in the immediate offshore waters. About a month ago, immediately after Easter, its crew spent two weeks much farther north in the western part of the Mazurbine Ocean." He stretched an arm out to encircle an area just offshore of where the Nannalt Delta system protruded into the sea. "Tarrent's Rise, I think, is the main feature there. It was, for the most part, a routine trip—surveying water temperatures. As most of you know—and certainly Forester D'Avanos—we have been concerned about the trend of falling average winter temperatures over the last five years. Although the weather was unseasonably bad and it was not a pleasant trip, they returned to port safely."

He paused, and Merral sensed that he was watching Corradon carefully, as if taking his cue from him. "At least, physically. Then we had a private message passed to us from the director of the Oceanography Center. The crew had made a curious proposal. It was simply this: Because of hardship, for the duration of such trips, they wanted their allowance to be increased." He paused again, looking around carefully for the reaction.

Vero sat upright with such speed that he nearly fell over. "Increased? Their allowance *increased?*" he said, in a voice whose pitch seemed to have risen several tones. "But the allowance is *fixed*. For everybody in the Assembly . . . For you, for me." He stared around with astonished brown eyes and then, with an "Oh dear, oh dear," fell into a troubled silence.

"Just so," noted the representative, in a tone that conveyed that he too had been shocked.

Clemant nodded. "When we had established it was a serious proposal, I was sent over. I had an interview with the captain, a Daniel Sterknem. He—*they*—apologized and dropped the matter. In fact, he seemed a bit puzzled where the idea had come from. I felt there had been more to the trip than he wanted to mention. But he now no longer wanted to pursue the matter. It worried us for a time."

"As well it might," said Vero. "It could unravel the Assembly very quickly if we started recompensing people by financial means. We would be back in a pre-Intervention mess very fast. How do you decide who deserves what? Who is worth more? A Farholme representative or a park keeper on Ancient Earth?"

"Our thoughts too, of course," Corradon replied. "But to me—to us—it sounded similar to some aspects of what you have described or hinted at."

Merral, trying to come to terms with the unpleasantness of a situation in which everybody was demanding compensation for what they did, was aware of the others' nods of agreement.

As Clemant returned to his seat, Corradon glanced around with a solemn expression. "So, now we need to decide what to do." Then his gaze fixed on Vero. "But before that, I want to ask our sentinel a question. From what I remember of the purpose of the Sentinel Order, you were set up to look for any new outbreak of evil. Correct?"

"Yes, sir. That was Moshe Adlen's desire at the inception of the sentinels. Having served throughout the fighting that ended the Rebellion, his desire was to ensure that such events were avoided."

"Yes. It is as I remember. And this is clearly an outbreak of evil. So, in the light of all the evidence, what do you think we are dealing with?"

Vero stared at his hands for a moment and then looked up at his questioner. "I should say, sir, that most of my guesses have been badly wrong. And some of my actions have, it seems, been unwise. But you are right that this is a sentinel matter. Indeed, I am convinced that it was precisely to look out for this sort of thing that we were set up. That I failed to spot it in time to prevent the Gate loss I think reflects badly on me. But it also reflects the fact that these events are not how we as an order had envisaged such a threat."

"If it is in my power to do so, I excuse you." Corradon's voice was little more than a murmur. "Anyway, any evaluation of your role and that of your order must await our reunification with the rest of the Assembly. But please, what do you think is going on?"

Vero opened his notebook, glanced at a page, and then leaned forward. When he spoke, the words seemed to be almost painfully drawn out of him. "I feel there are three elements here. The first is this: there is so much of this matter that suggests the work of our own troubled species."

Corradon's eyebrows lifted in surprise. "With the breach of so many of the Technology Protocols? No one in the Assembly could do this." There was a hint of outrage in his voice. "And there is no other humanity."

"Indeed," Vero agreed, without raising his eyes from his notebook. "That is what we have always known. But, even without Merral feeling that he glimpsed a man, I would still guess that there was something human here."

"The use of human DNA suggests that too," interjected Anya.

"Perhaps," said Corradon as he sat back in his chair and stared at Vero. "So your first element is a human component. But, Sentinel, please continue."

Vero gazed ahead. "Th-the human element is important. I think we can eliminate any idea that we are dealing with aliens here. The second element is also another puzzle. It is that, even before you told us about the request of the crew of the *Miriama,* I felt that there were just so many aspects of this that echoed the times before the Assembly. Or some of the proposals the Rebellion's instigator, William Jannafy, made long ago. It's almost as if something—or *someone*—is turning back the clock."

Vero looked at his notes again. "So that is the second element. I feel that there is an air of lawlessness, of rebellion, about it. Of rebellion . . ." He nodded, as if agreeing with himself, and then went on. "And if it is to do with mankind, then they have pushed beyond all the boundaries we have defined, whether they be in genetics or robotics. . . ." He hesitated, his expression becoming still more solemn. "Or, I fear, in other areas."

"I see," Corradon noted in an unhappy tone. "A terrible thought. Your third strand?"

Vero grimaced and twisted awkwardly on his seat. "Ah. That, sir, is the easiest by far. There is something evil about this. You can see it in the spiritual contagion. At its heart, this is evil."

"I see," said Corradon after a long, drawn-out silence. "Yes, I will not argue with that at least. Human, rebellious, and evil—worrying verdict. Lucian, what do you say?"

The advisor stared at his fingernails for a moment as if thinking carefully. Then he looked up at Corradon with his unfathomable eyes and said in his low, dark voice, "Sir, I would not argue with that view. But I would say that—by themselves—the adjectives *human*, *rebellious*, and *evil* do not greatly help us. Not without defining exactly what the nature of the threat is."

Merral was troubled by the brittle, almost antagonistic, edge to Clemant's words.

Vero looked hard at the advisor and then flung his hands wide. "D-Dr.

Clemant, I do not dare be more precise. I was asked to comment and that I have done."

"Please," Corradon said, rubbing his forehead. "I take Sentinel Enand's comments in the spirit they were offered. But I have a more practical question for our forester here." He sighed. "You see, we meet with the other representatives tonight and tomorrow. Do I pass on to them what you have told us over these meetings? What do you say?"

"I would think so," Merral answered, "but I am open to other advice."

"I would agree," Vero said, "but it should be done privately and face-to-face. They must be told not to tell anything about this matter to anybody else. And not to use a diary to talk about it or to store anything about it."

"To keep it private." Corradon stared at him with a perturbed expression. "Yes, you think they can read our diaries." He cast a brief, unhappy glance at his advisor. "This is very difficult, Vero. You think all our lines of communication are being intercepted?"

"No. But for the moment, I think it is wisest to assume so. I want to research how we may make them secure."

Corradon made no reply, and instead Clemant spoke. "Forgive us, Vero," he said, his voice so deep that it almost seemed to rumble, "but perhaps we find it harder to take such a view. To put ourselves in—what shall we say?—a *suspicious* frame of mind."

Vero hesitated. "I can sympathize. If I had not seen what I have seen in the last few days, I would be of a similar mind."

Clemant tilted his head slightly, stroked his chin with a finger, and frowned. "But we are an open society. The idea of not transmitting views is very odd. I mean, we have a policy of transparency here." Merral felt certain that there was a slight, but unmistakable, emphasis on the word *here*.

"As elsewhere in the Assembly," replied Vero slowly, phrasing his words with an almost deliberate politeness. "But I have to say, from my studies of the ancient past, when faced with enemies, almost the most vital information we could give them is what we know about them."

"Yes, I could see that," Corradon said slowly, "but, Vero, should we not circulate a general warning for people to be on their guard?"

"I have agonized over this and I think not. I think, for myself, there might be a risk of panic."

Merral saw Clemant shift uneasily in his seat, and the representative looked at him. "Lucian?"

"Panic," Clemant said, with a deeply troubled tone of voice, "is the worst of all possible responses." He stared at his hands, neatly extended on the table, for a moment and then looked up with what Merral thought was a barely suppressed expression of alarm. "With widespread panic, Farholme could become ungovernable."

"Sorry, Vero," Corradon said, "what you want really is, I believe, secrecy. *Secrecy*." The representative pronounced the word emphatically and slowly, as if testing an unfamiliar sound. "A term I do not like. Any more than I like a world without a Gate. But I sense its logic. I take it you agree, Merral?"

"Sir, I agree, most reluctantly, with Vero's suggestion of keeping this private. For the moment."

"Very well. Lucian?"

"Reluctantly." Clemant tapped a finger nervously on the table. "*Most* reluctantly."

"I see." Corradon's dislike of the situation was plain from his expression. "Very well. We will tell the other representatives that we have a problem. And that they must keep quiet. But, Forester, what do we actually *do*?"

Merral recognized that the time they had expected had come. "I—we—feel that above all, we need more information. The conclusion we have come to is that we all want to work on this. In different ways." He waited to be sure that his words and tone registered. "I would suggest that you authorize the four of us to investigate various aspects of the problem. We would, of course, report to you."

"I see," Corradon said with a pause. "A sort of research group. And you, Forester, would personally do . . . what?"

"Sir, we have agreed that I should look at the satellite imagery to see if I can find out where the intruders are based. To find the ship they came in. That seems a priority."

"It's an incredibly large area," Corradon said, staring at the map on the wall.

"Around three million square kilometers," Clemant said, with the air of someone who had calculated it.

"That's a maximum. But it is big and rough."

"But you know the area as well as anybody does, I suppose," Corradon said. "And the others? Dr. Lewitz, for instance; what about you?"

"Me?" Anya said, fixing the representative with her lively blue eyes. "I want to rerun those DNA tests. And I want to model and compile everything we know about the two creature types."

Corradon gave a grunt of approval. "Captain Lewitz?"

Perena hesitated a moment and then spoke in her low and intense voice. "Sir, I would like to look at any reports produced by the team investigating the destruction of the Gate."

Corradon stared at her. "We are putting our best people on that. Will you be able to add anything to what they can do? I have no doubt about your piloting abilities, Captain. But this is, surely, Below-Space and gravitational physics?"

Perena's face expressed the gentlest disagreement. "Sir, I know things that they do not. They, I presume, are looking for a mechanical failure. I will be looking for a destructive act from the outset. I also know that Gate calls were being intercepted and modified at least a week ago. I know that there was an incursion into Farholme space as long ago as just before Nativity. In fact, I want to look at the astronomical data for that time to see if we can work out where the ship came from. And, sir," she said, and paused briefly, "I also want to set up a watch."

"A watch?"

"We know one intruder ship entered the Alahir System. But are there other ships there too? We need to scan the skies."

"So we are not caught out again?" said Clemant.

"Exactly."

"Hmm," Corradon said, sharing a knowing look with his advisor. "I can see this has been thought out carefully." He turned to Vero. "And so, what does our sentinel want?"

A good question, Merral thought.

"Sir," Vero said in a cautious voice, "my request is one that I alone am responsible for. It is somewhat radical, and I would be grateful if you and Advisor Clemant would not reject it out of hand."

"You will have our most careful consideration of it."

"Thank you." Vero looked grave. "S-sir, I would like to put together and train a team."

Puzzlement swept across the representative's face. "A team of what?" he asked. "I thought the four of you *were* a team?"

After a moment in which Vero seemed to be summoning courage, he simply said, "Sir, I want a team of people who will work on the defense of Farholme."

There was an interchange of surprised glances, and Corradon turned to Merral. "Do I gather that this is news to you?"

"Er, yes," Merral answered, aware that Clemant was staring at Vero with an expression of open misgiving.

"Hmm, I see," Corradon said. "Vero, *defense?* You'd better expand."

Vero's fingers twitched. "Well, for a start, investigate—and then make—anything that we think will protect us. Against the intruders. I'd like to look at ways of making secure communications." There was uncertainty in his voice, and Merral realized for the first time that for all his cleverness and insight, Vero was not very good at verbal persuasion. "I b-believe, well—for instance—that if the intruders are looking into our diary system, it ought to be possible to detect how it's done. And stop it."

"I can see the value of that," Corradon murmured. "What else?"

Vero looked uncomfortable and bit his lip. "And, sir, I want to research some, well . . . defensive equipment."

"Defensive *equipment?*" The bushy eyebrows nearly met. "Can you elaborate?"

Vero's dark face became strained. "Well—shall we say—er, military things."

"Military?" Corradon repeated, leaning forward as if he had misheard something. Merral caught a low gasp from Clemant.

Vero hesitated and then, apparently aware that he had already committed himself, spoke again with more confidence. "Yes, I mean, can we produce weapons? Should we need them."

"Weapons . . ." The chair creaked as Corradon sat back in it, looking thoroughly confounded. "I see . . . ," he said, glancing at his advisor, who was staring intently at Vero.

"Well, I agree with Vero," Anya said in a determined tone of voice. "Reluctantly. You can't realistically keep tackling these things with bush knives and exploding diaries."

"But, Anya—Dr. Lewitz," the representative replied with an air of gentle and dignified exasperation, "we are Assembly. Or we were. I remind you what you all know: the time of peace we have had from Jannafy's rebellion to now is over twice as long as that from the building of the Pyramids to the start of the Assembly. We have given up war."

"But, sir, respectfully, our enemies haven't," Merral said and was surprised at the force of his words. "And while, sir, I share your unease, I too agree with Vero and Anya. We need at least the possibility of weapons. Last time we were blessed with an undeserved success. Next time we may not be able to rely so much on a kindly Providence."

Perena's voice, as quiet and undemonstrative as ever, broke the profound silence that followed Merral's words. "And if I must declare my preference—and it seems I must—I also back Vero and Merral. We nearly lost a general survey craft and an inter-system liner the other day. We *did* lose a Gate."

The advisor, who had been staring from one to the other with a look of careful and unhappy evaluation, turned to Vero.

"But, Sentinel," he rumbled, "this issue of weapons. Surely, it does go against every principle of the Assembly?"

Vero shook his head. "No, sir, I would disagree. The Assembly has always had a small defensive force at the insistence of the sentinels."

"It took twenty years of debate for it to be approved," Clemant grunted, "if I remember correctly. We could start that process here if you or Brenito wished."

Vero's dark skin seemed to pale. "No, on the contrary, sir," he answered, his voice unsteady but defiant, "I-I would like it *now*. If you want me to justify it, I would say, if necessary, that Farholme now forms a little Assembly, an offspring of the greater Assembly. And what was decided for the parent applies to the child. And I don't want two frigates in twenty years; I want twenty-four men and women tomorrow. Or the day after. Quietly. But I do want them." Then, as if taken aback by his own boldness, he added, "P-please."

The advisor, apparently surprised by the force of Vero's words, blinked, shook his head sharply, and turned to Corradon, as if seeking his help.

"I note your disapproval, Lucian."

"Sir," he said slowly, "we know so little about these intruders. I mean, we may be misreading their intentions."

Corradon raised an eyebrow. "But surely, Lucian, they don't *seem* friendly. We have the holes in Perena's general survey craft and our forester's wounded ankle as very tangible evidence of that."

Clemant looked around, his face troubled, and shrugged. "Perhaps, sir. But I maintain that we need to be cautious. By everybody's admission—even that of our visiting sentinel—we do not know what is going on. At all. I agree that these things seem hostile. But so might our dogs. There may be other explanations. For us to act in a hostile manner . . . it might be a capital mistake; it could give a misleading impression of the Assembly. Possibly a fatal one. It is a heavy risk."

Corradon put his large hands on either side of his nose and rocked his head backward and forward, clearly weighing up what he was hearing. "Perhaps, Lucian. *Perhaps.* But they *did* destroy the Gate. And as for risk? All our choices have a risk."

There was an awkward silence, and everyone seemed to turn to Vero who, looking discomfited, blinked and then shrugged. "I simply believe," he said, "that it would be wise to prepare for the worst. I am not asking to use weapons, only to have them made ready."

Clemant shook his head. "But the very act of preparing weaponry could destabilize an already precarious situation."

"Maybe," Corradon said. "But only maybe. Anya, Perena, and Merral—do I take it that you are all in agreement that Vero's proposal is the way forward?"

"Reluctantly, yes," Merral said, and as he spoke, he heard agreement from the sisters.

"Very well," Corradon replied. "Lucian, we must leave. We can talk about this later. I can make no decision now, anyway. I have a lot to think about."

The representative rose to his feet stiffly and moved toward the door. Then, his hand on the door handle, he turned to face them. Merral was struck by how hidden any traces of alarm or disquiet had become.

"Thank you all for coming," Corradon said, in such an untroubled tone of voice that Merral felt they might have been discussing nothing more serious than some plan for a forest extension.

Then he caught Vero's eye. "Sentinel, if—and only *if*—I was to authorize this, how many people did you say you would want?"

Vero seemed to take a deep breath. "Twenty-four, sir. W-well, actually I'd prefer thirty-six. Of the best students you have in around twelve disciplines. I have details—"

The representative raised a hand to silence him. "Later, maybe. Well, I will give you my answer as soon as I can. The other representatives are on their way here, and there are many other issues for me to weigh in the balance. I imagine most of you are going to be staying in Isterrane. Merral, now, what are your plans?"

"I hope to take the two o'clock flight back to Ynysmant, sir. Unless I hear from you otherwise, I will return to work as a forester."

"I see," Corradon answered. "Well, whatever happens, I hope that your return to your vocation can be soon. But let me get someone from the office here to take you to the airport. Where are you staying?"

"Narreza Tower."

"Very good. Say twelve-thirty?" He looked around and smiled. "Thank you all again. I would covet your prayers for the decisions I have to make."

Then he and the advisor left, and as the door closed behind them, Merral could hear animated conversation starting up as they walked up the corridor.

There was a long silence in the room.

Finally Anya spoke. "Hey, Earther," she said, looking at Vero with a grin, "next time you want us to agree with you about forming an army, can you give us some warning?"

24

At Narreza Tower, Merral and Vero parted from the sisters and returned to their apartment. With sunlight pouring in through the windows, the place seemed brighter and more welcoming. Merral persuaded a subdued Vero to sit outside on the balcony.

"Do you think that we will get what we asked for?" Merral asked him.

"Yes," came the response, "I think we will. But I am worried about that discussion."

"Yes. I felt the opposition from Clemant was striking. I put it down to the shock of the loss of the Gate and the seriousness of what we were discussing."

Vero looked at Merral, his brow creased. "Yes. Perhaps that is it. 'The Gate Loss Syndrome'—a state of mind which you have never heard of before because I have just invented it. I think you will soon. But what do you think lay behind Clemant's attitude?"

"I felt he was afraid."

Vero nodded. "I agree. I have started doing a lot of reading in the pre-Intervention files. It is instructive, even if alarming. We tend to think of fear as an isolated evil. But when you go to the past, what is striking is how often it is fear that triggers other things. Anger and hatred, for instance, often come from fear. 'When a man is terribly afraid he may do terrible things.' It's a quote."

Then, after a few moments, Vero looked at Merral. "I was shaken by the news of that ship, though."

"The *Miriama?*"

"Yes. I am wondering if the evil may not be spreading faster than we had feared. And even whether our conversation today may not have reflected something of the decline we are undergoing."

"Maybe."

"Merral, we must watch. Close at hand and far away."

Then he pulled out his notebook and, with a plea that he wanted to think through what had been said at the meeting, leaned back in his chair and closed his eyes.

Half an hour later, there was a sharp knock at the apartment door. Merral got up from his seat on the balcony and walked to the door. "Come in," he called out.

The door opened and a tall, large-framed woman in her early thirties came in. Merral stared at her, simultaneously struck by her height, the long, wavy mane of black hair that flowed over her shoulders, the bright but rather sad dark brown eyes, and an unusual sense of energy. He instantly decided that he had never met her; she was not a woman you would easily forget.

"Excuse me," the visitor said, in a sharp, no-nonsense voice, "Representative Corradon said to call here. Are you—?"

"Forester Merral Stefan D'Avanos." Merral turned. "And this is—"

But Vero had joined him. "Verofaza Laertes Enand, sentinel. Or Vero."

The visitor's smile was open and toothy. "And I'm Gerrana Anna Habbentz, Research Professor of Physics, Isterrane University. You can call me Gerry."

Vero shook her hand and gestured to the balcony. "Welcome, Gerry. Come and join us; take a seat. I'm afraid my physics is rather decayed. What sort of physics, anyway?"

"Stellar physics," she said, walking out onto the balcony with a grace that seemed surprising for such a large woman. Yet as he looked at her, Merral was aware that, for all her vigor, she was troubled.

"We have a good little department, really," Gerry said, taking in the view. "Or *had* . . . before the Gate went. Fifty years of isolation isn't going to help." Suddenly she looked glum.

"I'm sorry. Can we get you a drink?" Vero said.

"Thanks. Water's fine," Gerry said, lowering herself into a chair and stretching out long legs. "And we will lose lab access. Of course."

"Lab access?" Merral asked.

"Far Station physics lab and solar observatory. Thank you," she said, as Vero offered her a glass of water. "Yes, flight cutbacks."

"Ah," Merral said.

She shrugged wearily. "That's the least of the issues." She sipped the water. "Look, guys, sorry to come here without warning, but I have something that *may* be of value."

Vero smiled—Merral decided that there was something about Gerry that invited smiles—and said, "Let me guess: you have a faster-than-light-speed ship all ready to launch?"

Gerry returned his smile, but Merral felt there was pain in it. "Now wouldn't *that* be nice?" She sipped at the water again. "But you are pretty close. I may—mark the word *may*—have a way for you to contact the Assembly."

"Surely not." The smile left Vero's face and his eyes widened. "You'd need a Gate link of some sort."

"No. We may be able to send a message by quantum-linked photons."

Vero looked at Merral with a baffled expression; Merral felt sure that he returned it.

"Gerry," Vero said, "go slow here, please."

She shrugged. "It's been known since the dawn of physics—well, Einstein anyway—that you can link subatomic particles so that if you separate them, what happens to one happens to the other." She looked inquiringly at them with her big dark eyes. "'Quantum entanglement?' No? 'Spooky action-at-a-distance'?"

"Sorry."

"Oh well . . . Anyway," she said, "trust me. Einstein got a lot wrong, but not this. If you had some linked photons on Ancient Earth and brought some of them here, what you did to those here would instantly be duplicated on Earth. Okay? So, in theory, if you released them as flashes of light here, matching flashes of light would occur on Earth. Instantly. So you could send a message."

"But—," Vero began.

"Why isn't it used? Because it's horribly complex to set up. And there's noise. And conventional Gate links work well, are simple, and 100 percent reliable."

"Until now," Vero added.

"Exactly," she agreed, and Merral heard a tinge of sadness in her voice.

"But, Gerry," Vero said slowly, "if I understand you—you'd need two things: A supply of linked photons here and someone somewhere else watching their—*entangled,* you said?—counterparts."

"Exactly. And it turns out that we have a limited supply of the first and we may have the second."

"Go on," said Vero, his face a picture of eagerness.

"As part of advanced physics, post-Einsteinian physics part three—never the most popular course, by the way—we demonstrate the principle. We have a twinned department—at Zacaras University on Tahmolan—two hundred light-years away, and we have a small supply of entangled photons they sent us. And, at a prearranged time, we send them simple messages."

"It works?" Vero asked.

"Of course it works," she said sharply. "That's why we do it. So, theoretically, we could send them a message. And if someone is watching—expecting a signal—then they might see and decode it."

"And *would* anyone be watching?"

Gerry colored slightly. "The professor there, Amin Ryhan, is a good friend. Well, more than that—"

Suddenly, Merral understood exactly why this woman was troubled. "I'm sorry," he said. "I'm very sorry."

Gerry's face wrinkled. "Yeah. Well, it happens. We were committed and going to get engaged. Amin wanted me to leave Farholme. . . . Sorry, that's all personal stuff—" For a second, Merral thought she was going to cry, but she blinked and began again. "I was going to try to send a message to him. Then I thought that was selfish. So I had a chat with Anwar—Representative Corradon—yesterday; he's a distant relative. And he said to talk to you. Straightaway. I suppose he wants me to send a message to the Assembly saying that we are okay and that the casualties are low. To list the seven dead on the ship."

"No," Vero said, with a fierce shake of his head. "Gerry, we have a far more important message. How much can you send?"

She hesitated. "Not much. Forty words sent a hundred times, or a hundred words sent forty times. And there's no guarantee. We may not even get an acknowledgement. I'd go for repetitions over length. Send them on the hour, Universal Assembly Time."

"Merral," Vero said, his face a confusion of emotions, "we need to talk. Gerry, will you excuse us?"

Merral followed Vero into his bedroom.

Vero closed the door. "My friend, if this works, it's a gift of God," he hissed. "We have to use it now."

"Shouldn't we get it approved by the representatives?"

Vero shook his head. "No. Definitely *no*. Corradon's given us the go-ahead. They could spend months debating the wording. Or that's the way I read it. Besides, the warning needs to be sent now." He clenched his fists. "Merral, my caution caught me out last time. I will not risk another delay."

"But do we let her in on the secret?"

"Of course. We have to. She's a useful ally." Vero pulled out his notebook. "But what to say?"

After a few minutes of scribbling and crossing out, they had agreed on three sentences:

> *Farholme Gate destruction not an accident but sabotage by non-Assembly forces. Evidence of genetically modified humans, superior technology, and hostile intent. Intruder presence associated with a corrupting spiritual evil.*

Vero hesitated, looked at it again, and shook his head.

"No point in messing about, is there?" he said quietly. He took a deep breath and added three words: *Arm the Assembly!*

"I can't believe I wrote that," he said in an awed tone and looked at Merral. "Do you have a better idea?"

"No," answered Merral slowly, feeling—yet again—out of his depth.

Vero signed it. "There," he said. "That will put the cat among the pigeons."

"The what?"

Vero shrugged. "A twentieth-century Ancient English idiom. It was one of their sports; they would chase pigeons with cats. They were odd like that."

"Are you sure?"

"No, not really. But it's a confident guess. They *were* odd—" Vero slapped Merral on the back—"but let's see what the prof says."

They walked out to see Gerry leaning on the balcony rail and staring out to the western headland where the fluffy clouds still hung over the plateau.

"Gerry," said Vero, handing her a sheet of paper from the notebook, "you'd better sit down and read this. You should add some words of your own to Amin."

She sat down and read it, shook her head so her dark hair flew about, and read it again. The color drained from her face. Then, without warning, she slammed her fist down on the table so hard the glass bounced off it, scattering water on the floor.

"I knew it!" she snapped, her voice bitter and angry. "I knew it. It wasn't an accident. These . . . animals!" She glared at the paper again, then looked up with wild and angry eyes. "You'd better tell me what's going on."

Over the next ten minutes, Merral and Vero explained to Gerry what had happened. As they did, Merral felt that Gerry's mood seemed to harden. When they had finished, she got up from her chair, paced around for a moment, then stood against the wall and stared at them, a picture of defiance.

"Okay, I get the picture," she said. "It's *war*. I'll send the message this evening. But what else can I do? These things are our enemy. The Assembly's enemy. They are evil."

"I think we can use a physicist," Vero said. "I'd like you to think about how these things got here. These creatures have come a long way. By a ship, not a Gate. Hibernation? Colony ships?"

She nodded. "Or faster-than-light travel. Autonomous Below-Space travel, perhaps." She paused. "Okay. I'll go and send the message. It will take time to set up the equipment. It should go tonight. But no guarantees, right? We may not even get a confirmation back."

"Gerry, do what you can," Vero said. "I'll be in touch."

"I hope so," she said, and there was determination in her voice. "I'd like to do something to fight back."

As they strode to the door, Merral felt Gerry's shoulders had straightened, and her eyes glittered with a new purpose.

"Oh, Gerry," Vero said, "you know Perena Lewitz?"

"The captain? Yeah, she's flown us to the lab before now."

"That's her. Get together and talk with her on the travel issue. She has some orbital data."

"Okay, I'll do just that."

"Anything else you can think of you might want to look at?"

"Yes," she said, fixing Vero with brown eyes from which any softness had fled. "I'm surprised you didn't mention it."

"What?"

"Weapons." There was a cold anger in her words.

"I'm not sure—," Merral began to say, but Vero silenced him with a gesture. Merral said, "Okay, Gerry. You look into that too."

As their visitor's footsteps faded away down the corridor, Merral turned to Vero. "Was that wise? To talk of weapons?"

"It was her suggestion," said Vero defensively. "And it's only research."

"And shouldn't we have warned her not to get too deep in exploring Below-Space?"

"My friend, it's only a theory. But I'll mention it when we meet again."

There was a knock at the door. Merral opened it to find a man in an official uniform who introduced himself as the driver sent to collect him.

"My apologies for being early," the man said. "There has been a change in schedule. Are you ready to leave now?"

Vero followed Merral as he went to his bedroom to collect the few things he had.

"I leave it up to you what to say to people in Ynysmant and Herrandown," Vero said with quiet insistence. "Thankfully, in a strange way, the destruction of the Gate has wiped our trip north out of most people's minds."

"True, but I will have to talk to Henri about it at least." *And Isabella will want to know.*

"Yes, it's difficult. But you could, I think, just say that there may be some genetic anomalies up there. If people want to think that they are natural mutations, just let them think so."

"So we tell the partial truth and not the whole truth?"

"Oh, I suppose so." Vero sighed. "It's all so difficult. Remember: what is said cannot be unsaid; what is unsaid can yet be said. But encourage some precautions, though."

"I will."

"I will be in touch as soon as I hear anything. It may not be direct; I will have to find ways of communicating with you securely. But be careful."

It came to Merral that, even without the approval of Corradon and the representatives, Vero was already making plans.

"You are assuming that you are going to get the go-ahead, aren't you?"

"Yes." Vero nodded. "I understand the reluctance, but there is no option. I felt it before the meeting, but with the news of the *Miriama,* I feel it is a certainty. I see their reasons. I feel that both Corradon and Clemant are reluctant to authorize a defensive team. But they have no choice."

"I wish we could have the time to discuss this with everybody."

"I agree. But we do not have that luxury. Indeed, I fear we are already wasting time waiting for the approval. And so, I am making plans already. Gerry is the first. She will not, I think, be the last."

Merral stared at him, sensing an immense determination breaking the surface. "I see. You seem very resolved on this."

"I am." Vero paused. "Merral, if there is one man on this planet who feels responsible for the loss of the Gate, it is me. I made a bad mistake in not bringing in a threat evaluation team earlier." He clenched his fist. "I do not intend that such a mistake will happen again."

"We'll be early, won't we?" Merral commented to the driver as he got into the vehicle with its neat emblem of Farholme Planetary Affairs on the side.

"I'm to swing by the office with you," the driver said, pulling out into the street. "There's a message for you there."

It was more than a message. As they arrived at a rear entrance, Merral was surprised to see the tall figure of Representative Corradon himself emerge and beckon him over to a porch.

"Forester," he said, with a soft and apologetic tone, "I am sorry to do things this way, but these are odd days." He frowned. "Very odd days. I needed to speak to you. I think I can promise you that you will be getting the approval on those images. But it will take some time to set up. Do nothing until you hear from me in writing."

He paused, another frown sliding over his tanned face. "But, before you get them, I want you to do something for me. I have a task for you."

"Whatever I can do to help," Merral said, puzzled at both the setting and the tone of the meeting.

"Thank you. Instead of going direct to Ynysmant, I would like you to take the early afternoon plane to Larrenport. I want you to talk to this Captain Sterknem about what happened on the *Miriama*."

"Certainly, sir . . ." Merral hesitated. "But I thought that the matter had been handled already by Dr. Clemant."

The expression on the representative's face was one of total noncommitment. "Lucian did a good job. But I'm not sure now he got to the bottom of what caused it. How could he? We had no reason to believe that it was anything other than a rather odd sociological phenomenon. Not *then*."

"I see," answered Merral, realizing that the representative was revealing a gap between himself and his advisor.

"Yes, I want a second opinion and I value your judgment. I've written a letter requesting that the captain tell you everything." He reached into a side pocket of his jacket and carefully pulled out an envelope with a handwritten address on it. "He's in Larrenport. I'd like a written report; send it by courier over to me."

Merral took the letter slowly. "So what do you want me to ask?"

"I want you to find out exactly what happened—from your viewpoint. To see whether it matches with what you have experienced."

"I see. Who am I to tell about this?"

"I'd keep it between us, I think." He paused. "Yes, between the two of us—for the moment." He turned his tired eyes on Merral. "Is that all right?"

Merral hesitated. "Yes. I'll do it. There's a place on the flight?"

"Yes. I took the liberty of booking you on it. It goes at two."

"I see," Merral answered, feeling unhappy about this most irregular commissioning but unable to express his concerns. "Oh, we had a meeting with Professor Habbentz."

Corradon gave a gleaming smile. "I'm glad. Gerry is a remarkable woman. Very determined." Then he glanced at his watch. "More meetings, I'm afraid." He extended a hand. "Thanks, Forester."

"I'll see what I can do, sir."

As a result of the disruption to flights caused by the suddenly announced Day of Prayer and Fasting, the short-haul flier to Larrenport was full of people and cargo. Merral was pleased to get a seat by a rear window, even if it did mean he was squeezed in next to a crate of engineering equipment.

As he stared out of the window at the view, he realized that he was rather relieved at not having to talk to anyone. It was, he decided, another disturbing implication of no longer being part of an open society: silence and isolation had become desirable.

As they flew on, Merral stared down at the wild and often savagely indented coastline. Despite having just seen his world from space for the first time in his life, he still enjoyed seeing it from this altitude. *Is it,* he wondered, *because from this height, you can see not just the physical features but also the human elements: the farms, homesteads, and orchards?* And yet this was an artificial division. *After all, on the Made Worlds, human beings made everything except the rocks.*

He had been to Larrenport twice before, both times on conferences, and had, each time, been struck by the town's geometry. The town was on a half circle of steep cliffs facing south and was split into two almost symmetrical parts by a sheer-sided gorge. On one of the best-protected bays of eastern Menaya, Larrenport had long served as a port and provided vital ferry links to the few communties scattered around the long Henelen Archipelago of over a thousand jagged-peaked islands that stretched almost as far as the equator. *In other words, it is a quiet town on what was once the quietest part of the Assembly.*

As he thought about Larrenport, Merral remembered that his aged Great-Aunt Namia, having outlived her expectations of dying in early spring, was still in an intensive nursing home there. *Well,* he thought, *if I get the time I will visit her.*

What with two stops and a two-hour time-zone shift, it was just before six o'clock local time when the descent into Larrenport began, and Merral caught a glimpse of the deep and precipitous-sided gorge that bisected the town. The airport was on the western part of the plateau, and after a struggle against wayward wind gusts from the sea, the plane landed gently.

"Felenert Terrace?" Merral asked a blonde clerk at the reception desk, reading the address off the envelope Corradon had given him.

"Top end of Sunset Side," she answered, with a ready smile.

" 'Sunset Side'?"

"Oh, sorry," she said, giving him an apologetic look, "you're from out of town. *Sunset* is the eastern side. *Sunrise* is the western side. You're one or the other in Larrenport."

"I see," he replied, feeling that the last phrase sounded like some sort of local idiom, and walked over to where a bus with "Larrenport (East)" marked on its destination screen stood waiting. Ten minutes later, having crossed the five-hundred-meter-long suspension bridge, it paused at the crest of the plateau and Merral got off. He could carry what luggage he had in one hand and felt that after the hours in the plane, he needed the exercise.

As the bus disappeared down the first of the hairpin bends into the town,

Merral went over to the stone wall and leaned on it, looking down at the rows of neat, gray-roofed houses broken up by clusters of trees that, in a dozen rows, dropped down to the blue sea nearly three hundred meters below. He looked beyond the houses at the white-flecked waters stretching out ahead, at the clustered shipping in the harbor complex and the white wakes of the vessels entering and leaving. In the middle distance, the great black snake of Fircorta Isle that gave the town its natural protection against storms and tsunami stretched across the waters. Beyond that lay the white-tinged waters of the open ocean that stretched out into the hazy distance, and on the very horizon a dark peak like a broken tooth rose out of the water; Merral recognized the nearest island of the Henelen Archipelago.

I love this world. I've fought for it before and I'll fight for it again.

Then—mindful of his recent ankle wound—he walked slowly down a line of steep steps between the houses, enjoying the early evening warmth and salt air. The steps were almost empty; a gull perched on a wall flew away as he approached and a cat scurried silently for cover at the sound of his feet. As he descended, Merral became conscious of the stillness of the town. He listened harder, hearing only the voices of children playing behind walled gardens, the soft chatter oozing out from behind opened windows, and from far below, the melancholy hoot as a heavy freighter made its way out of the harbor.

Merral felt troubled. There seemed to be something wrong about this town, but he found himself unable to say what it was. There was not the bustle he had expected; for all the brilliant evening sunlight, Larrenport seemed like a town over which a shadow hung.

My own strained imagination, he told himself. *Anyway, why shouldn't a town be subdued days after the greatest calamity in the planet's history?* Yet these thoughts did not reassure him.

Eventually, Merral found a street of three-story, balconied houses labeled "Felenert Terrace" and, at the number he had been given, stepped inside the weather porch and pressed the doorbell. There was no answer. Merral opened the door.

"Anybody home?" he called.

As his words echoed along the white walls of the hallway with its carefully hung seascapes, his eye was caught by a slip of card displayed on a message board. The handwritten note, signed by Daniel Sterknem, simply said, *While my wife is away visiting her family, I'm staying down on the* Miriama.

Closing the door carefully behind him, Merral walked on and turned down a new set of winding steps. After a few minutes of descent, he began to feel again that there was something oppressive in the town's silence. It was almost with relief that he saw four youngsters sitting on a wall at the bottom of the next flight of steps, swinging their feet idly.

"Evening," Merral called out as he approached.

One of the boys, no older, Merral guessed, than thirteen or fourteen, stared inquisitively at him. "You from Rise Side?" he asked in a sharp voice.

Rise Side? It took Merral a moment before he realized that he was being asked if he was from the Sunrise Side, the western half of the bay.

"Does it matter?" he inquired, slightly perturbed at both the nature and the tone of the question.

The answer was sharp. "You're one or the other."

"Actually neither," answered Merral. "I'm from Ynysmant."

"Ah, let 'im pass," muttered one of the other boys, and they returned to kicking their feet against the wall.

Merral shrugged and walked on, his feeling of unease deepening. A few minutes later, he came out by the lowest line of houses. The seafront lay ahead of him. He began walking eastward along the promenade, heading toward the harbor and the boats. He passed a few people walking in the evening sun, but they gave him no greeting other than rather formal nods of acknowledgement and distant, cool smiles. *How strange,* he thought, beginning to wonder more about this town. *Is it subdued, or is there something worse going on?*

In the port area, the first vessels Merral came to were small sail craft, each labeled with the school, street, or even congregation it belonged to. As he walked by them Merral, still troubled by the *something* that hung over the town, caught the sounds of the wind rattling cables and cleats, of the hulls creaking, of the small waves slopping against sides, and of chains clinking. There was, he reflected, something timeless about ports. Jason, Ulysses, Columbus, and Cook would have, with only the slightest adjustment, soon been quite at home here. *True,* he decided, *they would wonder at our sea's lower salinity, marvel at our artificially generated tides, and doubtless be frustrated by the strangeness of our moonless night sky. Yet surely, on whatever world it occurred, the sea is the sea?*

Passing beyond the sail craft area, Merral came to the main part of the harbor. Here larger vessels were moored to a maze of quays and hoverers, and smaller boats lay beached on ramps while an extraordinary array of cranes, gantries, and servicing engines worked on them. Ahead of him, he saw a big, silver, six-legged transporter leaning at an odd angle against a large red cylinder on wheels. There was a cluster of men standing around peering at the interlocked machines, and Merral decided that he would ask them the way to the *Miriama*.

"Evening," he said.

Heads turned toward him, and there was a ragged chorus of greetings in response. Yet despite the words, Merral felt strangely aware of looks that did not seem as welcoming as he would have expected.

"What's up?" he said, trying to make conversation.

"Machine's amiss," a man said. "This spider here hit the tanker."

"That's odd."

"Telling me," a second man said. "Could have been nasty, only Malc here hit the manual override. Shut it off before it did any real damage."

"Has it ever happened before?" Merral asked.

"Nah," the first man said. "Machines always work, don't they? That's what they're designed for."

"That always used to be the case."

How very odd, thought Merral, trying to resist the temptation to look up to where the Gate should have stood if it had not been destroyed. But someone else made the connection for him.

"It's 'cause of the Gate," said a third man.

"What do you mean?" asked someone else.

There was a shrug. "Dunno. But if the Gate can go, so can a spider. Figures, right?"

"An interesting thought," Merral said, oddly anxious to move on. "Anyway, I'm looking for a ship called the *Miriama*. Where can I find it?"

"Can't miss it," someone said, gesturing with a jerk of a large thumb. "Over there. The only orange vessel round here."

Ten minutes later, after skirting the area where the big cargo and passenger ferries for the islands were berthed, Merral came to the *Miriama*. As he got closer, it seemed to him obvious that this dumpy, businesslike ship with *OCEANOGRAPHY* written in man-high black letters on the lurid orange sides could only be a research vessel. The strangely smooth hull—he presumed of some high-strength dura-polymer—was broken by a sharp, titanium alloy, ice-breaking prow; the masts had an abundance of strange aerials; and aft of the cabin the deck was covered with an array of drogues, submersible samplers, winches, and davits. A small launch under a pair of davits hung above the ship's stern.

The ship appeared deserted, and Merral climbed up the gangplank onto the deck, feeling the high-friction flooring surface grip his feet and noticing the numerous dents and scratches on the surfaces.

"Hello?" he called out. There was no answer and he looked round, seeing the terraced houses of the town staring down at him.

"Hello?" he called out more loudly.

Suddenly he saw a face at the window of the bridge, and moments later, a doorway swung open. The head of a man with unruly but sparse and receding gray hair, wild green-blue eyes, and a thin, stubbly gray beard peered at him from the top of a stairway.

"I'm looking for Captain Sterknem," Merral shouted.

"Wait," the figure called out. He clumped down the stairway and walked over. The man's bulky frame was dressed in old, stained blue overalls that were held in place by a wide belt from which an array of tools hung.

Merral found himself staring at the man's face, noticing the etched lines round the eyes and mouth, the rough, reddened skin, and the small white scars visible beneath the beard. *He must be in his fifties, and I'll bet he's spent most of those years at sea.*

"Captain Sterknem?"

"I suppose that's me," the man grunted. He came a few steps closer, and Merral saw that his eyes showed both intelligence and caution. *A closed and reserved man,* he thought, suddenly reminded of his troubled uncle, Barrand.

"Merral Stefan D'Avanos, forester," he said, extending his hand.

"Daniel Klaus Sterknem, captain, Farholme Oceanographic Service," was the response, and with it came a brief but powerful handshake. The hands were large and marked with numerous tiny scratches and cuts.

They looked at each other for a moment, and Merral decided that there seemed to be something strangely wintry about the man, as if long years among ice floes had transmitted their character to him.

"Not from these parts, are you?" the captain asked, tilting his head slightly as if to give him a better view.

"Ynysmant," Merral replied. "But does it matter where I come from?"

"Not to me," was the terse response, "but some people seem to think so these days. But how can I help you?"

"I have a message from Isterrane for you."

Merral handed over the letter from Corradon. Shaking his head, Captain Sterknem took the letter with reluctance and slit it open with a knife from his belt. He read the single sheet silently and then, without comment, folded it up and put it in the breast pocket of his overalls.

There was a pause and then he turned to Merral. "Look," he said, his weather-beaten face reminding Merral of some wave-washed piece of driftwood, "excuse me for being blunt—even rude. I told Dr. Clemant everything that was significant weeks ago. We, the crew, apologized. It's all over. I'm trying to forget it. It was a bad move."

As the green-blue eyes locked with his, it suddenly came to Merral in a flash of certainty that this man had seen something that had troubled him and still did. Merral uttered a little prayer under his breath and then began talking, groping for words as he went on.

"Look, Captain, I'm here because I know there is a problem. A few of us do. We know that there is something bad up north. Really bad. Something that we in the Assembly have never met before. *Things.* And to counter it—to counter *them*—we need to know. We need to know what you know. Please?"

For a moment, the only acknowledgment that Merral had even been heard was a faint widening of the sea-colored eyes. The big man gave a soft sigh so deep it was almost a groan. Then he gestured toward the cabins. "Follow me," he said. "I suppose we'd better talk."

25

The captain led Merral through the watertight doorway into the lower part of the bridge, where Merral glimpsed a complexity of screens and consoles that reminded him this ship was as much a laboratory as anything at his own Planning Institute. Then they descended a ladder and went aft along a corridor with the names of the crew on the doors.

As if answering some unspoken question, the captain said over his shoulder, "I have lots of work to do at the moment. We are supposed to be listing all NFS parts that may need replacing in the next fifty years."

"NFS?"

"Not heard it yet? Oh, you will. It will haunt you and me to the end of our working lives. 'Non-Farholme Sourced'—NFS—the problem bits."

The door at the end of the corridor opened to reveal a low-roofed kitchen with a mess room attached. Two open portholes let in light.

Merral glanced around the mess room. In the best Assembly tradition, a good deal of effort had been made to make it pleasant and even homely, with genuine wood paneling and a collection of decent landscape paintings on the walls. He presumed that in the bad weather and short days that the *Miriama*'s more northerly winter voyages must encounter, an attractive eating room was considered a vital feature.

"You hungry?" the captain asked, with an abrupt gesture of a big hand toward the cooker complex. "I normally eat about now, even without having days of fasting. I get up early."

Merral looked at his watch. "Why not?" It felt early, but he hadn't yet adjusted to Eastern Menaya Time.

The captain nodded as if to himself, then turned his rugged face to Merral. "Look, I'll tell you what happened, right? All of it, including the stuff I didn't tell Advisor Clemant. But after supper. Not before. That all right?"

"Fine by me. I may be able to help you."

"Hope so," Captain Sterknem muttered. "It's bugged me." He looked around. "You got somewhere to stay tonight?"

"No. I was going to knock on a few doors when I had finished talking with you. As usual."

"Of course." The captain paused. "Better still, I'll give you a cabin. The company won't hurt me. Meantime, come and choose some food out of the store."

He stopped and twitched his back as if troubled by an old injury. "Personally, I ain't eating any crayfish or lobster, though."

"I've never heard of a sailor refusing to eat invertebrates. We kill them humanely too."

The captain's tight-lipped expression seemed to hint at something hidden. "Forester, I'm just being humane to myself. But let's have a look at what we have."

In the end, they agreed on a bean, vegetable, and cheese casserole recipe, and after finding the ingredients in a well-stocked freezer, Merral started the cooking while the captain went off to close down hatches on deck.

A quarter of an hour later, just as Merral was deciding that the food was ready, the seaman came back.

"I've closed everything up. Oh, and if you try and leave in the night, I should warn you I've pulled up the gangway."

Merral detected a hint of embarrassment in his voice. "Any reason?"

"Same as the lobsters, Forester," he said with a strange, deep, and injured look. "Let's just say I feel better that way." They sat down at the table and, after giving thanks, began to eat. Captain Sterknem began to thaw out as the meal progressed, and soon it was "Merral" and "Daniel" rather than "Forester" and "Captain." The barriers, though, did not drop entirely, and Merral felt certain that there were things that his host was not ready to talk about. So he let Daniel lead the conversation in his clipped, almost staccato speech, and for a long time they talked only about the loss of the Gate and its probable effects on Farholme life and culture.

Sitting opposite the captain at the other end of the thin table, and aware of the ever-present gentle sway of the ship underneath him, Merral was struck by how nearly it was an enjoyable meal. Yet despite the cozy nature of the room and the increasing openness of his host, he did not feel at ease. *There are shadows about,* he thought, *both around this man and this town.*

As they ate, the sun went down and the evening light flooding in through the west-facing porthole reddened, making the room glow and casting long, distorted shadows across the table. Finally, with the fruit pie dessert over, Daniel began, at last, to talk about the work of the *Miriama.*

"Extraordinary, really. The rest of these ships—" here he gestured with a big hand toward the rest of the harbor—"avoid storms, currents, unstable water masses, gas seeps. We seek them out. That's why she is built like she is. Capable of surviving even if we capsize. Not that I want to try it."

He rubbed his sparse beard, sipped his drink, and stared into the distance. "This is the last ocean, Merral. If there are any oceans beyond here, beyond Worlds' End . . . they will be different. Funny," he sighed, "that idea always used to excite me. To be the sailor navigating the farthermost ocean. To sail the ultimate edgeward sea."

I sympathize, thought Merral, recognizing the common challenge of the Made Worlds. But he noticed the past tense. "Does it still?"

"No," the captain answered after a long time. "Not after what happened. . . . I am now afraid of what I may find."

Then he stood up and, walking heavily, went over to the portholes and slid covers smoothly over them. As the crimson light went and the room slipped into a soft darkness, a low yellow illumination came on around the room.

"Night is coming," the captain said and seemed to shiver.

Then in a slightly unsteady way, he sat on a corner seat. Merral rose from the table, sat opposite him, and waited. Finally, with a grimace, the captain spoke. "The trip. You really want to know all about it?"

"Yes. That's why I'm here. Take your time."

Daniel sipped his drink. "A ten-man crew. No women on this voyage. A two-week trip. Our orders were to sail a precisely defined course—north to the Nannalt Delta and then eastward over Tarrent's Rise. A series of zigzags. No, I don't plan the course. Rassumsen in the Institute does that. *Stop.*" He raised a hand. "You know about Made World oceanography?"

"A little."

"The oceans are the most important thing on a Made World. Most overlooked. Transmit energy, water, nutrients. Switch a water current off and the climate goes crazy. Very delicate, almost chaotic. So we have to watch them carefully. That's what we're about. Physical oceanography. The physics and chemistry of seawater and the seafloor. We were mostly looking at seawater chemistry. *Not* biology. Got that? That's important to my story."

"Go ahead."

"So we were up at the delta mouth first. We knew from the color of the water there had been flooding as soon as we got near. So much mud in the water, we were sailing red-brown seas. From the lavas. You've seen it?"

"Only from the air."

"Yes, well, it often occurs at that time of year. But this year, of course, it was particularly bad because of the wet winter. Anyway, our task was to put out a kilometer-long array of sensors. Across the area where the fresh water from the delta was mixing with the seawater. Thirty-meter-long sensor tubes, each separated by forty-meter gaps, all linked by optic fiber. Leave it out for twenty-four hours. You get the picture?"

"Yes."

"But when we got there we realized there was going to be a problem. There was a lot of debris in the water. Wood, tree trunks. All that stuff washed out to sea." He shrugged. "So we anchored, put out the array in the afternoon, and kept a watch for anything striking it. That was hard, as it was misty. And cold. The only good thing was that it wasn't raining and the sea was smooth."

Daniel paused. "Anyway, I got woken about two in the morning by one of the men on watch. Lemart, Billy Lemart, lives on the Rise Side. A whole tree had got caught in the outer sampling array." For a long time he said nothing, his lips moving silently. "So I dressed and we looked at it. We agreed that we needed to clear it before it wrecked the equipment. So I left the officer on watch in charge, and three of us decided to go and try and free it with the launch.

"I want you to understand what it was like. Cold, mist patches rising off the water. A faint starlight. A cone of silver light from the ship on the water. We get out there—seven hundred meters out—and we see this tree wrapped on the cable. Massive thing, half as long as the ship, big roots. Fir of some sort. . . . Sorry, Forester, I don't know the name." He paused again and closed his eyes for a moment. "The plan was easy. Get out to the far end, free it, and tug it away. I got out the all-purpose cutting-saw tool we have. The combination arc-and-vibration P20 unit. You know the thing?"

"For trees? Never use it. The fire risk is too great."

"Ah—of course. Well, that's not a problem twenty kilometers from land. Anyway there's me, Billy Lemart, and Lawrence Trest. Trest takes the cutting tool, I manage the launch's lighting, and Lemart has the helm. You have to be careful. If he cuts the tree so it rolls the wrong way, we could lose the launch. And us." He stopped, sipped his wine again, and wiped his lips with his tongue. "You've got the picture, then?"

"Yes," Merral answered slowly, feeling a prickling of unease.

"It's dark and cold. Anyway, Trest cuts away one branch. *Splash.* Then suddenly he yells out, 'Cap'n, there's an animal in the branches!' "

Merral felt himself go rigid.

"I point the light at the tree and—" Daniel swallowed and closed his eyes, as if in pain. "In it . . . is a *thing.* Moving. At first I think it's a bear. Then I realize it's like nothing I've ever seen. Perhaps half my size, brown, and shiny."

"Shiny?" Merral heard himself say, his own voice sounding strange.

Daniel opened his eyes wide in a look of acknowledgement. *"Ah,"* he said in a long, ragged whisper as their eyes met, "so you have seen it too?"

He stared at his glass, seemed to realize that it was empty, and put it on the floor with an exaggerated carefulness. "It was hard to see, really. Ten meters or so away. But it was shiny; glistening in the spotlight. The weirdest, most horrible thing. You could make out plates on it. Brown, gleaming—some sort of strange limbs. An odd brown head. Moving very slowly. Toward us . . ."

"Go on," Merral said as gently as he could.

"Like a big insect. A fifty-kilo cockroach. You could hear the thing hissing. None of us liked what we were seeing.

"Lawrence steps back and starts praying. Weird thing was, I could see its breath. Weird—for an insect, that is."

Suddenly the captain exhaled noisily and the words began running out. "Then, all of a sudden, this *thing* leaps at the boat. Just like that. Weird arms up in the air, clattering. As if they were mechanical. Billy screams. The thing lands in the prow, rocks the boat, and lashes out at Lawrence. An attack. Lawrence runs back, nearly overturns the boat. Drops the cutting tool. Now this thing, brown plates, scales—whatever—is in the boat. Like a lobster the devil's made. Then it's coming at me. So, I do the only thing I can think of and I pick up the cutting tool. And as the thing moves toward me, I flick the beam on."

Merral shuddered, imagining all too clearly the cockroach-beast in the boat held at bay by a meter-long, pencil-thin beam of glowing, high-temperature gas.

"For a moment I thought it was going to back off. Then it jumps. Waves its arms at me and then moves at me. With these weird hands that look like they are crossed with an electrician's wire cutters. And—"

He stopped and stretched out his arms on either side of him as if to brace himself against the cabin walls. Then, with his voice slower, the captain spoke again. "And I hit it with the beam. There's an awful scream and a smell of burning. The flames are all round its face and it leaps in the air, screaming. I keep the beam on it because I'm terrified, and it lands on the edge of the boat. Thrashes around there in flames. Then it crawls over the edge and drops into the water."

His jaw trembled. "And Billy is yowling and Lawrence is yelling at me and I realize I've still got the cutting tool blade on. So I turn it off and I see that we're all shaking like leaves in a gale, and I focus the light into the water where this thing is thrashing about with steam coming off it. And there's blood all over the side of the boat. And then this thing stops moving and just lies there, bobbing up and down. Facedown, with this strange corrugated brown back. And there's blood in the water."

Far away a ship's siren sounded. When it had died away, the captain began again. "So we stare at the body. Lawrence is just saying 'mutant insect, mutant insect' over and over again. Billy is gibbering, and I'm wondering what to do."

He sighed. "But I figure now we did the wrong thing. We should have hauled it back onboard, piled it in a big sealable bag, thrown out half our food, and put it in the freezer. Let Biology look at it. Well, you can guess what we did, can't you?"

"Yes. Easily." Merral realized his mouth was dry. "Just let it float away and washed off the blood?"

Daniel nodded, and Merral could see his pink tongue wrap round his lips. "Yes." His voice was thickened and slow now. "We said we were *physical* oceanography, see, not biological. And we just decided that it's some insect thing, right? Some mutant, Made World arthropod, some crustacean monstrosity. That's why I don't eat the things now. Only, as I stare at it, it begins to roll over. 'It's sinking,' says Lawrence, and his teeth are chattering. And as it does I see the head properly."

He rubbed his cheeks with his hands as if rubbing soap into his beard. "This is the worst bit. You see, it's the head—the face—that's burned the most. And as it sinks, slowly, I can see that it has a skull. White bone, braincase, jaws. A skull. Like you and me."

"Ah."

"Yes." A muscle twitched in the side of Daniel's face. "It wasn't an insect. So that's why we decided to keep quiet. We figured—well, I figured—that I'd killed some poor mutated human. We swilled out the boat, got the tree trunk free of the cable in double-quick time. Promised secrecy to each other. By dawn, we were kilometers away. So there you are. I killed it."

Merral stood up and stretched himself, more to give himself a chance to think than because he needed to. He walked to the window and then back to his seat.

"Let me try and put your mind at rest," he said after a moment. He took out his diary, found on it an image of two cockroach-beasts, and showed it to Daniel. "Is this it?"

The seaman gasped. "Two more?"

"Yes. I think there are still others left." He switched the image off and sat down. "I have also met these creatures, and under circumstances like the one you described, I too killed one. It was either him or me."

The eyes widened. "You're serious? You are not just saying that?"

"Can you imagine what a nip from those hands would look like on an ankle?" Merral lifted his right trouser leg and rolled down his sock, exposing the red line of the still-healing wound. "My boot protected me a bit, but it still cut in."

He covered his ankle again and looked at Daniel, who was shaking his head in disbelief. “No, Captain, whatever you killed was not human. It had human elements, but it was, in a way that we do not understand, a fabricated creature. And evil. I think it would have killed you and all your crew if it had had the chance. I think you can rest in peace about your action.”

“Thank you. Thank you!” The captain seemed close to tears. “Thank you very much indeed. You have no idea—” He shook his head.

“I do,” answered Merral, feeling an intense pity for this man. “Oh, I do. Actually I can guess your feelings better than most people. After all, I did the same as you. But in my case it was very obvious that these were hostile, evil things.”

“So . . . what are they?”

Merral hesitated, then decided that this man had earned the right to know far more than he knew already. So, omitting the details of the spiritual malaise that seemed to have affected Barrand and the Herrandown community, he described as much as he knew of the two types of intruders seen near the Lannar Crater. At the end, they agreed that it was perfectly likely that a creature, unfamiliar with the way Farholme’s rivers could suddenly rise, might all too easily have been caught in a flash flood and washed out to sea.

Daniel shook his head in disbelief. “I was horrified about what I had done. Now I am less so. Instead, I am appalled at what has been done in the making of these things.”

“Yes,” answered Merral, “and there many questions lie.”

“But are they a danger? with the Gate gone?”

“We do not know. Their losses have been heavy. They have not been reported much beyond the area of the Lannar Crater. We are working on the problem. That is why I came here.”

“Altered *humans,*” Daniel muttered in disgust. “And the Gate gone. These are strange days.”

“Indeed,” answered Merral. “But it’s as well that as few as possible know how strange they are. And if I may ask you more questions—what happened on the rest of the trip?”

“Ah,” Daniel sighed and shook his head. “Yes, well, from then on it seemed like things went wrong. Only the three of us knew, and we said nothing, which was hard. We cleared the delta and then the wind got up. Even with stabilizers running at full compensation it was rough. The wind was from the north and it was bitter out; there was spray lashing over the prow, night and day. The ice covered the deck and the equipment; the antislip surface was useless. Then we got the main submersible sampler snagged on a recovery and had to send a diver down. He got his suit cut and nearly froze from exposure. Then we had a storm and a big wave that almost swamped the ship. And somehow a ventilation hatch was open and we got water all through the ship. And the electrics started playing up. Oh, and everybody started going down with colds. It was a dreadful trip. Worst I've known. And the thing was, they all started blaming me or each other."

"I see." Merral looked around, imagining ten people in this room with the floor tossing and heaving and all arguing with each other. "And that's when the allowance idea came up?"

"Yes."

"Who thought it up?"

"No one will admit it. Each side blames the other."

An insight flickered in Merral's brain and he tried to grasp it, but the captain continued speaking and he lost it. "Anyway, when we got back, someone asked me to raise it as a suggestion and—like a fool—I did. I can't think what came over me."

He gave another deep sigh. "So the rest of the voyage felt like a curse. There is an old sailor's poem, from before the Intervention. I only know it in the Communal translation as 'The Venerable Sailor.' The original is Alt-Dutch or Ancient English."

"English. 'The Rime of the Ancient Mariner.' "

"That's it. Anyway, you remember how in the days of sail, the sailor shoots an albatross with an arrow and the ship gets cursed as a result. Strange poem. You never know with the ancients whether they really believed these things. It kept coming back to me." He gave a tired smile. "But tonight I think I can sleep as a more relieved man. I will tell Lawrence and Billy when I see them. Privately, of course."

"So," Merral asked, as gently as he could, "you think it's all over now?"

"Yes," came the answer. "It was a temporary aberration. A bad voyage. It's over."

I hope so, thought Merral but stayed silent.

The silence that followed was broken by Daniel stifling a yawn. "Excuse me!" he said. "I was up early. But come, let me show you your cabin."

He led Merral beyond the mess room to a cabin so wide that it seemed to extend across the width of the ship. There was a big wallscreen on one side and a variety of sporting and exercise gear.

"The recreation room," Daniel commented. "You can hardly run around the deck in bad weather. Your room is through here."

"Very nice," observed Merral. Then his eye was suddenly caught by a notice board. On it was a large white sheet divided in two, with columns of marks underneath. *A score sheet,* he thought idly, then stopped, his eyes riveted by the twin words at the top: *Sunrise* and *Sunset.*

Trying to make his voice sound unconcerned, Merral turned to the captain. "You divided the crew into two teams?"

"Have done for years."

"And it's easy enough to divide the crew up? I mean on the basis of where they come from?"

"Yes, we've been split neatly into Rise Siders and Sunsetters for some years."

"So 'you're one or the other in Larrenport'?"

The captain smiled back in a tired manner. "That's what they say. I gather you've heard the phrase?"

"Yes."

Daniel shrugged, walked over, and opened a door, revealing a small cabin with a single bed. "I hope it's all right?" he asked.

"Fine," Merral answered, glimpsing the town's lights visible through the porthole. "Can I ask you another question, Captain?"

"Why not?"

"Yes, you see, I couldn't help wondering—really it's none of my business—why you sleep on the boat when you have a home not far away?"

A soft "hmm" was all the answer that Merral received.

"Is it," he suggested as sensitively as he could, "that you feel safer with the gangway up and the hatches closed than in a house with open doors?"

"Yes," came back the tentative answer. "That's it."

Merral, staring at him, discerned a look of embarrassment in his eyes.

"But I think I'll go back tomorrow. My wife will be back then anyway." Then, with a wish that Merral would enjoy a good night's sleep, he left.

By the time that Merral awoke, showered, and dressed the next morning, Daniel was already up and working in one of the cabins beyond the mess room. The captain joined him for coffee and breakfast and then led Merral up into the deck. Above the town the sun was shining between gaps in patchy gray clouds. The captain lowered the gangway and stood by it.

"Thanks, Merral," he said, giving him a firm handshake. "Thanks so much. I guess I can now try to forget what happened on that voyage. I can put it behind me."

Merral stared beyond him at the twin halves of the divided town before them, the left-hand side gleaming in the morning light. *Sunrise and Sunset*, he thought, remembering that he had one more question.

"Yes, Daniel, try to do that. Put it behind you. But something comes back to me. Yesterday you said about the crew problems on the voyage—what was it? 'Each side blames the other.' Did you mean that this sports division, well, sort of spread into everyday matters?"

"Yes, I suppose so," Daniel answered, his voice charged with reluctance.

"But only really during the trip we've been talking about? Never before?"

"No—I guess not. All the bad weather seemed to make things worse. We were more cramped. And the colds—but it's over." He hesitated. "Isn't it?"

Merral glanced at the captain and saw he was gazing with a troubled expression at the split town. In a flash of intuition, he realized that Daniel was worried that it wasn't over. Had he, perhaps, sensed something of the atmosphere of the *Miriama*'s voyage in his own town?

"I don't know, Captain," Merral said. "Let's pray that it's so."

As he had expected, Merral found a bus stop at the gate of the harbor. A number of people who looked as if they had come off an overnight shift greeted Merral in an affable fashion and, when they learned he was a visitor from Ynysmant, offered him advice on how to get to the High Cliff Intensive Nursing Center where Great-Aunt Namia was.

"Easy enough to find," said one woman. "Straight off the bridge. Turn right and it's at the top of Rise Side at the cliff edge. Looks down on us. Typical." The tone of disapproval in her voice caught Merral's attention.

"Why, er, typical?"

She waved a hand dismissively to the west. "They don't have the docks and harbor, see. Risers pride themselves on being better because of it."

Merral tried, with difficulty, to bury his alarm. "This feeling they have—or you think they have—of being superior. Has it always been like this?"

She looked at him warily. "Oh no. Only the last two months. Suddenly."

"I see," he said, and he was going to ask whether there was any reason, when a bus turned the corner.

"Here's your bus," the woman said sharply. "Yes. Ever since Easter they have been getting so above themselves. Well, I really don't know where it will end."

As the bus went up over the last of the hairpin bends, Merral looked back down to the ships, trying to see the orange dot of the *Miriama*.

"It's over," the captain had said. But Merral knew he hadn't believed it.

Now *he* didn't either.

26

High on the western side of Larrenport, Merral bought some lilies from a flower shop and then, his mind preoccupied by events, strolled over to the High Cliff Intensive Nursing Center. The center and its grounds, embraced in a protective semicircle of beech trees and evergreens, lay tucked just below the plateau edge. Looking at it, Merral felt that this elevated setting on the edge of the cliff was almost symbolic, as if it were easier to pass from earth to heaven from up here.

Halfway along the gravel driveway he stopped, gazing beyond the rosebushes and down to the town and the bay far beyond. Far out to sea, beyond multitudes of turning gulls, a belt of cloud was broken at the horizon so that a line of brilliant silver etched out the boundary of the sea and the sky. With an effort, Merral pushed his concerns out of his mind; in this twilight of her long and profitable earthly life, his great-aunt deserved his full attention.

He walked on to the reception office.

"Good morning; I've come to see Mrs. Namia Mena D'Avanos," he said to the fresh-complexioned nurse with a blonde ponytail who sat behind the desk.

She smiled up at him welcomingly with round, nut brown eyes. "Oh yes. Are you a near relative?" she asked, in the sort of smooth and soothing voice that Merral felt was entirely appropriate for dealing with the elderly.

"Fairly," he answered, wondering how near you were when a hundred years separated you. "She's a great-aunt. I bring her family greetings. You know her?"

"Of course. We know them all." She smiled again, but something at the edges of her mouth hinted at some difficulty. "But let me call the doctor to take you over to her," she said and pressed a button.

"Do I need to talk to the doctor?"

Her smile was disarming. "I'll think she'll want to talk to you." She nodded at the flowers Merral was carrying. "Nice bouquet. But you aren't local, are you?"

"No, visiting from Ynysmant. Came in yesterday."

"Ah, up on the lake, eh? Stay anywhere nice last night?"

"On a ship in the docks, funnily enough."

"A pity. You should have stayed over on Rise Side."

There it was again.

"Rise Side. Is it better?" he asked, peering at the smooth face and the brown eyes.

"We think so. Quieter. Of course, they make all the fuss about East Side being the real heart of Larrenport. But West is best."

Reluctant to answer, Merral replied with what he hoped was seen as an equivocal nod.

A paneled door opened and an elegant, auburn-haired lady in her forties, wearing a white jacket with a Diagnostic Medical Unit poking out of a pocket, came over and introduced herself. She and Merral exchanged greetings, and then she led him down a covered walkway to a cluster of rooms.

Outside a doorway decorated with hand-painted creeping red roses, she stopped and beckoned Merral close to her.

"It's an odd case," she said, in a low, confiding tone. *"Odd."*

"Is it?" he answered. "I thought she was just, well, *old*. One hundred and twenty-four. I presume all sorts of things start packing up at that age."

"Hmm. Yes and no. Physically, she's remarkable; you'll be blessed if you have some of her genes. No, it's just that Mrs. D'Avanos is suffering from an odd set of psychological symptoms. Very strange . . ."

"What sort of things?" Merral felt a shadow of unease fall across him again. *But this,* he told himself, *must surely be something else. It has to be.*

The doctor frowned and adjusted her jacket. "A sort of depression. Anxiety attacks. The pastor and I have a dossier. . . ." She hesitated. "No, I think it's better you talk to her. Then—if you want—you can talk to me. But I just thought I ought to warn you."

"I see."

She looked at him carefully. "When you last saw her . . . was she fine?"

"Yes. I saw her last autumn. I was here for a conference."

She paused and he was aware of her green eyes scrutinizing him. "May I ask," she said gently, "how did she view her death?"

Merral felt himself staring back at her. "Well, we barely discussed it. But she had a perfectly normal view of it." He was tempted to add *of course,* but somehow *of course* didn't seem to apply as much as it used to.

"Great-Aunt Namia was," he said, remembering what they had talked about, "looking forward to going Home, to going to be with Jesus. Which she expected to be in the spring. She was awaiting the Resurrection and the new heaven and the new earth. And a new body—she was particularly looking forward to that. She had been active well into her nineties, but that was a long time ago."

She nodded sympathetically. "So we have heard. We had her in just after Easter and didn't expect her to stay. Most people come here for the last few days or weeks of life. She was slipping away, as they do, but then something happened. Now she's fighting it." A look of troubled perplexity crossed her face.

"Look, I'll leave you with her. But, if you get any insights, see me on the way out? Please?"

Then she turned and walked up the corridor, looking deep in thought.

Merral knocked and, hearing no answer, slipped into the room. His aunt lay propped up in bed, facing away from the door and apparently staring at a painting of a mountain landscape on a wall. Hesitating to disturb her, Merral looked around the room, noting the pastel blue walls, the discreetly hidden medical equipment, the readout panels high above the bed, and the framed family images on the chests. The windows stretching from floor to ceiling at the end of the room looked seaward and were open a fraction, so that the white gauze curtains swayed gently in the breeze.

"Great-Aunt?" Merral called out softly, and as he walked over to her, she turned slowly and stiffly and looked up at him.

He was immediately struck by how delicate and pale she had become. It was her paleness that struck him most, and it occurred to him that an artist could have painted her faithfully using only a palette of grays, whites, and blues.

Her wan lips twitched and tired bleached-blue eyes smiled at him.

"Merral, dear! How lovely. Come and kiss me." The voice was slight and brittle.

Merral carefully put the lilies on the table where she could see them, pulled a chair up to the bed, bent over the fragile figure, and kissed a powder-dry cheek.

"Let me sit up more. Sit back a bit," she whispered between bloodless lips. "Bed, more upright, please."

There was a faint whine of motors and the top part of the bed tilted. "Bed, stop!" she called and the motion ended.

"Merral, now turn off that camera, please." She gestured at a small wall-mounted lens. "I can't order that."

He rose and tapped the switch below it.

"Why, thank you, dear. I don't like being watched all the time."

He was suddenly aware of the sensor bands on her neck and wrist, of the way her white hair was tied back, of the soft embroidered white nightdress.

His great-aunt gave another thin, forced smile. "So tell me all the news. About everything and everybody."

"Are you up to it?" he asked.

"Ah," she said, with almost a snort of amusement. "Look at that book on my side table and tell me what you think of it."

He picked up the white book, opened it, and was faced with pages of strange characters. "Let me guess," he said. "Your Old-Mandarin Bible?"

"Indeed so. And I still read it daily. Keeps my mind going. You have to keep up your Historics. But—" a frown crossed the lined face—"it doesn't help. . . ."

She grimaced as if struck by pain. "Later. Tell me about Ynysmant. And the Gate exploding. I can hardly believe that. The family, though, first . . ."

After spending twenty minutes recounting matters to do with his father and mother in Ynysmant, his sisters and their families elsewhere, and other news, Merral looked searchingly at his great-aunt. "But how are you?"

She gave a wheezy sigh. "Not good," she whispered in a faint and pitiful voice.

Merral held her fragile, bony hand gently, watching as she screwed her old eyes up in misery. Suddenly the novel thought came to him that in his great-aunt, he saw a malignity in old age. At its best, he had always seen old age as a mellow autumnal ripening, and at its worst, as no more than a gentle fading out. It was the slow, soft draining of physical and mental powers; the yawning and dozing before the onset of that long sleep of the real person that extended until the Great Awakening. But now, as he looked at his great-aunt's pained face with a fierce stab of pity, Merral could see aging as the ancients had seen it: as some cruel force that ripped and gnawed at the very essence of what you were.

Namia spoke slowly. "Merral, I need to be honest with you. Can I?"

"Of course."

"I'm scared." Her hand shook.

"Of what?" he asked.

"Of dying, Merral. Oh, I know it's crazy, but I'm scared."

He squeezed the almost fleshless hand gently. "But you know the truth. Jesus loves you and died for you. Dying is going home to heaven—to the Father's house. He is waiting for you."

Her eyes watered, and he reached for an embroidered handkerchief and dabbed her eyes. There was something contagious about her tears, and he felt like weeping himself.

"I know it in my head," she said to him in a peculiar and distant tone. "But I can't feel it. I have no confidence. Supposing it's just dark forever? or that I just cease to exist?"

Merral stared at her. "It isn't dark. And you go to be with the King of the worlds. But, Great-Aunt, you have trusted him in the past for well over a century."

"Yes," she said weakly.

"I'm puzzled. I've never come across anything like it. You've prayed about it?"

"Yes," she sighed, but it was nearly a sob, "but I seem to get no answer."

"I see," Merral answered, feeling utterly inadequate. "When did it start?"

"I had been here a few days. I was expecting to go. Waiting for him to lift me away. I remember rather looking forward to it. It was the first spring day. It'd been such a long winter. I was sitting down there, in that chair, just watching the ships. Always liked that. One boat attracted my attention. A little thing coming in past the island. *That's like me,* I thought, *nearly ready to get into port.* But as I stared at it I felt there was a dark cloud over it. . . . And then the cloud came and hung over me. And I suddenly had a terrible fear that has never left me since. They gave me tablets for it."

She gave what was almost a whimper, and on the console above the bed Merral saw that a red light was flickering. "The tablets hide it, but it's still there. That's why I've held on till now." Her pale eyes seemed to widen, and her frail hand stiffened in his. "It's worse at night. I sleep with the light on."

There was a tap on the door and a male nurse glided in and came behind him.

"Sorry, Mr. D'Avanos," he whispered in his ear, "metabolic monitors indicate her stress levels are very high. We'd prefer to let them drop a bit. A mild sedative—"

"Very well," Merral answered, feeling suddenly angry with whatever it was that had so terribly afflicted this old woman at the end of her life, "but let me pray with her."

As the nurse retreated to the window, Merral prayed audibly over his great-aunt and was rewarded by a faint "Amen" from the pale lips.

"God bless you, Great-Aunt. Trust him."

She squeezed his hand feebly.

He rose to his feet and gestured the nurse over. Then slowly he walked to the door. Just as he was opening it, a thought struck him. "Oh, Great-Aunt, one question: the boat you watched. What color was it?"

The nurse looked at him, his face full of bewilderment.

"What a *strange* thing to ask, Merral," his great-aunt said slowly and faintly. "It was orange."

At the reception desk the nurse with the blonde ponytail and the round, dark brown eyes looked up at him. "I hope it wasn't too upsetting."

For a moment, Merral felt lost for words. "Yes," he answered. "I mean, it *was* alarming. I think I ought to talk to the doctor about what she said."

She nodded. "Thought so. Follow me."

As they walked along, Merral turned to her. "By the way, Nurse, I was struck by a comment you made earlier. That the Sunset Side believed it was the real heart of Larrenport. Since when have they been making a fuss about that?"

He caught an expression of mild embarrassment. "Six weeks, eight weeks maybe. It just seemed to start as the weather got warmer. But I was going to say to you that I've been wondering whether I should have said that."

"That's interesting. How so?"

"I was just thinking about it and it struck me that—well, if you let the business about one side of town being better or worse continue, then there was no telling where it would end."

Instinctively, Merral patted her gently on the arm. "Nurse, that's about the most sensible thing I've heard all day. You're right. *Don't* pass it on. Try and stop it. We have to fight it."

She turned to him, pale eyebrows raised in something close to alarm. "What's going on? Your great-aunt . . . ? The mood in the town . . . ? And now the Gate?"

"I don't really know," he answered. "But, hard as it may be to believe, the Lord still reigns."

After a moment's thought, she smiled slowly back at him. "I guess so. I never felt I needed reminding of that before." She gestured to another room. "The doctor is in there."

The doctor was reclining in an old armchair, drinking from a mug of coffee and staring into space.

"Ah, Forester D'Avanos. I thought I might see you. Do you want a drink? coffee, tea?"

"No, thanks. I'd better get over to the airport soon."

She scanned his face. "You saw the problem?"

"Oh, indeed. She's scared of dying. No," Merral corrected himself, "not of *dying,* but of being dead. She's scared of *death.*"

"Exactly. It's very sad. Very disturbing."

"Is she the only case?"

There was a long pause in which the doctor sipped her coffee and gazed ahead. Then she looked up at him with a frown. "No, there are others in the town. She was one of the first, but she was—*is*—an unusual woman. Very sensitive, perceptive, intuitive."

She looked at Merral as if comparing him to his great-aunt. "Yes, you have something of that. But any ideas about treatment? I was intending to call Central Geriatric Care on Ancient Earth." She shrugged. "Not a lot of hurry now. I can find nothing like this in our files. Nothing so deep or so permanent. It's not death as we have known it."

Merral shook his head. "Oh, you can find references to it," he said, and he was aware of her look of surprise. "Go back before the Intervention. You'll find it there. My guess is her symptoms were not atypical then. My memory suggests that there are hints of her mood in the Psalms."

The doctor gave a little start, her face squinting in thought. "Yes . . . I suppose so. But that is *very* odd."

"Yes. It is odd. My suggestion is to get the brightest spiritual advisor or counselor you can find here and let them dig some of the pre-2050 pastoral counseling material out of the Library."

He suddenly realized that he had already told her too much. "Look, I'd better go. You have my details with the nurse. Keep in touch."

She put her coffee down and rose slowly to her feet. "Yes, I think that's a good idea. But, surely—" She looked perplexed. "Surely, that age of humanity is long over?"

"Hmm," Merral said, moving toward the door. "That's what I used to think too."

He got to the airport earlier than he had expected and easily found himself a spare place on an early afternoon ferry flight to Ynysmant. Then, while the freighter was loading and being refueled, he found a quiet corner, took out some sheets of paper, and began writing his letter to Representative Corradon. Merral had never been one for using pen and paper, but now he felt it was time to get used to it.

He began by outlining, as precisely as he could, Captain Sterknem's account and suggested that Anya be informed of the relevant biological details. Then he recounted the curious divisions appearing in Larrenport and mentioned the problem he had heard of with the machines at the dock. Finally, he summarized his visit to Great-Aunt Namia and her frame of mind. Then, after a long time thinking and choosing his words, he wrote the final sentences:

All these phenomena worry me in different ways. If they are interlinked—and the timing suggests that they are—then the implications are extremely disturbing.

Yours, in the Service of the Assembly,

Forester Merral Stefan D'Avanos

Then he sealed his letter in an envelope, addressed it to Representative Corradon at Isterrane, marked it "private and personal," and handed it in at the airport office with a request for it to be urgently sent by courier.

Merral arrived back at Ynysmant in the late afternoon and, deciding it was too late to go into the Planning Institute, walked into town along the causeway. Hearing the energetic chop-chop of the waters against the walls and feeling the wind and sun on his cheeks, Merral stopped to look at his hometown rising on its steep, dark mound out of the lake. Seeing its curving lines of red roofs, spires, and towers bathed in the spring sunshine, he was seized with a sudden, intense affection for Ynysmant. *It's very good to be back.* It seemed quite extraordinary that less than two weeks ago he had left there with Vero for Herrandown. His life before then already seemed to be distant and dreamlike.

He walked on, and as he approached Ynysmant, the long, steep-pitched roof of the hospital caught his eye and an idea came to him. Instead of going straight home, he turned up the street that led to the hospital, and walking in through a side entrance, he made his way to Administrative Affairs. There, in his office dominated by potted plants, he found Tomos Daynem, the junior administrator.

Tomos, lean and muscular, seemed to bounce up from his seat when he saw Merral at his doorway.

"Hi, Merral! Come in. Heard you were out of town." He shook hands. "Welcome back. Take a seat."

Merral sat down, stared at his friend, and gestured to the image on the wall of the winning side at last year's Ynysmant Team-Ball championship.

"How have we done lately?" he asked, knowing that particular image well. On it, Tomos, as captain of the Blue Lakers, one of the three best teams in town, was holding the cup high while Merral, who had merely played as a winger in a semifinal match, stood at the back.

Tomos gave a theatrical groan. "Oooh, don't ask. We lost against the Western Lake College First Team. Those boys are good. And we need to improve our passing. You ought to play more."

"I ought to. I just don't seem to be in the right place at the right time. Any repercussions from the loss of the Gate?"

He shook his head. "None I've thought of. I mean, it's hardly as if we had inter-system championships, is it? It's all we can do to get a northeastern Menaya tournament organized every three years."

Merral felt a sense of relief that something at least seemed to be unchanged. In fact, it was hardly surprising; Assembly sports were informal, localized, and frequently haphazard.

Tomos leaned back in his chair. "But you didn't come to talk Team-Ball, I presume."

"No," answered Merral, choosing his words, "I have an odd question. I was in Isterrane recently, and there was some discussion about some regional medical anomalies. Then, this morning, I visited a rather aged great-aunt in Larrenport, and I found that she and some others were having problems at the end of their lives. They were fighting it, afraid of death. Anxiety. All very disturbing. It had just started within the last two months. So, I thought I'd ask you if there were any oddities you had heard of concerning the terminally ill."

Tomos's mouth made an expression of surprise. "Odd. I've heard of nothing. Not here. And I meet with all the medical sections regularly, so I'd know. In the last two months?" He shook his head. "No. Same as usual. A couple of heart attacks when the Gate went, but that's not the same thing."

Merral felt a surge of relief. The idea that his hometown was unaffected was a relief.

"Thanks. I'm glad to hear it. *Very* glad. Forget my question." He rose to leave. "I'll leave you to get on with your work."

"Thanks. In fact, I am pretty busy. The Gate loss has had a major impact on the hospital's work. We'll have to make do without some equipment, some organ replacements, and some drugs." Tomos got out of his chair in a fluid motion and walked to the door. "It's going to be a very challenging half century. About the only plus point is that with no visitors we should have fewer stray viruses."

"Nice to hear something positive."

"Ah, but the difficulties may come when the isolation is over and we get exposed to any new strains that have developed." Tomos smiled. "But that won't be my concern. Anyway, Merral, I'm glad I've put your mind at rest." He opened the door. "Mind you, if you'd asked me about the beginning of life, I'd have had a different story to tell."

"The *beginning*?" Merral asked, suddenly feeling as if a lump of ice had been placed against his back.

"Yes. The delivery problems. But that, I presume, is another thing."

"What?"

"The labor difficulties we seem to be encountering this year."

Merral held on to the doorframe. "We have problems with *babies*?" He was aware that his voice sounded strangely muffled.

There was a nod. “Yes. But you didn’t ask about that. You look a bit pale, Merral, are you okay?”

“Sorry. I’ve had a stressful few days. Can I talk to someone about it?”

Ten minutes later, Merral was sitting in another office staring across a fussily tidied desk at Dr. Edgar Meridell, a short, plump man with a smooth, bald head framed by tufts of white hair sprouting above his ears, and prominent white eyebrows. Just behind him a holographic womb and baby were displayed on a floor stand, but Merral tried to avoid looking at it. He remembered that it was an unease about dissections and anatomy in his early biology courses that had been partly responsible for diverting his career into forestry.

“The best index,” the obstetrician was saying in his dry, rather scholarly voice, “is the use of painkillers in childbirth. We use a substance called OA25. That’s obstetric anesthetic 25. Do you need the formula?”

“No.”

“Assembly standard. Has been for, oh, five hundred plus years. We have it on standby; the mother can ask for it if she feels excessive pain. Now, the figures—” he consulted his diary with slender fingers—“yes, last year, ’851, we had just over two hundred babies born here, and it was used twice. Say, less than one percent take-up. Now this year—” he tapped the diary screen carefully—“ah yes. We have the figures for the first four months, as a percentage; January—2 percent; February—6 percent; March—15.8 percent and April, well, 29.4 percent. Our projections for May’s figures are looking—” he gave a low whistle— “higher still.”

Merral thought about the figures. “Very odd. So it’s doubled every month, more or less. You will soon be at over a half take-up.”

The doctor gave a reluctant nod of assent.

“So what’s happening? Labor is getting more painful?”

“Well, now,” came the wary answer, “that’s not scientific language, Mr. D’Avanos. It’s not easy to measure pain quantitatively. All we can say is that midwives are reporting an increasing demand for painkillers during childbirth. I’ve done a memo on it.”

“I see,” Merral answered, trying to keep his emotions from showing on his face. “Can you do me a favor? Send me a copy. No hurry. But by hand, not by diary.”

The eyebrows rose. “It’s a bit out of the area of forestry, isn’t it?”

Merral shrugged. “Yes. I’m collecting oddities. It’s becoming a hobby. Any idea why this is happening?”

"Embarrassingly, we have no idea. The possibilities are a virus, but there is no evidence of that. Some dietary issue, perhaps. Some sudden variation in a trace element. Or it might just be some factor to do with the dreadful winter. Lack of exercise . . . that sort of thing." He shrugged his shoulders and looked mystified. "But I'll send you that memo."

Suddenly, feeling that he had taken as much bad news as he could bear, Merral decided that he needed to get out of the hospital. He found a secluded site that looked westward over the inlet of Ynysmere and the rolling ground beyond it and sat down on a sun-warmed bench.

There he sat staring into the distance for some time, his mind distracted by events. Words and phrases seemed to circle round and round in his mind. *Birth and death; Herrandown, Larrenport, and Ynysmant; not death as we have known it; that age of humanity is over.* Linked with the phrases were images: his great-aunt's tears, Daniel Sterknem's face as he remembered his terror, the eyebrows of Dr. Meridell raised in puzzlement. Plainly, some subtle, vague, and spreading evil was abroad in the land, and its occurrence was clearly related to the intruders. And what he needed to do was equally plain: he had to observe and report, and when he was given the go-ahead, do everything he could to find the intruder ship. In the meantime, his duty was to not alarm anyone.

A cooler gust of wind spiraled past him, and to his surprise he realized that it was nearly six o'clock. It was time to see his family. He got up from the bench and walked out of the grounds, up through the sinuous streets to his house.

"I'm back," he called out as he entered the house. His father, starting at his voice, stood up suddenly from the general room table where he was writing on sheets of paper. Brushing crumbs off his chest, he came over and hugged Merral.

"Why, Son! Good to see you. Excuse me—" Stefan gestured to a half-eaten sandwich on a plate by him—"I started eating. I wasn't sure when you were coming. Your mother is next door, just having a chat with friends. As she does—"

Merral sat at the table opposite, relishing being back home. "You look tired, Father."

"Me? Oh, it's been a long, weary day," his father said, running his hands through his straggly hair and stroking his unruly silver beard. "We have been making new guidelines about even stricter recycling of anything with rare earth elements."

"So you are working on it now?" Merral pointed to the sheets of paper covered with blocks of neat handwriting, lines, and arrows. It was one of the characteristics of his father, consistent with his often-winding way of thinking, that he preferred to scribble on sheets of paper rather than use a diary.

"This? No, it's my Historic. We Welsh speakers are having a discussion meeting next week." He paused, then read the title. *"Am fater y Porth a'r oblygiadau ar gyfer dyfodol y Cynulliad a Farholme,* or *On the matter of the Gate and its implications for the future of the Assembly and Farholme.* I said I'd open it with a presentation of some of the issues. But oh, Son, it's hard work." He sighed and stroked a rogue strand of hair vaguely back into place over an ear. "It gets harder as you get older. A lot of future tenses. And concepts. I find Welsh so much less clear-cut than Communal and, of course, a lot more difficult." He sighed again and his finger intertwined with his beard. "But I wonder really—"

"You wonder really *what?*" asked Merral, feeling almost too scared to ask.

"Well, I don't know. I just feel, somehow, this emphasis on us all pursuing these old languages—sorry, that's not a sentence."

Merral, dismayed by what he was hearing, tried to keep his face blank and nodded encouragement for his father to continue.

"Yes, I've just been thinking now about the whole issue of preserving Historics. Perhaps this business—" he gestured upward to where the Gate would have hung if it had not been in a billion fragments—"will give us a chance to think things through. . . ." Then, as if struck by the implications of what he was thinking, he fell silent.

Before Merral could make any reply, the door opened and his mother bustled in and surrounded him with her arms.

"Merral *dear.* How *lovely!* Let me look at you."

She clutched him to herself.

"It's been *ages.* And the Gate *gone.* We have missed you. Has your father got you some food?"

"Well, we've just been talking—"

She turned to his father. "Oh, Stefan! The boy's traveled hundreds of kilometers! You could have started getting *something* for him." Merral found her tone strange; jocular, yet also with a sharp and critical edge.

His father's face clouded. "Oh yes, sorry. I mean we were talking, weren't we, Son?"

He rose to his feet, shedding more crumbs off his pullover.

His mother frowned. "Oh, Stefan, just look at you! Those crumbs—all over you! The *men* of this house—" She gave a sigh and then hesitated, as if struck by her own reactions. "Sorry," she said in a quiet, introspective tone. "I'm not feeling quite myself lately. I suppose it's this awful Gate business."

But is it? Merral thought as they ate their supper and his mother discussed the practical repercussions of the loss of the Gate in her life and that of her neighbors and colleagues. Was his mother's critical mood a reaction to that event, or was there something else at work?

After supper, Merral called Isabella to apologize for being back a day late. From the diary screen, he could see that she was sitting in her bedroom.

"Can we meet tomorrow?" he asked. "It's the Lord's Day, and we can meet in the afternoon or the evening."

Isabella's face showed an expression that was close to a pout. Then she brightened and turned her head slightly on one side, smiling. "But you could still come over now," she said in a voice of warm invitation.

Struggling with his emotions, Merral did not immediately answer. *I care for Isabella,* he thought. *I find her invitation appealing, yet I want to keep my distance. Something is going wrong between us. Time was, we controlled our relationship; now it seems to control us.*

Suddenly an excuse came to mind. "Isabella, it's a bit late and I'd like to spend some time with my parents. Tomorrow's better."

The response was a brief moment of silence.

"Yes," Isabella said slowly and smiled again, but Merral felt there was effort rather than spontaneity behind her expression. Then, after making arrangements to meet on the following evening, and further pleasantries, they ended the call.

That night, before he went to sleep, Merral lay awake reviewing the day. What he had worried about on the hospital grounds now seemed terribly confirmed by the hints and nuances from within his own family.

The intangible shadow that had fallen over Herrandown and Larrenport was now falling over his own town.

27

The following morning, Merral tried to put his concerns out of his mind. He felt it wrong that on the Lord's Day matters of evil should preoccupy him. Yet it was a struggle. Everything seemed to draw his mind back to the nagging shadow that now appeared to loom over everything. Indeed, as he left the Congregation Hall, high at the top of Ynysmant, Merral paused and looked north through the clear air. He could just make out in the far distance the snowcapped summits of the Rim Ranges. *How many days would it take,* he wondered, *for those cockroach-beasts and ape-creatures to reach here?* Could he be certain that, even now, they were not slowly advancing through the greenery of the orchards and woodlands that he could see? In spite of the warm sunshine, he shivered.

In the afternoon, Merral played a full game in the Blue Lakers' B squad. He had no great success, and his injured ankle was throbbing at the end of the match. But it took his mind off matters and gave him some exercise.

That evening Merral and Isabella walked down to the Waterside Center. The sun was setting by the time they got there, and it was still too chilly to sit outside, so they went into the center. Most people were downstairs where a local string-and-wind band was playing, so they went upstairs to an almost deserted lounge. There they got some drinks, found a quiet corner by a window, and made themselves comfortable. As they sat there together, Merral felt his concerns about their relationship slip away. Indeed, he was soon thinking about the kiss they had shared, a recollection that seemed to tingle with promise. Yet, as he thought about it, he realized that while that memory thrilled him, it also troubled him. *There are times and places for every stage in a relationship,* he thought, *and that, somehow, was out of place.*

Then Isabella started speaking, and he pushed his troubled thoughts away. "I have a new job," she said with excitement. "I am starting work this week in Warden Enatus's office. He is setting up a crisis team using people like me who have nothing to do now that the Gate is gone."

"Looking forward to it?" Merral asked.

"Absolutely." There was no mistaking the enthusiasm in her dark eyes. "It's going to be very stimulating. I feel like an explorer."

"I'm glad someone is positive."

"It's not all bad, you know."

She leaned over the table. "So, Merral D'Avanos," she said in a secretive voice, "tell me all about your trip north. You have been very evasive. Did you see that insect man-thing that Elana saw?"

It suddenly came to Merral that this was going to be very different from the conversation with Henri. Isabella would not be content with platitudes. And, as he realized it, he felt a horribly strong temptation to deny everything and to say that he had seen nothing. The attraction of the lie made him feel almost nauseous. Sensing his hesitation, Isabella murmured, "Go on. You can tell me."

"Isabella, dear," Merral said after a moment, "I'd just rather not talk about it. I really would."

The sort of relationship that Isabella and I have, he thought in alarm, *should involve progressively greater openness; that is what the whole sequence of commitment, engagement, and marriage involves. Yet instead of going forward, I find myself wanting to hold back. She demands to know more of me, yet I find I am reluctant to do so.*

A darkness seemed to cloud her face. "But I ought to know, really. It might help you to talk about what happened."

There was the usual gentle softness to her voice, but underneath Merral sensed a hard core of insistence.

"Perhaps," he answered, "in time, I may be able to talk about it fully."

Isabella looked out of the window into the dusk as if trying to hide her impatience and then turned sharply back to Merral, her dark hair swinging over her shoulder. A strand landed across her face, and almost with irritation, she flicked it back.

"Merral," she said softly, "I was up there at Herrandown with you. I *know* the problems already. I really ought to be told the end of the story."

Her tone was gently imploring, and Merral found that somehow it irritated him. And the fact that her insistence irritated him made him feel both miserable and alarmed.

"Well, I said I'd rather not—"

"And at least," she said, giving him a forced smile, "I want to know how you got from presumably well north of Herrandown to Isterrane, over a thousand kilometers away. Oh, come on, tell me!"

After a moment's further hesitation, Merral spoke. "Look, Isabella, all I wish to say—at the moment—is something like this: Over three days, Vero and I walked up the Lannar River as far as Carson's Sill, which is a rock ridge just before the Rim Ranges proper. There . . ." He paused, puzzling exactly what to say. "Well, there, we saw what shouldn't have been there. That we cannot explain. We asked to be pulled out and were picked up by a general survey craft and taken to Isterrane."

Isabella stared at him. "So it does exist. I thought so. From the way Elana talked."

"Well, we think . . . that whatever they are, they are gone. At least from that area."

"They?" Her thin eyebrows arched upward.

"There was more than one of them."

"I see." She shuddered. "And you are doing something about it?"

"Of course. There is an informal group of people working on it."

"Who? You and Vero?"

"And Anya Lewitz, the biologist who looked at the samples. And her sister, Perena, who piloted the craft that picked us up."

Isabella took a sip from her glass before speaking. "I see. But how does she fit in? Perena, I mean, to the group? I mean, I can see how you and Vero fit in, and I can see how Anya fits in. But a pilot? And if she's flying a general survey craft, she has got to be a Near-Space pilot."

Merral stared at Isabella, realizing that he had underestimated her.

"Well . . . we think it possible that these things may have come from outside Farholme. By ship."

"You think they are aliens?" Her eyes widened.

Merral hesitated, realizing that he had been dragged into saying more than he had intended. "Well, that may be going too far. We are looking into every possibility, but obviously we need to keep it quiet. We do not want to panic anybody, and as you would be the first to appreciate, now is not the time to release speculations."

As he spoke, it came to Merral as a fresh insight that while he was capable of being firm in his dealings with captains, advisors, and even representatives, in his dealings with Isabella he was weak. The insight irritated him.

"That is *so* scary. But what I want to know—"

Suddenly, Merral felt he had said enough. "Look, Isabella, I've told you as much as I can at the moment. That's all I want to say. The rest is, for the moment, private."

As the words came out, he realized how brusque they sounded and was appalled. "Sorry," he said.

Isabella blinked and then she just reached out and stroked his hand for a second in a placatory gesture.

"I'm sorry; it's been a difficult few days—for us all."

"That," Merral said, sitting back, shaking his head, and sighing, "is what everybody says." *Perhaps,* he thought, *we can work something out between us. What we once had was so good that we ought to be able to get it back.*

"But it's true, Merral. It's an unprecedented shock."

"But is it, in your view," he said, thinking how relieved he was to turn away from the subject of the intruders and his trip north, "an unmitigated evil?"

"What do you mean?"

"Well, I was talking to someone at the hospital who was saying to me that at least we might be free of those viruses that come in with travelers from other worlds."

"Like the Carnathian flu we all had to be inoculated against last year?"

That's it. Stay away from the intruders. "Yes, I suppose so. . . . I mean, have you found any silver linings in the black cloud? I could use them."

"Me? Well, I did have one odd thought—"

"Which was?"

She creased her brow and gave him what he always thought of as one of her intense looks. "Well, the Assembly has always valued stability. As you know, Assembly society doesn't change very much in space or time. It has been said that if you could—somehow—transport one of the founding generation here across those twelve millennia, he or she would fit back into our society with barely a murmur."

"It's almost a truism," Merral said, feeling more relaxed. "Or if our society does change, it changes within only tiny limits."

Applause drifted up from the room below.

"Yes, well, that is partly due to planning. But there are also sociological reasons why that has been the case. The Assembly is just too big and too open for innovations to take hold."

"Yes," he answered, realizing that part of her charm was the way her intelligence and analytical ability stimulated him. "Genetic systems work in the same way. It's hard to modify large populations as the new genes just get swamped."

"That may be where the idea came from. Well, you see . . ." She paused, a slender finger tracing a meandering pattern on the table. "I was thinking that in a small, isolated society, which is what Farholme will be for the next fifty years, change can happen."

"I see. . . ." It was an interesting insight.

"And," she went on, "when we get reconnected, we may be very different."

"And this change . . . ," Merral asked slowly, watching her delicate face, "would be good?"

A flicker of uncertainty crossed Isabella's face. "Well, of course, not all change is good. We need to be careful. That's what we will be looking at. But—and it's a tentative thought—the Assembly may, for the best reasons, have kept us back."

"Kept us back?" Merral felt suddenly tense.

"Don't sound so surprised, Merral. What I mean is this: To be an adult you need to make choices. We have not had the choices. We have been kept in a moral kindergarten."

"Go on, Isabella," Merral said, feeling unease. "I'm just a plant person really. All this social analysis stuff is new."

She stared at him. "Well, you see, societies may be like people. Perhaps we too need to go beyond kindergarten."

Merral felt cold, as if the lake waters were seeping into his veins.

"I see," he said, trying not to express his disquiet. "I would need to think about that. It's a new idea."

Isabella touched his hand again. Far away, the band struck up a new piece.

"Maybe," she said, in a low voice that seemed somehow to make all Merral's concerns trivial, "maybe *we* need to think about it."

Merral, feeling both longing and alarm in equal and conflicting amounts, tried to speak in as smooth a way as he could manage. "Yes, but not just now. When things settle down."

Then to cover his confusion, he took another sip of his juice. *I wish Vero were here. I need to talk with him about how she perceives the situation.*

Then, in order to restore balance to his mind, he switched the subject to the plans for a new sports tournament for the Ynysmant schools. After an hour, pleading genuine tiredness, he walked her back to her house.

As he donned his night-suit for bed that night, Merral still found himself troubled. He took down imaging glasses off his shelf, went to the table, and carefully picked up the small crystal egg that was perched on a stand. He placed it on the personal creation reader by his bed, lay down, put on the glasses, and ordered that he be logged on to the castle tree simulation.

He closed his eyes as the optics adjusted and opened them to see that he was standing a few meters above a thick snowfield that was lit by late winter's afternoon sun. Data hanging in the air told him that in the fortnight since he had last visited his world, over three years of simulated time had elapsed.

Merral paused, adjusting himself to the sterile, noise- and odor-free brightness of his world. Then he flew effortlessly over the gleaming ground until the vast, snow-streaked brown bulk of his castle tree loomed up before him. He stared at it, admiring again its towering mass, twice the volume of Ynysmant town, before slowly spiraling up around the outside, examining its surface. At the completion of his survey, he found himself pleased; the simulation was progressing well. There was new growth, and despite the heavy snowfall, only a few branches had snapped under the snow's weight.

Now, at the top of the tree, Merral turned and floated down into its enormous hollow interior. Here, protected by the vast wall of the tree, a quieter, milder climate prevailed, and he found that parts of the lake at the bottom had remained unfrozen. He was not surprised to see no sign of life; the only creatures he had created so far were insects, and they were overwintering as larvae in the crevasses of the trunk.

Satisfied, Merral ascended again until he was high in the air above his creation, and as the sun set, he put himself in a slow circular orbit around the tree. There he toyed with the questions his simulation raised. When should he let the tree breed? Should he make another tree anyway? And what other life-forms should he create? He could, of course, just let the insects evolve, but that would take time.

Normally, unless he was going to make adjustments to the program or take images, Merral would have exited his created world fairly promptly. But today, somehow, things were different. As the darkness gathered under and inside the tree, Merral found himself lingering. He had always been fond of his world and proud of his castle tree, but he had never had any illusions that it was anything more than a pure fiction of electrons and photons created and sustained by enormous processing power. Yet now it held an attraction for him that it had never had before. There was something clean, simple, and undefiled about this world that he found alluring. "If only it was real," Merral said with longing, and he marveled at the strangeness of the thought.

The following morning Merral walked across the two-kilometer causeway and went straight over to the office of his director, wondering what Henri was going to say to him.

Henri gestured him straight to one of the chairs in front of his desk. He flung his own wiry frame into the facing seat.

"Man, I'm glad you are back," he drawled. "*Ach*. You chose a momentous time to be away." He gave Merral a bewildered, almost stunned smile.

"Yes. Pretty momentous."

"Momentous. Isn't it?" Henri toyed with his beard, and Merral noted that it had lost its usual neatness. "A week ago the job of this Institute was to slowly and steadily expand the forest and the settlements. Then, out of the blue, the Gate goes, and everything is changed. Now our job is ensuring survival." He breathed out a heavy sigh. "*Ach,* man, we haven't a clue how to do it. So it's endless meetings. But I think we will have to let much of the north go to wildwood."

Merral groaned. "Wildwood? Oh, let's hope we can avoid that."

Henri looked sympathetic. "I know. Foresters see wildwood as a mark of defeat. But what else can we do? Our overstretched resources won't allow for more. And remember, it's merely a fifty-year setback. Think of the ten thousand years we have already spent on this world."

"I suppose you are right, Henri; take the long view."

"There's no other way." Henri paused, raised an eyebrow in inquiry, and leaned toward Merral. "But we can talk about that later. Your Herrandown trip. What can you tell me?"

Merral thought for a few seconds. "I'm glad you put it like that. The answer is, not a lot yet. . . .We have got a lot of data in Isterrane, and it's being studied. But there does appear to be something up north, beyond Herrandown. Something that is genetically odd."

There was a sharp, quizzical look. "What? The Antalfers may be your family, but they are my responsibility. Some sort of anomaly?"

"Yes, something like that . . ." Merral paused. "A mutation or mutations. Perhaps."

"Hmm. I gather from the quarry team at Herrandown that you sent a message advising more precautions?"

"Yes, people to work in pairs, not to work at night. To avoid the woods."

"Man, I'd like to know more. . . ." Henri's dark eyes seemed questioning.

"I'd like to tell you. But we just want to be careful. I'll tell you when we have firm data and a decision on what to do. But I take it no one is intending to visit the Lannar Crater area?"

"Not for a month. Assuming that the schedule holds. Which I doubt. But you have a suggestion?"

"I think the area should be left alone. We shouldn't send anybody north of Herrandown until things are clearer." Merral heard a sharp edge to his voice.

Henri rapped slender fingers sharply on the chair arms. "Well, I'd normally request your reasons, but it's now an unusual situation right across the board." He sighed. "And to be frank, man, the development of the extreme north was always going to be the first casualty of the Gate loss. Okay, we'll veto the extreme north. We may boost some of the southern colonies instead. They are less demanding."

"Thanks. So tell me, what have I come back to?"

Henri leaned back and gave a chuckle, but it was one without any happiness. "*Ach*, a fluid and fast-moving situation. I don't even know whether your tropics posting is going to come off."

"It can wait," Merral answered, and he meant it.

"Sorry. Anyway, the initial directives are for categorization; we have to look at all our plans in terms of what equipment and resources they need and whether they make use of non-Farholme-sourced material."

"Any specific guidelines?"

"Two specifics: Delete no data files unless you have first checked that the Library holds a copy. And just today I have had a direct order from Representative Corradon's office telling me that we are not to use machines with gravity-modifying engines. All available Farholme GMEs are prioritized for medical, rescue, and other such work. So, if you need a low-impact machine, use a hovercraft, not a GM sled."

"Makes sense," answered Merral, wondering what else would be affected.

"Yes." Henri rubbed his forehead. "I suppose we must be positive and see it as a challenge. There's a pile of things on your desk."

"Yes. I saw it."

Henri rose to his feet. "Yes. But, man, it's good to have you back."

Seated in his office, Merral began to sort out the memos and files that had accumulated on his desk and on the in-tray of his deskscreen.

A lot of the material awaiting him dated back to before the loss of the Gate, and Merral was able to simply consign it to either a digital or real recycling bin. It was when he stared at his personal calendar with its list of forthcoming virtual conferences across the worlds that he had been planning to attend that the isolation his planet was now under came home to him. He closed his eyes and issued an order. "Diary, delete all reminders re inter-system conferences from today onward."

The metallic tones came back to him. "Diary query: Your request normally requires an end limit. Until when am I to delete them?"

"Diary, unlimited deletion. All of them. Until further notice. Forever."

The words "request completed" echoed around the office.

"Good-bye, my old life," Merral said aloud, and suddenly struck by the enormity of it all, he put his head in his hands.

For the next few days, Merral threw himself vigorously into his work. He heard nothing from Isterrane and part of him began to hope that Vero's proposal for teams was going to be refused. *Perhaps,* he thought, *I can return to my old life.* Yet every meeting he went to was dominated by the changed priorities they all now faced and reminded him that his old life was gone beyond recall. And at any meeting, whenever a map was produced, he found his glance straying northward to where the broken circle of the Lannar Crater appeared.

Midmorning on the last day of the working week, there was a knock at his door. Henri walked in carrying a large carton and two long white envelopes, one of which was open.

"Morning, Merral," he said in a strange, unsettled tone. "May I talk to you privately?"

"Of course."

Henri closed the door behind him and, putting the carton down on the floor, pulled up a chair at the other end of the table.

"Our world is changing isn't it?" Henri's voice expressed how uneasy he was with the idea.

"Yes. And it worries me, very much." *I can guess what is about to happen. It is what I have been expecting since I got back.*

Henri waved the letters. "These were couriered to me today. And this carton. Both marked 'urgent.' One letter for me personally and one for me to hand to you. From Representative Corradon."

"Ah."

He handed an envelope to Merral, who glanced at the front, taking in the linked crests of Farholme and Menaya and the embossed emblem of the Assembly, the words *Private and Confidential,* and the two-line address *Forester Merral Stefan D'Avanos, Ynysmant Planning Institute.*

"I think you'd better read it now," Henri said. "*Ach,* it's private, but we need to discuss what it says."

Merral opened the heavy envelope with a knife and unfolded the two sheets of paper. The heading on it said simply *Anwar Corradon, representative for northeastern Menaya,* and underneath the previous day's date was a neatly handwritten message. Merral read it carefully through twice.

Dear Forester D'Avanos,

I have carefully considered both our discussions and the letter I have just received from you on the state of matters in Larrenport. After meeting with the other representatives, I am hereby authorizing your release from your duties at the Ynysmant Planning Institute to work specifically on some of the questions raised by the appearance of the intruders. I have written separately to your manager requesting your immediate release. You are authorized to use such resources of Farholme as needed. You may wish to use the Planning Institute as your base for the time being.

In an accompanying package you should find the datapaks of all the imagery you need. I would like to be made aware of any significant developments in this matter as soon as possible by personal or written communication alone. No contact of any form with the intruders is to be sought without my permission. I have written similar letters to Captain Perena Schlama Lewitz and Dr. Anya Schlama Lewitz.

Furthermore, after further discussion with Sentinel Enand, the other representatives, and Advisor Clemant, I have, most reluctantly, authorized the creation of a Farholme Defense Unit that will interlock with the research work authorized above. Sentinel Enand has been authorized to instigate and organize the development of the Defense Unit, again with the strict ruling that no contact with the intruders is to be made without my approval.

In a break with Assembly tradition which, we must pray, is a temporary measure, the nature of your research and the existence of the Farholme Defense Unit is not to be made public knowledge.

These arrangements will be reviewed on a monthly basis.

Please keep this document private and secure.

Be assured of all our prayers and support.

Yours in the service of the Assembly,
Anwar Corradon, representative

Merral closed his eyes as the import of the letter sank in.

"You okay, man? You look like you need some fresh air."

For long moments, Merral could not answer. "My responsibilities are now heavier than you can imagine," he said finally. "Sorry, Henri. What do you know?"

"A bit. The representative says that he has appointed you to be—how did it go?" Henri looked at his letter. "'To be in charge of a special project of vital importance to the future of Farholme, centering on some of the oddities that have been occurring within Menaya. Rather uniquely'—*I'll say*—'this is not to be made public. I would ask you to assist him in whatever way you can. If you wish to discuss this matter, please do it either by a hand-couriered document or by face-to-face contact with me. I am anxious that no mention of this matter is made on either diary links or the Admin-Net.'" Henri looked up and shook his head. "I'm still trying to work out the implications of that. And the rest. But I don't like it. Not at all."

"Me neither."

"Anyway, he goes on to say, 'I would be grateful if you would not press Forester D'Avanos on any matters to do with this project. Yours, *et cetera.*'"

"Does it say to keep this document private and secure?"

He smiled ruefully. "*Ach.* Man, it's worse. At the bottom it says, 'Please commit the above to memory and then have it destroyed.'"

Henri looked intently across the table at him. "I have no real idea what this is about. I have never heard of anything like this happening. But, Merral, you have my support. Anything I can do to help, I will do."

He extended his hand and Merral shook it.

"Thanks, Henri," he answered, his mind still adjusting to the arrival of what he had both hoped and feared. Then he walked over to the window and for long moments stood there, resting his fingers on the sill. He looked across the lake where the sun was breaking through thin, ashen clouds and lighting up the tops of waves in the distance. *My days of being a forester are ended,* he thought. He tried to console himself that, weeks or months away, he might be fully able to resume the work he loved. Yet it was a consolation that now seemed hard to believe.

Finally, he turned round to Henri. "Thanks. I need to sit and think. And pray. Then, if I may, I will come back to you, probably with some requests."

"I'll do everything I can, Merral. May God help you."

"May he help us all, Henri."

An hour later, Merral walked into Henri's office with a piece of paper in his hand.

"Okay," Henri drawled, "tell me what you want."

"I need some things to start with. A big cupboard, big enough for maps and papers."

"Done."

"And I want another computer, able to handle map data for the whole of northeastern Menaya."

"Again, done."

"Thanks. But there may be a problem. I want that machine isolated from the network."

"Isolated?" Henri's jaw sagged slightly. "But, man, to state the obvious, if you do that no one will be able to interface with it."

"That's the point."

"*Ach.* I see," Henri said, his face showing evidence of a brain working double-speed to handle new ideas. "So I get to lose you? That's bad news for me."

"I've been thinking about that. I don't think I can work all day on this project, anyway. I'll need a break. And if I dropped out of all forestry work, everyone would be very curious. So why don't we cut my workload, and I'll see how much I can do?"

Merral found the happy look that came to Henri's face gratifying.

"Excellent. Anything else?"

"I want to see if one of the maintenance people can modify my office door in some way."

"Let me guess. The same as Herrandown. You want a bolt?"

"No. More complex. A device so that I can bolt and unbolt the door, but from the outside."

An uncomprehending stare slid across Henri's face. Merral paused and then reluctantly said, "The design will be in the Library files. It's called a door lock."

"A door lock . . ." Henri stared at the map on his wall for a long minute in a perplexed manner and then turned to Merral. "What, in the name of the Assembly and all it stands for, are we up against?"

There was a long silence, and then Merral said, "The problem is, Henri, I don't know." He paused, struck afresh by the dreadful responsibility that had now been thrust upon him. "And it has become my responsibility to find out before it's too late."

28

Within hours, Merral had started on his task of finding the ship. And by the end of the day, he had realized that he faced a daunting task. Not only had he a vast area of incredibly rugged terrain to search—his estimate was that the Lannar Crater alone covered around a million square kilometers—but he didn't know what he was looking for. What shape was the ship? What color? What size? Would it show up on gravity or magnetic data? Could he eliminate swamps, screes, and mountain summits? The answer, he realized, was, in every case, that he simply didn't know.

Over the next week, Merral's doubts deepened. One promising technique had failed completely. He tried getting the computer to compare last year's images with this year's and to flag any changes. The problem was that the crater area was so dynamic that every square kilometer turned out to have something new, whether it was a fresh stream, some fallen trees, or a new landslide. So for two days he turned the images into a digitally created landscape, put on imaging glasses, and cruised across it at a variety of altitudes. But he found no trace of any ship.

In the end, Merral divided the imagery into blocks of ten square kilometers and began to look at each in turn, cross-checking the visual data with any geophysical oddities. It was slow work, and he found he could only concentrate for so many minutes at a time before he had to take a break. As a change—and to try and freshen his mind—he took to running along the lake edge at lunchtime. But after a week's work, the verdict was inescapable: he had discovered nothing.

One of the few consolations that emerged during that first week of the search was that Merral found his relationship with Isabella seemed to be running more smoothly. For one thing, her new job seemed to occupy her energies. It soon emerged that she had been made the deputy leader of the warden's crisis team. For another, she seemed to have made a decision not to push Merral to say anything more about the intruders, and he was spared more troubling questions. But the topic didn't go away. Merral felt that, like a rock under the surface of the water, the subject was always there. In the end, Merral found the whole thing so awkward and irritating that he decided to tell Isabella almost everything. So, one evening, they went for a walk in the woods south of Ynysmant and there, in a clearing a long way from anywhere, Merral told her—on the condition she told no one else—what had happened.

"That's as much as I know," he said at the end. "So I'm hunting this ship while Vero is busy organizing things in Isterrane."

Isabella had followed the account in an attentive silence. "Thank you for explaining this," she said. "I could guess the Gate destruction was linked to these intruders. It stands to reason. You don't get oddities in a world like Farholme. When you get two oddities, it figures that they must be related. But I had no idea that it was this bad. It has awesome implications."

She fell silent again, and as they walked back together, he felt he could sense her mind working away, putting the pieces into place.

As he left Isabella at her parents' house, she turned to him and hugged him tightly. "Thank you, Merral. I wanted to ask, but I preferred for you to tell me in your own time. Thank you so much for telling me."

But as Merral walked home, a troubling thought seized him: had he genuinely volunteered the information, or had Isabella somehow manipulated him into giving it?

At the start of the next week, he had a terse handwritten note from Vero announcing that Perena would fly him and Brenito out in two days' time to see Jorgio. The letter concluded with *Very busy here; be good to talk with you.*

Merral immediately set about making arrangements for the trip. The real problem turned out to be ensuring Jorgio's presence. In fact, Merral found it frustratingly hard to even find him. The central files listed Jorgio Aneld Serter as a "noncorrespondent," the curious term used for people—like honeymoon couples and those seeking the discipline of solitude—who decided to forgo diary usage for a few days. Only in Jorgio's case, it seemed that he hadn't used it for twenty years. Eventually, Merral got hold of him through Teracy, the assistant manager at Wilamall's Farm, and managed to extract a promise from Jorgio that he would be there. In contrast, arranging to get a rotorcraft and pilot from Henri proved simplicity itself.

Two days later, Merral was at the strip at nine o'clock peering into the cloudless skies for any sign of the plane. It had crossed his mind that Anya might come with the party as well, and he was disquieted at finding how much he hoped that this was the case. Shortly after nine, a small courier plane flew in from the west, made a perfect landing, taxied toward him, and stopped.

Vero, carrying a briefcase, was the first to get out, followed by a tall, muscular, blond-haired young man who helped the slow and heavy figure of Brenito down the steps. Moments later, Perena and another woman in a pilot's uniform emerged. There was no Anya.

A few steps away from the plane, Brenito stopped and pulled a broad-brimmed hat down over his large head, then extended a hand to Merral.

"Well, we meet again, Forester," he said slowly as they shook hands.

Looking at his pale, drained face, Brenito seemed to Merral to be badly shaken by events.

"Sooner than we had expected, Sentinel Brenito. But I welcome you nonetheless. There's a rotorcraft waiting over here."

Vero came over. They hugged each other and stepped back to look at each other. Merral wondered whether his friend was thinner.

"Oh, it's good to see you, my friend!" Vero said, his brown face displaying transparent pleasure. "It really is. I have missed your insights and your leadership. And there's so much I want to show you." Then he looked at Merral. "Is there any news?" he asked in an urgent tone.

"I'm sorry. No."

Vero bit his lip. "Ah. I was afraid of that." He paused. "We will talk later. Introductions first."

He beckoned the young man forward. "Merral, this is Zachary Larraine. He's one of the team: an aide."

Zachary, who had the sort of physique that Merral associated with those who took their athletics seriously, gave him a knowing smile.

"It's Zak. I'm from Kelendara. Heard a lot about you," he said, his sharp blue eyes radiating a quiet self-assurance. He gave Merral the firmest of handshakes. "I'm just delighted to be involved, sir."

Sir? thought Merral with something approaching alarm, as Zak joined Vero in walking on either side of Brenito as he made his slow way toward the rotorcraft.

Perena then hugged Merral and introduced the second woman as Lucinda, the pilot. Lucinda smiled, shook hands, and said she was staying by the plane.

"So, Perena," Merral said, "whose is the plane?"

She smiled. "It was going to go to the Mazarma geographic survey. It's been reallocated to us."

"Us?"

"The Farholme Defense Unit."

"I see."

"It is useful. We don't have to try and squeeze on existing flights."

"Makes sense. But how did you get it?"

They began walking slowly over to the rotorcraft.

"With some help from Gerry, I persuaded Corradon and Clemant that the intruders almost certainly had some sort of ability to travel faster than light without using a Gate. And as we all face a very tough future, the idea of having access to that ship or its technology is very attractive."

"I can imagine."

"But there was more. They are also fearful of the risk the intruders pose for the Assembly."

"For the rest of the Assembly . . . ?" Then, as an understanding of what she meant came to him, Merral felt a sudden stab of alarm. "Oh! How silly; I hadn't thought of that. I had assumed that, with the destruction of the Gate, the intruders had been stopped from infecting the rest of the Assembly."

"No, we do not have that consolation," Perena said. "If they can achieve, say, just thirty to forty times the speed of light, then they could be at Earth within a decade. Faced with that prospect, they have given Vero more or less everything he has asked for."

"I see. And Dr. Clemant agreed? I'm amazed; I thought we had some serious opposition there."

"Yes, he agreed. Our doctor has taken a long, hard look at the way things are going. And he has realized that, of a number of evils, Vero's approach is the least objectionable."

"Interesting. I am impressed at what he has achieved."

"You have only seen the tip of things," Perena said, gesturing toward Vero. "He's doing an amazing job. Generating orders and paperwork from dawn till late at night. Ten days ago, the FDU was just a few bits of paper and some ideas. But now, it's an organization. I'm impressed." She paused. "Mind you, it's all a bit scary. So much is happening."

Merral looked at her, sensing something. "Do I detect caution?"

"Ah." She glanced at him and he caught a concerned smile. "A bit. I only wish we knew more about what we face. But that's just me. I'd see it as being like playing chess with an unknown opponent; you're careful first. But Vero . . ." She hesitated. "Vero has decided that we must move fast. We can't wait for them to make another move. And actually, I think he's right. This isn't chess."

"No."

The others had reached the rotorcraft, and Perena and Merral stopped just out of earshot behind them.

"And you . . . ?" Perena inquired.

"I'm sorry. Nothing to show. I've just had a long, tiring, and so far fruitless search."

"A pity."

"Yes. And Anya? How is she?"

"Busy. She sends greetings. The intruder genetic code is being unraveled." She shook her head. "Unpleasant."

"It's a pity she wasn't able to come out."

"Yes. It would have done her good. She has been working long hours. They all have."

"So, are you getting much flying done?"

"A little. I've got my first space trip next week. I am taking Gerry and some colleagues out to Far Station."

"I thought her research had been cancelled."

"It's been redirected," Perena said, looking at Vero with an expression in which Merral felt respect and amusement were mixed. "He's got most of the physics department working for him now."

Half an hour later, they landed at Wilamall's Farm. Merral felt relieved to see the lopsided figure of Jorgio Serter waiting patiently by the landing pad.

Jorgio wore faded green trousers and an old white shirt, and had a single red rose stuck in his breast pocket.

As if the others didn't exist, Jorgio came over to Merral and gave him one of his big and clumsy embraces. "Why, Mister Merral!" he said. "Arriving out of the sky like this." He shook his tanned and twisted head. "*Tut.* You'll forget how to ride like that."

"No, my old friend," Merral answered, "I will not forget how to ride, and one day I'll come up here for a weekend and do nothing but ride."

"And how is Graceful? You're not too busy to look after your horse, are you?"

"She is fine, stabled at the Institute, but she gets little riding from me. But let me introduce you to everyone. Vero, you know."

In turn, Merral introduced Jorgio to Perena, Zachary, and finally to Brenito, who bowed slightly.

"If you please," said Jorgio, with a wave of a large hand, "do come over to my cottage. I have some tea and cake. Mind you, it will be a tight fit for us all. But we will do it."

In the end, after Zak had taken a quick look around the room and volunteered, with quiet tact, to take a walk instead, they did all manage to squeeze into Jorgio's small, sparsely furnished living room with its low wood-beam roof and its walls hung with gentle pastel abstracts.

As they drank tea and ate the cake, Brenito said, "Jorgio, I want to thank you for your help and advice to my friends, Merral and Vero."

"Just part of my service to the King, that's all," Jorgio said in his rough voice. "I just wish I could have saved the Gate. There've been a lot of people I heard of as are separated from loved 'uns."

"Indeed. It's very sad. But, Jorgio, please tell me about your family. Go back as far as you can."

So, for the next ten minutes or so, Jorgio talked in his roundabout way about his father and his grandparents, while Brenito sipped at his tea and listened carefully, occasionally making such comments as "indeed," "really?" or "how interesting."

There was, Merral decided, an odd affinity between the two men. It was as if they were two related plants: Brenito, the cultivated variety; Jorgio, the wild form.

Then, as their host paused for a moment, Brenito raised a finger. "Now tell me, this gift of 'seeing things' you have. Does that run in the family?"

Merral saw Vero stiffen. Perena, squeezed unobtrusively into a corner of the room, tilted her head as if anxious not to miss a word.

"I reckon so. My grandfather—on my dad's side—could sense the weather. So they said. People would go to him 'bout that. Reckoned he was better than the forecasts. Least for this part of Menaya; forecasts don't work right here sometimes."

"So was he considered a prophet?"

Jorgio pouted. "Now, the local congregation did say that. Crops, seasons, missing animals—they felt he knew that sort of thing. In fact, now as you mention it, I remember when I was young him saying as his grandfather had something similar."

Brenito nodded. "So that would take us back, what? Almost two hundred years? Intriguing."

Merral wondered why such an inherited gift should have gone unnoticed. Then it occurred to him that, in a world where nothing much happened, the gift of seeing the future was hardly one to be prized.

"So," Brenito said, his voice oddly resonant in the small room, "Jorgio, Merral, and Vero have told me about your visions, about the Assembly, about what's happening. Can *you* tell me about them?"

Jorgio rubbed his smooth, bald head and stared at the table. "*That.* That's why you're here, isn't it? 'Cause old Jorgio sees things."

"I think God has given you a gift that we need."

"*Tut*. We all 'as gifts," Jorgio said dismissively and looked around. "Lots of gifts here."

"I think so too. But we want to hear about yours. Tell us about your dreams, your visions. We need help and you can give it to us."

So, prompted by Brenito, Jorgio recounted his dreams and visions. Although Merral had already heard what his old friend had to say, he still found his words both compelling and troubling. And from the tense, rapt expressions on the faces of Brenito, Vero, and Perena, he knew that the others were similarly gripped. And as Jorgio told them of his awareness of cold, creeping shadows under the northern woods, Merral felt as if the sunlight somehow faded and the day's warmth left the room. And when Jorgio told of his two specific visions of a threat to Farholme and the Assembly, Merral felt there was an almost electric tension to the room, as if a summer storm were brewing.

"Hmm," Brenito said in the long silence that followed. "Extraordinary. Tell me, when the Gate went, Jorgio—when you heard the news—what did you feel?"

"Now that was odd. I felt anger." Jorgio's forehead creased into a frown. "Yes, if you please, *anger*. It was almost as though it was the Lord's anger, if you like."

"Would it surprise you to know that it wasn't an accident?"

Merral was aware that every eye in the room was turned to Jorgio's face.

"Accident?" His thick lips smacked in indignation. "Surprise me? *Tut*, I knew it weren't that. It was them in the north that was behind it."

"Ah," Brenito said; it was a single, long, slow word of discovery. "And who," he continued, as delicately as if his words were on tiptoe, "are *they*?"

"I don't rightly know." The leathery face wrinkled, revealing uneven teeth. "But I know as they aren't good. That's obvious anyway. And there's something there that ain't flesh and blood either, if my dreams are right. Or, at least, not *natural* flesh and blood. Not warm, living, flesh and red blood, like what you and I have under our skins." He chewed his lip. "And I think this something is old—"

"Old?" Brenito's question was barely a whisper.

"As old as the hills. No—older. Older than the stars."

"I see." Merral caught Vero's glance.

"And they don't like us, Mister Brenito. They hate the King's people. Always have."

"Hmm." Brenito shifted awkwardly in his chair. "What else do you know about them?"

"Know? Oh, I know little. It's what I reckon, really."

The old sentinel smiled. "Go on. I'm very interested."

"We all are," added Vero quietly.

"For instance, where are they?" Brenito asked "Exactly? Do you know?"

"Up north, I reckons. Beyond the mountains." Jorgio shivered. "I get cold at night thinking about the north. The ice, the frost. But it's colder than that now. Now it has them."

Jorgio fell silent, looking at the floor and twisting his gnarled fingers.

"Why are they here?" Brenito asked.

"It's 'cause the barrier is down."

"The barrier is down?" Merral echoed and received a cautionary glance from Brenito.

"Yes," Jorgio said, scratching his uneven nose, "leastways, that's how I look at it."

"What barrier, Jorgio?" Brenito said in a soft voice.

"Well, see, I don't say as I'm right or I'm wrong. But I always reckoned there has been a barrier. Like a wall, see?" He tapped a finger on the masonry beside him. "I expect it's invisible except to the Lord and the angels. It's his handiwork, of course. Round the Assembly. And it keeps 'em out. Or it did."

"Did?"

"Well, I reckon. No, I *knows*. But either they have been let through, or something—*someone*—has made a hole in the barrier. And they're getting through. Now."

"This barrier—where does it lie?"

Jorgio gestured sharply upward at an angle. "Beyond Farholme. We're at the edge. We are Worlds' End."

There was a long silence.

With a loud creak, Brenito leaned back in his chair. "Well, thank you, Jorgio. I think what you have said is very significant. I am delighted to have heard it from you personally."

"Mr. Serter." The sound of Perena's quiet voice made everyone turn toward her. "Just before the Gate went . . ." She paused. "I met a strange figure. A man—only he wasn't a man. He warned me that night was falling and the war was beginning. He told me that the Gate was under threat—" she swallowed—"he said he was an 'envoy' sent from 'our Lord the King.' I was wondering if you knew anything about him."

Jorgio looked at her, then broke out into a broad smile. "Well, bless his Holy Name, I am glad to hear that." Jorgio gave a little clap of pleasure. "Best news I heard in a long time. 'Course, it's not surprising. The King never leaves his people on their own."

"So you know who he is?" Brenito asked with a raised eyebrow. "This envoy?"

"Oh, I don't know *who* he is but I can guess *what* he is: one of the King's warriors, he is. There's old stories as all the worlds have angels. He'll be ours."

"Thank you," Perena said quietly. "Thank you very much indeed."

There was a long silence, a silence deep enough for Merral to hear the sound of Brenito's heavy breathing. Suddenly, the old man gave a sharp little gasp. Merral saw the look of concern on Vero's face and understood his expression perfectly; this was not a well man.

Jorgio rose slowly. "Mister Brenito, would you like to lie down on my bed while I prepare lunch?"

"P-please," said Brenito in an unsteady voice. "Thank you—I don't mind if I do. . . . And a glass of water? Thank you."

Helped by Merral and Vero, Brenito managed to get out of his chair and into Jorgio's bedroom, where he lay down. After taking some water, he seemed to improve and asked that he be left on his own.

Perena insisted on helping Jorgio with lunch, so Merral and Vero left the cottage. It was turning out to be one of the first really warm days of the year, and they went and sat down on a grass bank in the shade of a big western oak that faced the cottage.

"Brenito's ill, isn't he?" Merral said.

"Yes," Vero said and shook his head. "It was a risk bringing him today. But, I think, a worthwhile one. What do you think of what Jorgio said?"

Merral thought for a moment. "It's scary. The barrier being down, I mean. But it makes sense, doesn't it? The idea of something outside the Assembly managing to get in."

"Yes. I just think it makes what we are doing even more urgent."

"Perena told me that the FDU is growing."

"Yes, I think it is, gratifyingly fast. And then I hear Jorgio and I wonder what we are up against."

"No news on Gerry's quantum communication device?"

"None." Vero shook his head. "She sent the message repeatedly; we have used up all the linked photons. There was no reply. Gerry wasn't surprised though. I guess I don't understand the physics. 'We will know in fifty years whether it got through,' she said. But Clemant was *not* happy about it. 'It should have been approved, Sentinel.' He didn't care for your account of what had happened at Larrenport either, when that got out." Vero shook his head as if trying to shake off a troublesome fly.

"But he has come around to supporting you?"

"Yes. He is fundamentally a pragmatic man. It took him some days for the gravity of the situation to sink in, but when it did—" Vero shook his head—"he became very helpful. He doesn't care for what we are doing, but he acknowledges it is needed. But, Merral, tell me about your hunt for the ship. You really have found nothing?"

"Nothing."

The look of disappointment on Vero's face was unmistakable. "I had assumed from your silence that that was the case."

"Vero, I'm spending six or seven hours a day on it. I can't do any more. I'm now going over it square by square at a scale where I can make out individual trees. But it's slow."

"How slow?"

"It could take me another three months to do the entire area."

Vero gave a cluck of dismay. "I'm not blaming you, of course, but can it be speeded up?"

Merral explained the difficulties.

"I see," Vero said. "It's like 'looking for a needle in a haystack.'"

"Not heard that one. Is that another of these pre-Assembly sayings?"

"Yes. All my reading is in that period now. When I find time."

"'A needle in a haystack' raises lots of questions; I mean, why bother trying to find it? Couldn't they have used a magnet?"

"It was probably a ritual." Vero thought for a moment. "But are you staying fit?"

"I try and run every day. Why do you ask?"

Vero frowned. "Because when you—when *we*—find this ship, we will need to mount an expedition to it. You'll have to lead—"

"Vero," Merral interrupted sharply, "you aren't serious?"

"Of course."

"I really don't fancy turning up and knocking on the door, you know. Not at all."

Vero laughed. "My friend, the work of almost my every waking hour is to ensure that if, and when, we do meet them again, we meet them on very different terms than we did before. But let's not talk of that now."

Merral noticed that, by the cottage, Perena and Jorgio were putting out lunch on a table set up outside the door, and Zak was unrolling an awning from the cottage wall.

"Where did you get Zak from?"

"As soon as the FDU was approved I sat down with all the university academic and sports listings and looked up the best of the recent graduates in both areas."

"Why sports?"

"I wanted them fit. If we have to go for the ship—" Vero left the sentence unfinished. "And I was also looking for the good team players. But Zak Larraine's one of the best. He learns fast. I think he could master anything very quickly. He was in the first thirty-six I had."

"The first?"

A sheepish expression crossed Vero's face. "Oh, well. As I got them, we made plans and I realized we needed more than twenty-four. So we recruited another twenty-four. And so on—"

"'And so on'? How many more are there?"

Vero peered intently down at the ground by his side. "Currently I have around a hundred people—all busier than these ants."

"That was fast."

Vero looked up, his face gloomy. "But we may not be fast enough. Things are happening and it's not good."

"What sort of things?"

"At Larrenport the annual Team-Ball match between the Sunrise and Sunset sides was cancelled last week. There was abusive language between the supporters. Unheard of. 'Stupid Setters.' 'Risers are slugs.' Amazing stuff. And there've been problems in the Library."

"The Library?"

"I'll tell you about it when it is confirmed. But, Merral, I fear that time is not on our side."

By lunchtime, Brenito seemed to have recovered, and he and Jorgio engaged in quiet and close conversation. After lunch, Merral and the others drifted away to allow them some privacy. As he walked around Wilamall's Farm, Merral was disturbed to find how rapidly the complex was being run down. Shortly after two o'clock, they all returned to the house. The intense conversation between Brenito and Jorgio had ended, and Merral felt that the old sentinel had an oddly subdued air about him. They made their farewells to Jorgio and left.

On the rotorcraft journey back to Ynysmant, Merral noticed that Brenito barely said a thing but instead stared out of the window with a distant expression on his face. *It's his ill health,* Merral decided.

At Ynysmant strip, they clambered out of the rotorcraft and walked over as a group to the courier plane. Midway, Brenito raised a large hand. "A moment," he announced and gestured Merral over. "I need to have a private word with our forester."

The others withdrew out of earshot.

"Hmm," Brenito began, paused, and then began again. "Merral, over lunch and afterward, Jorgio said more than he had said earlier. He told me some things that I did not especially wish to hear." The big man paused again, wiping a bead of sweat from his forehead with the back of his hand. "He is an extraordinary person. There are depths to him that I really cannot fathom. His counsel is of great value. Not always easy to understand, of course. And he may be wrong. . . ."

Brenito paused again, staring at the spires and roofs of Ynysmant. "A pity. A town I never visited—" Then he seemed to focus back on Merral. "Yes, Forester, two things: First, guard and protect Jorgio. I have played my part, but I feel he has yet a great part to play. What part, I do not know. But our stable hand and gardener is not just someone who sees things; like you, Merral—but in a different way—he is a warrior. Do not neglect him, but at the same time do not expose him."

Merral found Brenito's gaze oddly disconcerting.

Brenito's slow voice continued. "You know, if I were the enemy, the person among you I would most fear would be Jorgio. So keep an eye on him."

"I will do that, sir, as best I can," Merral answered, struck by the sentinel's solemn tone.

"Thank you. And secondly, a warning: I fear that you will all have many dangers to face. Jorgio sees the testing of the Assembly as being not just of an organization but also as a testing of people. I think he is right. You will face dangers. Some of those dangers may come from nearer at hand and in stranger fashions than you suspect. Jorgio warned me that not all who are drawn into the fight against the intruders will win. Some, alas, will be lost."

"I see," answered Merral, feeling very uncomfortable.

"That's all, Forester," Brenito said, extending a hand. After they shook hands, he said, "Thank you, Merral, it has been good to see you."

"I hope to see you soon with the results," Merral said.

"Do you now?" A quite unreadable expression crossed the heavy face. "Perhaps—I would appreciate your prayers for the next week. I have much to do. Good-bye, Forester."

Then he turned and, with Zak at his elbow, walked with a slow and unsteady gait to the plane.

Vero came over. "I won't ask what that was about. But he is in a funny mood."

Merral, touched in a way he couldn't understand or express by what Brenito had said, just nodded.

"But thanks, Merral, for arranging this today. And as soon as you get something, get on a plane and fly over."

"I will, trust me."

Vero smiled. "Look, do what you can, as fast as you can, but don't worry. Even if we had a location, we aren't ready for an encounter yet. Realistically, we need three weeks." He turned and looked northward beyond the strip and trees. "And will we be ready even then?" he said in a voice that was barely a whisper.

29

Eight days passed.

Merral's life remained dominated by the search. There were just two breaks: the Lord's Day and the annual holiday of Landing Day, traditionally marked by the first picnics of the year and a great deal of good-humored fun. This year, though, the picnics were not a success; they were blighted by a sudden rainstorm, and somehow the fun never really happened. And the next day, Merral was back again at his desk and staring at images on the screen.

Midmorning on the ninth day after Vero and Brenito's visit, an envelope was brought to Merral. He recognized Vero's handwriting on it and tore it open with a strange sense of foreboding.

"Oh no," he heard himself say as he read the first line.

Dear Merral,

I'm sad to tell you that Brenito went Home a few hours ago. He was taken into Eastern Isterrane Main Hospital yesterday morning feeling unwell and had a series of heart failures which culminated in his death around three. They could have kept him alive longer, but we all knew it was the end. In the end, death—ever the King's servant—took him Home gently.

I was there, and he said to me toward the end, "Vero, I have done my bit in this business. I would have wished to see the matter through to the end, but that is not to be. You play your part." He said other things, some of relevance to you, that I will pass on to you when we meet.

You can imagine my feelings. Since the loss of the Gate I had come to see him as part of my family. I had hoped that he would continue to be around to help us as we enter difficult days. I shall miss his bluff wisdom and his common sense. He discouraged some of my wilder ideas, and without him around, frankly, I fear for myself.

He told me over the last week that Jorgio had told him—in effect—to put his affairs in order. We agreed therefore that, contrary to usual practice, the funeral would be soon and private. We decided, and Corradon agreed, that as a matter of strategy, news of his death would not be made public. As you know, he had no family here. He will be buried in the Memorial Wood on the headland by his house. I will leave the planting of the tree till later. An oak perhaps?

He fought the fight well. May we do the same.

Yours in the service of the great Shepherd who protects all his sheep,
Vero

Merral sat back in his chair, suddenly realizing how utterly expected the news was. Yet it was a loss, and the idea that there was one less person to offer guidance was a hard blow. He left his office and went for a walk up through woods behind the Institute. There he found a quiet spot and gave thanks to the Lord for the life of Brenito Camsar, sentinel, formerly of Ancient Earth, and the man who, in summoning Vero to Farholme, had set in motion so much.

So much, Merral thought as, half an hour later, he walked back to his office, *but so much unfinished business too.* He wrote Vero a letter of condolence and then, telling himself that it was what Brenito would have wanted, he sat down at his imagery again. Perhaps today, he told himself, he would find what they sought.

But he didn't.

Over the following days, Merral found that success continued to elude him. A week later, as he stood at the window of his office staring at the grayness of Ynysmere Lake, he realized that he was very close to despair. *Nearly three weeks of searching,* he thought gloomily, *and I have found nothing.*

His unhappiness was not just because the ship was still hidden. It was also because things were changing—and changing for the worse—in Ynysmant. Joylessness and dreariness now seemed widespread, grumbling and criticism were now common to be heard, and even Team-Ball matches were marked by grumpiness and bad temper. Even the weather seemed to conspire to depress him. The delayed spring weather had only just arrived and yet already they were having those dry, dusty days with the winds buffeting out of the interior of Menaya that normally only came in summer.

At home too Merral had found things emerging between his mother and father that he was uneasy about. In particular, his mother now seemed—almost as a matter of habit—to be telling his father to tidy up either himself or whatever he was doing. Surely, Merral wondered, she had been more tolerant in the past? Or was his father getting more slovenly? There too something was wrong.

The situation with Isabella also troubled him, although Merral was not sure whether this was part of the general malaise or something purely personal. He had not seen much of Isabella because both she and he had been so busy. But when they did meet there were problems. True, the matter of the intruders was no longer an issue between them, but the matter of their "understanding" with each other had replaced it. Merral preferred to see this as merely an informal agreement that they had a serious relationship. Isabella, though, clearly saw it as something else: as an unofficial statement of commitment, the formal public precursor to engagement and marriage.

It was not that Isabella regularly mentioned the matter of their commitment; it was just that she always seemed to hint at it. Merral preferred not to raise the subject, hoping against hope that it would go away. Yet it didn't; the question of their commitment always seemed to be there between them. In his darker moments, Merral wondered if Isabella was doing, by accident or intent, what she had done with the intruders and employing slow, subtle pressure on him to yield and agree with her point of view. The effect was a renewed tension between them.

One other oddity was that he had spent more time than usual in the simulated world of his castle tree. Frequently, Merral entered the silent realm where his great tree stood before going to bed. He found a strange relaxation in drifting around in between the branches as, in speeded-up time, the clouds flew by overhead and the sun glided across the sky. He had decided that it was time for the tree to breed and had prepared those modifications to the program that would allow his tree to bear male and female flowers that his insects could pollinate. Eventually, he decided, he would make both male and female trees, but for the moment, his only specimen would have to be a hermaphrodite. Yet something about the growing intensity of his involvement with his personal creation troubled him. The sense of relief and release Merral felt as he entered the simulation was something that he had never experienced before. Was it, perhaps, an escape?

"Time is not on our side," Vero had said, and his words seemed to haunt Merral. Yet the one thing he could do that might change matters—find the ship—seemed to be impossible.

Merral frowned. Despite all his hours of poring over images on screens and printouts of various sizes, shapes, colors, and resolutions, he had made no progress. Indeed, in strange and unpleasant moments of mental darkness, he had even begun to wonder if what he sought existed. Clearly, if there was anything, it was hidden. Such a situation was, of course, quite logical; if the intruders were warlike, then one of the skills they would have mastered was camouflage. Satellite surveillance was a very old art and, he presumed, proficiency in avoiding it equally ancient.

Deeply troubled by his thoughts, Merral looked over the water to where, at the edge of his view, the outer houses of Ynysmant clustered round the lake margin. *I'm losing the battle; things are going downhill fast.*

He turned away from the window; this was getting him nowhere. He wondered whether he should travel to Isterrane to talk with Vero. He had heard nothing from him since the announcement of Brenito's death. He needed to clear his mind. Sticking a note on his door, he left the office complex, walked past the stables, and paused at the paddock fence, watching the horses. After a minute, Graceful came over to see him, and he stroked her head for a few minutes, feeling the grit in her mane and wondering at the changes that had happened in the months since he had ridden her into Herrandown that cold winter's evening.

Then Merral walked slowly up the grassy rise, trying to minimize the intake of dust into his lungs. Halfway up the slope he found an empty wooden seat overlooking the lake. He sat on it and tried to think. *What am I doing so wrong that I cannot find this craft?*

As he struggled with his thoughts, his attention was caught by the slow elevation of a hydraulic access platform down by the engineering complex. It was the time of year when the equipment that would be used over the summer was checked. He sighed; all the equipment and technology that he had used had failed him. Then, as he looked over the dust-tinted clouds of white and pink blossoms on the trees below him, the idea came to him that it might be the technology that was the problem. He gnawed away at the idea, progressively becoming more enthusiastic about it. After all, he had to recognize that it was in the area of technology that the intruders were superior. If there was a way of masking a ship's presence, they would know how to do it, and he, novice that he was, was not going to penetrate such a mask.

Merral sensed a glimmer of progress. *Perhaps, I now know what I have been doing wrong.* He tried to think of an alternative.

His thoughts were interrupted by a handsome male Menayan bullfinch that landed on a nearby apple tree bough and began to nip at the blossom. Merral leaned forward to watch it, struck by its confident manner and its glorious breeding plumage of glossy red and black.

The animals could detect them.

Merral sat bolt upright, his discouragement suddenly ebbing away at the thought. He remembered how he and Vero had found the woods so quiet and lifeless on the way up the Lannar River. Other birds had fled the dreadful buzzard—half machine and half corpse—that had watched them as they made their way northward. He remembered how Barrand's dogs had been uneasy at Herrandown and how Spotback had pursued the two creatures northward and paid for it. *Perhaps,* he asked himself with mounting eagerness, *the intruders' weakness lay here?*

Agitated, Merral rose and walked to the summit of the hill overlooking the Institute, trying to pursue this line of thought. He smiled at the idea of leading a team of dogs across the length and breadth of the Lannar Crater. That was hardly practical, yet there might be something in the principle.

It was a pity, he reflected, as he finally stopped on the smooth, grassy summit, that the wildlife of the crater area was so poorly known. He looked northward thoughtfully, hoping to see the Rim Ranges in the distance, but the grimy air had hidden their peaks. He went through what he knew: herds of caribou migrated across the area, their numbers kept in balance by wolves. There were brown bears, beavers, long-tailed otters, and many other smaller mammals. Of course, there were also various birds, and many ducks and waders migrated in and nested in the swamps. The problem was that few people ventured regularly up to study them. There was just too much to do farther south. Yet there was *some* data and some of that, Merral realized, was in the Institute itself.

He hurried back down and went straight to the office of Lesley Manalfi, the ornithologist.

Lesley ran his fingers through his wide, straggly, and graying red moustache as Merral asked him about any bird oddities in the Lannar Crater. One of his fingers bore a large pink bandage.

On a shelf above them, a female chaffinch hopped about watching them cautiously. In the background Merral could hear chirping and cawing from the adjacent room. Lesley had a reputation for being able to heal injured birds, and in spring and autumn his laboratory was often the home of exhausted migrants that had been brought in.

"Oddities, my boy? What sort of oddities?" Lesley asked.

"Signs that animals are avoiding an area. Please don't ask why."

"Avoiding an area?" Lesley repeated in perplexed tones. "Well, the Lannar's not really my patch," he said, looking at Merral with good-natured puzzlement. "The only studies are by remote means. But, strange to tell, I did see something from a satellite run only the other day. Where was it?"

He flicked his bandaged finger over the touchpad below the deskscreen. "Yes, that's it. There's a lake; formally unnamed as yet, but it's Fallambet Lake Five on the maps. There's always a lot of *Cygnus cygnus*, that's the Whooper Swan—the Farholme subspecies, of course—breeding around the northern tip. You see, we can keep a tag on them because they are big enough and white enough to be easy to count on remote imagery."

He muttered under his breath quietly as he looked at the screen. Above them, in a flutter of wings, the chaffinch flew unsteadily across to the other side of the room.

"And?" asked Merral, aware that Lesley had turned to watch the bird.

"Now that *is* good; it's only today that she has been flying at all. And what? Oh yes, this year the image shows none breeding. Not there."

Merral felt a tingle of excitement. "Which means what?"

Lesley twirled the end of his moustache and smiled up at Merral. "Well, without checking on the ground, it's hard to say. And you know, probably better than all of us, that the area is rapidly changing. Perhaps the water quality may have altered in some way that has affected the ecology. Whatever the cause, they've moved elsewhere."

"Could it be, perhaps . . . disturbance?"

"Disturbance by *what,* my boy?" The brown eyes glinted.

"Oh, anything," Merral said, realizing as he spoke that he was deliberately trying to sound vague. "A methane seep? hot springs?"

"Hmm. But yes, it's possible."

"How long have they been breeding there?"

"Oh, regular records go back three hundred years. Plus. This is the first year with no breeding pairs."

"And could it be the bad weather?"

"Possibly—" Lesley checked the screen—"but . . . no, elsewhere they are still nesting farther north."

"Do you have an image of the lake there?"

"Yes, certainly. Here." He swung the screen around.

Merral glanced at it, recognizing a dumbbell-shaped lake near the center of the crater that he had already looked at in his search. He checked the scale; along its longer northern axis it was barely ten kilometers long and less than half that at its widest part. In the middle, where a small delta had built out from the western side, it was no more than a kilometer wide. There were extensive reed areas around the northern margins and clumps of firs elsewhere; otherwise the surroundings were rolling sands with coarse grass patches. There was nothing striking in any way about it.

Merral, conscious that Lesley was looking at him, tore his glance away and got to his feet. "Thanks. Well, I must go. . . . Fallambet Lake Five . . . very interesting. And that's the only data you have for the area?"

Lesley looked curiously at him. "Well, we have the bird migration pathways, of course. A lot of species breed in the Lannar area."

"Of course. I should have remembered that."

"Well, we don't do too much with the data. At the moment. We plot them as routine; there're, oh, probably about a thousand tagged birds of a dozen species. As you know, the rings transmit the position fairly accurately, so we have a good idea of the flight paths."

"Could I interpret the data?"

"Even a forester can do it, my boy. It's in standard map format; the routes are for spring and autumn each year. You want the files? I'll send them over to you." His finger moved over the touchpad.

"Yes . . . but wait. I'll call them up from you."

"As you wish. But can I ask—?"

I'd better get used to this. "Sorry, Lesley, it's a special project. It's confidential."

Lesley's expression was suddenly one of surprise. "Confidential? That's a strange word. Who says it's confidential?"

"Uh, I'm probably not supposed to tell you that."

"Huh?" The eyes widened further. "You mean the reason why it's confidential is confidential itself?"

Struck by the logic of the question, Merral hesitated. "Hmm, I hadn't thought about it that way. It is a bit odd. Sorry, I really am." He moved toward the door.

The ornithologist shrugged. "You know, five weeks ago this was a normal Made World. Now I'm really beginning to wonder. Things are going crazy here. The Gate. You. The hawk."

"I'm sorry," Merral said, feeling unhappy that he couldn't explain to a colleague more about what was going on. Suddenly, Lesley's final word registered with him. "The hawk?"

The ornithologist grimaced and waved his bandaged finger. "Oh, I thought everybody knew. One of the Levant sparrowhawks I was checking on yesterday suddenly had a go at me. It took a chunk out of my finger with a claw."

"I'm sorry, Lesley. Serious?"

"No, but I'll have a scar. . . . But I felt stupid, really. Thirty years of handling birds, I know what I'm doing. Or I thought I did. Weird though. It behaved as though it was scared of me. They don't do that."

"They didn't—," Merral sighed. "You know, Lesley, I'm hearing—and using—the past tense far too much these days."

Before he had to explain any more, he left the ornithologist and walked past his office to the empty teaching lab. There, without giving his name to the network, he accessed Lesley's data.

Feeling as if he was holding his breath, Merral scanned the migration routes of the twelve species over the last dozen years. Of the twelve species he had the data for, ten regularly migrated north over the feature labeled Fallambet Lake Five.

But not this year.

This year things were different. Most species had swung west round the lake, while a few had gone east. None had gone over.

An hour later, Merral had acquired from one of the mammal biologists the remotely tracked caribou migration routes in the Lannar Crater and was plotting them on his computer. When he overlaid this spring's routes on those of years past, he saw a sudden, sharp, and unprecedented diversion near the middle of the crater. When Merral flicked on the underlying topographic map, it was with an enormous sense of relief and satisfaction that he saw a blue figure-eight shape with the words *Fallambet Lake Five* printed next to it.

His search area was now down to under a hundred square kilometers, and Merral knew that, if necessary, he could map every boulder and tree of that.

On the following evening, Merral found the Intruder ship at last.

He felt it was a strange irony that, in the end, the final thing that allowed him to pinpoint the precise site was not the birds or animals, but his own trees. As he scanned the image of the eastern lakeside for what he felt was the fiftieth time, a clump of five firs next to the water's edge arrested his attention. Their tops had snapped off—a common enough result of an ice storm. In this case, though, the broken crests all pointed northward, and Merral knew that no ice storm ever came out of the south.

He then focused on the rock- and boulder-strewn area of the lakeside to the north of the five decapitated trunks. Visually, he could see nothing unnatural, but juggling and merging images of thermal, magnetic, and gravity data at maximum enhancement showed a smooth and regular ellipse, some hundred meters long and forty wide, just to the east of the water's edge and running parallel to it.

Examining the images in visual wavelengths, even with those that had a resolution capable of picking up a boulder the size of a man's head, Merral could see nothing unusual. Rubbing his weary eyes, he peered again at the visual images taken before and after the landing, trying to spot differences. He stared at the earlier of the two images, taken ten weeks before the landing date, trying to register every boulder and shrub in his mind. The features were simple: there was the lake strand, and some hundred meters away, and more or less parallel to it, a steep cliff the height of a three-story house that had been cut in the gravels. Eroded, Merral decided, by the lake at some higher water level. He turned to the subsequent image, taken nine weeks ago, and saw the same cliff. With a sudden thrill he realized it had moved. But his excitement quickly ebbed as he realized that it was probably nothing more than natural erosion.

Discouraged, Merral flicked the image backward and forward on the screen. Then it dawned on him that the cliff had indeed moved, but *toward* the lake and not away from it.

"It can't do that!" he said aloud.

The cliff was now only fifty meters from the shoreline. Somehow, between the taking of the two images, an extension to the cliff had been created. He rapidly superimposed all the other data on the images and found that the new extension to the cliff exactly covered the long ellipse of the anomalies.

"Thank you, Lord," he said aloud.

Merral looked at the time and realized that he had missed the last flight of the day. Deciding that he would travel out on the dawn flight, he called the airport office, booked a seat for the earliest flight, and got them to call Vero and tell him the arrival time. Then he printed off the data, downloaded it onto a datapak, and locked everything else away in the cupboard.

It had taken him almost four weeks, but he had, at last, found the intruder ship. That, however, raised a new and troubling question:

What were they going to do about it?

30

The next morning the continuing dust storm delayed the flight, and Merral and the other passengers had to stand around in the terminal and talk as the latest meteorological data was checked. As he stood there watching a sun so muted that it was no more than a hazy, coppery glow in the clouds, Merral realized how impatient he was to be at Isterrane and to talk with Vero and the others. He wanted to share what he knew and to talk over his fears.

He also realized that he was particularly looking forward to seeing Anya. Merral found this feeling of anticipation troubling. *Surely,* he thought, *I ought only to feel such an excitement with Isabella?* After all, although Isabella clearly saw their relationship as being further advanced than he did, she and he *were* linked together. Yet Merral sensed that although he was still fond of her, he didn't delight in her presence in the way that perhaps he ought to. In fact, he realized he had been thinking a lot about Anya; indeed, over the past week or so, he had frequently found himself unfavorably comparing Isabella's subtle and roundabout manner with Anya's bluff openness. He found his pleasing thoughts about Anya perturbing. In what he now—rather worryingly— saw as his "old world," feelings and choices had worked in harmony; somehow you both chose whom you loved *and* fell in love with them. The two sides of a personality worked together. Now though, he sensed, a conflict was possible; the feelings of the heart and the choice of the head might not automatically come together.

Merral walked around to the window overlooking the landing strip. Through the heavy air, almost brown with fine dust, he could see the tanker filling the short-haul passenger flier with hydrogen. As he stood there, he was suddenly aware of a conversation from two men seated a few meters away.

"Yes, it's the very weirdest thing," he heard one man say in a tone that made the hairs on the back of his neck prick up. "You know I'm now doing the health certificates for the employment check on the sixty-five-year-olds?"

"Of course," said the other man, whom Merral felt he had seen around the hospital. "I sympathized, remember? It's one of the worst things about being a doctor. People often get unhappy at being told to ease up on work."

"Well, that's the thing. See, in the last six weeks, I have had three—really—*three* people, all thanking me for failing them."

"Seriously?" Merral, held spellbound by the conversation, noted the genuine surprise in the voice.

"Absolutely. The last guy said, 'Well, Doc, truth to tell, I'm glad. It's all been a bit of a strain lately. I reckon I'm glad to go and do part-time work.' The other two said much the same."

"Extraordinary. But I've heard other things too. . . ."

At that point, the navigator came over and called them to the plane, and Merral never found out what other new and ominous novelties had transpired in Ynysmant. He could have asked, but he was already worried about becoming known as the man who was asking too many odd questions. As the plane rumbled up into the dusty air, he knew that there were some very serious decisions to be made in Isterrane.

Two hours later Merral landed at Isterrane airport to find the sun shining through an atmosphere swept free of dust by the coastal breezes. The terminal was full, as two flights from the west had just come in, and he could not see Vero. To his surprise, a tall, well-built man came over to him. He was in his early twenties, with short, pale brown hair, a chiseled face, and green eyes.

"Forester D'Avanos? Sentinel Enand sent me for you," the young man said in a musical voice.

Merral stared at the young man and decided that they had never met. "Yes, that's right."

"My name's Lorrin, Lorrin Venn." An open smile broke across the face, and there was an eager and enthusiastic handshake. Lorrin Venn, Merral decided, was another of Vero's team, just out of college.

"This is good," Lorrin announced with enthusiasm. "I am really delighted to meet you, sir. I'm in the FDU, and I'm under instructions to take you to the Library Center to meet Mr. Vero. Straightaway. Do you need a hand with the bag?"

"No, it's light."

The young man, already moving toward the exit, shrugged in an easygoing manner. "Okay, sir."

"But why the Library Center?"

"Sir, I wasn't told and I didn't ask. But over here, please. We have a vehicle."

At a pace so fast that Merral could barely keep up, Lorrin walked through the main doorway and out to where a small, blue, four-seat urban machine was parked.

"But can't we find a lift?" Merral asked.

"No need, sir," was the quick and buoyant response. "The FDU has its own vehicles now. Priority."

"I see," Merral answered, wondering exactly what else Vero had acquired for the Farholme Defense Unit. He gestured to the people waiting at the terminal exit. "But shouldn't we offer a lift to someone? We have two spare seats."

Lorrin smiled. "No, sir," he said. "The FDU has priority here too. Orders are to take you straight there and not to wait. Speeds us up no end. It's neat."

"I see," said Merral, noting Lorrin's enthusiasm for the privilege. "I was expecting Zak. What's he up to?"

"Zak Larraine? He's in the contact team. I'm in support."

"What's the difference?"

"Contact's gonna be more exciting." There was a note of regret in his voice.

Lorrin whistled softly as he drove; it was a tuneful and happy sound, and Merral found it soothing. Halfway to the Library Center, the young man turned to Merral with a curious, almost awed look. "You know, sir, we've all heard about you."

"About me? What—?"

"That you fought the creatures. On your own. 'Hand to hand' was the old term." His tone was respectful.

"Oh . . . ," Merral said, feeling embarrassed, "you know about that?"

"Well, Mr. Vero told us. See, we don't have much else to go on, really. Your information is hard data. But it sounded well, heroic." He looked encouragingly at Merral. "I'd love to know more. Be neat."

Merral looked out of the window for a moment, turning away from this man who seemed to think he was a hero. "Lorrin, I would give a lot to be able to forget all about it. Forever." Then he realized that his words might sound rude. "But, well, if you need me to talk about it, then I'll do it. But only once. And then under pressure. And, if it's all right with you, not now."

"Mr. Vero said it was nasty," Lorrin said, glancing at him. "But I figured it might just be him. Well, sir, when you tell it, I hope it's not just for the contact team."

"Lorrin, if you don't hear it, you won't miss much. It was nasty. *Very.* Fighting is nasty. Period."

Lorrin seemed to consider the matter and then, moments later, began to whistle again.

They parked at the rear entrance to the Library Center, and Lorrin, still whistling, led Merral in through an unlabeled door and hurriedly down a dusty metal spiral staircase that vibrated under their footsteps. From the faint hum from the wall beyond, they were at the back of the data storage units that formed the core of the Library Center. And as he thought it, it occurred to him that what he was hearing was no longer just the sound of one small extension of the Library, the vast information network that spanned the Assembly. As far as Farholme was concerned, it was *the* Library and would be until today's young men and women were elderly.

At the bottom of the ladder, Lorrin turned, pushed open a door, and walked through into darkness. The automatic lighting switched on slowly after him, almost as if it were reluctant to believe that anyone was actually there. Ahead of them lay a narrow, bare, and unpainted brick corridor with a feeling of neglect about it.

"Mind your head," Lorrin called back, gesturing to the sagging cabling festooned along the roof. With energetic strides, he set off down the sloping and curving corridor. Merral followed him as fast as he could, hearing their footsteps echoing all around. After a hundred meters or so, they stopped before a solid dark door in the side of the wall.

The door swung open a fraction to reveal Vero's brown face. His look of caution was suddenly transformed into one of pleased recognition, and he flung the door wide. "Welcome. Do come in!"

Clasping Merral's shoulder in a friendly grip, Vero led him into a tiny, white-painted, brick-walled chamber with a low, curved roof and the air of having been recently cleaned out and painted. It was sparsely furnished with a table, a few chairs, and a wallscreen, and in one corner a number of cables snaked down from an open ceiling duct to the floor.

Vero waved a hand at the young man. "Thanks, Lorrin! Can you find Harrent and tell him our guest is here? Quietly, though. Don't shout it out. Then get the truck ready."

"Right, Mr. Vero," Lorrin replied, in what Merral felt was a strangely formal way, and turned and walked swiftly back up the corridor. As the door closed, they could hear him beginning to whistle.

Vero closed the door firmly behind him and turned to stare at Merral.

"My friend!" Vero said, pleasure stamped across his face. "It's been too long. I have missed you. Especially with Brenito gone. I wanted to be in touch with you, but I thought it best to leave you be."

Then he paused, swelled out his cheeks, and exhaled with a loud sigh. "Oh yes, such a lot has happened since we last met! But take a seat." He gestured to a chair and then bobbed over and sat on the other side of the table behind a pile of datapaks and a battered yellow notebook with a neat *5* inked on its cover.

"And I'm glad to see you, Vero," Merral replied.

He was struck by the odd feeling that Vero seemed at home in this subterranean room.

"But you've found it." Vero stared expectantly at Merral's backpack.

"Yes. On the eastern edge of Fallambet Lake Five; the Fallambet is in the north of the crater. It's a tributary of the Nannalt River."

"Ah. It was off the Nannalt Delta that the *Miriama* found the cockroach-beast."

"Yes. I made that link too."

"Splendid! I can't wait to see it. But I'd better. Anyway, Lorrin looked after you all right?"

"Yes. Happy fellow. Where's Zak?"

"Oh," said Vero rather vaguely, "out with the contact team. But Lorrin was fine?"

"Yes."

"He's a great guy. One hundred and ten percent enthusiasm. The top student last year in Library Science at the College at Baandal. Loves working with the FDU."

"So it seems. I think he's happier than me about it all. But Library Science?"

A sudden look of deep intensity came into Vero's eyes. "Merral, I have realized many things over the last few weeks." He shook his head as if awed by events. "I decided early on that I could create an FDU from first principles, but that it would take about twenty years. And your news from Larrenport and your doctor's alarming report on obstetric problems suggested to me that we might not have twenty months, or even twenty weeks. I realized that the only way of speeding things up was by using the past. So Lorrin—and others—have been working in the Library. And we have found more than we expected." His expression was suddenly pained. "Ah. And also less. But Harrent will explain that."

Then his troubled look lifted and he smiled again. "But it is good to see you."

"I was sorry to hear about Brenito. I'd like to visit the grave."

"I'll try and find the time."

"Do you miss him?"

"Yes. I keep saying, 'What will Brenito counsel?' and then—" Emotion welled up in Vero's voice, and for a few moments he was silent. "But then I tell myself he would have told me to decide for myself."

"Are you living at his house?"

"No. I have been tempted. But it's too far out to run a secure communications link to. And I've been working very odd hours. I have two people staying there, though. Cataloging all that he left behind. It's quite a collection of objects. They have instructions to look for anything that has a bearing on the rebellion." Vero's expression brightened. "But how is Ynysmant? Isabella? your parents?"

"Troubled, Vero. All of them. There are problems in Ynysmant. The mood—whatever we call it—is spreading. I'm sure."

"So quickly?" Alarm flooded Vero's face. "I have heard hints of problems. I don't think we have any time to spare at all." He paused. "Anyway, I've brought you here first because I want you to hear what Harrent the librarian says about a problem. He's not part of us—not really—so don't reveal anything, right? Then we move on to the base."

"The base? I thought this was it."

"This?" Vero seemed amused at the thought. "You don't understand. The base is very much larger. You remember the new water transport project for Isterrane, based up in the Walderand River?"

"Vaguely . . ."

"Well, the project was frozen; the pumps were being brought in through the Gate. So they've given us—that is, the FDU—the pump chambers. It's ideal. But secret." He tilted his head, listening. "Ah, that will be Harrent now. But remember, don't say too much."

There was a knock at the door, and a very tall and elderly gray-haired man in a dark official suit came in, stooping carefully and rather stiffly to avoid hitting his head on the doorframe. Inside the room, he straightened himself up carefully, eyeing the low ceiling with suspicion. He shook hands in a rather ritualistic way, first with Vero and then with Merral.

"Harrent Lammas, Assistant Librarian of Isterrane," he said in polite, formal tones. His air of reserve seemed to Merral to be heightened by the dark eyes and a rather stern expression.

They sat down and Vero turned to Merral. "Let me start by explaining that Lorrin and I wanted to do research in the Library, but I was worried that we might be watched. So I consulted Harrent here and, well, together we found some interesting things. Harrent, please explain."

The tall man rested his long arms on the table, exposing neat white shirt cuffs beyond the dark, precisely turned-up sleeves of the jacket. *This is a man,*

Merral thought, *who is everything I would imagine a librarian to be: precise, knowledgeable, retiring.*

"Very well," Harrent said, his expression suggesting that he was far from being at ease in this setting. "Hmm, Merral, I'm not sure how much you know about how the Library works. I take it you have some understanding?"

"I know that the Library is modeled on a fixed geography of rooms, corridors, and stacks which goes back to the days before virtuality when libraries really were repositories of books. So wherever you are in the Assembly and whether you access it by a diary or a computer, you get the same pattern." Harrent nodded encouragingly, and Merral continued. "What else? I also know that there are rules and protocols of Library use, which, to my limited knowledge, have always existed. I suppose they go back to the era of the Technology Protocols?"

"Actually they started to be subscribed to over a hundred years earlier. Anything else?"

"No, not really. It's just there for whatever we want—words, text, images, programs."

Harrent nodded in a rather restrained way. "Hmm, in some ways I am pleased by your ignorance. It is a maxim of Library usage that the system and the librarians should be transparent."

A cautious smile flickered across his face. "Sometimes, in our case, literally."

He tapped his diary and the wallscreen opposite lit up with the familiar picture of a grand vaulted Gothic interior with multiple levels of floors, along which book-lined corridors stretched off on either side as far as the eye could see. As Merral looked at it he remembered the pang of disappointment he had had as a child when he had found out that there had never been a real building as grand and glorious as this.

With a smooth and practiced speed, Harrent slid the viewpoint confidently along the main aisle and then down a side corridor. As he did, he passed gray, stylized human figures, devoid of detail, that were either standing by shelves or moving along purposefully. The librarian nodded at the screen. "The Library at the moment. Very familiar and part of all our lives. Every member of the Assembly has grown up with this exact version since 2170, with only minor software tweaks since. And a billionfold more data." His tone was so dry and formal that Merral wondered how much contact with real human beings his job involved.

"Now for various reasons," Harrent continued, "some practical and some psychological, it has always been found helpful to indicate other users graphically. As we just saw. It's really just a convention."

"But you never know who they are or what they are reading," added Merral.

"Just so. Hmm, privacy. But—and it's a little known fact—the on-duty librarians have a different view. Diary, librarian mode."

The figures on the image were now suddenly marked in multicolored bands, and as Harrent approached a form standing nearby, Merral saw that superimposed on the color bands were long sequences of letters and numbers.

"See now, this coding allows us librarians to help a little if needed. I can walk down the library, quite invisible to other users, and see all this. Thus I can tell you from the color codes that this, hmm—yes, is a male academic from Qarantia, that he studies language acquisition, and that he is a regular user of text files and familiar with the Library. In this case, he is unlikely to need help. I can even check, if I wanted, from the data displayed on him, what he has ever examined or downloaded."

"I had no idea," Merral said. "You have more of a supervisory role than I suspected."

A strange, rather awkward smile slid onto Harrent's face. "Hmm, I take that as a compliment, Forester. The ease of Library use is only achieved by a lot of hard work behind the scenes. And anyway, why should you? What we do is only to help users. Though it's also, to a lesser extent, useful for us. It's so much easier to get an idea of what is popular in the Library, and with who. Hmm, actually very usefu—"

"Harrent," interrupted Vero, glancing at his watch, a finger raised in partial admonition, "could you explain the oddities? Please?"

"Hmm, sorry. Ah, I am beginning to fear that in this new era some of the relaxed traditional customs may go. Yes, well when Vero here asked for my help, I realized, after the initial surprise, that he might be able to shed light on some anomalies that had recently occurred. And which were, in my long knowledge of library work, unprecedented."

He delicately tapped a corner of his diary screen. "Now, in order. This is a data record, taken eight days after Nativity Day last year. A remote librarian recorded this view."

There were the multicolored figures again but, in the middle of them, a figure shaded black stood examining a data file on a shelf.

"Harrent," Merral asked, hearing the alarm in his voice, "who is it?"

The librarian gave a little sigh of bewilderment. "Hmm, we really don't know. We at first assumed a data error, or a software glitch. The figure has no code identifiers, no records, no identity. We named him, her, or it, 'the ghost.'"

Vero gestured at the screen. "Please tell Merral what the ghost is downloading."

"It is in the History rooms and it is scanning Lyonel's *Introductory History of the Assembly of Worlds.*"

"The basic high school text?"

"Quite."

"Is that all?" Merral asked, remembering having read Lyonel's work when he was around thirteen.

"Odd, eh? But watch, it moves on and we lose it. It was leaving no trail for us to follow. We can't call it up. Very irregular." Merral thought that it was the untidiness of the matter that outraged Harrent. "Not at all the sort of thing one likes to have in a library."

"Was the ghost ever seen again?" Merral asked. As he spoke the word *ghost,* it seemed eerily appropriate.

Harrent nodded stiffly. "Briefly, a day later, which was a Lord's Day."

"But," Merral exclaimed, unable to hold back his surprise, "surely, no one uses the Library then?"

"A few people: doctors, engineers, and, hmm, a surprising number of preachers who need to check some last-minute sermon illustration. Anyway, this happens to be a routine survey frame of the main aisle."

Harrent tapped his diary, and the new image showed the central Library aisle from a high point of view by the main entrance. Apart from two forms heading in the direction of Medicine, there were no figures to be seen. Suddenly the black figure appeared at the entrance, glided along the main aisle, turned down a side corridor, and then stopped and seemed to retrace its steps until it was back in the main aisle. There it appeared to look around.

"Our belief is that it has just realized that it's on its own," said Vero.

The figure rotated again, abruptly headed for the exit, and vanished before it got there.

"After that unhappy incident," Harrent said, "where, incidentally, the ghost seems to have been again heading for Assembly History, it was never seen again."

Merral heard himself speaking, the incredulity thick in his voice. "What sort of being is it that is surprised by the Library being empty on the Lord's Day?"

Harrent looked at him quizzically. "Hmm, I'd like to know too. Very much . . ."

Merral caught a cautioning glance from Vero. Clearly, he felt that it was a question that could be better discussed later. Besides, there was an obvious but disturbing answer: Only a creature from quite outside the Assembly could make that sort of a mistake.

Vero leaned forward toward the librarian. "Now, Harrent, tell Merral why we think it is still there."

"Ah yes. Our guess is that it soon realized how the Library worked and either became invisible or adopted another person's identity. But since then there have been other oddities. It was Vero's idea to set the trap."

"Oh, it was hardly a trap," Vero said, his tone slightly defensive. "It was perhaps a test. It was just that—after I heard this story—I was worried. So, when I went to check some data files, I got Harrent to watch me while there was a virtual camera running." He gestured to the screen and a new image appeared of colored bodies walking and standing in a library corridor.

"There I am," Vero said. "The green hue at the top is because I'm from Ancient Earth, the purple base is for a sentinel. Now watch as I skim through the contents of a file here."

The image focused onto a line of thin, vertical gray files with glowing green lights on their bases. "Now watch as I consult the volume."

On the bottom of one file, the green light turned red.

"The accessing light glows; Anatheon on *The Causes of the Jannafite Rebellion,* for your information. I put it back." The green light came back on. "It's not being accessed. But, on my suggestion, Harrent kept the virtual camera on it. Watch now!"

Abruptly at the base of the file, the light went from green back to red.

"Hey!" Merral cried. "But there's no one there!"

"Exactly—no one we can see. But I was expecting something like it and had Lorrin ready. Watch now as he races across and tries to access the same file. Even in a virtual library our Lorrin is fast."

A figure with yellow and blue bands on its head moved over swiftly and stood by the file with the glowing red light. As the figure representing Lorrin reached for the file, the light instantly changed back to green. A black shape, vaguely human in outline, appeared briefly, flickered, and then vanished.

"Our ghost knew he'd been discovered, panicked, and fled, losing invisibility on the way." Vero's voice was serious. "To use the expression of the ancients, he 'pulled the plug.' "

" 'Pulled the plug'?"

Vero shrugged. "As in ending a bath. I suppose." He looked solemnly at Merral. "Well, that's it. So the Library has a ghost."

"A most unhappy state of affairs," said Harrent, his somber expression endorsing his words.

"I agree," Vero said, "but it gets worse."

That, Merral noted with alarm, *is another expression I'm getting used to.*

"Yes, the losses," Harrent muttered in an irritated tone.

"Quite so," Vero agreed. "When I started looking up some works last week, I was surprised to find that they were not there. Not being familiar with library nodes on the Made Worlds, I wondered if they were ones that normally would have been asked for through the Gate. But I checked with Harrent. . . ."

The librarian's face had acquired a look of deep vexation. "Hmm, I checked the index banks and they were not listed. Then, after a suggestion by Vero, I checked an older index that was on an unerasable archive and, well, there they were." He looked at his big hands as if to hide his emotions. "In all my years, I have never heard of titles being erased deliberately. But for them to be erased and then to have the matching records removed too is yet another thing. I have to use the word *wicked.*" He paused and repeated to himself softly, "Wicked."

"Can you stop the losses?" Merral asked, suddenly horrified at the prospect of the Library having all its billions of irreplaceable files deleted.

"We are trying to," Harrent said. "Based on what has gone missing we have established a profile of what the ghost is seeking. I have taken the unusual step of having the remaining titles in those areas digitally transcribed to indelible archive format. We think any further erasure impossible." The librarian shook his head in a gesture that conveyed dismay and regret. "But I am appalled. *Most* appalled. Is there anything else?"

"No, my friend. But thank you; now go and watch carefully."

Harrent stood up cautiously, shook hands again with Merral and Vero, and left. As the door closed behind him and the steady footsteps receded into the distance, Vero leaned back in his chair, put his hands behind his neck, and exhaled heavily.

"So, my friend, what do you make of that?"

"Very worrying."

Vero nodded. "But also, in a strange way, encouraging."

"I found no encouragement."

Vero smiled. "Yes. But they made mistakes. *Again*. They are not totally beyond us. Let us be grateful for small things."

He rose. "Let's go. We have a meeting at the base. It's about half an hour's drive, but Lorrin will take us. We can sit at the back of the transporter, and you can tell me about Ynysmant and where this ship is exactly. Corradon and Clemant will be up later, and we need to decide what to do then. But action is urgent. You see we face a double attack: The intruders are getting themselves into the heart of Farholme, and the evil associated with them is spreading in our society. Time is slipping away faster than we realize."

Merral stepped into the corridor. "It's scary. By the way, what data files were missing?"

"Oh, you can probably guess," Vero said, closing the door behind them.

"No, I can't. Not easily. You tell me."

"Well, a lot of things to do with Jannafy's rebellion; mostly those that talked about how it ended."

"Another common theme."

"Yes, isn't it?" Vero's face bore a knowing look. "And the name of William Jannafy will doubtless arise later on today. Also missing, interestingly enough, were a lot of technical works on late twenty-first century military techniques and weapons."

As he motioned Merral onward he said, in a casual way, "It is almost, my dear Forester, as though they were preparing for us to fight them."

When they got to the transporter—a big four-wheeled, open-backed LP4 with fading yellow paint and piled high with cases and boxes—Vero led him to the back of the vehicle.

"We can talk here," Vero said, clearing a space to sit. "I want you to tell me all about Ynysmant and the ship as we drive. Lorrin knows a lot, but the fewer that know about this the better. Besides, I think a forester like you may prefer the sun and the fresh air."

Merral sighed. "Indeed, I've had little enough of it lately."

"I find it bright," Vero said. "I spend my life indoors now." He took a blue-peaked cap out of his briefcase and pulled it over his head.

After checking that they were strapped in, Lorrin leapt back into the cab, and they drove steadily westward through Isterrane on the main coastal avenue. As they drove out of Isterrane into the countryside, Vero plied Merral with questions about events in Ynysmant and how he had found the evidence for the ship. For the most part, Vero listened to his account without comment, merely giving encouragement with nods and looks.

Faint snatches of Lorrin's whistling drifted back from the front of the vehicle, causing Merral's spirits to lift. The sky was a brilliant, flawless spring blue, the sun warming, and he could smell the sea salt in the breeze. It was the sort of day that brought to mind thoughts of climbing hills, taking picnics with friends by turbulent and wayward streams, and sitting on new green grass, or lying out, reptilelike, on warm stones. Then it came to him that today he could do none of those things but must talk of darker things, of intruders, sin, and evil. And the contrast saddened him.

Suddenly they turned up from the coast road and climbed northward on a narrow, uneven track along the side of the Walderand River. From the swaying transporter Merral could see the bubbling white waters of the river along the valley bottom. Lorrin, evidently enjoying himself, had shifted to loudly singing a string of folk songs.

Suddenly Vero, who had said nothing for many minutes, looked at Merral. "The landing site; is it accessible?"

"I think so. You are thinking about the expedition?"

"Yes." Vero bit his lip and frowned. "I suppose I need to look at the maps first." Then he gestured back toward Isterrane. "The ghost in the Library . . . Can I guess what you found the most striking thing?"

Merral shook his head. "Too easy; the idea that this thing could be unaware that the Library would be empty on the Lord's Day."

Vero nodded. "Yes. Mind you, reading Lyonel is weird too. It just confirms to me that whoever the intruders are, they are not Assembly."

"Exactly."

"Or if they are of the Assembly—" Vero's face darkened—"then things have gone very badly wrong somewhere." Then he shook his head and fell silent again.

Merral was glad of the break in the conversation, and as Lorrin drove them upward on the winding road, he stared at the scenery, trying to clear his mind from the notion of something unpleasant prowling in the Library. They had gained some height now, and Isterrane was stretched out below them, the white blossom of the orchards and the verdant spring grass breaking up and isolating the red and white patches of buildings. Beyond them and the high gray seawall was the dazzling blue of the sea, where Merral could make out white lines of the waves breaking in the spring breeze.

Now Lorrin turned off onto an even narrower track that showed signs of the recent passage of many vehicles. Ahead Merral could see how the hillsides were closing in as steep cliffs of purple-gray lavas swung across the valley, almost sealing it off. They passed a sign on which the words *Walderand River Project: Site Road Only* were written, and Merral noted that above it had been posted a smaller, newer green sign on which the letters *FDU* had been marked.

As the road became rougher and steeper, the swaying of the transporter became more pronounced, and Merral saw that Vero was starting to look uncomfortable. Then they rode over a crest in the road and Merral was able to see that, a kilometer or so away, the road stopped below the sheer cliff that ended the valley. As he stared at the rocks ahead, Merral was suddenly aware of men and machines working away below them. A small cloud of brown dust drifted slowly upward.

"I thought the water project had been stopped?" Merral asked, gesturing at the construction work.

"It has. That's ours," Vero replied.

"All of it?"

"All of it." Vero sounded almost embarrassed.

"But it's vast." The rumbling of the wheels beneath him was now so loud that Merral almost had to shout.

Vero hesitated for a moment and then exhaled noisily. "Yes—it needs to be." Then he smiled. "But my manners fail me." He made an expansive gesture with his hand. "Welcome, Forester, to the FDU base."

31

As they drove ever closer to the end of the valley, Merral could see what was being constructed: a semicircular earth wall with a narrow access gap for the road. Nearer still, Merral was surprised to see that the gap was closed off by a moveable metal barrier.

They stopped in front of the barrier, and Vero gestured that they get out. "Let's walk through!" he shouted over the noise of the earth-moving machinery. "It's quicker."

As they walked past the transporter, Lorrin, whistling happily, beamed at them and raised an outstretched hand sharply to the side of his head.

A salute. I've been saluted. The world seemed distorted again. *We only ever salute the emblem of the Lamb and Stars, and that on special occasions.*

Merral tapped Vero on the shoulder. "Lorrin just saluted us," he whispered. "Is that supposed to happen?"

"Ah. Saluting. A problem, that. At the moment, it is voluntary. But we need to make a decision. I should say—perhaps warn you—that while we have made a lot of progress in some technical areas, there are some things we have not resolved. Such as discipline."

"Can't we make it voluntary?"

"A voluntary discipline?" Vero gave a strained smile. "Give that idea some more thought, Forester."

Merral noticed men unrolling metal wire mesh to put up along the top of the earth wall. *A month ago, I would have assumed it was to keep animals in; I can now guess it is to keep things out.*

A young man with a databoard came over, gave Vero an abrupt but somehow deferential nod of the head, and then, with polite efficiency, took Merral's name and date of birth.

"Sadly necessary," muttered Vero, as if embarrassed by the procedure, and walked on briskly.

Feeling perplexed, Merral followed him to the foot of the towering cliff. There, by the side of two great tunnels, a new wooden building had been erected.

"Excuse me a moment," Vero said. "I just need to check on deliveries."

While he waited outside, a still-bemused Merral watched the noisy activity going on around him. By the perimeter wall there were three earthmovers and a dozen men putting up the wire mesh, while inside the compound two LP4 transporters were being unloaded by another half dozen men and a lift truck. From deep inside the tunnel came noises of further mechanical activity.

Vero returned clutching papers and motioned Merral urgently toward the larger, right-hand tunnel.

"Merral, things are moving fast," Vero said in an impatient tone of voice. "But it's a race and I'm not sure we are winning."

He led Merral past another observant young man with a databoard and a sign that proclaimed "FDU Personnel Only" into the darkness of the tunnel. As they walked carefully along the side of the tunnel, Merral became aware of an increasing volume of noise ahead of them. About eighty meters from the entrance, the tunnel opened out into a vast four-story cavern lit by bright cones of light and the flash of electric and plasma beams.

Merral stopped, gazing around in awe. Ahead of him, in an area the size of a Team-Ball pitch, perhaps fifty or more people were at work at a dozen sites. Some were packing crates and containers, others were working busily on vehicles and machinery, and still others were assembling equipment. The warm and heavy air was filled with sounds: hammering, shouting, clanking, all reverberating off the bare rock walls.

Merral grabbed Vero's arm. "Is all this . . . yours?" he asked, barely able to believe that his friend had been able to organize so much.

Vero stopped suddenly. "It's not mine; it just sort of grew," he said loudly as a new burst of hammering broke out beyond them. "I'll explain how later. Up here." Then, before Merral could ask him any more questions, he was clambering up a metal stairway that led to a walkway along the side of the cavern.

"Just a minute!" called out Merral, catching up with his friend. "Look at those things!" he said, pointing at the two familiar gray vehicles being worked on under spotlights. "Those are gravity-modifying sleds!"

"True," Vero replied in a matter-of-fact way.

"But we were told—in Planning—not to use them. Gravity-modifying engine technology was for urgent and emergency use only. It was a case of priority."

Vero inclined his head in evident agreement. "True, true. But this is why there was that restriction. We needed them. Ours is 'urgent and emergency use.'"

"But—"

Vero, however, had walked on and, opening a door off the walkway, beckoned Merral into a gloomy corridor. He closed the door behind him and the noise of the cavern vanished. They walked a dozen meters along the corridor before Vero stopped in front of another door and turned a handle. The door opened, revealing a room so well-lit that Merral found himself blinking.

"Welcome to the office!" Vero announced.

"Greetings, Tree Man!" cried a familiar voice, and Merral found himself being given a disturbingly welcome hug by Anya. Behind her, a smiling Perena rose from a table covered with datapaks and maps.

Vero took a seat at the table and gave a theatrical cough. "Everybody, please! Representative Corradon and Advisor Clemant are on their way. I suggest we get our own business over first."

Still taking in his surroundings, Merral sat at the table, gratefully accepting the coffee and biscuits Anya passed him. As he looked around at the bleak, white-walled room and its harsh artificial lighting, he couldn't help contrasting it with the glorious, open, sunlit countryside that they had driven through. *Is this going to be the pattern for our future meetings? Is the price we pay for security to be that of a permanent existence in windowless rooms underground?*

But his meditations were short-lived.

"Merral," Vero said, "with you here we can start to move forward. This is the base, and it is here that we are preparing for what may lie ahead."

"I'm impressed. Awed. That you have done everything in the time you've had."

"The original team designated projects and appointed leaders for them; then those leaders set up subteams and squads to tackle the projects. For once, the structured and disciplined nature of Assembly society has worked in our favor. And the representatives offering us a free hand was a great help."

Then Vero looked at his watch and shook his head. "But we must move on. I want Perena to speak first. And then Anya. I think that will help put you in the picture and perhaps answer some questions. Captain Lewitz?"

"Merral, I'm glad you are here," Perena began in her quiet, unruffled voice. "We've missed you. Now, on the issue of how the Gate was destroyed, I have made little progress. It seems certain that two things happened. First of all, the various safeguard programs were overridden and then a pulsating gravitational imbalance was established between the Gate segments. No amount of modeling has been able to achieve either phenomenon accidentally."

"So it *was* sabotage?"

"Even the official investigation team is beginning to use that most unfamiliar of words as a hypothesis."

"And the ship?"

"Ah. The ship." Perena paused, as if taking stock of her thoughts. "I organized the checking of all the astronomical data sources we have—every bit of it—to see if I could trace the origin of the ship. Those results are now coming in. As you know, the Guardian satellites monitor all incoming debris heading for Farholme so they can destroy or divert anything that poses a risk. A check of that data looking at what we now believe was the intruder ship has allowed us to trace it back as far as the orbit of Fenniran. But beyond that is a problem—there is no trace of it. None at all."

"So, what have you concluded?"

"Well, all the data is consistent with it emerging from a Below-Space Gate just beyond the orbit of Fenniran. Not close, of course; you don't put a Gate near a gas giant."

"But there is no Gate there."

"Well observed," she said with gentle irony. "But the data would also fit a ship which had traveled through Below-Space on its own and emerged into Normal-Space there."

"Hence your belief that the intruders can do what we can't. That they have . . . what did Gerry call it? 'autonomous Below-Space travel'?"

"That's right," Perena said. "It increasingly seems like a reasonable supposition."

Vero raised a finger. "A reminder, Merral. The Assembly, it seems, could have done that. Our forefathers were just uneasy about the spiritual side effects of doing it."

"Except General William Jannafy," Merral added.

"Ah," Vero said and gestured for Perena to continue.

"Indeed, Merral, the suggestion Vero made that, during the Rebellion, Jannafy went on to pursue Below-Space exploration also seems entirely reasonable. Anyway, we believe that the intruder ship has a Below-Space drive."

Vero caught Merral's eye. "And that is certainly the hope that Corradon and Clemant have. So before they get here, let's have a look at what you have found."

Merral took the various maps and images out of his holdall and put them on the desk. Together they all peered at the images and carefully marked the identified location on an enormous map of northeastern Menaya that Vero had hung on a wall. Merral watched as Perena carefully measured off the length of the anomalies and copied them down in fine handwriting into a notebook. Another idea of Vero's that was catching on, he noted.

After a minute, Vero looked at her. "So, space expert, is this it?"

"Yes . . . ," Perena said slowly, continuing to stare intently at the image. "I think so. There are aspects about it that I'm unclear about. . . . But it fits." She frowned slightly. "Merral, I need to talk to Gerry on this. Can I have a copy of the data?"

"Of course."

A bell-like tone sounded. Vero picked up from the floor a handset attached to a thin silvery cable and put it to his ear.

"Good, good. Send them up when they come," he said, nodding at Merral, and put the handset down.

"Corradon and Clemant are getting near. We are using an optic-fiber link from the entrance, Merral; we are getting a line laid to Isterrane." He shook his head in wonderment. "Doing that will use 10 percent of the whole annual optic-fiber cable production of Farholme. But it's secure." He paused. "*Secure* . . . It's a word I'm getting used to." He sighed. "And I wish I wasn't." Then he turned to Anya. "Anya, tell us what news you have."

"I wish I could skip this," Anya said, sweeping a strand of red hair from her face and looking around. "I think these creatures are the most loathsome things you can imagine. But I suppose I have forced myself to come to terms with them. To distance myself . . . After three weeks plus of DNA work, I suppose you could say that we have made some progress in understanding these creatures. Although actual specimens would, from the scientific point of view, be preferable. But let's deal with the general features first." She pointed her diary to the projector on the table, and above it a meter-high, three-dimensional ape-creature appeared and slowly rotated.

Merral shuddered and caught a flash of sympathy from Anya.

"The images are from the DNA cross-checked with visual information. The ape-creatures have human and gorilla DNA with some artificial code segments. They have good eyesight, good hearing. They are probably omnivores and are potentially very strong. There is a lot of musculature."

She tapped the screen and a hunched figure of the cockroach-beast hung over the table. As it turned round, Merral felt its reptilelike head seemed to look accusingly at him.

"Despite the superficial arthropod-like appearance, we now know that this is a modified human being: a more or less ordinary skeleton, but with a thickened insectlike cuticle instead of skin and modified hands capable of cutting between the thumb and the fingers; deep-set eyes with, incidentally, extended sensitivity to short wavelengths—they can see in ultraviolet; some ingenious work to adjust for the rigid exoskeleton—they must molt periodically. Another feature—and this may be significant—is that there appear to be modifications to allow for resistance to radiation."

"What about intelligence?" Merral asked.

"It's hard to be specific; *intelligence* is a tricky term. The best guess for both is that they have a patchy intelligence—good in places. There is little evidence of an ability for complex language, but some areas are specialized: hand-eye coordination in them both is probably good. I'd guess that—overall—their intelligence is probably in the lower part of the human range."

"Can you do me a favor, Anya," Merral asked, "and switch the pictures off?"

The image faded.

"That's better. What else?"

"I think the key thing is that these creatures imply something else. They cannot breed, so they must be made in a laboratory as clones. They have limited intelligence; I don't see them making a ship."

"But serving on one?" Vero asked.

"Perhaps," Anya said.

There was an awkward silence, and Vero made a small gesture with his hand. "You'd better tell Merral what you told me. Your speculation . . ."

Anya stared at Vero as if considering defying him and then turned to Merral with a face clouded with unease. "Very well, although you may not like this. These, then, are clearly designed creatures, even if we can only guess what they are designed for. But I am certain that they weren't designed to be predators."

"But they fought—" Merral stopped, struck by the sense of what she said. "No, I see what you're thinking."

"A true predator—a designed animal—would be faster, smarter, have better senses, and have claws or fangs. But having seen what they have done with these, I can imagine what they might produce in that area." She paused. "And it scares me."

Me too. "Let's hope we never meet such a beast."

Vero nodded. "It remains only a speculation. But Anya is right; we need to be aware of the possibility that the enemy may have more creatures than we have met."

As Merral was digesting that uncomfortable news, there was a knock at the door. Representative Corradon and Advisor Clemant entered. They were in casual clothes, and as greetings were made, it occurred to Merral that, unless you knew who they were, you wouldn't have realized their offices. In a disturbing flash of insight it occurred to him that, perhaps, that was the point. *Are we too learning the arts of disguise?* As he framed the question, he knew the answer. *To fight the intruders, we must risk becoming like them. But how dangerous a risk is that?*

"Thank you, Representative, Advisor, for coming," Vero said.

As they sat down, Merral gazed at the new arrivals. He felt that Corradon had subtly changed; the blue eyes seemed tired, the streaked hair now appeared to be more gray than black, and the bronzed complexion seemed paler. Clemant too seemed to have changed: his round, smooth, pale face seemed even more like a mask than ever, and Merral felt that the watchful dark eyes were more deep set than they had been.

"Merral," Vero asked, "I wonder if you would start by outlining what has been happening in Ynysmant?"

"Oh, right. But I thought the location of the ship was the most important thing?"

Vero nodded. "It is, but your story tells us why exactly it is so vital that we find it."

So, as briefly as he could, Merral recounted the various incidents he had observed or heard of within the town, from the bad-tempered Team-Ball game, through the emerging irritability and difficulties within Ynysmant, to the incident with Lesley Manalfi and the sparrowhawk. He ended with the conversation overheard at the airport that morning. As he spoke, he was aware of shared, uneasy glances across the table, and it seemed to him that the already heavy atmosphere in the enclosed room became still more oppressive.

There was a long silence when he had finished. He noticed Corradon looking at him as if judging something.

"Thank you, Forester," Corradon said. "Something of what you have said has reached our ears, but not, I feel, the depth or breadth of it. Your first-hand report is helpful, if alarming."

He looked at Clemant. "And there have been other incidents, eh, Lucian?"

"A number," he admitted. "It's very disconcerting."

"For instance," Corradon said slowly, "I have it on good authority that there will be at least one rather odd birth in Larrenport this year. The baby will be born only eight months—or even less—after the wedding."

"I'm sorry, sir," Merral interjected, "that's different from Ynysmant. We have painful births. Not premature ones."

Corradon's face acquired an expression as if he had eaten something that disagreed with him.

Anya nudged Merral in the ribs. "There's another explanation," she hissed quietly. "Think!"

"Oh . . . I see," Merral said, suddenly embarrassed. "You mean that . . . they just didn't wait?"

Corradon merely grunted assent and Clemant shook his head, as if in disbelief.

The representative looked hard at Vero. "So, Sentinel, do you have any comment on all this?"

"I think it just confirms all that we have felt and discussed. With the coming of the intruders, evil has returned to the Assembly, and it is confronting us here on two fronts. We have an external, visible enemy in the ship and in these creatures." The anxious expression on Vero's face gave the lie to his calm statement. "And we also face an internal attack; a subtle spiritual malaise which, it seems, is spreading. That is linked with the intruders, but we do not understand how."

Suddenly, Merral glimpsed Clemant's fingers twisting against each other on the table. *He's afraid. That's why he's supporting Vero. He sees our world slipping away into chaos unless we act.*

"We are addressing the first problem but not the second," Clemant said in his rumbling voice. "Is that wise?"

"Mainly, sir, because we *can* address it. I'm not sure how we can tackle the second problem."

"Surely, Lucian," Corradon said, "the hope is that with the intruder issue—how shall we say?—*resolved,* the second problem may vanish."

"And," Vero quickly added, "their ship or its technology may allow us to seek help."

Clemant stared at him. "This is the hope. Unless there are any other options . . ." He looked around slowly, as if seeking some new suggestion. But there was only silence.

Vero gestured to Merral. "It's time for you to show us what you have found."

Merral slid forward the images on the table and, for the third time in the day, began to talk about what he had discovered. As he spoke and displayed other images, he sensed the total attention of Corradon and Clemant. But as he continued, he was increasingly aware of their disappointment.

Eventually, Corradon turned to Perena. "Captain Lewitz, what do you make of this? I confess I was rather hoping for something more obviously a spacecraft than these rather abstract shapes and lines."

"I agree," said Clemant, his expression leaving no doubt that he too was unimpressed.

Perena stared at the image before answering. "Yes, sir," she said in a voice that, while firm, was barely audible, "I think that this is the ship."

Clemant looked sharply at her. "Captain, we need to be sure. If we go for the wrong location it could be disastrous. I see little hope of a second chance."

"I know, sir. But the data fits. The combination of anomalies is consistent with a craft comparable in size and mass to one of our in-system shuttles."

"Yet, Captain," Clemant said, with a creasing of his forehead, "I thought you had proposed that this vessel goes between stars?"

Perena looked at the advisor carefully. "Sir, there is, as you know, data for that hypothesis. I agree this ship seems smaller than I would have predicted. But we have no idea how a mobile Gate system might look, and this ship might be big enough. It's certainly large enough to carry a ferry craft."

"We are on the point of mounting a risky venture based on scanty data," the advisor said.

Corradon shrugged. "Lucian, we have been through all this. Is this an objection?"

"Sir, it is not an objection. But it is a statement of disquiet."

Corradon said nothing and shifted his gaze to the images. He gestured at the sheets. "Captain Lewitz, Sentinel, can't we get more detailed images?"

Vero scratched his nose. "I-I agree, sir, that they would be nice. But that too is risky; we might alert them."

Perena nodded assent. "Yes, I agree. It might frighten them. And if they were to take off, we might never find them again." She looked around with her keen blue-gray eyes. "There is something else I want to say here. I'm struck by the way that the disguise has been done. After examining all the images, especially comparing the ones taken before and after the landing, I think that all they have done is put a simple metal-frame structure up and drape a polymer fabric cover with reactive paint over it."

"So how else would you do it?" asked Clemant.

"Well, camouflage is not a specialty of the Assembly, but I would imagine that if you had a sufficiently advanced technology you could produce a holographic field or create some deformation of the light around the ship to give it invisibility. This looks far simpler. Even crude. But then—" She hesitated and seemed to be having a debate with herself. When she spoke again, her voice was so quiet that Merral had to strain to hear her. "Yet it doesn't use any energy and it doesn't emit any stray radiation. So it has merits. Indeed, it may not even be that crude, ultimately."

Corradon, who had been gazing at the wall map, turned to Vero. "So, Sentinel, the plan you had suggested to approach the ship . . . now that we have found it, will it work?"

"Yes," Vero answered. "I should say I have not yet discussed it with Merral. But, yes." He gestured to the images on the table. "It needs detailed planning, but I believe it could succeed."

Corradon looked at his advisor. "Lucian?"

Clemant shifted in his seat. "Sir, the decision is a hard one. We are faced with hard choices. . . ."

"Tell me what I don't know!" Corradon said. He was smiling but his voice was empty of humor.

Clemant stared at his hands for a moment and then looked at the representative. "Sir, my decision is that we go with the sentinel's plan."

Corradon closed his eyes for a moment, as if overwhelmed. Then, his face the picture of steady control, he looked around the table. "Thank you. If the rest of you will excuse us—Lucian and I would like to talk with Merral here alone. I realize that this is somewhat unusual. But these are unusual days."

As the door closed and Merral found himself alone with Corradon and Clemant, he felt troubled.

Corradon stared at him with a look of intense scrutiny. "Very well, Forester D'Avanos, the situation is this: I am—no, we as representatives are—convinced by the analysis of the path of the intruder ship that it is indeed possible that it has some sort of independent Below-Space capability. If it has, we need that technology and we need it badly. There are a number of scenarios for the future we are concerned about."

"More than concerned," grunted the advisor, in a response so rapid that it was almost an interruption. "Each day brings new evidence of problems."

"So, you see, we *have* to approach the intruders." Corradon's tone was confiding. "We will send a negotiating party."

"Remember, Forester, our preference—on every ground—is for dialogue." There was no possibility of mistaking the seriousness in the advisor's voice.

"Agreed," Corradon said. "The negotiating party will approach openly and without weapons. With nothing that could remotely arouse any suspicions. They will approach slowly—with banners, flags—that sort of thing." Clemant nodded as Corradon continued. "Now, hopefully, they will want to talk. But if they don't . . . if there is—what shall we say?—a negative response, then, well, we will have no option but to try and seize the ship."

"You mean, sir, *attack* it?"

There was a pause. "Yes, Forester. Attack it with the intention of taking it in working order. But *only* after diplomacy—if I may use an old word—has failed."

Before Corradon could continue, Clemant had spoken. "We must not underestimate the risks. We do not know what weapons they have."

Corradon waved a hand with a hint of impatience. "Absolutely. And that is why we agree with Vero's suggestion that we need to be in a position where, if diplomacy fails, we can move to a capture strategy instantly. Surprise may be one of the few weapons we have. We can't squander it by summoning a council of the representatives."

Clemant gave a slight and unenthusiastic nod.

"Exactly," Corradon said. "Vero wants to have a second group standing by so that, if negotiation fails, they can disable this ship and prevent it from taking off. And achieve a seizure."

"That raises a lot of issues. . . ." Merral spoke slowly, his mind struggling to cope with ideas of attack and seizure.

"Oh, indeed," Corradon replied, and Merral marveled at how assured he appeared to be. "But we've read twenty-first century law—of course, the matter has not been discussed since—and that suggests that we have a legitimate right to ask for their surrender as they are on our sovereign territory."

"I see, but respectfully, sir, there are practical issues too."

"Oh, we know that. Vero has been working on a plan for the last few weeks. But this is where you come in."

"I see." *Of course,* Merral thought, recognizing with alarm something that had been hinted at all along.

"Yes," said Corradon. His blue eyes seemed weary. "We want *you* to carry it out. To lead. That is the big gap. We have the decision, we have the equipment, to some extent we have the personnel; we even have the inklings of a strategy. But we need a leader to bring these things together."

Merral swallowed, his mouth suddenly and unaccountably dry. "Me?"

"You. Yes, there was a unanimous feeling among the representatives that, in this respect, you are marked out as the man of the hour. That we should appoint you as captain of the FDU."

"I am less sure, sir," Merral replied, oddly aware of his heart beating heavily. "And surely my opinion counts?"

"Well, only to a limited extent," Corradon countered.

"To be blunt," Clemant added sharply, "there are precious few contenders. And we can't risk the luxury of an experiment."

Merral suddenly felt an irresistible urge to stand up. He rose, walked to a corner of the room, then turned and faced the two men.

"Gentlemen, I am not at all positive about this. In fact, I'm very skeptical."

"Forester, there is no one else suitable to lead."

"What about Vero?" Merral gestured at the room. "He has put together an organization in very short time. Remarkable."

Corradon shook his head. "No, not Vero. Not at all. He is a strategist, and I agree a remarkable one, but he is not a leader in battle. It is not his gifting. You and he complement each other."

"Our sentinel is also from outside," said Clemant. He seemed, to Merral, to be ill at ease. "And you, of course, have fought already."

Suddenly, Merral felt a great desire to just say nothing and walk outside, to get out of this room and its claustrophobic, subterranean atmosphere and see the sun. He struggled against his desires.

"That is why I am so reluctant. I will not readily go back to fighting again. Nor would I wish it on others."

As he said it, he wondered if his answer was so frank as to sound disrespectful. Should he try and justify it by talking of the horror he had felt at the fighting? But he felt inadequate to express what he had experienced, and anyway there seemed little point. Their minds were plainly made up.

Corradon's look seemed sympathetic. "Oh, I know, Forester. But we *must* deal with these intruders, whoever they are. If we do, we must prepare for the possibility that we have to attack them, and as Vero has repeatedly pointed out to us, we cannot go halfheartedly into such a matter. We have only one chance, one possibility of surprise. Any attack must be done as efficiently as we possibly can."

"I want to confirm that," said Clemant, looking at Merral with his dark gray eyes. "We may have a single chance. A window of opportunity, perhaps only a few minutes."

There were long seconds of silence. "I see that," Merral answered. "But you must realize that any action like this would carry with it a certainty of death and injury on our side. We had an almost miraculous escape last time. If I was to lead it, I would feel responsible for what happened."

Corradon looked up at him solemnly. "Yes, but if I authorized it, Forester—if I asked you to do it—why then, *I* would take responsibility."

The silence returned. Eventually Corradon broke it. "But you see, Merral, we have a responsibility whether we like it or not. If we attack, we take risks. If we don't attack we also take risks. I bitterly wish it was not my decision. But what can we do?"

Clemant gave a nod of grudging agreement.

How had this happened? Merral asked himself. How had it come about that he was being asked to lead a battle?

He suddenly knew, with unarguable certainty, that he could not agree there and then.

"Representative Corradon, Advisor Clemant," he said, "I have to think this through. It is without precedent. Yes, I fought before, but it was defensive. I had no choice. This is different. Now we are planning an attack. And . . ."

For a moment, Merral closed his eyes, trying to think of the words; then he opened them and spoke slowly. "There is another factor. The great achievement of the Assembly has been peace. With this we would end that."

"I know," Corradon said, sounding distressed. "But we need a decision. I need you to lead these people."

"I agree," Clemant said. "This is a perilous venture. Your presence increases the chance of success. Your absence . . . " He shrugged.

Suddenly, Merral knew what to say. "My decision is this: I need to think more about it."

Corradon and Clemant exchanged unhappy glances.

"Very well," Corradon said, shaking his head, "but Vero has suggested we act within a week. In fact, he is working to have the contact at dawn a week from tomorrow."

"So soon? We have no more time?"

"No longer than that. We simply cannot afford to have the ship leave, and neither can we risk it heading into Assembly space spreading contamination. Midsummer approaches when the crater will never be in darkness; now, at least, we have some darkness to approach in."

"But only a week? Can it be done?"

Corradon did not immediately answer but rubbed his face between his hands as if weary. Then he looked at Merral, his face showing concern. "Done? I would be lying if I said I had any assurance over the matter. But it has to be attempted. And that is why we need you. Even if we knew what to test for, we do not have the time to test men or women to lead in battle. You are the one man who we know can lead."

"Perhaps."

"No." Corradon's tone was blunt. "Merral, if you do not take this, we appoint someone else. But for all we know, when they are faced by these things, they may run. Only two men have fought for the Assembly in eleven thousand years. You are one; Vero is the other. He is eliminated. The equation is simple."

"Sir, I appreciate that," Merral answered, feeling under an intolerable pressure. "But surely we believe that a man must volunteer for such a position?"

A long, pained sigh came from the representative. "Yes. I cannot order you. We are Assembly still. The Assembly does not force." He looked intently at Merral. "But I can plead," he said, "and I do. But please talk to Vero about the plans. Perhaps advise him. Then let me know before, say, the evening of the day after tomorrow, what you choose to do. On the eve of the Lord's Day. If you will not lead, then we will find someone else. But I would prefer you."

"And I agree," Clemant said.

He and Corradon rose.

"We must return to Isterrane," the representative said. "I wish you peace with your decision. We will pray for you."

As their footsteps faded away, Merral sat down heavily in a chair.

"I do not want to do this!" he whispered, and his voice seemed to echo about him. His memories of the battle at Carson's Sill came flooding back. He even half wished he had not found the ship. *Why am I so reluctant? Is it cowardice or something else?*

Suddenly, the answer came to him abruptly and clearly. It was not cowardice, or not entirely. *I'm reluctant because with this we would lose our innocence. With this action we will put the clock back twelve millennia. At a stroke, we would unleash all the ghosts of the past: the deceitful vocabulary of war, the dreadful concepts we have forgotten, those horrors disguised as "chivalry," "patriotism," or "valor" that lurked in the very oldest books, the laments like that of David over Saul and Jonathan, the grieving of the widows and orphans.*

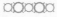

Then a new and darker thought struck him. If it happened, he could become known to posterity—for however many ages there were yet to run—as Captain Merral Stefan D'Avanos of the Farholme Defense Unit.

The man who brought war back to the human race.

32

Suddenly anxious to talk to Vero, Merral strode out of the room to the walkway in the cavern. At the railing, he paused and gazed into the space beyond. He stood there, his eyes caught by the angry flashes of yellow and white light and his ears assailed by the cacophony of noises: the conflicting rhythms of hammering and the roar and hum of engines and machinery, all echoing and reechoing off the rock walls. Now all this bustle of activity made sense. Vero was preparing to launch an attack against a vastly superior foe in a week's time.

As Merral stood there, he found that all this activity buried in this vast, half-lit cavern saddened him. *Where is our openness and our innocence? Have we lost it so soon?*

He looked around for Vero and found him standing by one of the gray hulls of the gravity-modifying sleds in insistent conversation with a man in overalls. He clattered down the stairway and walked over to the sled.

As he approached, Vero dismissed the engineer, then came over and took his friend's shoulder in an understanding grasp.

"I'm sorry," Vero said, speaking loudly to make himself heard over the scream of a drill that had just started up.

"Yes, so am I," Merral answered, feeling a strange mixture of emotions. "They want me to lead the fighting."

"I know," Vero said, his face lit by flickers of light. "Have you agreed?"

Merral said nothing for a few moments. "No. I'm thinking about it. There are lots of issues. It's not an easy decision. But you think it will come to fighting, don't you?"

Vero gave an almost imperceptible nod. "I fear so."

Merral looked at the gray sled perched on trestles, noticing the benches that were being welded to the frame.

"Let me ask: what do you plan to do with these?"

"These? The two sleds are the main attack vehicles. Thirty men on each. The hoverer—over there—we will use for the negotiating party. These sleds are quieter and we may be able to get in faster. We are working on them to make them more suitable."

Merral was suddenly aware of his ignorance. "Tell me, Vero, what's supposed to happen. If I am to lead people into this attack, I ought to know."

"Yes," Vero agreed, leaning back cautiously against the polished hull of the sled. "Well, once the order is given—"

"Wait, who gives the order?"

"You . . . or whoever the commander on the ground is. We can't assume that we will be able to keep a link to Isterrane going. They may be able to block it, just as they did with our transmissions."

"So the decision to fight—that may be mine?"

"Yes. But, I mean, there is hardly time for the representatives to debate the matter. Is there? Seconds may count here."

"I see. So if—or when—I say go, what happens?"

Vero's face acquired an unsettled look. "Well, it's still fluid. The idea is to get in quickly and disable the ship somehow. Perena suggests we blow open a hatch or some doorway. All we have to do is stop it from leaving the atmosphere. The intruders can't breathe in a vacuum. Of course, it would help if we knew exactly what the ship looked like, but there must be doorways, landing gear, that sort of thing. . . ." He pointed a thumb over at a nearby pallet where some lurid red boxes lay. "We have had some fast-expanding polymer cut into wedges; when you trigger the reaction, they triple their volume inside a second. They will stop a door from closing. There are also some planar explosives safe down another tunnel. With them we can blast off an entire landing leg."

"I see. You know that they aren't going to stand by while you put these charges down?"

Vero pursed his lips. "No. Of course not."

"So have you weapons?"

"Nothing fancy, but we have some things. Better than just bush knives. Although we will be issuing those—it's a tried-and-tested weapon. But the new weapons . . . do you want to see them?"

Merral suppressed his dislike. "No . . . But I'd better, I suppose."

"Over here," Vero said, motioning him to the corner from where Merral had seen the flashes of light earlier. In the corner, two men and a woman in thick overalls were working on some tubular parts at a bench.

As Vero introduced him, Merral was struck by the look of recognition that his name drew. *They know who I am; my reputation has gone ahead of me.*

Was this also why they wanted him to lead? A man who had already fought and won once. Yet the next time might be different.

Cautiously, Vero picked up one of the dull gray tubular objects off the bench. "Recognize this?" he asked. "Careful, the barrel's hot."

"Yes, it's a rock cutter," Merral answered, seeing the handle and the shoulder rest. "I've seen my Uncle Barrand use one in the quarry work."

"Exactly," Vero answered. "The XM2 model. We have been modifying some to give a pulse of energy. We have adjusted the beam focus and put an easy-to-operate switch on. What's the range now, Salla?" Vero asked the woman.

Merral, glancing at her, noticed the beads of sweat on her face, the stains on her hands, the disheveled and dusty blonde hair.

Salla nodded at the rock cutter in a detached way. "Well, with the hundred millisec pulse we have settled on, we can get fifteen meters with a tight beam and fifty meters on the broad focus. Broad focus is lower temperature. Below a thousand Celsius at the center. It's the best compromise at the moment. . . ."

Her tone seemed as clear and precise as if she expected Merral to take notes. He wondered what she had been previously; an engineering lecturer, perhaps?

"I see," Vero said, standing back. "I'd like to show Merral how it works. Give him a demonstration, please."

Salla picked up the weapon. "It's too heavy really, but the XM2s were not designed to be carried about quickly. I wouldn't like to carry one for a long time." She slid a toggle on the side. "Another innovation—a safety switch. Technically, a fascinating compromise." Merral noted her keen gray eyes staring in his direction. "You have to balance the need to stop it going off accidentally against the need to switch it on fast."

Merral merely nodded, his mounting unease warring against his urge to understand.

She pointed it toward the chamber wall, and Merral noticed for the first time a series of colored concentric rings painted on a plastic screen perhaps twenty meters away.

"With the safety switch off," she said, lifting the gun up and squinting along the barrel, "the power comes on instantly with the first pressure on the trigger." There was a faint hum and a red light on the side glowed. "A further press and you fire. *Thus.*"

There were three soft hisses from the barrel and three small crimson flames flared briefly in the center of the target. As the wisps of smoke faded, three blackened holes appeared in the target, each large enough to put a finger in.

As Salla lowered the gun carefully onto the bench, her smile seemed uneasy, almost guilty. "And then, you put the safety back on. Always."

"Impressive." As he said the word, Merral realized he wasn't sure what he meant by it.

Vero nodded. "Yes, these are the final adjustments being made. We have over a hundred of these ready. What are you working on now?"

"Calibrating the focus switch," one of the men said.

"A focus switch? Why do you need it?" Merral asked.

Salla answered him. "A tight-focus beam will cut through most metals and polymers," she said, "but it's got to be precisely aimed. The broad focus gives a wider burn zone: say a hand's width."

Merral looked at her, suddenly curious whether this woman was married or not, and if she was, whether she had children.

"You'd use that for what?"

Without hesitation came the answer. "For soft targets."

"For soft targets," Merral echoed, trying to conceal his feelings. "I see. Thank you for the demonstration, Salla. You have worked hard. Excuse me."

He turned sharply and walked away a few paces, urgently gesturing for Vero to follow him.

"Let's go back to the room with the maps. We need to talk."

Back in the room, Merral closed the door and sat at the table. Vero sat opposite. "You seem upset," he said.

I am *upset.* Merral tried to contain his emotions. "Vero, let me ask you a single question: What is a soft target?" His voice sounded hard and cold.

"Ah. Yes, well . . . a soft target . . ." Vero seemed to stare at the desk as if an answer was inscribed on it. "Well, it is . . . what shall we say? An objective . . . an opponent perhaps, that is, well, unarmored."

"Who."

"Who?"

"You used the word *opponent.* An opponent is not an *it,* it is a *who.* Opponents are personal."

"Ah yes," Vero replied, intertwining his fingers nervously, "we mustn't lose our grammar."

"The grammar is not the point. As well you know." Vero stared at his interlocked hands in embarrassment, and Merral thought that he was blushing.

"Vero," Merral said, almost horrified at the sharpness of his own voice, "let me suggest that a soft target is unprotected organic tissue. Right?"

"Er, right."

"Do you see what worries me?"

"Yes . . . I'm sorry."

"Vero, that charming woman, Salla, who is, for all I know, a wife and a mother beyond reproach, and the men with her, were happily talking about maximizing the potential for efficiently burning holes in the flesh of living, intelligent creatures. Is this what we have come to?"

Vero rose to his feet and paced the room before stopping, turning, and answering.

"I suppose so," he said, clearly discomfited. "It's just that we have been in a hurry; we've only been going perhaps four weeks here. We have been just too busy to consider some of the issues. Like ethics. And, I suppose, you have to distance yourself. Really."

"But I would prefer not to."

Vero stared at the table, a range of expressions flitting across his face. Then he looked up, his brown eyes wide. "Look, Merral, let me turn it round. You believe that what we face is evil?"

"Yes."

"You believe we are right to be prepared to fight?"

"Yes, I suppose. If negotiation fails."

"Then tell me," Vero said, his voice suddenly hardening, "would you have us use our bare hands or stones?"

Suddenly, Merral was aware that his position was hopelessly undermined. He stood, as much to cover his awkwardness as for any other reason, and faced Vero across the room. As they looked at each other, there was a tense silence.

Unable to avoid the inevitable, Merral blurted out, "I apologize—"

"I apologize too—"

Their words came so close together that they found themselves smiling.

Vero made an apologetic gesture. "You are right; I have been blinded. I should have known better. It was in all the old literature that there was a danger of this."

"Yes," Merral added slowly, "but I see that there is a fault in my thinking too. I have been too idealistic. I accept the idea of fighting, but not the reality of it." He sighed. "Oh, what a horrid, horrid business this is."

"It is so dirty that we must, to some extent, get our own hands dirty," said Vero sadly.

"I suppose so."

Abruptly, Vero sat down.

It's no good. I must now pursue Vero's plan. "So then, the thing I saw is your main weapon?"

"Yes. I'm pleased with what Salla's team has done with the XM2s. . . ."

Merral sensed reservations. "But?"

"I am worried that they are only short-range weapons."

"So you have nothing for a distance?"

"We toyed with projectile weapons. Guns that fire explosive charges, bullets, that sort of thing. But we have nothing to adapt for that. We'd have to start from scratch to make them. It would take months."

"Yes. But doesn't that leave everybody vulnerable?"

"To some extent. We are putting together jackets that may give some sort of protection, a dense, impact-resistant synthetic with a broad spectrum reflective layer under the surface coating, but it is hard to give more than token protection."

"So you will have to get in fast to the target."

"Yes." Vero frowned. "I'd like your thinking on that. Here now . . . pass me those images and I'll show you what I am thinking of."

"Please," Merral said, sliding them over, "if I am to seriously consider leading this party, I have to have all the information I need."

"Yes." Vero flexed his fingers. "I—we—have been envisaging a three-way approach, and your news has helped me clarify that. My working proposal is as follows: We send the diplomatic party up from the south. Up here." On the map, Vero's finger moved along a river toward the lake. "When they come to the lake, I would want them to come up it in the middle, in full view of the ship. They will be using a hoverer and will be fairly slow. It's noisy and I don't think it can be mistaken for anything warlike. We will have the banners on it. But before they move out we will have brought up two assault parties with the sleds. They are silent, so I think that they ought to be undetected until they can be seen. Now with a location to work from, I suggest that we have one that comes from the north." He gestured to the map again. "The other from the west, as close as we can get." He tapped a finger on a stream on the western side of the lake. "Hmm, possibly approach down in this valley here, where they will be out of sight."

Vero measured across the lake with his fingers and checked the scale. "Say two kilometers. So, if the negotiation fails, then both assault parties attack at once. You see the strategy?"

Merral hesitated. "Vero, this is a new area for me and a very unwelcome one. Yes, I think so. Their attention is attracted to the south with the diplomatic party. Then the attack—sudden and unannounced—comes from two other points of the compass. I suppose you might get close enough without being seen. Thirty people in each?"

"Yes. All men, by the way. That's because, as Salla implied just now, the weapons are so heavy. If we had time we could make them lighter."

"But sixty men—is that going to be enough?"

"Probably not. But as soon as the attack starts we bring in reinforcements. A ship flies in and lands an extra sixty or so troops."

Merral shook his head. "And you have the hundred-plus men? And this ship?"

"Actually, yes. A hundred and forty men are being trained. The old texts always said to have extra in reserve. And as for the ship, well, Perena has been given an old subspace freighter that has been unused for over a century: the *Emilia Kay*."

"A freighter? Your ability astonishes me. But why not just come in with the ship?"

"We discussed this. It's too obvious and too vulnerable. This way, the *Emilia Kay* will bring the sleds and the hoverer up to the crater margin the night before and wait there just over the horizon for whatever happens. If we do have to go for the assault option, then she flies over and lands. It would be easier if we had specialized landing ships: fast, armored machines. But we don't. We can make guns, but not ships. We will have to manage with what we have."

He fell silent as he stared at the images; then he looked at Merral. "So what do you think?"

Merral found himself reluctant to speak. "I have never assessed anything like it. No one living has. It all sounds risky. What if things go wrong?"

"It is risky," Vero said gloomily. "The whole thing is risky."

"I need to think about it."

"Please do, but quickly. We do not have much time."

Suddenly Merral realized that he could make no decision here. "Vero, I am going to go back home and think about all this. For no more than forty-eight hours. I want to stand back from all this. I have to be convinced that what I'm doing is absolutely the only possible way forward. To get a feel for whether the risks are needed."

Vero looked disappointed. "Ah. Well, I can understand that. But be careful not to give anything away. This is not a sports match. If the intruders hear of our plans at all, then we are in trouble. Surprise is almost all we have. That's another reason why I want to move soon. So far we have kept what is happening quiet, but we can't disguise it forever. There are too many people involved."

"Yes, I understand." Merral picked up his bag. "Let me leave you the images. I have copies."

"Thank you; we will study them, I assure you." He stared at the sheets. "I wish that we had better shots of the ship. So much is just guesswork."

"So do I, Vero. Anyway, I want to get out of this underground world and see the sun."

"Very well. But let me come with you to the entrance."

On the way out of the cavern, Merral met Anya and Perena. While Vero went ahead to organize transport to the airport, Merral explained to the sisters what he planned to do. After expressions of sympathy and support from both of them and farewell hugs, he walked out to the tunnel's entrance. There, he stepped out of the shadow of the cliff and stood in the afternoon sunshine, enjoying the air and trying to ignore the ceaseless activity all about him.

Vero soon returned. "There is a driver who will take you straight to the airport," he announced.

"Thanks."

"No, thank *you* for coming. But I do hope you agree to lead. We need you."

"If I don't, who does?"

Vero shrugged. "Someone like Zak, I guess. He seems to be doing well in training. But he is unproven."

A young man hurried out of the hut and motioned Merral over to a vehicle.

"Have a safe journey, my friend," said Vero, clapping him on the shoulder.

"Thank you. I will be in touch with you the day after tomorrow."

The direct afternoon flights to Ynysmant were full, and Merral could only find a seat on a late and slow circuitous route that took him through Ranapert and Halmacent Cities. He stared out of the window as the purple dusk darkened into night, watching the pinpricks of light underneath him, recognizing towns, tracing roads, and locating vehicles. Each point of light, he reminded himself, represented a person or a family. And within a week, all of them could be affected by his actions or his decisions.

As he thought about it, he acknowledged that Vero's plan seemed reasonable, logical, and necessary. Yet, it was perilous. If the intruders had the power to reach out and destroy a Gate high above them in space, what could they not do on the surface of the planet? Even hundreds of generations ago, mankind had had the power to destroy entire cities and even planets, and had—if the stories of pre-Intervention times were true—come close to destroying Ancient Earth on more than one occasion.

No, planning such an action so quickly, against an unknown enemy, was risky. It was not only an issue of whether he led the forces. Perhaps the operation itself should be stopped. He could probably demand the whole thing be cancelled, and they would probably listen to him; for some reason, people respected him and his views. After all, that was why they wanted him to lead the attack.

Merral stared hard out of the window, watching the lights of a big road vehicle far below, winding its way along a curving trail. He weighed his options. Perhaps he could go to Corradon and Clemant and say that it was too risky and try to persuade them of a less hazardous alternative.

They were starting to descend. Ahead, visible as fine and delicate points of silver in a sea of darkness, lay the lights of Ynysmant. So much seemed to revolve around him and his decisions, and in under forty-eight hours, he had to make his choice.

O Lord, he prayed intently as the pitch of the engines changed, *I must decide. Show me plainly what I must do.*

But there was no answer: no abrupt vision, no sudden certainty, no ringing affirmation. It was just a sort of spiritual silence.

Almost as if communications to high heaven had also been disrupted.

33

Less than an hour later, Merral reached his house. Only his father was in. His mother had, he was informed, gone to a women's meeting of some sort. Merral helped himself to food and then went and joined his father, who was painstakingly completing a picture puzzle on the table.

His father bent forward over the table, his thin elbows jutting down onto the puzzle, and stared with a pained gaze at the opposite wall.

"I really don't know what things are coming to, Son," he said in a troubled voice, his face somehow strangely aged and forlorn. "People just don't seem as . . . well, *nice* as they used to be. Maybe it's the long winter. Maybe it's the Gate going; some people say that. Maybe I'm just getting older and less tolerant. Why, even your mother now . . . I don't know." He gave a burdened sigh. "It's all 'Move this, Stefan,' 'Tidy that up, Stefan,' 'Oh, comb your hair, Stefan,' 'Those fingernails need cutting.' It just goes on. I don't remember that she was always like this."

He gave a pathetic little moan. "Son," he said, suddenly turning a lined and worried face to Merral, "I'm getting old and I don't like it."

Merral, almost too overcome to say anything, just patted him on the shoulder.

"It's not you, Father," he said finally. "Nor Mother either. There is just something wrong. But we are working on it. We are doing our best."

His eyes watering, his father nodded. "I hope so. Well, I'm tired. Have been for months. I'm going to bed. See you tomorrow."

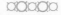

After breakfast, Merral walked over the causeway to the Institute with a heavy heart. There he sat down at his desk to try to plan what he wanted to do in the next day and a half. He decided he had to go to Herrandown. It was there that things had started, and Merral felt that what was happening there now might be some guide to how great the risk to Farholme was. He went to see Henri to ask him whether he could borrow a vehicle to visit Herrandown. Henri shook his head and smiled. "*Ach,* man, I can do better than that," he offered. "There is a rotorcraft due to fly near there tomorrow. It's been delayed by the dust, but the weather's supposed to be clear tomorrow. I can arrange for you to be dropped off and picked up on the return leg. Is a couple of hours long enough?"

After talking briefly about other matters, Merral left Henri and returned to his office, where he called Isabella and arranged to meet her that evening. He felt he needed to see Jorgio and called his brother to find out where he was.

"That's easy," said Daoud Serter. "He's over by you; probably at the stables."

"So he's not up at Wilamall's Farm then?"

"Didn't you know? Not now. But he'll tell you."

Merral walked out of the back of the Institute building, looking for Jorgio. He found the old stable hand stroking one of the horses in the stalls.

"Jorgio!" Merral called out.

"Mister Merral," said the old man, turning awkwardly. They embraced. "Good to see you."

"So you heard about Brenito?"

"I heard." He shook his head slowly. "A nice man. He'll be welcomed up there and missed down here." He made a soft clucking noise. "I hope as I helped him. The Lord told me as we were talking that he had only a few more days. So I felt I'd better tell him."

"I think it allowed him to sort things out."

"See, that was the point. I think *he* was ready; but I've no doubt folks like him have plenty of things to sort out."

"Indeed. But what are *you* doing here?"

Jorgio shook his head. "I've finished at the farm."

"Finished?"

"Yes," Jorgio said, and his distorted face bore a look of deep unhappiness. "Been a change of plan. It's a matter of resources, they say. No Gate now, so new priorities. They don't need people like me there; they need fewer, fitter people."

"I'm shocked," Merral said, genuinely astonished but remembering that Teracy had warned of changes. "I'm very surprised. I knew nothing of it. But then, I'm in the wrong part of forestry."

"It's a new decision," Jorgio added. "So I'm back down in the town with my brother. I'll move my things down soon enough."

Merral felt annoyed with himself. Having promised Brenito he would keep a watch on Jorgio, he now found that the man had been uprooted and he hadn't realized it.

"Of course," Jorgio continued, "I've still my allowance, the same as you. I just don't have anything to do. So I reckoned as I'd come here and see the horses."

"Welcome. But I had no idea," Merral said. *It is worrying. If we are no longer concerned about our weak, then what has happened to us?* Here was yet another small piece of evidence that Farholme was changing for the worse.

"It's the way things is. There's a shadow over us all now, Mister Merral. But what are *you* doing?"

"Me? I work here."

"*Tut.* If you please, Mister Merral, I know better than that. You are struggling over something."

Merral stared hard at Jorgio, wondering if his conflicts were that visible or whether there was some other gift at work. "Truly said, my old friend. I have a hard choice to make. I am hoping that before tomorrow evening I will see and hear enough to make my decision about what to do very plain."

"You're worried what to do about them, aren't you? I don't blame you. Fighting 'em can't be much fun. Not from what I knows about them."

Merral stared at the old man, wondering yet again how he knew so much. "No, it's not fun, Jorgio," he answered. "And do you have any advice?"

"*Tut!* You want me to make your decisions?" he said, raising a rough finger in warning, but there was both warmth and sympathy in his expression. "You must make them yourself."

Then, to Merral's surprise, the old man closed his eyes and fell silent, his big lips moving slightly. After a few moments, he suddenly opened his eyes.

"There. I've done what I can do. I 'ave just prayed as you'll find out very clearly what you have to do."

"Thank you."

"Oh, you may not thank me." There was a curiously distorted smile, revealing his displaced teeth. "You may find out more about the evil than you want."

Jorgio fell into a tight-lipped silence that seemed to discourage further questions.

"Thank you," Merral answered eventually, both gratified and disturbed by the conversation.

"My pleasure," came the response. "I'll continue to pray. And promise—if you decide to fight, let me know. I'll ask that you'll have help."

"Help?"

The look on the broken face became strangely intense. "If you please, you'll need help against them." He muttered to himself, "Knives and guns won't do. Not for *them.*" Merral found something oddly dogmatic about his tone. "Not for them all anyway. Not the one in the chamber. And that's the one that matters."

"I see; the one in the chamber, the one that matters," Merral said. "Can you tell me anything more?"

"No." There was a stiff shake of the head. "Don't know any more. Don't really want to. Nasty. But Mister Merral, don't be surprised at what you find there." He wrinkled his face. "And now, if you'll excuse me, I'm off."

"A moment, Jorgio. Brenito was anxious that I kept an eye on you. Please don't leave Ynysmant. If you have to travel, leave a message with Daoud."

"*Tut,* me travel?" Jorgio smiled. "Hardly. But may the Lord's blessings be with you, Mister Merral."

Then he shook hands roughly with Merral and in his determined, tilted way set off walking toward the town.

Merral watched him go, then, full of bewilderment and foreboding, walked back down to his office.

That evening, Merral met Isabella at her house and, after some discussion, they decided to take a stroll along the town's lake-edge walk. The walk was popular in summer when the nights were shorter and hotter, but this evening it was still too cool for many people to be about, and for much of the way, Merral and Isabella were on their own.

As they walked along, Merral sensed that Isabella was in a strange mood. There was a hint of a carefree, almost reckless frame of mind in the way she bounced down the steps and swung round lampposts. In contrast to her, Merral felt slow, leaden, and preoccupied.

"I was wondering whether you would make time to see me," she said in a light but purposeful tone. "You seem to be so busy." Merral caught a gleam of inquiry on her face.

"Yes," he answered. "I'm sorry. I hardly seem to know whether I'm here or there. I went to Isterrane just for the day yesterday."

"My! It must have been important," Isabella said, peering intently at him. "I wish I could do that. I find Ynysmant just so limiting. So what was it? Intruder business, of course."

Merral looked around, but there was no one who might overhear. "Possibly. But I'd rather not discuss it."

Isabella gave a girlish pout. "A *secret,* eh? We all have secrets now. Well, I suppose we can live with them. In fact, I quite like the idea. Openness can get dull, can't it?"

"Can it?" Merral countered, sensing that yet another area of difficulty was about to open up. "Well, I suppose a lot of worthwhile things can, in theory, get dull. But it was never something that worried me."

"Well, it did me." She grabbed his hand. "But I suppose I do feel uneasy at the way I am being pushed to the margins of your life. I mean, Vero and this Anya and Perena know *everything*. But I don't."

"I've told you lots. More than I should have."

"But there are limits. And there's lots I ought to know. I'm now heading up the new priorities team. Did I tell you?"

"No. That's new. I thought it was someone else."

"It was, but she didn't realize how much work there was, and she has two children. So I had a chat with her and she has stepped down."

"I see. So you now report directly to Warden Enatus?"

"Exactly. And I think we ought to be told about the intruders. I mean if they came south we'd be on the front line. Is that the term?"

"I think so; Vero would know. But you do make a point. I'll have a chat with Vero—I'm seeing him again soon."

"No doubt. But I'd appreciate it if you could raise the concern. I feel as if I am being cut out of your life. You seem to be so busy." There was recrimination in her eyes.

"I'm sorry," Merral answered, feeling her hurt and the validity of her argument. "Perhaps things will settle down. But what I'm doing is very important. As is what you do."

"Yes, of course," she said, but to Merral her response sounded very automatic.

Then they stopped and together leaned over a stone parapet, peering at the waters of the lake. Isabella was so close to Merral that he could feel her shoulder gently touching his. He was, he decided suddenly, really very fond of her.

"Merral," she asked, "when are you leaving again? And for how long?"

She isn't going to like this. He stared at the ink-dark waters of the lake. "Well, tomorrow evening. And I could be away maybe for a week or more." *Or forever, if I decide to lead an attack and pay the price.*

"Oh—," came the response, full of surprise and even hurt. "But there is a lot we have to discuss, you know."

"Sorry."

"Well, I just feel," she said, her words soft and tentative as if she was expressing something for the very first time, "that, in the light of our understanding, our relationship needs to be bonded more closely. And with you so—well—distracted, it's hard."

"Yes, it is, isn't it?" Merral said, choosing his words carefully. *So,* he thought with a pang of unhappiness, *she has reminded me again that she sees our "understanding" as a private equivalent of a commitment.* He wondered, for the hundredth time, how he could try and retreat from that position.

Suddenly there was a noise to his left and he looked up. A crowd of perhaps a dozen teenage boys, all in the same kind of light gray trousers and jackets, came by in an excited and chaotic circle. They were joking noisily, jostling each other and taking turns to run up and down the sloping wall with squeals and shouts. *Have teenagers always been so rowdy?* Merral wondered. *And why are they trying to dress so much alike? Or am I now seeing shadows that are not there?*

After they went past, he saw Isabella looking at him, her face strangely pale in the light of the streetlamps.

"Oh, Merral," she said in her softest voice, "you know Helga Demaitre, works over in Communications? Lives in Lazent Street by the market?"

"I know her elder brother better. Why?"

"She's just got engaged to some lad from the south side."

"That's nice," he replied, feeling that it was hardly news.

"The thing that's interesting," she said with a quiet insistency, looking at him intensely with her oval eyes, "is that she told her parents *after* they had decided."

"I see," he heard himself say in what seemed a rather distant and feeble voice. Somehow, the night seemed to have grown chillier. "That's . . . well, I've never heard of that. What did they say? The parents, I mean?"

"Well, after the initial shock, they agreed. Afterward they decided it was a good idea. Interesting, eh?"

"It is," Merral said, realizing as the words came out that what he found interesting was not what Isabella did. The news troubled him. *If we are to honor our parents at all, we must surely not present them with accomplished actions. Not in that area, at least.*

"Let's walk," he said. "I'm feeling cold." He started walking away.

Isabella followed him, putting her hand in his. "I admire her," she said with determination.

Merral, aware that Isabella was scrutinizing his face, felt he should not show any emotion.

"You see," she went on, "*she* took the initiative. Now that's sometimes important."

"Well, yes," Merral replied, forced onto the defensive, "there are times when you have to make a stand. But it's tricky to go against things that are—well—part of tradition."

"Yes, that's what it was, wasn't it?" Isabella said with enthusiastic confidence. "Just *tradition.*"

"Well, sometimes . . . ," Merral countered cautiously, "tradition is a good thing." He had a certainty that, whatever he said, he couldn't win.

"And sometimes," she said, her voice filled with something like defiance, "tradition needs to be challenged."

Under the light, he saw Isabella look at him with an oddly hard expression. "You know, Merral, the Gate going may actually be a blessing in disguise."

"It may?" he answered, barely able to keep the horror out of his voice.

"Yes. And it's not just me who says it. There's something of a feeling of release, freedom almost, in the air." She squeezed his hand. "It's subtly exciting. You can feel it with the youth especially. Like that group that just passed us."

So, it wasn't just me. Then the implications of what she was saying sank in, and something seemed to tighten around his heart. He was aware that she was staring at him, waiting for a response.

"As always, Isabella, you are stimulating," he said, in as mild a tone as he could manage, desperately wanting to lower the intensity of the conversation.

She squeezed his hand gently. "Oh, Merral, I hope I'm more than just *stimulating* to you." He saw her frown. "But I do think you, we, need to challenge our preconceptions. I think we are in danger of being trapped in a situation that no longer exists." She paused, and when she spoke again her tone was lighter and happier, as if a light had broken into her mind. "The past is over. There is a new world to think about. The horizons are open. Don't you agree?"

"Oh, I'm thinking about it. . . . Thinking very hard indeed. But I think there's something to be said for waiting. At least for us."

"You are *so* cautious, Merral. You really are." There was now a note of irritation in her voice. "Oh, do loosen up!"

Merral was aware that she was smiling, but somehow it seemed to be a rather artificial expression. He was still wondering how to answer her when they turned a corner and came across a group of his old school friends on their way to a café. To his relief, they insisted that Merral and Isabella join them, and he was spared any more difficult conversations until much later, when he walked back with her through the deserted and echoing streets to her house.

"So what do you think we should do?" she said, holding his hand firmly.

It's no good. I can't prevaricate forever. "Isabella, now you ask me, my decision is this: I wish to do nothing for a couple of weeks. Then, if things have settled and I know better what I am doing, well, you and I will have a long talk."

"And then?" came the rapid reply.

"Then, maybe, just maybe, I will approach my parents to reconsider things."

"Not before?"

"No."

"Oh, Merral," she said, disappointment filling her voice, "I thought we had a commitment."

Feeling peculiarly irritated that she saw their understanding as much more than he did, Merral replied sharply, "Well, Isabella, a starting point would be exactly what you think this wretched commitment means."

As he heard his words, he regretted them. But it was too late.

She dropped his hand and stepped back, staring at him, her mouth half open.

"So it's a *wretched* commitment now, is it, Merral D'Avanos?" she snapped.

"That's not quite—"

"Oh, you! You don't care at all!" Her eyes flashed in anger. "All you care about is your own *wretched* project with that outsider, Vero!"

Then she whirled round and clattered heavily up the stone steps to her house. A moment later there was the sound of a door slamming.

Merral was aware that he was shaking and that his stomach felt as if he was going to be sick. He slowly walked back to his house, his mind preoccupied with a single thought: he had had an argument with Isabella.

The next morning, as Merral landed in Herrandown, the matter still loomed over him. As the rotorcraft pilot lifted off and flew her machine eastward, Merral was met by his uncle and aunt who hugged him in turn.

"Good to see you, Nephew," Barrand said. "You just passed through last time. When was it? Yes, over a month ago. Ho, too quick."

"Yes, sorry about that. I've been so busy."

"Not good for you," Zennia said with a smile. "Come up and stay."

"Perhaps one day," Merral answered. "But today it's just a brief visit too."

He looked carefully at them, watching for anything untoward. Somehow, he felt reassured by the fact that they seemed healthy, if slightly weary.

"So how are things?" asked Merral, looking around the hamlet. Now, with the fresh vegetation, the new grass, and the blossom on the trees, Herrandown looked a tranquil and happy place.

"Better," his aunt replied. "Thankfully. Look, I'll go and put the coffee on. You men go and chat."

As she left, his uncle patted Merral on the shoulder. "Oh, come over to the office."

"So how do you find things, Uncle?" Merral asked.

"Hmm. Well, in some ways, Zennia is right," Barrand said. "They're better. The hounds aren't so nervous, for example." As if to make the point, one of the dogs came up and rubbed against Merral's leg.

His uncle continued as they walked along, "So we don't feel as physically threatened as we did. I mean, no one goes into the woods on their own. As you suggested . . . But, oh, I'm wondering if that was an overreaction."

He picked up a stick and threw it for the dog to catch.

"No," he repeated slowly, as if to himself, "not *physically* threatened."

"What about other things. In other ways?"

"Well," his uncle replied, "it's hard to express. Sometimes I think it's as if a dream has ended. I don't know whether it's the Gate going or something else. I only know that when I look back on how we lived before Nativity . . . it now seems it was almost a different world. I mean I used to really enjoy what I was doing here. But now . . ." He shook his head. "Now, it's all changed."

He fell silent as they walked into the office, which seemed to Merral to be more crowded and disorderly than he remembered it. Barrand pulled up a chair and lowered himself heavily onto it.

Merral lifted a stack of maps off another chair and sat down.

"I suppose it's not surprising," his uncle said after a minute's silence. "You see, now that they are cutting back on the expansion program, the whole purpose of being here has changed. I mean, if they do build a new Herrandown now, it looks as though it will not be in my lifetime." He tapped stout fingers thoughtfully on the chair arm. "I suppose you could say that we've really lost our purpose here. Maybe that's the problem."

How disturbing. His uncle and aunt had been carefully selected for this job and must have been assessed as having a resilient psychological makeup. Yet now it looked as though they were having trouble handling the changes that were happening to them.

Merral looked around the office, suddenly feeling that something was missing.

"Uncle, what's happened to the painting you had? The Lymatov? *A Last View of Hesperian.*"

Merral remembered the conversation they had had about it and how Barrand had felt that it symbolized everything the Assembly stood for.

"Oh, *that.*"

His uncle stared in a rather abstracted manner at the pale outline on the wall where the painting had hung. "That. Yes. Well, I took it down. It's safe in the house. I suppose it sort of irritated me in the end."

"But I thought you liked it?"

"Well, I did. But, I suppose, what with the loss of the Gate . . ." Barrand seemed vaguely embarrassed about the matter, and Merral decided not to pursue it.

The conversation turned to the recent departure of the quarry team and then his uncle, suddenly apparently uncomfortable, rose to his feet and suggested that they go back to the house. "The coffee will be ready and the children may be back from school. It's a half day, of course. When did you last see Elana?"

"Well, it would have been, what, a month ago? Then she was still under the weather."

"Oh, she's better now. But changed . . ."

Five minutes later, Merral was forced to agree that Elana had changed. It seemed that she had, at a stroke, crossed the boundary from an attractive girl to a rather pretty young lady. He tried to pin down how it was that she could have altered so much in such a short time. Physically, she seemed to have grown and could now, he thought, have passed for much older than her fourteen years. Perhaps it was the way she now wore her blonde hair, or dressed; certainly the tight blue woolen pullover left no doubt to her newly gained femininity. Yet he felt that it was more than just the physical changes. There was a look of mature self-awareness about her small face, and he felt that her manner and poise was now that of a woman.

When their eyes met, she smiled with a strangely warm, knowing, and oddly adult expression. But the smile disquieted him.

He looked away and concentrated on his aunt and uncle. He tried to distance himself and listen to what was being said and to watch the unspoken body language between his uncle, aunt, and Elana. In some ways, there now seemed to be no tensions just under the surface ready to snap. Yet in other ways, he was not reassured. Merral was disturbed to find that his uncle now played little music and that his aunt had unfinished canvases.

After finishing his coffee, his uncle ambled over to the window. There he rested his elbows on the sill, looking out. "You know," he said in a regretful tone, "I'm no longer sure about the artistic side of me. It's funny." He turned and looked at Merral. "I always used to enjoy being a quarry master *and* being artistic; the two things worked together. Now, it's one or the other." He sighed. "It's very strange. I think it's the long winter. Or the Gate going, of course. That's had repercussions." Then, he turned back and stared out of the window again. Soon after, the rotorcraft pilot sent a message that she would be landing in an hour. Merral, unhappy about the atmosphere in the house, decided to take a walk outside. There was much he wanted to think over.

He strolled behind the house to look over the sunlit hamlet. The air was buzzing with insects, birds were calling from within the woods, and there was a taste of the longed-for summer everywhere. Merral found a smooth grassy bank, lay down on his back, and stared skyward, enjoying the warmth of the sun on his face as he tried to relax.

He had barely closed his eyes when there was the sound of soft footsteps nearby. He opened his eyes and saw Elana next to him.

"Hi," he said blinking, rising to a half-seated position.

"May I join you?" she asked quietly, with a careful glance around, as if to see if anyone else was near.

"Of course—," he began, but she had already sat close to him.

He looked at her, catching an odd, fleeting look on her face. She smiled back, but it was a strangely joyless expression.

"Merral," she said in a low, urgent tone, her face close to his, "I want to talk. Privately."

Merral looked around, confirming that they were certainly out of sight and sound of the house. Deep inside him, he was aware of an uncomfortable feeling that he could not pin down. "Surely. How can I help?"

"I need to leave," Elana said abruptly, her blue eyes fixed on his. "I need to leave here." There was a note of desperation in her voice.

"Why, Elana?" he asked, feeling sorry for her.

"It's the atmosphere," she replied. She picked up a blade of grass and began to chew on it, her sky-colored eyes still looking into his. He was vaguely aware that he found her closeness very agreeable. He was also dimly aware that there was something perilous about this proximity.

"I want to escape. It's not a good place anymore. It's tiny and boring and the atmosphere gets me down. I want to live somewhere else. I want to *be* someone else. Can you help?"

"Me?"

"Get me out. Anywhere. Herrandown, Isterrane. The Southern Seas, the ends of Farholme. I don't care. Just get me out of here."

He tried to smile. "I'd love to help. How?"

She chewed a little more on the grass stalk, then took it out of her mouth. "There are ways. Get us relocated. Go back to your boss—what's his name?"

"Henri."

"Okay, now, I've been thinking. We've been here eight years. In two years, Mum and Dad's posting is reassessed. So you could, you see, just ask Henri to move us early."

"I can't do that. There are rules. There's a long transfer list."

"Rules can be bent. You could say that Dad's getting weird. Mum's—what's the word?—*unbalanced*. Get us reposted. South. Somewhere with beaches."

"I can't do that," he protested as he tried to think of some other way of helping her. He paused. "I could, I suppose, request a psychological survey of you all. Say you have been through a stressful time."

She gave a firm shake of her head. "No. I've read up on that stuff; it's in the Library. Dad would fight an assessment."

"True."

And you'd never get a verdict in your favor; you are all sane. Or at least as sane as anyone else on this increasingly messed-up planet.

"Merral," she said in a low, soft voice that he found extraordinarily compelling, "Couldn't you go to Henri and ask for us to be moved? Now. As a special favor. A private arrangement."

I could too, he realized with a shock. *Henri trusts me.* "But there's a list." As he said it he felt his protest sounded feeble.

"Please. As a favor. Just get us put on the top of it." There was a gentle, troubling tone of pleading in her voice.

"Elana, I can't do favors," Merral answered, aware that his voice sounded as if it belonged to someone else.

But I can, he thought. *There are vacancies in the new southern colonies.*

"Not even for me?" she implored, flicking her pale hair back and wriggling slightly, as if pressing herself down into the grass.

"Well . . ."

I could do it. Get them put on the top of the transfer list. And why not? She has *had a rough time. And who would be affected by one family moved to the top?*

She stared at him. "For us."

He was silent.

She reached out and stroked his hand gently. *"Please."*

Suddenly, Merral jerked his hand away. He started to his feet, conscious that his face was burning.

"No, Elana!"

She stared at him with a hurt look, as if something precious had been snatched from her.

Merral headed toward the house and then stopped.

He looked behind, relieved to see that she was not following him. He brushed the grass off himself, took a deep breath, and tried to settle his thoughts. He had been tempted and had gone a long way to giving in. In his mind, he began to pray for forgiveness.

A few minutes later, to his enormous relief, he heard the whispering of the approaching rotorcraft.

In his urgency to get back to Isterrane, Merral arrived slightly early at the Ynysmant airport terminal. He was walking around the waiting area trying to bring some calmer reflections to bear on what had happened when he saw Ingrida Hallet standing looking out of the window, a travel bag at her feet.

"Hello, Ingrida," he called out, welcoming the possibility of a conversation that would distract him from his guilty thoughts. "I haven't seen you since before Nativity." He remembered again that memorable evening, the night that he had first met Vero, when Ingrida had so warmly wished him well with the new job he was to be given.

"Oh, it's you," Ingrida said in a cold, hushed voice. Her face, framed by her long black hair, showed no trace of welcome.

"Yes . . ." Merral stared at her, alarmed at the lack of welcome in her face. "What's the problem? You don't seem very pleased to see me."

Ingrida bent down, picked up her bag, and then looked at him with a hard, irritated expression. "Frankly," she snapped, "I'm not."

Wounded, Merral shook himself. "Look, what have I done? I don't understand."

"Remember the rain forest job? The one *you* were offered?"

"Yes, you were the first to tell me about it."

"Oh yes. I was, wasn't I?" She snorted, as if furious with herself. "Well, it was a job *I* wanted, the job of a lifetime. And it went to you, didn't it?"

"But—"

She was unstoppable now. "So I had to take something else, didn't I?" she snapped. "And what a second best. They put me on lichens! A millimeter's growth in a hundred years. They are barely alive. Lichens!" For a moment, he thought she was going to spit.

"Well, sorry. But I don't see why you are so mad at *me*." Merral felt overwhelmed by this onslaught that, for all its fury, seemed to have no focus.

Ingrida gave him a look of contempt. "Why? Because I *now* find out you are not taking the job. Mr. Merral pick-and-choose, eh? Henri tells me when I pass through today that you are 'doing something else,' that you are 'no longer really in Planning.' It's wasted!" Her face was pale with anger.

Merral, appalled and sick to his stomach, felt he had never heard anyone be so sarcastic.

"Sorry, I mean—"

"Oh, keep your words!" she snorted. "I can't apply for it now. I'm stuck with my lichens."

"I'm sorry. I had no idea."

"Really?" she grunted, glaring icily at him in a way that no one ever had before. "To change your mind like that . . . it's rotten!"

Suddenly Merral was seized by a sense of how totally and utterly unfair it was. Here he was, prepared to risk his life trying to save Farholme, and this—this senseless woman—was attacking him! The total injustice of her assault irritated him beyond measure. He felt himself getting angry in response and could now no longer be bothered to rein in his feelings. The offense against justice was, he knew, so great that it required an appropriate and just response. He had to tell this stupid woman bluntly, and plainly, how idiotic she was.

Merral was just going to say, "Ingrida Hallet, you are a total fool and you have not the slightest idea what you are talking about," when he saw another passenger staring at them with a look of shocked curiosity. Ingrida followed Merral's glance then, with a toss of her head and a new snort of anger, turned her back on him and walked away.

For a fleeting moment, Merral considered pursuing her to tell her exactly what she ought to hear. Then, suddenly ashamed of his temper, he controlled himself and walked away in the other direction to the men's room. There, instinctively, he washed his face in cold water. When he looked in the mirror, he saw that he was as pale as if he had been sick.

Isabella, Elana, and Ingrida. Jorgio's prayer had been answered in triplicate with an appalling vengeance. One answer alone would have been enough. *Dear God,* he prayed, *have mercy on me.*

Ten minutes later, he got on the plane and made his way to the very back. Ingrida came in later and, without looking at him, sat down at the front. When they landed at Isterrane, she got up and exited as soon as the fuselage door had slid open.

To Merral's surprise, Vero was waiting for him at the terminal.

"How did you know I was on the flight?"

"It's hardly a stunning feat of intelligence to check the passenger lists." Vero stared at Merral. "You know, you look dreadful."

"I'll tell you about it. But not here."

His friend had a vehicle outside, and once they were inside and had closed the door, Vero turned to Merral. "Have you met them?" he asked.

"No. I found no trace of them. At least not physically."

"But . . . ?"

"I found enough evidence to make me know that I—*we*—have to fight."

"I am glad you now agree. But I am concerned. What did you find?"

"Let me be clinical," Merral said, trying to keep his voice level. "In under two days I found evidence of sin, to my knowledge, unparalleled in Assembly history. I found, among other things, a flagrant and open desire to dishonor parents, a gross outbreak of anger in public, and . . . something else I will not name."

"In two days?" Vero's eyes opened wide. "The rot is faster than I thought."

Merral stared out of the windscreen at the lights of town. Then he turned to Vero.

"The *rot?* Vero, you have no idea at all how bad it is. You see, I didn't find the rot in others; I found it in myself."

34

Vero drove Merral to Corradon's residence, an unremarkable single-story building at the edge of the lake that lay at the heart of Isterrane.

As they walked through the garden toward the house, a man standing by the door came over as if to ask a question. Seeing Vero, he nodded respectfully and stepped back.

"Who was that?" Merral whispered as Vero knocked on the door.

"A guard. One of Clemant's ideas. Justified, I suppose."

The representative, dressed casually in an open-necked shirt, answered the door himself. The sounds of family chatter and music drifted past him. "Welcome both," he said, looking unsurprised at their arrival. "Do come in."

Merral was briefly introduced to those members of Corradon's family who were present: his wife, Victoria; one of their three sons; a daughter-in-law; and two grandchildren. They were curiously formal introductions, and any anticipation Merral had had that here, at his home, he might meet a private Anwar Corradon evaporated. Merral had a brief conversation with Victoria, a graceful lady with short white hair, who made some warm comments about Ynysmant, recalling a happy visit there some years earlier. But as she spoke, Merral noticed that her eyes were constantly glancing toward her husband as if she had some deep worry for him.

Within a few minutes, Merral was shown to the representative's study. It was full of books of poetry and theology, family images, and statues, with one wall being devoted to a large map of Menaya, drawn and painted by hand with exquisite engraved scenes scattered across it. Beyond it was another glass door that led to a small conservatory full of plants.

"So, my dear Forester?" the representative said as he sat down behind his desk, his eyes staring at Merral with undisguised anticipation.

"Sir," Merral said, and he found himself swallowing hard, "I am now, very reluctantly, ready to lead the FDU contact party."

Corradon closed his eyes for a moment before looking at Merral. "Thank you. It is about the best news I have heard today. Daily, things get worse. Since I saw you, Lucian and I had a private visit from a senior member of the Farholme Congregations Committee; they are noticing it now. Other events have been reported. There are three focal points: Ynysmant, Larrenport, and Ilakuma."

"Ilakuma? In the Anuzabar Chain? It's at least five thousand kilometers away. Are they sure?"

"It seems the same sort of thing," said Corradon. "A lot of bitterness, but here it's centering on property disputes. They are talking about . . ." He paused. "What was the word? I had to look it up to be sure what they meant. . . . Yes, *lawyers.*"

"Lawyers?"

"Anyway," Corradon continued with a shrug, "it's getting messy. They blame the Gate going and I wasn't going to argue otherwise."

"I'm not surprised, sir."

Corradon opened a drawer, pulled out an envelope, and handed it over.

"On the assumption that you would take on the task, I had a formal letter of commissioning drafted for you. Lucian is, as ever, anxious that we do things right."

The envelope was marked "Confidential" and bore the seal of the Council of Representatives. Inside there were three sheets of paper. Merral took the top sheet and, aware that his hand was shaking slightly, began to read it.

> Forester Merral Stefan D'Avanos is hereby authorized to take charge of the Farholme Defense Unit as of the above date until such time as he is relieved of his office. He is to take the rank of captain and, under God, is to be answerable only to the Council of Farholme Representatives. His general duties are to carry out, to the best of his ability, the task of countering the intruders. His specific and immediate duties are detailed on the separate sheet. Captain D'Avanos is authorized to use such Farholme facilities and resources as may be required.

At the bottom was a signature and beneath it, *Anwar Corradon, Representative for northeastern Menaya; Chair, Council of Farholme Representatives A.D. 13852.*

Merral flicked to the next sheet, which was headed by "Confrontation Plans: Top Secret." Underneath were four short, numbered paragraphs:

> *1. A body of approximately one hundred and forty soldiers is to be assembled by Sentinel Enand. These are to be divided into four*

units as follows: a) One six-man squad to accompany the two-person diplomatic team. b) Two thirty-man teams for the possible assault. c) The remaining personnel to be kept in reserve on the Emilia Kay. Each unit is to be under a lieutenant and a sergeant.

2. *The diplomatic party will be unarmed and will advance openly without show of force. If, in your judgment, their approaches are rejected by the intruders, you are authorized to attack with all possible speed.*

3. *If such an attack becomes necessary, your goal—to be achieved at all costs—is to disable the ship. If at all possible, the ship is to be taken intact by the FDU.*

4. *In the event an attack is undertaken, all reasonable opportunity for the surrender of the intruder forces is to be given. Should there be a failure to surrender, then you are authorized to use whatever force is necessary to ensure the completion of the mission.*

At the bottom was Corradon's signature.

The third sheet was simply an acknowledgement form stating *I have read the above two sheets and agree to them.*

Merral paused. "Sir, what's a lieutenant and a sergeant?"

A sad smile crossed Corradon's face. "They are, I'm told, military ranks. The ever-knowledgeable Sentinel Enand will explain."

"I have no doubt."

Merral stared at the paper, struggled with a sea of emotions, took the pen off the desk, and with a silent prayer for help, signed his name.

Corradon took the sheet from him. "I'm sorry. I truly am. You and I are in the same unhappy position of having been given a task that neither of us wants." He rubbed his face before staring at Merral. "A task without precedent, a task that may not even be achievable. To lead a world without a Gate . . ." He stared darkly into the distance. "To lead a world without a Gate that is being infiltrated by evil?"

Merral felt that he had never heard such gloom in the representative's voice.

Corradon put his elbows on the desk, clasped his hands together, and leaned forward so his chin rested on his fingers. It was, Merral thought (and immediately felt ashamed for thinking it), a terribly statuesque pose that made him look rather noble. Yet there was something brooding about the way Corradon appeared that reminded Merral of some troubled king or president from before the Intervention, faced with leading his people through a time of strife or disaster. And then Merral realized such a parallel was all too apt.

"I know you are busy," Corradon said in a quiet voice, "but come through to the conservatory. There are things that need to be said and here is perhaps rather formal. But can I get you a drink?"

"A fruit juice, sir, please."

"I'll be with you in a minute. Go through."

The conservatory was full of anemones of many colors, most with their petals closed for the night. Merral was looking around, trying to identify the species when Corradon returned with two glasses of juice.

"Shall we?" he said, pointing to a pair of chairs in a corner.

"A fine collection of plants, sir," Merral said as he sat down and took the juice from the tray.

"Thank you. I have concentrated on the anemones of Menaya." Suddenly the representative's tone of voice changed, and Merral was all too aware of tiredness and strain in it. "But, Merral, let's drop the formality. Here, at least, please call me Anwar."

Merral was surprised to see that any trace of confidence had left the representative's face. The man who sat in front of him now seemed older and troubled.

"As you wish, Anwar," Merral said, feeling both sympathy and alarm.

His host sipped his drink and frowned. "Merral," Anwar said slowly, "I want to explain something. So you understand. Now that you have agreed to help, I can tell you."

He hesitated. "The post of representative—and even more so, that of chairman of the Farholme representatives—is not just functional, it is also public. Indeed, it is perhaps primarily a public role. You know: the opening of schools, the visits to processing plants, the endless speeches and dinners; that sort of thing." Corradon gave a pained smile and stared into the darkness of one corner of the conservatory. "It is harmless enough. A sort of perpetual theatrical performance. You understand?"

"Yes. But I had never thought of it that way."

"No, why should you? But since the loss of the Gate, my role has changed. People now look to me for help, for guidance, for encouragement. I sense them hanging on my every word. They are hungry for me to reassure them that it's all going to be all right. It is almost idolatrous. But do you see the problem?"

"I'm not sure I do, sir—Anwar, I mean—you'd better spell it out."

"It quite simple. I can't show any doubt or concern. I have to deliver what they want."

"I see."

"And increasingly, Merral, I find that my private views are so much at variance with what I have to say in public that I feel a fraud." His face seemed to sag, and Merral felt the blue eyes were close to tears. "I think we are in trouble. I'm worried. But I can't say it. I have to pretend."

"Ah," Merral said, reeling at the situation that the representative had exposed. "I see. I'm sorry; I hadn't realized."

"You weren't meant to. That's the problem. I'm caught every way; I can't even resign. That would be bad for morale. At times, I feel I am putting on an act. As if I am a circus clown, with a fixed smile."

"That must be hard."

"It is." Corradon shook his head bitterly.

"Who else knows?"

"Victoria, of course. And Lucian. He misses very little. He is concerned about it. He wonders how long I can keep up the act. That's another reason why he backs you. I—*we*—need you. And we need a victory. Of some sort. But he has been very helpful."

Merral sipped his juice, aware that the burden on him had just been increased. "I understand. I will do what I can."

The gaunt face that stared at him seemed to brighten slightly as if some burden had been lifted. "Thanks," Corradon said with a long, weary sigh. "Anyway, I just thought you ought to know. I'm the wrong man for this job."

"I think there're at least two of us in that position," Merral told him. "But thank you for your honesty. I will pray for you."

As Merral watched, he felt that somehow Corradon's face regained something of the smooth assurance that it had had before. *He has put back on the public mask,* Merral thought, and the idea appalled him.

"Thank you," Corradon said and sipped his drink. "Incidentally, Merral, it has been agreed that, despite the rush, we and you would all take tomorrow off and keep the Lord's Day."

"Seems sensible."

"Well, we thought not to do so would be a lack of faith. And besides, it would be rather noticeable." The representative shrugged and took another sip. "Anyway, I'll let you go. You'll have a lot to do before you go south."

"South?"

There was a pause. "Ah, hasn't he told you? The ever-inventive Sentinel Enand? Well, he will." Corradon rose. "And we'd better not keep him. But let me show you out. I may try and see you before you go, but Vero is anxious that I keep up a normal schedule. Not to alert anyone who is watching."

He ushered Merral to the conservatory door. "Thank you again for listening."

"It's a privilege. I'll keep it confidential. But I have a question. You see,

Brenito told me—it was almost the last thing he said to me—that we must all play our parts."

"True."

"And surely to play a part, we have—at least sometimes—to act?"

There was a thin, tired smile. "Ah, how interesting. Yes, I think you are right. We may not like the parts that the Most High has written for us. And sometimes we may not even feel that we can do them. But we must do what we can."

He patted Merral on the back. "Thanks. But do me a favor, Captain? If it comes to a fight, seize the ship! Please?"

As Vero drove him to Narreza Tower, Merral mentioned nothing of his conversation in the conservatory to Vero. But he did mention other things.

"And on Ilakuma," Merral said, "there are disputes; they are talking about lawyers."

"Lawyers!" The vehicle swerved and a red light flashed as the auto-steer circuitry took over and directed it away from the curb. "The people of Ilakuma want lawyers?"

"That's what he said."

"We are in big trouble." Vero shook his head. "Bigger than I thought."

"And he also talked about us going south. Where and why?"

Vero suddenly looked rather sheepish, "I meant to tell you. Do you know Tanaris Island?"

"Tanaris? In the Henelen Chain. A bit lonely, isn't it? Five or six hundred kilometers southeast of Larrenport. There have been various plans for forestry work there, but they never got very far. Why do you mention it?"

"Because Tanaris is our forward base. Zak and many of the men are already there, building a camp, beginning to practice. The rest will be there soon. The day after tomorrow—all being well—you and I will take the *Emilia Kay* to Tanaris."

"But why there?"

"Because the men need to practice and Isterrane is just too public. People will see and maybe talk. If they do that over diary links then the intruders may know. Besides, there are always ships landing, and they get in the way. So Tanaris has become the assembly point; it's uninhabited, isolated, and has a good landing strip."

"Makes sense. You *have* been busy."

Vero sighed. "Yes. Everyone has; that's another reason why we are going to take tomorrow off. Anyway, this is the plan. We have three full days of training at Tanaris. Then the *Emilia Kay* flies due north on the evening of the fourth day, drops the teams off, and lands at the southern edge of the crater overnight. So, all being well, six days from now at dawn, we make contact."

"That's soon."

"I know."

"But what do I need to start work on?"

"I have a folder ready for you."

"Good."

Vero parked at the base of Narreza Tower.

"And, Vero, I also need to talk with Perena urgently. There's a problem with the sleds."

"A serious one?"

"Probably. I was thinking about it as I flew over. It took my mind off things."

In the apartment, Vero took a thick box file off the shelf. "In this you have three things. We recovered a number of texts from the Library and had them printed out. Some of them are for soldiers and that is a help, as we are using them to start getting the men trained. So you have a military leadership handbook from the 2020s, and it may be a help to you. Mind you, it is in a very peculiar form of Ancient English. There are whole sentences of abbreviations whose meanings are hard to uncover. There is another file of the technical details of the weapons and the *Emilia Kay*. Finally, you have a folder of the men you will give orders to."

"'Give orders to?' That has a strange sound to it."

"Well, the ancient wisdom was—and they had lots of battles—"

"In that context it is questionable how much wisdom the ancients did have."

"Point taken. But their maxim was that if you want to win a battle, you don't stop to take a vote."

"Oh, Vero!" Merral sighed as he accepted the folder. "Are you trying to make me change my mind already?"

"Sorry," Vero said, "but it's the way it must be." He hesitated. "There is one other thing for you. Brenito left you a package."

"For me?"

"Yes. I know a bit about what's in it. And I didn't feel it was right to give it to you before you made your mind up."

Vero went into his bedroom and returned with a small package wrapped in blue paper with an envelope attached.

Merral opened the envelope.

My dear Forester,

If you are reading this then I have indeed—at long last—been called Home. Although I shall appreciate getting a new body, I feel it is rather a shame leaving things just as they get exciting.

I said most of what I want to say to you at Ynysmant. Basically, guard Jorgio and watch yourself. However, in thinking of you as I arranged to dispose of my considerable effects, a certain something came to mind which you will find in the attached box.

It seems all too likely that it will come to a fight. If, as I expect, you are summoned to lead the attack, I would like you to wear this in my memory. I could wish that it had some magic power, but, of course, it hasn't. But do consider it as an encouragement and a reminder, something like that. If you are tempted to flee, it may encourage you to stand firm.

With every best wish,
In the service of the Lamb,
Brenito Camsar, Sentinel

Merral opened the wrapping paper to find a small, dark wooden box. He looked at it. It was plainly very old; the wood was fine-grained, polished smooth, and blackened with age.

"Can I open it?" he asked.

"Of course. The box is recent. Relatively speaking."

Merral opened the lid carefully, wondering how ancient the contents were if a box so old was "recent." Inside, nestled on a soft black fabric, was a dull gray-brown titanium disk just big enough to sit in the curve between joined forefinger and thumb, attached to a fine but plain neck chain of identical metal. *It is jewelry,* he thought, then realized there was a functional air about the chain that proclaimed that it was never meant for display.

Merral lifted the chain and, as the disk spun before him, saw there was writing on it. He stopped it spinning and peered at the words. The script was Early Assembly Communal, slightly scratched and hard to make out. He read some words, then, as they made sense, found his hand shaking so much he could not read the remainder.

"Is it . . . is it the real thing?" he asked, finding himself almost overwhelmed at what he apparently held.

"Oh yes. May I see it?"

Vero came over, took the disk, and read aloud, "'Lucas Hannun Ringell, Space Frigate *Clearstar,* Assembly Assault Fleet. Date of Birth: 3-3-2082.'"

"His identification disk. Really?"

Very gently, Vero lowered the disk back into Merral's hand.

"He told me it had been kept in the family. Ultimately given to some distant ancestor by Moshe Adlen, to whom General Ringell gave it in his old age."

"But," Merral protested, "we must be talking, what—five hundred generations? This is older than almost anything else on this planet."

"Probably, but put it on."

Merral lowered the chain over his head and let the disk, oddly cool, slip down inside his shirt. *I could not feel stranger if they had put some crown on me.* "If I understand this correctly, I am now wearing the identification disk that was hanging around the neck of the man who, in killing William Jannafy, ended the Rebellion and the Last War."

Vero nodded. "He thought it would be appropriate. A symbol of our last war goes into the next. A continuity."

"Yes . . . ," Merral sighed. "And by giving it to me, he also placed a high burden on me: the burden of history."

Vero gave him a sympathetic look. "Yes, he did. And that was doubtless what he meant to do."

"Ah," Merral said, feeling unable to say anything more profound.

"Anyway," Vero said, "let me go and get Perena."

Ten minutes later, Merral's attempt to understand the manual's alien concepts of imposing discipline were interrupted by Vero's return with Perena.

"Sorry for the delay," she said, amid a gentle hug. "I was showering. I've been busy all day supervising the work on the *Emilia Kay*. It's the only flying craft I have ever had where you've had to hose bat droppings out of the turbine scoops."

"That bad? Is it going to work?" asked Merral, abruptly realizing that the whole strategy hung on an ancient ship.

"Yes, it will be fine." She frowned slightly. "Probably. It's just that they never really expected to use it again, so for ten years or so the protective storage coat was breached on the port side. Anya reckons we could have done an ecological study on the wildlife inside. We have removed rats, mice, a dozen scorpions, and a couple of snakes. And the bats." She ran a hand through her short hair.

"I thought it was an operating ship."

"No, it had been put in mothballs," Vero said, sitting down at the table.

"What?" Perena asked.

"Ignore him," Merral said. "It will be some sort of Ancient English phrase."

"Okay, but what does it mean?"

"Well," Vero answered rather defensively, "it means . . ." He frowned. "Hmm. I don't actually know. A mothball was a small ball of naphthalene." His frown deepened. "How could you put a ship in them? You'd need tons of the things. Very odd."

Merral interrupted him by asking for the images of Fallambet Lake Five. The three of them gathered round the largest image. Silently, Merral measured distances on the sheets and then looked up at the others. "As I thought, we have a problem."

A new frown crossed Vero's face. "You'd better explain."

"It's the sleds. When you first envisaged using them, you were planning to do it over land. Right?"

"Pretty much so."

"Sneak up close and then race in. Right?"

"Again. Yes."

"But how fast are they?"

"Say, eighty kilometers an hour."

Perena muttered something under her breath, but it was Merral who answered. "Vero, that's a maximum. Try sixty when laden. So how long to cover two kilometers?"

"Two minutes. Ah."

"It's too long. There is no cover. They will have a clear shot in that time. The last kilometer is open water. And we know that they have beam weapons of some sort."

Perena nodded. "I should have thought of that," she said.

"No, it's my mistake," Vero added. "You've been busy on the *Emilia Kay*. And this is new territory for us all. Merral, I hadn't realized that the lake position is far more open than I had hoped."

Merral looked at Perena. "So, Captain, a technical question. How can we increase the speed of the sleds?"

She returned his gaze, and he felt he could almost hear her mind calculating. "How fast do you want them to go?"

"Oh, so fast they can't be hit. See this lake stretch? I would want them to cover that last kilometer in well under thirty seconds. So, say about one hundred and fifty kilometers an hour. Oh, and as close to the water as you can get. Under a meter?"

Perena shook her head. "Tricky. And you want it within two to three days, eh? Well, the simplest solution is the oldest: bolt a rocket booster propulsion unit onto the back and strap everybody in. Glide down the valley silently under normal GM power, then when you hit open ground, just fire the motors. A small motor will give you that acceleration. Of course, at that speed, handling will be a problem. And then you have to decelerate on the other side. Hmm." She paused, evidently doing mental calculations, then looked hard at Merral. "And you want it close to the water too? Well, you'll have to have the controls automatic. Human reflexes can't handle those speeds. Still, you know where you are going, so it's a simple program. And the surface, apart from waves, is fairly flat. I'd say it's possible to modify the circuits that control the altitude and course."

"So," Merral asked, "it could be done?"

"Yes . . ." Perena dragged the word out slowly. "But you'd have to calculate how many g's you'd pull though."

"Is a straight-line course the best thing?"

She thought for a moment. "Probably not. You could write some swerves into the control program. But then it could be a wild ride. Lots of strains."

Perena looked at Merral, "So you want me to try and get it organized? I have enough work to do with the *Emilia Kay,* but I can find engineers who would like the challenge. They will have to work very hard, though. And there're no guarantees."

Vero nodded assent.

"Okay, Perena," Merral said, "can you try and see if you can get someone to do it? Please?"

Vero tapped him on the shoulder. "You could order it."

"*Order* it?"

"You're the Captain of the FDU. You could say, 'Captain Lewitz, I hereby order you to get it done.' Only snappier. And no tentative 'please' is needed. It's the sort of thing you ought to practice."

"Are you serious?" Merral asked, staring at Vero. "She's a friend. I can't order her."

Perena gave him an intense look. "He's right, Merral. Sadly. You have to give orders. In this context, I'm your obedient pilot."

"But this is horrible."

"Oh, just do it!" Vero snapped.

"Now who's ordering who? Oh, very well . . . Perena . . . . No, *Captain Lewitz,* I hereby order you to get it done."

"Yes, sir." There was a nod, a smile, and she left.

After the door closed behind her, Merral turned to Vero. "This is hopeless," he said. "I'm not up to it."

Vero smiled and clapped him on the back. "The orders thing is—I think—easy enough to pick up. The more important thing is that you have identified a tactical problem that I had overlooked. You've just shown why we need you. You have a flair for this sort of thing."

"Perhaps . . ."

"No, definitely. Now let's get to work."

The next day Merral rose early. Normally on a Lord's Day he would have lain in bed until later. Now, though, he felt that he had no mandate for any such luxury. Instead, he spent time praying and reading his Bible.

Then he sat on the bed and called Isabella on his diary. She seemed to stare at him for a few moments before answering. Slowly and painfully, Merral made an apology for what had happened when they last met. Isabella seemed only reluctantly to accept his apologies. "The trouble is," she said rather sourly, "you're never around for long enough to talk to properly. And when are you back next?"

"I really can't say, Isabella, I'm afraid, but that is the way it is. I may be out of touch for a few days."

"There we are again," came the sharp response, accompanied by an exasperated shake of her head. "As I said, you're never around. Look, I have to go. Good-bye."

Then, before he could say anything more, the screen went blank. He stared at it for a moment or two, then, in exasperation, slammed his fist onto the bed.

35

Early the following morning Merral and Vero drove to the airport but went on past the main terminal to the western extremity of the complex.

Merral soon spotted the *Emilia Kay*. She was a large vessel, the gray of a winter's sky, hanging low to the ground, with a swollen belly and stubby wings. The ship reminded him of some animal—perhaps a whale—but it lacked any sense of the harmonious unity of an organism. It was too easy to see that it was made of individual components: wings, fin, four engines, fuselage, and load module. As they approached, Merral decided that the intention had been to conceal the ship by parking it at the extreme end of the western runway system. But to him, particularly in the absence of the regular Gate shuttle traffic, it still seemed glaringly prominent, and the dozen or so vehicles in attendance around it seemed to highlight the fact that something unusual was going on.

Vero drove onto the service track outside the earth ramparts that marked the runway edges. As they turned a corner and went out of sight of the terminal, he slowed the vehicle and brought it to a stop in front of what was clearly a brand-new barrier of sand-filled containers and wire mesh.

Two men in matching blue overalls stood by a gate in the barrier. They nodded in recognition at Vero and walked round to Merral.

Vero leaned over. "Show them your letter," he whispered.

Merral pulled it out and let the men examine it. They glanced at each other, stared at Merral again, and then turned quizzical looks to Vero before raising their hands in tentative salutes.

"Welcome, sir," the taller said. He glanced at Merral's belt.

"Oh yes," Vero said, "can you let him have your diary?"

"What is this?"

"A new program that restricts use of the diary. No location of position, no signals out except emergency ones or ones on a coded FDU band. You'd best get it done. A temporary measure."

Noting that Vero had taken action on a problem that had emerged in their last dealings with the intruders, Merral handed his diary over. The man slid it into a downloading interface slot, pressed a button, and passed it back.

"Thank you, Captain D'Avanos," he said with a salute. He lifted the barrier and Vero accelerated through toward the *Emilia Kay*.

"So this is how it is to be," Merral said, as much to himself as to Vero as he put the diary back on his belt. "*Sir* this, *sir* that, *Captain D'Avanos, sir* . . . And the salutes."

Vero looked at him out of the corner of his eye. "Merral, in the past no one invented a better way, and there's no time to try and find it now." He seemed to consider something. "My friend, if I may suggest something?" Vero's tone seemed guarded. "You have to play the part whether you like it or not. Among the men and the few women you will command, everyone is confused, and some are scared. All will be both at some point. They will look to you to hold them firm. I know it's hard because you have no models to base yourself on. But then neither have they. In Tanaris you will have to work hard. But I think you will do it."

"And supposing I can't?"

Vero slowed the vehicle to a crawl and looked sternly across at him. "Don't ever even think that!" There was rebuke in his voice. "I believe—*we* believe—that God has called you to lead us. If he has called you to play the part, then he will equip you for that. You mustn't doubt that!"

Then, as if to soften the rebuke, he punched Merral on the arm. "Come on Captain D'Avanos," he said as the vehicle sped up toward the confusion of activity around the ship. "You'll do it."

They parked a hundred meters from the ship. Given that so much was going on around, in, and on top of the vessel, Merral decided any closer would have been risky. A quick glance suggested that there must be at least a hundred people and fifteen vehicles clustered about the ship. He counted six LP4 transporters alone, each in various stages of being unloaded, their contents of boxes, bags, and drums lying next to them and being checked off. There were other vehicles too: a hydrogen tanker parked at a safe distance, numerous smaller four-seater vehicles, and even the odd bike. Everywhere there were businesslike noises—hammering, the whine of lifters, the hum of motors, the shouting out of requests—all merging into a continuous hectic buzz of activity.

While Vero was detained by a man with an inquiry, Merral walked on, a robotic lifter pausing to let him pass with a bow of its head, and threaded his way past two men earnestly comparing databoard lists. Near a wingtip, he stopped and stared at the ship. The vessel was larger than Merral had imagined; he could easily believe that it would swallow the sleds, the hoverer, and a hundred or more men with room to spare. Merral cautiously identified it, from a memory of a model he had once made as a child, as a Series D Freighter. The phrase *the flexible workhorse of the Assembly* came to mind but, he decided, if it was after all to be compared with an animal, it was not a horse. Particularly not in this mode, where the massive landing legs were bowed so that the flat bottom of the cargo module that made up half the fuselage was now within centimeters of the ground, making the whole ship look squat and low-slung. It was as if someone had started by modeling the ship on a toad and then, at the last minute, had decided that it had to fly.

As he approached he saw that the long, curved, slablike doors that ran along most of the length of the cargo module were open, allowing him to see inside. On the floor of the module, the two sleds were already in and the hoverer was being winched aboard. Trying not to trip over piles of equipment or get in the way of the numerous workers, Merral walked into the shadow of the wings of the *Emilia Kay* and looked up at the gray bulk hanging above him. There were scratches and dents on the body, and the paintwork was dulled and locally peeling. Two high gantries had been erected under each rear engine, and on them people were standing, peering into panels, and inserting cables and tubes.

"Awesome, isn't it?" Vero's voice sang out behind him.

Merral glanced at him, then looked around at all the activity. On the high single tail fin with the faded Lamb and Stars emblem, the rudder was swinging backward and forward in some mysterious test procedure.

"Yes, it is. How did you get all this organized?"

"I just set it in motion, my friend."

"What am I supposed to do here?"

"Nothing much. Most of the men are already at Tanaris; there was another flight this morning. But you may want to familiarize yourself with the ship. I suggest you go and see Perena. Here, as captain of the *Emilia Kay,* she is almost more important than you."

Careful to avoid getting in the way of either people or machinery, Merral made his way into the ship and, after asking directions, found Perena in the spacious three-seat cockpit high at the front end of the ship. At least, Merral concluded, it would have been spacious had it not been filled with six people wrestling with cabling in access panels, squinting at flashing screens, and calling out incomprehensible codes to each other.

Perena, in T-shirt, baggy jeans, and worn running shoes, was leaning with apparent nonchalance by the cockpit door, looking at a databoard in her hands and ticking off lists on it. It occurred to Merral that with her relaxed air, casual clothes, and slight build she looked insignificant—the very last person in the room who one would expect was the captain.

Perena glanced up and winked at Merral. "So, Captain, stealing aboard without ceremony?"

"I'm afraid so, Captain Lewitz. I'm enjoying the anonymity while it lasts. How's it going?"

"Not bad; I think it will be late afternoon before we take off. Come back here; there's more room and it's quieter."

She led him to the bare and shabby passenger compartment just behind the cockpit that had twenty or so rather austere seats. There was no one else there. Merral noticed the faintest remains of a spider's web in a corner.

Perena looked around and nodded. "Scruffy, eh? For an Assembly ship. But it will do."

"Are we on schedule?"

"No. We will be two hours later than planned, but as the camp is already set up for us at Tanaris, arriving in the dark isn't a problem. We still have to repaint the ship's exterior. That's the last task. That and fueling."

"A nice color scheme?"

She grinned. "I've ordered a nice, pale, eggshell blue."

"You're not serious?"

"Yes. But only for the underside—matches the sky. On a good day. The top is a disrupted green-and-brown camouflage."

"Camouflage! No, I suppose it makes sense. I hope they can't see us now."

"We don't think so. We have monitored Farholme local space for satellites and found none. And just in case they are planning to use our own, one of Vero's people arranged a widespread satellite communications malfunction for today. All signals are being lost."

Merral found himself marveling again at his friend's inventiveness. "Smart move. I'm glad he's on our side."

"He is very ingenious. I have played him at chess."

"Is he any good?"

A smile with a hint of disquiet crossed her face. "Ingenuity, Merral, is fine, but it has its limits. Vero's strategies are cunning, but they can be overambitious."

"Ah," Merral said, suddenly alarmed at the thought that such a weakness might extend beyond the chessboard.

As he saw the expression of tender unease cross Perena's face, Merral realized something.

"You care for him, don't you?" he said, wondering if he was intruding into private matters.

Perena seemed to think hard. "Yes. But is there anything more? Any possibility of a deeper relationship?" She gave a slight shrug. "There could be, perhaps. But, for the moment, I have put it to one side." She stared into an infinite distance and her voice became even quieter. "By temperament, Merral, I am a dreamer. And for someone who plays chess—and flies ships—that can be dangerous. I handle it by being focused, by pushing everything to one side. So might there be anything with Vero? Maybe, when this is all over. 'For everything there is a season,' and I'm afraid our season is war. Or at least we must be prepared for that." Perena's eyes seemed to stare at Merral with a new intensity. "So 'anything more' assumes a lot."

"That we survive, for a start."

"There is more than that."

"What do you mean?"

A strange tautness seemed to come over Perena's face. "You have recognized that our world is changing, Merral?" At his nod, she said, "Where there was sunlight, there are now shadows. Where our paths were once straight and smooth, they are now winding and rough. And as our world changes, so do we."

Perena's voice had become hushed and distant, and Merral felt he was being given access to her most private thoughts. He said nothing as she continued. "Some people are adapting to the new world. Clemant, for instance, has realized the way the wind is blowing and, although he hates it, is trimming his sails to suit. Corradon? I think he senses the changes but can only hope and pray that they will go away. But we are all reacting to it." She gave Merral a smile whose meaning he found impossible to fathom. "But will any of us be the same when the storm passes?"

"A good question," Merral replied, feeling troubled.

Perena fell silent.

A heavy knocking reverberated through the hull. Perena winced.

"And are you happy with this ship?" asked Merral, feeling a pressing need to talk about practical matters. "I mean, I gather it's not been used for years."

Perena looked around as if anxious not to be overheard. "Only partially," she said in a confidential tone, "but I'm not shouting about it. It's not the age either—that can be fixed. And the test flights showed she was fine. No, I've read up on ships of war, and this is a long way away from being one."

"I can imagine. What's the problem?"

She smiled, but it was a severe and joyless smile. "*Problems,* plural. Too slow, too unmaneuverable. There is no armor whatsoever; the hydrogen tanks in the hull are very vulnerable. Ironically, my general survey craft is better equipped: that at least has thermal plates and an ability to take some impacts. But *Emilia* was designed as an atmosphere-only ship, so the hull is barely two mills thick. There is little that counts as defensive sensors, nothing that acts as electronic countermeasures. The ability to accept different modules in the load bay is a great feature for a freighter but it weakens the structure; it can't take severe stresses. And the doors cannot be opened quickly. Do you want me to go on?"

"Definitely not. But practically, what does it mean?"

"Good question. What, as Vero would now say, is 'the bottom line'? Well, it means I can't take risks. There will be no dramatic rescues for you under fire with this old lady." She tapped a girder near her.

"Thanks for the warning."

"But I like her all the same. The test flights yesterday were encouraging. Typical Series D. Slow, steady, stable."

"Good. And this is all the equipment?"

"Not at all." She shook her head. "There is much already at Tanaris, and there will be a series of supply flights almost every day. There's a lot of gear outstanding: uniforms, medical gear, that sort of thing. The booster jets for the sleds and their controllers. All being well."

"I see."

A figure appeared at the door and beckoned Perena. "Sorry," she said. "Nathan, my chief electrics man. Have a look round but watch your step. To have your captain break a leg tripping over a wire might be seen as, well . . . inauspicious."

Then, with a light pat on his arm, she was gone.

Merral wandered back along the upper hull of the *Emilia Kay,* in a corridor that he found hard not to think of as the spinal column of the great misshapen toad. He was trying to get a feeling for how the ship functioned, but not being an expert, found the various labels on the hatches and doors confusing and felt disinclined to ask explanations from the men and women who were preoccupied with cabling and circuits.

Halfway down the corridor, he heard footsteps behind him, and a familiar voice called out, "Tree Man! Or should I say *Captain* Tree Man?" Then an arm was linked playfully into his.

He turned. "Anya!" he said, pleased more than ever to see her freckled face. "I thought you would be elsewhere. . . ."

"No," she said wrinkling her nose, "I played my part in this affair starting and I will see it through. But come and see what I've been working on."

Anya led him down to the very end of the corridor, where there was a door with a small window in the middle. There were bolts at the top and bottom and a complex box with a keypad in the middle. All the features had the air of being recently fitted. Merral peered in through the thick glass to see a sizeable room with padding on every wall. Puzzled, he looked at Anya. "What's this for?"

"Prisoners," she murmured, with a strange note in her voice. "I am preparing to be a zookeeper."

"And if they aren't alive? What then?"

She gestured below. "We are fitting a freezer unit down there. And we have bags and disinfecting agents. We have to be prepared."

"I'm glad *you* are! So you are coming?"

Her blue eyes seemed to flash. "Why not? You may need a biologist. And I'm hardly going to miss the biggest bug hunt in history, am I?"

"No," Merral said.

Anya looked cautiously at him, as if concerned that he would veto her accompanying the ship. "Besides," she declared firmly, "my first aid isn't bad, and I can act as a medical orderly if needed."

"And we have those facilities?" Merral asked, suddenly realizing that this was yet another thing that he had overlooked. The gloomy thought struck him that there were probably many other oversights that he might make.

"Two doctors, six orderlies. A lot of equipment. Enough synplasma to replace everybody's blood. On our side anyway. The moment there is any contact, a hospital vessel will be mobilized. It will be there in an hour or less."

"Let's hope it's not needed," he said and then added, "But welcome on board, Doctor." And as he said it, he realized he felt both pleased that she was coming with him and also slightly guilty that he felt so pleased.

They walked back down the corridor and into the cargo module, where at least a dozen people were either hoisting things on board or fastening them down with straps and cabling. Merral was conscious that a number of those in the hold were staring at him and that whispered comments were being passed around. *They know who I am.* He looked at the growing piles of equipment being assembled.

Outside the cargo unit he could see more activity. By a wing, the complex structure of a robot painter with its multiple tubular limbs, flexible pipes, and nozzles rose like some strange insect emerging from a chrysalis.

"You look worried," Anya said to him.

"The scale and complexity of all this intimidates me. Vero has done a superb job. But I'm worried we will get there and find something missing."

"That's why there is the time in Tanaris to—"

There was the clatter of footsteps on the metal floor behind him. A voice shouted, "Captain D'Avanos here?"

For a fraction of a second, Merral thought that the reference was to someone else. Then he turned to see a young man dressed in blue.

"Yes, I'm Merral D'Avanos. Can I help?" As he said it, Merral realized that a decisive "What do you want?" would have been more in keeping with his rank. Oh well, he would learn.

"Sir!" The young man saluted again. "Sentinel Enand wants to see you, promptlike. There's a problem. This way."

With a nod and a shrug to Anya, Merral followed.

An evidently agitated Vero was waiting by a four-seater. "We have a difficulty at the entrance. It can be handled, but I'll need your help. Get in. I'll explain as we go."

Carefully, Vero turned the vehicle through the equipment and set off toward the line of wire they had come through earlier.

"The problem is," Vero said, "that two people from the Menaya news team have turned up. They have seen the *Emilia Kay* and the activity and—quite naturally—want to see what is going on."

"Vero, that could be disastrous! I mean, everybody on the planet will know." Merral looked at the activity behind him. "We can't disguise this. What can we do? Can we make them promise not to tell?"

Vero frowned and shook his head, "They would still know and it might get out. We could get it banned temporarily through Corradon. But that raises monumental constitutional issues. There is another way."

"How?"

A look of cunning flickered over Vero's face and then disappeared beneath a bland gaze of innocence. "Ah, *secret*. No, you introduce yourself as the 'head of what is going on here'—now use that exact phrase—and then designate me as the person who will talk to them. With my accent they may be uneasy about me, but if you back me that will be acceptable. Then get back to the vehicle and stay out of earshot."

"Why?"

Vero winked. "I just don't want you standing by when I talk. Trust me."

Merral had seen enough reporters at sports matches, weddings, and festivals to recognize the type, especially when they carried the trademark recording gear on their belts as this young man and woman did. The way they were sitting cross-legged on the ground suggested the sort of dedication associated with reporters who refused to leave the stadium without interviewing the losing captain.

Merral walked over, shook hands, and introduced himself by name, but without mentioning his rank, and then introduced Vero to them. As he walked back to the four-seater, he saw that Vero had gotten the reporters into a huddle with him as if they were discussing something confidential. A few minutes later, the group broke up with the shaking of hands, and Vero walked back with an awkward smile on his face.

"Back to work," Vero said and then, whistling tunelessly, lowered himself into the driving seat and switched on the engine.

"So what did you say?"

Still whistling, Vero set the vehicle rolling back toward the freighter where the painting machine had now risen above the wings. Only when the four-seater had sped up did he speak. "Promise you won't be angry?"

"No," Merral replied suspiciously. "I will probably be furious. What did you say?"

"Ah . . . I told them the truth. In a, well . . . modified form. I told them that there was a group being set up to carry out rescue operations within Farholme, in the event of forest fires, earthquakes, volcanoes, and other perils. To do the sort of things that the Assembly would normally send ships for."

"Good grief—"

Vero continued as if he hadn't heard Merral's expostulation. "But, I said, we were keeping it secret because we didn't want to alarm everybody. As everybody was already concerned about the Gate loss, we didn't want to make it worse. So I asked them not talk about it. Not yet. And they were persuaded."

Merral could barely believe what he was hearing. "Vero! You *lied* to them!" he shouted. "Completely and utterly!"

The response, when it eventually came, was thoughtful and restrained. "Hmm, that's open to debate. You see my definition of 'perils' was sufficiently broad that it would allow for the invasion of hostile aliens. Or similar. And my definition of 'rescue' was, likewise, broad."

"But, Vero, you fell well below the standards of openness and truth that we have always held to. Far below."

"Yes, well, remember Rahab the whore in Joshua, chapter 2—one of those Old Covenant stories we pass over quickly with children?"

"That? . . . That was in the bad old days."

"Merral," Vero replied, with a tone of exaggerated weariness, "wake up! See those robot arms climbing over the top of the dear old *Emilia Kay*? It's painting her in camouflage. We are loading her now with explosive charges and guns. These are the preparations for war. As captain of operations it would be a help if you acknowledged this." Vero threw Merral a look that was somehow both critical and sympathetic. "See, my friend, the bad old days are back."

Back at the *Emilia Kay,* Merral decided the best thing he could do was stay out of the way and try and master what he was going to be responsible for. So he made himself comfortable in a patch of shade in the back of an empty LP4 and spent some hours alternatively reading the leader's handbook and then flicking through the folder with its details of the men he was commanding. Some things, he was glad to see, had already been done. The assignment of seven lieutenants and sergeants and the heads of medical, logistics, and communication teams had also been made. Vero, he saw, had even made a choice of someone as chaplain. As a starter, Merral decided to memorize those names, faces, and details.

So, as the afternoon passed, he tried to get his mind around the immensity of what he was shortly going to have to undertake. The only relief he took was that, every so often, he emerged from his shaded seat to walk up to the ship and see how progress was being made. On one visit, Vero came over to him accompanied by a man with a familiar open face, carrying a holdall.

"Lorrin Venn," Merral said, extending his hand to the tall man with the pale brown hair and green eyes. "Nice to see you. Still working in support?"

Lorrin smiled, as if anxious to please. "Sir, that was what I've come about. I was wondering if I could be released from that, just for a week, and come and join a team. It was my first choice. I know it's late. But I have my gear with me." He looked plaintively at Vero, as if for support.

"He meets the physical requirements," Vero said. "And we could use some spare men. But it's up to you."

"So, Lorrin, you know that it may be unpleasant. Even dangerous?"

Lorrin nodded urgently. "It's really what I want, sir. It'd be neat. I know Zak. Maybe I could be on his team?"

Merral stared at Vero, hoping for assistance, but found that his friend was looking away. *He wants me to make the decision myself.*

"Very well, Lorrin. I would imagine we can use you. Get Sentinel Vero here to assign you to a squad when we get to Tanaris. See you on the flight."

"*Yeah!* Thank you, sir!" the man said, eagerness written across his face. Then he gave a sharp salute, turned, and beginning to whistle happily, left the ship.

Merral, watching him depart, shook his head in amusement, and turned to Vero. "Was that okay?"

"Yes. I suppose so."

"You don't sound convinced. Why wasn't he put on one of the contact teams first? He's a nice guy. There's a contagious happiness about that man."

"Yes, isn't there? I refused because he's an only child. We have made no ruling on it. But I thought . . ."

"I see . . . ," Merral responded slowly, realizing that Vero expected not just fighting but also loss of life. Chastened, he returned to his seat in the back of the transporter and, preoccupied with unhappy thoughts, stared blankly at his notes for some time.

Late in the afternoon, Merral looked up to see Dr. Clemant, his neat dark suit and carefully parted hair making him conspicuous among the sweaty, dirty, and increasingly disheveled men and women laboring around the *Emilia Kay.*

The advisor stared at the ship in a thoughtful manner for some time before coming over to Merral.

"Good afternoon, Captain," he said.

"Advisor, good afternoon." Merral said, leaping down from the transporter. "How are you?"

"Well, thank you. I thought I'd come and have a look at the preparations. I have followed the planning closely."

"I'm sure," Merral said. "I don't know about you, but I'm awed by everything that has been done."

Clemant's eyes scanned the busy scene ahead carefully before answering. "Yes, it is a remarkable achievement. But—alas—it is not here that the plans will be tested."

"True."

There was a long silence. "I came to see you, Captain. I thought it right to do so." Merral felt there was a stiffness in the way Clemant spoke that hinted he wanted to say something.

"Thank you."

"I am truly delighted that you have accepted the task of leading the approach."

"I am less enthusiastic."

"I understand." Clemant continued to stare at the *Emilia Kay*. "Captain, let me say that no one is more anxious than me that this operation succeed."

"Thank you again," Merral said.

"You see . . . I know this planet well. It is my business; my life. I have my finger on its pulse and . . . " The advisor paused, stared stiffly at the ground, and when he looked up, Merral could see the fear in his eyes. "And frankly, I am scared."

"By what?" Merral asked, surprised by Clemant's candor.

"By the sense that it is all unraveling."

"I see. . . ."

"Do you?" Clemant said, and Merral was struck by the bluntness of the question. The advisor's pale face colored slightly. "I'm sorry," he said awkwardly. "I find it hard to express myself properly these days; it seems to come out wrong. No offense meant. What I mean is . . . " His words faltered for a second. "What I mean is this: as a world we have been bound together by grace and goodwill. But faced with a return of evil, that may not be enough. In the last month, I have been reading about the past." His eyes closed briefly as if he was in pain. "I have read and watched horrors. The Plague Wars, the destructions, the burning cities, the victims . . ." The advisor shook his head and fell silent. As he continued, his eyes bore a strangely intense expression. "And each new incident here is another point on a graph that marks out a trajectory. And, Captain, I have seen where it is heading."

Somewhat shaken by the analysis, Merral found himself denying it. "It may not be that bad. There is an enormous resilience here."

Clemant gave him a cold, shrewd look as if to say, *I know you don't believe that.* "Perhaps. I hope you are right. But you do see that we have no barriers? no defenses? no structures to protect us?"

Merral struggled with the concepts. "I suppose so. We don't have such things."

Clemant's dark eyes stared at him. "I am from Kelendara. In your former profession you will have heard of our town."

"Indeed, the big forest fires of '22."

"I was a teenager then and I watched the hillsides burn for weeks. You know the verdict of the investigation?"

"I read it at college. The firebreaks weren't wide enough; the first fires weren't tackled fast enough."

"Yes." The advisor's expression suddenly showed a deep concern. "Farholme is like those forests, only worse—there are no firebreaks. We have seen sparks: Larrenport, Ynysmant, Ilakuma, and who knows where else? If they catch . . . " His eyes seem to stare into an infinite void. "We will lose everything. Everything."

Merral, troubled by the vision, said nothing.

"You talked to Anwar last night, I gather?" Clemant said, and Merral knew he referred to something more than an ordinary conversation.

"I did."

"I worry about him. I think he's close to the limit of what he can take. In a storm, some trees bend and recover while others snap, do they not, Captain? And which is our representative?"

"I've never applied the analogy to human beings, Dr. Clemant."

"Perhaps wisely so. But if this tree breaks, we are in trouble." Clemant shook his head, and the expression on his face returned to one of inscrutability. He looked at the ship.

"So," he said, and his voice was less intense, "I came to encourage you. To urge you on. We need that ship. More than you can imagine. We need to be reconnected to the Assembly, and fast."

"I will do what I can," Merral said. "Everyone I have met here is totally committed to doing their task."

"Good." Clemant stared at the ground, and Merral felt there was something else he wanted to say. "There is one other thing," Clemant said finally, looking up at him, a new expression in his dark gray eyes.

"Please."

"I don't know how to say this, but I have a concern."

"Go ahead."

"I hope—as we all do—that diplomacy will work. That they, whoever they are, will say, 'Sorry, it was all a misunderstanding.' " He paused, and Merral knew that he didn't have the slightest faith that this would be the case. "But, Captain," Clemant continued, "if you do have to attack, I want you to be firm."

"I see. In what way?"

He shrugged. "I cannot say exactly; I do not know what will happen. But I don't want you to be overly cautious. Increasingly, I see this evil as a cancer in our world. It needs to be dealt with." He hesitated. "You may need to be a surgeon, Captain."

"Another interesting image, Advisor," Merral said, thinking that, in fact, he found it a very disturbing one.

Then, apparently embarrassed by what he had said, Clemant opened his hands wide in a dismissive gesture. "Well, that's just my view. But I do apologize for taking up your time."

"Advisor, it was very helpful to hear your concerns."

Clemant seemed slightly embarrassed. "Thank you. I felt I needed to express them." He looked around. "Oh, I was also looking for Zachary Larraine. You know him?"

"Zak? He's on Tanaris."

"Ah, I should have checked."

"But how do you know him? Oh, wait, he's from Kelendara too."

"That's right. I know his parents slightly. That's all. Incidentally, Professor Habbentz is at the ship and mentioned she would like to see you."

"Gerry? I'll go and find her."

"Do so. Well, I must go." Clemant's smile as he extended a hand seemed weak. "I will be praying for your success."

They shook hands and the advisor walked away. Merral found himself watching the neat departing figure with a great deal of unease. He sighed and then turned and made his way to the ship.

Gerry Habbentz's tall frame and long, flowing black hair made her easy to find.

"Hi, Merral," she said with enthusiasm as he walked over to where she stood staring at the ship. "Good to see you again. I hear you are a captain now."

Merral shrugged. "I am still working out what that means."

"You'll learn." She grinned, and Merral felt that some of the strain she had borne when they had last met had lifted.

"What are you doing here?" he asked.

"I was at the airport and I came to say farewell to Perena. She flew us to the lab last time. And we've talked about this intruder ship. If you seize it, I'm down to view the engines."

"I'm hoping we are going to have a guided tour from the crew."

"Yeah. Really. You don't believe that, do you?" Her dark eyes glinted.

"I try to, Gerry. But it's hard. How's the physics?"

"Well, your message went. As you know. Whether it was received is another matter." Her face clouded. "Like a lot of other people, I am coming to terms with isolation." She wrinkled her face in an expression of dislike. "And separation."

"Sorry. And the research?"

Her face brightened. "The research is, well, promising. Yeah, *promising* will do."

"Good. Any progress to understanding how the intruders got here?"

"Perhaps. We have been working on the math of the Normal-Space to Below-Space boundary. It is very technical, but we have been trying to see how you could make a ship that could enter and leave Below-Space without using a Gate. We have some ideas. Let's say no more at the moment."

"Just be careful about exploring Below-Space. Please?"

"The *Argo* business, right? Perena told me." Her hair flew about as she shook her head. "No problem. We are a long way from creating any physical model. But anyway, this is a fine place and time to talk about risk, right? Look at that!" She gestured to a box marked *Explosives!* in big red letters being wheeled carefully past them.

"Point taken."

Gerry looked longingly at the *Emilia Kay*. "Oh, I wish I was going with you guys. Incidentally, did Lucian Clemant find you?"

"Yes. How do you know him?"

"Easy; our research has to go through him. He approves most things. But he keeps an eagle eye on what is going on. He's been very encouraging."

"I can imagine."

"Hey, look who's here." She pointed to Vero, picking his way between the few remaining boxes.

Vero came over and hugged Gerry.

"Good to see you, Prof. But it's a brief meeting. Merral, it's soon going to be time to get on board."

"Okay, guys, I must go. I find my hair responds badly to rocket exhaust. But do me a favor, Captain."

"What?"

"I hope, like you, it's a peaceful encounter, but I kinda doubt it." Her brown eyes seemed to become frosty. "But you take that ship. I want to see it. I want to know how they do it, and I want to ride that ship back out of here. Please."

"It seems a popular request," Merral murmured.

Gerry's fingers clenched tight. "And if these animals get in the way, don't be too squeamish. You give it to them from me. Okay?"

As she walked away, Vero and Merral looked at each other.

Vero shrugged. "That is one mean lady."

"Mean?"

"Just an expression. But I wouldn't like to be the cockroach-beast that walked into *her* lab."

There was a further delay, and Merral walked back to the LP4 and resumed his studies. Finally, around five o'clock, the robot painter finished. The *Emilia Kay* now looked very different, but Merral decided he felt ambivalent about the effect. It was splendid to see Perena's "old lady" now dressed up in new paint, and the color scheme of blues and greens gave her a real sense of purpose, but seeing a ship in camouflage was too evocative for him of the ancient wars. He found a slight assurance in the fresh gleam of the Lamb and Stars emblem on the nose and tail.

The fueling was completed, and Perena and an engineer walked around making last-minute external checks.

Merral looked up at the sky, sensing a slight breeze. Sure enough, high above them, fine wispy clouds were sweeping in from the southeast. They would be on their way before any rain came in.

Vero, whom Merral had seen busy consulting with people and checking lists, strode over with a sense of purpose. He scrambled on board the LP4 and sat next to Merral. "Everything all right?" he asked.

"Pretty much. I feel nervous," Merral confided.

"Yes. Me too. Anyway, I have some good news. Possibly."

"Go on. I need it."

"You know how we have been worried about the poor data on the intruder ship?"

"Of course." One of many vague and dreadful scenarios Merral had considered had been that they would land at Fallambet Lake Five and find a perfectly elliptical—and perfectly natural—lump of iron ore.

"Well, I think we may have images in two days."

"Really! How?"

"Well, I was much struck by the dreadful business with that surveillance buzzard, the thing that was a machine but with the dead bits." There was a look of disgust on his face. "And I felt that something like that was what we needed. Only not exactly like that, if you follow. So I wondered if we could train a living bird to fly over and image the ship; like you can steer a horse."

"With a micronic camera and transmitter system? Interesting idea. Possible, but not in the time."

"Exactly what the two people I put to work on the idea said. But not impossible with a horse. So a day ago they landed a horse equipped for signals on the southern edge of the Lannar Crater and are now nudging it slowly northward. I've just heard from them on the secure link; it seems to be working, and the horse should be going along the other side of the lake the day after tomorrow."

"*Whose* horse?" Merral asked urgently, suddenly concerned that Vero might have enlisted Graceful.

"A small, wiry, and shaggy gray mare called Felicity. From Isterrane stables, but originally from high along the rift flanks. Sure-footed and looks wild, so she shouldn't be suspicious. The transmission is a low-energy directional burst signal southward. That should be undetectable."

"And you are looking after her?"

Vero gave him a cautious smile. "Merral, try not to be too suspicious. The guys are taking it very slowly and have a metabolic monitor on her to check stress levels. She's doing fine."

"Good. I wish you'd told me, though."

"I started it off when you were in Ynysmant, and anyway, I wasn't sure it was going to work. It may not."

"I don't mind it failing. It's a good idea, typical of you. But I'm worried it will alert the intruders. It may be risky to Felicity and maybe to us. But look, just keep me in touch on it."

"Yes, I will do."

Another vehicle drew away from the ship. "Oh, Vero," Merral said, "I've been thinking. About what to do when we get to Tanaris. My feeling is that the best thing I can do is to start off with a meeting of all the leaders you have set up. The lieutenants, the chief of logistics, communications, etc. Perena, of course, as ship's captain, Anya as chief of intruder studies. Get them to introduce themselves and give me status reports. You agree?"

"Yes, that would be a good idea."

"Good. But, by the way, what are you?"

Vero chewed his lip and turned his brown eyes toward the ship. "A title for me? I have thought about it. . . . There's an old term, but it describes what I want to do. Intelligence."

"So you will be chief of intelligence?"

"Yes, why not? Chief of intelligence—" he made a slight bow—"at your service."

"Very well, but I will expect you to define exactly what you do."

"Terms of reference, *et cetera*. Yes, you will have it."

"And so, Chief, at this meeting, what else do you propose I do?"

"Oh, announce a provisional timetable for the next few days. Show them you are decisive."

Merral sighed. "But I gather the trick is to be sure that your decisions are right."

"True. That as well. But to be indecisive is to be wrong before you start. You must be decisive and decisively right."

"Help! And I suppose also at some point I must address the men? As soon as possible?"

"That would be wise. They are expecting their leader."

While he was considering an answer, Merral caught a glimpse of Perena waving at them from the side of the *Emilia Kay.*

"Well, time to fly, Vero. Tanaris beckons."

Vero left to get his bags while Merral started walking to the bulk of the *Emilia Kay* with his holdall. As he paused on the runway, waiting for Vero to catch up, he felt suddenly daunted by all that lay before him. He was strangely reminded of the Lymatov painting that, until recently, had been in Barrand's office; he could imagine a similar painting of him, now in that same genre of historical realism. He would be a small, vulnerable figure with a large bag walking across the empty black runway to the looming, freshly painted bulk of the ship. And the *Emilia Kay* would be so depicted that the name and the emblem of the Lamb and Stars would be clearly visible, as would be the late-afternoon sky in which clouds were ominously gathering. What would the title be? *Captain D'Avanos leaves Isterrane? On the way to Tanaris*? or even *The War Begins?*

Then Vero caught up with him, and Merral curtailed his imagination. The present reality was more critical than any fantasy of the future.

Besides, he reminded himself, if he failed, there might be no one to paint pictures.

36

Inside the *Emilia Kay,* gently throbbing and humming with new life, Merral and Vero found seats in the passenger compartment behind the cockpit. There were eleven other people there; most appeared to be technicians and engineers. Merral realized that all of them seemed to know who he was. *This will be the way now; the title "Captain" hangs round my neck like Lucas Ringell's identity disk.*

As if sensing his unease, Anya smiled warmly at him. "Preflight nerves, eh?"

"The flying, Anya, is probably the easy bit."

Then the engines coughed and rumbled to life, the airframe began to vibrate softly, and they rolled forward onto the main runway.

There was a long pause and then, without warning, came a sudden ear-jarring blast of thrusters and the ship began accelerating forward until, after what seemed an uncomfortably long time, it shuddered free of the ground.

Ten minutes later Merral slipped forward into the cockpit and stood quietly at the back. The view ahead out of the expansive windscreen caught his attention immediately; whatever vices the Series D might have had, poor pilot visibility was not one of them. Through the broad, bronze-tinted screen Merral could see a mosaic of small, white, fluffy clouds hanging over the brilliant blue-green sea, the golden rays of the late-afternoon sun illuminating the clouds and casting vast black shadows on the ruffled waters below. The effect was one of great beauty and charm, and Merral felt uplifted and somehow soothed. *It is a view I could watch for ages.* Then he reminded himself that today—and for the foreseeable future—preoccupying himself with the admiration of creation was something for which he and others might pay a high price. It was yet another disturbing thought.

He dragged his eyes down to look around the spacious cockpit. Only once or twice had he been in a similar position in any atmosphere craft when it was flying, and he didn't know what to expect. But he saw nothing in either the many screens and lights or the language or attitudes of Perena, the copilot, and the flight engineer to raise any alarm. All seemed ordered and calm.

Perena glanced back and motioned him to her side.

"Everything okay back there?" she asked, keeping her eyes on a multicolored display of daunting complexity.

"Fine. Noisy though."

"Yes. Ideally we would have replaced the acoustic insulation, but there were other priorities."

"And everything is all right here, Captain?"

"So far fine, Captain," she answered, an amused irony in her tone. "Barely two hours' flying time. But she's doing okay. Some fine-tuning needs to be done."

He watched her eyes flick carefully across the screen. "But no, *Emilia Kay* is one nice old lady. I have a good feeling for her."

Perena gestured forward with her head. "We are flying due south for another few minutes. Mainly to mislead anyone watching by giving the impression that we are going to one of the Farakethan Islands."

"Deception again . . . ," Merral remarked, as much to himself as to her.

"Yes, sorry. I think we shall all be forced to retake Basic Ethics when this is over." As she said it, she gazed up at him with a troubled expression. *I too am worried,* it seemed to say.

She looked back at a screen. "But, more immediately, I'm concerned by the weather. There's the tail of a storm belt coming in, and we will probably intercept it in forty minutes."

"How bad?"

"I don't know." She shrugged. "That's the fun. Vero's ensuring that all the observation satellites, including the weather monitors, were down today was clever, but it has left us blind too."

"You can't fly above it?"

"No. We are staying pretty low to keep well over the horizon from anything watching in northern Menaya."

There was a gesture from the copilot.

"The turn coming up. Watch out ahead." Perena's voice was flat.

The ship banked left gently, and as it turned, the vista ahead changed. The isolated clouds seemed to suddenly cluster, thicken, and darken, and as they did, they lost their innocence and became threatening. As if to add emphasis, the ship was buffeted slightly, and Merral reached out to hold a strut.

When he looked forward again, there was just a wall of black dense cloud ahead stretching from the sea below to a level high above them. Staring at it, Merral could make out swirling and boiling billows within the cloud barrier. A flicker of lightning illuminated the interior of a cloud column.

Although he could hear the quiet but urgent discussion occurring among the three crew members, Merral felt unable to take his eyes off the scene before him. The view seemed somehow symbolic of all that had happened over the last few months—how his life and that of Farholme had gone from an infinitely open and benevolent landscape to one over which a turbulent darkness loomed.

Perena, her voice cool and tense, interrupted his thoughts. "Merral, we are going to risk flying between the cells of the front. Sensors say it's a thin but violent weather unit. As you can see. We have about ten minutes before it gets really rough. Better make sure everybody is strapped in back there."

With a final glance at the impending cloud mass, Merral slipped back into the passenger cabin as another shudder struck the ship.

"Captain's warning," he announced as he took his seat. "Storm ahead. Fasten belts."

Merral caught a shudder of expectation from Vero and remembered that he was a bad traveler.

"You're serious?" he said, peering nervously at him.

"'Fraid so. She's says it's all your fault, switching off the weather sats."

"Ah. It seemed a good idea at the time. I have antinauseants. Oh no, they're in my bag."

"Where's that?"

"In the hold. Oh, the moment you get a new Gate here I'm back to Earth. The weather on the Made Worlds isn't for me. Not—"

"Alert! Imminent turbulence!" proclaimed a mechanical voice from above their heads.

The ship suddenly dropped as if the air had been removed from underneath it.

For a second it seemed to Merral as if his stomach had been punched skyward, then he was crushed down in his seat.

All around a great rattling and slithering erupted as unsecured objects flew around the cabin and crashed against the floor and walls. Someone's diary flew past Merral and struck the side with a crash. There were exclamations and groans around him. The *Emilia Kay* banked and then nosed slightly upward. There was more shuddering and creaking.

Above the noise, coming vaguely from somewhere below and behind the cabin, Merral was aware of a strangely ominous rumble. Perena's voice, now insistent and tense, sounded through the speaker. "Captain, Anya, can you come forward, please?"

Merral released his belt and made his way forward carefully as the ship jolted again. The worrying rumbling below them continued. As Anya joined him, he caught a glimpse of Vero reaching for a sick bag.

The strained and tense atmosphere in the cockpit and the flashing red light on Perena's screen confirmed Merral's unease. She didn't look up but gestured to an ancillary monitor.

The image on it was a wide-angle view of the hull interior and, as Merral watched, he saw a large yellow drum roll along the floor and strike a crate. He now knew the source of the rumbling.

"We have something loose among the cargo," Perena announced in a coolly precise tone. "It shouldn't have happened, but it has. Anya, is it one of yours?"

There was a cluck of distress from her sister. "Yes. It's the fifty-liter drum of disinfecting agent. Thyrol 56."

"Full strength?" Merral asked, remembering the care enforced when they used it in the lab for sterilizing equipment. There was a new, violent shuddering, and he clutched the seat back. Out of the window, he could only see a swirling blackness ahead now. Raindrops were splattering on the windscreen.

"Yes," answered Anya. "The concentrate. We assumed a potential major biohazard risk. But it should have been secured properly."

"Results if it breaks open, Sister?" The anxiety underlying Perena's level and controlled tone was all too obvious.

"Not good. It's horribly oxidizing; it will dissolve strapping and maybe insulation."

Perena didn't look up. "And if it meets explosives?"

There was the briefest of pauses. "Guess . . ."

A new jolting began. Ahead, a flash of lightning sliced through the darkness.

Perena flicked an urgent finger at the engineer next to her. "Pierre, start rehearsing the routine for ejecting the cargo module."

Merral caught the engineer's eyes widen. "Ejecting? Yes, Captain."

Perena glanced at the hold image, where the yellow barrel was still careering around.

"Merral, if I feel it's leaking I have no option but to shed the whole cargo module. It won't do the aerodynamics or the mission any good, but we may land in one piece. Better get a couple of men to try to secure it. Fast."

She flicked a switch. "The hold microphone is on for anybody to communicate with me. I'll give you warning once we start the ejection sequence. Sister, get back to your seat; there's more turbulence to come."

The ship bounced around again as Merral made his way back to the passenger compartment. Ten faces with various degrees of anxiety on them looked up at him; an eleventh was too busy burying itself in a large brown bag. For a brief moment, Merral paused, realizing that, as captain, he could just order them to do it while he stayed up with the others. Somehow, though, he felt that wouldn't be right.

"Lorrin! You!" he yelled at the two men at the end of the row of seats. "Follow me!"

As the men unbuckled themselves, Merral made his way down to the hold. As he went down the spiral staircase, further jolts bounced him off his feet, throwing him against the walls.

The rumbling noise was louder at the bottom of the stairs. As he triggered the hatch switch, he saw for the first time the multiple seals around the door to the cargo module. It came back to him that on the model he had made in his childhood, part of the fun had been sliding the specialist load components in and out.

As the hatch door slid open, a pungent chemical aroma struck Merral. *We have some leakage already.* He paused, peering across the darkened cavern of the hold as he tried to evaluate the scene. The ship was buffeted again. Ahead the yellow drum rolled angrily backward and forward.

Perena's voice spoke from above him. "Okay, Merral, I have you on camera. Is it leaking?"

"Well . . . there's a smell."

"Okay. It's leaking. We'd better start preparations for ejection."

There was a jolt. Everything in the hold seemed to lurch and creak. The drum struck a crate with a loud crack.

"Perena, wait. I think it's a minor leak so far."

"Negative, Merral. Pierre has pointed out that we can only safely eject on the straight and level. We have to do it before we hit the main belt of turbulence."

Merral looked at the hold. "Give me five minutes. Please."

"Three." There was a note in her voice that forbade further negotiation. Through a porthole a flash of lightning flickered.

"Okay. Perena, can you put her into a smooth climb? Say, five degrees. I want the barrel to slowly, *slowly* roll to the rear."

"Okay."

Merral turned to the men behind him. "We have to get that barrel upright and secure it. And quickly. Try not to get any fluid on your hands."

The ship began to tilt gently nose upward. After a moment's hesitation, the barrel began to roll backward. Then it accelerated and for a horrible moment, Merral thought it was going to smash against the far wall, but the tilt eased off and it thudded to a stop.

"Now!" Merral shouted. He ran across the hold, winding his way past the boxes and the edge of the hoverer. The hold seemed full of bouncing and clattering objects. Under the lights, he could see glistening smears of fluid on the barrel. On the floor, though, there were only a few small drops. So far, at least, any leakage had been minor.

Handling the barrel, he realized, was going to be difficult, and he wished he had gloves. Trying to ignore the now persistent shuddering, he steadied himself against a sled, looking around for something to handle the barrel with. There was another flash outside, and he glimpsed the window smeared with rain.

To his right Merral saw a pile of familiar gray fabric cylinders in a box labeled "Tents." He jerked one of them out and threw it to Lorrin, who caught it.

"Open it!" he shouted. The shaking was almost regular now, as if the ship were bouncing over a corrugated surface.

Lorrin tore it open and folds of green fabric spilled out. "Use it to push the drum upright!" Merral yelled, trying to make himself heard over the noises of the lurching ship.

As the two moved to the bouncing drum, Merral moved back, searching for something to lash it against the wall. Spotting the end of some line protruding from a holdall, he pulled out a coil of rope. He ran back with it to where the men had managed to get the barrel upright, smelling the chemical again and noticing that the floor around them was slippery. The hold was humid, and Merral was aware that he was sweating profusely.

Perena's voice echoed about them. "Merral! We have to initiate separation shortly. Is it secured yet?"

Merral looked at the barrel, aware that the rope was still in his hands.

"Almost. Can't you wait?"

"No. I need a decision. Can you guarantee it's safe?"

Lightning flashed, so close that even through the portholes it illuminated the hold. An instant later, a peal of thunder rang through the hull and the lights above them flickered briefly.

Merral glanced at the men by him, aware of their pale, sweat-beaded faces watching him. *Lord,* he prayed, *give me wisdom.* He was aware that his options were few. If he told Perena to stop the ejection sequence and he couldn't tie the Thyrol 56 safely in place, they might well blow up and perish. Yet if he let the cargo be ejected, they might never get another chance against the intruders. Merral wanted to shout, *I've been captain for less than twelve hours and already I have to make an appalling decision!*

"Perena, cancel the ejection procedure," he said. "Repeat, cancel the ejection procedure. On my orders. If we blow up, I'll take responsibility."

"Cancelled on your orders," came back the quiet voice. There was a further jolt. "So if we blow up, you'll apologize as we wait to enter heaven, eh?"

For once she sounds like her sister.

With the two men pushing the barrel against the wall through the fabric, Merral looped the rope round a strut. Trying to ride with the bucking of the ship, he thrust the other end round a hole in a girder on the other side. With each jolt, Merral half expected to be thrown free. Somehow he managed to wrap the cord outside the tent fabric and pull it as tight as he could.

The barrel stiffened upright and Lorrin, his face running with sweat, gave a cracked cheer.

"See if you can find the leak," Merral snapped as he tightened the knot, desperately hoping that the barrel was not irreparably cracked. He tied off the rope awkwardly and started another loop across the barrel.

"Sensors say severe turbulence coming up in less than a minute," Perena's insistent tone sounded from above them. "We can't turn back."

"The cap has been loosened, sir," Lorrin shouted as the second loop was tied.

The ship lurched again and Merral could hear the Thyrol sloshing about in the drum tank. As he caught a fresh waft of its acrid fumes, his eyes watered. Now he grabbed a corner of the tent, found the cap, and twisted tight. For a desperate moment the fabric, greasy with liquid, would not grip the cap. Then it caught and Merral felt the lid tighten under his grip.

"You guys—get back! I'll finish this off."

They looked at each other, hesitating.

"Let me do it, sir!" Lorrin shouted.

"No! Get back! That's an order!"

The ship seemed to fall again. Merral held on, and when he had stopped being jolted about, he screwed the cap further, until it would go no tighter.

Gasping, he stood back, bracing himself against a strut and another crate. Out of the corner of his eye, he could see the others now exiting the hold.

Without warning the ship dropped.

The force was such that, for a moment, Merral realized that every part of him was off the ground. Then he crashed down, his shoulder jarring painfully against a crate. Yet, although the barrel had bounced up and down, it had stayed lashed against the wall.

Ignoring the pain in his shoulder, Merral stepped back and braced himself against a crate as further jolts struck the ship. It would have to do.

He wiped his forehead with the back of his hand and carefully, mindful of his throbbing shoulder, he turned and made his way back to the hatch.

Back in the passenger compartment, aware that he smelt of disinfecting agent, Merral lurched back into his seat and strapped himself in. There was the sound of clapping, and he looked up to see everyone applauding him. Embarrassed, Merral shrugged and gestured to the beaming Lorrin and the other man.

"Very nice, Captain. And you two—many thanks," Perena commented.

"So we may survive, eh, Vero?" Merral said, turning to his friend.

But Vero, his head deep inside the bag, was preoccupied with being violently sick.

An hour or so later, the appalling bouncing and shuddering began to wane and, shortly afterward, Merral felt the ship descending in a slow, low-angle flight path. Despite the limited illumination on the landing strip, Perena brought the *Emilia Kay* in smoothly to land on the wet surface. Or maybe, thought Merral, it just seemed smooth after what he had passed through.

"Welcome to Tanaris," announced Perena. "Sorry about the flight."

One by one, Merral and the other passengers filed down the stairs, picked up their bags, walked out of the ship, and stood on the gritty basalt runway. Under the thick purple-black clouds that hung overhead, a premature night was setting in. Here at least, though, the storm seemed to have already passed over, and there was only an occasional flurry of heavy raindrops. Far away, westward over the seething sea, the lightning and thunder still erupted spasmodically.

Merral, rejoicing to have his feet on the ground, said a silent but heartfelt prayer of thanks. He looked around in the humid gloom, aware that, by his side, Vero was feebly propping himself up against the fuselage. Beyond the strip, the lights of the runway showed a somber landscape of bare and jagged black rocks broken only by the occasional low tree. From the other end of the runway, a line of paired lights revealed a column of approaching vehicles.

Merral saw that Perena was next to him. "Is Vero all right?" she asked in a voice of quiet concern.

"Yes," Merral said, "but it's the last time he will switch the weather sats off when there is a risk of him flying. Nice landing, though."

"It wasn't hard, really. The Tanaris strip was made originally for emergency landings for in-system shuttles if Isterrane was closed with bad weather. I think it's the longest on the planet. I could have come down vertically, but you need to be absolutely certain of your equipment to do that." Then she lowered her voice and whispered to Merral. "Look—while the vehicles are arriving—come into the hold with me."

Inside the ship, the smell of the disinfecting agent was still powerful and Perena sniffed dubiously. "Nasty stuff. Anyway, full marks. We survived. So you made a bold and decisive decision."

"Thanks. And if we hadn't survived?"

"It wouldn't have been bold and decisive; it would have been rash, foolhardy, and badly judged. We won this one. But you got a lot of credit for your action, and you made the right decision."

"It wasn't easy." Merral was surprised at the emotion in his voice. "Would you really have ejected the module?"

Perena shrugged unhappily. "Under the old rules, yes. By letting you do this I broke with Standard Operating Procedures. But do those old rules apply in what is, effectively, a time of war?" She sighed. "You see, Merral, we are all having to learn new things and new attitudes."

Making no further comment, Perena walked over to the barrel and peered around it.

"What are you looking for?" Merral asked.

"I want to find out why it broke loose," she said, squatting and staring to one side of the drum. "Under normal conditions we'd have a full inquiry. There's no time here. But I'd still like to know. It's very odd—almost unprecedented—for a load to break free. But see, here's where it was attached." She leaned forward and lifted up a broken strand of silvery webbing. "Okay, so it snapped. But why, eh, Merral?" She looked at him, her face angular in the hold lighting.

Merral shrugged.

"Well," she said, "we have an imaging record of the loading, so we will find who was responsible. And I'll get this looked at in daylight." She peered closely at it and muttered, "You know I think this is old. It's got an orange safety thread in it."

Merral bent down and looked at it, noting that he, too, could make out a fine orange line along it. Safety threads occurred in most critical rope or straps, whether for climbing or for lashing down equipment. Green indicated pristine condition with full strength, but over time and use that shifted to yellow, orange, and then red to indicate a progressive weakening. It was a well-known ruling that, for critical tasks, you never used less than green. He turned to Perena. "Okay. Let me have a full report. We nearly lost the mission before we started."

"We could have lost us."

There were noises at the hold door. A tall, green-clad man with a long face dominated by a hooked nose climbed into the hold. "Captain D'Avanos? Captain Lewitz?"

"Indeed," said Merral, struck by the way the man's wide smile was accentuated by his thin dark moustache. There was an awkward salute and smile on the broad face.

"Lieutenant Ferenc Thuron, sir. Welcome to Tanaris."

"Thank you." *Thuron,* Merral thought, going through the list of names in his mind. "Ah yes. You're a team leader?"

"Yes, sir."

"Your team will come in from the west. Right, Ferenc?"

"Yes, sir, but I am afraid everyone calls me Frankie." The gentle brown eyes were apologetic. "The Ferenc was because my dad was into the Old Hungarian at the time I was born, but it's confusing to spell. So it's Frankie. But only if it's no trouble. You're the boss."

Merral found it hard not to smile back. "Trouble, Lieutenant, is a relative thing, and you going from Ferenc to Frankie does not really rate in the scheme of things. Not now. Does it, Captain Lewitz?"

She grinned. "Hardly. Not now."

Frankie looked around and sniffed. "If you don't mind me saying, sir, you haven't half had the ship cleaned out, have you?"

"A leak, Frankie."

"Yeah. I guess that explains it. I'm ready to take you to the base. Any immediate instructions, sir?"

"Only that I want to have a meeting with you, the experts, and the other team leaders later. We need to get started here fast."

"Sounds okay, sir."

As he exited the hold, Merral saw, by vehicles, other men wearing green. With a shock of recognition, Merral realized they were in uniform, and suddenly the significance of what he was about struck him. *We have made soldiers, and I must lead them.* It was all he could do to stop himself from trembling.

Zak, smartly dressed in a green uniform, was waiting for Merral at the main tent.

"Sir," he said, with a smart salute, "good to see you here. Welcome to Camp Alpha."

"'Camp Alpha'? I thought this was Tanaris?"

Zak looked nonplussed. "We figured, sir, we ought to give it a name that wasn't on maps. So if anyone overheard they wouldn't know the address. That's what they did."

"I see," Merral said, trying to ignore feelings that he was utterly out of his depth. "Camp Alpha, it is. Everything okay, er . . . Lieutenant?"

"Good, sir. Do you want me to brief you now?"

"I need to change my clothes."

"Yes, sir, your uniform's in the tent there. There are a couple of tunics and trousers; we weren't sure of your size. You'll want to put them on straightaway."

"Thank you, Zak." Merral forced himself to smile. "Let's have the briefing later. I want to meet all the lieutenants, in half an hour, say, at seven-thirty."

"That's 1930 hours, sir?"

"Nineteen—? Yes, of course, Lieutenant, that's what I meant to say. Pass the word around."

"I'll give the order, sir."

Merral hesitated. "Yes, well, whatever. Go on and do it, Lieutenant."

"Yes, sir!" Zak said with a snap in his voice, saluted, turned, and left.

Merral walked into the tent, closed the flap, and stared at the uniforms on his bed. He sat on the folding chair and put his head in his hands.

"Oh, Lord, they've picked the wrong man," he said in quiet prayer.

Less than an hour later, the last few of the ten men and women Merral had summoned came into the office tent and took their seats around a long collapsible table. As the chattering and introductions slowly died away, Merral, feeling a little more sure of himself, gazed around again.

On his immediate left were five men in the same uniform that he now wore. All were in their mid- or late twenties, and Merral, whose twenty-seventh birthday was still six months away, felt slightly encouraged that he would not have to order men about who were much older than him. He reviewed again who they were and what their responsibilities would be if it came to fighting. Closest to him was Zak, sitting bolt upright in his chair as if he found it perfectly natural to be on a remote island wearing a military uniform and preparing to do battle. It wasn't just pretense either, Merral reminded himself. By all accounts, Zak had excelled in organizing the setting up of the camp and had been designated as the leader of the team that was to approach the ship from the north.

Next to him was the lean, tall figure of gentle, apologetic Frankie Thuron, who, it turned out, was a chemistry research student and a long-distance runner. Beyond Frankie sat Fred Huang, a large, long-limbed man who wore his thick and lengthy dark hair tied back and who seemed to have a permanently fixed grin and loud, cheery voice. Fred, Merral knew, was a marine biologist and an accomplished diver from one of the smaller islands of the Mazarma Chain. It was Fred, Merral reminded himself, who would go with the diplomatic team and attempt first contact.

Forcing himself not to think about whether Fred's mission could succeed, Merral moved his gaze to the tall figure of Barry Narandel slouched in a chair beyond him. Barry, down to lead the reserves, had his hair cut so close that it was almost stubble and thoughtful blue eyes that seemed to drift around in a lazy scrutiny. The fifth of the line of uniformed men was Lucas "Luke" Tenerelt, who had been designated chaplain, his green uniform marked with improvised bronze clerical flashings. Merral knew from his folder that Luke, whose almost gaunt face and piercing dark eyes were accentuated by the basic lighting in the tent, was in his late thirties and had, after an outstanding dual-track theology and engineering degree, become a leader in his home congregation in Maraplant.

As the silence deepened, Merral turned his gaze to those on his right. There was Perena, the still-gray-faced Vero, and next to him, looking unusually solemn, Anya. Beyond her was the head of communications, the short but strikingly blonde Maria Dalphey, and next to her, Lucia "Lucy" Dmitri. Lucy had been seconded from the Farholme Atmosphere Transport Board and made responsible for the logistics; she was a willowy brunette with green eyes, and Merral was struck by her look of quiet competence.

So, the solemn thought came to Merral, *this is my team.* Well, his first impressions suggested that Vero, Corradon, and Clemant had chosen well. Merral opened his folder to a blank piece of paper. "Gentlemen and ladies," he began, wondering even as he said it whether it was the right mode of address, "I just have a few things to say, and then in half an hour we shall adjourn for the evening meal."

He caught the grimace on Vero's pallid face. "For those who feel like eating, that is. But I thought it would be good if Luke, as our chaplain, would pray for us."

Luke nodded, got firmly to his feet, and as everybody bowed their heads, prayed clearly in a loud, confident, and booming voice. "Lord of the Assembly, we pray that You go with us in our planning and preparations. We pray too that we do not forget You in the urgency of the hour and that You protect us all through the blood of Jesus, the Lamb of God, from all the powers and principalities of evil that we face. In the name of the Father, the Son, and the Holy Spirit. *Amen.*"

Merral felt that if Luke had any doubts about the task ahead, he kept them well hidden.

As Luke sat down, Merral looked around. "By any reckoning," he said, "the last meeting like this happened in the Rebellion. So I suppose this is, very sadly, a historic occasion." He watched heads shake in agreement, then went on. "The schedule is this: After the meal, I want to address everybody briefly. Then we have three days of training ahead. Tomorrow I want an early morning meeting of us all for a progress report. At eight." He caught a glance from Zak. "That is, 0800 hours. I would like to see you individually during the rest of the day. Is that okay?"

There were glances and nods of agreement. "Fine then. I want us now to go around. Briefly say who you are, what you see your job as being, and what stage you think your work is at now. Then we shall go and eat after that."

There were more nods.

"So then, let's start with Zak here. . . ."

When they all went to eat, Merral felt so preoccupied about his forthcoming speech that he found he had lost his appetite. After picking at the first course, he made an apology and went and stood outside the mess tent. His shoulder still ached.

In the darkness above him he could glimpse patches of fierce stars where the clouds had been ripped open. The air was still moist from the rain. Just beyond him, in a dip in the ground illuminated by a delicate spiderweb of silver lights, stretched the accommodation tents. Seventy tents, Merral reflected, perhaps two hundred people in total. Over half preparing to fight, the rest to support. All puzzled, all uncertain, and all looking to him for decisions and wisdom.

Merral watched the scene as he tried to rehearse his words, noting the tents with their eerie internal glow, the reflected glitter of the lights off the muddy pathways, and the shadowy figures padding to and fro. The sight in itself was not novel to him; he had camped a lot, but those campsites had never sounded like this. There were sounds aplenty here tonight, but there was no laughter and no noise of children, and all the voices he could make out were serious. Slowly, one by one, the men and women drifted toward a broad, level square that must once have been an extension of the runway.

A tall figure came over to him from the tent; it was Frankie. "Sir, sorry to disturb you. But it'll soon be time for you to say something. There are a few guys we've posted as what they call perimeter guards and a couple of guys in the Comms center, but otherwise everyone will be here soon and waiting to hear you. And we are recording it for posterity. If that's all right?"

Merral shook his head. "Why not, Frankie? Okay. Let's go."

They had made him a low platform out of stacked containers and turned lights onto it. Merral went and stood silently to one side, just out of the arc of illumination, watching the company as it gathered and half wondering whether he should have arranged for amplification. The dazzle of the lighting was such that he knew he would be unable to make out more than silhouettes facing him. Perhaps it was best he could not see their faces; he was nervous enough already. He had spoken regularly at conferences and meetings, but never at anything like this. Indeed, it occurred to him with a tingle of strange excitement, the last person to do anything exactly like this was the man whose identity disk hung cold and light against his chest. And he had been dead for a hundred and twenty centuries. Perhaps, Merral suddenly thought, he should have found the famous clip of Lucas Ringell briefing his men before the attack on the Centauri station.

Frankie nodded to him, teeth shining in the glare. "I'd say that they are about all here, sir. So whenever you are ready."

Merral clapped him on the back and walked up slowly onto the platform. There he paused briefly, tensing involuntarily, as an expectant silence fell on the crowd before him. He was uncomfortably aware that they were all staring at him. He paused. *So, help me, God.*

"Ladies and gentlemen; troops and technicians; colleagues and comrades; above all, brothers and sisters in the Lord." Merral paused, listening to his words die away in the silence, reassured that he was loud enough, that the words had come out at all. "I am unclear which of these titles I ought to address you with. So I address you with them all. I am Merral Stefan D'Avanos. Of Ynysmant, Menaya, Farholme."

Take your time. Don't fumble it out of nerves, keep making pauses. "Until yesterday I was Forester D'Avanos. My present title, given to me by our representatives, is that of captain of the Farholme Defense Unit. It is my hope to return shortly to my former title."

Merral paused again, weighing his next words, relieved that nerves had not caused him to dry up. The stress was lifting; he felt more at ease. "Indeed, it is my real hope and prayer that all of us will shortly be able to return to our old professions. I would wish nothing more than that this extraordinary episode we have become drawn into be ended. I look forward to it being a footnote on one of the many pages of the history of the Assembly. However, our wishes are one thing and our duty is another."

He stopped, let the words register, and continued. "I want to say to you that I have not taken up this task lightly. Indeed, I refused the commission for two days while I returned to my hometown to think it over. But what I found there convinced me that, however great the many risks of this operation are, the risks of *not* confronting the intruders are greater. They must be faced. If they are not, then all that we are may perish."

The electric silence continued. "We do not know entirely what we face; all we know is that the intruders are from beyond the Assembly and are hostile to us. As some of you have apparently heard, Sentinel Enand and I have encountered them and were forced, reluctantly, to fight them for our lives. I plan to have a full briefing with the leaders on everything we know about them tomorrow. Now I will only say that they are strange and frightening and hostile, but also vulnerable. By the grace of God, our first contact resulted in substantial losses to them. I should warn you, though, that this may simply have been because they were caught unawares. They demonstrated the possession of weapons that we do not have. I have since learned that they have tried, and to some extent succeeded, in entering our data files in the Library at Isterrane. It is also almost certain that it was they who caused the destruction of the Gate."

He heard someone say, "Told you so," and a ripple of angry whispering ran through the crowd. Merral paused, letting everyone quiet down. An almost tangible silence returned. "Above all, I should warn you that there is a good deal of evidence that they are evil . . . and that they can transmit evil." Merral felt hundreds of eyes staring at him. "If I may speak of something which is almost beyond my understanding, I want to warn you all that we may be moving into a spiritual atmosphere that is like nothing any of us has ever known. Or that anyone in the entire history of the Assembly has known since the Rebellion was ended."

There were mutterings of agreement here and there, and Merral wondered if others had felt it. "All I can say," he said, "is that of late I have been reading those parts of the Old and New Covenant writings that deal with the struggles against evil with a greater interest and a greater sense of reality and relevance than ever before. In the past when I read them, I, like you, always saw them largely as a sobering history. They recorded a time that we could rejoice was behind us. I have now come to realize that they may not represent just our past, but also our future. To every one of you I say this: watch; be mindful of your thoughts and words."

He stopped for a moment. There was total silence. In the western distance, where a faint purple glow marked the remains of sunset, a fork of lightning flashed. He had planned to end here, but for some reason, he found himself continuing.

"In this present conflict, we have all been given a part to play. Some of us may find we dislike the part we have been given. Yet that is irrelevant. I, and you, must play the part we have been given as best we can."

Merral caught his breath, aware of the tension all around him, and continued. "According to the present plan, we have just under eighty hours before contact. We need to make the most of every minute between now and then. I'll take no questions now. I'm going to hand over to the chaplain to lead us now in prayer and a hymn." He hesitated, suddenly overawed almost beyond bearing by the situation. "God be with you. With us. With the Assembly," he said, his voice suddenly thickening with emotion.

As his words died away, Merral had no idea what reaction he would get: neither clapping nor prayers would have surprised him. Then a voice sang out, shaky at first but growing in strength:

"Lord of all worlds, whose mighty power

"Sustains your people hour by hour . . ."

One by one, others joined the voice until everybody was singing the great anthem, and the air seemed to vibrate with the words as if they were a challenge flung at the darkness.

Along the horizon, silver lightning flickered again. In support or in defiance? wondered Merral.

37

Over the next two days, Merral found that he had very little time to reflect on how things were going. It was not for want of trying. As a matter of the highest priority, he endeavored to make time to be alone and to evaluate progress. Yet, no matter how carefully he scheduled events, he found it impossible to make the space. Something else always seemed to seize any time slot he left vacant.

Although he delegated as much as he dared, he felt obliged to keep something of a personal eye on what was happening. Everything was so new that he felt it essential to participate to some extent in order to learn what the tasks involved. So he took part on the firing range with the modified XM2s, or "cutter guns" as the soldiers now called them. He strapped himself into the sleds with their newly added boosters and was buffeted with the teams over the waves of the nearby lagoon that they used to simulate Fallambet Lake Five. If he wasn't the fastest out and up the beach from the sled, he was up there with the leaders. He flew with the reserve team in the hold of the *Emilia Kay* and rappelled with them out of the open doors and down the swaying thirty-meter-long ropes to the ground while the hot engine thrust bellowed and roared just meters away from his kicking legs.

As a point of principle, he took part in the training drills with the explosive charges and the expanding wedges and, amid cheers, personally felled an isolated and ailing palm tree—standing in for a landing leg—with a circlet of planar explosives. He even took part on one of the cross-country runs carrying gear after a hint that some people were finding it tough. In the course of all these activities, which had left him bruised and tired, he had become better acquainted with the men. Now, after two days, he knew most of them by name, and they all knew him and seemed to respect him. And, as far as he could tell from his reading of that long-dead world where war had been a way of life, these were all good things for a military leader.

Yet Merral's time was not just eaten away in activities; it was also taken up by the need for discussions and decisions. There was also a lot of debate over strategy, and the plans for the assault were slowly refined. After consultation with Vero, it was decided that Merral would go with Frankie's team, which was approaching from the west. From the western side of the lake, he ought to have a good view of the intruder ship and—critically—be able to observe first-hand the response that the diplomatic team received.

The decisions Merral had to make seemed endless. Everything was so new that the team leaders were always coming to him to clarify some point of protocol, a safety ruling, or an issue of discipline. Strangely, the one leader who bothered him least was Vero. He was now almost permanently surrounded by three young men of his "intelligence group," and the four of them were often closeted together in an isolated tent where animated discussions could frequently be heard.

One of Vero's contributions was, however, a disappointment. On the afternoon of the second day, the sentinel had announced that the progress of Felicity had been slower than expected and that the horse was still ten kilometers away from the lake. Privately, Merral wondered whether they would be at the lake before she was.

Urgent and unpredictable incidents took up time. Despite a reduction of the battery power on the cutter guns to 5 percent strength, a persisting habit of firing before aiming had resulted in an unacceptable level of minor burns. More seriously, two men broke limbs because of overzealous assaults out of the *Emilia Kay*. Following consultation with Dr. Felix Azhadi, the grizzled veteran trauma-care surgeon who had been persuaded to be the medical officer, they reviewed procedures and sent a message to Isterrane, asking for a dozen extra men to be sent. In one of the personnel shifts that resulted, Lorrin Venn found himself shifted from the reserves to Frankie's team. When Merral saw him hours later, he was whistling through a broad grin.

In the end, after two days of hectic busyness, Merral decided that he had to make time to think. Noting that he was exactly forty-eight hours away from the planned contact, he set his alarm for just before dawn and, after a quarter of an hour in prayer and Bible reading, put on running gear. He briefed a bleary-eyed Frankie, yawning apologetically over his cup of coffee, and then, as the first rays of the sun struck the craggy rocks, set off jogging up to the rocky crest of the ridge that dominated Tanaris. He ran slowly, aware that, even by Farholme's low standards, the island's bare and rocky landscape was unforgiving.

Twenty minutes later, Merral gasped his way past a sentry onto the summit ridge.

Regaining his breath, he slowed to a labored walk and strolled out onto an overhanging rock slab that formed a viewing point. Here, with the emphasis granted by the low-angle sun, he could see the *Emilia Kay* at the southern end of the runway, the tents where lines of people were assembling for breakfast, and the lagoon where they practiced to the north. *So, tomorrow evening we fly, and this make-believe practice world of Tanaris gets replaced by the reality of Fallambet Lake Five. Are we prepared?*

It was, he realized, an unanswerable question. Prepared for what? How could anyone make any prediction when faced with something as totally unknown as this? Warfare, he knew, had always been a reckless and uncertain business. Yet even in the endless wars of the far past, men had always known that they faced other men or the machines of men. *Now, though, we do not even know what we face.*

Merral sighed. Realistically, he knew, all they could aim to do was the best possible. With regard to the men of the assault teams, he sensed everywhere a rising confidence coupled with a growing discipline and skill. But were any—or all of them together—enough to outweigh the total lack of experience?

As Merral thought about the probable conflict, he was aware of something that tugged at a corner of his mind, something outstanding that he had to do. While he was attempting to pursue the thought, he heard a call of "Sir!"

The sentry approached, clutching a low-power short-range communicator.

"Yes, Lennis. What is it?"

"A message, sir. The freighter *Henrietta Pollard* is coming in to land. In fact, I reckon you can see it." He pointed at a small black dot low above the western skyline.

In addition to bearing the remaining supplies, the flight carried the dozen replacement men as well as the pair who were to try diplomacy with the intruders. Was there to be no chance of escaping his responsibilities?

"Thanks, Lennis," he sighed. "I'd better go on down."

Merral had barely had time to shower and change before two visitors were shown into his office and the fabric flap lowered behind them. They were a man and woman, both of late middle age, and the first thing that struck Merral was how elegant they looked. Perhaps, he thought as they shook hands, the smartness was especially marked because of the new world of sweating, uniformed men that he seemed to now dwell in.

"I'm Erika Nateen," the lady said with a polite, tired smile. Her accent was not quite that of Farholme.

"Van Denern. Louis Van Denern," the man added in a rather precise way as he looked around the tent with cool, evaluative gray eyes. He had a rather pale complexion, and Merral wondered if, like Vero, he was a bad flyer.

"Welcome," Merral answered, uncomfortably aware that, despite the shower, he was still sweating from his run. "Merral D'Avanos, recently forester, now—by an act of Providence—captain. And yet hoping to be forester again very shortly. Please take a seat. You had a good flight?"

As they sat on the chairs, they looked at each other as if for reassurance. "Yes," Erika answered. "An early start but otherwise fine. Representative Corradon—who sends you his greetings—was anxious not to obviously disrupt the flying schedule. The best way of doing that was to squeeze in the early morning flight for us on the—whatever it was called."

"Henrietta Pollard," Louis added in a tone that suggested he liked accuracy.

Merral realized he was overlooking hospitality. "Can I order you a drink? or breakfast?"

"Just a coffee, please," Erika said with a formal smile that reminded Merral of one of the teachers at his junior school.

"Water," Louis said firmly. "Just water. I presume it is sterile?"

"Oh yes."

Merral gave an order to one of the guards and then sat back down in his chair. "So," he said, looking at his guests, "you are our diplomatic team?"

The visitors looked at each other and Erika seemed to sigh slightly.

"Yes," she answered with what Merral felt was a lack of enthusiasm. He stared at both of the newcomers again, feeling slightly puzzled. Somehow, they were not what he had expected.

"Can I ask something?" Merral said. "Why did you volunteer for this? You do realize that this is likely to be risky?"

Again, he caught a shared, confiding look passing between them. It was almost as if they were married to each other, something that he knew wasn't the case. Erika gestured for Louis to speak.

"I am a language teacher," he replied in his rather stiff way. "Isterrane University. Grammar is my specialty. I have five historic languages, plus Communal and Farholmen, of course. And I am an old friend of Anwar Corradon."

"I see," answered Merral, wondering whether he would answer the second question.

Louis put his head slightly on one side for a moment. "Now, as for the risk . . . I am sixty-five, a widower, and I am—I suppose—one of the few medical casualties of the loss of the Gate. Other than those on the *Schütz*."

"I was not aware there were any."

Louis nodded in a slight but precise way. "Oh yes. I have a degenerative liver disease coupled with an oversensitive immune system. A tailored prosthetic liver was on order. My hepatic specialist assures me that if we have a new Gate in fifty years, it will be around forty-eight too late. More or less."

That, thought Merral, *is as elegant a circumlocution as I have ever heard for saying "I have two years to live."*

"We are honored to have you with us," he said.

"Thank you, Captain," responded Louis with a little bow of the head.

"And, Erika, what about you?"

She gave him a pained look. "I'm not from Farholme; I'm from Bannermene."

"Our next-door neighbor. We say here that it's the next best thing."

"And we say the same about you. Well, I work on Assembly government protocols for our sector. I was caught here by the Gate's loss—*destruction.* Call it what you will."

"Ah, I see."

"Yes, all my family are—" she glanced skyward—"over there. I too know Anwar Corradon, of course. He asked if I would volunteer for something difficult. If these intruders do have the technology to go through Below-Space, then I would certainly like us to get it."

"So you can go home?"

"Of course. But equally, if they are evil, which I gather we suspect, then I don't want them going on to the next system and wiping out their Gate. I don't want what happened here to happen there."

"A fair point."

Merral was thinking what to say next when the drinks arrived.

As Erika drank her coffee and Louis cautiously sipped his water, Merral outlined the plan for them to approach openly. He watched them carefully for their response.

Louis just shrugged in a polite way. "What you've said is about what we were told. How many people are there with us on this hoverer?"

"Fred Huang—your lieutenant—suggested four. The only arms I can offer are bush knives, which are now slightly modified and probably more effective."

"Do they work?" asked Erika.

"Oh yes," Merral replied, rather reluctantly. "They work. At close range." He tried not to think about his own experiences. "And we are also giving you smoke canisters. If there is trouble, Fred will tip them overboard. They float, and they may give you a screen to escape behind." The smoke canisters had been Vero's idea.

Erika bent over to whisper something in Louis's ear. Whatever it was, Merral decided it was well received, because he nodded agreement.

"Captain," Louis said, leaning forward, "Erika is suggesting that we reduce the crew going with us. To the minimum. Two, I would think. A pilot and this Lieutenant Huang. As you gather, we are not particularly concerned about our own lives. But I am—no, *we* are—about those of others."

Merral evaluated the request for a moment before answering. "Very well, I accept that suggestion. I will talk to Lieutenant Huang about that. So you are not very optimistic about a negotiated settlement?"

"No," Louis said firmly, and he put down his glass with a look of slight distaste. "I've talked with Anwar, and I can make my own deductions. If they wanted to talk they would have done so earlier."

He peered into the empty glass and then looked up with sad eyes. "If I were you, Captain, I would prepare for the worst."

After Erika and Louis had gone to the tents assigned to them, Merral sat down to check the manifest from the *Henrietta Pollard* and was encouraged to see that it had brought the dozen men needed and the outstanding equipment. As he put the manifest down on the table, he heard the sound of the freighter taking off on its way back to Isterrane. *The next time engines like that roar over this island, it will be us on our way north.*

A few minutes later, his guard admitted Perena, accompanied by a pale-faced young man in civilian clothes whom he did not recognize.

"Sorry to interrupt you, Captain," she said as she saluted, her face stiff.

"You are always welcome, Per—Captain Lewitz," Merral said, rising and saluting back. He was wondering at her formality when he noticed the worried look of her companion.

"Have we met before?" he asked, extending his hand.

There was a look of hesitation in the man's face as he shook hands. "No . . . sir. Not so as you'd remember. I was loading the *Emilia Kay* the other day when you came through. I'm Leonas Vorranet."

"Loading, eh, Leonas?" There was something about both his and Perena's manner that allowed Merral to guess at what was to come. "Take a seat, both of you."

The young man sat down and stared at the floor as Perena began to speak. "After our problems with the barrel I made inquiries. Leonas very kindly volunteered to come over from Isterrane in the *Henrietta Pollard* and tell us what happened. Exactly."

Leonas tilted his head up enough that Merral could see his eyes, deep blue and tinged by guilt.

"Sir, I've come to apologize," he said, his voice faint and strained. "It's my fault. Somehow, I used old strapping. Stuff that was already on the ship. Not the new stuff."

Perena looked hard at Merral. "That's what tests confirm," she said. "The strapping was decades old and decaying inside. We thought we had removed it all, but there must have been bits lying around."

"I see, Leonas," Merral said, already wondering whether he was supposed to discipline this man and, if so, how. "But wasn't it obvious that it was outdated? It's color coded."

There was a long pause and the blue eyes looked down at the floor. "Well, it was really, sir. But I was . . . careless, I suppose. I didn't think it mattered. There was the hurry. I suppose I thought that Assembly standards are always overcautious." There was a pitiable tone in his voice. "I'm sorry."

Merral walked round to the front of his desk and sat on it. *What do I do with this fellow?* He saw that Perena was frowning.

"And, Leonas," Merral asked, "I take it Captain Lewitz has told you how she nearly had to eject the cargo module because of your stupidity?"

"Sir," interrupted Perena, her diffident tone suggesting how unhappy she was about intruding, "if I may make a distinction; I have had a longer time to think about this. It was *not* stupidity. Leonas is not stupid. It was *negligence.* In some ways that is more worrying."

"I see. . . . Negligence, eh?" Merral wished he'd had a chance to look that term up in the dictionary and also in the section on military discipline in the handbook. "As in carelessness? Perena, I suggest we send this fellow off to Luke while we have a talk together."

"I think that would be very wise," she said. "Very wise indeed."

Merral turned to Leonas. "I accept your apologies; I will decide what to do with you later. In the meantime go and find the chaplain and tell him why you are here."

Leonas bowed his head in a way that Merral thought was possibly indicative of gratitude. "Thank you, sir," he said and rose to his feet.

As he went to the tent door, Perena called out, "Oh, Mr. Vorranet. One last thing. Would you just tell Captain D'Avanos where you are from?"

"I don't see as—," Leonas began, but Merral saw Perena's thin eyebrows rise in irritation and he seemed to change his manner. "Yes, sir. Larrenport . . . sir."

"Larrenport?" Merral said loudly as the significance sank in. It had to be coincidence. "I don't suppose you know the crew of the vessel *Miriama?*"

Leonas gave a weary grunt. "*That* again. Yes, one of the crew stays with us. Lawrence Trest. But I fail to see . . ."

Lawrence Trest, Merral remembered: one of the men who, with Daniel Sterknem, had met the cockroach-beast on the floating tree trunk.

"You fail to see, do you?" Merral replied, rather more sharply than he had intended. "There's a lot we fail to see too. But I suggest you go to the chaplain."

When Leonas had gone out of earshot, Merral stared at Perena. "So what do you make of it?"

Perena ran slender fingers through her cropped hair and shook her head sadly. "Merral, I'll be honest; as a pilot it scares me rigid. Of everything that has happened here, including those holes burned in my ship, this is the worst."

"I think I see why, but go on. Explain."

"Certainly. Negligence of the type perpetuated by Leonas is almost unknown. There have been odd instances in Assembly history of accidents caused by the coming together of minor acts of forgetfulness. You know, X forgets to put in the right computer code, Y is away, and Z forgets to check it, that sort of thing. But that is basically it. Nothing like this. Ever. And we are very vulnerable to negligence. If it breaks out on a large scale, we could be in a lot of trouble. We may have accepted the Technology Protocols, but an awful lot of our technology—diaries, ships, Gates and so on—are very complex machines. And we have very few defenses against negligence."

"Forgive my stupidity, Perena, but how *can* you defend against it?"

"Oh, ask Vero. The ancients did in the old days. Before the Intervention and the Assembly. They double-checked things for a start. They trusted nobody—least of all themselves. So in this case there would have been a loading supervisor in the module who checked Leonas's work, and there would have been a specific list to check it off against. There would have been rules and instructions and discipline for any breaches."

"I see." Merral felt his mind reeling. "So is this another manifestation of evil?"

"Yes. And one we had not expected. Evil is proving more complex and subtle than we had anticipated." She stared into the distance, rubbing her face with her hands. "You see, Merral, think of evil and you think of murder, rape, and war. Yet there are lesser manifestations, and they may be just as dangerous. Fear, grumbling, pride, and yes, negligence. All could be our undoing."

"A depressing but valuable thought. But the Larrenport link again? I wonder how many—"

"Three." She gave him her severe introspective smile. "You have three men from Larrenport in the existing teams."

"You guessed my question. What do I do? Pull them all out?"

Perena gave him an odd look. "Aren't you forgetting something?"

"What?"

"There is another center of infection. If you pull out the Larrenport men, then you'd better be consistent and remove the Ynysmant men too. You'd lose a man from the reserve unit—"

"Jonas Trinder . . ." Merral snorted as the implication sank home. "And also the captain himself. I can hardly discriminate against them except by discriminating against myself."

Perena looked at him in knowing sadness. "Just so. You must be fair. But the implications are, Merral, that we all need to be on our guard. To check and double-check."

"So what do I do with Leonas, then?"

"Your decision. But seeing as he resulted in a tent being ruined, why not have him sleep out in the open?"

Just after lunch, as Merral was reviewing the plans for the following evening's deployment of forces, one of the young men who worked with Vero came into the tent with an air of urgency and handed him a piece of paper. He unfolded it to see Vero's fine neat handwriting.

Felicity is approaching the ship!!! We are getting images! Can you assemble the team leaders? I will bring the printouts over. Get a screen fixed.

It took twenty minutes for Merral to find and assemble the leaders in the humid meeting tent and get a wallscreen hung up at the end. No sooner had everybody sat down than a sweating Vero pushed his way in through the flap, clutching a datapak and a roll of large prints. The sentinel's face bore such an intensity of consternation and unease on it that, for a moment, Merral thought he had failed. Vero nodded clumsily to everybody, pulled up a chair, and sat down.

"H-here it is," he said, with a hint of a stammer, and let the sheets unroll on the table. "Th-there's a copy each."

Perena leaned forward and, in her enthusiasm, almost snatched a sheet. The others followed. Merral pulled off a copy and stared at the image, barely conscious of the hum of excited chatter developing around the table.

They were large, grainy color prints. At the limit of resolution for a micronic camera, thought Merral, trying to assimilate what he was seeing. At the bottom of the image lay the blue lake waters, and in the upper part, above a rugged slope, were the hazy gray hues of the sky. In between the two, not quite horizontal, lay the shoreline on the other side of the lake, and on that rocky shore was the ship.

Merral's first impression was of a giant matte black slipper stretched out under some sort of extended awning.

"Brilliant!" cried someone in the room. "Just brilliant!"

"Marvelous, Vero! Well done!" called another.

Merral did not look up but stared at the image, trying to pull out as much information from it as he could. There was a sharp rear end and smoothly rounded front. The rear section was supported by two massive legs, apparently paired, while the front was held up off the ground by a high, single column. The only other features appeared to be long, lateral, finlike protrusions on the sides and top and, three-quarters of the way along, a ramp that sloped forward onto the ground. Below the ship, and dwarfed by it, were four small bipedal creatures and three taller creatures of a broadly anthropoid form. Neither was human, and the sight of them gave Merral a sick and fearful feeling in the pit of his stomach. He realized how much he had hoped not to see them again.

Merral looked up to see that Vero was leaning forward on the table, his head supported on his clasped hands, staring darkly into the distance. *Funny. I would have expected him to be excited about these images. But perhaps he feels the same as I do on seeing these creatures again.*

Merral saw that Perena was measuring off the size of the ship with her fingers.

"Perena, your initial thoughts?" he asked. "Please."

She looked up, her face thoughtful and wary. He saw the others look at her.

"Only very initial. Size—bigger than predicted. The shape is less ovoid—your computer smoothed it too much, Merral. From the tactical point of view, my guess would be for the teams to go for severing the nose leg and blocking closure of the gangway ramp. The rear legs look too solid."

Frankie and Zak nodded agreement.

"Seen anything like it before?" asked Maria Dalphey.

"No." Perena's voice was sharp. "I'm fairly certain no production Assembly craft has been designed like that. If we had the time, I'd compare it against any of the prototypes. But it's not like anything I recollect seeing. And it looks all wrong. It's *ugly.*"

That's right, thought Merral. *No Assembly ship looks this unattractive.*

"But you reckon as there's any evidence of Below-Space technology?" It was Zak's voice.

Perena looked at the image again, pursed her lips, and shook her head. "No . . . not that I can see. Looks like a chemical or ion engine at the rear. I think I can see evidence of where a hatch for a ferry craft hold may be. On the top. The closest thing would be, oh, one of our inter-system liners. Say the current 20D series."

Anya caught Merral's attention with a gesture of her hand. "The creatures we can see. Cockroach-beasts and ape-creatures?"

"Yes. I'm afraid so."

There was a moment of silence as everybody looked at the images again.

"Funny thing there," Luke said. "The dark object. On the water . . . Or above it? Just to the right of the ship. Debris?"

Merral looked at the image again, seeing, not far from the ship, a black object that eluded immediate identification. *A bird,* he thought, before he remembered that birds shunned the ship. He stared at it, wondering how big it actually was.

"It's n-not debris," Vero said with such a tone of numbed assertion that everybody turned to look at him. Seeing his strained face, Merral wondered whether he was ill.

"So what is it?" Merral asked, somehow unable to restrain a shiver of unease.

"I-I don't know," Vero said in a distracted tone. "It's in other frames. . . . It is s-something new."

Suddenly a thought came to Merral. "Vero, the horse—Felicity? Is she all right?"

The brown eyes blinked. "No," Vero said eventually, and his expression told of some awful fate. Then he breathed in deeply and seemed to regain some measure of control.

"I'm sorry, Merral, ev-everyone. We'd better watch the whole clip. I should warn you that it is not . . . not easy watching."

People looked at each other, their faces openly expressing alarm and bewilderment.

Vero started speaking. "This morning Felicity reached the southern end of Fallambet Lake Five." His voice was now controlled, but under its flat tone Merral was aware of a real anxiety. Vero tapped his diary and the wallscreen flashed on with a tilted and grainy image of the lakeside.

"Part of the problem was that increasingly we had been having problems motivating her. She seemed reluctant to go north. Anyway, this morning she did. F-frame rate here was once every ten seconds, so we can fast forward."

A flickering and shuddering succession of images filled the screen. The pointed end of the lake got progressively nearer and nearer as the mare moved slowly and hesitantly northward. She seemed to stop every so often. *Presumably,* Merral thought, *to eat.* Now the images looked across the lake waters toward the other side.

"It was about at this point that the metabolic indexes of stress started to rise," Vero said, his voice drenched with unhappiness. "Heart rate, adrenaline or its equivalents."

The images jerked onward, and for the first time they caught a glimpse of the ship. Vero paused the display, freezing on a tilted image with the lake leaning strongly to the right.

"We haven't printed these yet, but I don't think they will show too much more than you have seen already."

He unfroze the screen, and as the new images flickered past, Merral decided that the horse was no longer stopping to eat.

As the imagery became increasingly like the printout they had studied, Vero spoke again. "The idea," he said, "was to get Felicity opposite the ship and then get her to veer away westward. Then she could make her own way back south. Or we could have picked her up in a couple of days' time. That was the idea. . . ." He trailed off into silence and more images flashed up. "By the time we got to this point she was under severe stress. The control team was very worried."

"Why?" asked the dry, worn voice of Dr. Azhadi. "Why was she scared?"

It was, Merral thought, a question a doctor would ask.

Vero looked at him. "We . . ." He paused, looking at the table. "Doctor, we have noticed that animals seem sensitive to the intruders. We think she was afraid. But she was so disciplined that she kept going northward as she was trained to do on the appropriate sound stimulus."

With a look of guilt on his face, Vero turned to the screen. "Anyway, the new frame rate is now one every second."

The images still jumped, but the transitions were smoother. Finally they got to the one they had all examined, and Vero paused on it.

"By now the control team was very concerned about her. I gather they were on the point of switching off all commands. They had the images they w-wanted. But then—No, you watch. See the black mark? Let me go back a bit."

There was a flicker, and as Merral watched, he saw the black object move back to the landing ramp.

"Now forward."

The thing seemed to bound and jump through the air. Merral decided that, even allowing for the time lapse between the images, it still flew in a very strange manner. Aware of gasps around him, Merral tried to focus on the object, trying to interpret what he was seeing but struggling because it was so totally unfamiliar to him.

His first impressions were of some kind of black sheet that undulated through the air as if it were a rug or a blanket carried by the wind. But the lake was calm, and there was a purposefulness to the thing's motion that told of it moving under its own power.

After a few more frames, Merral decided that it was an animal, but like nothing he had ever seen. It seemed to change course, and as it turned, it tilted and he glimpsed that its profile was kite shaped. There was even—and suddenly he was sure of it—a long tail.

Merral was aware of Anya beside him, shaking her head in disbelief. "How's it doing that?"

There was no answer.

Vero let the frame jump forward and froze the image. "Now," he said in a strained voice, "we get a better view."

Merral noted new details. Unlike a bird or a bat—and it was surely much larger than either—there was no separation between body and wings; there was just a single smooth unit, thicker at the middle and thinner at the edges. Equally, there was no distinct head.

"A flying wing," someone said, horror in his voice.

"It's like a ray; you know, the sea fish." It was Fred Huang's voice, and Merral was reminded he was a diver.

"A manta ray," said someone else.

"Yes, but this thing's flying, like a sheet," said another voice, full of incredulity and fear.

Vero pressed a button and more images flickered by. Merral could now see that the creature moved by slow but steady wing beats. There was something unnervingly determined in the way it moved.

It was getting closer, Merral realized, and he was able to see the black shadow of the creature on the water. Then it came to him with a spasm of horror that this thing was speeding toward the horse.

"Yow, it's big," said an apprehensive voice.

Suddenly the creature went off the screen, and the scene became an angled one of rocks and scrub with little patches of grass.

Vero paused the images. "Th-the controllers released her here. H-heart rate was far too high. She was panicking. Image quality goes here too. There was s-signal loss; she was moving too rapidly."

The images shifted again. There was another frame, also at a bizarre angle, of a stream valley and white flowing water. *She's running away,* Merral thought. *She has seen the creature and she's fleeing it. And I don't blame her.*

There were disconnected images of sky and distant ranges. Now there was a new image, and a gasp of horror came from someone. Was it from Anya?

Most of the image was sky, with just a patch of ground in a corner. But protruding into the right side of the image and tilted as if it was banking to swing parallel to the horse was the front half of the creature. On the underside of the black sheet, running lengthwise as if below some spine, was a long pale slit with strange appendages hanging down on either side. *A mouth,* Merral thought. The next frame showed it more clearly. It was a mouth and the appendages either side of the long jaws were now eight or so pairs of tiny clawlike limbs.

Merral, suddenly holding the table edge tight, was aware of a smell of fear in the sweaty and sticky air of the tent.

"Oh, Lord," someone said quietly in a horrified prayer.

Vero froze the screen. "At th-this point the decision was taken to jettison the equipment," he said in a voice that was unnaturally calm. For a fraction of a second, Merral tore his eyes off the image to look around the table. Every face bore an expression of utter horror.

The image changed. The shot was now clearly from a lower angle; the creature had gone, and all that could be seen was a pile of rocks.

"Any more?" asked a voice, heavy with distaste.

"Just one that is relevant . . . ," Vero answered. "A few minutes later."

The new image screen showed the rocks again but now there was the thing flying above them, tilted again, allowing a glimpse of the underside. But this time the pale slit of the mouth was a different color: the wet bright red of fresh blood.

Merral was aware of voices all around him, of cries of horror, of a chair leg being scraped as someone got to their feet and moved unsteadily to the tent door.

"Switch it off!" someone ordered angrily. Merral realized that it was his own voice, but who he was angry with, he could not say.

The image vanished.

Merral swallowed, his mind awhirl with fears and worries. He was aware that outside the tent, someone was sobbing.

"One question, Vero," he said.

The sentinel looked guiltily at him, as if bracing himself for a rebuke. "Yes?"

"Can you guarantee, *absolutely guarantee,* that the equipment—the micronic camera, the transmitter, the biosensors—have not been picked up by the intruders?"

There was silence for a moment. "N-No . . . ," Vero replied after a pause, the words seemingly dragged out of him. "The camera failed shortly afterward."

"In other words," Merral said, aware that everyone was looking at him, "there is the possibility that these . . . that they now know we have found them?"

Vero interlocked his hands and stared blankly at Merral. When he spoke his voice was barely audible. "I-I think . . .Well, there is no evidence for that. But I must say—I suppose—that it is conceivable. . . . A possibility."

Suddenly Merral realized there was a decision that needed to be made. He closed his eyes, partly trying to focus on the issues, partly praying. The answer came easily and he opened them. He looked around, seeing ashen faces, noting people dabbing their eyes.

They were all watching him. He was strangely conscious that his lips were dry and that there was sweat dripping down his back.

"Everybody," he said, thinking as he said it that he sounded more confident than he felt, "we must now bear in mind the possibility that we have been

discovered. We are at approximately forty hours before contact. Unless, in the next minute, anyone of you can give me an absolutely unassailable reason why we shouldn't, I want to change that to put us at sixteen hours before contact."

"Huh?" grunted someone in surprise.

"Yes, I want to bring the mission forward a full twenty-four hours."

There were gasps from around the table, but Merral continued. "I want us to fly in six hours' time. Tonight. And I want to make contact at dawn tomorrow."

There was silence.

"Very well, the decision is made." Merral glanced at his watch. "So everyone bring forward all times by twenty-four hours. We will shortly be at contact minus sixteen hours."

In the silence that followed, Merral spoke again, slowly. "And Luke, I want you to make sure that every man and woman among the contact teams has recorded a final message for his or her family. And that we have a copy on file."

The chaplain closed his eyes and nodded.

Merral got to his feet and leaned forward, his hands pressed down on the table. Again, he scanned the faces.

"Maybe God will grant us a diplomatic miracle. . . . I think not." He saw pale, taut faces staring blankly back at him. "On the basis of what we have just seen, I think we will have combat tomorrow. And we must expect casualties."

38

Five hours later, Merral sat wearily back in his seat in the passenger cabin of the *Emilia Kay* as they prepared for takeoff. He wanted to relax, but he knew the effort was futile. Since the decision to move the mission forward a day, the afternoon had been a frenzied whirlwind of activity. He had barely had time to record two brief messages: one for his parents, the other—full of apologies—for Isabella.

Outside the window, the sun was sinking into the sea and casting an orange glow on Anya as she leaned back in her seat at the very end of the row. She smiled at Merral. "Tired?" she asked sympathetically.

"Yes, but I don't mind being tired. It's just not the right sort of tiredness."

Anya nodded and gazed at him with a soft and caring look. *What is going on between us? Does she care for me beyond an ordinary friendship? Or am I simply imagining this because that's what I would like to believe?* On and off through the chaotic afternoon, he had caught her watching him. Or had he been watching her, and had she just caught his glances? He wondered whether she had a special friendship with any other man. He would have known if there had been any commitment, everyone did, but was there, perhaps, something less formal? At the memorable meal at her apartment the night before Vero and he had left for their trip up the Lannar River, she had seemed to be very friendly with Theodore, the extroverted oceanographer. However, he realized that he hadn't heard anything of him since. As he thought about it, his troubled relationship with Isabella prodded his mind, and he suddenly felt guilty.

Perena's voice from the loudspeaker overhead announced an imminent takeoff, and Merral put Anya out of his mind.

Here in the passenger cabin, we can at least belt ourselves in. Down in the cramped hold, the men could only brace themselves as best they could, but at least there was so little space that they were unlikely to be thrown about.

He surveyed the others around him. Vero, sitting on his own, was trying to stretch out, but his expression and movements proclaimed an inner agitation. Merral felt sure that it was not just the prospect of more flying. Ever since the images from the doomed Felicity had come in, Vero had been withdrawn and pensive. Merral felt that he must find time to talk with him before the flight was over, but now was not the time. Louis and Erika were also silent, both staring ahead. Among so many uniforms, they seemed strangely incongruous with their smart, pale fawn jackets with the Lamb and Stars emblem neatly affixed to the breast pockets and their matching trousers and polished shoes. Maria Dalphey, with a bag full of communications gear at her feet, was absorbed in studying sheets of paper. "Logistics Lucy," as Lucy Dmitri had become known, was slumped back in her seat with her eyes closed. Merral felt certain that not only was she not sleeping, but that she would not sleep.

Could anybody?

As the noise of the engines began to build up behind him, Merral reviewed the planned flight path of the *Emilia Kay.* The first part, keeping low over the sea, would be a wide arc southeastward to clear the rest of the Henelen Archipelago. Then, having swung wide around Cape Menerelm, they would fly out into the Mazurbine Ocean before flying northwestward at as low an altitude as possible, to make landfall on Menaya just east of the Lannar Crater margin. From there, the three teams would be progressively dropped off clockwise around the margins of the crater.

With a frame-rattling engine roar, the *Emilia Kay* lifted off heavily from the runway. Perena, anxious to stay low, leveled off quickly and then banked gently southeastward. *Fortunately,* Merral thought, *the forecast is for fine weather.* With a maximum flying altitude of under two thousand meters, there wasn't going to be much space for sudden drops in altitude.

As soon as the *Emilia Kay* had become horizontal, Merral left his seat in the passenger cabin and went down to the cargo module. As he slid open the door, the smell of sweat and anxiety greeted him. He paused in the shadow of the doorway, surveying the scene. Even after having left everyone—and everything—that wasn't essential behind at Tanaris, the hold was still almost completely filled. There were people everywhere: squeezed together on the floor, sitting in the seats inside the sleds and the hoverer, and standing, braced against the equipment or the walls. All were uniformed in the new green armored jackets with their embossed Lamb and Stars emblems, but only a few were wearing helmets. The hold was too warm for that. Beneath and behind the soldiers, Merral could make out the two camouflaged sleds on their handling trolleys, the hoverer painted an innocent white, and various stacks of equipment.

There was surprisingly little noise for well over a hundred people, but a lot of them were silent, seemingly engrossed in their own thoughts and prayers. The few that were talking were doing so quietly. Merral, trying to understand the unfamiliar atmosphere in the hold, sensed expectancy, uncertainty, and fear.

As he surveyed his men, the *Emilia Kay* made a small course adjustment, and the rays of the setting sun shone into the packed compartment, throwing a weird, ruddy light on the men and machines. *Like blood,* Merral thought unhappily.

The soldier nearest the door looked up, saw Merral, and with a tense smile on his face, tried to salute. *Philip Matakala,* Merral thought, remembering his name.

"Oh, forget it, Philip," Merral said more strongly than he had intended as he squatted down next to him, feeling a sudden revulsion for the whole business of orders and rank. *What do I really know of this man?* Philip was the sergeant and sled pilot with Frankie's team, so Merral had had more contact with him than with many of the other men. But even so, all he really knew was that Philip was an agriculture graduate, a sailor, and a single man from Caranat, one of the smaller coastal settlements. And the thought came to Merral with no pleasure that he was in some way accountable for this amiable but retiring man's safety.

"You're ready?" he asked him, trying to say something to cover his feelings.

"I suppose so, sir," Philip replied, then looked up inquiringly with thoughtful eyes. "Are you?" He paused. "Sorry, am I supposed to ask that?"

Merral, bracing himself against the doorway, thought hard. He realized that he faced Corradon's dilemma.

"Why not? Am I ready? A good question. I vaguely feel—from the depressing ancient stuff I've read—that I should be confident and so fill you with confidence."

"And you aren't?" Philip asked, his words tinged with sympathy.

Merral hesitated. "I don't feel confident. I simply don't know enough to know whether we are good enough. I think we—especially the teams—have worked wonders to get so far, but how good we really are is something hard to determine. Especially when we don't know what the opposition is like. I wish we had some old soldiers here."

"Old soldiers?"

Merral laughed. "I'm getting like Vero. It's an expression. Veterans. In the Dark Times, wars were so frequent that when an old one ended they seemed to start a new one. So there were generally soldiers in the ranks who had fought in the last one. It gave continuity."

"Yes. I remember. But it sounds like a crazy way to run a civilization."

"Well, it was. But we don't have any veterans. I'm the nearest we've got. So we just hope and pray and stay prepared for anything."

Philip winked reassuringly at him. "We'll do our best, sir."

"Yes. I have no doubt about it."

Merral patted him on the back and rose to his feet. The hold was too full for him to walk around in, and he knew he ought to get back to the passenger cabin. He looked around, catching thumbs-up gestures from the men and noticing Lorrin Venn grinning at him. He forced a smile back in response. *I suspect he's going to see his action. I only hope he likes it.*

He saw Chaplain Luke and Dr. Azhadi squeezing their way through the press of men as they did their rounds. They had more defined and easier tasks, and for a brief moment, he felt utterly overwhelmed by what he faced. He was aware of Lucas Ringell's identity disk around his neck, and he felt that somehow it mocked him. He found himself wondering why he had accepted this whole monstrous task. *It's too late to argue. I'm here, I have been called to be here, and I must do my very best.*

Full of thought, Merral returned to the cabin, which seemed surprisingly roomy after the hold. Anya, who seemed to have been watching for his return, gestured him over to a seat next to her.

"Merral," she said in a soft tone as she leaned over toward him, "I need to talk to you." Her eyes were wide and bright.

"Go ahead," he answered, realizing again that the urgency of the hour could not suppress his feelings of a growing attraction for her. In fact, he realized that, in some bizarre way, the impending action seemed to heighten his feelings for her.

Anya put her diary on her knees, bending closer to him so that her words would not carry beyond the two of them. "I suppose I really need to talk to you about that creature. Whatever we call it." She looked up at him with a strange concentration as if trying to read his mind.

"I have no name for it. A flying sheet? A two-dimensional dragon?" Merral said, tearing his mind away from other, more pleasant things.

"A two-dimensional dragon? A sheet-dragon?" She seemed to weigh the words. She tapped her diary and a still image of the creature came on the screen. She looked at it and seemed to shudder.

"Anya," Merral suggested, "you don't have to talk about it if you don't want to."

She gave him a stern smile. "I was shaken when I saw it. And I don't want to talk or think about it, but I have to. It's my job. I'm a biologist, and I am supposed to be your expert. So I've looked at the images and cleaned them up."

"So what is it?"

"I don't know. This 'sheet-dragon' is, I presume, a vertebrate; there's got to be a skeleton under that. But what sort of a skeleton . . . ? Ah," she sighed, "I think it's very lightly built. The feature on the underside is, of course, a mouth—there are teeth visible on the enhanced images—and it has these members around it, feeding palps, claws, limbs, mandibles; whatever you want to call them. Two small eyes inset on what my sister would call the leading edge. It's like no creature that we know of."

"Is it made of other things? Like the other creatures? A bit of bird, a bit of lizard?"

"I can't see it." She shook her head. "I just think it has a sort of elemental quality."

"By which you mean . . . what?"

She grimaced. "It seems quantitatively different from the cockroach-beasts and ape-creatures. They can be considered as bits and pieces of different organisms put together. This is something else."

"Could this sheet-dragon be a genuinely alien creature?"

"Maybe . . ." She stared at him, her eyes wide in the darkness of the cabin.

"Any advice if we meet it?"

"Fire first. No, I have a few thoughts. Size, first: We think the wingspan is just below two meters; say the width of your outstretched arms. And the way the mouth is structured, it's not going to be a great biter. The gape isn't that wide. But if it got a chance at exposed flesh . . ." She shivered.

Like the back of a horse or a human face.

Anya stared at the images again. "What else? Oh, and the tail could be nasty; it might be able to use it as a whip."

"Ah . . . In other words, keep your distance."

They exchanged glances, and Merral felt that there was more being transmitted between them than just thoughts about this strange and dreadful creature. Silently, she tapped the screen off.

"I see," he said after a while. "But you are worried, aren't you?"

Merral received a confiding glance. "Yes, yes I am. I have no idea what is in that ship. I hope we can immobilize it, seal it up, and deal with what's in it at our leisure." She glanced around the cabin, and Merral, following her gaze, saw that no one was looking at them. She reached out, touched his hand briefly and shyly, then withdrew it.

"And, my Tree Man," she said, with an affection that was no longer concealed, "I'm concerned that something may happen to you."

"I see," Merral answered, his mind already clouded with all sorts of strange thoughts. Suddenly, finding Anya's unmistakable expression of affection too overwhelming, he realized that he needed to focus on other things. He could not afford to be distracted, and anyway, the unresolved matter of Isabella still hung over him. With a flustered apology, he got up and went forward into the cockpit.

There the lighting had been turned down so low that it was hard to see anything at first other than silhouettes of the three people in the cockpit outlined against the multicolored lights of their screens. Merral was trying to regain his composure when he saw Perena's head turned toward him.

"Okay, Captain?" he inquired.

"Yes . . . ," she said, turning back to look ahead. "The ship's fine. Fully laden and we are flying too low for comfort, but we are in good shape."

"Where are we?"

She gestured to a glowing map nearby. "Still going north, well over the horizon from the most northern coastal settlements. In fifteen minutes, we cut due west toward the coast and come in just north of the Nannalt Delta. So we will have the first landing in about an hour."

There was a catch in her voice. He bent his head forward so that he could talk to her without the others hearing. "Are you all right?" he whispered.

"Yes," she murmured back. "I suppose so. . . . I'm just in a strange mood. Am I worried? Is that it?"

"Understandable. I mean—"

"No," she interrupted, apparently realizing something. "It's not worry. Or not entirely. It's a feeling—I suppose—of awe. That we are, somehow, on the edge of something immense. Something momentous? Is that the word?" She paused. "Sorry, I guess I'd better focus. This is not the time for reflection."

She fell silent, and Merral decided to take the small spare seat at the extreme back of the cockpit. He tried to run through everything in his mind to be sure that he hadn't overlooked anything. Had he done everything that he had to? There was so much to manage. The idea nagged him again that he had forgotten something, that there was something that he should have done but hadn't. But what was it?

His thoughts were interrupted a few minutes later when a low bell tone chimed, and then he heard Perena's voice on the speakers. "Captain Lewitz here. Just to say that we are nearly as far north as we get and very shortly I'm going to start flying due west to put us toward the northeastern edge of the crater. From now on, we will be at a very low altitude, and I want to reduce the possibility of us being seen by dimming the interior lights even further. I should warn you that as we go overland, the ship is going to bounce around. So be prepared. Fifty minutes to Landing Site One. All being well, my next message will be just before the landing maneuvers."

Behind him, Merral saw the corridor lights fade out, and a moment later the ship started to drop in height and began a leisurely turn. Out of the small window to his side, Merral peered into darkness. *I should go back to the passenger cabin.* But if he went there, he had to choose to sit next to Anya or not. Part of him badly wanted to sit next to her, but he was somehow uneasy about what might happen between them. *There seems to be the potential for things to happen between us that I ought to think hard about. There are matters too that I must sort out with Isabella first.*

There were footsteps beside him, and he looked up to see Vero, bracing himself unsteadily against the wall. Vero bent down so that he could speak to Merral and not be heard by anyone else.

"Merral," he whispered in a strained, hesitant voice, "I just want to say that I am sorry about the business with Felicity. I really am." His unsteady tone suggested an intense unhappiness. "I am very worried that I may have jeopardized things. At the time, it seemed a good idea. . . ."

"Oh, Vero, stop it!" Merral whispered back, clapping him on the shoulder. "Have I blamed you?"

"No, but I blame myself," he murmured.

"Well, better not to," Merral answered. "I need you with your mind alert here. We are entering unknown territory. All our actions have a risk."

"Yes, you are right," he said a few moments later, a renewed resolve apparent in his voice. "Sorry . . . But I was just shaken by what we saw earlier."

"Me too. But it may have done us a service. We have learned a lot more about the intruders. We know there is another type."

"Yes. And it is carnivorous. Each new thing unsettles me more," Vero responded. "I can only hope and pray that we have not gotten involved in something too big for us to manage."

"That's out of our control now. We must just do what we have to do."

"I guess so."

Perena turned her head toward them. "Coastline coming up," she called out in a low voice.

Vero tapped Merral on the shoulder. "Many thanks. I'm going to get strapped in. See you when we land."

Merral stared out of the window into the darkness, and a few minutes later, he was rewarded by seeing a faint line of starlit white breakers and then a pale ghostly strip of the seastrand. Then they were flying over ground, low enough for him to sense the rough fabric of the forests racing away underneath and to distinguish the raw, ash-colored rocks around. They were so low—perhaps barely five hundred meters above the ground—that although he knew Perena had slowed the speed down, they still seemed to be going appallingly fast.

As Merral peered down, seeing starlight glimmering on dark lakes, the ship began to sway laterally and vertically in a sickening motion. *It's the computer, nudging us over and around the oncoming landscape.* In the cabin ahead, he could make out the crew scanning their sensor screens, trying to detect anything unusual. This far north there would be no one to see them. At least, he thought ruefully, that was what he had once believed as a certainty. Now though, that—as so much else—was in doubt.

Time passed as the *Emilia Kay* swayed this way and that and the shadowy landscape slipped by underneath. Suddenly Perena was talking to him, her voice terse. "Captain D'Avanos, no anomalies ahead at Site One. Do we go for landing?"

"Yes," he said, "or rather, affirmative."

Seconds later Perena's voice came over the speakers. "Landing maneuvers starting in thirty seconds. Brace yourselves. On my command, Lieutenant Larraine's team begin to disembark."

The *Emilia Kay* started to reduce speed even more, and a new whispering whine indicated the vertical thrusters were firing. As Merral watched out of the window, they sank down into a river valley and then in a series of fierce turns began to veer from side to side as they followed the meanders. Outside in the darkness, he could now see silhouettes of crags above him. There was a hissing and a soft clanking noise as the landing gear was extruded, and the speed dropped to what he judged was little more than walking speed.

A moment later, the ship slowed to a dead stop, dropped slightly, and then, with a thud and a gentle bounce, settled slowly down to a horizontal angle.

"Stable," Perena pronounced over the speakers. "Location correct. Team, you are clear to leave. God be with you."

Even before she had finished speaking, Merral was already heading for the hold. By the time he arrived, the port-side door was raised, a ramp had been lowered, and in the dim lighting, men were already working on unloading the sled.

Carefully, Merral clambered down the ramp and stood on the ground. Here there was a cool, fresh breeze on his cheek. The smell of pinewoods wafted past him, clearing away the stale and all-too-human air from the hold. The night air seemed to speak to him of the past, of the unsullied days before the intruders arrived, and for a moment, Merral felt he could almost weep. He was aware of Zak giving low, curt orders to his men as they manhandled the sled out on its trolley and then the whispers and grunts as the men pushed and rolled it down the ramp.

Merral looked at the stars above the ragged tips of the firs. *I would give a lot to see the hexagon of the Gate again. And a lot more still to be camping out here with no cares except that of filling in my trip report.* As if to deepen his mood, there came the call of an owl from within the woods.

A few minutes later there was the faintest of whines as, safely distant from the ship's electronics, the gravity-modifying engine came on and the sled floated up and free. As they loaded the trolley back into the hold, Merral saw someone come over and stand by him. In the starlight he recognized Zak.

"Sir," Zak said in clipped tones, and it came to Merral that no one had acquired the trappings of soldiering better than Zachary Larraine, "my team is clear and the sled is operational."

"Good work so far, Zak," Merral said. Then he realized that he didn't know what else to say to a man who, in all probability, he would next meet at the scene of a battle.

Merral hugged him.

"For the Assembly, sir," said Zak, returning the hug.

"For the Assembly, amen and amen," Merral answered, feeling surprisingly moved.

Zak stood back, and in the darkness, Merral made out a salute. Merral returned it and clambered back on board. "Perena," he announced, looking toward the wall microphone, "Zak's team is clear. Ready to go."

"Okay," came the response, and even as the hatch door slid down, the faint hull vibration trebled its force. Within seconds, the *Emilia Kay* was airborne and turning on her axis.

Merral climbed up out of the hold, which now looked much less crowded, and returned to the cabin. Exchanging smiles with Anya, he went over and squatted by Louis and Erika who were making desultory conversation.

"Twenty minutes or so going south and then we drop you off," Merral said. "You're ready?"

The diplomatic team had seen some of the images from Felicity, but only Fred Huang, the team leader, had seen the awful final frame. Louis looked at him. "Yes. I'm trying to maintain my faith that negotiation may work. But now, after those images, I expect otherwise." His voice was calm and resolute, and Merral found himself with a new respect for this man.

"I also," returned Merral after a pause.

Erika just nodded an obviously reluctant assent. Then, after a short silence, she turned to Merral and spoke in a confiding tone. "Captain, I just want to say that if our mission gets in trouble, I expect you to put gaining the intruder ship as a priority."

"Thank you," Merral answered slowly. "I know that, but I am grateful for you saying it. Fred and Nate will do their best. They are under orders to get out as soon as there are any hostilities."

Louis merely nodded with an air of resignation.

"Not long now then," was all he said.

Shortly after, Perena set down the ship on a bank of rough sand on the side of another river valley, and as they manhandled the cumbersome hoverer onto the ground, Merral clambered out again. Unlike the sleds, the hoverer had conventional hydrogen turbines and could have been switched on in the hold, but it was still too crowded and there was too much sand and dust about. As they heaved and slid it out down the ramp, Merral walked some paces clear from the ship and peered around in the darkness.

At first, all he could see was the dull sparkling silver water of the river as it tumbled down out of the crater on its way to the sea. Then, his eyes adjusting to the gloom, he began to make out towering cliff walls on either side, with dark gray forests draping their flanks. Behind him stood the great mass of the *Emilia Kay,* with little figures moving below it holding shielded flashlights as the pale hull of the hoverer emerged on the sandbank. They were a hundred and fifty kilometers away from the intruder ship here, but it had been estimated that it would take most of the rest of the night for the sluggish machine to make its way up the river and across the rough ground to the southern part of Fallambet Lake Five.

As a cool gust of air blew past him, Merral shivered slightly. Even with the start of summer only a few weeks away, here in this windy valley it was still barely warm. Merral looked up at the thousands of perfect twinkling diamonds of the stars and was strangely reminded of that fateful night before Nativity when he had first met Vero and had seen the stars on the journey south from Wilamall's Farm. As he thought about it, Merral was reminded that it had been that night that he had had the first strange conversation with Jorgio Serter.

Jorgio!

With a start, Merral realized what it was that he had forgotten to do. He had made a promise to contact Jorgio before there was any fighting. He was halfway to switching on his diary before he realized that it was disabled. He jogged back across the coarse, gritty sand to the *Emilia Kay,* where Vero was standing quietly in the hold doorway.

"Vero!" Merral said. "I've just remembered. I've got to call Jorgio. Can I use your diary?"

Vero, his dark face lit only by the dull gleam of the dimmed interior lights, appeared to hesitate. "Is it really needed?" he said. "I'm trying to keep communications to the minimum."

"He said that he would pray for us if it came to a fight."

"Ah." Vero nodded in the darkness. "I suppose you'd better tell him. After what I have seen today, I feel unsettled. I think we will need all the help we can get. But—please—say as little as you can. Be brief."

Fortunately, Jorgio turned out to be with his brother Daoud and had not yet gone to bed. "Jorgio! It's Merral."

"Why now, Mister Merral!" said the old man, staring at the diary from such an odd angle that Merral wondered whether he had ever used one. "And where might you be with so little light, eh?"

"About the King's business. On a task we discussed."

"Oh, *war.* So it has come to that, has it?" The old man scratched his crooked nose leisurely. "About time really. Well, I suppose I'm glad of it. Hmm . . ." He seemed to drift off into his own thoughts.

"You asked me to tell you. I—*we*—need your prayers."

"I thank you. I knew it would happen, but I appreciate not being forgotten. And I will pray."

"Thank you," Merral replied.

Jorgio looked at him with his thick eyebrows raised. He smiled strangely. "Off to war! Just like Lucas Ringell in the old days. You remember him?"

Merral shivered, and as he did, the cold metal disc tingled against his chest. "Yes, Jorgio. I know of him. But that was a long time ago."

"Quite so. And things change. . . . Or do they?" There was now a strange, wild look on the old man's face. Out of the corner of his eye, Merral saw Vero watching him and gesturing urgently with his hand.

"I must go, my friend. But do you have any counsel?"

"Me?" There was a tilted grin. "Oh, hardly. Only I'll pray. But I think you'll have some help."

"From who?"

"Well, I'd say as the King will send whoever he sees fit. And who it is will depend on who *they* are. But I hardly think he'll let you be outmatched. Mind you, he sets his own terms."

"I see," Merral answered, trying to memorize the words so that he could puzzle over them later. "Well, thank you."

"Fight well, Mister Merral. And remember there are many enemies. Fight well."

Merral ended the transmission and handed the diary back to Vero.

"So was he helpful?" his friend asked.

"In a way, yes. He thought there would be help."

"I hope so," Vero said in a low, self-pitying voice. "The nearer we get, the worse I feel about it."

There were the sounds of the hoverer being pulled and pushed free of the landing gear.

"Ah, we're ready," Vero said, pointing to where, by the faint, bleached shape of the hoverer, a man was gesturing. They walked carefully over in the darkness to where Merral could hear the flags on the hoverer making weak fluttering noises in the breeze.

Merral shook hands solemnly with Fred Huang, Nate the pilot, and Louis. There was a lot that he wanted to say to each of them but he felt he couldn't. Then he turned to Erika, and by the metal hull of the hoverer they faced each other in the near total darkness.

"I hope," he said, "that we shall meet by the lake tomorrow."

"Perhaps," she replied in a solemn way. "But I am less sure. I fear our diplomatic efforts are doomed. But they must be done. If we perish . . ." She faded away into uncertainty. Then when, moments later, she spoke again, Merral was heartened to hear that her tone had acquired a new, thoughtful confidence. "And so, if we do perish? What better way than in the pursuit of peace? After all, we would follow a good example."

In the darkness, Merral could vaguely see her reach out and trace something on the fluttering flag by her side. Then a gleam of starlight caught the fabric, and he was able to discern that, in the symbol of the Assembly, she was touching the Lamb.

A few minutes later the *Emilia Kay* lifted off and, keeping as low as possible, made its way southwest round the crater rim to the third and final site. Merral stood at the back of the cockpit for the approach to this last landing zone where Frankie's team would be unloaded and the ship and the reserve team would wait until dawn. As slowly as she could, Perena flew in a winding path up a rugged river valley broken by waterfalls, rapids, and vast boulders.

When the scan of the area revealed nothing untoward, Merral approved a landing. From the images he had seen in the planning stages, he knew it was a difficult landing zone, a deep hollow set amid high cliffs. He held his breath as Perena took the ship down vertically, nudging it gently sideways in a series of little taps until it came to rest.

After long seconds of scanning screens and readouts, Perena stroked switches and the ship's engines became suddenly silent. Amid a flurry of orders to the engineer, she got up from her seat and, stretching her arms wearily, came over to Merral. "We can still take off within five minutes if we need to," she said. "But I want to check our site. Let us survey it together."

Merral found his armored jacket under his seat and put it on. It was an action he had left to the last moment not just to give him more comfort—it was hard and inflexible—but because he felt that putting it on was symbolic: it was an admission that fighting now seemed inescapable. *And when will I get to take it off?*

Leaving Frankie and his men to get the sled out, Merral climbed out of the ship with Perena and peered around in the intense darkness. This was by far and away the darkest site so far, and it was only with difficulty that Merral could make out anything at all. Here they were so deep down into the dry gorge that the sky above them was just a torn, star-filled strip between sheer black walls of rock.

Perena switched on a powerful flashlight and pointed it around the cliff sides.

"It will do," she said, her voice seeming to echo around the gorge. "There are bits of loose rock above, but the ground is stable and the night is dry. I think we are safe here. We'll await your signal. I'll have the engines ready to fire up from six. All being well, I will be with you within fifteen minutes."

"I hope that's fast enough," Merral said, feeling that down there the air was as still and heavy as if it hadn't moved since the Seeding.

"The old lady will do her best," Perena said. "But there are limits. I can't just pull up straight out of here. I need to check all systems are working acceptably. And I will have to approach you carefully."

"Well, take no more risks than needed. You know the rules we agreed to."

"Yes. And as soon as I know it has gone to a fight, I'll summon the medical support."

"Thanks."

Through the still darkness, Merral heard Anya call out his name lightly.

"Over here!" he answered.

"Well, I'd better go back to the ship," Perena said, reaching out for his hand and squeezing it.

In the darkness, Anya came over and stretched out an arm to touch him softly.

"A strange night," she murmured.

"One of the strangest in the history of the Assembly," Merral replied, feeling strangely tense and excited.

"Indeed so, but I was—I suppose—thinking more personally."

"I see," he said, trying to sound matter-of-fact but suddenly aware that all his feelings were in total confusion. Here in this dark, still cleft with the stars so high above, it seemed that he was in another world from the rest of Farholme.

Anya grasped his arm tightly. "Look, I'm worried about you, Merral. I've come to care about you." She paused, and he could hear her breathing. "Of course, now is the wrong time to say this. And you probably don't want me to say it."

I do. But he didn't say anything.

"But it's just now," she said, "facing what you face, I, well, just wanted you to know. . . ."

If only I could freeze this conversation until after everything is over. Then another voice within him said that she was right, and that when you were faced with the prospect of death, there were things that it was appropriate to discuss.

Merral was suddenly reminded of his meeting with Theodore, the man from Maritime Affairs. It had been that odd evening, the night before Vero and he had left for their trip up the Lannar River. The night before his world changed.

"I thought . . . ," he answered, "that, er, you and Theodore were . . ."

"Him?" In the darkness, he knew she was smiling. "No, he's not my sort really. Or so I've decided. *Now.*"

His heart seemed to bound, but with the surge of excitement came a cloud of unease about his relationship with Isabella back in distant Ynysmant. Anya—and suddenly Merral realized he was thinking of her as *his* Anya—was talking to him. "And you? I thought there was something with this Isabella?"

Merral felt a stab of awkwardness at hearing Isabella's name mentioned. She seemed so far away now, so remote from this present, very private moment. She and Ynysmant might have been on the other side of the galaxy from this dark, secret cleft. She was, he felt, so much a part of the past. And surely, he told himself, that past, like his title of Forester, was gone.

"Once . . . there might have been," he whispered. "But not now. There is nothing special between us."

As he said the words, Merral reassured himself that what had happened there had a been a lifetime ago, before the world went to bits. Besides, he told himself, it had never been with parental approval. And it only remained for him—for them both—to sort out the final details of their return to being merely good friends. And with that, he pushed Isabella out of his mind.

Merral looked at Anya's dim outline. Suddenly he snatched her into his arms, his armored jacket strange and stiff against her yielding softness. He ran his fingers through her wild hair, sighing at the touch of her arms around his neck. He wanted to hold on to her and be with her. There was nothing sweeter he could think of than Anya. And this night, with its threats and tensions and its brevity of time, seemed to make it all much more precious, just as darkness heightens the smallest light.

For an immeasurable time, he stood there holding her, until a low voice called out his name from somewhere by the *Emilia Kay*.

"Look, it's nearly time," he said quietly, wondering why everything had to happen at once.

Their lips gently kissed.

With an extraordinary reluctance, he forced himself away from her, telling himself that there was much to be done. Then, his mind in turmoil, Merral walked carefully back over to where the sled was now hovering just above the ground with a gentle whisper. In the darkness he could make out the men moving against each other as, weighed down by equipment, they settled clumsily into their seats. Between the sled and the *Emilia Kay*, he could vaguely make out the men of the reserves spilling out of the ship and stretching themselves.

From the front of the sled, Frankie called out in a muted voice, "Captain, if it's all right with you, I think we ought to leave."

Suddenly Vero quickly embraced Merral. "Come back safe," he said.

"I'll do my best," Merral replied, feeling that he sounded utterly feeble.

Then after Maria, Lucy, and Perena hugged him, there was a longer and more meaningful hug from Anya.

"See you at the lake," she whispered.

"Maybe it will all work out," he muttered. "Perhaps we will be invited to breakfast."

He felt, rather than saw, her wrinkle her face in amusement. "Given what we know of their eating habits, I'd say it'd be a good time to fast."

Then, after a brief but precious grasp of her fingers, he clambered on board and was tugged toward a bench seat near the front, just behind Philip and Frankie. With a chuckle, someone that Merral decided could only be Lorrin Venn passed him a helmet, and he put it on. He tightened the strap and fastened the security belt around his waist, took the offered weapon, and put its cold metallic mass carefully down between his feet.

Then the chaplain was praying over them.

"Amen," came a low chorus of voices from the sled's occupants and the bystanders.

Then switches were flicked and the whispering of the sled's engine grew to a slight hum. There was a soft tug underneath him as the vehicle began to move at little more than a fast running pace over the ground.

His heart torn by a dozen emotions, Merral looked back as they slid northward out of the gully, and one by one, the faint lights of the *Emilia Kay* vanished behind him. Then he swiveled round on his bench seat and faced forward.

Ahead of us, in less than seven hours, lies a confrontation about whose outcome not one of us has any certainty. We face unknown foes of unknown powers with unproven weapons and untrained men.

It was not a comforting thought.

39

The sled moved steadily northward toward the Lannar Crater in almost total silence. It was so dark that Merral could make out very little clearly. There was a constant sense of trees and bushes racing past, and occasionally branches and leaves would whip against the sled and rattle off helmets or hands. Almost the only noises were the soft whistle of the air, the low hum of the engine, and the gentle rustle of grass and small shrubs against the sled's underside. Their passage was so quiet that more than once they startled animals. Once, a herd of deer bounded away as leaping shadows. Another time they stopped abruptly, and ahead of them Merral made out the shape of a large bear lumbering irritably out of the way.

Normally Merral would have found the journey invigorating, particularly after being enclosed inside a ship. He had always loved being out in the open, and this journey with the stars above and the fresh clean air with its scents of pine and heather all around should have been enjoyable. Tonight, though, everything seemed to conspire against any enjoyment. He had to keep his head down to avoid being lashed by branches, it was impossible to find a decent position for his legs in the cramped space, the armor made his spine ache, and soon, as they climbed higher, he was very cold. Repeatedly, memories of his fight with the intruders at Carson's Sill came back to him, and he found himself quailing at the prospect of battling against those terrible creatures. And what he fought against then had now been supplemented by this new flying monstrosity. Unease also nagged at his mind about what had happened between him and Anya. The memory of her embrace left a warm glow. Nevertheless, in another part of his mind, he told himself that he could perhaps have handled it in a better way. He had somehow allowed himself to be caught unawares by events. It would have surely been better to have resolved matters with Isabella first.

After ninety minutes, his troubled reflections were broken when they stopped in the midst of a pile of gravelly dunes overlooked by a high, saw-edged line of summits. With groans of relief, everybody clambered out and stretched to restore circulation.

Merral checked the dimmed digital map with Frankie and Philip. He saw that they had slowly climbed up from the landing site but still had the main part of the southern Rim Ranges to negotiate.

After ten minutes they set off again. Over the next hour, they wound their way through the mountains, climbing ever higher and going round great fragments of rock beside which patches of snow still persisted. Above them the stars seemed to burn ever more brightly, and in the deep cold everybody huddled next to each other, grateful for even the slight warmth transmitted from the man on either side. They slowly descended into the crater proper. The high, sharp-edged blackness of the bladed peaks was now behind them. They descended gulches and ragged screes to the crater floor, and as they did, Merral found himself ever more troubled. He tried praying, but that gave him no peace, a fact that unsettled him still more. He sat there shivering, trying to keep warm and wishing that, one way or another, it was all over. Slowly, the bare angular rocks gave way to a flatter and more swampy area, and for some time the sled pushed through tall reeds, while in the waters below, unseen creatures plopped and jumped as the sled glided over them.

On the other side of the marsh, they stopped again amid clumps of dwarf willows and, on a bank covered with thin sparse grass and moss, stretched out trying to massage cramped muscles. Frankie sent a brief coded message, compressed into a fraction of a second's tight directional transmission, southward to the *Emilia Kay*. A few moments later, the terse acknowledgement came back from Maria Dalphey. All parties, the message said, were on schedule.

They continued on, and as the ground rose again, Philip was forced to steer the sled in an increasingly circuitous route in order to keep them low in valleys. Merral tried to doze but found that he could not.

An hour later, there was a final stop in a barren, gravel-strewn depression. Everyone dismounted, did more stretching exercises, drank water, and ate biscuits. Here, Merral noted, all the men seemed subdued, and an air of unease hung over everyone. At least two of the party kept their guns with them, and in the darkness he could sense people looking around warily.

Merral was lying down, trying to bring life to stiff legs, when one of the men came over to him.

"Sir, a question: You were a forester, right?" Merral recognized Lee Rodwen from his southern Varrend Tablelands accent.

"Yes, Lee," Merral sighed, "and at this moment I would like to be one again. As you would want to go back to your farming studies."

"Aye, true enough. But is it always this quiet up 'ere?"

Merral listened beyond the low whispers of the men and realized that he had heard no sign of either bird or animal for a long time. *I have been too preoccupied. I must concentrate more on this undertaking.*

"You feel something is missing?" he asked.

He sensed Lee looking around, sniffing the air. "*Life*, sir, is what's missing. Birds, rabbits, foxes—anything. I'm no forester, but I am a countryman, and this is a funny place 'ere. *Bleak.* As if round 'ere, the Seeding went wrong."

Merral listened again, hearing only the tense silence, as heavy as the air before a summer storm.

"No, Lee, the Seeding went right. But, if I can make up a word, perhaps it's been unseeded."

"Unseeded?" There was a pause and then the man spoke again. "Aye, that about feels like it. But sir, who—or what—unseeds what the Assembly seeds?"

"A good question, Lee."

Then behind them there was a murmur of activity, and Merral was aware that people were starting to climb back into the sled. It was time for the final lap.

Forty minutes later, the sled glided to a halt in a shallow but steep-sided river valley. It was still dark; indeed, the night was now thicker and more impenetrable than ever before.

There were whispered commands from Frankie; the sled sank slowly to the ground, and the faint hum of the engine died away. Stiffly, but with great care, the men dismounted from the sled and, trying not to make the slightest noise, began taking out their weapons and their packs.

In low whispers, Frankie assigned duties. "Three hours sleep, one hour on guard. If you're not on guard now, go and sleep. Everyone keep your weapons next to you." Then he turned and touched Merral on the arm. "If it's all right with you, Captain, shall we go and take a look?"

Putting on light-enhancing goggles that, in happier days, Merral had used for monitoring wildlife, he and Frankie grabbed their guns and picked their way down the stony valley bottom. There was little vegetation, just straggly thistles and wiry grass clumps around the flanks of the sluggish shallow stream. After a hundred meters, they began climbing up a slope, trying not to slip on the loose stones. A few minutes' labor brought them to just below the rounded summit, and there they hesitated for a moment.

If we are in the right place, Merral thought, *then just over the top will be the lake and, on the other side of that, will be the ship.*

Frankie gestured him forward. They crawled up on their hands and knees and, lying uncomfortably on the cold and pebbly ground, peered eastward.

With the image distorted in color and texture by the goggles, it took time for Merral to work out what it was that he was seeing. Before them was the rough descent down to the lake edge, and beyond the dark, immobile waters he could see the other shoreline. In the middle of that, like some sort of strange reclining ebony sculpture, was the intruder vessel.

"The ship." Merral's whispered words rang with soft wonderment and fear. At first, all he could make out was the general shape of the intruder craft. Even when Frankie passed him a fieldscope, he could still make out little more than he had seen on Vero's images. There was the single front leg, the paired and larger rear legs, and between them, the forward-descending entrance ramp. He could see no sign of life but felt that in the irresolvable blackness around the ship there could easily have been any number of sentries.

Merral put down the scope. Although actually seeing this vessel added little new to what he had already observed on the images, there was nevertheless something almost overwhelming about the experience. The intruder ship had been progressively an abstract theory, a computer image, and a crude piece of imagery. Now, at last, it was a solid and tangible reality, and with that the whole operation had assumed a dire immediacy. After all, with a real ship went real battles and real deaths.

Frankie tapped Merral's arm and together they slid down below the crest of the hill.

"Well, it's *there,*" Frankie said in low, awed tones, and Merral knew that he had, in his own way, felt the same arresting intrusion of reality.

"Did you expect something else?" he asked.

"I don't know," Frankie answered, and Merral could make out his shrugging his shoulders. "I suppose, sir, that's the thing about this business. I've given up knowing what to expect. I was concerned, I suppose, that it might have gone. To have been a bad dream."

"No, it's there. But that may be the bad dream."

"Yeah. So it's as we planned then, sir?" Merral identified disquiet in the voice. "It looks awful big. To try and blast that front leg and maybe get a hole in the ramp doorway?"

"Yes," Merral answered, sounding more confident than he felt. "We can do it. That's what Perena preferred. Her argument was that we were more likely to disable the ship by concentrating on the front. I think she was also worried that there might be fuel at the rear."

Frankie seemed to chew on that. "Yeah, sir. It makes sense. Right; I'll make sure we keep a continuous watch on the ship from here. Get us an optic fiber communications link down to the sled. What watch do you want, sir?"

"Me? I'll take the last hour before dawn. I need to be here to watch the diplomatic team approach anyway."

"Yeah, I worry about them," Frankie said in a sad voice. "I feel they are going to be in trouble."

"Yes, I think so too. And I think they know it. I think they are the bravest of the lot of us."

"True. Anyway, Captain, if it suits you, let's go and get the cable set up to here. Then you can go and snatch some sleep."

Down by the sled, Merral settled down on a more or less flat spot, put his cutter gun within reach, rolled himself in a thermal blanket, and tried to switch his mind off.

Despite his tiredness, he found sleep elusive. The cold, pebbly ground and the inadequate blanket were factors in keeping him awake, but what ultimately kept sleep at bay were the wild swings of emotion he felt. He struggled against the near certainty of a battle and the unnerving possibility that, in the darkness, a sheet-dragon creature circled above them. To seek relief, Merral turned his mind to warm thoughts of Anya and again felt excited that she cared for him and that he cared for her. Yet from that peak of exhilaration, he would soon slide into guilty feelings about Isabella, and then the fear would return. Eventually sleep came, only to be broken after what seemed mere seconds by a gentle shaking and Philip Matakala's apologetic voice in his ear asking him to wake up.

Stiffly, Merral pulled himself to his feet, yawning and rubbing his face, aware he was covered in a cold dew. His watch told him it was almost five. Now, an hour before dawn, the dark of the western sky was already becoming lighter.

Philip had prepared him a cup of coffee, and Merral gratefully drank it and ate some biscuits. Then putting his armored jacket and the goggles back on, he picked up his gun and walked slowly back down the stream valley. Ahead he could easily make out the figure of the watching soldier on the ridge, the circuitry of his goggles painting his warm body orange against the cold blue of the ground. Carefully, Merral climbed to the summit of the mound and crawled forward to get alongside the man who, hearing his footsteps, turned toward him as he approached.

"Morning," Merral said quietly.

"Morning, sir. Good to see you. Very good." Merral recognized who it was and noted the relief in the voice of Lorrin Venn.

"See anything, Lorrin?"

"No, sir, but I feel it." Merral sensed him shudder. "Nasty-looking ship. Gives me the creeps." Merral found it hard to remember the bubbly young man whom he had first met and realized that he hadn't heard Lorrin whistle at any time during the night.

"Wish you were back working in Isterrane?"

There was a faint pause. "I won't say, sir, that in the last hour, the idea hasn't come to me," Lorrin answered; then Merral felt he smiled. "But I asked for this. I asked you to get me in on this. And I'll stick with it. . . ."

"That's the spirit, Lorrin. I can't say I'm very happy about it."

"Yes. Well, I suppose back in Isterrane it all seemed . . . well, exciting. Like a sort of grand sports event. Know what I mean, sir? I couldn't miss it, could I?"

"No, I guess you couldn't," Merral replied.

"I've been thinking about this. I mean this is the—I don't know—*strangest* event in the history of the Assembly. This is history in the making. And when it gets talked about in the future, I want to be able to say, 'I was there.' Yet I'm still a bit scared, sir."

"I don't blame you, Lorrin. The key thing is, I suppose, to do what you have to do. That's what I tell myself."

"I'll do my best, sir."

Merral suddenly felt sorry for Lorrin. "I know you will. Now, any signs of life?"

"I think they vented steam a few minutes ago. A cloud of something warm, but otherwise it's quiet. I thought I saw something move around just now below the ship, but I couldn't be sure."

"Nothing on this side then. No birds or bats?"

"No, sir," Lorrin said with just a hint of hesitation. "But I find your eyes play tricks after a while."

"In what way?" Merral asked, feeling that something lay behind his words.

"Well . . . I thought I heard footsteps earlier. Lee Rodwen was with me and he agreed. But there was no sign of anything. Or anybody. But we felt, well . . . watched."

Unsettled by his words, Merral glanced around with the night goggles but saw nothing but cold ground and a gnarled pine tree to his left.

After dismissing Lorrin, Merral stared again at the ship for several minutes but saw nothing new. He found the silence odd; it was a strange and tense quietness, as if some colossal storm was brewing. He slid his goggles up and squinted into the darkness with his unaided eyesight. Above him, the stars were glowing. In the sky ahead, the pure blackness of night was now turning into shades of indigo, and above the jagged horizon the stars were fading out.

Indeed, by straining his eyes, Merral could make out the silhouettes of the eastern Rim Ranges standing black against the purpling sky. Wreathes of mist drifted this way and that in the slight westerly breeze.

Merral slid the goggles back down and examined the ship again with the scope. There was no sign of activity. He gave up looking and concentrated on listening, stretching his senses as far as he could, swinging his head this way and that. He wondered whether Lorrin and Lee had really heard anything. Or had it simply been their imaginations?

He listened carefully, but all he could hear was the faint rustling of the breeze in the branches on the solitary pine tree nearby and the feeble gurgle of water in the stream behind. There was no sound of animal life: no birds, not even the buzz of an insect. Merral felt ill at ease.

Then he looked again at the distant ship and felt suddenly almost overwhelmed by its power and menace. In contrast to that machine, his own force for the initial attack seemed pathetic; a mere sixty men, mostly dragged from college studies barely days ago, with almost every piece of equipment improvised from quarrying, farming, or forestry. True, they had courage and dedication, and Merral knew he could rely on them to do their best, but what he had seemed so puny. *Our only real asset is surprise, and even that might have been compromised. . . . Surely, we are like a bunch of village children suddenly thrown into playing a Team-Ball game against the Isterrane champions.*

As Merral stared across the still, dark waters of Lake Fallambet Five and considered the sheer inadequacy of his forces, he slipped into silent prayer. Yet, here and now, it seemed that prayer was not easy. Merral was able to say the words in his mind, but as he tried to pray for the day ahead, words were all that they seemed to be. Irritatingly, Anya's form and face seemed to teasingly pop up into his prayers and distract him with guilt and desire. Finally he ended his praying, feeling that there was no answer.

As he considered the situation, Merral felt himself drifting toward self-pity and even anger. Here he was, on the verge of awesome events and about to lead men to possible—even probable—death, and badly in need of God's support. Yet instead, he had silence. *Say something, Lord!* But the silence only continued.

Suddenly Merral heard the tiniest of noises off to the right. He knew with certainty that another man had joined him. He felt a spasm of irritation that he had been so absorbed in his own struggles that he had missed his arrival. Merral swung his head round but, to his surprise, the goggles showed only the cold ground and the single forlorn pine.

I must have imagined it.

As he looked back across the lake to the ship, there was another slight sound from his right. It was as if one of the men was adjusting his position on the ground. Mistrustful now of his goggles, Merral slid them up and peered into the darkness toward where he had heard the sound.

He stopped breathing.

A mere arm's length away from him, a large, dark shape was lying on the ground.

Slowly, taking strained breaths and aware that his hands were shaking, Merral put the goggles back over his eyes. To his surprise, he could make out no form there and no hint of any heat source disturbing the uniform chill blueness of the ground. Alarm threatening to flood his mind, Merral slid the goggles up again and stared to his right. Were his senses playing tricks on him?

The shape was still there and Merral peered at it. He shivered, certain now that something was lying next to him—something the size and shape of a man.

The dark form next to him stirred, and abruptly Merral felt under a gaze that seemed to go right through him. Suddenly he felt terribly exposed, as if he was being examined. An almost irresistible urge to run and hide descended on him.

In the silence the figure spoke. "Man, a time has passed. The war deepens."

"I'm sorry," Merral replied, hearing his voice wobbling with fear. "I can't remember your name."

Even as he spoke, he knew what he heard was not the voice of any man he knew. Indeed, he realized, with a strange and chilling certainty, the voice was not human. It was in one way characterless and neutral, and yet in another it had an extraordinary and unassailable authority.

"You do not know my name."

Merral's throat was suddenly dry. "I mean," he said, swallowing nervously, "you, er, are one of my men?"

"One of *your* men? In no sense."

The words held a rebuke.

"Then who are you?" Merral asked, his hand inching toward his gun. Perhaps, he thought, the enemy was already among them. His fingers closed around the stock. "Who are you?" he repeated.

The voice broke the silence. "Man, you are right to be concerned. I have come as the representative of the King."

Merral felt that the word *King* reverberated strangely, as if it had its own special resonance.

Before Merral could answer, the voice spoke again. "The King who was, and is, and is to come. The one who was slain as a Lamb and rules as a Lion. Does that answer your question?"

"Yes," quavered Merral, realizing that whatever this creature was, it was not an enemy. He felt at once relieved, chastened, and terrified. "But—but, who are you?" he asked.

There was another pause. "I am an envoy. I am sent to you from the Highest."

Suddenly it came to Merral in a flash of comprehension that this had to be the strange being who, only hours before the Gate was destroyed, had appeared to Perena.

"You—you are the one who spoke to Perena Lewitz? the one who warned her about the Gate?"

Slowly, and with only the faintest rustling sound, the dark form seemed to rise up from the ground and stand upright, obscuring the waning stars. Merral peered up at the figure, knowing with a hard certainty that the being that stood before him was gazing down at him with stern, cold, invisible eyes. He suddenly felt small and exposed, as if he were a mouse under an eagle's gaze.

"I did," the voice said.

Merral sensed, with a deepening fear, the head move as if to stare more closely at him. He cringed. *I ought to thank him. I owe him my life.*

"Man, whom do you serve?" the voice asked suddenly, its tone cutting and sharp.

"The King, of course," Merral answered. "It goes without saying. I bear his badge."

In the darkness, he reached out to his shoulder and touched the embossed Lamb and Stars emblem on his armored jacket.

The voice spoke again. "Nothing goes without saying. It never did. And least of all now, with the enemy unchained."

The blackness that marked the figure's head seemed to bend accusingly over him. "So you are his servant?"

"Er, yes. Yes, of course," Merral answered, shivering and wondering why he sounded so guilty.

"So you obey him in all matters?"

The word *all* seemed somehow to have a universal feel to it, as if there was nothing it did not include. Merral felt a new stab of discomfort, as if somewhere, some raw nerve in his soul was being probed.

"Why, yes," he answered, desperately wishing that the conversation might move on to other subjects.

"In *all* matters, Man?" Merral found the coolly knowing tone to the voice profoundly unnerving.

"Well, yes . . . ," Merral answered slowly, aware of something like acid eating into his mind and etching around thoughts of Isabella and Anya.

"So there is nothing that has happened this night of which you are ashamed?"

There was a terrible ring to the words, and Merral quailed at them. He felt as if a spotlight had illuminated the innermost parts of his life.

"Well, I . . . I suppose I may have . . . made an error of judgment."

The only answer was a strange and terrible silence in which Merral felt he had to speak. "I was confused," he said, almost spluttering his words, feeling his face flush. "It's, well, been an awful time. *Awful.*"

"Man, did I ask for your excuses?"

"No . . ." Merral fell silent.

"You broke a promise."

"But that . . . ," Merral hesitated, feeling transfixed by the invisible gaze of this visitor. "Well, you see, Isabella extracted it from me. . . ."

"And what has that do with breaking a promise?"

"Ah, things have been changing in Ynysmant. It has been very hard."

There was a heavy silence before the dark figure spoke again.

"I was sent on the basis that you wanted help. Is that still the case?" Now the words seemed to have a ring of impatience in them.

Suddenly, Merral felt a surge of defiance. He had to resist. "I'm sorry," he said, "but I must say that she manipulated me."

"Really?" There was a strange weariness in the voice. "Your first ancestor used a similar excuse. In the beginning."

"Well, I do feel that Isabella—"

"Man, I was sent to deal with Merral D'Avanos. Not any Isabella."

Merral suddenly felt that being apologetic might be more profitable. This terrible figure had to be placated. "Look, I'm sorry," he said. "What must I do?"

"Man, you must resolve to repair the wrongs you have done. The commitment you made must stand until it is ended—if it is to be ended—by agreement between you. You must also explain the true situation to the one you lied to and encouraged unfairly. And apologize. And apologizing, I must remind you, is not the same as making excuses."

It suddenly occurred to Merral that both actions were horribly unattractive. "Look, is this important, I mean, right now? *Really* important?"

There was a sound like an angry intake of breath. "Of course!" The words were charged with displeasure. "Do not add folly to dishonesty. You have invoked the King's help this day of battle because of his covenant agreement with his people. At the heart of all covenants lies obedience and faithfulness. Yet in these last few hours you have despised both of these in your own life."

From nowhere came the wild thought that he couldn't let Anya go. *I must fight for her.* "But—"

"Enough, Man!" The envoy said, and his dark form loomed over Merral so that the voice almost seemed to buffet him physically. "Choose. If you wish to fight these things in *your* strength, then you may do so." Merral, pressing himself against the ground, found the pause before the voice spoke again as menacing as any words. “But I warn you, you will not win. Not against these foes.”

Suddenly the voice sounded as if it was retreating into the distance. “Or if you do win, it will be such a victory that men and women will wish until the end of time that you had lost.”

Merral sensed the figure seemed less substantial now, as if it were merely smoke or mist.

“Which will it be, Man?” asked the quieter, fainter voice. He could see a star now where the figure had stood, as if the envoy was fading away.

His mind buffeted by a tumult of emotions, Merral hesitated, unable to choose between his fears and his desires.

“Decide,” the voice said, but now it was a drained echo coming from a vast distance. Where the envoy’s figure had been, more and more stars were becoming visible.

Suddenly a great and awful fear came into Merral’s mind, a terror of an unspeakable darkness and grief. In the fear, he saw that there was only one way forward.

“Please! I’m sorry. I choose the right way,” he cried, and this time he was aware his contrition was genuine. “I am truly sorry and I repent. I will try to sort out things with Anya and Isabella.”

“Try?” The voice was nearer now and the figure more solid. Stars vanished. “That is inadequate, Man. *Do.* Make things right whatever it costs you. And watch yourself, Merral D’Avanos. The enemy delights in using a man against himself.” The voice seemed to resonate strangely. “He seeks your ruin. For him, there are more satisfying and useful ways for your destruction than fire, sword, or tooth.”

“I can imagine.”

“Imagine?” The rebuke in the tone was tangible. “Man, I have *seen.*” There was a knife’s edge to the words. “I saw Saul, son of Kish, go from mighty warrior over Israel to the haunted wreckage of a man. And many after him. Lesser and greater. I am an envoy and I am a witness.”

Merral, now utterly appalled at the idea that he had tried to withstand this being, felt unable to speak.

“Now listen, Man,” the envoy went on. “We have wasted time. The hour of battle is almost upon you. I am to warn you of the thing on the ship.”

“The dragon thing?”

“That? That is a servant, no more. It is its master you must fear. That is a spirit, released from the utter depths and now housed in a body crafted for it by some of your race.”

“Mine?”

“Yes. But listen. Such beings are powerful and not easily vanquished.

They remain linked to their own realm and derive their power from there. Even were that ship to be utterly destroyed, that being would shed its body and persist here as a disembodied form. Your world would not care for that."

"Like a ghost?"

"Their kind has had that name. And others. To destroy it completely, the link with its realm must first be broken. Then, while it is weakened, you can consign it back to the abyss."

Merral felt a cold sweat on his forehead. "And how am I to do that?"

"You, and you alone, will enter the ship. You will need courage and arms. Take your gun, a blade, and a charge. I will meet you inside to give you instructions. There, Man, you must fight, and there is no certainty of victory. I do not know the outcome. Only the King does."

Against the lightening sky, Merral felt that he could make out limbs and a head on the envoy's form.

"I want to know—please—will there be casualties?"

"Man, if you want to battle evil without loss, then evil has already won."

"I see. I just wanted to know."

"You have the only guarantees that there are, and those have existed since the founding of the worlds. Have faith in the King, and be true to him and his Word and, in the end, all will be well."

"In the end, yes. But what about in the meantime?"

"That? *That* is mere curiosity." There was almost scorn in the words. "Play your part. See, the sun rises."

The voice had begun to become more distant again. The figure suddenly began to fade away as if it had been merely vapor.

"Merral D'Avanos," came the whisper, "I trust we will meet in the ship."

"Wait!" Merral cried, but there was only silence, and he knew he was now alone.

He stared across the lake, his mind reeling both at the contact he had had and the dreadful revelation about his own behavior. He found himself humbly asking God for forgiveness. *How appalling,* he thought in a mood of bitter astonishment, *that I could have ever behaved like that.*

Then, suddenly aware that dawn was about to break, Merral forced himself to consider the task ahead. Across the western sky the stars were fading out; in the predawn glow he could make out the difference between the lake and the rough land beyond and see the ship with his naked eye. Looking at his watch, he saw that there was just twenty minutes before the hoverer would start its journey up the lake.

He peered again at the ship through the fieldscope, seeing slightly more details of it now. As he looked at it, he felt that Perena's insight had been right: this could never have been an Assembly ship. Not that all Assembly vessels were beautiful; the *Emilia Kay,* for a start, was hardly stunning, but she had a plain functional harmony that was pleasing. This intruder ship, by contrast, had an unattractiveness that seemed almost to be deliberate.

Realizing that dawn was only minutes away, Merral took off the night goggles and laid them aside. From now on, there would be enough natural light. He turned his gaze back to the ship. With a shock, he realized that something was different. He snatched up the fieldscope to see that around the ship there were creatures moving like ants around a fragment of food. It took him a few seconds to work out exactly what was happening and a few more seconds for the implications to sink in. Above the long black hull, camouflage sheeting was being rolled back, and down on the ground, he could make out creatures working on the supporting frame.

Merral grabbed the microphone, fumbled for the call button, and pressed it.

"Frankie!" he snapped, hearing agitation—if not panic—in his voice. "They are preparing the ship for takeoff. Get the men ready for action. Alert Perena and Zak's team, now!"

"Are you sure, sir?"

"Yes!"

"Okay, will do!"

As Merral turned back to the view of the ship, he could hear orders being given. Desperately, he tried to weigh his limited options. Was he to wait for the diplomatic team? Or should they launch their attack now? It was a complication he had not envisaged.

He looked across again to the intruder vessel, hoping against hope that he had been mistaken. Yet, in the growing light, there could be no doubt that they were indeed removing the camouflage. As he watched, Merral noted that the tall, dark ape-creatures were doing most of the lifting with their long forelimbs, while the smaller cockroach-beasts scurried around at their feet, apparently working on lesser tasks. The shapes and characteristic movements of the two intruder types dug up hateful memories to Merral that he tried to suppress.

There was a bleep from beside him and he picked up the handset.

He could hear Frankie breathing heavily. "We are now ready, sir. I guess we can launch within seconds."

"Okay. I don't think they are going to leave just yet. There is still work to do. But it definitely looks like they are getting ready to move. I'll get on board as you come past."

"Fine. I'll have a helmet ready for you, sir." Besides Frankie, Merral could hear men moving.

"Oh, and I want an explosive charge too."

"For you, sir?" Frankie answered, his tone filled with doubt.

"Yes," Merral answered, hearing the reluctance in his own voice. "I'm going to get inside the ship. I may need it."

"Inside?" There was a pause. "Er, sir, did we discuss that?"

"No, Lieutenant, we didn't," Merral said, surprising himself with the sharp authority in his voice.

"Yes, sir," Frankie answered. "A kilo charge with an intermolecular cement pad and a sixty-second fuse—will that be all right? That's all we have."

I have no idea. I haven't a clue. "Ideal. Thanks, and keep the line open."

A sliver of brilliant red light suddenly rose over the horizon, and the rays of the new sun cut through the mist patches on the water. Even as Merral watched, the world seemed to change. The light lit up the hill around him, and he felt grateful for the warmth of its rays. He was suddenly awed by the realization that, with the exception of the space conflicts that ended the Rebellion, this was going to be the first true battle of mankind under a strange sun. Then he pushed the thought aside, telling himself that in reality it wouldn't make the slightest bit of difference.

Merral switched his gaze back to the ship. Here it was now plain, even to the naked eye, that the camouflage was being dismantled. With the fieldscope, Merral could see piles of metal tubes and fabric sheeting accumulating on the sand and stones at the foot of the strange vessel. It must, he decided, be more than coincidence that this was happening only a day after the attack on Felicity. If they knew they were discovered, were they then also prepared against any attack?

Merral tried to count the figures opposite. There were perhaps a dozen or more of the ape-creatures and at least the same number of the cockroach-beasts. Of the winged creature or men there was no evidence. *We are at least matched in numbers, and there may be many more inside.*

Without warning, the creatures burst into action. The fabric sheets and metal frames were hastily thrown aside, and the antlike figures began running about at the foot of the ship. A faint mechanical noise drifting up from the southern part of the lake explained the new activity. The hoverer was on schedule and had already been seen.

Merral stared down the lake. Far away in the middle of the water, the frail white dot of the hoverer was moving up toward them. He reached for the microphone, hoping that, away to the north, the other team was ready.

"Frankie," he said, marveling at how steady his voice sounded, "the diplomatic team is in view and has been seen by the ship."

"They said they were moving, sir. Everybody here is ready to go. Ready for your word."

Merral turned his gaze back to the ship, where there was renewed activity. Some of the creatures had returned to packing the camouflage sheeting while others were bringing a tubular apparatus on a tripod down the ramp and out onto the lake strand.

A weapon, Merral realized with a feeling of horror. He was tempted to call Frankie and have him order the hoverer to turn back. In the end, he resisted the idea. The rules they had agreed upon were plain. There had to be clear evidence of the failure of diplomacy and preferably active aggression by the intruders before any Assembly attack could take place.

With the fieldscope, Merral looked south down the lake, seeing the hoverer moving straight and steady toward the Intruder ship. He could make out the flags flying, the creamy V-shape of the wake behind, and could even make out dark forms of two people standing erect by the hoverer's prow. He lowered the scope, trying to gauge the present distance between the hoverer and the ship. Contact must only be minutes away.

There was a yellow flash on the other side of the lake.

A large, dirty orange sphere of flame rolled from below the ship across the water straight at the approaching hoverer. Trailing white steam behind it, the ball crossed the gap between the ship and the hoverer in under a second. As the burning sphere was on the point of engulfing its target, the hoverer lurched abruptly sideways.

The evasive action came too late.

The flaming ball, almost half the size of the hoverer, struck the side of the hull and rolled over the vessel in a explosion of oily golden light.

Merral, already speaking into the handset, had a confused impression of the white craft being thrown up and sideways, and of tiny figures being flung into the water.

"Hoverer attacked! Hoverer attacked!" he shouted. "Everybody start immediate operations!"

As he spoke, the boom of the explosion reached him. Waiting only a fraction of a second for Frankie to acknowledge his order, Merral flung the handset aside and grabbed his gun.

As he did, out of the corner of his eye he caught a glimpse of another smoking ball of flame being fired from below the intruder ship. Whether it struck what was left of the hoverer Merral never saw, because he was already slithering down the stony slope toward the stream and his men.

Two thoughts hammered together in his brain as he raced down: a cold fury that the intruders had attacked an unarmed boat and a cloying fear that the sleds would suffer the same fate before they were halfway across the lake.

"Let it not be!" he gasped under his breath as he slid down, sending a volley of small stones flying around. "Lord, let us at least have a chance to fight!"

40

As Merral reached the bottom of the slope, the sled, full of men in uniforms grappling with gear and weapons, came silently skimming down through the shadows toward him. It slowed down briefly. He clambered clumsily on board, and outstretched hands guided him roughly into a seat near the front.

The sled renewed its acceleration down the valley. All around him, Merral glimpsed anonymous-looking, pale, stern-faced men bracing themselves, holding guns, and checking webbing and straps. Lorrin Venn, scared excitement written across his face, passed him a helmet, while someone else fastened a belt around him. As someone passed him a small package labeled with ominous red symbols, Merral heard Frankie, sitting at the front of the sled, yelling into his helmet microphone. Merral, unable to make out his words, presumed he was talking either to the *Emilia Kay* or Zak's team.

Suddenly he turned to Merral. "What happened?" he shouted, tightening his helmet strap.

"They fired a big ball of flame without warning!" Merral yelled back, aware of the men around him on the sled listening. "It exploded over them. They didn't really have a chance! Then they fired again!"

Frankie shook his head angrily and turned to face forward.

The rock-strewn valley was opening up on either side of them now as they raced down, and then suddenly they were out onto the flat delta surface and into the full glare of the rising sun. Philip slowed the sled down to align it with the exact coordinates for the computer-controlled approach.

To the south of them, Merral glimpsed a turbulent column of dense white and gray smoke spiraling up from the waters of the lake. He tried to derive some comfort from its quantity, telling himself that it looked as if someone at least had survived long enough to trigger the smoke canisters.

"Now!" Frankie shouted. Merral caught a glimpse of Philip hitting a red switch newly welded on the control panel.

The booster pack ignited.

There was a surging, booming roar from the rear of the sled. Merral, pressed back against his seat, felt the hull beginning to vibrate like a beaten drum as the sled raced, with growing speed, over the desolate ground and green reed clumps.

They were still accelerating as they came to the water's edge, and Merral found himself holding on even tighter as the slipstream began to whip past him and snatch at clothing and straps. The sled was impossibly low, and he felt that there was barely a handbreadth between them and the wave crests. Every so often they clipped the top of a wave with a hissing slap and the sled gave a little bound that made Merral's tense stomach quiver again. At any second, he expected the sled to overturn. Glancing back at the shoreline they had come from—already diminishing into the distance—he could see the wake of spray and fumes trailing behind them. *They will have seen us now,* he thought, looking ahead to where the great dark silhouette of the fuselage of the intruder ship was now rising up above the approaching shoreline.

Merral braced himself again, remembering that at any moment the computer would use the gravity-modifying engine to flick the sled sharply to the side. A maneuver, he unhappily reminded himself, that they had never done at anything like this speed and that the sled had never been designed for.

Now!

The sled jerked a dozen meters to the right, bobbed sharply, and struck the wave crests with a great slapping noise. Merral felt that if he hadn't been strapped in he would have been thrown free of his seat. Yelps of exhilaration mixed with alarm went up from the other men. Over the roar of the motor, Merral could hear the creaking of the titanium skin and girders under the strain of the jump. The sled wobbled, smacked the water again, recovered its equilibrium, and raced onward.

Merral peered ahead, squinting into the dazzling sun, his eyes fixed on the intruder ship still visible only as a vast silhouette.

They were still accelerating but no longer at such a fast rate. Merral saw that they were already halfway across the lake.

They hit a wave. Water flew up everywhere into the sunlight, and for a second, a faint, ghostly rainbow appeared. *A covenant sign,* Merral told himself, his mind numbed by the wild vibration. *We must have hope and have faith.*

The sled shot sideways, this time to the left, and again he found himself pounded back against the seat frame.

Now there was spray all around him, and Merral felt cold water on his face and seeping into his clothes.

From under the rear of the intruder vessel came a bright yellow flash. Then, like an infant sun, a glowing orange disk of fire came streaking straight toward them.

There was shouting around him. Everyone ducked.

Just as it seemed that they would be engulfed by the spinning fireball, the sled suddenly shot to the right. Barely two meters away, the fiery sphere—a man's height or more in diameter—flew past them with an angry hissing noise. The smell of steam and smoke drifted past from its wake.

Merral was suddenly aware of a new grimness on the faces of the men around him. Any remaining exhilaration had been removed by the realization that they had been fired upon. The beach was fast approaching, and there were other questions to ask.

Merral wiped cold spray from his eyes and tried to focus on the bouncing image ahead. The black ship now dominated the view, and below it Merral could make out distinct shapes of the long-limbed, slouching ape-creatures. At their feet, cockroach-beasts with their restless rocking movements scuttled around. Merral had a worrying impression that there were more of them than there ought to be. The ship, too, was bigger than he had imagined.

We've miscalculated. His stomach lurched. *It's too late to turn back.*

There was another flash, but this time it came from the nose of the ship and the sphere of flame flew north over the waters. *A second gun,* Merral thought in alarm as he traced the projectile's motion. Its target, another dark dot trailing spray and fumes behind it, was racing onward to the intruder ship.

He jabbed the man next to him. "Look! Zak's team!" he shouted, and as he watched he saw the second sled jink sideways. A moment later, the ball of flame sprinted harmlessly past it.

His own sled lurched violently to the left again, and water flew around them.

He could hear Frankie and Philip shouting together, their voices barely audible over the roar of the booster, the hiss of spray, and the booming slap of the hull against the waves.

Frankie leaned toward Merral, bellowing at him with exaggerated movements of his mouth. "Sir, Philip wants to go straight at the gun! A smoother landing there. Better hang on tight!"

Then there was another burst of light from the rear of the great black ship, and Merral saw a new flaming sphere coming toward them.

No! He suddenly saw with relief that it was aimed to their right and would easily miss them. Then he realized that it had been so directed that when—as must happen any second—the sled made the next lateral slip, their rightward slide would take them into its path. Their tactics had been deduced and already countered.

"Down everyone!" Merral screamed, pressing himself down against the hard wet metal and expecting at any second to be thrown into the water.

Suddenly the sled lurched.

But to the left.

The flaming globe hissed well away from them. Merral made a mental note to praise whoever had written the program. If he got the chance.

As he looked at the shore, his relief was short-lived. They were barely seconds away from the water's edge, and they were clearly going too fast. The beach was rough and boulder strewn, and the cliff face beyond it seemed horribly close. They had to decelerate.

Merral watched Philip maniacally flicking switches. He was struck by the fact that there was now water slopping around inside the hull and that his feet were already soaked.

The booster cut out.

At that precise moment, Philip tugged on a control panel lever. The nose of the sled rose up into the air and the rear end struck the water with an awesome, shuddering crash.

For a fearful instant, Merral, flung viciously against his safety belt, was aware of boiling white water below and pale blue sky above. From all around him came the awful noise of creaking and flexing metal. Just as he was sure they were going to tip over, the nose came down and cracked onto the water in a bone-jarring blow. A fountain of white spray gushed up all around.

The sled ploughed on.

They were slower now. Yet a glance at the shore ahead where the sands were glittering in the new sunlight showed they were still not slow enough. On the intimidating, charcoal black bulk of the ship he could make out details of the fins, ramp, and legs. Beneath the ship, creatures of both sorts were running around across the gleaming sand like animated black paper cutouts, their legs kicking up little sprays of sand as they ran. With a ghastly feeling in the pit of his stomach, Merral realized that there were far too many intruders. They had indeed badly miscalculated.

There was a screaming whine as the engines were thrown into reverse. Out of the corner of his eye, Merral glimpsed red lights flashing furiously on the control panel.

Philip was turning the sled now, swinging it toward the rear of the ship, tilting it like a racing yacht. Now they were aiming straight for where two of the ape-creatures, their odd shapes warped still further by vastly elongated shadows, were swinging the barreled gun toward them.

Sensations now came in so fast that Merral had barely time to assimilate them: rippled sands under the water, little waves breaking against the strand, spray in his face, intense black shadow under the ship, Philip suddenly flicking the gravity-modifying engine switch, the knife edge of fear in his stomach.

The sled struck the water again with a ferocious, deafening smack.

For a second it bounced up and then, lunging forward, thudded heavily onto the shore.

There were now new sensations: the scream of metal on sand and rock, the hissing spray of grit flying everywhere, the mountainous rear of the ship sliding above them like a vast black roof blocking out the sun, and the dull brown pebbly cliff racing toward them.

At the gun, black animal shapes were suddenly trying to throw themselves out of the way.

They struck the gun.

There was a prolonged grinding crash of metal upon metal. With an appalling soft, liquid thud, something large and black and as limp as a child's toy flew overhead, its outstretched limbs flailing against the sun.

The sled slewed and jolted crazily and then, with an insane ear-piercing screech, they came to a halt in a cloud of dust and sand.

For a brief, stunned instant there was a numbed silence.

Then, apparently from everywhere at once, furious shouts and cries erupted. Some—familiar and human—were from the sled as the men tried to leap free. Others—wild and animal—came from underneath the intruder ship.

Merral, partly dazed by the impact, fumbled for his belt release catch and clambered free, trying to orient himself. They had stopped just behind the intruder ship. As he stood unsteadily on the sand he could see, towering above him as high as a five-story building, the curved, blackened rear surface of the ship broken only by three inset thruster nozzles.

The foot of the cliff was less than ten meters to their right. As he realized how close they had come to hitting it, he heard a sudden, bellowed warning.

Something the size of a small man, brown and shining like wet wood, was racing toward him. On the edge of his vision, Merral saw another cockroach-beast coming from his left. Behind that was another. And another.

Merral raised his gun and, trying to steady his shaking hands, flicked off the safety switch. There was a gratifying hum from the stock as the electronics came to life. He sighted on the heaving chest of the cockroach-beast and fired. The gun hissed. Merral saw the hard central ridge of fused plates become momentarily illuminated with a red disc of light. There was a faint wisp of smoke. With a rattling and spluttering scream, the creature toppled over.

As Merral trained his gun on a new target, there were bellows, screeches, and yells all around him, and he was suddenly aware that he was in the midst of a bitter and chaotic hand-to-hand battle. All about him soldiers, ape-creatures, and cockroach-beasts were locked into a melee so intense that it was impossible to work out what was happening. Immediately to his left, a yelling man was kicking wildly at a cockroach-beast slashing at his legs with its bladed fingers. Barely thinking, Merral reversed his gun and swung the butt as hard as he could against the creature's plated head. There was a sharp and sickening crack, and the beast was flung backward onto the ground.

The soldier the beast had been attacking aimed his gun and fired repeatedly at it. There was a smell of blood, steam, and fear.

Another cockroach-beast, its carapace the color of old leaves, leapt ferociously at Merral, who dodged desperately to one side. Its pincer-like digits slid a handbreadth away from his face and clattered harmlessly on his armored jacket.

For a fraction of a second, Merral glimpsed dark eyes glaring at him and the moist, twitching slot of a mouth opening and shutting around yellowing, needlelike teeth.

Thrown off balance, his attacker tumbled to the ground beyond him. With a leap of surprising energy and speed, it sprung back upright and turned to face him, chattering angrily as it flexed its armored legs.

As Merral raised the gun, it jumped at his face. Instinctively, Merral jabbed with the barrel, striking the creature in the neck while it was in midair. The beast toppled back and hit the sand. As it tried to rise, Merral, aiming the gun by intuition, fired twice. With an uncontrollable rattling of limbs, the cockroach-beast fell back onto the bloodied sand.

Almost at his feet, a soldier, his helmet awry, was rolling on the ground, locked in a bitter embrace with a thrashing black ape-creature that almost dwarfed him and whose arms were clamped round his throat. A fellow soldier danced around the struggling pair, stabbing and slashing away with his bush knife at the hairy limbs whenever he could. Beyond him, another man, screaming in fear or anger—or both—was furiously hitting a further ape-creature in the face with the butt of his gun.

As Merral ran over to help, he saw two more ape-creatures running toward him with their elongated arms held high and their teeth bared. He turned, fired, and missed. He found the focus beam switch with wet fingers, slid it to the "wide" setting, and fired again and again. The shots seemed to have no effect and the creatures were almost upon him. Then, as suddenly as if it had been a machine, the leading ape-creature stopped dead in its tracks. Its jaws opened wide in a howl of pain and it began slapping its shoulder, from where Merral saw a trickle of smoke emerging. Suddenly a line of yellow flames flickered along the massive chest and leapt across to the wrist of the beating hand. With a series of pitiful screams, the creature turned and loped frantically toward the lake where it plunged its smoldering body into the waters. The other creature fled back under the hull of the ship.

Suddenly Merral was aware that the men around him were looking for new enemies. The attack was over. Around the sled were strewn the bodies of their attackers; perhaps seven cockroach-beasts and three ape-creatures, looking far less human in death than in life.

Frankie, his face streaked with blood and looking this way and that with a wild-eyed gaze, was gesturing frantically to a stack of metal struts and plates some way back against a pile of boulders near the cliff.

"Back! Over here!" he shouted, his voice hoarse. "Take cover!"

Slowly, their pale faces proclaiming their shock and horror, the men followed his gesture, picking up weapons and helmets as they went. Two were limping, one badly. A sobbing man was led away past Merral, clutching a hand shorn of fingers. An ape-creature writhed momentarily and then lay still.

Guns, chest armor, and surprise gained us this brief victory, Merral thought, a part of his mind marveling at his ability to analyze under stress. A glance around suggested that all of his men lived, but that two at least were injured to the point that they could take no further part in the fighting. *Next time, it may be different.* As the thought came, he realized that the next time might be only seconds away.

Frankie, his trousers torn and dirtied by red smears, ran over to him. "Sir, better take cover with us. . . ." He looked ahead under the ship. "There's dozens more there!" he cried, his voice ringing with alarm.

Merral looked over to see more dark forms emerging off the ramp and gathering in the deep shadows under the hull. Instinctively, he ducked down behind the tilted sled, gesturing to Frankie to join him. As the lieutenant squatted next to him, Merral looked around, trying to take stock of the situation, noting that the remaining men were running or limping to take cover behind the equipment pile.

Frankie stared at Merral, his hands shaking. "I could never have imagined it, sir." He swallowed and looked at Merral with astonished and troubled blue eyes. "Sorry, I'm kinda shaken up. I ended up sticking my gun barrel in the mouth of one of those ape things. I had to pull the trigger. . . ." He closed his eyes and shuddered. "Sir, can you imagine what happened?" he asked.

"Take it easy, Frankie," Merral said, patting him on the arm, feeling faintly ridiculous as he did it. "You've a done a good job so far. Any ideas for the second half of the match?"

Frankie shook his head. "Sir, I'm afraid . . . well, I don't think we can go ahead with the plan—" He looked around. "We are down to twenty-seven, twenty-six men. There's another twenty or so of them and more coming. And that front leg's past them. What do we do, sir?"

There was such a pathetic note in his voice that Merral felt a spasm of pity for him. The exercises at Tanaris had been so simple. This was reality. A situation they were unprepared for, a location away from where they were supposed to be, and an enemy that was more horrible and more numerous than they had expected.

"Zak's team?" Merral asked. "Did you see what happened to them?"

"Zak's team? Oh yeah. I think I saw them land north of the ship, sir. They were being fired on too. And there was a bay there."

"Let's hope they made it," Merral said

Frankie glanced down, saw a smear of blood and black hair on the Lamb and Stars emblem on his armor jacket, and began to rub it clean with a finger.

"Sorry, sir. I guess I look a mess, eh?" Frankie's jaw began moving up and down as if he were chewing something. Then he seemed to snap back into reality. "Sir, there are too many for us to attack."

Merral glanced back to the rest of the team, who were taking cover behind the equipment piles and enlarging depressions in the sand. "True, Frankie. Let's go for Game Plan B."

"Game Plan B, sir? What's that? I don't remember that."

"Easy, Frankie, easy," Merral said, feeling that by trying to calm Frankie he was calming himself. "You get your men to take cover by those boulders. Dig down into the sand like they are doing now, but get them as deep as they can. And use that equipment for cover. If you can keep firing and hitting one or two of them, that will help. Slowly whittle them down until we get more people here."

"Sir, is that okay?" Frankie asked, his eyes wild. "I mean we *are* supposed to take the ship. Orders."

"I know, Frankie. But they aren't going to fly away with everybody outside. Keep everybody there. If they show signs of taking off, then you can risk everything and run and attack the legs."

Frankie's eyelids flickered, then he swallowed, turned around, and began shouting instructions to the men to dig down and make defenses.

Merral looked ahead to the ship. Beyond the massive rear legs with their pipes and pistons, he glimpsed creatures running and hiding behind some of the piles of metal and camouflage sheets near the ramp. He turned his gaze to the lake, taking in the smoke still hanging over the water behind him. Where was the other sled?

Frankie nudged him. "Sir, should I call Perena and warn her?"

"Good idea. Hadn't thought of that. If there are more of those guns around the ship, she could be in trouble." He looked around. "Tell her to come in from the east and land the men on the slope above the ship. But not to approach from the lake."

"Yeah. Land on the cliff top . . . Makes sense. It'll give us some protection from an attack up there. Okay. I'll do it."

"Good," Merral answered, relieved that, in spite of being traumatized, his lieutenant showed signs of being able to think. "If these things get up top, we'll have a problem."

"Yeah, sir. Right. We don't need another attack from there."

As Frankie took out his diary and talked into it, Merral examined the ship further and wondered how he was supposed to make an entrance. The ramp itself was out of the question. It was almost a hundred meters away, and he could see dark forms edging out cautiously in front of it. It would take at least a hundred men to assault that entrance.

But was the ramp the only possible access point? Merral turned his attention to the complex lattices of discolored pistons, struts, and pipes that made up the rear legs. Stained by grease, they ran up some twenty or more meters from the great square feet and extended up inside the fuselage. On the back of the right leg was a narrow metal ladder that ran up from near the ground into fuselage wells where it was screened by some sort of hanging bay doors.

Merral decided there was a reasonable chance that it connected with the ship's interior. Anyway, there seemed no other option. He planned his actions. A short, rapid dash would bring him to a leg; once there, the leg would give him cover as he climbed, and at the top, the hanging doors would give further protection.

Frankie's voice, now slightly brighter, broke into his thoughts. "Sir, I got through. She'll be with us in fifteen minutes and will off-load the men to the east as close to the ship as she can. I guess we stay down here and wait and fire at the creatures, I suppose." He seemed to catch Merral's gaze. "Sir, you're not still going to try and get inside?"

"Yes," Merral answered. "That's what I've been told to do. Can you and the others make a distraction? get those intruders to keep their heads down?"

"Sir, if you think it's wise . . ." Frankie's expression suggested he was of another opinion.

"Wise? I'm not sure," Merral replied, aware as he spoke that someone had run up to join them from where the men were taking cover. He turned, recognizing Lorrin Venn and feeling a great relief that he was not badly injured. However his pale, fraught, and bloodstained face suggested that what was left of Lorrin's enthusiasm had died in the fighting.

"Sir," Lorrin spluttered to Frankie, revealing a torn lip and a chipped tooth, "we reckon there are men there. Under the ship. Wearing some sort of armor and with guns."

As Merral peered into the shadows at the far end of the ship, something whistled past his head. There was a dusty explosion on the cliff wall.

"Lorrin, get down!" he bellowed, ducking down below the sled.

Aware that Lorrin had remained standing, he reached up and jerked the uniformed leg. "Get down!" he repeated.

There was a further whistle and, with it, a soft splattering noise.

The leg shook violently.

Merral stared up to see Lorrin clutching his throat, blood oozing through the closed fingers. With an expression of stupefaction on his face, Lorrin sagged slowly down to his knees as if in slow motion and then collapsed forward. Merral was suddenly conscious of Lorrin's chest heaving under his armor and of Frankie gasping in horror beside him.

Treat it as a logging accident, Merral ordered himself. *Go into the automatic first-aid mode you have been trained for.*

"Lorrin," he said, his voice thick and distant as he fumbled for his medical pack on his belt, "Perena's going to be here soon." He tore the pack open, his fingers jamming against each other. *The ship has good facilities, and Felix Azhadi is a trauma-care expert.*

As he pulled out the bandage, Lorrin thrashed sideways. Merral knew that it was too late for Felix or anybody to save Lorrin now. All he could do was clutch his thrashing wrist.

An only child, Merral suddenly remembered with a deep and piercing bitterness, as Lorrin twitched and kicked his way into death.

There were more fierce whistles overhead now. Something hit the cliff and stone chips flew out in a spray of fragments around them. Behind him, Merral saw some of the remaining men frantically digging deeper into the sand with bare hands and improvised tools. Others were heaving up metal struts to give them more protection.

Frankie, his face a ghastly white, was gaping at the body. He looked at Merral. "Sir, Lorrin's dead?" he gasped, swallowing hard and blinking. "O Lord God . . . Sorry, sorry . . ."

"Yes, Frankie!" Merral said, trying to suppress both guilt and anger. "Now get back there and shoot back!" *Return fire,* the manuals had called it.

"And, Frankie, I'm going for that right rear leg and going up in from there. Tell everybody to aim for the men, not the creatures. The men are the ones with the guns. After you start shooting, I'll count to five slowly, then run." Merral was surprised at how cool his voice sounded. He looked at Frankie, wondering if his words had registered.

"Okay, sir; the right leg. A count of five. And Lorrin?"

Merral stared at the body by him, struck by the bloodied hand lying on the gray sand, its fingers wide open as if ready to receive something.

"Later. He's gone Home."

"Oh, what a mess. Sorry," Frankie muttered, his fists clenching and unclenching, and Merral glimpsed tears in his lieutenant's eyes.

"It is, Frankie. Better get back to your men. Stay low, and when I give you a signal, fire at the intruders. The men mainly."

Frankie seemed to take control of himself. "The men. Okay. Be careful, sir."

"I will be," Merral answered automatically before he realized how stupid it sounded.

He saw Frankie touch Lorrin's outstretched hand. "Sorry," he said in a tone of immense sadness. Then, bent double, he raced back to his men.

Merral stared at the ship, forcing himself to concentrate on the task ahead and not think of Lorrin next to him, dead and silent.

There were shouted orders behind him, and more whistling sounds and small explosions broke out against the cliff. Something, somewhere, clanged off a piece of metal. Merral slung the gun across his shoulder and prepared to run.

He turned and caught Frankie staring at him with an inquiring look from over a bulwark of gray metal plates, stones, and camouflage fabric.

Merral crouched into a running position and raised his thumb.

"Fire!" came the shout, and there was a jumble of hissing sounds behind him. Bitter, angry shrieks came from under the ship. Merral slowly counted to five.

He ran.

He had intended to dodge from side to side, but in the end fear drove him to run as fast and straight as he could. Ducking as low as possible, he raced across the sand, expecting at any moment to feel something hit him. He was aware of the grit under his feet and things whining and whistling past him.

A stone or a ricochet bounced off his armored jacket with a harsh clipping noise. Sand spat up around him. Something seemed to skim by his helmet, and from somewhere there was the smell of burning.

Now, though, the ship's leg was in front of him. Gasping for breath, Merral ran gratefully behind its protective bulk. But he knew he dare not stop.

Urgently, he began pulling himself up the ladder as fast as he could. He was under no illusions that the foot of the leg, midway between his men and the enemy massing around the ramp at the front of the ship, was safe.

Rung by rung, his chest heaving under his armor, Merral clambered upward, aware of the heavy gun tugging at his shoulder and the bush knife clattering against the ladder.

He was no more than a dozen rungs up when he felt the ladder vibrate sharply. He glanced down to see an ape-creature, its black hair lank and wild, climbing up after him with fluid movements of long arms. It turned its face up to him, showing bottomless dark eyes and pale flaring nostrils.

Merral redoubled his speed but, in a second, his ankle was grabbed in a ferocious and tightening grip.

Barely thinking, Merral slipped the gun off his shoulders, grasped the strap and let it drop butt first.

There was the sharp crack of metal on bone as the gun's butt struck the creature's skull. Merral heard a soft groan. The pressure on his ankle was suddenly released, and something large and heavy tumbled down, striking the ladder as it went.

There was a deep thud from the landing leg pad.

Without looking down, Merral shouldered the gun and resumed his hectic scramble upward. Weighed down by his weapon and encumbered by the stiff armored jacket and helmet, he found the climb difficult. Twice he felt his feet slide on the oil-stained rungs. Below him, and from under the ship, he could hear renewed firing and wild screaming in response. Trying to ignore it, Merral kept on climbing.

Suddenly he found himself inside the dark sanctuary of the undercarriage cavity. There, gasping for breath, he paused and listened to the shouts and noises from below. He glimpsed, far below, the still figure of the ape-creature sprawled on the sand at the foot of the ladder. It could almost have been asleep, but the pool of glistening crimson fluid around it denied that interpretation. There had been deaths all round this morning. Merral felt a spasm of pity for the creature he had slain. He wished it were all over. He glanced back to where, beyond the tilted sled and the intruder bodies, he could see his men behind the piles of metal tubing and rocks. They were feverishly scooping and pushing away sand to make their position more fortified. With their backs protected by the cliff, it seemed a reasonably secure position. If there were no further direct assaults, they might be safe until the reserves arrived.

He pulled himself up onto a narrow mesh walkway at the top of the ladder and stood up cautiously, catching his breath and looking around in the gloom. There was a strong smell of grease, and from somewhere came the humming of pumps. Panting from his exertions, he glanced around at the untidy complex of piping and cabling about him. He saw a number of labels in a red spidery script that he had never seen before. Despite the incomprehensibility and ugliness of the lettering, he was struck by what he saw, sensing that there was something about both the writing and the labels that spoke of humanity. Indeed, as he looked around, he felt that the whole structure, with its tubes, pistons, nuts, and bolts, seemed in some way, of human origin. There was nothing here, he was sure, that was alien. *Wrong* perhaps, but not alien.

Pushing such thoughts to one side, Merral concentrated on trying to enter the ship. To his relief he saw that ahead of him the gangway extended to an oval, polished, gray metal door. He approached slowly, fearful that it would be locked or that it might open to reveal attackers. He held the gun at the ready in case the door should suddenly open.

To the right of the door Merral noticed two triangular buttons. A tentative press of one of them caused the panel to slide sideways with a hissing noise. Beyond it was an ill-lit, green-painted corridor that seemed to run sideways across the vessel. As the door opened, Merral was assailed by a stale organic smell, reminiscent of old garden compost but somehow more acrid, that made him wrinkle his nose.

So, I can now enter the ship. Yet he paused.

Somehow, he was reluctant to trade the fresh air and indirect daylight of the undercarriage bay for this fetid, dark tunnel. He steeled himself to enter, but with one hand gripping the edges of the doorway, a thought suddenly struck him.

He could, he realized, simply place his charge here, trigger it, and slip back down the ladder. With this hatch blasted away or—at very least—rendered useless, the intruders would have to stay in the Farholme atmosphere. To Merral, the idea suddenly seemed a compellingly sensible proposal. It avoided the risk of his entering the ship at all. Indeed, it had the great advantage that he could be back with his men in moments. And wasn't that where he belonged? The only problem was that the envoy had ordered him to enter the ship and do battle with the creatures inside. Yet as he thought about that command, a doubt surfaced. After all, he told himself, the envoy had not stated exactly *when* he had to enter the ship. Could it be perhaps that they were to achieve surrender first?

In a second, his initial doubts had multiplied. Who really was the creature that had appeared to him earlier? In fact, was he so sure it was right to obey him? After all, did not the Scriptures say that the devil himself could appear as an angel of light? Perhaps—and the idea came to him forcibly—it was a trick to lure him to his destruction.

Anyway, even if the envoy was not some demonic phenomenon, Merral told himself that it could not be ruled out that he was merely some sort of vision, a figment of his imagination as it labored under the stresses of the day. As he reflected on the idea that the envoy was either an illusion or a demonic visitation, he became aware of an appealing corollary to such interpretations. In either case, he had no obligation to keep the unwelcome promises he had made concerning Anya and Isabella. It was an attractive idea. And yet—

Torn by uncertainty and trying to stave off a decision, Merral leaned farther inside. As he did, he caught his finger on something sharp and felt a sudden stab of pain. He snatched his hand away and sucked the gashed fingertip.

His attention painfully drawn to the door, Merral glanced around the frame, noticing that there were in fact numerous rough metal edges. He was surprised. Assembly practice was always to round and polish smooth all surfaces, whether visible or invisible. Such carelessly raw edges would never have been allowed on a finished product.

In a moment his perspective changed, and he now realized that there was something about this ship that he hated to an intense degree. Fueling that hatred was a certainty that this vessel was at the heart of the corrupting evil that had descended on his land. And as his hatred blossomed, he felt that every one of the dreadful events that had happened since Nativity had ultimately originated from this ship.

Merral suddenly became aware how strange his delay at entering the ship had been. Could it have been that he had been somehow influenced? tempted? Well, he decided, if that was the case then the attempt had failed.

With renewed determination and a new anger, Merral set the cutter gun beam on wide focus and checked that the status light was on red.

Then with a brief prayer and a final glance at the ground far below, he entered the ship.

41

The moment Merral set foot in the intruder ship he felt that something had changed. It was as if he had left his own world and passed into another—one that was strange and unfriendly. He found it impossible to define why he felt that this was so. The interior of the ship was dark and foul-smelling, and there were strange noises, but it was more than that. He was aware that there was something else: something too subtle to be instantly pinned down, but something that was wrong.

His hands clenched on the gun, Merral stood still, looking cautiously around. The dully lit corridor stretched to either side of him, with metal ribs protruding out along each wall and casting deep shadows on the floor. At each end, the corridor appeared to join larger longitudinal passageways that ran along each side of the ship. The corridors were higher than he had expected, as if made for giants. Or, he thought darkly, monsters.

Nothing moved. He took another step forward. With a hiss, the door closed behind him. The light and distant sounds of the outside world abruptly vanished.

Merral was suddenly aware of being isolated—more isolated than he had ever been in his life. Struggling to suppress an invading fear, he listened carefully, trying to make sense of the noises that he could hear from within the ship. Some of the noises were mechanical: a faint electrical hum, the sloshing of fluid in pipes, a distant vibration from some pump. Yet there were also other noises less easy to assign an origin to. There was a soft, high-pitched chatter, like that of far-off animals in a zoo, and a low, irregular, insectlike chirping whose source was impossible to locate.

There was a chillness to the ship, an odd, clammy coldness, different from the fresh cold of a Farholme winter. There was something about this austere green corridor and this bleak ship that seemed to speak to Merral of wild, deep, and hostile space. He felt the hairs on the back of his neck rise, and for a moment, he shivered uncontrollably.

"Okay, now which way do I go?" he asked quietly, his voice echoing in the stillness. He realized that he expected no answer.

"Go right, Man."

The voice was just there. Clear, audible, and unmistakably the same voice he had heard on the other side of the lake. Merral looked around, trying in vain to find the source of the voice. Against one of the bracing girders ahead of him was a deeper shadow that he was sure had not been there a moment earlier.

"So you *are* here."

"Man, the King's servants keep their promises," the strangely flat voice said, and Merral sensed the hint of a rebuke. Yet despite it, Merral felt curiously relieved at hearing the envoy's voice.

Then, catching a glimpse of Lorrin's blood, still wet on his sleeve, Merral turned to the shadow. "Lorrin Venn's dead!" he said, and he could hear the bitterness in his voice. "The others are at risk."

"I know. They are my concern too," the voice stated. "Yet evil must be fought, and battles cost. If you want to serve your men and their families best, do what I say. Lorrin played his part and is safe in the Father's house. You are not yet there and there is much to do. This is a most dark and perilous place, and there are many dangers. As you have just found."

"Yes," Merral answered, disturbed but somehow not surprised that the envoy knew of his hesitation.

"Now go right." The tone did not allow for argument.

"Envoy," Merral said, "can you go ahead first?"

"Man, do you not understand?" The voice was sharp. "This is your race's war."

"I see. But I thought you had the power."

"Power has nothing to do with it, Man. It is what is right. Only those that are human can fight for humanity. Even the High King bowed to that law. Or have you forgotten what you learned about the Nativity?"

"I see. I just hadn't seen this as the same. . . ."

"Man, I can only advise you. Am *I* human? Now go right."

The urgency in the voice was such that Merral instantly started right along the corridor.

As he padded along the floor, Merral glanced around constantly, trying to take in his surroundings. The contrast with the *Heinrich Schütz* could not have been more marked. That had been an artistic masterpiece of light and smoothness; this, he sensed, was a coarse, even brutal, assembly of parts.

He had now come to the passageway. Here he stopped and peered cautiously around the corner. As he had suspected, it was a major corridor and seemed to run the entire length of the vessel. It too seemed to be deserted. He listened, aware of a strange, twisting soft breeze that moved around him as if there were pulses of air in the corridor.

"To the front of the ship," came the order.

Merral was suddenly struck by the way that the voice sounded exactly the same here as it had out by the lake. It was as if it was unaffected by the local acoustics. Perena had described how the words of the envoy sounded as if they had been "pressed out of the air." Now he understood her description.

Merral turned left toward the nose of the ship and began moving along the corridor as rapidly and quietly as he could. The light was all wrong: it was not just dull; it was as if it was somehow drained of energy. He thought longingly of sunlight.

In this part of the ship, the outer fuselage was supported by large protruding girders, and feeling that they might provide him some cover, he walked close to them. A hasty glance over his shoulder gave him the impression that a dark shadow glided along after him in the dark margins of the corridor.

Merral, his nerves on edge, was aware of new noises in the ship: a distant clattering, muffled thudding sounds from below, a high-pitched scratching somewhere. A small, eddying spiral of dust flickered around on the floor ahead of him. Despite the coolness in the air, Merral realized that he was sweating profusely.

As he moved down the long, dark passageway, staring nervously into the shadows, his initial impressions about the ship hardened. In addition to the crude, rather unfinished workmanship that was all around, nothing seemed to be as neat as on an Assembly ship. In one place, an indecipherable label seemed to have been slapped on the wall in such a hurry that it was not horizontal. In another place, a panel had been put back so carelessly that a bolt head still protruded. He passed a crumpled fragment of plastic on the floor and the Ancient English word *litter* came to mind. He had a growing feeling too that there was something fundamentally wrong about the whole way the ship was constructed. On Assembly ships, the framework and supporting structures were always hidden. Here they were standing visible. It was almost as if the designers hadn't cared how things looked.

Midway down the corridor Merral stopped, suddenly struck by a new phenomenon. At his feet the metal floor had clearly been badly damaged and then patched up. The job had been done in such a rough and untidy manner that he could feel the join through his boots. He saw that the hull skin and the roof were heavily scarred; through the uneven paint, the sheen of bare metal could be seen in places. Something traumatic had happened here, and sensing it might be important, Merral wondered what. He glanced at a girder nearby to see that fine silver globules were speckled on its surface. Gingerly, mindful of the sharp surfaces, he ran a finger along a raised edge, pulled it away and looked at it. A number of tiny, perfect, shining metal spheres were stuck to it. Rolling them between his fingers, he puzzled briefly over what they meant. Merral walked on a few more steps and paused. Just ahead of him, he heard a fragile metallic tapping sound, like the noise of a tiny hammer striking pipes.

A little more than a meter beyond him something moved. Two gray tendrils, like enormously elongated fingers, crept round a wall strut at the height of his head.

He froze as a dull metal egg-shaped structure, perhaps a meter long, followed after the fingers. Its surface was made up of dozens of facets, almost as if it was some strange crystalline growth.

Merral felt he was being stared at. He raised his gun.

"Wait!" came the sharp command from the envoy, and Merral eased his finger a fraction away from the trigger.

Suddenly the egg-shaped body seemed to rotate on its fingers and, in a fluid, precise movement, swung down two impossibly long legs behind it onto the floor. Then, letting go with the front limbs, it dropped free. With delicate and economic movements of its four extraordinary limbs, the thing moved to the center of the corridor in front of him.

There it rose up so that the body was at the level of Merral's face. *A mechanical insect,* Merral thought, before realizing that the four legs, nowhere larger than a child's wrist, were without visible joints or segments. Indeed, they seemed to have both the suppleness of tentacles and the rigidity of limbs.

The machine—Merral had not the slightest doubt that it was a machine rather than a living thing—moved closer to him with smooth, impeccably coordinated leg movements.

Merral stared at it, trying, through his fear, to make sense of something so totally unfamiliar. As he looked at it, he saw that high on a front facet were two small, glassy black circles that stared at him. The machine bobbed and swayed as if trying to get a thorough look at his face.

As it did, Merral realized, with a further strange assurance, that what he faced was not simply a remote surveillance machine but something with an intelligence of its own. He stared back at it, now able to make out details on the body panels. There was an array of small green lights on one surface, a series of sockets along another, and fine lettering on a third.

The machine spoke, but Merral could make no sense of the jagged syllables. He knew, though, that they were words rather than noise.

"The machine says it doesn't recognize you. It wants your identity." The envoy's steady voice seemed to come from just over his shoulder.

"What do I do?" Merral whispered back, wondering how you dealt with an intelligent and probably hostile machine, barely an arm's length away from your face. *We should have predicted this,* he told himself with a spasm of recrimination. *We knew the intruders had worked without restrictions. We should have guessed that they would have ignored the notoriously complex Technology Protocol Two about creating autonomous-sentient machines.*

"Man, show it the identity disc you bear," said the envoy.

"But the disc isn't mine. We don't have them."

The machine swung its head as if it was trying to find out who he was talking to.

"Do it!"

Merral found the chain around his neck and, jerking it out, held the disc firmly up in front of the machine.

A panel flicked down on the underside of the body, and a tendril, as fine as a man's little finger, uncoiled smoothly out and extended to just in front of Merral's chest. Four delicate digits flowered on its end and grasped the disc with a gentle firmness.

The machine seemed to stare at what it held. "Lucas Hannun Ringell," it pronounced in slow tones. Then, after a moment's hesitation, it carefully enunciated the date of birth, "Three *dash* three *dash* twenty eighty-two."

There was a pause, as if it was thinking or consulting with something.

Suddenly the digits released the disc. The limb whisked back inside the body and the machine stepped back sharply with a simultaneous movement of all four legs.

"*Captain* Lucas Hannun Ringell?" it said, and there was no mistaking the note of questioning in the voice.

Along the length of the corridor, bright red lights began to pulse and a wailing siren sounded.

"Now shoot it," said the envoy.

Merral aimed at the body and squeezed the trigger. There was a brief cherry red glow on an underside plate, and a puff of smoke belched out. A flurry of thin, pale gray shards whistled outwards, clattering against the walls and floor. Fragments of metallic and plastic circuitry popped out. Amid thrashing limbs, the creature banged against the wall and crashed to the ground.

"Sorry," Merral muttered, wondering if he should apologize to intelligent machines. Then, stepping carefully over a still-flicking leg, he moved on down the corridor. He began to stride quickly forward. There was no point in stealth now; the alarm had been triggered, and the next machines or creatures he met would know that he was hostile.

"I should have shot it first," he protested. "The alarms have been sounded."

"No. The ship's defense systems think that Lucas Ringell is loose on the ship. They will divert forces to deal with this most serious threat."

"You mean," Merral spluttered, "you *want* them to come after me?"

"It is necessary. Your men cannot handle the Krallen pack they now face."

"The *what?*" asked Merral, struck by the menacing sound of the term *Krallen pack.*

"You will find out."

"Thanks," Merral said, recognizing in some distant and neutral part of his mind that he was being sarcastic. "I hope you can handle them. But—another thing—how can they imagine Lucas Ringell to be here? They must know that he died millennia ago."

"They think you are like them," the voice said but did not elaborate.

Suddenly the lights flickered, and Merral heard a faint click from his gun. He glanced down to see that there was no status light of any sort on. He stopped, tapping the various switches. But no light turned on. It was as if all the power had vanished from the machine; his weapon was dead.

"My gun's malfunction—," Merral began and stopped, jarred by the realization that the status light on his diary had gone off as well.

The indefinable shadow spoke. "The being at the heart of this ship has power over such things. Shoulder your gun; you may need it later. Move on."

Despite feeling a need to protest, Merral did as he was told. He found his knife, grasped the handle firmly, pointed it away from him, and pressed the release button. With a smooth click, the meter-long, dull gray blade extended. He pressed the retract button, and the blade hissed back into the handle. *At least my knife works.* The idea gave him little reassurance.

He strode on down the corridor. Suddenly he heard distant noises from ahead of him. A cold chill swept over him as he realized that the sounds were getting louder and nearer. The growing noises were matched by the rising vibrations he could feel in the floor. In an instant, Merral had a terrifying vision of something—no, many things—bounding up stairs and along corridors as they raced toward him. He looked around for somewhere to hide.

In seconds, the noise was clear enough for him to make out that it was made up of a collection of strange whistles, hoots, and the clattering of many feet. *The Krallen pack,* he thought, and considered turning and running back the way he had come.

"W-what do I do?" he said.

"Stand still against the wall and say nothing," said the voice close behind him.

Merral turned around to try and see the envoy, but all he could see was a tall, oddly vague blackness behind him. It was as if the envoy existed on some plane that was either too close or too far away for his eyes to focus on.

The noises became louder and the floor rang. Trembling with fright, Merral pressed himself behind a protruding girder on the inner side of the corridor. Resisting the temptation to close his eyes, he peered forward down the corridor.

The lights at the far end were suddenly obscured, and in a second, the passageway was filled with strange gray, athletic creatures racing toward him, some bounding along the floor, others—no less fast—swinging along the roof, whistling and hooting to each other.

Merral's first terrified impressions were of four-legged creatures the size of the very largest dogs but with very un-doglike legs. A pack indeed, he thought, like hounds or wolves. Suddenly, just as the leading creatures were barely a few meters away, Merral sensed the shadow on the edge of his vision moving, and he had the impression of an arm being thrown up above and in front of him. He blinked; he could still see, but everything before him was hazy, as if some gauze sheet now hung in front of his eyes.

"I will hide you," the envoy said. "You are not ready to face these things."

Merral had a sudden vision of himself standing pale faced and wide-eyed behind a wing of the envoy's cloak.

With astonishing speed, the pack came to an abrupt halt just in front of Merral. Conscious of his frantically pounding heart, Merral stared at the things that confronted him. There were ten—no, more—a dozen of them. The overriding impression he had was of an overwhelming, intelligent, and disciplined hostility. *These Krallen are not dogs,* he told himself, *they are way beyond that: there is intelligence here—coordination and language.*

Indeed, they didn't really look like dogs. They were too big—they stood chest high to Merral—and their tails were short, muscular, and passed smoothly into their bodies. The limbs were striking, apparently having something of an apelike flexibility, so that the three creatures hanging from the ceiling seemed no less at ease than those standing on the ground. In fact, as Merral stared at them, he decided he wasn't even sure that they were mammals. There was a cold, almost reptilian air to their actions, and their gray skin was hairless and thick. Their heads were roughly triangular, both in cross section and profile, widening to the rear and the bottom. Two small, dark eyes were inset in the upper part of the face and were protected by prominent ridges above and below them. The lower part of the head was dominated by a strong-jawed mouth.

As Merral watched, he saw their heads moving this way and that as if scanning every square centimeter of the corridor for the slightest trace of him. The whistling and hooting they made through half-open mouths kept changing pitch and tone, and Merral sensed that they were sharing puzzlement. His eye was caught by one, which had a wide black depression along its flank as if some flaming object had struck it. He found himself puzzling over why there was no blood and why the creature seemed to be unaffected by such a major wound.

At he stared at it, the nearest Krallen moved closer. It stopped and extended a forelimb, waving it slowly this way and that as if cautiously checking to see if there was something invisible before it. As it did so, Merral was suddenly struck by the feet—or were they hands? They had five big, fingerlike digits, three facing forward and two facing back, and as he watched, Merral saw sharp silvery blades extend from the fingers. *Like a cat,* he thought but checked himself when he realized that not even a lion had claws this long or this sharp. It was strange too how metallic they looked. It opened its jaws and Merral saw, with a strange lack of surprise, that its mouth was filled with sharp, knifelike silver teeth. Hadn't Anya warned of the possibility of designed predators? Surely, Merral decided, these were they.

Seemingly baffled by Merral's disappearance, the creature stopped still and seemed to stare at or through him. Then it spoke—and Merral was in no doubt that the whistles were words—and suddenly two Krallen sprang forward—they were surprisingly light on their feet—and bounded down the corridor in an oddly regimented action. Perhaps ten meters away, they spun round in a perfectly coordinated maneuver and, with their noses to the ground, began to sniff their way toward him.

As Merral watched, horror-struck, peculiarities registered. There was a precise smoothness to the way the Krallen moved that puzzled him. There were curiously regular features on the skin at the shoulders and wrists that almost looked like sockets or mounting brackets. And Merral was certain that there was something else about them that was odd, something that was very obvious. But he couldn't identify what it was.

What are these things? he wondered in a mixture of terror and perplexity as the two creatures came to within a handbreadth of his feet and began to look up at him with their cold eyes.

Yet as they moved their heads toward him, Merral became aware of the envoy reaching out his hand—he felt he could make out faint fingers—and gently touching the nearest creature on the back of the head.

"Az izara hamalaraka," the envoy said in a soothing tone, and the strange words seem to vibrate quietly in the air. Merral sensed that it was an order.

The Krallen that he was touching gave a slight shudder and uttered a long, descending whistling note. As if it was a mechanical device, it smoothly bent its knees and lowered its head so that it crouched low on the floor. As if some sort of contagion was spreading through the pack, one by one the others followed suit. The three creatures hanging from the roof sprung lightly down to the floor and did the same. Then, as if it was part of a carefully choreographed routine, the strange eyelids on the beasts simultaneously closed shut.

With an astonishing sense of relief, Merral stared at the twelve identical forms lying still on the floor in total silence.

"What did you say?" Merral asked.

"You could translate it as 'go into system shutdown mode.' "

"Oh."

"Forward," said the envoy and seemed to drop his hand. The haze that had been in front of Merral suddenly cleared.

Merral remembered something. "Daniel . . . , " he said. "Didn't God send his angel and shut the mouths of the lions for Daniel?"

"There are precedents. But lions are easier."

Merral stepped forward, gingerly tiptoeing between the still forms. He glanced down, noticing for the first time that the gray skin of the creatures was finely scored so it looked as if was made up of numerous straight-edged patches. *Like tiles.* He noticed another one that had a marked but bloodless gash on it.

"Are they dead?"

"They were never alive."

"What do you mean?" Struck by a thought, Merral glanced back at the others. *Yes, how very odd; they're all identical.*

"They are not animals," the envoy said.

"They aren't?"

"They are made beings. Synthetic creatures. Made of artificial bone and tissue."

Of course, Merral thought with a flood of realization, *that's what was odd about them: they weren't breathing. They had been running and weren't panting.*

"But why?"

"Why make them, you mean? Their makers wanted things that had none of the weaknesses of flesh and blood. The Krallen are stronger than any animal, they are hard to destroy, and they never sleep or tire. A Krallen pack would run across Menaya before it even slowed down."

Merral saw that they had come to some stairs.

"Are there more—"

"Enough! Now ascend, up to the next level. There is much to do."

Merral looked up and down the stairway, realizing that it must go up vertically through most of the ship. The siren was still blaring, and he could hear far-off, angry noises, but there were no noises from nearby.

"Very well," Merral answered, and he began climbing the stairs, keeping close to the wall, aware that close behind him something followed him. Somehow he found the envoy less alarming now. There was still something disconcerting about him, but in this hostile ship he seemed to be almost a friend.

Near the top of the next flight of stairs, Merral stopped and peered carefully over the top of the final step. Another lateral corridor stretched out before him. It was empty. He moved forward along it, hoping that if he was going to meet any opponents, the envoy would protect him again. Against the likes of things such as these Krallen, Merral felt his bush knife would be of little use.

Nearly midway along the corridor, he passed a wide doorway to his right. From the presence of a button pad at its side, he decided that it was an elevator. Next to it and aligned, as far as Merral could determine, with the central axis of the ship, was a large and strangely ornate alcove. He looked at it and saw that it had been blackened, as if a fire had been lit in it. In it was a strange statue made out of a dark gleaming metal.

Merral stepped toward it, realizing as he looked at it that it was a large cast of a human head. Or rather, it had been. Something had happened to make it melt, flow, and drip so that the original features of the face were now impossible to determine. Yet as he looked at the marred sculpture, Merral felt certain that it had been intended to portray strength, power, and authority. For a second, he wondered how such a mishap had happened, before he realized with a shock of identification that the damage might not have been accidental. Indeed, as he gazed at the sculpture, he felt suddenly certain that someone had willfully blasted the bust with some sort of weapon.

Puzzled, Merral stood back and saw, below the recess, an engraved label. The top line of writing was in the unattractive cursive script that he had seen earlier. Here it had been defaced, scored through several times by a knife so that even if he could have understood the letters, he would have struggled to read it. *They have tried to disfigure it*, he thought, puzzling over the oddness of the concept. Then his eye was caught by a second line of text below it, which had escaped damage. It was in a different, more familiar script, and Merral gasped as he realized that it was written in Communal.

"Zhalatoc, Great Prince of the Lord-Emperor Nezhuala's Dominion." He spoke the words aloud, feeling as he did that the strangely discordant names seemed to linger in the air.

He turned, trying—and failing yet again—to focus on the envoy. "What does this mean?" he asked.

"Everything. And, for the moment, nothing. Your business lies within the chamber."

Merral turned and looked at the entrance doorway on the other side of the corridor. What new horrors lay beyond? He walked over to it, noticing an odd-shaped handle and a notice to the right of the door. The first three lines of the notice were in the ugly, wiry red font that he had seen before. Yet below it was a three-line inscription written with a neat electric blue script in Communal. Merral read the words.

Warning!
STEERSMAN CHAMBER
Out of Bounds!

Merral frowned. Although the individual words made sense, the overall meaning eluded him completely. Warning, he understood, but what was a *Steersman? Chamber* was plain, reminding him of Jorgio's ominous caution, but what the last three-word phrase meant was utterly beyond him. As Merral stared at the writing, he felt certain that the odd way the letters were shaped and spaced was one that he associated with the earliest period of the Assembly.

"And what does this mean?" he asked aloud.

"You will learn. But you must go on. Open the door."

Merral turned to the door and grabbed the handle. He hesitated for a second and then tugged at it.

As the handle rotated down, the door beside it slid quietly sideways to reveal a small but high compartment illuminated with a dull green light. Apart from another door on the opposite side, it was empty and featureless. *It's an airlock,* Merral thought.

"Leave your gun here. It will only hinder you."

Merral hesitated for a second and then slipped the useless gun off his shoulder and placed it against the wall as, with a hiss, the door slid closed behind him. His fingers moved toward the bush knife on his belt as he tried to hold back a feeling of panic and oppression.

"Now go through the next door. But remember, there is more than one danger in this place."

Merral walked to the door facing him and grasped the handle beside it.

"Okay," he said, his voice shaking. "Let's get this over with."

42

The door opened vertically. It had lifted only a fraction before Merral saw a mist seep out from the chamber and felt cold air round his ankles. With the chilled air came a dreadful smell. The whole ship smelled, but this was something stronger: a putrid, rancid combination of a hundred separate odors of death and decay. It was so overwhelming that, for a moment, Merral wondered if the air was breathable.

As the door opened fully and the mist swirled around his legs, he looked around, feeling every muscle tensed for action. He stood at the edge of a large and gloomy chamber. Although the chamber was surprisingly high, wide, and long, it was crowded. Poking through the mist, like islands in some sea, was a scattered miscellany of dark structures—pillars, columns, and slabs—some rising to more than his height. Around the sides of the chamber, numerous fittings—perhaps cabinets or lockers—rose up to the roof, where large beams spanned the ceiling like the ribs of some gargantuan animal. The only lighting came from a dozen or so small, spherical lights of different sizes, ranging in color from orange to an icy blue, that were apparently randomly arranged below the roof. The combination of these strange lights, which seemed to be floating in space, the numerous structures, and the mist made the gloom of the chamber uneven, giving pools of inky shadow and patches of gray twilight. There were sounds too: a soft rattling and chattering, and Merral felt certain that, beyond the range of his hearing, there were other noises. In these sounds, he sensed a strangely tense and expectant tone.

I am awaited.

Shivering from cold and fear, Merral looked around urgently, sensing that he was being watched and aware that any one of a hundred places in this dreadful room could conceal peril. There was far more to this chamber than what he could see, feel, and touch. The darkness was not just the absence of physical light; it was an icy shadow that seemed to cloud his mind. He tried to think of Ynysmant, his family, Anya, and sunlight and open fields and woods, but here they were all distant memories, faint and muted. *Light and life have faded here.* He shuddered.

"Where am I?" he asked aloud and he heard his voice tremble. "Where have I come to?"

The voice behind him spoke slowly. "You have come to the edge of your world and to the entrance of that realm where the light does not come. Now go forward."

Merral took a step forward, and as he did, he crunched something underfoot. He glanced down, kicking with his feet to try and clear the mist, glimpsing white and gray fragments on the floor.

"It's dirty," he said under his breath and stepped forward again, wading through the mist as if he were fording a stream.

Merral saw before him a wide passageway that ran between some of the structures to the center of the chamber. There was more light there, and he could make out a short, strange column rising up out of the vapor. Beyond it was a series of steps that led up to a platform on which there was a seat.

Something sat on the seat; something that he wanted to look away from; something that instead dragged his unwilling eyes toward it. It was tall and thin and had the color of a dead leaf. Its form was human, but as Merral stared at it, he saw it move and knew, with a sure stab of dread, that it was not human. As he gazed reluctantly at the thing at the heart of the chamber, he saw it slowly raise a gaunt brown arm and make some sort of gesture. A command, he realized.

"Be careful," warned the voice behind him.

From somewhere ahead there came the faintest of noises: a soft, rhythmic, swishing sound. Suddenly, in an agony of fear, Merral saw something moving through the vapor toward him from the center of the room. A thing that moved in an unhurried way with a slow rippling of wide wings that caused the vapor to flow off its dark back.

Merral spun round, looking for somewhere to flee.

"Stand firm," came the order.

Merral turned back to face the oncoming creature, realizing through his fear that he faced the same being that had attacked Felicity. Behind the wide wings he could make out a long tail swinging from side to side.

Wanting to run but knowing that he had to stand his ground, Merral pressed the button on the bush knife and the blade shot out. *The teeth are on the underside,* he reminded himself, trying to work out the implications for defending himself.

The thing came closer.

Guided more by instinct than reason, Merral grasped the bush knife's handle firmly in both hands and swung the blade high above his head.

The creature slowed down until it was barely moving, suspended in the midst of the vapor as if it were treading water.

It's planning its attack. I must let it get close, but not too close. And I must strike at just the right moment.

Perhaps two paces away, the sheet-dragon came to a dead stop. Then the wings began to beat slightly faster and the broad front of the creature bent slowly upward so its front edge rose up out of the vapor.

A widely spaced pair of dark beady eyes seemed to survey him. He tensed, barely breathing, and considered stepping forward and striking the creature but held back. The eyes continued their cold gaze and on the upturned tip of the underside he could make out the start of the bleached slit of the long mouth. As the creature bobbed up and down, he could see—just below the vapor's surface—the first pair of the clawlike limbs around the mouth.

Suddenly there was movement. The head turned to the right and the beast swung its body around, a triangular wing tilting high up out of the mist as it banked.

It was leaving.

As the dragon turned away, the long tail swinging leisurely round after it, Merral relaxed his muscles. He lowered the blade and began to breathe again.

The tail lashed out.

Merral felt something wrap itself round his knees. He was tugged forward and tumbled into the cold mist. As he fell, the blade flew out of his grasp.

The dragon's body rose up high into the air with surprising speed, twisting as it came up so that the long, pulsing crevasse of the mouth faced him. As he plunged under the cold vapor, it crashed down toward him.

As he hit the floor, Merral rolled to one side. Instinct—or panic—took over, and he scrabbled desperately to his feet just as a great wing lashed down past him, glancing off a shoulder. As it did, the vapor was thrust aside and he saw the blade lying at his feet. He bent down and snatched it. As his fingers closed round the handle, he looked up.

And froze rigid.

An arm's length ahead of him, lifted up by rapidly beating wings, the creature was rearing up vertically out of the vapor. It rose until it hung there, spread out like some monstrous kite, a mere pace away from him. Still bent over, Merral could feel the air from the beating wings brushing past him, was aware of the long tail hanging down into the vapor, the buttonlike eyes staring at him, and—above all—the obscene, wet, vertical slit of a mouth suspended just in front of his face with the eight pairs of claws around it scrabbling in frantic anticipation.

Frozen rigid by terror, he realized that, at any moment, the creature would slide forward and the mouth would be upon him. A part of his brain that had somehow resisted being immobilized by fear told him that, under the vapor, his right hand was holding his bush knife. And another part told him that the creature hadn't realized it.

There was a whisper in his mind: *If I can move fast enough and if my limbs work, I might have the advantage of surprise.* The creature gave an extra little flick of its wings and, as if about to embrace Merral, moved closer.

The mouth gaped wider.

Now.

Merral bounded upright, swung the blade high, and with all the force he could find, chopped downward.

"The Lamb!" he cried.

The blade struck the creature midway between the eyes and kept going, cutting down into the flesh. Merral reeled back under the impact, tearing the blade free.

The creature, nearly bisected by the blow, flopped down into the mist where it thrashed helplessly from side to side.

"And *that,*" said Merral in a loud but trembling voice, "was for Felicity." He was surprised at the bitterness in the words.

On the floor, the convulsions of the creature slowly died away, and the mist rolled back over the bloodless corpse.

"Well struck," said the envoy's voice, "but beware the desire for revenge. It has betrayed others. It may betray you."

"Point taken," Merral said, wiping his brow. "But I have a soft spot for horses."

There was a moment's silence. "Continue," said the envoy, as if passing over some matter. "There is still work to do. That column in the center must be destroyed."

"As you say," Merral answered, reluctantly facing the fact that he had yet to deal with whatever lay in the center of this ghastly chamber. He looked around it, hoping that this was the only such creature. As he did, the strange array of lights suspended from the ceiling caught his attention. They reminded him of something—but what? One pair of lights close together made him think of a binary star system.

Suddenly, he realized what the lights were.

"They are stars!" he said aloud. The central light was Alahir; the others were the adjacent stars. Suddenly, the chamber made sense.

"Of course," he said. "A steersman steers. This is a map. They navigate Below-Space."

"Just so," said the envoy. "A useful service, but one that comes at a price."

Merral walked slowly forward between the gray line of structures. What were they? Cupboards, lockers, consoles? He did not want to know what was inside them. Suddenly, out of the corner of his eye, he saw something pinned to a vertical surface. He stopped. It was a dead kestrel, its brown wings pinned out wide as if it had been crucified. Hanging next to it was a half-completed silver filigree frame that matched the bird's body.

Merral nodded in recognition. It seemed years since he and Vero had encountered the dead bird spying on them at Carson's Sill, but the discovery that such a monstrosity had been begotten here was so unsurprising as to be inevitable.

He walked on, the mist swirling around his legs, his footsteps echoing dully in the heavy silence. He was reluctant to even glance at what was ahead. Finally, aware that he was nearly at the strange column and that he had to face what lay beyond it, he lifted his eyes up.

Immediately ahead of him, now perhaps only five paces away, the column poked up out of the vapor. This close to it, Merral could see that it was different than the other structures in the room. Its multisided surfaces were neither dull nor dirty but had an odd gleam to them, as if the structure was made of some polished metal. The column was chest height, and immediately above it, the air seemed to shimmer and twist as if some strange energy flowed through it.

Keeping his eyes fixed on the column, Merral stepped forward again. It had six sides, he saw. Was it a sort of Gate? And if so, where did it lead? He could see too that the column had patterns engraved upon it, extraordinary loops and spirals that, when you looked at them, had an oddly unsettling effect. That this was indeed the source of some awesome and dread power seemed plain.

"Envoy," he asked, "is this science or magic?"

"Both," came the flat answer, "there are depths—and heights—where they merge. But your task is to destroy it." A faint noise came from beyond the column, and at last Merral summoned the courage to look at the seat and the form the color of dead leaves that sat on it.

Barely a dozen paces away, the large figure with elongated and twisted limbs and a misshapen head with empty eye sockets watched him.

A steersman.

Merral was struck by two successive and contrary impressions: The first was that the steersman was extraordinarily insubstantial. What stared at him from the seat was no more than a dry and hollow husk, something with no more solidity than the discarded carapace of some great insect.

The second impression was very different. Suddenly Merral sensed that he stood before a being of extraordinary age. The creature had seen mountains and even worlds form. And with that age came power and authority. He knew too that the being before him was a mighty king seated on a throne. As that thought came into his mind, Merral noticed that the monstrous head wore a small metal crown. In an instant, his first impression was overturned. It was he, not the steersman, who was ephemeral, and insubstantial. *It is I who am dust.* He trembled.

In that moment of vulnerability, Merral was suddenly aware of the envoy speaking from behind him. "It lies. Go forward in the name of the Lamb and do what must be done. Go."

Reassured, Merral took three steps forward. He closed the bush knife, clipped it back on his belt, and reached for the explosive charge.

As he touched it, he became aware of the steersman moving in its seat, bending forward with stiff limbs, as if turning to stare at him. As if he had opened a door into the face of a winter's gale, a bitter torrent of malice suddenly poured over him.

Overwhelmed, Merral stepped back.

"Man, do not be afraid," the envoy's voice said. "It can do you no harm unless you let it. Trust in him who is the Lord of all realms. Go forward. Plant the charge on the column and trigger it."

"I'll try," Merral said, finding words difficult and taking two steps forward. Another step and the column would be within reach.

Suddenly he was aware of the steersman rising stiffly from its seat like some monstrous, desiccated insect. With a lurching, brittle motion, the thing walked to the column.

Merral stared at the creature that faced him. The face, long and impossibly narrow, seemed paper-thin, and the eye sockets were spaces in which motes of cold dust circulated. In an instant, Merral's contrary impressions resolved themselves. The steersman had both power *and* emptiness: indeed, its very power lay in the emptiness. It was the being that emptied things of life and light and drained all that was good out of them.

Merral tried to suppress his terror. *I must do what I have to do.*

The steersman moved its fingers, and the sound was like the rustling of dead leaves. Without warning, the creature spoke into his mind.

Ringell . . . Ringell . . . they brought you back?

The words were as clear as if they had been spoken, but he knew the jaws of the steersman had not moved.

Merral said nothing but slipped the explosive charge off his belt and felt for the protective wrapping on its back. *I have a task to do, a part to play.*

But you are not Ringell, are you? I was misled.

Forcing himself to concentrate, Merral tore off the wrapping on the red package so the adhesive patch faced toward the column surface. There seemed to be a battle going on in his mind. Light and darkness strove against each other like the interplay of sunlight and shadows as clouds raced over a field. One second, Merral wanted to flee, and the next his desire was to complete his task.

I am the king, said the voice in his mind. *Stop! Obey me!*

"No, you're not," Merral said aloud. "The Assembly stands and her Lord reigns."

Fool! Both the Assembly and her King have forsaken you. I am your king now. Leave while you can.

"Go away," Merral said aloud. "I have a task to do, a part to play."

He pressed the charge against the column, feeling a slight and tingling vibration under his fingertips as the inter-molecular cement bonded. Three seconds would do it.

One, two, three.

Stop! You cannot win! Your isolation is over; the breach in the barrier remains. There will be others who will come in vast ships of unimaginable power. And we will come with them.

"I have a task to do, a part to play," Merral repeated. His stumbling fingers found the protective film over the trigger and he tore it off.

One by one your cozy little worlds will fall. Like leaves in autumn. We will start with Farholme.

Merral found the safety pin, pulled it out, and threw it away into the chill mist at his feet.

We will strip the flesh from your people, turn them against each other, and damn their little souls.

Merral's fingers looped around the firing cord. The words sang in his mind: *I have a task to do, a part to play.*

We will win. We are your inheritors. The uniting of the realms will take place. The end of the Assembly has come.

A task to do, a part to play . . .

Merral pulled the cord.

Nothing happened, and he stared dully at the package, expecting at least some flashing light to tell him the fuse had been ignited.

It's a chemical fuse. He turned and started to run back to the door of the chamber the way he had come. *A sixty-second fuse . . . I should have counted.*

As he raced to the door, the mist parted around him. It seemed thinner now.

The dragon must be just ahead of me. He ran to one side to avoid treading on the body.

Nearly there. Merral glimpsed the tail in the mist at his feet. He stepped over it.

"Look out!" the envoy shouted.

The tail lashed out and snagged his ankle. Merral stumbled and lurched painfully into the nearest structure. He slid to the ground.

Stunned, he lay there for a second before he realized his danger.

I must get up. He pulled his foot free and staggered back to his feet.

He ran on and lunged through the open doorway into the compartment. He turned, tore at the handle with clumsy fingers, and swung it upward. As the door began sliding down, Merral collapsed backward against the wall and slithered down to the floor.

With what seemed an appalling slowness, the door moved down.

"Come on!" he shouted.

The door began to seat itself into the slot in the floor.

A dazzling flash of white lightning shot under it.

There was a stunning clap of noise, and the whole ship seemed to vibrate. Merral felt things strike the compartment door and slide down. The lights failed and then with a few blinks came back on again.

As the echoes of the blast died away, he rose to his feet. His ears were ringing; he was shivering with cold and ached all over.

"You should have come back well away from the winged creature," said the envoy. Merral tried one more time to see him, but as ever, he was no more than a shadow on the periphery of his vision. *Like an optical illusion: present, but not present.*

"Yes," Merral admitted. "I assumed it was dead."

"It was, but beings such as your enemy can manipulate the dead."

"I see."

"Now, you have one last task."

For a moment, Merral wondered whether to refuse. As he hesitated, he noticed that on his gun the status light now glowed green. He glanced at his belt and saw that his diary was working.

"Okay," he said, aware of the weariness in his voice. "What do I have to do now?"

"You must return and slay the being. Even that blast only stunned it and stripped its body of its protection. Unless you destroy it, it will soon pass into an invisible spirit form. You must use your knife. But be careful."

Merral closed his eyes. *I have come so far. I suppose I must go on.* "Very well," he said.

Once more, he found the door handle and pulled down.

43

With a series of creaks, the door slid open slowly, letting in a wreath of hot, foul smoke.

Waving his arms to try and dispel the fumes, Merral stepped carefully over the wreckage by the door. He was surprised to find that the chamber was now much better illuminated; the strange lights had gone, and along either side of the roof, strip lights had now come on. The mist had fled and the temperature seemed warmer.

The chamber had been devastated. Almost all the structures in the room had been badly damaged. Paneling hung from the walls, doors of lockers swung open, blackened cabinets were tilted and twisted, and the floor was covered by every kind of debris.

Merral walked forward, stepping carefully around the fragments. The corpse of the dragon could not be seen and he did not seek it. He walked toward the shattered column, aware of the envoy following noiselessly behind him. Even with the gloom lifted, Merral had no desire to linger here; he wanted to be out of the ship and back with his men.

Something white on the floor caught Merral's attention. He shuddered to see that it was the limb bone of some creature. Looking around, he saw there were other bones lying about. Were these the remains of things the dragon had eaten, or had they been used in some dreadful rite? He didn't wish to know and kept moving on.

He found the steersman by the broken metal shards of the column. It was lying sprawled over the remains of the seat, its limbs extended in impossible directions. As Merral approached, he saw it move. As he stared, he was astonished to find that the motion came not from the body, but within it. The pale brown surface seemed to ripple as if an invisible hand was moving matter from one place to another. As Merral watched, he saw the spindly legs shorten and solidify.

"Quickly!" urged the envoy. "Slay it."

But Merral felt reluctant to act. The spectacle unfolding before him was so astonishing that he felt he had to watch.

The movement within the steersman had now shifted to the body: the cavernous abdomen seemed to enlarge and become smoother, as if being inflated, and the skin became softer and lost its dried-parchment look. The creature gave a little lurch and slipped against the ruined chair so that it now sat facing Merral in a broken-necked way.

"Man," came the urgent order, "strike!"

"I will," Merral said as he stared in wonder at what was happening, and he moved his fingers to the handle of the bush knife. But he did no more than that.

Before him, the chest of the steersman was changing in the same way that the legs and abdomen had, becoming smoother and more rounded. The movement shifted to the arms and fingers, and wrists were fleshed out.

Now the neck moved and the head twisted forward. Eyelids extended over the cavernous sockets, cheeks filled out, eyebrows grew. A nose suddenly bulged outwards as if molded by an invisible sculptor, and the dry brown lips became a soft and healthy pink.

"Strike!" the envoy ordered.

Impressed by the urgency in his voice, Merral pressed the button on the handle and the blade raced out. He raised the knife and squinted, aiming for the neck.

The lips moved.

"You have won," the creature said.

Staring at the being that was forming in front of his eyes, Merral relaxed his grip.

"No! Wait!" The voice was human; the words were ragged as if it was still learning to speak.

Merral lowered the blade.

"It was a mistake to come here," the thing said in contrite, apologetic tones. Its words were smoother now, as if the mouth and lips had learned to move in coordination. "You may exact your price from me. As in the old fables."

Memories arose in Merral's mind of the primeval fairy tales of his childhood with their fantastic goblins and sorcerers. The creature shivered, and with a ripple the flesh on the face seemed abruptly to slide into place as if it were a garment that was being adjusted.

"Name anything," the creature continued, almost pathetically. "What do you want?"

Merral, conscious of the dull, gray, metal blade held in his hand, found himself torn. He wanted to end this horrid thing's existence, and he yearned to hear more. He hesitated, and its form changed further; tissue flowed miraculously from one place to another, and the pale brown skin became softer, paler, and more alive.

Merral glimpsed the dried blood on his sleeve: Lorrin's blood.

A deep anger bubbled up in him. "Thing!" he shouted, his voice unsteady with rage. "The Gate is gone! We are cut off from the Assembly. Everything is—" Emotion choked his words. In his mind, he could see Anya and others: Isabella, Barrand, and Elana. And poor dead Lorrin. "Everything is . . . is rotten!"

"I apologize," came the cool answer. "But you know, these things can be undone."

Merral watched as the creature flexed smooth fingers.

"Undone?"

A golden fuzz of hair was extruding from the skull.

"Strike!" ordered the envoy again, but although Merral tightened the grip of his fingers around the handle, the blade did not move.

"Wait! Please." It was both an order and a plea. New changes flitted across the face. "This voice," the creature asked him, "the one you are listening to. Tell me, please, what do you know of it?"

"I trust him and I have seen what you look like."

"You have been misled by appearances," reasoned the smooth voice. "And after all, you have not seen him. How do you know what he looks like? No, he wants you locked here on Farholme forever. If you strike me, you will lose all hope of traveling back to the Assembly. And without help, your tiny world will never survive in isolation." There was a pause. First one, then both ears sprouted. "Spare me and we will leave your system, and I will give you the secret you want. Of finding help and getting back. I will give you this ship. I am a steersman."

"Strike, Man! Before it is too late!"

"Oh, Merral," the creature said, its voice now gentle, even humorous. "He just wants to stop you from learning knowledge."

Merral stared at the creature. It was a young man—no, he realized with a mixture of emotions—it was a young woman. The face was shy and graceful and had wide, dark brown eyes. The hair, still growing, was framing the face.

Smooth, pale red lips parted gently in speech. "Merral, this envoy thing is a spoiler. He is himself fleshless, and thus he hates everything associated with life. But then, you know that, don't you?"

The tone was amused, intelligent, and sensible. To his utter amazement, Merral realized how much sense the thing was making. *No, it is not a thing, it is a person—a she.*

The long legs now locked themselves under her body so she seemed to sit cross-legged. The face looked up demurely at Merral as if expecting him to automatically acknowledge the truth of what she said. There were faint flickers of motion along her back as if some invisible sculptor was putting the final touches to his creation. Her hands, finely nailed, came up in a gesture of helplessness and embarrassment over her nakedness. Merral was almost overwhelmed by the vulnerability of this girl.

"You know, he wants to stop your enjoyment," she said, her tone at once wise and sympathetic. She shook her golden hair and it caught the light. "To stop you from doing what is your right. After all, this is *your* planet. Not his." She smiled at him and he felt his heart tremble. "Look, let me help you rebuild your world. I will gladly serve you. Help you in every way." She smiled with a happy innocence. "We can do things. Together."

The single word *together* evoked an extraordinary excitement.

"Do you really promise?" Merral asked, telling himself that listening could do no harm. Indeed, he reminded himself, did he not have a duty to extract the best possible concessions for his world from this being?

"Oh yes," said the earnest voice.

I must give her a new name. Something beautiful, something fitting. As he was thinking about it, he caught another glimpse of the caked blood on his sleeve.

"But Lorrin Venn is dead," he heard himself say.

"I know," she answered thoughtfully, "but only a short time ago. There will have been little biochemical change yet. If you promise to spare me, I can bring him back."

"You can do that?" he gasped.

Then she gazed up at Merral, and he thought how he longed to be immersed in her timeless and beautiful eyes.

"Spare me. I can restore life."

Then she bowed her face toward him submissively, as if to indicate that she was his.

As she bent her head, Merral glimpsed beyond her fine hair something white that had rolled under the chair in the blast. It was a polished, smooth waxen object, like a bowl.

In a moment of appalling knowledge, he knew what it was: the skull of a child.

And in that moment, he knew that she was Death, not Life.

He screamed.

The blade arced straight down. With a terrible sucking noise, it sliced through the smooth flesh of the neck.

Merral closed his eyes briefly as the head hit the floor. Slowly, sobbing with emotion, he opened them. The slack-jawed face was upside down, looking up at him from the ground.

"Man, have it be gone." The envoy's words were formal and unsympathetic.

Then, aware that his hands and legs were shaking, Merral spoke words as they came to him. "Thing! Demon! Whatever name you are known by, I command you by the authority of Jesus, the living King of the heavens and the worlds, be gone, and return to your realm to await your judgment!"

The figure crumbled away as if it were made of sand. A faint column of dust spiraled up into air and then, in an eddy of air, it was gone.

Merral stood there shaking, full of shame, realizing how close he had come to disaster. He wanted to be sick. What was it that the envoy had warned him barely an hour ago? *"The enemy seeks your ruin. For him there are more satisfying and useful ways for your destruction than fire, sword, or tooth."*

"I'm sorry," he gasped. "I didn't mean to listen."

The shape of the envoy, although still at the margins of his vision, was somehow more substantial than it had ever been.

"You would have been far wiser not to. Again, you nearly fell."

"I'm truly sorry."

There was only silence in response.

"Is it destroyed?" Merral asked, still shaking.

"It has lost the body fashioned for it and gone back to the abyss."

The horror of the thing, and of what he had had to do to slay it, came back to him and made him shudder afresh.

"Envoy, what was it?" he inquired.

"I do not name it. Its name is best forgotten until the Judgment breaks. It and its kind had been set free. By explorations where mankind was not meant to go, and by men who thought that they could be harnessed."

"And would she have kept her promises?" Merral asked.

"Man, you know so very little," the envoy said, and there was a great sadness in his voice. "Not one of your race ever struck a deal with their sort and did not regret it. I think Lorrin's family would not have long thanked you for what walked in their midst and pretended to be their son. And the Assembly's rejoicing at your arrival through Below-Space would have been very short-lived."

The figure beside him seemed to sigh in an almost human way. "And troubled as your world is now, all this would have been a pleasant dream compared to what you and she would have unleashed together as Lord and Lady of Farholme. Let alone your offspring."

"I see." Suddenly Merral felt very small and very weak.

He turned to the envoy, now certain that he was much less indistinct than he had been.

"The other things. The things the steersman said, in my mind. The breach in the barrier, the end of the Assembly. *Those* things. Are they true?"

"There were lies there, as you know. Yet not all was lies."

"Which bits were true?"

"Ah, Man, that is for you to find out."

"I had a feeling you'd say that."

"But more importantly, next time, obey immediately."

"Next time? I thought it was finished?"

"Finished?" Merral suddenly heard a sound that might have been a laugh. "No, you will know when it is finished. There will be no doubt of that moment."

"What about the evil loose on my world?"

The dark shape at the margins of his vision seemed to suddenly become even more solid, and Merral thought he could make out a strange, archaic coat and a round, wide-brimmed hat that seemed to hide the face.

"No," the figure said slowly, "the war will go on. But with this gone, your world may have some measure of healing."

"Only some measure?" Merral asked sharply, feeling that the sacrifice of Lorrin and the diplomatic team and—for all he knew—another dozen more, merited a greater prize.

"The time for the mending—and ending—of things is not yet. Be content with what the day brings. But you must go."

Suddenly Merral realized that outside the battle still raged. He glanced at his watch; to his amazement he saw that he had been on the ship for only twenty minutes. "Yes, I must."

"You will face opposition outside the door, but they already fear you as Lucas Ringell. When they see you return alive and victorious out of here that fear will be greater. They may use terror, but they are not immune to it themselves. And your gun works now."

"Thank you," answered Merral, collapsing his blade and clipping it back to his belt.

"Man, save your thanks for him who sent me." He paused. "I too serve."

Then Merral turned, ran across the ghastly floor and through the doorway. Any sense of achievement in having killed the thing that had been the source of evil was dampened by the awareness that he had come so close to destruction.

He picked up the gun, and as he did, he turned and looked back. There on the floor of the chamber he saw a tall, straight-backed man, clothed in a black ankle-length coat over black trousers, whose face was hidden by the brim of his hat. He was poking tentatively and thoughtfully at the remains of the column with a black-shoed foot.

As if aware of his gaze, the figure began to turn toward him. Merral, curiously anxious not to see the face under the brim of the hat, turned away.

He slid the gun to "ready," saw the status light go to red, and tugged at the handle of the outer door. As soon as the door began to open, he heard the shrill noise of multiple sirens.

As the door opened farther, he curved his finger around the trigger.

He gasped.

Lined up in front of the defaced bust in two symmetrical and silent rows were at least twenty intruders. The back row was made up of towering ape-creatures, the front by a line of twitching cockroach-beasts.

With a sickening feeling, Merral realized that every single one of them was staring at him.

44

The door clicked fully open, and as it did, it seemed that for a brief moment time itself froze. As the forty or so weird and hostile eyes gazed at him, two thoughts came to Merral: The first was the bizarre one of how much the sight in front of him resembled some monstrous parody of a formal sports team image. The second was simply this: the time had come to die well.

Then, on the heels of that, came a third thought: He had, first of all, to announce the defeat of the monstrous steersman.

"The steersman is dead! Glory to God and the Lamb who reigns!" Merral cried, in as loud a voice as he could muster. And as he shouted it, he felt astonished at the calmness with which he faced his end.

Then he fired in the air, and amid the crash of falling ceiling panels, the twin lines of the opposition suddenly broke. With a terrible cacophony of wails and yells, the creatures fled left and right in utter panic. Merral fired again into the midst of the fleeing figures on both sides.

The result was an astonishing—and gratifying—mayhem. The smaller cockroach-beasts with their faster initial response were overtaken near the stairways by the longer-limbed ape-creatures. The result was that both sets of terror-struck creatures tried to get down the narrow stairs at once. To his right, Merral saw an ape-creature trip over a cockroach-beast and go flying, taking another of his own kind with him. To his left, two ape-creatures reached the stairwell at exactly the same time, their limbs becoming hopelessly enmeshed, while a cockroach-beast cannoned into the back of their legs. Fighting erupted between them, and he glimpsed a brown-shelled creature tumbling—or being thrown—over the rail.

Merral fired quickly once more at each side, to renewed howls. Noticing that the elevator door was open, he ran in and pressed the lowest of the six buttons.

The doors closed, and with a soft whine, the compartment descended sharply.

Merral realized how desperately he wanted to leave the ship. How many of his men had perished? he asked himself bitterly. They had achieved some sort of victory, but what had been the price?

Suddenly the elevator stopped and the door opened smoothly, revealing a low-roofed and gloomy lateral corridor. Yet for all its gloom, Merral rejoiced when he realized that he could smell fresh air. Furthermore, over the noise of the sirens and the sound of panicked, tumbling feet echoing from the levels above, he could hear sounds and cries from outside.

Merral exited the elevator compartment. As he did, he felt a new and powerful vibration begin. He knew instantly what it was: the engines of the ship were starting up.

"Time to go," Merral said aloud.

To his right, a fresher, cleaner light seemed to be flowing into the corridor. He ran to that end and carefully peered round the corner.

Beyond a pile of equipment and crates, he could see a ramp sloping downward. At its base was a strip of beach where a chaotic mass of cockroach-beasts and ape-creatures milled about.

There were other noises from the ship. Harsh, unintelligible words trumpeted from speakers, and a red strip light began pulsing rapidly along the ceiling. The vibrations reverberating through the ship began to rise in strength and pitch.

Merral moved forward, ducked behind an oil-stained container, and peered round at the ramp. Up it trudged a handful of the ape-creatures, some limping, others showing patches of raw red flesh amid their black hair. At their heels scuttled several cockroach-beasts, one with a severed arm, another trailing a limp leg. Merral noticed that on the ramp there was a trail of red smears. At the end of the sorry line, he caught sight of two heavy, dull gray metallic figures, shorter than the ape-creatures but much taller than the cockroach-beasts. For a moment, he thought that they were yet another race until he realized that what he was seeing was an encrusting armor that covered the figures from head to toe. Underneath their heavy protective suits he knew these were men. One, he noted, had a left arm that hung limp.

Halfway up the ramp, the men stopped, squatted down stiffly, and fired a dozen whistling blasts out at the beach beyond. Then they stood up, turned, and with a heavy, labored tread retreated back up the ramp.

As they passed him, barely three paces away, Merral heard a new noise, a deep mechanical groaning from within the ship. He looked to see that the ramp was beginning to rise.

Without thinking, he threw his gun down and rose to his feet. Then he leaped onto the ramp and began racing down its bloodied surface. Above the sound of his boots pounding on the metal he could hear the shout of harsh voices.

He had been seen.

At the very edge of the ramp, Merral dropped to his knees, grabbed the metal rim, and rolled himself over. He heard the sound of firing. Something whistled over the tips of his fingers so close that he felt its warmth. Aware of the fresh air around him and glimpsing the sand beneath him, he let go.

It was a long drop.

He struck the soft sand with a force that punched the wind out of him. For a moment, he lay there, dazed but grateful to God that he was not going to die on that foul ship. Then he caught a whiff of bitter smoke, heard the cries around him, and saw the shuddering corpse of a cockroach-beast in front of him.

Something hissed over his head, and Merral rolled himself down into a nearby hollow in the sand. High above him there was a clunking sound as the ramp seated itself into the vast black underside of the hull. All around him, the beach surface was shaking with the vibrations from the ship.

As his breath returned to him, he looked around, trying to take stock of the situation. About him lay a scene of devastation, with smoldering debris and the bodies of intruders.

Barely an arm's length away lay the half-burned corpse of an ape-creature, and beyond that another lay immobile at the edge of the blue-gray waters of the lake.

Despite the ramp's closure he saw there were two intruder groups left fighting, one between the twin rear legs and another—nearer to him—just in front of the nose strut. There three armed ape-creatures crouched behind a pile of equipment and fired clumsily.

Heartened, Merral realized that the ongoing defense suggested that both Zak's and Frankie's teams were still in place and attacking.

There was a booming noise from above, and he glanced up to see the sky-blocking mass of the ship visibly vibrating. Underneath him the sand shook in response, and around the legs, gravel and sand spurted up.

Suddenly he realized that, above the noise of the intruder ship, he could hear a new and weightier clamor. Abruptly, the line of sky over the lake darkened, and Merral glimpsed the clean, pale blue underside of the *Emilia Kay* sliding into place over the intruder vessel.

Perena's got them in check.

Suddenly there was shouting.

To his right, helmeted men in green were slithering down the loose cliff face on ropes. The reserve troops.

As if responding to their arrival, Merral heard the rising bellow of rocket engines behind him. The intruder ship jerked into the air a fraction. It hung there for a few seconds before thudding back to the ground. Ahead of him, Merral saw the ape-creatures swing their weapons toward the reserves.

It suddenly dawned on him that it was not yet all over. There was still resistance, all three legs of the ship were intact, and there was no sign of any doors having been blasted open. The mission remained unaccomplished. Aching in a dozen places, Merral rose to his feet, found his bush knife on his belt, and once more opened the blade. Then he charged forward at the nearest ape-creature, his feet sinking into the dark sand as he ran. Suddenly conscious of his approach, the creature swung the gun barrel toward him. Before it could fire, he thrust the barrel aside with his arm. He lunged with the blade at the creature's throat, feeling it strike home through fur and flesh.

With a spluttering cry, the creature fell back, its weapon crashing heavily into the sand.

Merral stepped back, trying to ignore the blood on the blade. Above him the entire hull of the ship was now shuddering. One of the two remaining ape-creatures tottered to the ground. The remaining ape-creature turned toward Merral, cradling a long-barreled weapon in the black fur of its arms. Then its head twitched; a ghastly red circle punched into its face.

"Sir, sir! Are you all right?" a voice shouted.

Merral turned to the soldier, recognizing Barry Narandel of the reserves. "Yes, Barry!" Merral shouted back. He felt he wanted to hug Barry and say how extraordinarily glad he was to see him and his men, but he didn't trust himself. Instead, he gestured to the front of the ship. "We need to get a charge on that leg!" he bellowed.

Barry nodded as a new and more sustained roaring began from the engines above them. Warm air thickened with flying sand and hot fumes billowed around them. Ahead, the front leg shuddered afresh, thrashing sand all around as the table-sized metal foot rose up and then bounded back down onto the sand.

"It's about to take off!" Merral shouted over the new roar of sound.

Seizing a red package from one of his men, Barry ran with it to the leg. Just as he was about to climb on to the pad, the entire leg jerked free of the sand.

As the massive metallic foot lifted, a dark gaping hole appeared. Barry's legs slid down into it, dragging him under the overhanging pad.

The charge he was holding flew free and bounced along the ground.

"Get him out!" Merral screamed to the men, over the mounting gale of the engines. He knew they couldn't hear him, but it didn't matter; they were already running to their lieutenant's aid. Merral ran to the charge and snatched it out of the layer of bouncing dirt that now carpeted the ground. Somewhere above him, more jet vents were opening up, and the mixture of dense white smoke and dust made it hard to see anything more than a few paces away. The lake and the cliff seemed to have vanished into a smeared haze.

Ahead of him, in a vibrating blur, Merral could see the landing foot hanging at the height of his waist. He ripped off the backing strip on the charge and, running around the men as they struggled to pull their leader out of the sand, grabbed the side of the foot.

With the flying sand stinging him in the face, Merral reached over and slapped the package as far in on the pad as he could. He tore off the protective film from the firing cord and pulled out the safety pin.

The moment Barry was pulled free he would pull the detonation cord.

Suddenly there was a new shrieking roar from the engines. The ship pivoted sideways, and the suspended foot of the landing gear swung wildly. It struck Merral against his chest armor and sent him reeling. Somehow, he regained his balance. He reached out to regain his hold on the detonation cord, and as he did, the foot dropped down again.

Barry gave a terrible scream and the ground shook.

In a new torrent of sand, noise, and fume the leg lifted up sharply. As it rose past him, Merral lunged forward onto it, catching hold of a metal strut with his left hand and pulling himself onto the pad.

There was a ferocious jolt.

The angular corner of the pad struck under the edge of Merral's armored vest and jerked upward into his abdomen. An explosion of pain engulfed his chest.

Merral gasped, overwhelmed by the agony. *I must hold on!* he told himself over the dreadful pain, the deafening clamor, and the hot, choking smoke.

The ship was moving up.

Merral glanced down, seeing a figure with a red smear around his crushed legs and green-uniformed men standing around him with their pale helmeted faces staring upward. The raging fire in his chest continued to burn, and he could feel a warm liquid trickling down his stomach.

Fighting off an almost irresistible desire to pass out, Merral reached out with his free right hand and with slow, painful movements, found the charge. Even the slightest move seemed to drive a cruel stabbing blade up into his lungs.

He moved his fingers up, centimeter by painful centimeter, until he reached the cord. Then he grasped it between two fingers.

I must be sure I have it firm, he told himself between spasms of pain.

Now was the moment.

Now. But his fingers, apparently part of another man's body, wouldn't respond.

Now! *Now!*

Then, stiffly and reluctantly, they tugged at the cord.

There was a new agonizing jolt as the ship abruptly tilted and slipped sideways. A numbed Merral realized that the Intruder vessel was dodging out from under the *Emilia Kay.*

Check, but not yet mate.

As the ship tilted, the sun shone into Merral's face, and blinking madly, he looked downward to see the ground underneath him covered with tiny upright figures, black bodies sprawled out on the sand, and gray plumes of rising smoke.

Suddenly he was aware of a new kind of vibration. He looked up to the dark cavity under the ship's nose and realized the foot he was clinging onto was sliding upward. He glanced back to see that the massive rear undercarriage legs were retracting as well.

Unexpectedly, the ship swung round and went into a shallow dive. To gain speed, he decided.

For a moment, there was blue water below him.

Merral let go.

The next moment he was aware only of the cold air whipping past him, the dazzling sun in his eyes, the Rim Ranges poking up their serrated peaks to the sky, and the awful pain in his chest. Then he closed his eyes.

Something smacked into him.

As he went under the icy water, Merral felt new and agonizing pains in his chest, as if someone was knifing his ribs.

He opened his eyes to see blue water around him and a yellow light far above. He tried to swim up to the light, but the pain was all too much. The coldness of the water made him want to gasp, but he couldn't breathe.

Somehow he rose up through the waters until he was bobbing up into the air and the sunlight.

Gasping in agony for air, Merral looked up and saw the dark bulk of the intruder ship flying onward. He could see the underside smoothing itself out as the legs were withdrawn into the hull. A sudden triple jet of orange flame burst out at the rear, and the vessel began to accelerate away southward down the lake, gaining altitude as it did.

Something is supposed to happen, Merral thought, his mind numbed. *There is supposed to be an explosion.* The ship became a small black pencil heading up into the stratosphere.

Perhaps, after all his efforts, the charge hadn't worked. *How disappointing after all that effort . . .*

A tiny yellow flash rippled under the nose, and fine fragments of dark debris rained downward.

The ship continued accelerating until it was only a charcoal-colored point trailing a dirty streak of smoke above the far end of the lake.

Good-bye. The cold water chilled him. *Good-bye.*

Then, in an instant so quick that it was almost nonexistent, the black point turned into a dazzling disc of clear silver light.

In that briefest fraction of time, the light seemed to equal the sun in its brightness.

Blinking, Merral heard a wild roll of thunder, and moments later a strange, unruly wind ruffled the choppy waters.

The disc of light faded to yellow and then leisurely transformed itself into a smudgy, dirty cloud. For a moment, it crossed Merral's wearied mind that the intruder ship had somehow escaped into Below-Space while still in the atmosphere.

Then he saw the first of the fragments splash down into the lake with a hiss. Soon the whole southern part of the lake was covered by a series of rising steam columns.

Destroyed, destroyed utterly. Perhaps it was best that way.

It hurt to breathe. Merral noticed a red color in the lake water by his jacket. *I am still bleeding.* The armored jacket seemed to be keeping him afloat. *Just as well. I don't have the strength to take it off.*

Perhaps he would drift ashore. He tried kicking, but he lacked the energy. Anyway, it hurt too much.

The line of the shore was some way away, and he could now see the bulk of the *Emilia Kay* where the intruder ship had once stood. A fair exchange . . .

There were other noises now, but Merral was too tired to bother with them. He felt like sleeping. *I played my part; not well, but I did it.*

Freezing water lapped into his mouth and nose, jarring him momentarily alert.

The wind was getting up. He was aware of a little semicircle of waves radiating out from around him. *Strange,* he thought, in a dreamy haze. *Beware the weather in the Made Worlds.*

Then there was a splashing sound beside him. He knew it was sharks coming after his blood. Why had they ever introduced freshwater sharks into Fallambet Lake Five? He must ask Anya.

How very silly.

Something was now grappling with him, a thing of soft blue plastic tentacles wrapping round his arms, legs, neck, and head. *An octopus,* he thought stupidly, too tired to resist. Was that better than a shark? He was aware of the tentacles becoming slowly rigid, and he realized he could no longer move.

Suddenly he was conscious of being lifted up, of water running down his chest, of his legs being pulled free from the lake, and of a chill and noisy wind whistling around him.

Still puzzled by the octopus, he looked up to where he could hear a humming. There above him was a white Assembly rescue craft with the cross etched in red on the underside, balancing itself on the four columns of hazy air at each corner. A dark doorway opened above him.

In seconds they were lifting him on board, and the octopus was collapsing and slipping away. Then there were white lights and soft, urgent voices and a delicious warm heat flowing over him.

Merral looked up to see a familiar dark face.

"Welcome aboard, Captain D'Avanos," Vero said with an expansive smile.

Merral cleared his throat, aware that he was safe. "Thank you, Vero. . . . I thought I'd go for a swim."

Merral was aware of conversation, and then an authoritative female voice spoke sternly to him. "Please stay quiet, Captain. Save your energy."

"But, Doctor, I give orders," Merral protested feebly, feeling lightheaded.

"But as my patient, you are outranked," she said without humor, and Merral realized that he really wasn't well.

"Vero," he whispered, "shouldn't I be with the men? My men?"

"Zak's taken temporary charge, Merral. But it's all over."

Merral was aware of the rescue craft swaying slightly.

"Did we win?" he asked.

There was a moment's hesitation, and when Vero answered, his voice was subdued. "Win? Yes. I suppose so." He sighed deeply. "It just doesn't feel like it. But the doctor's right; keep quiet."

Then the female voice was back and a bright light scanned his face. "Thank you, Verofaza. You have at least two broken ribs, Captain. Some possible internal damage. You haven't coughed blood?"

"No. I don't think so."

"Good. We will transfer you to the hospital ship. Dr. Azhadi will want to have a look. You'll be back in Isterrane in two hours. Now a slight sedative." There was a cool whisper against his wrist. A soothing feeling drifted up his arm.

Then the motion stopped and a door opened. Abruptly they were lowering him into the sunlight onto a trolley, and from his horizontal position he could see another large white ship nearby with a side hold door open.

As they pushed the hover trolley toward it, he saw a line of green uniformed men forming up. Merral looked at them and saw how they were dirty and bore cuts, scratches, and bandages. As he passed in front of them, a loud ragged cheer went up. Looking away to try and hide his emotions, he saw that on his other side was a line of still, horizontal forms, lying on stretchers with their bodies and faces covered by bloodied sheets.

He blinked away tears.

45

Merral awoke with infinite slowness, climbing up out of deep sleep into a world of whiteness. Gradually he realized that he was lying amid white sheets in a white-painted room and that sunlight was coming in through white gauze curtains. It took him longer to remember who he was and why his chest hurt. Then he smelled the sterile odor of the hospital and realized that his chest was encased in a light cast.

There was a faint noise to his right. He turned, somewhat stiffly, to see Vero, wearing casual clothes, working on his diary at a table. He looked up and gave Merral a tired but relieved smile.

"So how do you feel?" Vero asked, pulling his chair over to the side of the bed.

"As if I had exchanged one piece of armor for another."

"The two broken ribs. Some minor internal injuries, other wounds and blood loss. And incipient hypothermia. Fallambet Lake Five is not a place to swim, even on the edge of summer."

Merral lay there, images flashing through his mind. "I don't remember coming here. The battle was when?"

"Just over twenty-four hours ago. You were anesthetized to travel back. You were also exhausted."

He was aware of the equipment around him now. There were monitor screens at the edge of his vision, and he could feel the sensor straps on his ankle and neck.

Vero looked drained.

"The casualties?"

Vero shook his head and was silent for a moment. When he spoke, his voice was burdened. "T-twenty men dead. And of the diplomatic crew, three are missing, assumed dead. That includes Erika and Louis as well as Fred Huang. We recovered the pilot alive but with some burns."

"Nate," Merral said dully. "That was the pilot's name."

"Another twenty wounded, including you. Some more serious. One may die."

"Oh, dear," Merral said, and as he spoke, he realized how inadequate his words were. But then were any words adequate? One third of the attack force was dead or wounded. "I saw Lorrin Venn killed."

Vero nodded, and Merral thought there were tears in his eyes. "Yes. Philip Matakala told me."

"So Philip survived. And Frankie Thuron?"

"Yes, but with injuries. Zak made it too."

"I thought Zak would."

"He fought well, the men said."

"I'm not surprised. And Barry Narandel? I saw him get his legs crushed."

"We got to him in time. They say he'll walk again but never run."

Merral stared at the ceiling in silence for a long time. "I'm sorry. Desperately sorry. Sometime I want to see a list."

"Whenever you want."

"Thanks. And Perena and Anya are well?" Merral tried to keep his voice neutral.

"Yes. I'm sure you will see both later. The Intruder ship, of course, is in a million fragments." Merral looked at his friend and saw that he seemed to be staring into the distance. "I doubt we will recover much of value."

Merral realized how bitterly disappointed Vero was over the loss of the ship.

"Yes. I wish we could have taken the ship. But we misjudged things, Vero, my friend. There were dozens of things on board."

Vero sighed. "Maybe a hundred. And other creatures."

"They were seen?"

"Ah, you know something of this." Vero gave him a sharp look. "It seems that just after you entered the ship a pack of creatures emerged and began to attack Frankie's team. The reports speak of them as being like fierce dogs or lions, with claws and teeth. Intelligent, regimented, and quite unstoppable—"

"Krallen."

"What?"

"They are called Krallen. I met them. I will tell you about them. Another time."

"Ah. Anyway, just as they were about to overwhelm everybody, they suddenly turned and raced back to the ship. After that the resistance was only sporadic. When Perena arrived and the ship began to take off, what was left of the teams made a concerted attack."

"I see."

Vero frowned. "We—no *I*—made an intelligence error. The ship was bigger than we thought. We also assumed that their ships would carry the same numbers as a comparable ship of our own. But somehow there were far more. Their crew compartments must have been horribly crowded."

"Yes, I realize that. It was . . . an *evil* ship."

"So I imagine," Vero said. Then he paused, a look of guilt on his face. "Do you think they were alerted?"

Merral stared at the gauze curtains. "No. They may have realized that we were onto them, but thankfully, I don't think the defenses were especially ready. If they had been, I don't think any of us would have made it to the ship. We were very much the weaker party in numbers and weapons."

"I was worried that the business with Felicity might have been the cause of the casualties."

"Yes. But I'd say it wasn't."

"Thanks."

"But, Vero," Merral added, "we blundered into something that was beyond us all. There was worse on the ship than anything we feared. I met the thing in the chamber."

"The creature that attacked Felicity?"

"That was there. I killed that. But there was also a being there. . . ." Merral realized that he didn't want to talk about what he encountered.

"Yes, you said things in your sleep." Vero raised an eyebrow.

"It was only that I—that we—had help that we didn't have an utter disaster."

"That too, I gathered."

There was a knock at the door, and the tall, erect, and gray-suited figure of Representative Corradon entered the room. As he did, Merral caught a glimpse of two men in unfamiliar blue uniforms standing stiffly outside the door.

"Sorry. I see that this is not a good time," Corradon said with a tone of gentle apology. Merral felt that although the representative looked as if he had not slept for many days, his manner was composed and his expression very much that of a man in control. Vero stood up and made as if to leave.

"I do need to see you, Sentinel," Corradon said, clapping a large hand on Vero's slight shoulder. "Could you wait outside?"

Vero nodded and left, closing the door behind him.

Corradon sat down in the chair by the bed. "I had a long chat with Vero yesterday. He feels very badly about the attack. So do I. But it could have all been much worse. Much worse." Merral watched as the representative allowed himself the luxury of a faint, tentative smile of relief. "We didn't get all we wanted. But we did win a victory."

"Of sorts," Merral added.

"True, but, Merral, we could have had this thing festering in the heart of Menaya forever. Anyway, first things first. On behalf of the people of Farholme, I want to thank you now. There will be other occasions, I have no doubt."

He extended a hand, and more as a courtesy than anything else, Merral shook hands carefully. He was certain he didn't merit the gratitude.

Corradon gave him a half smile. "I gather I can shake your hand. I was told, though, I shouldn't make you laugh."

Merral allowed himself a sigh. "There is, I fear, sir, little danger of that."

The half smile faded away. "I'm sorry."

"So am I. There was a lot of bloodshed yesterday."

"Yes." Corradon's voice was soft and sad. "I gather that you should make a speedy recovery. How do you feel?"

"Drained. I need to think through what I saw. There are things to do. And you, sir? How are you?"

The representative considered matters for a moment. "I feel better than I did. *Reassured*, in some way. At midday today, I am broadcasting to the people of Farholme. And at least now I can tell them the truth: we were invaded and the Gate was destroyed, but the invaders have been routed." He sighed. "Albeit at a high and sad cost. But at least the burden of secrecy is lifted." He turned to look out of the window, and Merral saw his silhouette, confident and strong. *The public profile; if you are to receive bad news, then you would want it from such a man.*

"But there are other things I have to announce," Corradon said, sounding less assured. His strength and confidence seemed only skin-deep. "There are other things I have to say. Of new troubles . . ."

He paused, seemed to struggle with his doubts, and his voice brightened. "Yes, I still desperately wish that I didn't have this job. But I have it and I will try and do it."

Merral found the determination in his voice encouraging.

"Good."

"Thanks. The speech today will have about 100 percent attention. People are getting up especially for it over in Aftarena. And we are beaming the signal to Bannermene so that in a generation's time it will go round the Assembly. I should warn you that your name will be mentioned in it. I will have to say that a hastily summoned task force under your leadership managed to destroy a superior force of invaders—"

"Sir," Merral interrupted, "I would prefer to be anonymous. Unless you wish to reveal how badly I handled things. I think we must be careful that the glory goes to God."

There was a slight nod of his head. "I understand. But I'm afraid I refuse the first part of your request. You can hardly be anonymous. And as to the second part, this coming Lord's Day is to be a solemn day of gratitude for deliverance and for the remembrance of those who were lost. Today I will also give out the list of casualties."

Twenty dead, Merral thought bitterly and wondered if that would be any consolation to Lorrin's parents or anybody else's. But the implication of Corradon's statement troubled him; once it was made, he would no longer be a private person.

"But before I speak to our world," Corradon continued, interrupting Merral's thoughts, "I want to talk to you about what happened. On the ship. Are you willing to do that?"

"Yes," Merral said, after a moment. "But can I talk to both you and Vero about it? I don't want to repeat myself." He knew he had to speak about what had happened soon, and it might as well be to both Corradon and Vero at once.

"Very well. I will get him."

Corradon rose from his chair and went to the door. He returned with Vero and a nurse.

"Sorry, Merral," the representative said, "medicine takes priority. This gentleman wants to see you. Vero and I need to talk anyway, so please excuse us."

Together they walked over to the window and out onto the balcony. As they pushed aside the flimsy curtains, Merral caught a glimpse of the gleaming blue sea. He had a sudden deep longing to walk lonely beaches on his own.

The nurse helped Merral to sit up, asked him those questions that the machines couldn't answer, and gave him a glass of medicated orange juice. Then, with a respectful glance at Corradon, he left, closing the door carefully behind him.

With the nurse gone, the two men came back in and pulled up chairs around the bed. Vero's face was troubled.

Corradon turned to Merral. "Thank you. There are lots of questions. If we'd have known you were going to get on board we'd have put a shoulder camera on you. Now obviously at some stage there will have to be a full report. And an inquiry. But now . . ." He and Vero shared glances. "Only if you are up to it, of course . . ."

Merral breathed in heavily and instantly regretted it. "Yes, physically. Mentally, I'm not so sure. But it is important. I suppose I should start with the appearance of the envoy."

Then, with interruptions for him to drink, Merral went through what had happened to him and what he had seen on the previous morning. He did not discuss the personal matters that had emerged with the envoy, although he was aware that he had hinted at more than he said.

He was interrupted twice. The first interruption came from Vero when he described the shattered statue and its inscription.

" 'Zhalatoc, Great Prince of Lord-Emperor Nezhuala's Dominion,' " Vero repeated, taking down the spelling and entering it in his diary. He stared at the screen, a range of emotions crossing his face; then he looked up. "As I suspected: two proper names that we have no records of in Assembly history. And you don't need me to tell you that to use the language of 'Great Prince,' 'Lord-Emperor,' and 'Dominion' for anyone other than the Most High is alien to everything the Assembly stands for. But written in our script . . ." His face expressed a deep and worried perplexity. "Who are they? What do they want?"

"And why was the statue defaced?" asked Corradon, anxiety visibly eroding away his look of confidence.

The questions were unanswered, and Merral continued with his account of what had happened in the chamber. He hesitated when he came to what the steersman had seemed to say to him as he had stood before the column. *After all,* he told himself, *it was a voice in my mind.* Yet the words had been so significant and ominous that Merral felt he had no option but to share them. As he described what had been said to him, he was aware that uneasy looks were shared between his visitors.

"Stop!" said Corradon suddenly, and Merral felt that his composure had now all but vanished. "Let me get this right. He said—or you felt he said—'Your isolation is over; the breach in the barrier remains. There will be others who will come in vast ships of unimaginable power.' "

"Yes. 'And we will come with them.' "

"This is—" Corradon's face paled. "No," he said slowly, as if reasserting control over his emotions. "Later. Continue."

Merral ended his account with his wild ride on the leg of the intruder craft. "So I just jumped and hit the water and saw the explosion. And I don't know how long after that I was picked up by the rescue craft."

There was a moment's silence before Corradon spoke. "An extraordinary account," he said, and Merral heard fear in his slow words. "Quite remarkable and, in part, terrifying. There is much more I would like to ask you, but I'm grateful for what I have heard. I have . . ." He shook his head and turned to Vero. "Did you have any questions?"

Vero, who apart from his one interruption had listened in total silence, put his long fingers up around his cheeks. "Dozens. Most can wait. But I do have one or two that I need to ask. Merral, you said the ship was dirty and smelly. Did you see any signs of damage?"

"Other than the statue? Yes, there was one place. Just before I met the thinking machine."

"Go on."

"There was a large hole, oh, the size of that door, now mended, and there looked to have been a fire. Or an explosion. At a temperature high enough to melt metal." Merral paused, remembering the spherical silver globules that he had picked up. "And thinking about it, I'm sure the blast occurred in zero gravity. The melted metal had formed spherical droplets."

A subliminal gesture of acknowledgement seemed to pass between his visitors.

"Why do you ask?" Merral said. "I didn't make anything of it. Not compared to everything else."

Vero answered him. "It's just that the *Emilia Kay*'s cameras got some good images as they hovered over, and there were marks on the hull. Blast marks, someone thinks."

"I see."

"A second question: You said both notices, this odd title and the 'Steersman Chamber' warning, were in Communal?"

"Yes."

"And an early style."

"I'd say so."

"Hmm. How *very* suggestive." Vero's voice was almost inaudible, and Merral saw his expression twisting this way and that in thought.

Corradon looked at Vero as if expecting an explanation. Then he glanced at his watch. "Really, I must go. But briefly, Vero, what do you think?"

Vero nodded, as if agreeing with some unspoken deduction of his own. "Yes . . . sir, it is now absolutely plain that the tale we have of the ending of the Rebellion is inadequate. I was very taken with one incidental detail of Merral's account: the way the robot identified him as *Captain* Lucas Ringell."

"Sorry, Vero, I fail to see the significance of the rank. Other than the fact that it knew of him."

"Sir, as you know, Lucas Ringell is always known to history as *General* Ringell, the final rank he reached. He was promoted on his return to Earth, *after* the ending of the Rebellion." A pensive look came over his face. "Or, what we have always called the ending."

Merral began to understand. "You mean the last the ship, or the robot, knew of him was when he was a captain?"

"Exactly."

Corradon stared at him. "Extraordinary."

Vero nodded. "I am now confident that something—man, computer, or whatever—survived the cleansing of the Centauri base and fled beyond Assembly space."

"And has come back."

"Or its descendants have." Vero's unhappiness showed in his expression. "But in whatever way the forces of the Rebellion survived, the trends that

Jannafy encouraged have plainly been continued. There appears to have been no respect of any of the Technology Protocols. There has been a pursuit of all things banned: human genetic modification, machines with a humanoid intelligence, undoubted explorations of Below-Space. And somehow, an alliance with deep evil has been made."

Corradon shook his head as if trying to ignore what he had heard. "These are matters to be pursued at length later. I will mention little of them today. It is already hard enough to say what I have to. But after Merral's account, I am now reassured that this costly battle was worthwhile. And that what I will propose is necessary."

As Merral wondered what he meant, he saw Corradon and Vero look at each other.

"Shall I ask?" the representative muttered, but Vero shook his head.

"Very well." Corradon rose stiffly to his feet. "I must go and prepare for my speech. Anyway, I wish you a speedy recovery, Merral. There is more for us to discuss." He patted Vero on the back and walked toward the door.

"Sir—" Merral raised a hand—"before you go, I have a request. Another one." There was something that had to be said, and now was as good a time as any to say it.

"Which is?"

Merral took a deep and painful breath. "Sir, I wish to resign my commission. I want to return to forestry. To go back to Ynysmant." His voice sounded brittle.

Corradon took a pace back toward the bed, his face full of incredulity. "But why?"

For a moment Merral could not speak, and then the words flowed out in an unstoppable rush. "Because I made errors of judgment. Because there are men dead. Because we failed to secure the ship. Because I'm not good at it. And, above all, because I hate it. Utterly."

Corradon pursed his lips and stared at him before answering. "You hate it? I'd hope so." He shook his head slowly. "Not good at it? I'd hate to meet anyone who was better than you. And the ship was, at least, utterly destroyed. The dead are . . ." He hesitated and then exhaled heavily. "The dead are a grievous and lamentable loss, but they are hardly your fault. As for your claimed errors of judgment, well, I think they are far outweighed by your wise decisions, your courage, and your skill. But there will be a full inquiry on the battle over the next month. There has to be for the records. And for lessons for the future."

He turned, as if to leave, and then paused, staring at something on the bedside table. He bent over, and for the first time Merral saw the dull silvery disc and chain and realized that the identity tag was gone from round his neck.

"May I?" Corradon asked, and without waiting for an answer, he reverently picked it up and stared intently at it, mouthing the ancient words engraved on it. "'Lucas Hannun Ringell, Space Frigate *Clearstar*, Assembly Assault Fleet.' How very strange. How very strange indeed."

His blue eyes glanced at Merral. "Well, anyway, if heaven allows any knowledge of these worlds' tribulations, neither Brenito nor General Lucas Ringell will have been displeased with yesterday's events."

"Unfortunately, sir," interjected Merral, trying not to sound rude, "my conduct is judged by a higher authority than either. And there, I feel, I have blame, not just praise."

Corradon nodded, lowering the tag reverently down to the tabletop. "It is perhaps as well, lest this victory breed an overconfidence. But apportion blame fairly, Merral."

"I will, sir. But my resignation?"

"I don't accept it. Sorry." Corradon shrugged.

"Respectfully, sir, I believe that you have to accept it. It's over. The task I was asked to do is done."

"Really?" Corradon exhaled loudly. "Merral, Lucian and I have agreed that the FDU is to be closed down. In fact, I will be announcing that during my speech."

"Good."

"To be replaced by a larger and better-equipped Farholme Defense Force with a range out to the system's edge. With real weapons. And—I was not going to mention this now but I will—I'd like you to head it up. As Commander."

"I don't understand," Merral said, staring at him and Vero, struck by the solemnity on both their faces.

"I will be stating—" the representative seemed to weigh his words—"that we will be enlarging our defense capability. As much as our world's limited manufacturing and technical base can take. It would be an enormous help if you would lead the new force. Indeed, I think it would help stabilize shaken nerves across the planet if I could announce your appointment during my speech." He looked out beyond the curtained window with a burdened gaze. "It is my job to tell the whole of Farholme that not only are we isolated from the Assembly, but we have enemies. That is a heavy task. I would like, in the same breath, to give them the slight comfort of saying their defense is in trustworthy hands."

"No!" Merral snapped. "I see no reason for it. I want to be an *ex*-captain and an *ex*-soldier."

Corradon gave him a wry, sad, and sympathetic smile. "I'm afraid, Merral, you face the same dilemma I have faced. This world is in crisis and it looks for leaders. You and I must do our bit to provide them with what they need." He glanced at his watch. "Look, I must go."

He gestured to Vero. "I give you leave, Sentinel, to tell him what I told you."

Then he walked to the door and opened it. He turned to Merral. "Captain D'Avanos, it would be a great help to me—and to Farholme—if I could have your agreement by noon."

Then with a salute, he left.

Merral turned to Vero and was about to speak to him when the door slid open and an energetic female figure with a shock of tied-back red hair entered.

"Anya!" cried Merral.

Vero, beaming at her, got to his feet. "I'm off for a bit; I need some breakfast. Or lunch. Whatever is appropriate for now. We will continue our conversation, Merral." Then he slipped out of the room.

Anya bent over and kissed Merral lightly on the forehead, pulled up a chair, and sat next to him. She was wearing a rumpled navy waistcoat and unfussy, plain blue trousers, and he felt his resolve weakening.

"So, Tree Man, you survived," she teased him, laughing brightly. "I gather that you float. Hardly surprising." The joking tone did not conceal a deep relief. She took his hand and squeezed it hard.

"Yes," Merral answered slowly, "I survived. But I'm not unscathed." He tried to prepare the words that he had to say, but faced with her in person, he found the idea difficult. He played for time. "So did you catch any creatures?"

"No. Not alive." She wrinkled her face in expressive disgust. "They were all dead. Some of the men say that the few that were left alive committed suicide once the ship took off. But there are about a dozen dead specimens in all. Although being clones, I think we'll only need to look at one of each. And none of this very worrying new type. The predators."

"They aren't creatures. They are machines of some sort."

"Machines? That explain—"

"Anya," interrupted Merral, feeling that he had to speak now or her presence would persuade him to forget what he knew he had to say, "I have an apology and an admission to make."

She looked at him carefully, as if wondering whether it was a joke or not. "Which is what?"

"That, the other night, I wasn't entirely . . ." He could hardly bring himself to speak the word, it was so appalling. *"Honest."*

"About what?" she said, letting his hand drop.

"About Isabella."

Her face darkened. "But you said . . . you *denied* that there was anything."

Merral felt that this was a new agony. "Yes, Anya, I know. I'm truly sorry."

"You mean that . . . there *is* something?"

"Well, yes. It was, well, something that . . ." He paused. "Something that

I slipped into hurriedly, without thinking. An *understanding*. Without parental consent. So, well, I thought it wasn't really valid. And I have regretted it since. But—"

Anya had gotten to her feet now. "But *what?*"

"But, that I—we—never ended . . . Not *mutually.*" Merral felt his face burn with shame.

"So you are *not* free." Her words were biting.

He tried to smile. "But I would like to be. Very much."

"It was a *lie.*"

The word cut and stung like a lash of hail in the face, and the thought came to Merral that in the last twenty minutes he had been praised by the highest in the land and was now being utterly humiliated.

"Yes, I suppose . . . that's a legitimate word. But I was caught off guard. No, that's an excuse. . . ."

"I can't believe it!" Anya said, her expression a harsh mixture of pain and anger. Merral wondered if it might not have been better to have stayed on the ship and been blown into a billion atoms.

"So what are you going to do?" she snorted, her eyes wide with emotion.

Merral tried to look away. "I'm going back to Ynysmant, and I'm going to talk to Isabella. Ask her to agree to our commitment—such as it is—being concluded. *Mutually.*"

He could hardly bear to look at her now. He knew that she was glaring at him.

"And if she refuses?" Anya asked in a sharp, querulous tone.

"I hope that won't happen. But if it does . . . I have no idea," Merral said miserably, thinking that in the last twenty-four hours he had known war, death, and injury, and that this was almost as traumatic as any of them. "I now want to do what is right."

"Now . . . ," she said, and the scorn in her voice cut into him. "Oh, *now* you want to do right!" She stood there shaking her head, her hair somehow having come untied and flowing out wildly.

"Anya," he said, "I do love you."

"And why, oh why, should I believe that?" she exclaimed and then rounded on him. "And anyway, what *you* feel is irrelevant if I can't trust you."

"I'm sorry."

"I hurt," she said, wringing her hands. "I just feel . . ." She shook her head as she tried to find the words. She glared at him, her eyes glistening with tears. "I just don't have the vocabulary. I just feel that . . . I don't trust!" Then she turned sharply on her heels and stormed out angrily.

The door thudded heavily shut behind her.

Merral lay there, grasping the sheets with his eyes shut, wishing it had all never happened, and feeling very sorry for himself.

A few moments later, he heard the door opening, and he opened his eyes to see a young, male doctor looking at him in a concerned way. "Oh, Captain D'Avanos. The metabolic monitor system sent me over. Your functions were indicating high stress loads just now. You are, perhaps, in pain?"

Merral stared at him, not sure whether to order him out. In the end, an approximation to civility triumphed. "Thank you. It's not a medical problem. But you can help. Unhitch me from these monitor cables, will you? I want to walk. To the window. I need fresh air."

There was a pause. "Well, we were planning to keep you under observation until tomorrow."

"And what happens if I just pull them off?" countered Merral, hearing a strange brusqueness in his voice.

The doctor looked alarmed. "Oh, I'd rather you didn't. You'll probably damage the sensors, and they are made—*were* made—off system on Ticander. We have only a limited number."

Merral lifted up the sheet, painfully bent down to his ankle, and began undoing the covering bandage. "Well, let's not risk that, shall we? Get them off, please. And can you find me some proper clothes?"

Ten minutes later, the far-from-pleased doctor having departed, Merral walked stiffly over to the balcony rail and leaned against it, trying to avoid the tender part of his chest. As he had suspected, he was high—perhaps six floors up—on the tower that was the Western Isterrane Main Hospital. He looked out southward over the playing fields, green woodlands, and rolling pastures that ended abruptly at the sharp line of the sea cliff. Beyond that, the open vastness of the sea stretched onward to the horizon. Around one of the new sandbanks offshore, he could see the etched lines of white breaking waves, and he could just make out flocks of gulls wheeling. He breathed in and felt he could smell the sea air.

He had hard decisions to make.

He was still pondering them a few minutes later when there was a noise behind him, and he turned to see Vero entering.

Again, he glimpsed the two statue-stiff blue figures outside the door.

There was something in Vero's gait and look that told Merral he had met Anya. The sentinel walked out to the balcony and, standing by him, stared at the view.

"Sorry," he said, but the single word conveyed an intense empathy.

For a long time Merral did not answer. He felt the warm sunlight on him, stared at the curves of the ground ahead and the splendid beech trees clad in the green brilliance of their early summer foliage, and heard the excited screams of the swifts as they swooped around in the air catching insects. He wanted to be a long way away.

At length, he spoke. "Vero, I don't know about you, but since Nativity I have said 'sorry' to more people than in all the rest of my life."

"Me too. The world has changed in so many ways."

"It is broken, Vero. And I don't know how we rebuild it." Merral's sigh was deep enough to make his chest ache. "It is broken so badly, so thoroughly, that I could weep."

He caught a look of sharp, pained sympathy from Vero. "I know," he said, almost inaudibly.

Merral remembered something. "The men outside, the ones wearing blue. Who are they?"

Vero leaned forward, staring toward the infinite distance of the sea, and when he spoke his tone was distant and drained. "A new organization. Advisor Clemant has come up with it."

"Called what?"

"Police."

Merral closed his eyes briefly as he grappled with the significance of the word. "What?"

"It's not a Communal word. It's an old French and English word. A non-military law-enforcement body. For internal security." The staccato, reluctant phrases displayed his disquiet.

"Oh, I know what it means, Vero. But here? in the Assembly?"

"Yes; Clemant is no fool. He knows what we know. That the old world is gone. And that the new one will be a hard place. The police will be, he says, merely a precautionary and temporary measure. Maybe . . ."

"I know. He hinted at it. Oh, what a mess," Merral muttered, feeling that another new, discordant note had entered his world. *It was never Eden here. At best, maybe it was a sort of harsh New Eden. But it has gone. I miss it already and I fear for its future.*

The noise of schoolchildren playing a Team-Ball match on the fields below dragged him out of his sad reverie. He looked over to where Vero was silently wrapped in his own thoughts.

"What are you supposed to tell me?"

Vero looked up carefully at him, "Do you really want it?"

"It can't make things worse."

Vero's fingers tapped the railing thoughtfully. "It can. I heard a rumor last night and had it confirmed now by Corradon. While we were training at Tanaris, some of the Space Affairs orbital experts began to bring together some of the astronomical work Perena had started. On the records of objects within the Alahir system. They had lots of data that she hadn't been able to access, and they reprocessed all the old records." His voice was emotionless.

"And . . . she was wrong?" Merral asked, feeling that there was now a note of alarm ringing throughout the spaces of his mind.

"No. She wasn't. Her path of the Intruder ship was confirmed. Of the first ship."

The adjective exploded into Merral's brain. "The *first*?"

"Yes. The thing is, they found another trace. A few days later."

"Where is it?"

"Ah. The best analysis suggests it appeared in the system a day later and followed the first intruder ship at a distance, as far as the inner asteroid belt, where it changed orbit and stopped." He gave a profound sigh. "Now, as you know, there you—I suppose I ought to now say *we*—have good data and continuous monitoring. It stayed for a week and then headed back out of Assembly space. One day it was going fast toward Fenniran. And the next, it had gone."

The facts were easily absorbed, but Merral struggled to find meaning in them.

"What else can you say about it?" he inquired.

"Only that it was bigger. Much bigger."

Merral clutched the railing as hard as he could, as if by doing so it would somehow impart something of its stability into his own life.

"Jorgio said that the barrier was down. The steersman confirmed it."

"And warned of other ships."

"Indeed. This second ship—any ideas what it was doing?" Merral now understood what Corradon had meant about "lessons for the future," why he wanted an enlarged FDU, and why he had wanted Merral to lead it.

"We don't know for sure," answered Vero, looking up as if he expected a sign in the heavens. "But there is a suspicion that it was chasing the first intruder. That was the idea generated from the orbits alone. The evidence from the ship here, including your report about the damage, confirms that it had been attacked."

"So the inference is what? I'm still partially sedated, remember." *Or am I? Perhaps I am just numbed.*

"That the intruder—call it the first intruder—was fleeing."

"So, although it was hiding in the Lannar Crater, it was not hiding from us."

"Not *primarily* hiding from us. But you see the obvious implications?"

"No. Or rather, I think I do. But be gentle." Merral felt that a whole chorus of alarms was now echoing through his body.

Vero continued in a soft, factual tone. "The idea—the theory—is this: There was a chase, and the first intruder somehow made it into your—*our*—

system. The other ship followed it. Only to realize it had stumbled onto something too big. *Us.* The Assembly. It watched for a bit and then went back."

"From where it may return again at any time?"

For a long time Vero said nothing but just stared over at the tiny figures of the schoolchildren running around the ball.

"Yes," he said, and his voice was small. "That's the point. They may be our friends or our enemies. They may be this Dominion under this Lord-Emperor Nezhuala. But we know that they know how to fight. And Corradon and Clemant feel that we ought to be prepared for the worst."

"I see."

"Yes," Vero said, looking at his watch. "But we can talk about it later. Corradon is speaking in an hour. I was going to watch it with Perena." He paused. "And probably Anya. Are you all right here?"

"Me? Yes, I want to think about what I must do. Your news has added a new dimension to the problem. But you, Vero, what will you do?"

"What will I do?" Vero asked slowly, and Merral saw his brown eyes tracing a black swift, effortlessly scything through the air.

"I, like you, thought my task was over. It is not. I need to search every bit of data Brenito left me on the rebellion of Jannafy and see if we can find any clues as to what really happened. And I want to talk to Jorgio again. Oh, and I suppose I must prepare my statement for the inquiry." Then Vero touched Merral's shoulder briefly. "And you, my friend?"

"I have a lot to think about. I want to leave for Ynysmant as soon as I can. I want to write my report while it is fresh in my mind, and I have things to sort out with Isabella."

"Yes." Vero looked at Merral with his deep brown eyes. "I am sympathetic. I have been thinking. About the way we are." He paused. "Can I say something?"

"By all means."

"It is just this: Before all this happened, we took everything for granted. We did what was right because it was pleasing to us. We had, as it were, the wind behind us. Now, all that has changed. The wind is against us. Yet what is right has not changed; it has just become harder to do it."

Merral considered his words. "Yet we must still do what is right, even if it costs us. Yes, that makes sense."

"It's little comfort, I'm afraid. But I must go. I will be in touch."

"And me."

"Give my love to your family and Isabella when you talk to them. I will pray for you."

"Thanks. And I for you."

Then abruptly, as if wishing to conceal some deep emotion, Vero turned and left.

Merral watched him go and then turned back to stare at the view. *I never realized how much I had until I lost it.*

A final whistle blast from the Team-Ball referee drifted up to him, and as he watched, the children began boisterously trooping off the pitch. Merral presumed they were leaving in time to see the historic broadcast. He watched their colorful animated figures moving away to their changing rooms. They were unaware—and would be for a little longer—that a permanent shadow had fallen over their lives.

As Merral watched them, the decision made itself.

He walked slowly back into the room and found his diary among his possessions in a drawer. He took it and strolled unhurriedly back out to the balcony. It would be easier for him to say what he had to say with the view of the woods and the sea in front of him than in the anonymous and universal hospital room.

As Merral switched the diary on, he saw that the restrictions on its use had been lifted. He had had calls from his family and from Isabella. Well, he would answer them in due course. He tapped the screen. "Get me Representative Anwar Corradon please."

A moment later an image of a young man appeared, looking up from a pile of folders.

"I'm sorry. The representative is busy, I'm afraid. This is Jules, his office assistant. As you know, he's speaking in a quarter of an hour. Can you leave a message please?"

"I want you to pass on a message to him now. Urgently."

Jules's face acquired a look of profound disbelief at the idea that anyone could wish such an action at this time. "I'm sorry. But he is engaged in preparing for this rather important broadcast."

Merral tapped on the icon to transmit his name.

The man glanced at his screen and suddenly stiffened, his face flushing. "Oh . . . Captain D'Avanos, sir. I must apologize. I didn't recognize you. The message was . . . ?"

"It is very simple, but he must hear it before the broadcast."

"I'll take it to him now. He's next door. I do so apologize."

"Your apology is accepted. Just tell him this." Merral took a breath, closed his eyes, and then gave Jules the message.

It was just a single sentence.

After he had spoken it, the young man looked at him in perplexity. "Just that?"

"Just that. The exact words. He'll understand. Thank you," Merral said and flicked the diary off. He went into his room, put the diary down on the table, and turned the wallscreen on with the volume low.

Then he went out again on the balcony to continue staring at the view and feeling the sun on his face. There was so much he had to do, and so many perils he had to face.

He was still standing there when the "Hymn of the Assembly" sounded from the screen.

"Time," Merral said aloud to no one, and he turned to go inside and watch the broadcast.

Time for all Farholme to hear that the long peace of the ages was finally over.

Time for them to be told that they faced awesome enemies.

Time too for them to hear that Commander Merral D'Avanos had accepted the burden of being in charge of their defense.